T0365945

JOYCE
BRANDON

DIVERSIONBOOKS

Also by Joyce Brandon

The Kincaid Family Series
The Lady and the Lawman
The Lady and the Robber Baron
The Lady and the Outlaw
Adobe Palace

Diversion Books
A Division of Diversion Publishing Corp.
443 Park Avenue South, Suite 1008
New York, New York 10016
www.DiversionBooks.com

For more information, email info@diversionbooks.com

First Diversion Books edition July 2015.
Print ISBN: 978-1-68230-249-1
eBook ISBN: 978-1-62681-907-8

This book is dedicated to Kristina Lynn Wilson, child of my heart

This book is dedicated to my former Ballantine editor, Cheryl Woodruff, who loved it enough to eventually publish it, thereby giving me entree into the amazing world of novel writing. And to my agent, Abby Saul, who tracked me down and made this publication possible. And to the team at Diversion Books for their attention to detail and their professionalism. Thank you.

PART ONE

Then said Almitra, Speak to us of Love.
And he raised his head and looked upon the people, and there fell
 a stillness upon them. And with a great voice he said:
When love beckons to you, follow him,
Though his ways are hard and steep.
And when his wings enfold you yield to him,
Though the sword hidden among his pinions may wound you.
And when he speaks to you believe in him,
Though his voice may shatter your dreams as the north wind lays waste the garden.

For even as love crowns you so shall he crucify you.
Even as he is for your growth so is he for your pruning.
Even as he ascends to your height and caresses your tenderest
 branches that quiver in the sun,
So shall he descend to your roots and shake them in their clinging to the earth.

Like sheaves of corn he gathers you unto himself.
He threshes you to make you naked.
He sifts you to free you from your husks.

He grinds you to whiteness.
He kneads you until you are pliant;
And then he assigns you to his sacred fire, that you may become
 sacred bread for God's sacred feast.

All those things shall love do unto you that you may know the secrets of your heart,
 and in that knowledge become a fragment of Life's heart.

Kahlil Gibran
The Prophet

CHAPTER ONE

"El Gato Negro is coming! *El Gato Negro!"*

Squinting against the glare of the fierce afternoon sun, Tía stepped to the window of the small dress shop to peer through the dusty, fly-specked glass. On the wide, rutted road that divided the small town of Tubac, Arizona, three young Mexican boys—their faces contorted as if they had gone insane with their jubilation—ran, waved their arms, and shouted in Spanish, *"El Gato Negro* is coming!"

At the north end of town, between the faded wooden store fronts on one side and the yellow stone and masonry bank on the other, a fat, rust-colored cloud rose over the desert.

Tía pushed pink ruffled curtains aside to get a better look. She could have stood in the center of the window and had an unimpaired view, but she chose to shield herself behind the tied-back curtains.

El Gato Negro could not be coming here. Nothing ever happened in Tubac.

Outside, countless Mexicans appeared as if by magic to line the wide road, and their excited voices raised in a fluctuating babble of Spanish and English. Gesturing Mexican women craned their necks and tried desperately to verify their good fortune.

White men, women, and children ran for the safety of their homes.

A frown puckering her severe face, Mrs. Gaston, owner of the small dress shop, joined Tía at the window. "What's going on out there?"

"They say *El Gato Negro* is coming," Tía answered.

In Tía's circle of friends and acquaintances, the legendary figure called *El Gato Negro*—Spanish for *"The Black Cat"*—though never seen in this town before today, was a king, credited with defending and protecting poor Mexicans from their white oppressors. Tía was white by birth—what Mama called technically white—but for living purposes Mama had found it far more expedient for herself and her family to live as Mexicans. Their surname—Garcia-Lorca—was one of the finest

Spanish names in the territory.

"Good heavens!" Blinking her watery, pink-rimmed, green eyes and sucking in a hissing breath, Mrs. Gaston clasped her hands over the bulging bodice of her high-necked cotton gown. Eyes wide as saucers, she turned and fled, her plump body skittering past the carefully crafted wire mannequin in the plum-colored taffeta gown. She grabbed the money from her money box, ducked into the back of the shop, and then ran out the back door, her reticule clutched in one hand, her skirts in the other.

Tía turned back to the window and lifted the pink starched curtains and the white sheer so she could see out. Apparently *El Gato Negro* was not unknown to Mrs. Gaston.

Tía's fingers plucked at the wide-bibbed gray bonnet she had been trying on. A thousand unspoken dreams and wishes surfaced for that one moment. Wouldn't it be wonderful if *El Gato Negro* saw her and fell in love with her and carried her off? All her life she had heard about his wonderful exploits, how he protected the downtrodden Mexicans.

Tía realized what she was doing and closed her eyes in frustration. Lately, every time she rode, and other times as well, a strange feeling of excitement came over her—a fever, almost—that made her yearn to dress herself in the most frivolously feminine gown in Tubac and parade up and down until some man noticed her. Unfortunately, the kind of men she could attract in Tubac would smuggle her across the border and sell her to a bordello.

Very shortly, she feared, she might not regard such an end as unacceptable. She would have to give up riding! Last time this feeling had overwhelmed her she had spent her entire savings on a blue gown, scrubbed herself until she tingled, put the gown on, and sashayed over to the stable to exercise her charms on poor, scrawny-necked Elmo, the only relatively eligible man in Tubac at the moment. Availability was a changing thing in a town like Tubac, where men and women switched partners with relative ease, especially among Mama's friends. Since the women talked incessantly about their men, Tía knew too much about them to be interested. Elmo's sole virtue was that he had never lived with any of Mama's friends.

Tía picked up a fan, positioned it under her eyes, and practiced flirting at the mirror the way her sister, Andrea, did on occasion, just in case *El Gato* did notice her.

The fast-moving horsemen drew closer. At least fifty men, all heavily armed, emerged out of that reddish cloud. Crossed *bandoleras* gleamed darkly against their rough, dirty clothes.

The thundering pack galloped into the north end of the small town. Tía determined that the one riding at the fore, dressed as a gentleman rancher, was *El Gato Negro*. She peered through the curtains at him, but the cloud of dust and his wide-brimmed sombrero shaded *El Gato*'s face. His features were indistinct.

As a precaution, Tía deftly untied the sashes that held back Mrs. Gaston's frilly curtains. Pink ruffles cascaded down to shield Tía from the outside. While they were still far enough away…

With sure step she crossed the shop, picked up a straight-backed chair, positioned it under the lamp that hung in the center of the room, climbed up on the chair, and turned out the lamp. People outside, nearly blinded from the sun, would not be able to see into the shop, but she could watch them unobserved. Now sure of her invisibility, Tía again stationed herself at the big, curtained window to the right of the door.

Suddenly the door of the small shop opened, and a man, his attention riveted on the approaching riders, slipped noiselessly inside. Without seeing Tía, he stepped to the side and closed the door. His booted foot almost covered hers.

"You step down on my foot any harder, and I'm going to let out a yell heard all the way to Tombstone," she said evenly.

The man's head turned abruptly, and he glared down at her. Then a grin spread across his dark face. "Mighty glad I didn't step down harder, then." His voice was cautiously low but filled with easy humor. She liked the way it sounded—richly masculine but with some depth to it. She was sure from its undertones it could become instantly gruffer and more rowdy. She could imagine him the center of attention in a group of raucous cowboys, each trying to outdo the other in the outrageousness of their tall tales.

"So, you're what *El Gato Negro* is chasing…"

A scowl pulled the man's straight black brows down in a frown. "I ain't exactly running," he growled. His forehead was short, framed between a tan cowboy hat and the heaviest brush of black eyebrows Tía had ever seen. Separated by the bridge of his nose, his thick eyebrows formed a flat ledge over deep-set black eyes. An even heavier brush of mustache covered his top lip. When he grinned, the full swell of his lips flattened and pulled back to reveal straight white teeth, and deep smile lines spread out from the corners of his eyes. His cheeks were clean shaven, except for the crisp black sideburns that grew down to the bottom of his earlobes.

"Reckon it's just a matter of time."

"Do I look important enough for *El Gato* to lather one of his fine thoroughbred horses over?"

"Depends on what you did," she said dryly. From the stories she'd heard, *El Gato* would kill a dozen horses to track down a hated enemy.

The stranger's lips flattened in another grin. His dark eyes twinkled with mischief. Without taking his gaze from hers, he eased the door shut and leaned his broad shoulders against the wall between the door and the curtained, plate-glass window. A humorous light fairly danced in his cocky black eyes.

A gun fired outside. The stranger frowned and turned to peer out the window. He raised one arm and scratched the back of his neck. From behind, the smooth swell of his shoulders flattened and tapered into a lean waist. He would look wonderful on horseback. His neck and the curve of his broad back looked just like Papa's. Tía sighed. She felt sorry for men with scrawny necks and flat backs.

Looking outside, Tía saw *El Gato Negro*'s small army ride into the street in front of the dress shop. The man at the head of the plunging riders raised his gloved right hand. At this signal the surging knot of renegade Indians and dangerous-looking Mexicans—bearded and mustachioed, with high-crowned sombreros—reined in their horses. The rattle of stirrups and creak of saddles mingled with the stamp of the horses' hooves and the exclamations of the crowd as the riders fought the fiery horses to a standstill. Tía loved horses. She could tell these were wonderful, fast, strong-hearted horses. Her hands itched to stroke one of them.

The stranger turned back to look at her. Warm amusement sparkled in his black eyes. His straight black lashes were so dark and sooty, she nearly suspected he put coal tar on them the way some of Mama's women friends did. Grinning, he crossed his scuffed boots and hooked his thumbs in his gunbelt as if he had all the time in the world and intended to spend it looking at her.

"For a hunted man, you look mighty relaxed. With fifty *bandidos* after you, I'd think you'd be hightailing it out of Tubac." The stranger grinned his boyish grin, and the heat that had started when she'd ridden Cactus Flower that afternoon pooled in her belly and flushed upward to burn her cheeks. Such startling feelings confused Tía. She had known since she was fourteen or so that her body sometimes did things without her permission. It never seemed to wait for her head to figure things out. It just raced her along, and she had to hang on as best she could.

Usually these feelings were caused by riding bareback or taking warm baths or just lying on the warm ground in the sun. A time or two it had been brought on by waking up in the middle of the night and hearing her parents making love. Tía knew what men did to women. She had seen horses and other animals mate. Their frame house was too small to allow real privacy even behind a closed door. In the middle of the night on those rare nights when Papa was home, Tía had heard her parents creaking their bed and whispering gasped-out words. Certain times, when her own body got itself in a dither, she had dreamed of some man making love to her in that urgent, breathless fashion. One time she had even thought of Papa.

Mama would sure laugh at that if Tía ever told her, which she wouldn't. Tía knew her body had a way of stirring up its own problems, but the tingling sensation that nearly capsized her now had never been so obviously tied to a man before.

"What makes you think an important man like *El Gato* would be chasing a small fry like me?"

"Because I know everyone else in this town," Tía challenged. "And besides, you're hiding."

He glanced through the curtains—faded in all the places where the sun hit them and vibrantly colored in the protected creases. "You're hiding, too. All the white folks with good sense are hiding," he drawled.

Tía shrugged. He had the easy banter; he could be a drummer. But he was too relaxed. He looked like a cowboy, but most cowboys lived such a solitary life that they got tongue-tied talking to females. He took off his hat, wiped his forehead with his sleeve, and sailed the hat to the middle of the floor.

Tía couldn't begin to explain to him that she wasn't really white. People who considered themselves white had a hard time understanding how a blue-eyed blonde could be Mexican. "Something's different in the way you're hiding, though."

Still grinning he shook his head. "Mighty observant."

"I'm still alive, aren't I?" she snapped. Tía had lived in the Arizona Territory all her life. If a woman wasn't observant, she didn't survive. He looked like he'd grown up here, too. So why was he treating her as if she were a tenderfoot? Tía glanced back at the mirror. She didn't recognize herself immediately. She had momentarily forgotten the bonnet, and her cheeks were as richly colored as ripe watermelon. Not even Papa would recognize her with such fiery red cheeks and her telltale blond curls hidden.

"Is that really *El Gato Negro?*" she asked, edging closer to the window. But Tía had lost interest in the bandit. She merely glanced out, then let her attention return to the interesting stranger who must be awfully dangerous himself, else why would *El Gato* be chasing him?

The stranger squinted to see through the translucent curtains covering the window and nodded in answer to her question. Even if he hadn't nodded, she would have known by the way his dark eyes changed. For one brief second the smile died out of them, leaving them as expressionless as black buttons.

"You better get down," she whispered, and tugged the stranger's warm leather vest until he complied.

Tía knelt on the floor so only her eyes peered over the windowsill. The stranger knelt beside her. "You're gonna be wanting to put me in one of them contraptions next," he said, cutting his eyes upward to the rim of her bonnet.

Tía laughed at the thought of this big, strapping man in a bonnet. His face was the color of terra-cotta—a warm, sun-reddened color that shaded into bronze where the beard stubble showed through from midear to the base of his throat.

Outside, someone fired a gun. As the dust cleared Tía could see *El Gato,* dressed in the tight-fitting *charo* suit of a genteel Mexican horseman—dusty black cloth jacket with silver ornaments and toggles, dark trousers with rows of silver buttons on the side seams, and a white shirt with flowing cravat. He rode past the dress shop and stopped.

His back to Tía's window, *El Gato,* tall and sturdy on his shiny black horse, stood up in his stirrups and appeared to survey the townspeople lining the dusty road. Tía had never seen such excitement and loving admiration on the faces of her friends and neighbors.

"Find him and bring him to me," he commanded in Spanish. That jolted Tía. *El Gato* did not see the love on those faces. He was looking for the man who had violated his code. Tía glanced knowingly at the stranger beside her. He raised his eyebrows and started to crawl away.

On the street, Elvira Arrabella, as thin and stooped as a splayed donkey, stepped off the sidewalk. In her usual shapeless, faded black garment, she left the crowd and walked quickly to stand before *El Gato Negro*'s big black horse. Crossing herself, Elvira bent low as if before a king and began to cry loudly. *El Gato* held up his hand. His men, about to ride away to begin their search, stopped. Tía could not believe any woman would be foolish enough to bring herself to this man's attention unless she wore her Sunday best.

"*Gracias, patrón,*" Elvira sobbed, in her high-pitched, reedy Spanish, which was hard to understand because of her crying. All waited until Elvira could control herself. Tía sighed. They would be here awhile. Elvira had many problems.

"Thank you for coming. It is true that your powers are great! You have detected much evil here, *patrón.* The town marshal lies against us. My own grandson has been sentenced to hang for a crime he did not commit." The old woman burst into fresh sobs, unable to continue.

El Gato reached down and stroked her head.

In her mind, Tía could hear Elvira telling her friends and neighbors about the magic of *El Gato Negro*'s touch. They would hear of nothing else for years. *He touched me. Me. Elvira Arrabella. A lowly peasant. His hand barely touched me, but I felt it the length and breadth of my body...*

Tía wished she could see *El Gato*'s face. Would it be as handsome and fine as his lithe body?

"Thank you, *patrón.* Thank you," Elvira said, sobbing into her hand. Tears streamed down her face in a continuous sheet. Tía would be sick of hearing about this day long before Elvira tired of telling about it.

"*El Gato Negro,* as God is my witness, my grandson, though wild, is a good, hardworking boy. He is innocent. Save him, *El Gato Negro*! Save my boy!"

Racked by sobs, Elvira flung herself forward to kiss *El Gato*'s dusty boots.

Tía snorted and shook her head. Leather creaked and groaned as three sombreroed *bandidos* dismounted.

The stranger grinned over at Tía as if pleased she was not taken in by the wonder of *El Gato.* His deep-set black eyes twinkled with a look Tía thought was either admiration or appreciation. He swatted at a fly that had buzzed down. His arms, at least as much as she could see beneath his turned-up shirt-sleeves, were covered with silky black hairs. In so many ways he looked like Papa, a healthy animal himself—richly colored and fairly bursting with masculine vitality.

The stranger looked at Tía, and she turned her attention back to the street.

With the awkward stride of men crippled by too many hours in the saddle, the *bandidos* limped toward the jail. Mexican men near the jail pointed to the north. *El Gato*'s men hobbled back to their leader.

"Bring him to me!" *El Gato Negro* thundered, his deep baritone voice filling the town and sending a chill down Tía's back.

El Gato's men mounted their dusty horses, whipped their tired mounts, and disappeared beyond the cloud of choking dust they left behind. Tía gritted her teeth at this display of needless cruelty to the beautiful animals.

"I'd like to whip them until their own folks wouldn't know 'em from a stack of fresh hides," the stranger muttered.

Tía flashed him a look of gratitude. The crowd on the street waited expectantly, silently, except for the shuffling of feet against the rough wooden sidewalks and an occasional jingle of harness or stamp of iron-shod hoof on the dry, powdery surface of the rutted road.

The man beside Tía eased himself around, leaned his back against the window, and crossed his long legs. Within seconds his breathing evened out.

Tía poked him. "You asleep?"

One narrowed black eye opened slowly and looked at her with chagrin. "Not anymore."

"I can't believe you'd go to sleep with fifty men outside waiting to hang you."

"You'd believe it if you knew how hot it is out on that desert and how long it's been since I cooled my saddle."

"What's the heat on the desert got to do with it?"

"You see that coyote dun across the road over there?"

Tía rose up slowly and located the dun with a dark stripe down the middle of its back. "Yeah. He's a little coon-footed, isn't he?"

"He is not. Pasterns are a little low, but he's a clear-footed hoss if I ever had one. He's never once stepped in a gopher hole." He shook his head in disgust at her attempt to downgrade his horse. "Like a fool I left him out in plain sight. He's the sum total of all I own or love in this world, and he's too winded to ride another yard. He needs a long walk, a heap of rest, and water and grain. I'm damned sure not going to high heel it out of this town."

"What'd you do?"

"Nothing."

"They didn't chase you all this way to show you the danger end of their guns for nothing. Don't lie to me if you want me to help you."

"I can't even imagine anything you could do to help me against them. They spot a pretty little thing like you I'll have to kill a whole passel of 'em just to save your neck."

Tía grinned. "It isn't my neck they'd be interested in."

The honesty and lack of pretension in her statements caused Johnny Brago to look closer at the girl. Her sardonic eyes shone with a sassy light that tickled his funnybone. She lived in the same world he did. He'd suspected it when he saw how she reacted to the bandits whipping their tired horses. She had round blue eyes, the color he called flag blue, and the sweetest curve of cheeks and swell of lips he'd ever seen. A fringe of short blond hair poked out of the pretty gray bonnet she wore.

"It didn't seem like much, anyway. One of *El Gato*'s men rode into the saloon where I was having a drink, and I had to shoot him."

"You *had* to shoot him? How come?"

"He tried to drag a woman off on his horse."

"You were asleep then, too, weren't you?"

Johnny pondered how she knew he had been asleep. He'd dozed off in one corner of the saloon. Beer too early in the day made him sleepy. But he'd been so thirsty that nothing in the world had satisfied him but a beer. Some Indians he knew got mean, but he just got sleepy. To his way of thinking, sleepy was better. Of course he was only one-quarter Indian, which might not count for anything since he looked like a carbon copy of his father who had no Indian blood at all.

"I woke right up," he protested.

"He rode a horse upstairs?" she asked, raising one pale blond eyebrow.

"How'd you know that?" Johnny looked at the mouthy little blonde with new respect. She was either durned smart or one of the best guessers he'd ever met. The Mexican bandit had ridden his horse right up the stairs, snatched up one of the whores, and was on his way out the door with her when Johnny woke up and plugged him. Folks asked him why he'd done it, and he couldn't think why exactly except that he didn't think a woman ought to be carried off against her will. His friend Tom had said, "Hell, she was just a whore," but her being what she was didn't matter to Johnny. She hadn't wanted to be kidnapped. And he hadn't liked the look of the bandit anyway. Johnny hadn't killed the bandit. That was probably his mistake. If he had killed the drunken *bandido,* the man wouldn't have brought fifty more bandits down on his head.

Tía laughed at the young man's discomfort at her knowing what he'd been up to. Every town had some kind of whorehouse. According to the gossip around Mama's kitchen table, all the cowboys went upstairs at least once a week, more often if they could afford it and could find some way to get into town. They claimed some of the gamblers and bandits who lived in the hotel went upstairs every day if their money held out.

"What's your name?" she demanded.

"Johnny. What's yours?"

"Tía."

The blast of a shotgun rattled the window. Tía turned and peered through the curtain. She didn't dare call attention to them by moving the curtain. One of *El Gato*'s men lowered the shotgun he had fired into the air. Slender young *vaqueros,* rosy-cheeked girls, stoop-shouldered old men, smooth-faced, buxom women, and round-eyed children—barely breathing in their excitement—lined both sides of the road and crowded as close as they dared to their hero and protector. Tall and broad-shouldered, *El Gato* sat his horse like a king. Tía could easily fall in love with a man who sat a horse like that. She wished he would turn around so she could see his face.

A sharp biting sound—like the sudden yip of a coyote—caused Tía to look south. Belly down, arms folded over his face for protection, flailing at the end of a rope tied to the saddle horn of one of *El Gato*'s men, Bethel Johnson bounced over the rough, scorched ground. A funnel of red dust floated above him.

Tía had never liked Bethel—whenever she passed him on the street his gaze crawled over her body like ants over sweet bread—but her heart pounded with dread and fear for him now. Where were his deputies? Usually the three of them were inseparable. Tía looked at the stranger beside her, who had also turned to look out. His warm shoulder brushed hers. Tía felt that one spot of contact travel the length of her body.

Johnny glanced over at the pretty little blonde. Her look seemed to accuse him. Johnny shook his head. "He ain't done me no favors. That's how I got into this spot—minding other folks' business."

Two of *El Gato*'s men jerked Bethel to his feet. He staggered drunkenly as if from a blow to the head and faced the dress shop. For one moment his gaze—wild, drenched with fear—seemed to connect with Tía. She shivered helplessly.

Other men brought Elvira's son, Fidelio, from the jail. Now Fidelio and Bethel faced Tía and waited. In a stern voice *El Gato* questioned Bethel and then Fidelio until he seemed satisfied he had heard the full story from each of them. Then he raised his arms and spoke to the Mexicans, who crowded around his horse. Tía held her breath. *Turn around,* she prayed. *If I'm going to be in love, I want to see your face.*

"All those who believe this swine's story, raise your voices in his behalf," he yelled, pointing to Bethel. Raised in anger like that, *El Gato*'s voice sounded vaguely familiar to Tía. She strained forward, wondering where she might have heard that rich baritone before. Could *El Gato* be someone known to her? Perhaps one of the hunted men who rode in and out of Tubac?

On the street, silence reigned. No white man stood in this crowd, and no one stepped forward now to defend the trembling marshal. Tubac was a Mexican town, but the men who ran it were white, no doubt a holdover from the days when Tubac was a garrison town. The Mexicans were accustomed to being ruled by either the Spaniards or the Americans. Tía had mixed loyalties. Her father was Spanish, her mother English, from an upper-class family in Albany, New York. But the Garcia-Lorcas lived among the Mexicans as if they were Mexican.

Mama laughingly said that it allowed her more freedom. White women were trapped in what she called the "Anglo myth of virtue." Simple Mexican women were free of that stifling Anglo myth and could—outside the shadow of the Church—live almost as they pleased. So amazingly, even though she was as blond and blue-eyed as Tía, Rita Garcia-Lorca lived as a Mexican. People believed her rather than trying to explain to themselves how a white woman could live in such a fashion. Her fate was no different from that of Mary de Crow. Mary had been one of Mama's few white friends in Prescott. She'd come from Texas with a black man, lived with him for two years, then left him for a Mexican man. Respectable folks—brown, black, or white—had no trouble believing Mary was Mexican. Somehow only the unrespectable ones seemed to know she was white. That's how Tía knew Mary wasn't black or brown. When Mama moved back to Tubac, they'd lost track of Mary.

El Gato Negro turned back to Bethel Johnson and waved his hand. Bethel's knees buckled. Three *bandidos* stepped forward, caught him, and half carried him to a horse standing in front of the saloon. A *bandido* in a patched serape helped them hoist Bethel onto the passive horse, swishing its tail at flies. The other two rough men supported Bethel's weight so he didn't fall off.

The *bandido* with the patched serape put a rope around the sagging, dazed marshal's neck and led the confiscated horse nearer the saloon. He threw the free end of the rope up and around a wooden porch overhang and secured it. Then, without ceremony, he slapped the horse from under Bethel.

Tía shook her head and glanced meaningfully at the man beside her. "Maybe you better git."

Johnny's dark eyes flashed with humor and appreciation at her astuteness. "Reckon I better, but I doubt I can walk fast enough to outrun fifty bandits, even if their horses are a mite tired."

Outside, a glad cry rose from the crowd. Other justice was dispensed, but Tía preferred not to watch. While she wished folks no harm, she was practical enough to know she couldn't stop *El Gato*'s justice. She contented herself with waiting and sneaking looks at the man beside her. He'd been riding hard. His clothes smelled dusty and sweaty. Even his dark leather vest was covered with a fine mist of dust. At some point she noticed the noises from the crowd outside had changed.

Then *El Gato*'s voice rose to ask if the citizens of Tubac had any further cases for him to judge. No one responded.

"Now that the three oppressors have been dealt justice, we will have a celebration!" Whoops and hollers reverberated in the street.

Bandidos, firing guns into the air, spurred their horses toward the several saloons in town. Bullets zinged overhead, and the window above Tía was hit.

The stranger scrambled over her instantly and flattened her to the floor with his body. The window quivered for a moment, then shattered and fell. Pieces of glass hit the floor by Tía's face. Gunshots zinged overhead and ripped into the wall at the back of the small shop. Tía gritted her teeth and squeezed her eyes shut, dreading the feel of bullets slamming into her flesh.

Then, as suddenly as it had started, the firing stopped. Tía didn't move. The stranger felt too still. "Are you dead?" she whispered.

"Don't know." His voice sounded odd, sort of tight and harsh.

"Oh, damn," she muttered. Tía wiggled around until she turned over beneath him to face him. His eyes were open. The look in them reminded her of how she felt when she rode Cactus Flower and got herself all steamed up.

He raised his eyebrows at her in a look that seemed to fuel her agitation, then he sat up and carefully brushed the glass off her. A faint pulse rose and then throbbed insistently between her legs. Tía gasped and moistened her lips. She felt a shocking connection with Johnny. Looking into his eyes, she suddenly knew what men did to women and why. It must be this overpowering feeling of connection that drove men to spend all their money with whores. Only this feeling could explain why they made such fools of themselves over women. And why women found them so comical and helpless at times. Tía was relieved to have finally figured out the puzzle.

Johnny's face was too close. Her eyes felt as though they might cross from trying to see him plainly. His warm breath fanned her cheek. She wanted to look away, but something in his eyes had captured her interest and would not let go. Tía licked her lips nervously. His gaze darted from her eyes to her lips and back again.

His mouth opened, as if to speak, but then without seeming to move, his warm, open mouth touched her lips. A spear of heat rushed inside her, and she was shocked by the feel and taste of Johnny's tongue, tantalizing her and moving inside her, causing a rush of feeling that made her knees as weak as water.

An involuntary shudder rippled through her body, and she felt herself somehow moving from not touching him to being pressed dangerously against him. Her arms slipped up to tighten around his sturdy neck. Tía knew next to nothing about kissing, but this couldn't be kissing. Elmo had kissed her only last week. Elmo's mouth had felt wrinkled and dry. Johnny's mouth felt as smooth and hot as sun-steeped apricots after you got past the skin—all heated and ripe and soft inside. His mouth moved, and strangely her mouth did, too. She kissed him with a hunger so deep it would have scared her if she'd been warned about it, but since it was only happening this second, it didn't scare her at all. Something she'd never felt before guided her body, and she sighed, content that she would feed here until her body was satisfied. Her body was following its own wisdom now.

Johnny had rearranged Tía, so she was pressed against the length of him. Under her clutching fingers, his shirt and the incurving part of his back were wet with sweat. Freed up to move as she wanted, she still couldn't get either close enough or satisfied enough to let go of him.

Suddenly she heard a loud voice: "Find that *gringo* and bring him to me." In her mind's eye she saw the contemptuous curl of her papa's lips. No one said *gringo* with the same growl and snarl as Papa.

Jolted back to reality, Tía opened her eyes and tried to get loose, but she only managed to poke Johnny in the eye with the brim of her bonnet.

"Take this thing off," he protested, tugging at the bonnet. "You almost blinded me."

"No..." She held tight to it. It was the most elegant bonnet she had ever tried on. If *El Gato* discovered them, she wanted to be wearing it.

Johnny relented and kissed her again. Then Tía remembered where she was. And who was outside. That had not been Papa's voice. It was *El Gato*. Slowly she relaxed back into Johnny's arms.

Johnny expelled a frustrated breath. "I gotta go," he whispered.

"You sure do."

"You live around here?"

"Yes."

"Meet me tomorrow or the next day or the next. I'll get back here as soon as I can. Will you meet me?"

Tía nodded in agreement.

He touched her cheek. "Tía," he whispered. "It suits you. Here," he said, reaching into his pocket to pull out two dollars. "Buy that blasted bonnet you love so much."

Tía started to protest, but Johnny pulled her close and hugged her so hard she felt sure her ribs would crack. Even so, it wasn't quite tight enough for that hungry part of her.

"Stay here," he ordered. "Don't even look out there. They might see you. And I can't save you from all of 'em."

He let her go and crawled toward the back door. His booted feet disappeared into the alley. Unable to help herself, Tía struggled up and looked out the window. Now three *gringos* hung from ropes—three men who only moments before had been as alive as she.

As if the peasants had gone mad with the freedom that was theirs as long as their champion, *El Gato Negro,* ruled Tubac, the town filled with the sounds of revelry—laughter, music, loud bragging, and the shouts of jubilant children.

Tía stood up and walked carefully toward the back of the store. Cactus Flower was tethered to the hitching post two stores down, in plain sight of *El Gato's* men. She would have to walk.

The alley was empty except for a scrawny yellow cat that meowed loudly and plaintively when he saw her step into the alley. Staying in the middle, as far away from either side as she could get lest someone reach out and grab her, Tía walked as fast as she could without wearing herself out. It was a long walk home. Johnny was nowhere in sight.

Bright, hot sun beat down on her, and the alley gave way to a side street bordered by faded wooden shacks set back from the wide road. With the sounds of the revelers behind her and only the barking of dogs, whinnying of horses, and the soft, crunching sound of her boots pressing into the sand to keep her company, Tía quickly regained control of her self.

The alley smelled of burning lard, mesquite smoke, and refried beans. A whiff of corn tamales told her that not everyone had rushed to see *El Gato.*

A foot-long turtle gnawed a newly opened yellow blossom at the base of a prickly pear. It had rained yesterday. Summer was the rainy season, and all manner of creatures that usually slept in the daytime came out to feast on puddled water and tender new shoots and blooms. The turtle's lumpy, squarish, green-and-yellow head looked as if it belonged on a snake.

At the end of the dusty, rutted trail, beneath a tall stand of cottonwoods, the small rented house she shared with Andrea and Mama stood alone. A narrow stretch of desert separated Tía Andrea's house from theirs. Tall weeds and grasses sloped off, eastward, into a low sweep of ridges and mesas. Another stand of cottonwoods hid the schoolhouse where Andrea taught. Had Andrea and Mama also witnessed the events in town? Mama probably had. It was her day to work at the Blond Russian saloon. She must have seen everything. Andrea would still be at school. She might not have seen anything.

A long-eared jackrabbit sped across her path. It looked like a tiny antelope with extra-long legs. The fur on its flank flashed white, then brown, and Tía blinked. If she lived on this desert forever, she would never get used to the way the jackrabbits could change color while running. Papa said it was to confuse their pursuers.

Walking fast and looking back over her shoulder, Tía wished her Papa were there to protect her from *El Gato*'s bandits. She could imagine falling in love with *El Gato* or Johnny, and she could imagine them protecting her from bandits. She knew her Papa would protect her if he were there, but Papa just couldn't always be there when she needed him. Tía loved Mama, but she adored her papa. A good warm feeling filled her heart at the thought of Papa. Andrea might look like Papa, but Tía rode like him. Papa's pride in her riding set Tía apart, even from her sister. Papa said no one rode like his Teresa. The pride in his voice was all the incentive Tía needed.

Usually she liked being alone, but now she prayed that if Papa wasn't there, Andrea and Mama would be home, safe, waiting to greet her.

Its shingled roof glistening under the hot sun, the square, wooden house perched next to a small patch of garden. She and Andrea had planted peppers, corn, onions, melons, beans, and tomatoes. A faint, hot breeze flickered and rattled the white-woolly leaves of the cottonwoods. The flavorful aroma of beef stew greeted her on the porch, but she knew from the empty feel of the close, hot house that no one was home.

Tía stepped inside, looked around, and then hurried to stir the beef stew that simmered on a back burner. She breathed deeply of the aromatic smell. A sound drew her back to the door. A rider cantered toward the small house. Sunlight flashed off a silver bangle.

It was *El Gato*! Tía forgot her romantic hopes and dreams. Her heart leaped with fear. *El Gato* coming here?

Her gaze darted wildly, looking for help—for Papa or Johnny. Gray and olive green in the foreground, shading into the palest purple in the distance, the desert—dotted with clumps of sage, mesquite, creosote, ironwood, and cactus—shimmered under the hot sun. Except for *El Gato,* no human figure marred the desert scene.

The faint pounding of *El Gato's* horse's hooves grew louder, more insistent. Even from this distance Tía could appreciate what a fine figure of a man he was. He rode his enormous black horse as if he were an extension of the fiery animal. Straight-backed, broad-shouldered, and lean-hipped, he rode the way the men in her dreams rode—the way Papa rode, the way she imagined Johnny rode.

El Gato ran his horse almost up to the porch and then reined him in. Tía stood her ground. She could run, but on that horse he could catch her easily. She could hide, but he would have to look in only four rooms to find her.

Screaming, the black clawed the air with his great hooves and then slowly settled down. Beneath *El Gato Negro's* flat-crowned hat, her father's face stared back at her.

"Papa," she said dumbly. Her feet—accustomed to running to meet her Papa—rooted to the porch and would not move.

"Teresa? *Dios…*" Mateo Lorca cursed softly. He had seen a woman he'd thought to be Rita and had followed her. Teresa must have grown up more than he had remembered. Six months ago she could not have fooled him.

Rita would be angry he had revealed himself to Teresa, but Mateo was accustomed to his wife's anger. He would simply tell her that any young woman who could fool a man into not recognizing his own daughter is old enough to know her papa is *El Gato Negro.* Mateo patted Panther's heaving side and waited for Teresa to collect her thoughts. Her eyes were so blue and clear he could read every passing emotion—shock, fear, disbelief, and finally resignation. Slowly he dismounted and climbed the steps to the porch.

Tía backed away from him. Mateo shook his head and pulled her roughly into his arm. "Forget what you saw in town. I am still your Papa."

Tía struggled against him for a moment and then became still. He smelled like Papa. He sounded like Papa. But still part of her could not believe *El Gato Negro* was Papa. But he had sounded like Papa in town, and Papa always called her Teresa; when he was especially proud of her, he called her Teresa Garcia-Lorca, and his black eyes fairly snapped with pride. Papa disdained the nickname Andrea and Mama used. They called her Tía, Spanish for aunt, because she reminded them of Tía Andrea, the old woman who had cared for Mama since before Andrea was born. But Papa called her Teresa.

Tía lifted her face from his shoulder. "Why didn't you tell me?" she said accusingly, her eyes brimming with tears.

"Your mama would not permit it. She said you were too young to understand. I argued with her, but since it was not important..." He shrugged. "Women like to think they have won arguments. Where's your mama?"

"In town."

Mateo did not like that news. Rita had strong feelings about his role among his people. She would not be pleased at what she had undoubtedly seen today. Mateo blamed that damned *gringo*, Johnny Brago, for leading him here. Brago could have run anywhere else and not caused all this trouble.

The look on Teresa's face was so tense and miserable that Mateo shook her and pulled her close. "I missed you, little one. Every time I saw beautiful horses I thought of you, bareback, mounted on the fastest, strongest stallion, your hair whipping around your shoulders..."

"I'm surprised you recognized me with this bonnet on."

"You could not fool me," he lied.

His dark, hawklike face broke into a grin, and Teresa flushed and brushed aside the memory that she had been attracted, repelled, and frightened by him less than an hour ago. With his perfectly chiseled, sun-browned features, fierce black eyes, and glossy black hair, Papa was the handsomest man she had ever seen. She could not believe she hadn't recognized him, even from behind. But she had never seen Papa on horseback dressed in that fashion. Always in the past he just appeared at the house, usually while they slept. When he rode, he wore a brown serape that completely hid his body.

Stepping back from her, he pulled off his wide-brimmed sombrero, wiped his perspiring forehead, and pulled her toward the door. Tía put her arm around his waist and forgot everything except how much she loved him.

"Well," Papa observed, "my flower is blossoming, isn't she?"

"I'm almost eighteen. That's old enough to be an old maid." Tía laughed and then sobered instantly. If Mama didn't want her to know that Papa was *El Gato*, then Mama would be furious that she had learned the truth. And when Mama was mad at Papa, no one dared to offer Papa any kindness. No one dared even look at him if he was the cause of Mama's wrath.

Tía felt flooded with confusion—on the one hand she felt like a traitor, torn between upholding the family rules and loving Papa, who broke any of them whenever he liked. On the other hand she felt old enough to know. Poor Mama. All these years she had kept her secret—that Papa was *El Gato Negro*, a hunted man. Of course Tía understood. She was grateful she hadn't known. It was easier to know only that Papa dressed like a poor *gringo* in shabby black frock coats that never suited him the way this tight-fitting charo suit did. She would have hated knowing Papa was *El Gato Negro*, and if Papa were caught, the military would undoubtedly make good on their promise to cut off his head, put it on a stick, and parade it through the towns like a trophy of war. She was glad Mama had pretended he was a businessman who made frequent, long trips to Mexico City.

Tía tried to imagine how Papa's true identity must have affected her mother. Perhaps it explained why Mama didn't even try to be respectable. And then again it didn't. Tía knew that Papa's infrequent visits created tension in the house. Mama would be tense the first day or two Papa was home, and then she seemed to relax. Whatever went on between her parents was never put into words, the same way Papa's activities away from home had never been discussed.

Thoroughly confused, Tía walked to the stove. "Would you like something to eat? We have stew," she said, looking at the large iron pot on the back burner of the wood stove. She and Andrea had cut meat and vegetables into the pot before leaving for school. Tía lifted one of the stove lids. The fire was burned down. Mama must have added wood before she left for work at eleven. The meat would be tender by now. The vegetables had blended their flavors into a fragrant brown soup. Mama must have stirred the stew. It wasn't burned on the bottom.

"*Muy bueno, niña*," he said, switching to Spanish. "I could eat a string of donkeys." In midlaugh he turned back to the doorway as if he had detected some danger. Tía's gaze followed his.

Beneath a billowing, fast-moving dust cloud, a knot of riders approached the house.

"Who is it?" she asked, knowing his vision to be better than hers, better than anyone's. Now she knew why. Years of watching for enemies had honed every faculty to razor sharpness. Was this what had excited her about him? Made her so sure that no man alive was as wonderful and as special as her Papa?

"Just Patchy and some of my men," he said negligently. "Nothing to be alarmed about, *niña*." Restlessly he walked to the stove and lifted the lid on the stew. "Where's your sister?"

"Andrea's at school, correcting papers. She said next month, when I'm through with my last reader, I can be her assistant. Until then I just clean and wash clothes and iron. That's all they think I'm good for."

"Then why aren't you in school?"

"The older kids get out early." She shoved him aside with her hip to fill his bowl and set it—steaming with hot, fragrant beef, tomatoes, carrots, and peppers—on the table. He rummaged through cans and bottles on top of the tall iron stove, which also served as a makeshift pantry.

Knowing what he wanted, Tía leaned down and pushed the faded curtain aside, exposing a shelf where Mama kept a bottle of whiskey. She located a clean glass and placed bottle and glass beside the bowl of stew.

"Ahhh. You know your Papa." Smiling, he dropped onto the chair, lowered his dark head over the bowl, and ate hungrily. The sound of hooves grew to a clattering roar and then subsided abruptly as a dozen of Papa's men reined in their horses. Saddles creaked. Men muttered curses in guttural Spanish. Shortly the shuffle of booted heels accompanied the clink and jingle of one set of spurs scraping across the wooden porch.

Patchy stopped at the door, hat in hand, and waved his men to the water pump in the shade of the cottonwoods on the west side of the house. He walked in, nodded respectfully to his commander, and placed a letter on the red-and-white oilcloth that covered the table. It was addressed to Rita Garcia-Lorca. Still wordless, Patchy clumped outside to the porch and sat down on a chair as if he had been directed to do so. Tía looked questioningly at her papa, but he said nothing, just kept shoveling the food into his mouth. Occasionally he swallowed large gulps of the whiskey.

"What's your Mama doing in town?" he asked between bites.

"Working."

Papa put down his spoon.

Tía shrugged. "She works at the Blond Russian. It's a—"

Unexpectedly his fist slammed onto the wooden tabletop, clattering the dishes. Tía flinched. Usually she felt safe from his anger—it had never been aimed at her before—but now his dark face stifled the words in her throat. Looking into his furious eyes, she knew how poor Bethel must have felt before they hanged him, but she was not really afraid. Papa was frequently furious with Mama. Mama always survived.

"How long has she worked at this...place?" he demanded, his voice containing more fury than Tía had ever heard, even when he had ordered the marshal hanged. He had switched to Spanish. Always, Papa set the language. If he spoke Spanish, the rest of the family spoke Spanish. If he spoke English, they spoke English. Papa could be polite in English, but in anger he always spoke Spanish.

"A few weeks," Tía answered in Spanish.

His fist slammed onto the wooden table again. "Because I am not man enough to provide for her?"

"No, Papa! You're a good provider," Tía replied fervently. "Mama—"

"Then she does it to shame me in front of the town and my people!" he said, his voice tight with fury.

Papa rarely came to see them. Even when he did, he did not mingle with the neighbors. Tía had always wondered why he did not allow Mama's many friends in the house when he was home. Now she knew.

"Unless you made an announcement to the townspeople after I left, no one knows we are connected to *El Gato Negro*. How could she shame you?"

"She shames me with her friends and her working and her…" Papa swelled with rage. His bronze face reddened.

Tía had heard this or similar arguments before. Papa wanted Mama to be invisible, to melt into society, to live quietly and respectably. Mama would rather die. In any town they moved into, according to Papa, Mama became the undisputed queen of the misfits. Other women were content to be simple members of society. Mama needed to reign over at least a part of it, no matter how dissolute.

"Papa…she gets lonely." Tía stepped behind him, put her arms around his shoulders, and hugged him. In truth, Tía realized now that Mama probably did work to shame Papa. She probably knew how much Papa would hate it when he found out. Tía did not fully understand what went on between her parents, but she knew enough to stay out of their affairs. She had already said far too much.

"Pah! Rita is many things, but she is not lonely. See this! She gets mail from strange men."

Tía had forgotten the letter and thought he had as well. Now her gaze flew to the envelope. No name showed in the upper-left corner.

"It is not," she argued.

"I know a man's handwriting when I see it. Here, I will prove it to you."

Tía started to protest but suddenly realized Papa had probably gotten angry to justify opening Mama's letter. Now everything would be Mama's fault, for getting him mad by going to work.

Papa picked up the letter, tore off the end, and tapped out the contents. Without looking at Tía, he unfolded the paper and pointed at the bottom to draw her attention there. It was signed Bill Burkhart. Tía had never heard that name before. She read over Papa's shoulder.

> My dear Rita,
>
> I write this to let you know what is happening here. My doctor tells me I have only weeks to live. In contemplating death, I realize I must leave at least part of what I have accumulated to our daughter, Teresa.
>
> I know you have never asked for anything, and would probably prefer that this not become public knowledge at this late date, and I would like to accommodate you, but...

Tía stopped reading. Something about the feel of Papa had changed, become unpleasant under her hands. She stepped away from him. Papa's dark face seemed to drain of color. He read the letter to the end, crumpled it in his fist, and let it drop onto the bare wooden floor. Her heart pounded strangely. What did it mean—"our daughter, Teresa"?

"That cheating, *gringa* bitch!" he bellowed.

"What does it mean, Papa?"

Panting, too strangled by his own emotions to speak, Mateo looked at the girl. His chest heaved with each breath.

"That bitch tricked me," he rasped.

Teresa reached out her hand to touch him. Mateo recoiled as if her touch would burn.

In his thirty-year battle with the *gringos,* he had become a machine of destruction for his enemies. Long ago he had nurtured his rage against the *gringos* into a monster within capable of doing the things he, Mateo, could not. Now the monster within roared *Kill!* The command, a surprise to Mateo, was accompanied by such a hot flush of energy he could have killed a dozen men with his bare hands, but only Teresa stood before him, and his heart did not yet recognize her as enemy.

Mateo's arm raised of its own accord, but he could not strike the blow. He quivered like a man afire. His internal struggle went on for what seemed a lifetime, then his arm dropped to his side and hung like a drawstring.

Mateo sagged on his chair, suffocated by the sight of his "daughter." He had loved Teresa too long and too well. Hoarsely, he bellowed to his lieutenant. "Patchy!"

Patchy's boots scraped across the wooden porch. "*¿Sí, General?*"

"Find the man...at the Blond Russian...who hired my wife...as if she…were a whore…and let him join the marshal." Ominous silence filled the room for several heart-stopping seconds, then in a voice that chilled Tía to the bone, he added, "Bring my wife to me."

"No!" Tía cried. "No, you mustn't hurt Ludie or Mama. They've done nothing! She wanted to work there. Ludie didn't do anything wrong."

Patchy glanced from Tía to his commander. *El Gato Negro* nodded. Patchy sighed, turned on his heel, stamped off the porch, and yelled to his men. The men mounted quickly and whipped their horses into a gallop.

"Stop them!" Tía pleaded. "You can't hurt Mama!"

"They will both die!" His energy returned, and he knew he had found the proper outlet. Rita would die for her betrayal. He should have killed her twenty-five years ago.

"If you hurt Mama, I will hate you, and so will Andrea. I may no longer be your child, but Andrea is, and she will spit on you!" Tía cried, throwing herself at him. Before he could stop her she hit him hard across the face.

Mateo barely felt Teresa's slap. Normally no one could have hit him and lived to tell about it, but the monster within was as confused as he.

Teresa looked like a wild thing—trying to hit him, to kill him, anything to save her worthless mother. In that moment, with her teeth bared and her face flushed, she looked even more like Rita.

Mateo captured Teresa's wrists and pulled her close to glare into her frantic eyes. "Thirty years ago, when I was younger than you are now, I vowed to kill all *gringos*. Now I am married to one, like an ox in a yoke, and I find I have raised the blonde bastard she shamed me with." His fingers tangled in Teresa's blond curls and jerked her head back, forcing her to look at him. "If I had known, I would have smashed your head against a post…"

With her recently freed hand, Tía tried to hit him again, but he easily deflected the blow. Tears cascaded down her face. She swung again, blindly, awkwardly.

"She thought she had closed the snare on me forever, but now I am loose. Your mother will pay for this…"

"You can't hurt Mama. Or me. You love me!" Tía cried.

"No! I loved a child I thought was mine!"

"You love me!"

Somehow Teresa's fury stripped her of everything except her similarities with that bitch he had not killed when he should have. "I hate that *gringa* bitch I married, and I hate you," he panted.

"No! No! No!"

Blindly, she struck out at him. Mateo captured her flailing arm and pinned it between their bodies. She squirmed in fury and frustration, much as Rita had that first time. The girl even felt like Rita. A familiar stirring quickened within him. He had always exacted his revenge on Rita in this way. It suited her. And him.

"What's going on here?" demanded a shrill female voice.

Mateo whirled. Rita tossed aside a brown cassock, and her red taffeta dress blossomed from beneath it and filled the front door. As he watched, she stepped into the house and instantly took command the way she had always done, from the first moment he'd seen her.

A wave of energy flushed into Mateo, filling his loins with power.

He pushed Teresa aside.

"So, you dare to face me," he growled.

"Haven't I always?"

"Before, I did not know about...her."

Rita looked from her husband to her daughter. From the look on Tía's face, the hurt in her blue eyes, she knew that somehow Mateo had discovered her secret. Rita saw a piece of paper beneath the table, strode forward, picked it up from the kitchen floor, looked down at it, and saw Bill Burkhart's name.

Mateo did know.

"And now that you know?" she asked, shrugging her long blond hair out of her eyes with a flip of her hand and a little tossing movement of her head that always enflamed her husband. Even through his rage, she could see the reaction in him, as if a flame leaped and burned within him.

"Now I will kill you the way I should have..."

Rita laughed. "The way you couldn't have, you mean."

Rage fairly crackled in the air between them. Tía stepped away until her back touched the wall. Papa started toward Mama.

"When did you plan to tell me? Were you saving it for a special surprise? Or had you hoped to get away with it?"

Mama shrugged. "Nothing you can do now will change it. I lay with him," she said, crumpling the paper in her right fist and shaking it at him. "She is mine and his. She had nothing to do with you, and you were too blind to see it. You thought you could father a perfect blonde..." Mama shook her head and sneered. The look on her face caused the blood to drain from Tía's face. It was a look calculated to drive any man into rage. Papa needed less provocation than most.

Papa crossed the space between them in one step and grabbed

Mama by the throat. Tía screamed and flew at him, hit him on the back and head and face with her fists, but Papa seemed not to notice her. She hit him, pulled at his arms, and clawed at his hands to loosen them from around her mother's throat. Mama's face turned red and then blue, and Tía hit him harder, but he ignored her as if she were a harmless gnat buzzing around him.

In frustration and fear, Tía screamed. The sound was so bloodcurdling that Mateo let go of Rita's throat long enough to slap the girl away from him. Tía hit the wall, fell to her knees, and struggled to her feet to throw herself back at her father. This time he raised his booted foot, planted it against her belly, and pushed her away from him. Tía hit the wall so hard that her head filled with sudden darkness. Her knees buckled, but she willed them to support her and struggled up again.

But before she could reach her mother, limp and blue-faced, Andrea ran in the front door, saw her mother caught in a death grip, and grabbed the butcher knife off the counter.

Then, her lips pulled tight in a grimace, the butcher knife poised over her head, Andrea ran at Mateo and plunged the knife into his back. Mateo's eyes filled with surprise, his fingers loosed their hold on Rita's neck, and he fell.

Andrea rushed to her mother's side. Rita sucked in a breath and sagged to a sitting position on the floor beside Mateo, who lay still as death. Facedown, he sprawled on the floor in front of the bedroom door.

"I killed him!" Tía whispered.

Andrea looked up at Tía as if she had gone insane. "*I* killed him, and a good thing, too. Why didn't you do anything? Why did you just stand there? Why did *El Gato Negro* come here? I saw him in town…the children…I couldn't keep them in school…"

"Papa was going to…to…"

"Papa's home?"

Tía closed her eyes. Andrea had not recognized Papa, either, and she had been too stupefied to tell her. Now Papa was dead, and it was all her fault.

Puzzled at Tía's reaction, Andrea turned to look at the man lying on the floor. Her face contorted in disbelief and horror. "Papa!"

Tía slumped down beside Papa's still form. Part of her seemed to be watching from a distance, seemed to know what had really happened. Beyond that one word, Andrea seemed too stunned and too stricken to speak. Mama dragged in a deep breath, rubbed her throat, and knelt beside her husband's body.

Rita's throat ached where Mateo's fingers had tried to squeeze the life out of her. Blood welled up and soaked outward in a circle that covered Mateo's right side. Rita shuddered.

She had seen Mateo ride past, heading for the house. She had grabbed the brown cassock, a souvenir of Ludie Nabakov's, slipped down the back stairs, stolen a horse, and rushed home, barely avoiding Mateo's men.

Blood from Mateo's shirt ran onto the floor. Rita felt his wrist; a thin pulse beat there. She reached into his pockets, searched for the sack of gold coins, dust, or tiny silver bars he always brought for her, found it—a sack of coins this time—slipped it and the letter into her own pocket, and turned away.

"Hurry. Forget everything. We must escape before Mateo's men return," she said, her voice low and steady as she waved her stunned daughters toward the two horses waiting in the front yard, calculating how long Mateo's men would search the town for her before returning, how far the three of them could get on two stolen horses.

When neither girl responded, Rita stamped her foot in impatience. "Come!"

Tía shook her head. "I'm going to stay with Papa."

Rita stepped close and grabbed Tía's wrist. Tía shook her head. "I have to stay with Papa. It was my fault Andrea stabbed him." Grief swamped her. It was all a mistake. Papa wasn't supposed to die because of a letter that should never have been written. She wanted to throw herself across his body and howl her misery.

"I'm not leaving you," Rita said vehemently. "You come, or we all stay and die."

Tía looked at Mama and then at Andrea. They would be killed— all of them. She didn't care about herself, but she could not let Papa's men kill Mama and Andrea. Andrea had slipped into a waking sleep. Her beautiful brown eyes were dry and open, but unseeing. Andrea had never been able to cry, even when tears would be a relief.

"He might be alive," Tía whispered. She could not bring herself to touch him.

"He's dead," Rita lied. "Come, quickly, before they return…"

Tía remembered Bethel Johnson—his body limp as an empty sack—and her feet finally moved. No one had to tell her what Papa's men would do to them for killing their leader. She had learned about his justice that afternoon. She could only imagine with dread the justice of his men, crazed by the loss of their beloved *El Gato Negro*…

CHAPTER TWO

Her gaze fixed on the doorway to the corridor that lead to her father's bedroom, Judy Burkhart huddled in her father's favorite leather Morris chair. Knees pressed against her breasts, eyes downcast, she hugged her voluminous skirts and petticoats in front of her like a shield to protect her from the unaccustomed grief that hung over the room. Attended by Dr. Potter from Fort Bowie, her father lay dying. There was nothing she could do about it except cry; she was drained. They had known since yesterday, when Potter examined him, that her father would not leave his bed alive. She wanted to be with him, but the nurse kept making excuses to keep her in the parlor with the others.

From the corner of her eye she could see her brother, Steve. Next to him, Johnny Brago—tilted backward in a straight-backed chair, his booted feet resting on another chair—lounged in that particularly boneless, indolent posture that characterized him and all his actions.

Johnny glanced at her from beneath the sand-colored wide-brimmed hat pulled low on his forehead, his black eyes narrowed into handsome, cocky slits, and she felt a small jolt of shameful memory. He looked away and said something to Steve. The rich, husky sound of Johnny's voice resurrected a painful piece of the past. For a moment she thought she would be sick.

Judy closed her eyes to shut out the world, but she managed only to shut out the present. The past—hers and Johnny's—was there, and it was almost a relief to feel that old hurt. It was familiar, not frightening—while her father's impending death terrified her.

Almost gratefully, she allowed herself to recall that day three years ago.

Johnny had been in the barn, preparing to leave her and Rancho la Reina forever. She had stepped inside, dragging the heavy, creaking barn door shut behind her, her skirts swirling around her ankles. Like everything her father owned, the barn was large, sturdily built, and well organized. Occasional soft explosions of thunder rumbled from the distant mountains. Her nose twitched with the wild, wet-dust smell of the first raindrops. Cattle bawled outside, and horses shuffled in their stalls. The windows were lit with winter paleness; there was no warmth to it.

Her feet hesitated as she stopped behind Johnny and stood awkwardly, twisting her hands together. He cinched his horse's girth tight, not bothering to look around or acknowledge her.

"Hi, Johnny."

"Yeah," he said grimly.

"Why did you fight him?"

"Because I like the way it feels when I hit him."

There was such fury in that simple statement, and it was so much like Johnny, she almost smiled, but her heart pounded so hard that her mouth only twitched.

"Johnny…" She reached out, touched his broad back, and felt him stiffen and turn to stone under her hand.

"Don't."

The way he said the word—his voice so tight and flat—sent her mind spiraling. "I have to," she moaned. "I can't let you go…"

"Nothing can change that. If I stay here, I'm gonna kill your lover."

Judy flinched. She didn't love Morgan Todd, but she knew it wouldn't help to tell Johnny that. He would think worse of her than he did already—if that were possible. And Morgan—as tall and cocky as Johnny, and as capable with a gun—might kill Johnny instead of getting killed.

She felt like a fool, but she couldn't stop herself. "I love you, Johnny," she whispered to his taut back.

He turned slowly and stared at her as if he had never seen her before. One eye was almost closed; his lean, bronzed face was distorted and swollen from Morgan's fists. Always evident in his high cheekbones and the blackness of his eyes, Johnny's Cherokee heritage dominated his face at that moment. Although coldly controlled, his savage fury was evident in the level, contemptuous way he looked at her.

"Is that why you spent the night in Morgan Todd's bed? Because you love me?"

Tears burned in her throat and behind her eyes—hard, heavy knots of pain. Remembering the events that had led up to this moment, Judy swallowed painfully. Was life so simple for a man like Johnny that he never made mistakes? Did her one mistake give him the right to punish her forever? She'd made mistakes before. He'd forgiven her other things.

Would her life be changed forever because she'd left the dance with Morgan instead of going home where she belonged?

"Well," she said, forcing a smile. "You really wouldn't want to leave without kissing me good-bye. After all, everyone else does…"

Johnny's eyes narrowed, and a tiny starburst of light flashed in his eyes. Watching his lips curl in disgust, Judy stiffened with rage. Without thinking, she hit him as hard as she could across the face.

Johnny stared at her for a moment. Her open palm print on his face flushed with color. Where Morgan's fists had connected, bruises stood out against his rapidly paling skin.

Judy flushed with shame and remorse. "I didn't mean to hit you! I…"

He ignored her words and dragged her into his arms.

At first his kiss stunned her. But after the initial shock, when she finally realized that what he was doing—kissing her in this angry way—was far worse than what Morgan had done, she began to struggle against him, raining blows on his head and shoulders. But he seemed oblivious to everything except the terrible kisses he bestowed. She beat at him until her arms ached, and still he kissed her. Strength gone, sobbing with fury, Judy finally collapsed in his arms, unable to resist. Her arms lifted and encircled his neck, and she felt him grow rigid at her touch.

"Johnny…"

Breathing as if he had run three miles, Johnny drew away from her. Instinctively her hands tried to pull him back, but he pushed them aside. Usually so strong and steady, his hands trembled. Staring at them, her mind still numb from his terrible kisses, she suddenly remembered so many things. Those same hands, covered with blood, had cradled a newborn shoat only seconds after they had reached into the birth canal to extricate it before it suffocated. It had been the last pig in the litter, and apparently old Panbread, the last brood sow on the place, had just worn out after birthing twelve pink little piglets.

Judy loved Johnny's hands—their brownness and their strength. She had watched them stroke a kitten and lift a foal onto brisk, spindly legs. They were hands that had once cradled her face against his chest. Now, rejecting her, they trembled.

"No," he said, backing away from her. He towered over her. She expected him to say something more, something scathing that she would carry like a scar, but he only turned, walked to his horse, mounted, and rode away.

Unable to sit in the stuffy parlor surrounded by so many grieving people, Judy rose to her feet and paced to the window. Nothing moved outside. Looking back, that incident could have happened a hundred years ago. Was it only three? Now Johnny was back to stay. Steve and her father had written to him, asking him to take over as foreman, to replace Midas Curry, dead now, his neck broken by a wild mustang. Johnny had written back, saying he would come the week of the tenth, but he hadn't ridden in until the seventeenth. He had been home four days, but he had avoided her. Even his dark eyes avoided hers. He looked different— older, harder. His new mustache added aloofness and a cocky toughness. Rarely put off by any man, Judy now felt strangely intimidated by Johnny.

She had heard the riders talking about Johnny. They called him a gun shark. Slim claimed to have seen him in blazing gun play. Slim said that Johnny was a man who took his time. *No gun fanner,* he'd said. *Brago took his time. Only had to pull the trigger once.* The other riders had nodded their heads as if they'd understood exactly what that meant. She had questioned Grant about it, and he had said it meant Johnny didn't panic and fire wild shots that made him a risk to bystanders.

Curious, she had watched Johnny covertly, noting the quiet steadiness in his dark eyes and the purposeful way he moved, as if he had boundless self-confidence. He was not the same young man who had ridden away from Rancho la Reina.

Now he looked at her, and the way his eyes slid past hers—not lingering, not interested—caused a vise to tighten around her heart. She was nothing to him. Nothing! She hated him with every ounce of her being. A small muffled sob bubbled up from her stomach, surprising her. She covered her face with her hands, mortified at the pitiful sound that betrayed her.

His unwilling attention drawn back to Judy, Johnny squirmed in his chair. For once her passionate eyes displayed none of the fire and spirit that her father had complained of so frequently and with such bitterness. She had accepted her father's dying. He could see it in her mouth. Usually downturning and expressively mobile, her silken lips were now stiff with desolation.

Nothing showed on his own face. He felt sure of that. He had learned to control what other people saw there, but a pang of protectiveness formed a tight, hard knot in his chest, reminding him that even though he didn't love her, he still felt inexplicably bound to her. Judy felt everything passionately, and she expressed her feelings with the same unharnessed intensity. Other girls could cry, but only Judy could make crying a memorable event. Other women he'd known moved like stiff gray silhouettes against a pale background, with nothing sufficiently vivid about them to stamp his memory.

Except for Tía, who had disappeared so completely he would never find her again. Johnny had waited in Tubac a week for Tía to meet him, but she'd never returned. She'd just disappeared...

Johnny forced thoughts of Tía out of his mind. He concentrated instead on Steve Burkhart, Judy's older brother, who would bear the brunt of Bill's loss because the responsibility for running the ranch and the mine would fall squarely on his broad shoulders. Steve sat in a corner, keeping a morose watch.

Life wouldn't change much for the three Mexican women who shuffled their leather sandals and fingered their beads, whispering prayers for their *patrón*. Or for the other hands who lounged on the long shaded porch of the *casa grande* in sober and watchful postures. Johnny wanted to join them out there, to feel the slight breeze on his face, to smell the sage and enjoy that certain freedom not found inside a house, not even an expensive, sprawling, well-built adobe house. As foreman he belonged with the family. Protocol.

Dr. Potter and a nurse were also there, along with Amanda Adams, who had hoped to marry Bill. Probably so she could share some of the wealth from the Lucky Cuss silver mine in Tombstone. It couldn't be love. Bristling with prickly independence, Bill Burkhart did not inspire romantic love.

Johnny had no aspirations about inheriting anything from Bill. He was only the foreman of the ranching operation. Before he had left, he and Bill and Steve had worked easily together. That would not change. Steve was stable and hardworking—more engineer than cow man—and generally ready to take Johnny's advice on ranching matters.

Johnny was surprised when he heard his name called.

"Mr. Brago," the nurse said, her tone self-important. "Mr. Burkhart wants to see you now."

Every eye in the room was suddenly on Johnny. Coiling forward and then standing, Johnny glanced at Steve and took off his hat before he followed the nurse.

Bill's room was hot. One lamp burned beside his bed. Heavy drapes shut out the bright sunlight. Bill looked strangely fragile and small in the big bed. Was it because Johnny had never seen his boss in bed before?

"Bill."

"Bunch of idiots!" Burkhart growled. "Open those damned curtains. If that bossy nurse tries to stop you, pinch her on the ass. If you can find it under all that starch and sass."

Smiling, Johnny complied, more at ease now that he could see Bill hadn't changed all that much, even on his deathbed. The room filled with light.

"That's better!" Bill growled. "The only good thing about dying is those blamed hypocrites indulge me. I don't have to put up with that bunch of wailing women out there. They can just stay out of my way." He stopped suddenly. "I see you're not crying."

Johnny shrugged. He didn't know how to answer that. He hadn't cried since he was fifteen and returned home to find both parents murdered by Apaches. But Burkhart didn't wait for an answer. "Come over here where I can see you," he said, motioning to the side of his bed.

"How's this?" Johnny asked, complying.

"You in love with Judy?"

"Reckon that's between me and Judy," he said softly.

"Don't play the gallant with me, dammit. I'm dying. I got a right to know."

Johnny frowned. He wasn't being coy. His feelings for Judy were confused and not such that any man would feel comfortable discussing them with the girl's father. Even the reason that had brought him back had become confused and tangled in his mind. Even when he had clearly understood it himself, it hadn't been anything he could feel proud of…

"You gotta be the damnedest, stubbornest cuss I ever knew! You ain't gonna tell me, are you? And me dying." Disbelief mixed with outrage on his thin face; Bill shook his head in accusation. Small patches of whiskers missed by the nurse's razor sprouted like wild grass in the seams and creases of his wrinkled cheeks. Once Bill had been a handsome man— an older version of Steve—passing down the blond coloring and classic features of their Swedish forefathers. Now, at sixty-nine, that shock of flaxen hair was streaked with gray and silver, and his once handsome face was creased into an expression of testy sourness.

Doing a quick calculation, Johnny figured that Bill must have been forty years old when Steve was born, forty-nine when Judy was born. A little late for starting a family. He had already been too cranky to be a patient husband or father. Was that why his wife had run away when Judy was eight? That had been two years before Johnny came to Rancho la Reina, but already Bill had been filled with the bitterness that drove people away from him. Steve had coped by staying in the East as long as he could, getting his degree in mining engineering. Trapped on the ranch, Judy had avoided Bill when she could. Now Johnny was avoiding him as well.

Guilt twinged Johnny's gut. Bill have given him a job and a home after his parents were murdered by renegade Apache warriors. He owed Bill. He would like to give him an answer, but there was nothing he could say that would make Bill feel better.

"Damn!" Burkhart growled, slamming his gnarled fist onto the bed beside his thin form. "I thought you'd take care of Judy. That's why we brought you back here, tracked you down. Damn your lying eyes. I saw how you used to look at her. You cain't fool me there, you closemouthed cuss. You're just tormenting me, ain't ya?"

"*I* ain't tormenting you, Bill. Whatever *you've* done is tormenting *you*," Johnny said quietly. "I keep my broad Cherokee nose in my own feed bag."

"I don't need you telling me that…arghhhh!" Burkhart suppressed a groan. He strained forward tensely, his eyes reflecting an instant of pure agony, beseeching Johnny to help him. His lips worked soundlessly until he collapsed backward, exhausted.

"Johnny," he whispered hoarsely.

"I'm here, Bill," Johnny said gently, taking Bill's hand.

"Oh, God, Johnny, I cain't undo it. I want to change what I done, but I cain't. I'm not man enough. I done it in anger and spite, hankering after vengeance, but now when I don't feel none of them things, I cain't undo it. God knows I never hated that girl. I never did. I admit there were times when I looked at her, and I thought I hated her, but I don't. I swear it." Bill sagged back onto the bed, his breath coming in shallow pants.

"What girl?"

"Judy."

"You want to tell her yourself? She's waiting to see you."

"No. No. There ain't time…" Burkhart grabbed for Johnny's arm, missing it, his fingers tearing at the air as if he could hold himself back from the edge he slipped toward.

"It's okay, Bill. I'm here." Johnny took Bill's hand, holding it tight so Bill would feel it, wondering if he should call for the doctor. Burkhart's hand went limp, and Johnny felt a moment of panic as he realized Bill was dead. He continued to hold Bill's hand for a few seconds, then put it gently down onto Bill's chest, but he didn't feel like calling anyone or moving yet. He felt at once deserted and set up. He didn't understand how or why, but he knew that somehow the old schemer had fixed it so he would bear the brunt of whatever it was he had done to his daughter.

Judy. Her image came into Johnny's mind with the force of a body blow. Long brown hair, eloquent brown eyes, skin as pure and sweet as a baby's, and a mouth that would drive any man insane. Flirt, tease, hoyden, even a cheat and a liar, but never with malicious intent. Judy was a survivor. She had more needs than other girls. She needed more love and attention, and she was willing to pay the price. Only the men she rejected complained.

Johnny clamped his jaws against any more of that kind of thinking. Come what may, it was time to tell Bill's family he was dead.

That first second when Judy opened her eyes, everything seemed fine. As if today would be like any other day. Except for a headache that had formed deep inside her skull, throbbing into life as if nurtured by her waking heartbeats. Where had this headache been while she'd slept?

The sun must be high overhead; shadows on her floor were short. No one had come to wake her. She should feel grateful for the extra sleep, but part of her was scared, as if she had been abandoned in this house. She would get up and be all alone. She strained her ears for any familiar sound. A cow bawled in the distance, and then one of the Mexican women, probably Carmen, scolded someone in Spanish.

Relaxing back onto the bed, Judy closed her eyes. Usually filled with thoughts, today her mind was sluggish and balky. She tried hard not to remember, but with consciousness came the knowledge that her father was dead. As if her grief had been sleeping as well, it stirred and swelled into full-blown nausea. Tears welled in her eyes.

She needed to rearrange her mind, to accept a world without her father. She lay very still. They had not been close for a long time, but he had been the cornerstone of her world. She felt like a house that had lost part of its foundation. Perhaps if she could lie still enough, her thoughts would arrange themselves, but if proper thoughts did come, she did not recognize them.

Her eyes were tired and gritty. She was not ready for the simple burial ceremony that would be held today when her father's friends arrived from Tombstone and Fort Bowie.

• • •

Ready or not, somehow, with Carmen's help, Judy was properly washed, gowned, and combed in time to greet Jim Furnett, justice of the peace, barrister, and her father's friend. He presided over the solemn group of family, friends, and employees who assembled two hundred feet behind the *casa grande*, beside a gaping grave that had not been there yesterday.

Judy sensed the dull sanctity of the occasion in the small things: Furnett's slight self-consciousness as he read from the Burkhart family Bible, Carmen's sniffling, the pungent sweetness of the desert sage, the crackling of stiff yellowed grass as man and women shuffled from foot to foot under the hot sun. Furnett's words did not stick in her mind.

At last it was over. But then supper had to be cooked for all who had made the long trip from Tombstone and the short trip from Fort Bowie. Numbly, glad of anything that took her out of herself, Judy helped serve the heavy platters of food Carmen must have stayed up all night to prepare.

After supper Steve poured whiskey for the men, and then, gratefully, people began leaving, mouthing kind, awkward words of consolation to her and Steve.

Amanda Adams and Furnett stayed. After the last guest departed Furnett asked the family to assemble in the parlor. Needing his strength, Judy sat beside Steve, pressing against his warmth in spite of the heat that still bore down on them.

Furnett read the will as he had read from the Bible, in a stern and solemn voice:

> I, William Zetta Burkhart, of the town of Tombstone, County of Cochise, Territory of Arizona, being of sound mind, make this my last will and testament. After the payment of my just debts I devise and bequeath as follows: To my son, Steven William Burkhart, an undivided one-half interest in Rancho la Reina and the Lucky Cuss silver mine. To my daughter, Teresa Garcia-Lorca, an undivided one-half interest in Rancho la Reina and the Lucky Cuss silver mine. These two bequests are granted with one condition: that each of them live and work together on the ranch or at the mine. If either of them leave the ranch to establish any alternate residence, except as is made necessary by the mining business, he or she forfeits his or her interest in both for all time.

Too surprised and stunned to speak, Judy sat like a stone. Unblinking, as if unaware he had dropped a bomb in the midst of the little group in the parlor, Furnett droned on.

> To Judith Elaine Burkhart, my stepdaughter, I leave the sum of
> five thousand dollars. To Johnny Brago, I leave the sum of one
> thousand dollars. All the rest and residue of my property and
> estate are to be divided equally between my son, Steven, and
> my daughter, Teresa, with the same condition stated above,
> that they live and work together. I hereby appoint my good
> friend, Jim Furnett, Esquire, to be the executor of this will.
> In witness whereof I have set my hand this 10th day of June,
> 1879.
>
> William Zetta Burkhart

"What the hell does this mean?" Steve demanded. "And who the hell is Teresa Garcia-Lorca?"

Furnett cleared his throat. The action, like small explosions that puffed his cheeks out three times, fascinated Judy. Smoothing the parchment between his hands and looking strangely pleased with himself, Furnett fidgeted.

Suddenly everything about this man interested Judy. Smiling at her when they met, asking polite inane questions men ask women and children who do not really exist for them, he had kept his terrible secret for two years, maybe longer. Now his simple, florid face, so impersonal in the past, looked treacherous to her. It was the face of a man who could look simple and uninteresting, but could harbor hurtful, ugly secrets and could write them down in stilted, legal documents, recording them for all the world to know.

Furnett was talking again, but the words were not registering in her mind—it had become resistant to new words. Steve pulled Judy to her feet to stand beside him, his arm holding her trembling body close. What did the will mean? My *stepdaughter*? Bill Burkhart was her father...

Furnett cleared his throat again. "I reckon this is kind of a rough way to find out, but Teresa Garcia-Lorca is your half sister."

Looking up at Steve, Judy flinched. Heat flushed his handsome, usually calm face. His jaw was set, angry. "Like hell she is! Judy is my sister. If my father didn't have the guts to own up to his bastard when he was alive, he can't expect us to do it now."

Seated beside Furnett, Amanda Adams shook her head. "Not only his bastard, but apparently a half-breed as well," she said, her pale gray eyes flashing with righteous indignation. "It's never good—a man like Bill living alone all those years after his wife run off. Mark my words. I

41

told that to Bill himself. Told him a fine-looking, virile man like himself shouldn't be living alone, with only low types and Mexican women. Too many Mexican housekeepers in and out of here all the time..."

Amanda turned on Judy, who was clinging to Steve's arm lest her trembling legs gave way and buckled beneath her.

"Seems strange your mother would leave you with him...him not even being your own pa and all. I sure Lord didn't know you were only Bill's stepdaughter," she said as if regretting the pains she had taken to impress Burkhart with her motherly warmth.

Steve questioned Furnett about ways to break the will. Furnett's answers blurred in Judy's head. Slipping out of Steve's embrace, unnoticed, she walked quickly to her room. Once inside, she stopped at her vanity and stared at her reflection. Her face was pasty white. Her eyes reminded her of her horse, Dervish, after he had broken his leg and she'd had to shoot him. Dead, his eyes had been open, but the light had gone out of them.

She had been disinherited. Her father had left her half of the ranch and mine to his *real daughter*, Teresa. That might have meaning later, but at the moment all she felt was a terrible, all-pervading emptiness. She had felt like his daughter. She had never doubted it for a second. Daddy—Bill Burkhart, she corrected herself—*he* must have known for years.

If he were alive she could reason with him, beg him to see that she really was his daughter. Many times she had charmed him into doing things he didn't want to do. She had loved him as if she were his real daughter. She had put up with his moods and his occasional meannesses and bouts of temper as if she were his real daughter.

It seemed odd that all her years of loving him counted for nothing. Her stomach felt sick with grief, her world was black with it, and yet it counted for nothing. It seemed odd to hurt so bad and be declared *illegitimate* by a few words written on paper.

She would be thrown off the ranch by Teresa, *the real daughter*. Teresa's grief, if she felt anything at all, would be the *real grief*. Judy would be known by everyone as the bastard stepdaughter, an accident left by a woman who also counted for nothing.

The weakness in her legs grew so great that she sagged against the bureau. She could not stay here, and yet she had no place to go. Rancho la Reina had always been her home.

Judy forced herself to look at her room. Usually so cheerful and pleasing with its canary-yellow walls, white rugs, and yellow coverlet, the room now seemed to mock her with its cheeriness. Or was it only that the knowledge that her father—the man she had thought her father— had never loved her, had probably actively hated her, stunned her? Now she understood so many things…so many things…

Understanding the past bewildered her but also pointed out the senselessness of her life, living at the mercy of people who were supposed to care for her but carried out secret acts against her when she was most vulnerable, making her hate herself and her own intense emotions.

She walked shakily from the bureau, slumped onto the edge of the bed, and huddled there, holding herself against the cold ache in her stomach.

Her heart pounded hard and fast in her chest. Judy hugged her fists to her chest. Between two creases, a pulse in her slender wrist puffed up like a worm jerking under her skin, trying to hide. Her thoughts were disconnected by all those heartbeats. There were too many of them. How could she think with so many heartbeats? How could she get control of so many nerves with all that blood surging through her so wildly?

The small worm of her blood that writhed against her pale wrist pulsed rapidly as if trying to push through her.

Alien blood coursed through her veins. Bastard blood. Her chest felt suffocated. Judy wished she were dead. If she were dead, no one would ever be able to surprise her with their spiteful acts of viciousness. Not Mommy, not Daddy, not even Johnny…not loving her.

She sat up and walked down the hall, past the parlor, where they still talked, and around the corner into Steve's bedroom. She slipped inside and opened his top dresser drawer. The straight-edged razor he shaved with gleamed in the near darkness. She slipped it into the deep pocket of her gown and walked quietly past the parlor again.

They would not come looking for her until morning.

Voices raised in the parlor. Judy heard the word "bastard" clearly. They were talking about her. Amanda had finally realized Judy's mother had been married to Bill Burkhart for two years before Judy was born, that if she wasn't Bill's, she had to be Ellen Burkhart's love child, foisted off on Bill all these years as if she'd been his. "Why, I declare," Amanda said, her voice hushed. "Judy is a bastard."

Judy heard Steve's voice, deep, and angry, telling Amanda to get out of the house.

She closed her eyes. Running off Amanda would do no good. All that information was carefully recorded in the Bible that lay on the table in the parlor. The date of their marriage, the date of Judy's birth. Now, her father's rejection of her had been recorded as well. Steve had been fortunate. His mother had died when he was four. *Bastard. Judy is a bastard.*

Shame filled her from within and pushed like a fist against her throat, suffocating her. It was not bearable. She would die of it.

Bastard, bastard, bastard.

Judy slid the razor out of her pocket. She held her wrist and bent it toward her. A tiny bluish vein writhed visibly beneath the surface. That would be the one to cut—the one to pump out her traitorous blood.

She'd accidentally cut herself once. It had burned like fire at the time and hurt for days as if to punish her for being clumsy.

Judy closed her eyes and pressed. It stung like fire. A tiny cut oozed droplets of blood. The knife had moved, probably flinched of its own accord, and only nicked her beside the vein she had wanted to cut.

Sobbing in frustration and frightened determination, she positioned the razor over the tiny vein.

A place on her foot where she'd stepped on a nail when she was ten years old started suddenly to burn. It pulsed with pain and heat as if the injury were only a day old. She remembered how it had gotten infected, and red streaks had started up her leg. Carmen had soaked the injured foot in a solution of epsom salts and hot water every hour for days.

Frustrated, Judy put down the razor. She was not only a bastard, she was a coward.

Bastard. The word evoked a memory in her—something she had forgotten or that had remained hidden in her head the way that terrible secret had hidden itself in Jim Furnett. Now it had become dislodged from its hiding place.

It was about her mother. She could see her clearly. Pretty and busy, her mother wore a blue gown, the same color of blue as her eyes. Her soft golden hair, pulled back over her ears, hung in springy gleaming curls that Judy liked to squeeze when her mother would let her.

Usually her mother would smile at her, but that day she would not.

"Get outside and play!" she said, her voice cross.

"I want to help, Mommy."

"Leave me be!"

"I can help. See?" Judy picked up one of the gowns and tried to stuff it into the satchel that lay open on the bed.

Her mother grabbed the gown out of her hand. "I said leave me be!"

Judy turned her back so she could not see her mother's angry face. A buzzing started in her head. She hummed to shut out the sound of her mother's jerky movements and angry breathing. Judy pressed against the bed and watched her mother fling clothes into the satchel. When she could stand it no more she ran to the closet and picked up a pair of shoes. "These are the ones you like best, aren't they?" When her mother frowned, Judy changed her tactics instantly.

"Oh, drat!"

Careful not to look at her mother's eyes, Judy talked to shut out the sound of her mother's voice. "I washed my face and my hands real good. I ate all my dinner. I cleaned my plate. I'm a good girl, Mommy. See?" she said, holding out her hands so her mother could appreciate how clean they were.

"Leave me be! Just leave me be! Child, can't you see I'm busy?"

Judy tasted wetness on her lips, salty wetness. Seeking comfort, trying to burrow into the soft fullness of her mother's gown, she pressed close. Her mother always smelled nice and wore gowns that felt cool and smooth against her skin—smooth and silky and cool.

"Get away from me!" her mother screamed.

But Judy would not turn loose. She could feel her mother's hands frantic and clawing at her arms, but, screaming to shut out the sound of her mother's voice, she buried her head. Then her mommy screamed. Strong hands pried Judy loose. Sobbing, trying to find her mother again, Judy stumbled and fell. Above her, Daddy towered over Mommy and her. Mommy backed away.

"Don't take it out on the girl, you slut!"

"If it weren't for her, you'd never have known."

"You mean if he hadn't turned up here, like a dog sniffing out a bitch, don't you? It ain't her fault. You hit her again, I'll kill you."

Their voices beat at her ears. Judy covered her ears, but she could still hear them.

"Pack your war bag and get while the gate's still open!"

"Including her?"

"Suit yourself about that."

"You feel so protective, you keep her!"

Judy covered her ears. As hard as she tried she could not shut out their voices. They were like dogs, tearing at one another. Judy pressed her wrist into her mouth until the pain in her arm screeched along her nerves. Blindly she changed position and bit against a different place.

• • •

"Lawsy, chile, what done happened? Why, your pore little arm is all bloody."

Through a haze of tears, Judy could see Mary Sue's round black face. "I want my mommy," she wailed.

"Your mama's gone, chile. Done gone away for good, I reckon."

"I want my daddy."

"Your daddy ain't in no fitten mood. That pore man done gettin' hisself drunk as a lord. Reckon you better stay with old Mary Sue in the kitchen for a spell."

"He hurt my mommy. I hate him."

"Reckon your mama deserved it, chile."

"No." Judy could feel her face twisting out of shape. "She didn't. I was bad. She had to spank me. I was bad. My mommy loves me. She had to spank me. I was bad."

Mary Sue shook her big head. "The onlyist thing you done, chile, was in lookin' too much like your pa."

"My mommy loves me, doesn't she?"

A queer look of pity brightened Mary Sue's luminous dark eyes. She picked Judy up and hugged her against her big, warm body. "Yes, chile. Your mama loves you a whole bunch."

"My daddy loves me, too, doesn't he?"

"Yes, chile." Mary Sue stood Judy up, straightened her dress, and brushed the wet hair out of her eyes. "Now you all pretty again. You come with Mary Sue to the kitchen. We'll get some salve for that pore little arm. What a mess, chile! Lawsy!"

Judy turned slightly on the bed. Her window was open. Scrawny ornamental trees she had gotten from a mail-order catalog stood in dark outline against the late afternoon sky. The trees would die. They raised their pitiful limbs and dipped their hungry roots into the dry soil in vain. Even the water Steve's irrigation system gave them would not help. She had known they would die when she planted them. They were too pretty. Only ugly, gnarled things could live in this heat and dryness.

Shame was such an ugly, overwhelming feeling. Shuddering with revulsion, she closed her eyes. God, how she hated it all, wanted it to be over. All her life she had been sheltered from the ugliness of women like Amanda Adams, sheltered by her father's money, prestige, respectability. She had been proud to be a Burkhart, with all that the name implied. Now she had been stripped naked in front of her enemies—vulnerable to their vicious tongues and condemning eyes.

Judy curled into a tight little knot on the bed. She should get up and take off her gown, but her limbs felt like lead weights.

An involuntary shiver moved through her. A queer, chill mist filled her head. She had been disowned. Everything she loved and wanted now belonged to Teresa Garcia-Lorca. Tears of frustration and shame burned in her but would not come out. She didn't even have the courage to end it.

CHAPTER THREE

"Tía, where are you?"

Tía looked up from the book lying open unread in her lap. "Out here, Andrea. On the sun porch."

Andrea opened the French doors that separated the sun porch from the rest of the spacious, expensively appointed Caldwell house. "Heavens! It's hot out here. What on earth are you doing here?"

"Wishing I could find Mr. Burkhart," she said, closing the book. She wanted to call him "my father," but she felt too shy to say it so bluntly. *Grieving for Papa and all we lost that day. Hoping Mr. Burkhart can hang on to life long enough so I can find him and get to know him, to find out if he loved Mama enough to make all this trouble worthwhile, if he might even love me...*

Andrea's pleasant, slightly bored expression changed instantly to one of displeasure. "I thought you liked it here."

Liar! You haven't cared whether I did or not. Andrea was peddling a load, but Tía stopped herself in time. She might as well be talking Chinese to a pack mule. Andrea had kept to herself since they arrived in Albany. And because Tía had been grieving for Papa and feeling guilty about letting Andrea stab him, she had let her. They hadn't really talked since the stabbing. When they talked they could work out any problem. When they didn't...But there had never been a time before when they didn't talk. So Tía hadn't immediately figured out what to do about it. Something felt blocked between them now, as if too many assumptions had been made that no one acknowledged.

"I hate it here," Tía finally blurted.

"You seemed to be having fun."

"When I was riding, maybe. I ain't town-gaited the way you are."

"I'm *not* town-gaited," Andrea corrected.

"Yes, you are. You love it here. You could wallow in velvet all day. No one could have fun *here*."

Andrea lifted her chin. "I've enjoyed myself. I won't apologize for that."

"Are you going to forgive me?" Tía asked abruptly.

"For what?"

"For letting you stab Papa."

Andrea looked quickly away. In profile she reminded Tía of Mama. She had Mama's perfect cameo profile, except her complexion was colored by Papa's duskiness and her eyes fringed by the blackest, sootiest lashes Tía had ever seen. Except maybe Johnny's…

"I didn't stab Papa," Andrea said hotly. "I stabbed a man trying to hurt Mama. It just happened to be Papa. I don't blame you. If I hadn't stabbed him, he would have killed her." Abruptly Andrea stood up. "It's time to eat dinner. Mrs. Lockwood sent me." She turned and walked into the house.

Tía watched her sister's slender back until it was out of sight. Andrea lied. She would never forgive Tía. Mama had not bothered to speak of Papa again. Everyone else seemed to think it was over. Tía wanted to talk about it, to understand it, but no one wanted to listen. Just as Andrea had today, they became angry with her, as if by bringing it up she violated some unwritten law.

She did not feel hungry; even if she did, she would not enjoy eating at their table. Her uncle and his housekeeper were grim company. The look in their eyes was cold enough to make a polar bear hunt cover. They caught every mistake, and her manners, learned at Mama's loving but careless elbow, were anything but elegant. Even though they had the same upbringing, Andrea, eight years older than Tía and of a different temperament, managed well enough to keep herself from becoming the center of attention.

Andrea was so different that at times Tía could not believe they were related. Even in Tubac Andrea had lived at a different, more elegant pace. She enjoyed *a soak* in the tub, which meant fragrant bath salts and lighted candles. Tía took as many baths, but she could not sit still long enough to *soak*. Papa had said some horses were built for speed, some for style and looks. Andrea's womanly figure was softly curved, while Tía's was slender and angular. Andrea was a showpiece, and Tía was wiry and fast. Papa's rich voice still haunted Tía. *My Teresa can outride a Comanche.*

The dining room was one of the most beautiful rooms in the house. One entire wall was opened to the backyard by six tall windows. The long mahogany table gleamed in the sunlight.

Uncle Tyler waited until they were seated. Then he stared at Tía, somehow without looking into her eyes. He looked in her direction, his slate-gray eyes cold and glazed as if not allowing images to penetrate to any significant depth.

"Teresa, you received a letter from Tombstone, Arizona," he said, his voice accusing, as if she had somehow solicited the unwelcome letter.

For the first time in months, Tía's blood raced with excitement. Arizona! It must be from Mama. Surely not Papa. But why wouldn't he have said it was for Andrea, also? Tía's impulse was to rush forward and claim her letter, but two months in Uncle Tyler's house had taught her caution.

"May I have it, please?" Tía prayed he would not sense her excitement. Uncle Tyler did not approve of excitement, especially in young ladies. He approved of hard work, strict rules of conduct, impeccable table manners, and frugality.

Over the noise and jostling of the stagecoach Mama had shared with them as far as Douglas, the last segment of their narrow escape from *El Gato Negro*'s enraged men, she had warned them about Uncle Tyler. *He's nothing like the people you're used to in Tubac. These people live close to the earth. They are rough and crude in many ways, but they are honest, and they know a person for their true worth, not for their family, wealth, or social status. I don't envy you this trip or your stay in my brother's house, but I have no choice. I want to know you will be safe. And I trust Tyler in that. He's never turned loose of anything or anyone he's ever owned, except me, and I had to practically tear his arm off to get away from him.*

Uncle Tyler was a full twenty years older than Mama. He called her "Rita," saying it as if Mama's name made his mouth feel tight and soiled. *Probably because he blames me for our mother's death,* Mama had said. Charlotte Caldwell had died giving birth to Mama. With the help of the household staff, Tyler had raised Mama, because their father had been too busy chasing younger women to worry about a baby. When Rita was three, her father was pushed out an upstairs window, reportedly by a terrified maid who had not known her employer would insist on the right to sleep with her.

Uncle Tyler had hired a succession of nannies. When Mama had endured all of her brother's parenting she could stand, she had packed a small satchel and run away.

After two months in her uncle's house, Tía understood perfectly. Compared with Papa, who had been a playful bear with children, Uncle Tyler seemed a cold fish. His hair and whiskers were gray, like new steel wool. With his muttonchop sideburns and his heavy mustache, parted in the middle over tight thin lips, he was a pompous walrus of a man.

Tía waited to see how angry he was. Since they had arrived at his house, he had managed to find something to irritate him at each meal, usually her lack of manners.

"Eat your meal, and then we will read the letter," he said sharply.

"Uncle Tyler, may I ask who the letter is from?"

"No, you may not. We will have our dinner now."

Frustrated, Tía picked up her fork. Sarah Polansky, one of the kitchen maids, deliberately leaned between Tía and her uncle to serve a steaming plate of peas and tiny white onions. Sarah flashed Tía a reassuring smile.

Tía smiled her gratitude. Everyone except Mrs. Lockwood seemed sympathetic to Uncle Tyler's "wild sister's tomboy daughters." Tía knew he was probably not an unkind person, inside. It was just that she and Andrea were more of a nuisance than an old man wanted to deal with at this time in his life. Childless, he and his wife had probably lived quite contentedly until her death. Now, to have two nieces dumped off by an "ungrateful sister," who had "flaunted her reckless life-style" in his horrified and disapproving face and married "a common Mexican," was too much for him to endure.

"Teresa, that is the wrong fork!" Mrs. Lockwood's stern reprimand caused Tía to jump and drop the fork onto the lush Oriental carpet beneath the enormous mahogany table. She leaned sideways to pick it up. In triumph, she swung her arm around and up. Too late she saw Sarah turning to see what the problem was. Tía's arm caught Sarah's tray. The entire bowl of peas plopped onto the immaculate maroon pile.

"Now see what you've done!" Mrs. Lockwood shouted.

Squeaking an apology, Sarah knelt to clean up the carpet. From her toes to her hairline, Tía flushed as hot as a fresh-baked biscuit. Mrs. Lockwood turned to Uncle Tyler. "I do not know what I shall do with her! She absolutely refuses to learn anything. I could make a lady from corn silk easier than from this Arizona trash."

Smacking his lips in chagrin, Uncle Tyler sighed. "Perhaps a good school is the only reasonable answer to the problem. Do you suppose Altadena Herkimer could fit Teresa into one of her classes? She's years too old, but perhaps Altadena would make an exception." He fixed a cold, unfocused gaze on Teresa.

Face burning with embarrassment, Tía thought of herself trying to fit in among twelve-year-old girls learning manners, that thought quickly followed by the certain knowledge that she would never be a grand lady, and that she didn't care. Tía clutched her hands in her lap and tried to remember her promise to be polite and respectful. Tightness constricted her throat. She burned to stand up and walk out of the room, but she knew that would only make the next encounter worse—for her and Andrea. Mentally chanting her promise to Mama, Tía glanced at Mrs. Lockwood, who let her eyes roll upward, shook her head, and looked askance at Uncle Tyler, who said, "Mrs. Herkimer is very selective about whom she accepts, but perhaps if you asked her as a special favor…"

Tía did not dare look at Andrea. If Andrea supported her in any way, she would stand up and walk out of the room. If she did not, Tía would be crushed.

The moment passed. Tía pretended to eat. Her body went through the motions her uncle demanded, but her mind was two thousand miles away in Tubac, Arizona. She longed to be there. The industrialized city of Albany was a shock to her system. She appreciated the modern conveniences—indoor toilets, electricity, telephones, trolleys, swimming pools—and the wide variety of entertainments, but she hated the stifling rules imposed by "polite society." In Uncle Tyler's circle everyone had been respectable so long they had become intolerant. In Tubac, even after one of Mama's friends became respectable by marrying some miner, cowboy, or rancher, she still seemed to remember how she'd gotten where she was.

Here even men had fewer choices. Jack Polansky, Sarah's husband, worked in a factory all day. Separated from nature and from any vestige of satisfaction in his work, he felt no connection at all with the pulley he helped produce. He tightened a bolt on a wheel. Someone else assembled the pulleys for engines that would later be installed in hotels. Jack hated his supervisors, and they hated him. Tía shuddered at the thought of becoming one of those laborers, stifled and cut off from nature.

Here only the rich owned horses. It seemed a living death to her. In Tubac she had been free to ride when she wanted. Here she had to sneak away to the stables to keep her sanity. Without telling anyone, she had taken a job walking horses the young nabobs and debutantes rode. She sneaked away every morning for three hours. In exchange the stable owner let her ride any time she wanted, which worked out to any time she could get away. She pretended to take naps, to be sick, to have a headache. It was easier than trying to explain to Uncle Tyler why she needed to ride those "filthy horses."

Usually she was required to sit in the parlor and pay attention while Uncle Tyler entertained boring people whose sharp eyes flicked over her the way tongues of snakes flicked onto startled flies. Now she understood why women said "Please excuse me. I have a dreadful headache."

"Teresa!"

Her uncle's voice jolted her so, Tía almost dropped her fork again. "Excuse me, Uncle Tyler. I wasn't listening…"

"That was quite obvious, young lady. Sit up and pay attention," he said sharply.

Andrea exchanged a quick glance with Tía. The servants cleared away the dishes. Uncle Tyler made a big production of opening the envelope of her letter; it looked as if it had been opened previously. Tía barely breathed lest he change his mind. As if he were performing a duty that was unpleasant and possibly unwise, Uncle Tyler read the letter in a deep, portentous voice.

> Dear Señorita Garcia-Lorca:
>
> It is my sad duty to inform you of the death of your natural father, William Zetta Burkhart, and to tell you that he has provided for you in his will. Your father owned the Lucky Cuss silver mine in Tombstone and Rancho la Reina in the Sulphur Springs Valley. His will left half interest to you and half interest to your half brother, Steven Burkhart. The only condition to your inheritance is that you must live and work on the ranch. If for any reason either of you finds this unacceptable or intolerable, the entire ranch and mine will revert to the one who remains on the property.
>
> In addition to being his attorney, I was your father's friend and confidant. His greatest fear was that all he had worked for would be thrown away or allowed to fall into decay. There is much more I could tell you, but I will save the rest for a more appropriate time. Please wire me of your expected arrival time, and I will notify Steven so he can meet your stage in Tombstone.
>
> Your servant, James R. Furnett, Esq.
> Attorney-at-Law, Tombstone
> Arizona Territory

Tyler Caldwell folded the letter and inserted it back into the soiled envelope. The skin around her eyes burned and puckered the way it did when Tía was going to cry. She struggled to keep from crying. Mr. Burkhart had died. Ever since she'd reached Albany she had prayed for him and blamed herself for not getting his address from Mama so she could have written to him. Now he was dead. A feeling of darkness and loss filled Tía. Now she would never see him.

"Well?" Uncle Tyler demanded.

Tía looked up at him. "I beg your pardon?"

"We are waiting for your response."

Andrea stood up. "She is crying!"

Uncle Tyler glowered at Tía. "Get control of yourself, young lady. That is unacceptable behavior at this table."

"What do you expect her to do? You just told her that her father is dead." Andrea looked as if she wanted to leap across the table and shake him by the scruff of the neck.

"I will not tolerate your disobedience and disrespect," Uncle Tyler said coldly. Andrea glared at Uncle Tyler. Mrs. Lockwood looked shocked at such unladylike behavior.

Tía quickly stood up. "May I please be excused?"

Chunt, chunt, chunt. Uncle Tyler cleared his throat and looked around the table. His cold gaze settled on Tía.

"You may all sit down. I think you may as well know exactly how I feel about this whole sorry mess," he said gruffly. "First I will take the liberty of clarifying what was not too lucidly stated by this Mr. Furnett, who purports to be an officer of the court.

"If we can believe his almost illiterate letter, I suppose this explains how Teresa was able to retain the Caldwell blondness. It is difficult for me to appreciate which could be worse: that Teresa be the daughter of a living Mexican bandit or the illegitimate daughter of a dead coward." He paused. His gaze slid coldly past Andrea, who did not bother to hide her dislike for him. "Apparently there is no end to your mother's calumny. I find this whole business revolting. Revolting and disgusting! Harumph!"

Teresa glanced from Uncle Tyler to Andrea. Uncle Tyler had no right to condemn Mama. He had driven Mama to run away. She might never fit into his world, but Mama fit very nicely into Tubac's version of "polite society." Vivacious, clever, and gracious, Mama commanded respect from her friends and from every man who knew her. She was probably one of the few women in the world who could work in a saloon and still command that respect. Of course Tía would not divulge that information to Uncle Tyler. He would neither believe it nor be impressed by it. But Mama was worth ten Tyler Caldwells.

Uncle Tyler directed his words to Tía. "Next, young lady, I would like to know your initial reaction to all this. Pray tell us what, if anything, you think of this presumptuous proposition."

Tía did not hesitate. She had a half brother whom she wanted to see before something happened to him. "I want to go home to Arizona, Uncle Tyler." Her tone was respectful and firm. Andrea smiled her approval.

A queer look of satisfaction gleamed in Uncle Tyler's slate-gray eyes. According to Mama, once they had been pale blue, but the color had faded out of them as real vitality had faded out of him. Probably squeezed out...

"I was afraid of that," he said heavily, looking at Mrs. Lockwood as if he had already discussed this with her. "Well, you may as well know, so there will be no misunderstanding later. If you choose to go off on this wild-goose chase, spurning my hospitality as your mother did twenty-five years ago, I will not be amenable to receiving you here again. As diligent as I am in fulfilling my obligations to my relations, no matter how vilely they return my generosity, even I can be pushed only so far. I do not condone your chasing off into the wilds on the *chance* there is some substance to this so-called inheritance of yours. The man says very little, actually. He gives us no estimate of what this Lucky Cuss mine or this so-called ranch might be worth, if anything. Even if there is value there, I doubt if you would be allowed to share it with any dignity. People do not take kindly to having a dead man's bastard suddenly thrust upon them. No decent woman will have anything to do with you. I warned your mother before she ran away, but it didn't stop her. She was headstrong as well. Now look at her. Married to a common Mexican bandit who would as soon kill her as look at her. And with good reason, as it turns out. Harumph!"

Looking at them with fierce, satisfied eyes, as if pleased with the way their mother's life had turned out, Uncle Tyler cleared his throat again.

Tía bit back angry words. It would do no good to antagonize him. Not as long as they were dependent upon him. Tía Andrea had written one letter to tell them Mateo was going to recover from his wound. She had warned Rita, begged her to stay away from Arizona and never let her husband find her. Poor Tía Andrea. Torn between her love for Mama and her much older love and loyalty to Papa. Unfortunately Uncle Tyler was right about too many things.

"Even if this were not all true," Uncle Tyler continued gruffly, "and even if there were considerable value in these acquisitions, I still could not condone two young ladies returning to a savage environment in which they had not even learned the rudiments of proper manners. For a young lady, manners are absolutely vital if she wishes to make a proper marriage. Is that not correct, Mrs. Lockwood?"

Continuing without a breath, he shook his head. "Manners which should distinguish young ladies of your birth and breeding—at least on your mother's side of the family."

Tía glanced at her sister. Andrea's lips tightened; her eyes flashed as if she were going to say something, but she only straightened in her chair.

"But Uncle Tyler, it seems like such a wonderful opportunity. We would have a home of our own. We wouldn't have to impose on you," Tía blurted.

"Poppycock! Only the sheerest ignorance could cause you to think such balderdash. There is nothing for you there except more shame and trouble. Your half brother already has control, and he is not about to take kindly to having a worthless, interfering female thrust upon him in addition to all his other responsibilities. If he is no fool, why should he do all the work and settle for half the profit? Unless he is a child or an idiot! Perhaps it runs in the family!"

Andrea bit her tongue to keep from butting in. What was their uncle doing now? she wondered. He had never wanted them in his house, not for one second. Their presence had been the gravest imposition. Mama had known it would be and had apologized to them when they'd parted in Douglas, her pretty face pinched with worry. *I'm sorry, but I have no place to send you where I will know you are safe. Please try to get along with your uncle until I can earn some money and join you or send for you somewhere away from here,* she had ended, shaking her head, the customary vibrant life quieted in her so she looked like a different, more ordinary person.

Tyler Caldwell's face was set in righteous indignation. Andrea frowned slightly: was this only to insure that no matter what happened they would not return to upset his prim and proper household again? She glanced at her sister. Tía's eyes were watchful. Did she know? Probably not. Tía was so eager to love everyone. A surge of protectiveness and love for her sister swelled and ached in Andrea.

"Uncle Tyler," she said quickly before he could say anything else to hurt Tía, "could I talk to Teresa before we give you our answer?"

"Harumph!" He looked at Mrs. Lockwood and lifted one bushy, slate-gray eyebrow. "Very well."

Tía sneaked into Andrea's room after the lamps were out. Andrea lifted her covers, and Tía scooted under them.

"I've been thinking about it for hours, Andrea. I want to go."

"Then we will go."

"Aren't you afraid that Uncle Tyler will be right? Maybe Steven won't let us stay." Saying her half-brother's name caused her heart to pound. To have a brother!

Tía felt Andrea shivering against her. "What's wrong?" she asked. "It's not like you to be cold. I'm the one who gets cold at night."

"Would you want to go back to Tubac if we could?"

Tía yawned. Sleep was quickly overcoming her. "I don't know. But I don't think we'll have to. I want to live with my brother."

A pang of jealousy stabbed Andrea. Tía had gained an inheritance and a brother, and Andrea had lost Mama and Papa.

"I thought you were happy living in that mess."

"I was."

"You liked Mama's crazy friends. You liked Papa's coming and going all the time."

"I miss Mama and Papa," Tía said. "Don't you?"

"Maybe." To Andrea it was not such a simple matter. No matter how unaccepting or disapproving Steven might be, if they returned to the Arizona Territory, they would have more to fear from Papa than from Steven Burkhart.

Almost as if Tía had read her thoughts, she asked, "Papa would never hurt us?"

"God only knows, Tía. We never stabbed him before." Andrea was suddenly weary—tired of worrying about her father. Her family hadn't been easy for her. She seemed to know far too many things she didn't want to know. Countless tensions, conflicts, and moments of covert hostility had left her confused and afraid. Sometimes she questioned her own sanity. Did her parents hate each other? Or did they love each other? Watching them, no one could be sure. Andrea felt as if she had been holding her breath for years, afraid to say or do the wrong thing and not sure what that might or might not be.

It had been a shock to find out Papa was *El Gato Negro*. But part of her had seemed to know already. Maybe at one time she had known and then forgotten. She remembered a time when she had heard soldiers talking about how, when they captured *El Gato Negro*, they would cut off his head and parade it all over the territory on a stick. That night she'd dreamed about her father's head shriveled up on a stick. She'd woken up crying, but Mama had laughed at her fears, saying that she had confused Papa with *El Gato Negro*. Papa was a businessman who could trace his ancestry back to Juan the Second of Spain. His lineage was impeccable.

Papa was safe. Even *El Gato Negro* was safe from the soldiers. He had a hundred men and could raise another five hundred just by giving the order.

Andrea loved Papa desperately, but momentarily at different times she had filled with fury against him. Perhaps it would not have mattered even if she had recognized him in time. Knowing he had wanted to kill Mama confused Andrea. Long ago Papa and Mama had fought about something Andrea didn't understand, and that time Andrea hid in her bed and cried. They slept, but she did not. She lay awake crying and finally walked into their bedroom and hit Papa as hard as she could. He opened one eye, smiled at her, and told her to get back to bed.

"I hope my brother likes me," Tía said softly.

Andrea could tell by the quaver in Tía's voice when she said "my brother" that Tía had already started to love him. Andrea pulled her sister into her arms. Guilt twinged at her. She had withheld her comfort from Tía all these weeks. Perhaps she *had* blamed Tía, but watching Uncle Tyler and Mrs. Caldwell mistreat Tía had reminded her she was still the little girl Andrea had more than half raised, that their mutual love was more important than which one had stabbed Papa to save Mama. When she thought about it, she realized Tía loved him too much. Tía could not have done it, even to save Mama. Only she herself could have done it.

Andrea kissed Tía's forehead. "He will, Tía. How could he help it?" Hearing her own words of reassurance, Andrea flinched. How could she say that, given all she knew about human nature? Tía had always wanted a brother. She would go back to Arizona Territory no matter what threat Uncle Tyler held over her head. She would go even though Steven might not want her once she got there. Tightness closed Andrea's throat. Tía had suffered enough. If anyone tried to hurt her again…

"Oh, Andrea, I hope you're right. I want a real home for us! I want a place where we'll be safe."

CHAPTER FOUR

"Johnny!"

Johnny recognized Judy's whisper and slowly sat up on the side of his bunk. The room was dark, but he hadn't undressed. He should have been sleeping, but he had been restless, almost as if he had known she was going to search him out tonight. This afternoon she had deliberately gotten in his way as he'd tried to leave Steve's office. Dark and searching, her eyes had held his, commanding his attention.

"Just a minute," he said, walking to the door.

"May I come in?" It was barely a question. Johnny sensed that the Judy he knew was back. She had been wounded by her father's death and more listless than he had ever seen her. But over the last month Johnny had watched the vibrant life in her slowly reassert itself. The part of him that loved Judy had been pleased, but the part of him that feared the consequences to him had watched with dread.

"I'll come out." Leaving the door open behind him, he stepped outside. The warm June night was heavy, fragrant with the jasmine Judy had planted several springs before. The moon was high over the mountains to the east. Crickets chirped in the tall grass behind the cabin.

Johnny leaned against the column that supported the porch roof and fished in his shirt pocket for his makings. The Burkhart *casa grande* west of his cabin was dark and quiet. To the south, on one of the platforms, a man stood outlined against the lighter sky as he guarded the front gate of the compound. Burkhart had built a fort.

"Will you roll one for me?" she asked.

"What'd you do, run out?" Johnny had forgotten Judy smoked. Outside of two dance hall girls he had seen years apart, Judy was the only decent woman Johnny had ever known who smoked cigarettes. Decent women—even most dance hall girls—did not smoke. But Judy was not like other women. No decent woman in her right mind would come to his cabin alone after dark. To still the wagging tongues, any other lady of the spread would have sent for him or had him meet her someplace distant but clearly visible so anyone who cared could watch them. Even her father had given up trying to make Judy conform; it was a battle one could only lose.

"I hate these kind, but I'm out of the others. I'll get some when we go into town tomorrow."

Johnny rolled it for her. With the cigarette in her mouth, she watched him with dark, luminous eyes as he struck a match. She waited until he blew out the match to speak.

"She'll be here day after tomorrow. I wonder what she's like?"

Johnny shrugged. That same question had plagued everyone since the reading of the will. It had taken Furnett over two months to find Burkhart's daughter.

Judy inhaled, expelled a choking breath, and dropped her cigarette on the porch. She ground the offending butt under the toe of her shoe. In the faint moonlight the blue gown she had worn at supper looked black. "I hate your tobacco," she muttered.

The main bunkhouse stood behind Johnny. Judy's face, illuminated by the yellow lanterns from the bunkhouse windows, was a pale, lovely oval. Her dark eyes reflected tiny squares of light. She was so beautiful it made Johnny ache to look at her, but he wasn't sure if it was a new ache or the memory of an old ache in his loins.

"Don't be so grim all the time, Johnny. Relax, loosen your cinch a little." As if she realized the hopelessness of her advice, Judy took his arm and squeezed it. "So don't relax. I'll settle for your not snarling at me." She giggled, a deliciously naughty sound—as if she were either thinking something wicked or doing it—that caused Johnny to smile in spite of himself.

"I hope she's as ugly as a mud fence. And fat!" She let out another lilting trill of mischievous laughter and clapped her hands. "A fat stump of a body and a big round flat face! Wouldn't that be wonderful!"

"Not for her."

"Oh! You're just thinking of yourself. Besides, you're not allowed to look at other women. You belong to me, and I don't share. Do I?"

Johnny didn't reply. He had been home over two months, and this was the first time they had been alone together.

Now, if her words could be trusted, Judy acted as if nothing bad ever passed between them. For Judy life was pig simple. The only thing a man could count on was not being able to count on anything.

Judy tugged at his vest. "Life's too short to spend all your time snarling and snapping." She giggled, then sighed at his lack of enthusiasm. "Oh, Johnny...don't be so sober. Smile! Be happy."

She started to flounce away, seemed to think better of it, and stopped. "You're as tense as a hen in a pack of wolves, Johnny." Reaching up, she ran her hand along his shoulders and neck, then down over his muscular chest.

Johnny took her hands and held them away from him. "It's late," he said, his voice gruff, unnatural.

"You never used to be like this." She expelled a frustrated breath. "Are you *ever* going to forgive me?"

"There's nothing to forgive."

"I hurt you, didn't I?"

Johnny shrugged. "That's smoke up the chimney."

"Kiss me, Johnny, please." She sounded like a child asking for reassurance, not a woman asking for a kiss.

Johnny leaned down and kissed her forehead. "Go to bed. We have to get up early tomorrow."

"To ride in so we'll be there to meet Miss Garcia-Lorca...Lord, what a name." She sighed.

"She might be a lot like Steve," he said.

Anger flared in Judy. "And I'm not?"

Johnny had no answer for that. Judy went back to the subject he hated. "You're afraid of me, aren't you?"

"Beside you, Apaches look like house pets."

"I never promised you anything before..."

"Don't rile yourself up, Judy. This woman who's coming can't hurt you. Steve won't let her."

"Maybe you'll fall in love with her."

He laughed softly. "Maybe."

"I hate her! She has no right coming here," she said, her dark eyes flashing with anger.

"You set your mind to it, I don't reckon she'll last long," he drawled.

"You're blamed right she won't," she said darkly. "I've got everything all planned out. She won't last a day."

Judy stepped close to Johnny, and a strange look kindled in her dark eyes. A pulse began to pound in his temple, and an ache started low in his loins. This was no memory. It was the real thing. He turned away toward his door.

Judy caught his vest. "Please don't be mean to me, Johnny. I'm older now. You'll see. I *can* be true to you. I wasn't exactly untrue to you, anyway..."

"Sneaking around with Morgan Todd was being *true* to me?" he asked, caught off guard by the sudden anger that welled within.

"I didn't sneak around," she said, indignant. "I just forgot to mention it to you ahead of time."

Johnny felt like hollering. *I didn't sneak around. I just forgot to mention it to you ahead of time.* The simplicity of it confounded him.

"Johnny, please don't fight with me tonight. Everybody's against me. I need you."

Desire lowered her sultry voice. Tears welled in her eyes. Sliding her hands up his chest, clasping them around his neck, bringing her downturning lips tantalizingly close to his, she pulled his head down and pressed her mouth to his as if testing how far she could push him. Her small tongue tip darted hotly until it made a place for itself in his mouth. Tiny rivers of flame burned down the length of him. His hands slid over her back, pulling her hard against him. Part of him had already given up—it would do anything she wanted—but part of him knew better.

But it was Judy who ended the kiss, who sighed with contentment. Her hands stroked his face and neck, mesmerizing him.

"Go back to the house." He tried to sound stern, but he was sure he only sounded like a man too affected to speak plainly, a man about to embarrass himself by succumbing to a young woman who generally had more important men to spend her evenings with, but who was making do with him.

"Tell me you don't want me, and I might," she said, tossing her long brown hair, her voice sultry and rich with her power.

He did want her, but even that feeling confounded him. He didn't want her the way she wanted him to want her, and he knew it.

Judy seemed to read his mind. "Does everything have to be forever?" she countered softly. "Maybe tonight is all any of us has…"

"Is that what you tell yourself?" he asked bitterly.

"I don't want to talk about it," she said, her face taking on a sulky look he had seen any number of times when she didn't get her way.

I don't want to talk about it. Johnny controlled himself with an effort. Naturally she didn't want to talk about her infidelities, but he had better remember them or he would be right back where he was three years ago: a callow boy, making a fool of himself at every turn.

He hadn't come back to fall in love with Judy Burkhart all over again. He couldn't remember why he'd come back. He had been at loose ends when Steve's letter came. He'd talked himself into thinking that if he did come back, he'd either win her love or get her out of his system.

"Then let's don't talk about it," he said, determined not to play the fool again.

Judy brightened instantly. Her sullen look was transformed to a provocative smile. "That's better. Let's don't talk about anything..."

She pulled his head down. Her warm, sweet lips closed over his. Her kiss vibrated through him like a red-hot stake driven through him lengthwise, searing from his mouth to his loins.

Judy felt the slight vibration in his lean form and sighed with the closest thing to contentment she'd felt in years. Johnny's hands tangled in her hair and pulled her head back so she couldn't resist even if she'd wanted to. It hurt. A thrill tingled through her. Johnny was back. Really back.

"Love me, Johnny," she whispered.

Talking was folly at a time like this. Johnny lifted his head, wishing he hadn't heard her words. Because they reminded him he couldn't spoon with Judy if he wasn't going to love her and marry her. He had hoped to forget that fact. It meant he was going to have a miserable night. Morgan Todd had spooned with Judy, and he hadn't married her. But Johnny knew he was no Morgan Todd.

Something changed. Judy opened her eyes.

"How come you stopped kissing me?"

"'Cause I don't want to kill your brother."

"You'd never kill Steve. He's your friend."

"Any man comes after me with a gun ain't my friend."

Judy could not believe the turn of their conversation. One minute Johnny was about to make love to her, the next he was talking about killing her brother. "Why are you so lathered up all of a sudden?"

"If I make love to you, Steve would have every right to come after me with a whip or a gun. I'm not a kid. I can't let a man whip me or shoot me without a fight."

"Then those things we heard about you...they're true, aren't they?" she asked.

"Don't know what you heard," he said, his voice husky. "Don't care."

"That you're a gunfighter. That you killed Billy the Deuce and other men, too."

Johnny shrugged, a small negligent movement of his manly shoulder, and Judy knew it was all true. She'd known from the first day when he'd ridden in and hadn't come looking for her. He was *the* Johnny Brago, a gunfighter like Dusty Denton, Lance Kincaid, Sam Bass, Curly Bill Brocius...

Moon and starlight silvered the sand in front of Johnny's cabin. The cool night breeze felt good against her damp skin. A thin curving sliver, tilted crazily, the moon had moved out of sight. Moments ago it had nested between two limbs of the tree beside Johnny's cabin. A horse whinnied, and another answered. Steve's dog, Red, bayed at the moon.

"It's late. You better go back to the house before Steve misses you."

Judy knew the moment had passed, but somehow she couldn't give it up. She laid her head on his chest and felt the beat of his heart against her cheek. "We're good together, Johnny, aren't we?"

"We ain't together," he said.

"Oh, Johnny, don't buck so hard. Now that you're back everything is going to be so wonderful. I've changed; why, I'm nearly perfect. You'll see. I clean and cook and plan meals. I practically run the whole household. Steve is proud of me, too. And now, with you here, I'll be even better…"

Johnny closed his eyes. Judy rattled on about all the new leaves she was going to turn over, but he'd stopped listening. He'd heard them all before. She'd be the best everything in the world: cook, housekeeper, lover, mother. She'd be endlessly faithful, hardworking, clever, pretty, loyal, thrifty…

Judy was in her own private reverie, recounting how wonderful everything would be, and Johnny was in torment. He had forgotten how appealing she was—the childlike innocence in her that was so uniquely Judy. Every day brought a fresh slate. Yesterday's mistakes didn't count. Judy didn't hold grudges, so she couldn't fathom why anyone else would. And now she was determined to be good, so she had always been good.

Judy—my little dreamer. There were no lies in her world, he thought bitterly. No betrayals, only some promises that should never have been given.

Sadness settled into him. He shouldn't have come back here. He couldn't punish Judy or marry her. That had been the sheerest insanity— an idea dreamed up in the cold dark hours of a lonely night to trick himself into coming back. How else could he justify deliberately walking back into a tornado?

He'd known three years ago there was no hope for them. She was too fickle, too impetuous. Judy was quicksilver, and he was lead— as unmoving and unforgiving as she was fluid. He couldn't forget the past, and she couldn't remember it. That was why she could act like she hadn't ripped his insides out. That was why she could act like he was still twenty-two, still in love with the girl he planned to marry. For her nothing serious had happened. She made love to the man she wanted, and the other one got sore about it. They fought, and the sorehead rode away. End of problem. Now he was back, and she could pick up where she had left off...

Except it wasn't that easy for Johnny. He had kissed her, and now she was talking about love and marriage.

"Well?" Judy demanded, smiling expectantly.

"Fine, but I'm not here to marry you," he said.

"That's it?" she asked incredulously. "I tell you how wonderful your future is going to be, with one of the best-looking females in the territory, and you say fine? I'm insulted."

"Guess I'm off my feed."

"You're different now, Johnny. You know that?" she asked suddenly. "You hurt me," she said almost proudly.

"Did I?"

She searched his face and waited for his response. "There was a time," she whispered, "if I said you hurt me, you would have apologized." Judy wavered between pique and a newly awakened feeling of submissiveness.

Submissiveness won. "I'm glad you don't feel sorry. That'd spoil it if you did." She paused. "Why *did* you come back?"

"Steve wrote and said he needed me."

"I thought maybe you missed me."

Shrugging, he didn't answer. He had been over all of this in his head. No answer he could give would satisfy her. A week after Bill died, he had gone to Steve to find out why the Burkharts had brought him back to Rancho la Reina. He had stopped Steve on his way out to the barn. The sun had set, and the sky was a bright backlit coral with brooding gray streaks.

"We need to parlay."

Steve smiled and patted his shoulder lightly. "You want a drink?"

"No."

"Sounds serious."

"Bill told me that the two of you brought me back so I could take care of Judy."

Frowning, his clear blue eyes level and unwavering, Steve shook his head. "I don't know anything about that. I brought you back to run the ranch."

Johnny nodded his satisfaction and turned to leave.

"But," Steve added, a slow smile spreading across his clean, square-cut Burkhart features, emphasizing the easygoing manner everyone liked and trusted, "if it should turn out that way, you can count on my blessing."

Soft and rich, Judy's voice brought him back to the present. "Did you miss me, Johnny? You were gone a long time."

"It's time I walked you back to the house, before your brother discovers you're missing and thinks you've been carried off by renegade Injuns. You'll need some shut-eye if you're going to be in top form to ride into Tombstone to meet your new sister."

"She's not my sister!"

"Stepsister, then."

"She's Steve's stepsister, not mine."

"Well, you heard what Steve said, whatever's his is yours."

"Well, some things I don't want any part of. If I have my way, she'll be sorry she ever set foot in Arizona Territory."

Johnny walked Judy to the back door of the *casa grande* and waited for her to step inside and close the door. Then he walked slowly back to his cabin. His bunk was hot. The cabin was hot. And he was hot.

Picking up a blanket, he carried it into the orchard to a spot between two of his favorite trees and spread it on the cool ground. It felt good to lie on the earth. Must be the Indian in him. No matter what ailed him, lying on the earth always helped.

Moon and stars filtered through the limbs of the peach tree overhead. The night was alive with sound: dogs, cows, horses, night birds, even men snoring. His body was alive with feeling.

Three years ago he had thought any woman who kissed him could cause the same reaction Judy had—that it was a natural response to being kissed—but he had been kissed a number of times since leaving Rancho la Reina, and only Judy and Tía had stirred him up this way. Tía, who had disappeared the day he'd met her and never showed up again.

What had happened to Tía? His mind instantly made a picture of Tía and wanted to know why she had run away. Had she known when she'd left him that she would not be back? He had talked to a number of people in the town. White people had seemed to know of Tía but thought she was Mexican, so they probably didn't know of her at all. Mexicans had seemed not to know anyone like her had ever existed. He had walked from door to door, asking folks if they had work. When they'd said no, he'd asked about Tía. He'd found the house she'd lived in. It had been burned to the ground. Only smoking rubble, a charred iron stove, a few blackened cottonwoods, and a wilted garden marked the spot. He'd asked the family in the closest house, almost a quarter of a mile away, about her. Their reaction—the cunning in their eyes and their blank-faced ignorance of anything having to do with Tía or her family—

caused him to ask the same question at the next house. The reaction there was different, but just as intriguing. At the third cottage he'd asked what had happened to Tía's house. One of the children started to tell him, but the old woman had backhanded the kid and sent him in the house.

What could frighten folks so badly that they'd pretend they had never heard her name before? Johnny had decided that *El Gato Negro* had taken Tía, burned her house, and terrified her neighbors. He had followed *El Gato Negro*'s trail until he'd met an old prospector who'd claimed to have seen them ride past one evening. *No womenfolks. Just a pride of bandidos that would scare the hair off a warthog.* Johnny had invited the old man to share his grub and a fire. After dinner the old man had dipped some snuff and settled back to relax. *Course they could get women any time they wanted 'em, but I don't reckon they was in the mood, what with their leader bunged up liken he was.* The old man had adjusted his snuff in his cheek and waited while Johnny cut off a plug from a piece of tobacco he carried to use as bait. Catfish loved tobacco. So did prospectors. An hour had gone by while the old man chawed on it.

Johnny had been about half-asleep when the old man spoke again. *They dragged him behind a big black horse on a travois, and when they was going past me, they stopped for a minute and this feller wearing a mess a patches gave the man on the travois a drink outa his canteen. When the injured man lifted his head up, the blanket fell off 'n I seen his fancy silver suit and knew who it was.*

El Gato's getting injured might explain why the *bandidos* had lost interest in Johnny. But it raised other mysteries. And no one in town had seemed to know he'd been injured. Just like no one in town had seemed to know Tía existed.

He'd lost *El Gato*'s trail in the Chiricahuas. In frustration he had turned north toward the Burkhart ranch. The cavalry had spent years trying to find *El Gato Negro*'s lair, so Johnny hadn't been particularly surprised when he couldn't.

The prospector's tale seemed to refute his theory about *El Gato* taking Tía. Johnny hoped so. But still his instincts made him suspect her disappearance had something to do with *El Gato* showing up in Tubac. Tía hadn't seemed to be especially afraid of the bandit. But Johnny had noticed almost no fear in the girl. Curiosity, maybe, but no unreasoning fear.

Frustrated, Johnny turned over and punched the sand into a more accommodating contour to fit his body. He'd probably never see Tía again.

CHAPTER FIVE

Andrea shook her sister. "Wake up, Tía. We're here."

Moaning softly, Tía pushed her hand away. Andrea shook Tía harder. They were so different. Tía was half-dead now, but she would be up at the crack of dawn. Andrea hated mornings. It was torture for her to get out of bed, but she could stay up all night and would, except for the threat of missing her schoolteaching.

"Wake up, Tía. We're here. We're in Tombstone."

"Oh!" Opening her eyes, Tía struggled awake.

The heavily sprung coach had stopped swaying, and the other passengers had already departed.

"End of line, ma'am," the driver said, leaning in the door.

"But…what time is it?" Tía mumbled.

"Eleven o'clock, ma'am."

"Why isn't everyone in bed?"

The driver laughed. "Tombstone don't sleep, ma'am. They's a day crew and a night crew working the mines, and the smelters are a goin' all the time—night and day, day and night. That's the sound you hear: the stamp mills. Got to where I don't think I could sleep, that wasn't going on." He waved his arms around to encompass the town. "This here's a boom town, ma'am, right and proper," he ended proudly.

Lights shone in every shop and store. As if it were broad daylight instead of almost midnight, people filled the stores and strolled along the sidewalks. A dozen saloons and bawdy houses added to the racket. Music and laughter in the foreground, the sounds of the stamp mills in the background, Tombstone pulsed with activity.

Andrea took Tía's hand and tugged. Reluctantly Tía stood and staggered down from the coach. Men had stopped to watch them, but no one came forward. Andrea searched the faces for one man who might be there to meet them. Seeing no one, she turned to the driver.

"Sir, can you recommend a good hotel?" she asked.

"Yes, ma'am. The Occidental has good clean rooms, locks on the doors, and hear tell it be decorated just like the Astor in New York City—hear tell, anyways."

"Thank you." The thought that one of these raw wooden structures could compare with the grandeur of a real hotel caused Andrea to raise an eyebrow.

"I'll take your bags, ma'am."

"Why, thank you. That's very kind of you," Andrea said, smiling with gratitude. Tía slumped as if about to fall back asleep.

Shouldering aside raucous men who had fallen silent to stare at the women, the driver lead the way. A carnival sense of abandon filled the air, fueled by a frenzy of gambling—faro, chuck-a-luck, roulette, and poker—which no doubt went on all night to relieve the lucky prospectors of their sudden wealth and the miners of their hard-earned pay. As Andrea walked past, half-drunk men on the wooden sidewalks drawled merry, semi-lewd remarks. The driver yelled them down, shouting that these were "nice women."

The Occidental was only three buildings away. On closer inspection it did appear sturdy and reassuring. New wood on the outside, the interior of the hotel lobby was surprisingly well appointed with plush carpets, marble counters, gold-framed mirrors, a fan palm in a wooden tub, and crystal chandeliers.

"On your feet, boy!" the driver barked good-naturedly at the man sitting behind the marble counter. Smiling from ear to ear, the man rose to his feet. Andrea deposited her still groggy sister on one of the gold velvet love seats and approached the desk clerk.

"Got some real special guests for you, Luke," the driver said protectively. "Treat 'em like you're s'pose to, ya hear?"

Turning the register with a flourish, Luke held out an ink quill with a white ostrich plume. A smile warmed his long face.

"Don't need Fargo trail trash telling me how to treat beautiful young ladies," he said, and winked at Andrea.

Hesitating, barely hearing the cheerful exchange that followed, Andrea took the pen and wrote "Teresa Garcia-Lorca," just in case Steven Burkhart came looking for them. She scanned the names above the one she had written, searching for his. No luck.

Watching her, the men fell silent.

"Has anyone been asking for Teresa Garcia-Lorca?"

Luke turned the register, looked at the elegantly feminine script and then at Andrea's lovely face. It pained him not to be able to help her.

"No, ma'am," he said with real regret.

Andrea shrugged. She had not expected to be met; she had only hoped. For Tía's sake, mostly. It would have been nice to dispel the fears Uncle Tyler had raised.

Apparently enthralled, the men watched her as if starved for the sight of womanflesh. She stopped and lifted a brow to remind them they were staring. "Our bags…"

"Oh! Sorry, ma'am. I'll get them bags." Rushing around the counter, the one called Luke picked up the brand-new bags, their going-away gift from Uncle Tyler, and rushed up the stairs. Andrea roused Tía.

The room looked clean. Luke assured Andrea that the lock on the door worked. The decor was overdone in the extravagant grandeur that was so popular back east. Andrea found a nickel in her reticule and held it out to Luke.

"Oh, no, ma'am. I couldn't take yore money. A smile from you is all the thanks I need."

Andrea led Tía to the bed and let her collapse across it. "Hey! Sleepyhead, take your clothes off first. You'll sleep better."

Groaning pitifully, groggily, Tía obeyed. Andrea turned the covers back and searched Tía's satchel for a nightgown. Dressed at last in a cotton shift, Tía collapsed into the wide bed. Andrea quickly followed her.

"We made it, little sister," Andrea whispered when they were settled into the big bed, its plump feather mattress closing around them.

Tía smiled sleepily and nuzzled closer to Andrea. "The worst is over," Tía murmured. "Nothing could be as bad as that dreadful trip. Except maybe Albany…I'll never go back…"

As soon as she closed her eyes, Tía slept. Neither the throb of the stamp mills nor the raucous sounds of the midnight marauders of Tombstone could penetrate the heavy mantle of sleep that enfolded her.

Kissing Tía's soft cheek, Andrea sighed. *I hope you're right, little one.*

Allen Street sported more saloons than the surrounding hills harbored silver mines. From their upstairs window it was apparent the town had sprung up almost overnight, like a sea of pale white mushrooms. A thousand tents lined the streets and spread out like the fingers of a giant hand, filling the flats between the hills that surrounded the town proper. Pale canvas fluttered in the morning breeze. Like milk flowing out and away from the main street of town, climbing partway up the sides of the ugly hills, tents wedged into the draws and gulches.

Tía hung halfway out the window, thrilled by everything she saw. "Andrea, look! Hurry!"

Groaning, covering herself with a towel, Andrea staggered to the window, not the least enchanted with the thought of seeing another ore wagon. Tía had awakened her three times before nine o'clock; now she pointed at a heavy ore wagon pulled by sixteen mules, two abreast along a trace chain half a block long. It was the tenth one to go rumbling down Allen Street since Tía had awakened that morning.

Yelling and cursing, the mule skinner cracked his whip.

"Tía, we've seen a dozen of those," Andrea protested. "If you show me one more…"

"But look at the name on the side of the wagon!"

Faded black letters proclaimed the ore wagon to be the property of the Lucky Cuss. They watched in silence until it had passed down the street.

"Well, at least the mine exists. Even if no one came to meet you." Andrea stumbled back to the dresser, where she washed herself in the big bowl. At least the water was not cold. Her skin was too sensitive and sleepy to deal with cold water.

"Well, maybe Uncle Tyler told him the wrong day. Anyway, we can't stay here. The money he gave us is almost gone."

Andrea could not think. Fortunately, Tía did not wait.

"I guess we had better make our own arrangements," Tía said.

Andrea groaned. "You go. I'm going to lie down for a minute. I think I'm sick."

"If you would go to bed at a decent hour, you'd feel fine." The look Andrea flashed Tía had an edge she could skin rabbits with. Tía laughed. "So go back to bed. I'm going out."

Tía could hardly wait to get outside, to become part of this craziness called Tombstone. She grabbed her reticule, took out her last dollar, and stuffed it in her pocket. "I'll go downstairs and see how to get to the mine. Maybe Steven Burkhart will be there. If not, they'll know how to get in touch with him. I'll bet the mine is close by, probably a lot closer than the ranch. I'm sure that once he sees me, he'll like me. He has to. How could he not like his own sister?"

From the bed, Andrea groaned and turned over. "I don't understand how you can be so practical about some things and so blind when it comes to knowing how families are."

"I know I'm right," Tía continued. When Andrea's eyes rolled back in answer, Tía smiled. At some point they would have to locate James Furnett as well. Better to let Andrea sleep. If Steven didn't like her and tried to send her away…She stifled the thought. No sense looking for trouble. They'd had enough of that. Papa could be anywhere…

She had wasted the better part of the morning trying to get Andrea up for breakfast. At the front desk Tía learned she would need a horse to get to the mine. Luke gave her directions to the livery stable.

Tía walked into the dining room and found a table by the front window. The hostess took her order, and Tía sipped the strong, aromatic black coffee slowly.

A pretty young girl in a white gown stopped in the doorway between the hotel lobby and the dining room. A woman seated behind Tía spoke to her companion. "That's her. Can you imagine? She showed up at church with her brother just like nothing had happened. And her a bastard…"

The man must have turned: his chair creaked. "I don't reckon she had anything to do with her being a bastard. Right good-looking if you ask me."

The woman scoffed. "She may not have, but water seeks its own level. You mark my words."

The girl's expression changed. As if she had heard, her lips tightened, and her chin raised slightly. Not looking at anyone, the young woman picked up the skirt of her gown with a dainty hand and walked gracefully away from the doorway. A few seconds later Tía saw her sweep past on the sidewalk. She did not look in either direction.

A rush of sympathy flushed through Tía. She could be the one they slandered next week. She too was a bastard.

The woman behind Tía put her utensil down with a clatter. "Well, I'm glad she didn't come in. I hate it when they try to bluff their way into places with decent folks."

Tía turned in her chair abruptly. "'Pears to me you need to learn the difference between decent, self-righteous, and hypocritical. Decent folks don't blab nonsense about a woman they don't even know. Self-righteous hypocrites are prone to, though. Some of them—the worst sort, usually—even do it in public."

The woman sucked air in through her nose and pulled her chin in as if doing so would protect her from Tía.

"Well, I never!" she said defensively.

Tía glanced at the man with her. "Me neither. But I don't believe in making fun of those that might have." The indignant woman stormed out of the dining room. The man dug money out of his pocket, laid it on the table, and followed her.

The waitress brought Tía's breakfast—scrambled eggs and pan-fried potatoes and gravy. By the time Tía ate and paid for her breakfast, it was nine o'clock.

Already a heavy, baking heat hung over the town. At street level the throb of the stamp mills felt like a giant bellows, vibrating the windows. The sky stretched from horizon to horizon—clear and blue—except for a patch directly over Tombstone that had turned pinkish with smoke from the stamp mills.

Out on the street a feeling of vitality and jubilation prevailed. Tía absorbed it happily. After five days on trains and stagecoaches, walking felt exhilarating.

From stereopticons to Paris fashions, shop windows displayed a vast assortment of goods. Tía was so engrossed in the bustle of activity—the rumble of carts and wagons, the laughing, shouting men she passed— that it took her twice as long as it should have to travel the three blocks to the corral.

Fronting on Fremont Street, the L-shaped corral was deserted. A Mexican boy sat next to a small red burro in the shade of a building.

"*Buenos días*," Tía said, stopping next to the boy.

"*Buenos días, señorita*," he said politely.

"Whom do I see about renting a horse?" she asked in English, testing the waters.

"Señor Montgomery rents the horses…in the back of the store… see the *muy importante gringa*." Dismissing Tía, he stood up and tugged on the burro's lead chain. "Come, stubborn one."

A sign facing the road read "Papago Cash Store and O. K. Corral, Johnny Montgomery, Proprietor." A tall, broad-shouldered man in dusty trousers and shirt, one gun on his right thigh, jammed his sand-colored hat down over his black hair with angry impatience and backed out of the store as if he were having the last word in an argument.

"Excuse me," Tía said quickly, stepping forward before he could brush past her and leave.

"Yeah?" the man asked, his richly masculine voice impatient and strangely familiar.

"I'm looking for Mr. Montgomery…" Tía stopped. Recognition flashed in the man's dark eyes and in her at the same instant. An unexpected wave of joy caused her to flounder in silence.

"You're a month late and a little too far north," Johnny drawled.

Tía grinned. He hadn't forgotten. "So are you."

A slow grin spread from his mouth to his eyes. He looked genuinely pleased to see her. "I waited a week for you to come back. I thought for sure I'd never see you again."

His black eyes accused her, and Tía flushed with pleasure. "I couldn't."

"Finally figured that out. What happened?" With the complexion of a true blonde, Tía's face was so transparent he had the feeling he could see beyond the pure, freckled skin and female prettiness directly into her heart. It pleased him that she appeared flustered.

"I had to leave."

"Finally figured that out, too. Where'd you go?"

"Back east."

Johnny frowned. That didn't seem to answer his questions about Tía's disappearance, but it appeared to be all she was willing to disclose. It had been a long time since he'd met a woman as closemouthed as he was. Forgetting how hot and tired he had been only a moment ago, Johnny leaned confidently against the wall next to the door as if he had all the time in the world—and meant to spend it looking at her.

"I don't think I've ever seen you stand up straight, all by yourself."

Slowly, deliberately, Johnny's lips curled into a cocky, handsome grin, and Tía realized she was grinning, too. She'd never met a man before it felt so good to insult.

Johnny felt better than he had in weeks. Previously covered by that damned bonnet that had almost blinded him, Tía's hair uncovered surprised him. Its fine gold curls glinted in the sunlight. The urge to run his fingers through the fresh ringlets, to bury his nose there, overwhelmed him. The thought of actually smelling her skin roused the memory of its fragrance. Her freckled, baby-smooth face—a creamy shade of pink, except for her cheeks, which flushed almost scarlet—seemed to change color instantly. He could not believe he had actually kissed those alluring, bee-stung lips that trembled now like petals. That seemed years ago.

"I'm looking for Johnny Montgomery," Tía reminded him, still blushing.

"You just get into town?" he asked, ignoring her question.

"Not just, but almost."

Delighted, hooking his thumbs in his back pockets, he rubbed his shoulders against the wall. "Did you keep that bonnet?"

"Bonnet?" Tía asked blankly.

"The bonnet I bought for you."

Tía flushed with embarrassment. "I kept it, but I forgot to pay for it."

Johnny laughed. Suddenly he felt wonderful. Tía reminded him of a little golden kitten with big eyes and a face that was pure innocence, the kind that made a man want to take it home and heat milk for it. He grinned at the thought and was almost instantly sorry he had. His kitten had suddenly changed into a lioness.

"Are you laughing at me?" she demanded.

"No, ma'am. I was just thinking how pretty you are."

"I happen to know exactly what I look like, thank you!" Tía snapped. "And I don't need anyone teasing me about it, either."

"Hey, I wasn't teasing. I like the way you look."

Johnny could not seem to stop grinning. Tía was accustomed to men teasing her, but she had no tolerance for it. Their teasing caused her cheeks to burn and reminded her how awkward she felt. "I guess I'll have to find Mr. Montgomery by myself. The most useful thing you've ever done was to take a long squint at the sun and a quick squat in the shade," she snapped.

"Why you getting all mad at me? I ain't seen you in a month."

"I'm not some little nester gal. I know when I'm being made light of."

Johnny's black brows almost crowded his eyes shut. "You been this full of trust all your life?"

"Not yet," Tía replied, lifting her nose.

"What the hell kind of answer is that?" he demanded.

Tía sighed with as much condescension as she could muster. "I haven't lived *all* my life yet."

Johnny laughed, and Tía pulled hard at the heavy door. Johnny put his shoulder against it and held it shut. He wasn't going to let her disappear again. "What'd you need a horse for?"

"None of your business," she said.

"You planning to run off again?"

Tía shrugged. She was probably going to *be* run off. At any rate she was in no mood to deal with Johnny's provocations until she found out where she stood with Steven Burkhart.

Frustrated, Johnny stepped away from the door and helped Tía drag it open. "Where you staying?"

"At the Occidental." Tía hoped she didn't regret telling him that, but he looked determined enough to find her if he wanted to. She gave him one last look and stepped inside, wrinkling her nose at the musty odor:

leather and dust predominated, smelling like the dried-up mouse she had found under their house in Tubac.

It was a store, but Tía wondered if she were seeing things. A dozen men in the back of the store appeared to be in various stages of undress. She blinked rapidly, but the men—painted like savages—were still there, shouting and laughing as if they enjoyed a wonderful joke. They hadn't noticed her yet. She turned to leave.

"Hey!" called a female voice. "Were you looking for me?"

Turning back, Tía searched the dimness for the source of that sweet voice.

"Are you looking for me?" Closer this time. Finally Tía spotted the owner of the voice. It was the young woman in the white gown who had stopped in the doorway of the hotel dining room.

"No, I'm looking for Mr. Montgomery, the owner."

"He's not here. I told him I'd look out for things. What can I do for you?"

"I wanted to see about getting a horse."

"For how long?"

"Not long, I hope. I'm going to the Burkhart..." Forgetting the name of either the ranch or the mine, Tía paused.

The girl laughed. "Then you *are* looking for me. I placed that ad in the newspaper. Are you applying for the position?"

"I don't think so..." Tía paused, confused.

"I'm Judy Burkhart. I placed the advertisement for the housekeeper."

Tía's heart lurched, and a pulse beat high in her throat. This sophisticated, aggressive young woman might be her sister. "I was going to the Burkhart ranch," Tía said.

Judy laughed. "No one's there. We're all in town preparing to greet an unwelcome visitor."

Tía's heart sank. "Is this part of the welcome?" she asked, looking at the men smearing paint on themselves and each other.

Judy grinned. "I can hardly wait! Señorita Garcia-Lorca is in for a *little* surprise."

Tía's heart flipped so hard she coughed.

"Hey! Don't look so stricken," Judy said merrily. "She's a tenderfoot. We're just going to give her a good old-fashioned Tombstone welcome."

"Are they going to kill her?"

"Lord, no. We're just going to scare her all the way back to Albany, where she belongs."

Tía avoided Judy Burkhart's eyes by pretending to study the men solemnly smearing paint on themselves and one another. Now that she had adjusted to the dimness, she could see the men were as brown as savages. That puzzled her. Most men were only brown at the face and arms.

"Are they real Indians?"

"No, silly. There's a tub over there. They soak in tea water. That makes them brown as little berries."

"Oh." Tía frowned. "Was the one who just left…is he going to be an Indian, too? I mean, he was so…"

Judy smiled knowingly. "That was Johnny…Johnny Brago. He is brown…all over."

As Tía blushed, Judy giggled, enjoying the reaction her outrageous admission caused in the younger girl. "Johnny won't help. He thinks it's mean to scare her, even if she is an interloper. Probably because he's part Cherokee…one-fourth, actually. He's always felt like an interloper himself, I guess," she ended airily. Suddenly she looked sharply at Tía. "Hey, don't go getting any ideas about Johnny. He belongs to me. And I don't share." She laughed. "Not that it matters. Johnny's been in love with me for years and years. I couldn't run him off with a bullwhip."

Ignoring Tía for the moment, Judy engaged the men in merry, teasing exchanges. Nodding her acceptance, Tía tried to smile, to overcome her surprise at this unexpected encounter. This self-assured young woman was her half sister. How incredible. A sister she had never even known about…as closely related as Andrea and still a stranger. And brave enough to watch grown men with their clothes half-off. She felt a little put off by Judy and her attitude about "interlopers," but in spite of her misgivings, a warm admiration tugged at Tía's heart for the girl…a feeling of kinship that had started back at the hotel, a kinship that made her feel proud that Judy was so pretty and friendly, even sophisticated. With her quick wit and obvious spirit, she was probably the kind of sister Andrea had always wanted—a lady.

Up close, Judy's beautiful white gown appeared to be crisp organdy, trimmed at the neckline and sleeves in brown ruching that perfectly matched her dark eyes. Her gown was expensive and flattering, showing off slender curves and high breasts to excellent advantage. Judy was obviously enjoying herself, and her high spirits were infectious. Somehow it didn't matter that she was up to her eyebrows in a plot to run Tía off; the mere fact that her half sister was the mischief maker made it seem almost acceptable.

"Johnny's loved me since the day he rode up to the house looking for board and beans," Judy continued, smiling with open friendliness, her brown eyes sparkling.

"You're lucky to have a man who loves you," Tía said, torn between her desire to feel genuine happiness for Judy and her confusion at Johnny's advances toward her. If Johnny belonged to Judy, what had he been doing kissing her that way in Tubac? Tía had overheard Mama and her friends tell stories of men who were unfaithful or had a wandering eye, but she had never understood their anger until now. Maybe this knot of pressure in her chest was the sort that caused women to talk so bitterly about men cheating.

Judy giggled—an infectious, lilting sound like notes climbing and descending a scale. "I know it. Hey! You're nice. What's your name?"

"Tía."

"I'll level with you, Tía. I have a problem. My father, or the man I thought was my father, used his will to announce to the whole world that I'm not his daughter—" Her voice broke, and her passionate brown eyes filled with tears she brushed at impatiently. "Anyway, that isn't important anymore. The problem is, she's Mexican, and all the household help is Mexican. I want someone on my side. Otherwise even the hired help will turn against me."

Tía realized Judy spoke out of hurt and embarrassment, not maliciousness. The part of her that had felt abandoned and betrayed by her papa, too, urged Tía to take Judy in her arms, to protect her from women like the one at the hotel dining room. Tía forgot her own problems, even who she was. "I'll be on your side," she said impulsively.

"Thanks," Judy said. Dragging in an exasperated breath, she gave another impatient, apologetic swipe at her eyes. "I hate sniveling, especially mine."

"Don't," Tía said gently. "It's a hateful thing to be treated badly by someone you've always loved." Tears welled in her eyes, and she turned away, trying to hid them.

"Hey, Tía, are you crying, too?"

Blinking, amazed at herself, Tía sniffed back tears.

"Hey, you are!" Judy patted Tía's shoulder, then put an arm around her and hugged her.

"Hey, aren't we something?" Judy asked shakily.

Tía sniffed. "Something," she agreed. Confused, mostly, she reflected.

"Hey, Tía, do you want that job? It's yours if you do."

"Uh, I don't know. What would I have to do?"

"Head housekeeper, over three bossy Mexicans. Just keep an eye on them and be sure they don't gang up on me when Steve's new sister tries to lord it over me. Just look out for me. You speak any Mex?"

"Yes."

"Great! You want it, it's yours."

Tía did not know exactly how she had gotten to the point of considering a job as housekeeper for Judy Burkhart. Nor could she figure out why she hadn't immediately told Judy who she was. "Can I let you know later?" Those were not the words she had planned, but they slipped out as if she knew exactly what she was doing.

"Sure. I'll be here until the stage comes in at eleven. We're staying at the Occidental. Let me know by then if you can."

"All right." Tía hesitated. "What are they going to do to her, to Teresa Garcia-Lorca?"

Judy snickered. She looked completely recovered now. "This is an old trick, reserved strictly for pilgrims. We meet her at the stage all nice and friendly so she doesn't suspect anything. Then, when we're ready to ride out, we put the *señorita* on a nag that couldn't outrun cold molasses. About two miles outside of town the Indians attack and start chasing us. Everyone runs off, leaving her at the mercy of the Indians. She heads back to town, with them screeching and howling like a pack of banshees at her heels. She just barely makes it. If we're lucky, she sells her part of the inheritance to Steve for a song and gets back on the stage and never sets foot west of the Mississippi again. Think it'll work?"

"Yes, unless she's very brave."

"Would you be, with a dozen bloodthirsty savages on your tail?"

"No," Tía said earnestly. "I'm not brave at all."

CHAPTER SIX

From behind a dusty, fly-specked window in the broom closet on the second story of the Occidental, Tía watched the street below.

Across from the hotel, down on the plank sidewalk, Johnny Brago stood next to Judy Burkhart. With his thick black hair, mustache, and heavy brows, Johnny was easy to spot in a crowd. Restlessly, his narrowed dark eyes scanned the faces of the people who passed on the sidewalks and those who had congregated to meet the stage.

Judy and Johnny stood in the shade of an overhanging canopy. Standing still, Johnny managed to look relaxed, almost indolent, but when he moved something about him reminded Tía of her papa. She still called Mateo Lorca "Papa"; habit was strong.

Watching Johnny intently, Tía groped for the words to explain the strange tingle that suffused her, even from this distance. Was it the way he moved—as if he were always aware of his body, aware of its strength and sturdiness? Just looking at him caused her to remember how it felt when he'd kissed her.

A warm thrill illumined hidden places inside her. Then resentment caused her to look away. A man who was practically married to Judy Burkhart had no right to kiss strange girls or to tell them he thought they were pretty. Remembering the heat that flared from deep in his eyes when he looked at her, something stirred inside her.

Down on the street a flurry of activity captured her attention. From the east, beneath a heavy cloud of dust, the stage approached. A showman, the driver whipped the team into a dramatic display. Halfway through town he hauled back on the reins and let out a yell. "Whoa, thar! Whoa, you ornery, mule-eared varmits!"

As the coach rocked to a stop, the crowd surged forward from both sides of the extra-wide boulevard. Judy Burkhart and her indolent warrior held their ground. Anonymous hands reached out to open the doors of the still-swaying coach.

Tía's heart leaped. On the opposite side of the street from where Judy and Johnny had their heads together, talking in conspiratorial closeness, Andrea stepped from behind the corner of a building. Blending into the crowd, carrying her satchel as if she had just gotten out from the other side and was circling behind the stagecoach, she made her way slowly through the throng.

"Damn!" Judy muttered. "I hope that's not her."

Grunting, Johnny searched until he found the woman Judy referred to. It didn't take long. Of medium build, she was blessed with the sort of slim voluptuousness that men killed for. She was definitely a beauty, but she didn't look especially Mexican. Her oval face was as finely etched as one of those women on cameo jewelry, no hint of the flattened Indian features of the *peónes*. Her dark gaze glided smoothly over him, barely pausing, as she scanned the crowd. The natural scarlet bow of her mouth arranged itself in a questioning look. In the sunlight her skin gleamed with the warmth of old ivory. Johnny suddenly had no doubt this was Teresa Garcia-Lorca. If the young woman were as spirited as she looked, Judy was in for quite a tussle.

Gathering her courage and tightening her grip on the satchel, Andrea affected a confused, searching look as she started toward the couple Tía had pointed out to her from the upstairs window. As she came even with them, she gave a tiny shake of her head and sighed audibly in frustration.

The man stepped forward. "Excuse me, miss…"

Eyes deliberately widening, Andrea blinked. "Yes?"

"Are you Miss Garcia-Lorca?" he asked politely.

"Why, yes, I am," she said, flashing her most charming smile at him. "And you are the first one in days to say it correctly, using both last names."

Nodding, he reached back and pulled his companion forward. "Miss Garcia-Lorca, I'm Johnny Brago, and this is your sister, Judy Burkhart." Holding Judy there, he stepped back as if his duties were finished.

"You'll have to excuse Johnny," Judy interjected hastily. "We're not related at all. Not really…You're Steve's stepsister."

"Pleased to meet you," Andrea said, smiling, with a carefully constructed look in her eyes that was three parts challenge and one part friendship, so Judy would know from the start that she would be happy to play it either way—Judy's choice.

Judy had been on the verge of giving up her plan to scare Teresa Garcia-Lorca, but the young woman's brown eyes shone with such pure self-confidence that she responded immediately to the challenge she saw there. If Teresa had been as ugly as a mud fence or even if she had looked cowed and timid, Judy wouldn't have been able to go through with it. But this woman looked quite formidable. Even Johnny could see that Judy would not be picking on a weakling. The prospect of some good wholesome fun revived her.

Andrea recognized Judy as a fighter. It showed in the quick smile that lighted her eyes. Lifting one arched eyebrow, Andrea let her own eyes sparkle just as provocatively. "How thoughtful of you to meet me!" she gushed deliberately. "I can't tell you how relieved I am." She threw in a touch of southern belle and enjoyed Judy's noticeable discomfort.

"We wouldn't dream of letting you make the dangerous trip out to our ranch without an escort," Judy drawled. "There are just too many bloodthirsty red devils in these hills. Why, they're everywhere! No one is safe from them. Isn't that right, Johnny?"

Reluctantly Johnny nodded. Her statement was true on the face of it, but he wanted no part of the prank Judy had arranged.

Andrea noted the tiny flicker of reluctance in Johnny's eyes before he nodded his agreement. "Oh! Are you still seriously bothered by Indians? I thought they were being kept on reservations," she said, addressing Judy.

"Oh, yes! They herd them onto the reservations, but the minute they turn their backs, those crafty red devils slip off...Why, Miss Garcia-Lorca—"

"Please," Andrea interrupted. "Could we dispense with so much formality? My name is Teresa Andrea de Mara Garcia-Lorca, but my friends and acquaintances call me Andrea. My mother was the only one who insisted on calling me Teresa," she lied with ease. "Andrea will do nicely, if you don't mind."

Judy nodded. "Good! Andrea it is. I'm sorry we didn't have more time to prepare a welcome for you, Andrea, but we only got your wire from Mr. Furnett three days ago."

"Please, no apologies are necessary. Your welcome is more than sufficient," Andrea purred.

Johnny shifted uncomfortably. Two women going at one another so politely made his insides jumpy. He noticed Andrea carried a satchel and held a long slender box and, remembering his manners, stepped forward to assist her.

"I'll keep the box," she insisted, holding on to the box as if it were very dear to her.

Smiling sweetly and insincerely, Judy took Andrea's arm and lead her toward the Occidental Hotel. "You must be starved," she chattered on. "We'll have lunch—something extravagant to celebrate your arrival. Then you can change into riding clothes so we can head out to the ranch. You do ride, don't you?"

"I must confess, Judy, I didn't realize I also had a sister…"

"Stepsister, almost. We're not related, actually," Judy reiterated coolly. "Where is Steven?"

"Oh, yes, Steve…he had business to attend to at the mine. That's his job, you know. Mining engineer. You'll meet him after dinner."

Tía watched them head across the street to the hotel. That was her signal. She picked up the satchel that held all her possessions and ran down the stairs.

Outside the hotel she stopped to orient herself to the street and the crowd that still milled around the stagecoach. Andrea and Judy walked toward the hotel. Tía let them pass her, stepped aside, and tapped Judy on the shoulder.

Judy looked around, and her pretty face broke into a real smile. "Tía! I thought you had decided not to come!"

"Is the job still open?"

"Of course! Oh, I'm so happy to see you!"

"All right, then. I'll take it."

Judy flung out her arms and hugged Tía. "Can you leave right away?"

Holding up her satchel, Tía grinned. "I'm packed."

Judy took her by the hand and pulled her forward.

"Tía, I'd like you to meet my very special friend, Johnny Brago. He's the foreman of my brother's ranch." A frown puckered her forehead; Judy paused. "Oh, and this is the lady I told you about— Teresa Andrea Garcia-Lorca. She very graciously gave us permission to call her Andrea."

Andrea nodded at Tía. Although accustomed to the sardonic glint in Andrea's eyes, Tía was not accustomed to seeing her sister look so regal and so very patronizing. It was apparent Andrea enjoyed her chance to play the grand lady. It was equally apparent that Judy was thrilled to have such a worthy opponent.

"This is Tía…oh, hey, what's your last name, Tía?"

"Marlowe," Tía said firmly, giving the name she and Andrea had decided on earlier—their mother's cousins's name.

Tía and Andrea nodded at one another, then Judy turned to Johnny. "Will you round up another horse for Tía? A good one, please?"

"Yes, ma'am." Johnny allowed his eyes to move from Judy to the slender, feisty blonde. Tía smiled at him. He had never seen so much frankness and innocence in one female in all his life—except in Judy, and then only when it pleased her. God help them all if Tía Marlowe was another Judy Burkhart.

Judy and Andrea walked into the coolness of the hotel. Johnny stepped between Tía and the others.

"Can yuh ride?"

"I ride well," she said firmly.

"Stayin'-on well or fallin'-off well?" he drawled.

"Staying on."

Grinning in spite of himself, Johnny put on his hat. He should let her go so he could see about that horse, but there was something infectiously appealing about Tía. He was enchanted by her small, pretty face surrounded by that blaze of golden curls. Freckles appeared and disappeared with the pulse of her blood, probably to show him she was a real female—not a porcelain doll dredged out of a weeks-old memory.

Tía pretended to search the faces of the riders passing on the wide, dusty street; she squinted into the glare reflected off the tin roof of a building catty-corner from them. She heard Johnny turn and walk away and glanced in that direction.

His tall form was lithe and surprisingly energetic looking, once he actually moved. She knew she should go inside and find the others, but Judy and Andrea, with their love of sparring, made her want to stand clear of the fireworks.

The sun felt as if it would bake the life right out of her in a matter of minutes, but she preferred it to them. Besides, Andrea didn't need her. She had cut her teeth on Mama and the rambunctious women of Tubac. Awake, Andrea was perfectly capable of handling anyone or anything, even Judy Burkhart.

Tía wiped her damp forehead and scanned the faces of the people on the boardwalk across the street. An old Mexican man in baggy pants and a voluminous serape walked with an oddly familiar gait. Idly scratching his chest, he wore a wide-brimmed, high-crowned sombrero. Shaggy white hair, wild and matted beneath the tattered sombrero, and bushy white beard and eyebrows...

On the stagecoach Mama had confessed many things, including the fact that she had lied about Papa being dead. She warned them of disguises Papa used to travel unnoticed in the white man's world.

Once Tía had seen that old man leading a donkey into Tubac only an hour before she'd ridden home and found Papa there. She had watched for the old man every day but had never seen him again. At the time she had thought it odd that an old man would show up and disappear the same day. Usually any prospector lucky enough to make it to town enjoyed himself for a while before walking into the desert again.

It might be Papa! Her heart lurched into an uneven rhythm. Gladness, confusion, and fear mingled and vied for supremacy. She had to tell Andrea! She turned and walked smack into Johnny Brago's outstretched arms.

"Rein in," he said softly. "You know that old man?"

"I thought you'd left…" How long had he been watching her?

"I forgot to ask what kind of saddle you ride. You okay? You look like you've seen a ghost."

Tía started to protest, but she had never been good at lying, and Johnny sounded truly concerned. The intent look in his black eyes made her forget about the old man who could be Papa.

"What are you afraid of?" he asked gently, putting himself between the old man and her.

"Tarantulas, sidewinders, and black-eyed men who can't remember their tethers."

"Now what makes you think I can't remember my tether?"

"I s'pose you can, when the one holding it is right in front of your face." She stepped back, brushed off her skirt, and started around him toward the hotel. "I ride astride," she said. "I can't abide a sidesaddle."

"Maybe I better walk you inside." Looking at her critically, he paused. "You worried about paying for dinner? Is that why you didn't want to go inside?" He had seen how eagerly she'd accepted the job Judy offered. "If that's what's bothering you, don't worry about money. You'll be Judy's guest. She takes good care of people she likes."

"Thank you," she said firmly. "I'm fine." The old man could be Papa, but he also could be just an old man, belonging to nobody.

"What were you afraid of?" he repeated. She was putting on a good act, but he knew fear when he saw it, especially in eyes as easy to read as hers. She'd covered it right away, but that didn't fool him into thinking he hadn't seen it.

"I get a little testy with men who keep me standing in the hot sun," she said pointedly.

Johnny nodded. She was a little stubborn, too. But he didn't mind that. He was a little stubborn himself. "I'll see about that horse now."

But he didn't move away or let go of her arm. Surprised, Tía looked up into his face. A quiet look of hunger in his dark eyes caused her to remember the feel of his mouth on hers. Without wanting to, she also noticed the warm, adhesive tingle where his hand held her arm. She was getting a little tired of the way her body took off on its own. It had started this unruliness in Tubac when Johnny had kissed her, and it was quickly becoming a habit she wanted to break.

"You'll see about my horse now?" Was that really her voice sounding so satiny and unfamiliar?

"Yeah." Still he did not move away or release that warm pressure on her arm.

Tía swallowed around the unaccustomed tightness in her throat. She should say something to show him that she did not appreciate being held on to, but her mind, usually so quick, was curiously unresponsive.

"Well! So here you are!" Judy's voice startled Tía. The pressure of Johnny's hand on her arm diminished and dropped away as he turned with her to face Judy.

"Shame on you, Tía Marlowe! Flirting with my fella! I told you now, Johnny's mine," she chastised, ignoring the scowl on Johnny's dark face. "And you, Johnny Brago. Behave yourself! Tía is too young and innocent for your shenanigans."

Before Johnny could think of a suitable reply, Judy took her by the hand. Tía let Judy lead her inside. At the hotel door she caught one last glimpse of Johnny, staring after her, his dark eyes strangely vexed.

CHAPTER SEVEN

Tía disappeared into the hotel, and Mateo Lorca resumed his ambling, uneven gait. Slowly he shuffled toward the corral at the end of town. No one paid any attention to him. At last, cramped and irritable with his chosen role, he stopped in front of the store. Leaning against the wood railing to rest, he caught sight of a tall man in the long brown cassock of the padres, and he sighed. At least that had not gone wrong.

Horsemen and buggies passed on the street, but no one appeared to notice them. Mateo straightened his back for the moment. "*Buenos días,* Esteban," he said to his cousin's son.

"*Buenos días, mon general.*"

"You have news for me?"

"Good news. It gives me great pleasure to carry news that should benefit all of us in the fight to regain our lands."

A surge of hostility choked him at the phrase "to regain our lands." Mateo Lorca turned away from the young messenger. After seeing Teresa and knowing that Rita would not be far away, the news would have to be good indeed.

Clenching his fists, Mateo allowed his gaze to follow the flood of tents that flowed like a dirty white river out into the ravines between the hills that encircled the town. Tombstone grew daily. It had since April of 1879 when that *idiota* Schieffelin filed his first claim, announcing to the world that he had found silver in the Tombstone Hills. Soon there would be ten thousand *gringos* living here—most of them under canvas. The greedy ones did not take time from their frenzied digging and drunken revels to build decent shelters.

To his furious eyes, the *gringos* and their tents were like a fungus—an ugly white fungus that would cover its host with a decomposing stench until the host died. Only then would this fungus move on to a fresh host. All his life he, Mateo de Mara Garcia-Lorca, had been victimized by that pallid white ugliness that devoured everything in its path.

All this land, as far as the eye could see, from the barren Tombstone Hills to the bountiful Sulphur Spring Valley, had belonged to his family since 1771, when his great-great-grandfather accompanied Juan Bautista de Anza from the mission of San Xavier del Bac. Francisco Garcia-Lorca, himself a close friend of Captain Anza, personally financed the long trek from New Spain, outfitting the wagons, recruiting the *peón* families, providing supplies and domestic animals. When their party reached the north end of the Sulphur Springs Valley, the spot with which he had fallen in love, he had personally financed the building of the chapel for the missionaries, providing everything needed to take over the Apache-dominated valley. The Garcia-Lorcas had owned and controlled that land for almost one hundred years. Until the *gringo* soldiers stole it from them, they had ruled with fairness and compassion.

Mateo straightened his cramped shoulders. In the years since that time, his life had changed a great deal. Fortunately his appearance had not. He was blessed with his father's aristocratic bloodlines and boundless good health. He did not grow lazy and fat as these stupid *gringos* did. He and his men rode hard, fought well, and still protected the poor *peónes, mestizos,* and *Mescaleros* from the dishonest practices of their oppressors. Because he, of all men, knew what the yoke of oppression felt like. Twenty-nine years ago, at the age of sixteen, he had learned all he'd ever needed to know about *gringos.*

He and his cousin, Antonio Amparo—the father of this young man who now posed as a Padre—had been returning to the Garcia-Lorca *casa grande* after a hunting trip to the Sonora Mountains.

Their horses, fine sleek animals from the Garcia-Lorca stables, were draped with mountain goats. They had been gone a week, and the solitude of the mountains had settled on both of them. They were tired. It was almost noon, and they looked forward to sleeping in a real bed again after seven nights on the cold hard ground.

They rode out of the hills and stopped on an outcropping of granite. Mateo's eyes narrowed as he looked north, up the long sweep of the Sulphur Springs Valley. A haze of smoke drifted low, close to the ground. The imposing adobe *casa grande* he had been born in would be there, behind that far stand of cottonwood trees. Was his father curing meat?

"Let's go, Mateo, my *cojónes* ache from sitting too long on this damned horse!" Antonio complained.

"Your *cojónes* always ache," Mateo said idly. Antonio complained about everything. His *cojónes,* his parents, his teachers, but most especially about the stupidity of the young girls who resisted his clumsy advances.

They reached the cottonwoods in two hours. The roofline of the *casa grande* did not jut imposingly as it should have from behind the trees. Mateo spurred his horse forward.

Antonio yelled after him, "Are you *loco*? Slow down! I am too tired to ride fast."

Ignoring him, a great fear growing in his chest, Mateo raced forward. Always before, from this point, the heavy tile roof had been a sturdy, welcoming sight.

Clearing the last obstruction, Mateo halted his horse, stunned. His heart was a heavy ache in his chest. From here he could see all that he needed to see.

What had once been whitewashed adobe was now black and smoldering. The entire second story had toppled into the first floor and become rubble. One corner of the *casa* still supported a small piece of the roof. His mind refusing to accept the evidence before him, he rode the last mile in a daze.

Smoke drifted around the ruins. Close up, the acrid smell burned his nostrils. Mateo walked his horse slowly around the scorched, crumbled walls. A large sign, posted to the trunk of a blackened tree, beckoned him.

GOVERNMENT PROPERTY. KEEP OUT BY ORDER
OF ANDREW R. ROUNDTREE, LIEUTENANT
COLONEL OF THE U.S. ARMY, WILLCOX, NEW
MEXICO TERRITORY.

Government property? Disbelief and anger were slowly submerged by fear—for his parents, his sisters, his aunt and uncle, the servants. Where were they?

Searching now for any sign of life, Mateo rode quickly around the charred remains of the house. The earth was torn by the hooves of shod horses. Many hooves.

"Mateo! Mateo!" Face white with realization, Antonio rode up beside Mateo.

North of the house, the chapel bell began to ring. Gesturing for Antonio to wait, Mateo urged his tired horse toward the chapel several hundred yards away.

The interior looked deserted. "*¡Hola!*" Mateo shouted, walking toward the belfry. His words echoed in the empty room. Halfway, the belfry door opened and Tía Andrea staggered out, her thin face working with joy at sight of him.

"Don Garcia-Lorca! *¡Madre de Dios!* Praise God you have come!"

"Tía Andrea, what has happened to my family? Where are they?"

Her eyes filled with a mixture of pain and pity.

"All dead," she croaked, her voice breaking.

Mateo's mouth fell open. "All?!"

Tía Andrea crossed herself, sobbing.

"How?" he croaked.

Her eyes were bright with the hard shine of tears. Throat working, her thin, wrinkled lips trembling, she looked away. "The soldiers," she said as if she still did not believe it herself. "They came…a great number of them. They said they were looking for a fugitive, a Mexican boy who had stolen an army horse. Your father greeted them and offered them water and shelter, but the colonel in charge, a large man, *muy gordo*, with a red face and blond hair, *muy rubio*, demanded that your father surrender the boy. *Patrón* explained that he had seen no such boy. Your father is very brave, very polite man—"

Breaking, she dragged in a shuddering breath. Mateo stroked her thin shoulder as if she were the child and he the adult. At last her strength returned, and she sighed. "Then…then the fat colonel said he would not tolerate such disobedience. *Give us the boy or we will take him!* he shouted. The man was very angry. Too angry for such a small offense.

"Then your father began to be angry, too. A more courteous, honest man did not exist on this earth, but he was not one to tolerate disrespect. He was a proud man, a good man, and this…this animal, a disgusting fat pig, no man—"

"Please, Tía Andrea," Mateo whispered, urging her to continue.

Reaching out, she patted his hand. "A thousand pardons, *patrón*, but much pain comes in the telling…"

Mateo led her to one of the pews and helped her to sit. So hard and yet so delicate, her bones were protected by the thinnest covering of skin. He had never noticed how slight she was until now.

Crossing herself, she began again. "Your father remained polite in spite of gross provocation. He was a saint. He informed the fat colonel that he was mistaken and asked the man to leave. But the colonel turned to one of his men and told him to arrest the *patrón* since he refused to cooperate.

"The soldiers dismounted, two of them, but before they could reach your father, your uncle appeared at one of the upstairs windows with a gun and ordered them to step back and leave at once. The colonel's face flamed with rage. He shouted for his men to shoot. At first they were reluctant, so the pig pulled his own revolver and shot at your uncle and then at your father. The poor *patrón* staggered inside and closed the door. There were guns in the house, but only your poor father and uncle to use them. They fought bravely, *patrón, muy bravo,* but the soldiers were of too great a number. They set fire to the house, and Don Garcia-Lorca, good man that he was, asked mercy for the women…" Shaking so hard that her body seemed to vibrate, she sobbed quietly. Filled with helplessness and dread, Mateo patted her thin shoulders. Shuddering, sighing, she continued at last.

"But the fat colonel was *muy* devious. He granted the *patrón*'s request, and the *patrón* sent the women to the chapel, but the soldiers…" Sobbing, she leaned against Mateo. "The soldiers…it was a trick…they dragged them outside…and…oh, your poor father! He saw what they intended to do. He saw them stripping your poor mother…stripping his wife, his daughters, his sister…He was like a madman. He ran from the burning house, firing with two guns, but they shot him down like a dog…"

Now she cried in earnest. Gathering her into his arms, too stunned to feel his own pain, Mateo held her close. "And the women?" he asked thickly. "Are they all dead?"

"All dead…all dead…after they…"

He did not truly hear the words. There was no need. A great sickness grew in him. The thought of his mother, usually so serene, so filled with gentleness, being humiliated in front of his father by fat *gringo* pigs. His sisters, who giggled and teased about holding hands, who had never even been kissed except when they were tucked into their beds at night…

A rage too deep for words seethed within him. "Where are they now?"

She moaned. "I was digging a grave. To bury them, *patrón,* but it is so hot, and I am so slow…"

"Where are they, Tía Andrea?" he asked gently. The woman was in shock, dazed by so much death. Her eyes stared at him as if they could still see the horrors she had recounted.

Forcing her eyes to focus on the present instead of the past, she pointed to a door off the main room of the chapel. "In there."

She pointed to the padre's quarters, when there had been a padre. He had been gone for two years. Another sign of the times.

Clumsily Mateo patted her hand. "You have done well. Where are the others…the servants?" He was reluctant to see his family.

A look of shame blurred the pain in her eyes. "They knew," she whispered. "My own husband knew, and he did not warn the *patrón.*"

"Knew? Knew what? The servants?" he asked dumbly.

"My own people!" Her lips curled with contempt. "They disgust me! They ran away, leaving the *patrón* when he needed them. I was in the stable. I started back to the house, but Pedro would not let me go. He watched like the thing without honor that he was. I have much shame, *patrón*."

"Was?"

"He is gone. They are all gone. If I had the power I would have killed him, though he was my husband for twenty years."

Mateo found Antonio in the rubble, stumbling about, half-mad, his dark eyes glazed. Mateo led Antonio to the shade of one of the trees that used to keep the blistering sun off the red tile roof of the *casa grande*. Pacing, Mateo told Antonio the story, then left him crying while he went to see the bodies of his family. He could not delay any longer.

He lifted each blanket in turn. Father, mother, sisters, uncle, and aunt were all there, but they were not real to him. Could these waxen, inert, already stinking corpses be his family? Insulated by shock, he could not relate these bodies to the people he loved.

Outside, he found the shovel and the pitiful hole that Tía Andrea had dug. While Antonio knelt beside his parents' bodies, Mateo dug a wide grave. At first Antonio would not touch the bodies, but Mateo insisted. They carried the bodies from the chapel. It was a bad thing, this carrying of dead loved ones. Antonio sobbed brokenly the whole time. Mateo did not cry, but it started a terrible sickness within him. Their bloodless skin and inert heaviness imprinted itself on his outraged brain. He could feel their deadness in his head, but he could not cry.

When they had covered the communal grave with dirt, Mateo explained to Antonio what he would do.

"You are insane! They will kill you, too." Cheeks wet with tears, Antonio shook his head. He did not want to lose Mateo as well. Then he would have no one.

"The colonel must answer to someone. I will find out who, and then I will report his crimes, and he will pay."

Antonio Amparo shook his head in vehement disbelief. Mateo was either a fool or in shock. Men who raped and killed did not report to anyone.

They unloaded their quarry in silence and left them with Tía Andrea. At least she would not starve.

Bustling with activity, the fort looked formidable. At least two hundred soldiers billeted there. Trappers came and went; wagons of supplies rumbled in and out. *Peónes* shuffled about their business; a dozen Indian scouts lounged around the stores.

"Let's go," Mateo said. They sat their horses on a rise in the road. The fort was about a quarter of a mile away.

"I go no farther," Antonio said. "I will wait here."

Mateo let his lips curl with scorn, but he said nothing. He kicked his horse forward.

A soldier supplied the name of the man in charge: General Whittier. Mateo found the general's office and told the sergeant at the desk that he wanted to see the general.

Smirking and leaning back in his chair, the sergeant eyed the young man, no more than a boy, really, in spite of his size. He was a pretty one… probably one of those goddamned haughty *criollos* who still thought the queen ran everything…

"The general is busy," he said flatly.

"Thank you," Mateo said politely. He walked purposefully to the closed door and opened it.

"Hey! You can't go in there."

Mateo stepped inside and closed the door after him.

"General Whittier, my name is Mateo de Mara Garcia-Lorca. I apologize for my impertinence, but some of your men have committed terrible crimes against my family."

"What the hell!" Blustering and turning red in the face, Whittier stood up. "Sergeant!" he shouted over Mateo's shoulder.

The sergeant opened the door and stepped in. "Sorry, sir. He just barged right in like he owned the place."

"I need to talk to you, General. My entire family has been murdered by your soldiers."

A look of recognition crossed Whittier's face, and he sighed. "Very well. I'll see him, Sergeant."

Mateo told the story as Tía Andrea had told it to him.

"And what do you expect me to do?" Whittier demanded.

Mateo blinked incredulously. All his life his father had preached to him about his responsibility to the law. Now he spoke to the man who represented the law in this region, and this man asked him what he expected.

"I expect justice," he said as calmly as he could.

"Ahem." The general sighed heavily, then stood up and walked to the door. "Send for Colonel Roundtree."

Exactly as Tía Andrea had described him, the colonel was fat and ridiculously blond for one so red of face. He saluted smartly. "General?"

"Sit down, Colonel. This young man tells me that you and a troop of soldiers from this fort killed his family," he said bluntly.

The colonel turned and looked at Mateo. "Well," he said with obvious satisfaction in his heavy bass voice. "I see you decided to turn yourself in." He turned back to the general. "This is the boy we were chasing, General. He's the horse thief you sent us after."

Mateo leaped to his feet. "That is a lie! My name is Mateo de Mara Garcia-Lorca. My father raises…raised," Mateo corrected himself, reminded himself, "the finest blooded horses in the entire New Mexico Territory. I have no need to steal them."

The colonel smiled condescendingly. "All Mexican are generals, and every *peón* raises thoroughbreds, General." Ignoring Mateo, he adjusted his bulk in the chair. "This is the boy, sir. I personally saw him take the horse. I would recognize him anywhere," he said flatly.

The general let his cold gaze flick over Mateo. He sighed heavily. "When will they learn? Very well, Colonel. Take him to the stockade."

Mateo's eyes widened in disbelief. "This man killed my entire family! He is lying! I have been hunting in the Sonora Mountains for the past seven days. I have a witness."

The general lifted his eyebrows at the colonel, and a look passed between them.

"Where is your witness? Is he here with you?" the general asked casually.

"He…" A warning prickle of fear stopped Mateo. Something in the general's eyes—a furtive animal cunning Mateo had seen only one time before, but it had been enough.

"I do not know," he said.

They exchanged another look, and now Mateo could see a glimmer of satisfaction in the general's eyes.

"Too bad," he said smoothly. "If we do not know where he is, he cannot testify on your behalf." He paused. "Would you like time to think about it? Perhaps you can remember?"

"No," Mateo said. Better to suffer alone. At least Antonio would be spared more *gringo* justice.

The trial was a farce that left Mateo stunned. The colonel testified against him casually, and the panel of officers blatantly ignored his charges as if he were a thieving child who was merely to be disposed of. The sentence was savage. He was to be whipped in the quad that afternoon, left to repent his numerous sins until daybreak, and then hanged by the neck until dead. To set an example for others who would steal from the army.

The whipping was excruciating. It was administered by a sweating, muscular soldier with a black snake whip that seared into Mateo's back like a branding iron. No amount of determination could save him from humiliating himself before the crowd of *gringos* gathered in the dusty, savagely hot quad. Mateo cried, then he screamed, and then at last he fainted.

Tied shamefully to an oversized wagon wheel for all the world to see, covered with his own blood, Mateo was more dead than alive. Flies bit his open wounds and buzzed around his face. Fortunately the sun set before it could burn the life out of his tortured body.

Sometime during the night he was awakened by an explosion. The fort was instantly in chaos. Yelling, pulling on pants, carrying buckets, men ran toward the north end of the compound. A dark figure raced across the quad and stopped behind Mateo. Warm hands fumbled with the rawhide stripes that cut into Mateo's bleeding wrists and ankles. The cool blade of a knife sawed against them, and at last they fell away. Looking back, Mateo recognized Antonio.

When the last soldier ran by, Antonio helped him to his feet. They ran to the wall, where Antonio had left a rope dangling down. Mateo stopped. "But how did you—"

"I stole some of their gunpowder," Antonio hissed. "Now, quickly, before they see us!"

A soldier who saw them described it later to an interested barracks. "He went up that wall and over it like a damned cat...a big black cat..."

CHAPTER EIGHT

Antonio managed to get Mateo to Tía Andrea, who had moved to one of the Garcia-Lorcas' line shacks in case the soldiers came back. She nursed him patiently and tirelessly, but Mateo de Mara Garcia-Lorca had died. Looking back on it now, Mateo knew that the young man—left pale and thin by a raging fever—who rose from that narrow pallet was not the idealist who had ridden into the fort asking for redress. Because he felt himself unfit to carry his family's name, this man called himself Mateo Lorca, and he vowed he would never ask for anything again. He would take. He burned from within, and the fire was fed by hatred so intense that Tía Andrea crossed herself involuntarily every time she looked into his eyes.

For weeks Mateo was too pain-racked and weakened by the fever to do anything except lie on his bed and think his bitter thoughts. Word came to him that the fat American colonel had bought the Garcia-Lorca lands at auction. That day Mateo vowed he would not rest until he had taken back all that had belonged to his family.

Helpless on the cot, Mateo tempered his rage on the forge of his hatred, turning it this way and that until he had killed the fat colonel in a hundred terrible ways. And a strange thing happened. As Mateo exercised his rage, it took shape within him. Where it was ugly, he made it uglier. Where it was soft, he made it brutal. The fierce hatred inside became so real to him that all he had to do was close his eyes and he could see the devastating monster rise up on his command. Then a stranger thing happened. By his thoughts, Mateo discovered that he could cause the hatred inside him to grow or to diminish. If he thought about the fat colonel, the monster swelled to enormous proportions and flushed his body with energy. If he thought about Tía Andrea, working so hard to heal him, to feed him, to provide for his needs, the monster slunk back into its corner.

From twelve years of age, Mateo and his cousin Antonio had been invited into the library with their fathers, Castillo y Lanzas Garcia-Lorca, Joaquin Amparo, and any guests who might be visiting the Garcia-Lorca *casa grande.* They had listened quietly and circumspectly while the men, smoking their fine Cuban cigars and sipping their imported brandies and liqueurs, discussed politics.

Now, slowly, as Mateo lay on the narrow pallet gathering strength, he remembered some of the discussions between his father and his uncle. Now he understood what they had been saying as they'd read their week-old newspapers and talked of war clouds forming on the eastern horizon from the border dispute between President Polk in the United States and the Parades government in Mexico City concerning the land between the Rio Grande and the Nueces River.

In 1846, when President Polk sent General Zachary Taylor to occupy the north bank of the Rio Grande, Mateo had not understood their concern. Texas was hundreds of miles away. How could a border dispute there affect them?

Discussing it, Mateo's father had been furious. His finely lined face seamed with worry and anger, but he spoke quietly, cautiously.

"General Taylor is a very hard man. His arrival on the scene can only make matters worse. His name alone jangles my nerves like a fire bell in the dark of night."

"It is bad...very bad," Uncle Joaquin agreed, shaking his head.

"They are deliberately pushing Mexico to war!" Mateo's father said angrily. "Nothing could be more obvious. They are like small boys throwing stones. They will precipitate a war, and then they will scream 'War! War!' and they will move in and take advantage of the situation to steal even more land than they have already stolen."

When war was declared on May 12, 1846, Mateo was twelve. By the time the war ended sixteen months later, the United States had acquired not only the disputed area, but half of New Mexico as well—that portion between the west Texas border and the Rio Grande all the way to Santa Fe. When word came that Archuleta had conceded Santa Fe without a fight, Mateo's father was livid. "Archuleta is a fool to surrender without a fight!"

Antonio's father nodded his agreement. "The man is too ambitious. He is making a pact with the devil. Kearny will let him pretend to rule the land west of the Rio Grande only until they can regroup. Then they will trample over Archuleta just as they did Santa Anna."

"Kearny is a ruthless man...a very ambitious man. He wants to be military governor of California. If he can consolidate his gains here and assure the fall of the entire New Mexico Territory into American hands, he will get what he wants."

When word reached them about an uprising of Mexicans in Taos, the frown lines had deepened in Castillo Garcia-Lorca's fine, broad forehead.

"If it is true that our people killed Governor Bent and more than twenty of his officials, then it must have been Archuleta's doings. And if it was Archuleta leading an insurrection, it could only be because he now realizes that the Americans are going to take the territory they promised him for keeping still when he should have been fighting."

"I fear you are right," said Uncle Joaquin. "And the Americans will not take this lightly. Reprisals will follow. Our people will be the ones to suffer for Archuleta's stupidity and his greed."

"I wish you were wrong, but I know you are not, Joaquin."

"Magoffin is an excellent example of their falseness and their hypocrisy! They use him like a Judas goat! Even now he is working his way westward, preparing our people for the American takeover, telling them sugar-coated lies, promising them that all law-abiding people will be able to keep their lands. He is a wicked, treacherous man! He entertains our countrymen lavishly, lulling them into a false sense of security. He does not bother to tell them that, once in control, the Americans will be the ones who decide who is abiding by the laws and who is not."

"It is an easy thing to change a law or to twist an interpretation. The Americans are very greedy, and their government is run by crooked *políticos* who line their pockets at every opportunity. They are too responsive to the voracious needs of their people."

"As are our own." Uncle Joaquin laughed.

"One does not complain about the hand from which one feeds," Castillo said, scowling at Uncle Joaquin, who nodded in agreement as Mateo's father continued to speak.

"For them, the law is an easy thing to manipulate. The *americanos* appoint the judges and the juries. In this land, we are the *emigrantes*. We are at the mercy of their honesty or lack of it. If the men who sit on the jury would like to see the land you own auctioned off...I do not need to say more."

"Too bad Magoffin does not mention these little details when he praises the *americanos* and assures our people that *law-abiding* citizens will be allowed to keep all they own."

"The man should be arrested," Mateo's father said, staring gloomily into the fireplace along the ornately paneled wall of the library. "But too many of our people have already fallen under his spell. He is a very devious man. He buys his way into our midst with fine wines and lavish celebrations, but only because we are fools. How many times must the Americans deceive us before we learn the truth of their treachery?"

• • •

When Mateo was strong enough to mount a horse, he rode from shanty to *pueblo* to shack, calling on the *peónes* who had worked for his father, seeking their help.

"No. I cannot." The man was always surrounded by the faces of his wife and children, poking from behind him like a bouquet of flowers, their dark eyes filled with curiosity, fear, and hunger.

"What will you do to eat? Who will employ you?"

"We will not need to eat if the soldiers kill us."

"You prefer to let the soldiers starve you to death?"

"It is better than instantly losing life itself."

Now Mateo understood his father's frustration. It was the same everywhere he went. The *mexicanos* were so afraid to die that they could not live. Even Antonio would not help him.

It was not until Mateo stole an army payroll, killing the three guards, that he picked up five followers—two *mestizos,* two renegade *Mescaleros,* and an outlaw from a Chiricahua Apache tribe. He had wanted his own countrymen, but half-breeds and outlaw Indians were better than nothing.

That was the beginning. With each raid he led against the army, he gathered followers. Now he could raise his own army—as many as five hundred men in a week's time—for anything he wanted them to do. *El Gato Negro* became the patron saint of the dispossessed. He could do no wrong. Even now. Once his band had terrorized the length and breadth of two territories, but for a long time now they had infrequently been bandits. Like farmers, they had been living in the relative safety of the *pueblos.* It was time to go back to the old ways, time to slough off the soft ways of women. Was this what trusting Rita and loving Tía and Andrea had done to him? Turned him into the leader of farmers?

Looking back over the years, he could see how it had happened. He had managed to steal a little happiness for himself with his daughters. He corrected himself: his daughter and his wife's bastard. ¡Dios! How that hurt him. The monster within sniffed the air as if checking for Rita's scent. At night, when Mateo slept, the monster twisted his dreams. Even his daydreams had been invaded. Part of him had realized that he could not kill Andrea's mother, but the old hatred had begun to insidiously dominate Mateo's thoughts. He would be riding his horse and find himself filled with the vision of killing Rita in some horrible way. And no matter how hot the weather, his skin would turn cold.

He had never actually seen the monster within, but he had talked to it, and it had talked back. Mateo had explained he would not kill Rita, but he was like a drunk who had sworn not to drink. The monster within could not be appeased by promises, and Mateo had nothing concrete to offer. The nights were the worst torture of all.

Even waking, as now, no matter how hard he tried to stop them, his thoughts tormented him, reminding him that he had been a fool. The *gringos* were still robbing him blind. Rita had pointed it out to him in the most graphic way possible. His false pride—believing he could father a blonde—had been the sheerest stupidity. He should have killed Rita the moment he saw Teresa. How she must have laughed at him for his stupidity.

The *gringos* were still making a fool of him. When he did not make a fool of himself. Shame flushed though him at memory of his last encounter with Rita. He did not know who had stabbed him and left him like a dog to die in the gutter. Probably her latest lover. Rita did well to hide herself. His one mistake was that he had not killed her twenty-five years ago before Andrea was born. The other men had killed the women they took in the raid on that wagon train. Only he had played the fool! The greatest fool. For when he'd learned that she was great with his child, he had gone to her and forced her to marry him.

How many times would he allow himself to be cuckolded? All because Rita had resisted and fought him to the end and won his grudging admiration. He could still see her as she had been that first time: so ripe and golden, so bursting with life, that to look at her was to feel more alive, more male. From the provocative tumble of her tawny gold mane to the shapely turn of her ankles, she was woman. And she had been his woman until…In truth, he did not even know if she had ever been his woman.

His mind flashed picture after picture of ways to kill Rita. Mateo controlled himself only with effort. At last the flush of energy stopped, and he almost sagged, his weakness as tangible and intense as the rage that had swept through him.

He could not continue to live like this. He imagined Rita, then, the following instant, Teresa. *Rita, Teresa, Rita, Teresa.* Then it came to him. Rita was fiercely protective of her cubs, as protective as any lioness ever born. He would kidnap Teresa, make her his woman, and then let Rita know what he had done. Rita would die with agony knowing that her husband had taken her bastard. Such devastation would surely assuage his wounds.

A feeling of power flushed into him. Mateo sighed with relief. If Rita stayed away from him, she could live. He could take joy in knowing Rita knew and felt great pain and humiliation that her baby was now his mistress.

It was good that he had decided on his retribution. He had held off too long. It was not like him. Remembering Esteban, who waited patiently, he forced his mind back to the present.

"*General,*" Esteban pleaded, "are you unwell?" The boy's face looked white.

Mateo wiped his forehead with his arm. "It is nothing. The weakness still flares over me from my injury. It will pass. Tell me your good news, Esteban. I could use words of encouragement, even if they do not come from a real priest."

The young man stiffened and pulled himself up proudly. "You insult me, *General.* I studied for the priesthood since I was twelve."

"A thousand pardons," Mateo said solemnly. "I was only remembering the small matter of the Wanted posters and the men who will hang you on sight if you should be recognized. I meant no offense."

Esteban Amparo shrugged. "A technicality…"

"I am also the victim of a technicality, but enough of this. Tell me your news."

"The *gringo* pigs who own the mine known as the Tough Nut have decided not to entrust their silver to Wells Fargo again. By themselves, they are moving one hundred and sixty thousand dollars in silver bars two days from now."

"To where?"

"To Silver City. By mule train. The Texas and Pacific Railroad has reached there. Word came only this morning."

"What route?"

"Through the Animas Valley."

"By Devil's Kitchen?" Lorca frowned. "Why would they use a smuggler's route?"

Esteban grinned widely. "Perhaps they think there is honor among thieves, and that if they pretend to be smugglers, the real smugglers will leave them alone."

"How many men?"

"Twenty men and ten pack mules."

"Ten? For how many bars of silver?"

"Four bars, *General.*"

"Why the other six pack mules?" Mateo demanded.

"It is part of their disguise."

"Are they also going to pretend to be Mexicans?"

"*Sí*, but of course."

"Who will be in charge?"

"A pompous *gringo* who makes no secret of his contempt for our people."

"And his name," Mateo prompted.

"Señor Russel Sloan, a *muy* self-important *gringo* who shows his wealth at every opportunity. He is building a house that will be almost as splendid as he thinks he is," Esteban said bitterly.

Mateo smiled, and now there was real warmth in his heart. He could see how this would work. "Thank you, my little cousin. *Vaya con Dios*."

"*Vaya con Dios, General,*" Esteban said solemnly, blushing at the honor his general had paid him, "little cousin."

Mateo turned away and then paused. "I would ask one more favor, Esteban."

"*Sí*, anything, *General*," Esteban said quickly.

"There is a girl in town I want you to follow."

"One of our people?"

"One of *my* people. Her name is Teresa Garcia-Lorca." In his disguise, Mateo had ambled into each hotel and read the registry until he'd found her. His request of Esteban was simplified and made less shamefully revealing by the fact that she had not adopted her new father's surname.

"Ahhh! Tía!" Esteban bristled with obvious pride and recognition. And well he should. Esteban was one of the few people in the world who knew everything about *El Gato Negro*'s family. Even Andrea did not know as much as Esteban Amparo.

"She is registered at the Occidental. Keep an eye on her. I want to know where she goes." Mateo knew Bill Burkhart must have died by now. Perhaps that was what had brought Teresa to Tombstone. She would go to claim the promised ranch, and when she did he would follow her.

"*Sí, General.*"

CHAPTER NINE

Steve Burkhart waited until the dealer had picked up his hand before he reached for the five cards in front of him. Slowly he spread the cards, noted the three queens and two threes, and thanked his lucky stars he had not been the one to deal himself such a pat hand. His luck was almost too good to believe today.

"How many cards?" Russ Sloan asked as he paused, a card poised in his right hand.

"I'll play these," Steve said, watching Morgan Todd's face cloud momentarily as he considered his own cards. Todd's shrewd hazel eyes narrowed as he leaned back and pursed his lips. Todd had a gambler's cold nerve and a successful man's easy arrogance; he was not foolish.

"I'm out," Todd said. "I think he's bluffing again, but I'm tired of paying to find out."

Sitting next to Todd, Jack Martin leaned back and stretched noisily. "Some men always bluff, others never. Steve only does it when he needs to or when he thinks he can get away with it. Since he don't rightly need to, he probably ain't bluffing."

"So are you in or out?" Sloan demanded.

"I'm out. I'm about bust, anyway," Martin said, pushing his cards to the center of the table. "Go get 'em, Ace."

"Thanks, easy money," Steve said, grinning.

"Don't rub it in, pal. Our friendship ain't guaranteed unconditional like them Wells Fargo shipments they been losing so regular like," Martin retorted.

Morgan Todd snorted in disgust. "Those bastards! Leastways we don't have to stand the loses, but the prices they're charging to ship! It's damned hard to tell whether it's Curley Bill robbin' us or Wells Fargo and Company doing it in Curley Bill's name. Hell, maybe Wells Fargo hired Curley Bill and the Clantons to rob their stages so they could charge us ten times what it's worth to carry our silver," he ended caustically.

Russ Sloan leaned back and surveyed Burkhart, Todd, and Martin with a condescending smile. "Funny you should mention it, but there just happens to be a man who does more than just grumble and complain. I happen to know a man who isn't willing to sit still for the kinds of prices Fargo is charging to do a simple transportation chore."

Morgan Todd expelled a disgusted breath. Tired of hearing Russ Sloan talk about himself as if he were two people, each fortunate to know the other, Todd raised his hands in exasperation. The only thing Sloan did that was noticeable was to talk too loud, too long, and too often. Russ Sloan was an egotistical bastard. If it weren't for the fact that he owned part interest in a couple of the richest mines in the territory, people wouldn't give him the time of day.

"What are you going to do?" Steve asked, more out of curiosity than to bait him. They were all feeling the pinch. Wells Fargo was charging far too much for what should have been a cut-and-dried service—if they could find and keep reliable guards.

A self-important smile on his ruddy face, Sloan leaned forward. With his ripple-waved hair and hard eyes, he could have been a politician.

"I've outfitted a mule train. I'm going to take my silver to the rail head...cut out the middle man," he said proudly.

"That sounds risky," Steve said.

"Not the way I'm doing it." Sloan folded his arms across his chest. "I've even figured out a way to make the trip pay for itself."

Morgan lifted his eyebrows skeptically. "How the hell can you do that?"

"Easy! I bought a whole mule train from Don Miguel," he said in a low voice, looking from face to face with an expectant expression. Seeing their blank looks, he shook his head in disgust. "Don't you know who Don Miguel is?"

"Should we?" Steve asked, controlling the urge to smile at Sloan's patronizing tone.

Sloan picked up his cards with a flourish. "Don Miguel just happens to be the leader of a band of smugglers. I bought his contraband. I can sell the goods in Silver City for three times what I paid for them here, in addition to beating Fargo's inflated fees."

"Well, bully for both of you!" Morgan said. "Now let's play cards. I want to see Steve run this bluff, and then I've got to see a lady about a problem."

They all laughed. Morgan's problem was well known by regulars in Tombstone. Sadie's Place on Allen Street was the headquarters for solutions.

"I happen to know the man who dealt these cards," Sloan said, referring to himself again. "And that means, unless he's dead wrong, that it's to you, Burkhart."

Steve winked at Morgan and pushed a stack of bills into the center of the table. "Five hundred," he said evenly.

Sloan choked on a sip of bourbon.

"That's more like it!" Morgan laughed, clearly beginning to enjoy himself. He loved to see Russ Sloan sweat.

Sloan squinted at Burkhart. "I don't have that much left. I'm short four hundred dollars," he said stiffly.

"You're good for it," Steve said, a deliberately challenging look in his eyes.

"Ahem," Sloan grunted. "Of course." Frowning, he hesitated. He didn't know how Steve had done it, but now he felt like he had to call him. He looked at his cards again, but they didn't warrant a five-hundred-dollar wager. How the hell could Steve's cards be so good? He had to be bluffing. He'd bluffed the last three hands. He was running another one.

Sloan nodded. "Okay. I'm in. Show us what you got."

Steve almost felt guilty. Sloan was a good-enough man, but he had such an inflated sense of his own importance that he deserved this loss. The mansion he was having built on the outskirts of Tombstone was testimony to that, if any was needed. Austere English Tudor with all the trimmings, the house looked as if it had been moved from the green, rolling hills of Vermont.

Grinning, Steven laid down his cards.

"Damnation!" Sloan blustered, his ruddy face turning as red as the Bloody Mary in front of Jack Martin.

Steve clapped Sloan on the back. "I know a man who'll buy us all a drink," he said, winking at Morgan.

"I can't," Sloan blurted, "I'm broke."

"I meant me," Steve said, joining in the laughter.

"Oh, okay," Sloan said, brightening. "I'll have that drink, and then I'll go get your money. You have a room at the hotel, don't you?"

"Sure. You know Judy. She shops awhile, and then runs upstairs and changes her gown and goes out to shop some more. Today we've got room number seven at the Occidental."

At the mention of Judy, Morgan Todd looked quickly away. Just the sound of her name sent threads of fire through him. He shouldn't have played cards with Steve. Hell! What was the matter with him, anyway? He could take her or leave her. Wasn't that why he had deliberately avoided her today? Didn't pay to let a female like Judy Burkhart get to a man…or even think she had. He'd been going out there entirely too often. Folks were beginning to talk about marriage…

"Drinks on me," Steve yelled at the bartender. A whoop went up, and Steve allowed himself to be half jostled, half carried, to the bar. Standing beside Morgan Todd, he bought two rounds for the boisterous crowd. The chiming of the clock over the piano reminded him of the time.

Between sips of whiskey, Morgan slanted a look at Steve. "What's the matter?"

"Damn! Judy's waiting for me. I forgot what the hell I came to town for. I should say, *if* Judy is waiting for me, she'll be mad as hell."

"What'd you come for?"

"To meet a stagecoach." He tossed down the last of his drink, the taste of it warning him that it was the first one too many, and headed for the Occidental so he could change into his riding clothes.

"You talk like a schoolteacher," Judy said resentfully.

Andrea smiled across the table at her. "I was."

Judy made a wry face at Tía. "It figures."

"That was a very good meal," Andrea said, ignoring the exchange between the two younger women.

"You sound surprised," Judy chided her, winking at Tía.

"I guess I am. I didn't expect to find a French chef in Tombstone."

Judy shrugged, enjoying her superior knowledge of the area. "Folks always follow money. If the silver veins peter out, Tombstone will disappear off the map. Place wasn't even here two years ago. Nothing was, except the hills."

"Amazing. It looks so…"

Judy laughed outright. "Just like a real town, huh?"

"Why, yes, how did you guess?" Andrea admitted, playing the big-city dweller quite well, Tía thought.

Judy smiled—a small condescending twitch of her rosy lips. "Why, Tombstone has all the luxuries: an ice-cream parlor, the Maison Dorée, which serves nothing but the best, the Bird Cage Opera, and three nice hotels. The saloons have imported bartenders who can make anything from a silver fizz to a mint julep. The bartenders in the more expensive saloons wear white starched aprons, *and* we have three newspapers."

"Amazing! Money will buy just about anything, won't it?"

"Except peace and quiet," said Johnny. "Cattlemen in these parts, your father included, mostly resent a mess like this smack in the middle of their grazing land."

Andrea smiled at Johnny. "That makes it even more amazing." Dabbing daintily at her lips, Andrea placed her napkin next to her plate. "Is there someplace where I can change into my riding clothes?"

"Upstairs," Judy replied. "Room seven. If you want to bathe…"

"No, I'll wait until we get to the ranch. You do have facilities there, don't you?"

Rolling her expressive brown eyes, Judy ignored the last question. "Good! We'll leave as soon as you change. We need to get to the ranch before dark."

Number seven was easy to find. After locking the door from the inside, Andrea put her satchel on the bed and took out the fawn-colored riding skirt and blouse she had packed on top. Unbuttoning the long row of tiny fasteners in front, she stepped out of her gown, shrugged out of her thin cotton chemise, and was just about to slide it down over her hips when she heard a key scrape and turn in the lock.

Startled, she pulled the chemise up over her bare breasts just as the door swung inward.

"What the hell?" the man said softly, his clear blue eyes widening at sight of her bear arms and shoulders.

Heart beating suddenly hard and fast, Andrea nodded. "You must be Steven Burkhart," she said, intending to introduce herself.

Steadying himself with a hand on the doorjamb, Steve gave a low, appreciative whistle as his eyes moved boldly up and then down the woman's slender frame. "And you must be about four hundred dollars," he breathed, realizing Russ Sloan had had the last laugh after all. Sloan had more class than anyone had ever suspected. Maybe the bastard did deserve the high opinion he had of himself. This female was the most desirable creature he had ever seen—wide dark eyes, skin like creamy gold satin with the faintest flush of pink in her sweetly curving cheeks, and lips that would tempt a saint. Slender, graceful arms clutched a thin shift and tried unsuccessfully to hide the lush swell of thrusting breasts, tiny incurving waist, and sleek hips. Long auburn curls caught the light from behind and shimmered with an aura of iridescent gold fire.

Russ had sent her in payment of his debt. Payment accepted. Steve almost wished he had waited until she was completely undressed, but that was not a problem. He didn't mind finding his own treasure. She was here. For four hundred dollars she would be willing. He strode forward purposefully.

Andrea poised herself for an explanation or a struggle, whichever seemed appropriate, but Steve Burkhart's arms closed around her. Ordinarily she would have struggled, but his energy overwhelmed her. A swift, keen sensation of helplessness rose up in her, shading out everything except a piercing awareness of him. In that breathless span of time from first touch to first kiss she was engulfed in the heady, masculine fragrance of his skin: part salt, part clean smell of lye soap.

His mouth claimed hers, and her feeble gasp of protest died in her throat. His terrible masculine heat stifled her will. Lost in the urgent desire of his arms, stunned by the shocking heat of his hands burning into her naked back, sliding up slowly and confidently to her shoulders, searing everywhere he touched, Andrea twined her arms about his neck.

She tasted whiskey. Was he drunk? Was she? Was that why she did not resist? Stabbing into her mouth, forcing an opening into her body, his tongue made small, harsh movements that vibrated throughout her. Andrea's head spun. Maybe a whiskey kiss and heat combined to form some debilitating mixture in a girl's blood. She could feel herself dissolving around his tongue, melting into his liquid heat...

The thin cotton shift was too flimsy to withstand the quick, remorseless movement of his hands. Amazingly, she was naked in his arms. Her knees buckled. Still kissing her, he picked her up and carried her to the bed. When Andrea felt the softly yielding surface beneath her, she could not remember how she had gotten there.

Their bodies pressed together with a fierceness that was pure instinct. A languid urgency of the blood—primitive and breathless—incapacitated her. His mouth devoured her, pulled streamers of pleasure from her loins and filled her body with a passion that somehow made her need match his. Was it her blood that pulsed and pounded to get out? Or his blood that tried to get in?

His mouth burned a trail to her breast, and her blood tightened into a heated pool at her loins, throbbing painfully.

Groaning, he came back to her mouth. They kissed for an eternity. Somehow he was naked, nudging her legs apart with his knee. His hand found her hand and led it to him. The shock of his smooth flesh—pulsing and heated against her fingers—caused her eyes to fly open.

His tawny blond hair, backlighted by the sun coming in the window, was the color of Tía's.

Tía.

Oh, God! She had promised Tía…

"Oh, no!" she groaned, her hand jerking away from him. "No. We mustn't!" Panting, she caught his hair with both hands and jerked.

"Owww! Goddammit!" Cursing, Steve raised himself up on one elbow. What the hell was she trying to do? If this was a trick of some sort, she would be almost as sorry as Russ Sloan was going to be. They'd come too far to back off now.

Instinctively Andrea clutched at the only lie that could save her. "Steve…" she panted, her breasts heaving with the effort it cost. "I'm… your…sister…"

Blue eyes hard with desire, one hand still caressing her breast, Steve looked too dazed to comprehend.

"Steve," Andrea gasped. "Steve…I'm…Teresa!"

His eyes registered both shock and recognition. She could feel his body stiffening, the lithe heat withdrawing. Stifling a moan, he rolled off her and turned over onto his stomach, eyes closed.

"Steve…"

Pressing the hard ache of his erection into the soft mattress, Steve groaned. The throb of his pain felt as if it shook the room.

"Steve," she whispered.

"Go away," he growled. "Before I change my mind."

"I'm sorry," she whispered, feeling rejected and abandoned. More than anything in the world, she wanted to touch him, to stroke those long, flat muscles of his back, to feel again the heat and urgency. Her body was clamoring for his. The transition had been too abrupt, too painful.

"Go!"

There was no mistaking how he felt about it. Embarrassed, Andrea scurried off the bed.

"I have to dress," she protested. "I can't leave like this…"

"Dress!" he ordered.

Riding clothes hastily in place, she came to stand beside the bed. He hadn't moved or covered himself or looked at her.

"Are you angry with me? You shouldn't be, you know. You really didn't give me a chance to tell you—"

"Out!" he shouted.

Like a thief caught red-handed, Andrea bolted for the door and stopped only when she was on the other side. Standing in the hall, heart hammering almost as wildly as it had been earlier when his mouth had devoured hers and his lean body had pressed fiercely against her, she wanted to go back in and explain. But even if she told him the truth, which was impossible because of her promise to Tía, it wouldn't change anything. He would never forgive her.

Remembering everything suddenly, she felt the welcome return of anger. He'd had no right to barge in there and try to make love to her. She wouldn't ask for his forgiveness. What a ninny she had been!

Andrea made a face at the door. She was suddenly glad Steve Burkhart was mad. He could just stay that way. But as she turned away from the door to go downstairs, a small voice inside her wondered what it would have been like if she hadn't stopped him.

CHAPTER TEN

A mile and a half outside of town, Tía breathed her first easy breath since seeing the old man in the serape. Reining her horse, she turned in the saddle to look back at Tombstone Hills, treeless, brown, and dreary. It was hard to believe they were filled to overflowing with precious silver. But in the hotel lobby, men—dressed in expensive, gaudy suits, like exotic, overweight birds—talked of fortunes made and lost. According to them, ore samples assayed at from $15,000 to $50,000 a ton. All day and all night ore wagons rumbled through town to the smelters. Still faintly audible from this distance, the heavy sound of the stamp mills sounded like a giant heartbeat.

Tombstone was different from sleepy little Tubac, but even Tombstone was not as different as Albany had been.

Ignoring the look Judy flashed him, Johnny turned his horse and rode back to where Tía had halted the gentle, easy-gaited mare he had chosen for her.

"You all right?" he asked, taking off his hat and wiping his forehead.

"I just wanted one last look at the first boom town I've ever seen."

"It's not Tubac," he agreed.

Tía felt uncomfortable. He watched her in that intent way that made her feel strangely insecure. As if his dark eyes could see her heart beating much too fast, and he thought it was caused by him. He was probably conceited enough to think that…

He had a way of tucking the corners of his smooth lips in that drew attention to his mouth, probably hoping to make a girl remember what it felt like when he kissed her. His lean cheeks were a rich terra-cotta color, the same color as on his hands.

Tía suddenly remembered how Johnny's warm hand had felt when he'd stopped her in front of the hotel. Heat flushed into those two spots on her cheeks.

He looked at her as if waiting for a reply to a question. His gaze flicked from her eyes to her lips. "How far is the ranch from here?" Tía asked, hoping to distract him.

"'Bout thirty miles. You'll be on Burkhart land in about five miles, but the *casa grande* is at the north end of the Sulphur Springs Valley, about three miles south of Fort Bowie."

Johnny pointed east at an imposing mountain range. "Those are the Chiricahuas. It's about two miles this side of the mountains. Probably the best cattle country in the territory. That isn't saying much, though. Bill bought it almost thirty years ago for a song. Heard he bought the whole valley for ten thousand dollars, from the widow of an army colonel who had bought it at auction after the army took it away from some Mexicans."

"Sounds like Steve and Judy have enough greenbacks to burn a wet donkey," she said, awed by people who owned the house they lived in and the land it sat on. She and Andrea and Mama had always lived on other people's land, in other people's houses.

"Yeah," he said dryly. "But not from ranchin'. Old Bill bought half of the Lucky Cuss mine from Dick Gird and the Schieffelin brothers before they knew it was worth a fortune. Paid ten thousand dollars for half interest, the price of the equipment to mine the silver. They pull out that much a week now."

"Ten thousand a week! That's amazing! What would anybody do with that much money?"

Johnny grinned. Her eyes were as round as the bottoms of teacups. "If it was your money, what would you do first?"

"First? Me?" Squinting into the sun, Tía shook her head. She couldn't comprehend that much money. "If it was mine to actually spend, I'd buy a real house for my mama…a fancy, two-story house with land and trees and a well. We've never owned a house. Do your folks have a house?"

His smile slowly faded. "No."

"Would you like to buy them one?"

"They're dead."

"I'm sorry," Tía whispered. Impulsively she reached out and covered his hand with hers.

Johnny knew he should tell her it had happened a long time ago, but he wanted her touch and her sympathy. Then maybe she'd stop trying to run away from him.

Johnny's hand felt wonderful under hers, but Judy might be watching. Tía cheek-reined her horse sideways. It stepped to the left in a small prancing movement that made it easy for her to let go.

It was time to get the conversation onto safer ground. "Does Steve live at the ranch most of the time?"

"No, Steve's a dedicated mining engineer. He's usually needed at the mine, but he's taking some time to referee Andrea's arrival. Probably hoping Judy doesn't kill her."

Tía searched his eyes to see if he was serious. Amusement warmed in their depths, and she relaxed. "What's he like?"

"Steve's a good man, but he's not the one for you."

Tía laughed. "And why not?"

"Because I am."

Tía started to reply, but Johnny craned his neck and narrowed his eyes at something. She turned to see.

"Over there," he said, pointing east of them.

It looked as if the desert were on the move. At first she did not trust her eyes. Then she saw it was a herd of something a rusty-brown color. "What is it?"

"Chulus," he said, reaching back to pull a spyglass out of his saddlebag. "Coatimundis."

"Oh." Tía had seen coatis in Tubac. They traveled in bands of a dozen or more. This looked like more than a hundred. She'd never seen so many before. Their long fluffy tails—ringed like raccoons—bobbed skyward as they ran. As the band neared Tía and Johnny, Tía laughed. The coatis were the most implausible-looking animals she'd ever seen, like small brown bears with long hind legs and a shambling gait. They had the noses of pigs, faces masked like badgers, and the lean, wiry bodies of coyotes.

The band passed within twenty yards of Tía, cutting across their trail. Soon the leaders disappeared among the cholla cacti that dotted the desert.

"They can climb a tree quick as a tomcat," Johnny said.

"I saw one in the alley behind the restaurant in Tubac once. It was going through the garbage."

Johnny shot her a cocky grin. "Must have been an old one. They get too old to keep up with the rest, but they make good scavengers. They're like coyotes. They'll eat about anything they can find or catch."

They looked a little like skunks with their tails up and waving overhead as they ran along. They made good time, ten or fifteen miles an hour, Tía guessed. The last of the band, the old ones and the little ones, passed, and Tía looked in the direction of the other riders. "Shouldn't we catch up?"

Glancing at the trail ahead of them, Johnny shrugged. The last packhorse had entered the ravine where Judy's phony Indians would attack. The same frustration he had felt when he'd tried unsuccessfully to reason with Judy was back now, burning like bile in his throat. He had wanted to take Judy by the shoulders and shake her until she rattled. This sort of stunt was usually reserved for pilgrims who had bragged too much about their prowess as great white hunters, not for an unarmed female, probably tired and scared, coming to a strange town under what could only be the most trying circumstances. Steve had shared Johnny's anger when he'd found out about the prank after lunch, but Judy had already dispatched her "Indians." It was too late by then to call it off, but Johnny couldn't help thinking that it was a damned shame. With her proud carriage and level gaze, Teresa Andrea Garcia-Lorca looked like a woman who deserved better treatment.

"Tía," he said, "you're safer here."

Tía's stomach gave a sudden, sick lurch. "Is Andrea in danger, then?"

Johnny gazed into her suddenly fearful eyes. Guns, arrows, scared people, and nervous horses were a volatile mix, but he couldn't bring himself to scare Tía any more than she already was. "Naw, the boys'll just run her back into town."

"You're lying to me, aren't you?"

Johnny shrugged. Her blue eyes might look as clear as a mountain stream, but they weren't that way to accommodate men looking in, they were for her to look out. She didn't miss anything important. At the same time her eyes called up something primitive and protective in him. He felt naked before her gaze—naked and hungry. He wanted to tell her to forget Andrea and Judy; they could take care of themselves. He just wanted to touch Tía again, and at the same time, he resented that naive longing. His life was complicated enough already. She was just a kid: a big-eyed, fresh-faced kid who didn't know anything about men—or she wouldn't be asking him questions and expecting the truth.

"Andrea could be hurt, couldn't she?" Tía demanded.

"Andrea looks like a woman who can take care of herself."

"Does her body look like it won't break if she falls off a horse on rocky ground?" Something that had been bothering Tía all day finally crystallized in her mind. Andrea was a good shot, but she was not capable on horseback. They had both forgotten that in their excitement at turning the tables on Judy. Now it suddenly seemed like insanity to risk Andrea for a slight advantage that would disappear as soon as Judy found out who was who.

Tía turned her horse back toward the rest of their party.

"What are you gonna do?"

"I like Judy a lot, but I'm not going to let her go through with this. Someone might be hurt," Tía said.

They were in a ravine now. According to Judy, it was the last one before they would break out onto the flat valley floor and head northeast toward the ranch. Glancing at Steve, who rode about ten feet to the left of her, Andrea tried to gauge the depth of his anger.

He rode well. Staring straight ahead, his posture a little rigid and military, probably because of his anger, he rode in silence; she remembered the way his eyes had looked when he'd finally come downstairs to be introduced to his new *sister*, his pupils narrowed to tiny pinpricks of black, the blue harsh and bright. He hadn't looked at her as Judy had handled the introduction with her customary sugar-coated contempt. Nodding curtly, his face closed, grim, he had said, "We've met."

"Your brother has a wonderful way with understatement," she'd said to Judy, who had glanced suspiciously from one to the other of them.

"Yes, he does," Judy purred. "He read the marquis de Sade, and all he had to say about it was that the marquis was capable of being slightly inconsiderate when he was intent on satisfying his own needs." Squeezing Steve's arm, Judy laughed.

Steve grimaced and said, "The marquis probably learned all about women from having sisters..."

"Think how fortunate you are," Andrea said, smiling at him, sure he wouldn't attack with Judy so near. "To have not one but two sisters from whom to learn."

But he hadn't looked as if he'd felt especially fortunate. Now, glancing over at him, Andrea sighed. His face was closed and tight. Was it because he was still furious at her? Or because he was not enthusiastic about the reception Judy had planned for her? Or because he was holding his breath, praying it worked? He did stand to double his inheritance.

A sound, like Tía yelling, caused Andrea to look back. A few hundred yards behind, Tía, followed by Johnny, whipped her horse and rode fast as if trying to catch up. Andrea glanced quickly at Judy to see if she had noticed that the two of them had dropped behind.

Still riding beside Steve, Judy had turned in her saddle. Her silky, downturning bottom lip snugged in with disapproval. Andrea strained to hear over the crunch of horses' hooves on the sandy ground. Tía waved wildly as she raced her horse forward.

Andrea looked back at Steve, who apparently hadn't noticed. Just as she did, she saw the "Indians." Sinister black silhouettes appeared at the top of each side of the shallow ravine; loomed darkly, threateningly, their long, feathered lances piercing the skyline; then started down the embankments, kicking up clouds of dust as their ponies slid on their haunches toward the level, narrow floor of the ravine. Andrea halted the sluggish mare and turned to look at Judy, who instantly became animated.

Judy pulled back on her reins, causing her horse to rear and paw the air. "Indians! We're hopelessly outnumbered! Run for it!"

Except for Steve, everyone reacted, causing a moment of sheer pandemonium—dust flying, horses whinnying their protests, men yelling.

"Head back to town! Hurry!" Judy screamed, putting spurs to her mount, leading the disorderly exodus.

Twenty yards away, tawny brows knit in a frown, Steve sat his saddle and watched. The other riders had kicked their horses into a run and raced past Andrea, following Judy.

Holding her lethargic mount with her knees, Andrea reached deftly around for the long, slender box she had insisted on keeping with her. Flinging off the lid, she lifted out a sawed-off shotgun. She broke it, checked for shells, and lifted it purposefully to her shoulder.

Steve jerked instantly alert. Cursing Judy and her half-baked ideas, he spurred his horse toward Andrea, who was taking aim at five close-knit Rancho la Reina riders in disguise.

"Don't shoot, dammit!"

Ignoring his shout, Andrea fired point-blank at the men twenty yards away from her and closing. The air filled with curses and screams. Horses panicked, men fell, and Andrea swung around matter-of-factly and broke the gun to reload.

Steve reached her side. "What the hell are you doing?" he demanded, grabbing the shotgun out of her hands.

"I'm holding off the Indians while the rest of you escape," she said coolly. "Why didn't you run?"

"Why the hell didn't you?"

"That is not the direction I want to go," she said flatly.

An arrow arched overhead and fell into the dirt a few feet in front of Andrea's horse. Looking at it with disgust, she reached for the shotgun, but Steve lifted it over his head, keeping it away from her. The "Indians" coming down the north side of the ravine had seen what happened to their accomplices and wisely turned back to scatter in all directions.

Furious, Andrea turned on Steve. "In spite of you, it looks like a rout."

Steve grimaced. "Where did you get this thing?"

"Works quite well, doesn't it?"

"Too damned well! You've killed innocent men!"

"Bloodthirsty savages, don't you mean?"

"It was only a joke!"

"A joke! Unfortunately, no one told me it was only a joke. I took it seriously."

Through a mist of rage, part of Andrea realized they were screaming at each other as if they needed to. And of course they did. At least she did. She would like to scream other things, even more revealing.

"If one of these men dies, I'm holding you personally responsible," he gritted.

"That's hardly likely!" she screamed, knowing damned good and well that no one would die from what she'd shot at them.

"See if I don't!" Enraged, he looked as if he might drag her off her horse and throttle her.

Andrea took a deep breath and searched for a rational statement to cool his temper and her own.

"Your men will be fine."

"Like hell they will," he growled, looking around at his crippled riders. Amazingly, one by one, half-naked savages struggled to their feet, hobbled to their horses, dusted themselves off, mounted, and rode away.

"Well, I'll be damned!" Steve muttered.

"Not bad for rubber pellets, was it?" she asked proudly.

"Rubber pellets!"

"Well, I didn't want to hurt any of Judy's friends."

Steve's mouth dropped open. Judy, who had ridden up just in time to hear the last remark, laughed merrily, completely undaunted.

"I thought you didn't know," he said, watching her.

Andrea shrugged. "One of the Mexicans told me. She saw Judy getting ready to give me a welcome." It was out now. They would know she meant Tía.

But Steve seemed to accept the information at face value, and Judy only laughed. "I guess she *is* your sister, Steve," she said. "She's smart enough to give us a run for our money, or, I should say your money!"

Andrea smiled serenely at Steve, then turned to eye her nemesis with newfound respect. Judy Burkhart was turning out to be more of an enigma than she had expected. The girl wasn't the least perturbed about her failure—probably because she knew she would have lots of opportunities.

Andrea had expected her charade to end, but it hadn't. Relief flooded her at the realization. She wasn't yet willing to let Steve know she had lied to him in that hotel room. And she was sure he was in no mood to have her outfox him again.

At least she had accomplished one thing: Steve and Judy both knew they were not dealing with a namby-pamby female who would turn tail and run every time they tried to upset her.

There was satisfaction in that, but not enough to dispel the sudden weariness that assailed her. She positively sagged in her saddle. Even in dusty little Tubac, a hangout for murderers, fleeing bandits, and prostitutes, she and Tía had always been outsiders. Mama disputed that. She claimed that all people were essentially insiders, inside the wrong groups, perhaps, but insiders nonetheless. Mama and Tía seemed to accept this odd philosophy, but Andrea hated being forced to live on the fringes of *polite* society.

Tía didn't understand. She had been content in a busy, active household that revolved around Mama's friends—gamblers, fancy ladies, rustlers, miners, and even hunted men passing through. Mama had certainly been content. She was the undisputed leader of her social circle of outcasts, but Andrea had hated it. Mama might think it better to be the queen of the misfits, but Andrea had wanted only to be accepted by respectable people. All her life she had felt like an orphan peering into her neighbor's window. She could see into the house, and sometimes the residents would tolerate her looking in, but she wasn't allowed inside. Periodically someone would notice her there and toss a dipper of water on her. Then she would stay away for a while, but she always went back. Here she was again, hanging by her nails on their windowsill, looking in Steve and Judy's window. God, how she hated it.

Now Tía was, if anything, one rung down the ladder—the admitted illegitimate daughter of a man so cowardly he had only acknowledged his bastard after his death, leaving his children to cope with his announcement as best they could.

Understandably they hated their new relation and would not accept Teresa Andrea Garcia-Lorca without a fight. And in any sort of fight, Steve and Judy had all the weapons. Tía had been lucky this time, as she had. But she and Tía were the intruders, the ones on the outside, and supposedly the "pilgrims." Judy and Steve had the money and the power that came with years of advantage and possession.

Judy and Steve turned their horses north toward their destination, Rancho la Reina. Andrea bit her lip and looked beyond them, across the vast valley that was now half Tía's. The mountains to the east—half-obscured by waves of heat—shimmered in the sun's glare. A massive flood of sand covered by sparse, yellowed grass and scrub bushes blending into the horizon seemed to go on forever. The valley was majestic and wide.

As Andrea watched, Judy turned in her saddle, said something to Steve, and he reached over and patted her hand. A heavy lump formed in Andrea's throat. She had won the battle and lost the war. Her little triumph had soured quickly. All she had accomplished with her show of bravado was to unite Steve and Judy solidly against her. Now neither she nor Tía would be able to win a place for themselves here.

CHAPTER ELEVEN

Relieved that no one was hurt, Tía relaxed and enjoyed the rest of the ride to her new home. They seemed to be going slightly uphill. The horses labored under the hot sun. At times the slope steepened, and they all dismounted and walked. Hours after leaving Tombstone, they rode into a valley. Johnny dropped back and waited for Tía, who kept lagging to look at everything.

"This here's the Sulphur Springs Valley. The altitude's a little higher here."

"It's so big. How far is the house from Tombstone?"

Johnny smiled at how her choice of the word "house" showed her limited notion of what she was going to find. "About fifty miles. The first twenty are the roughest, through the Dragoons and the Pinalenos." He waved at the hills behind them.

Tía noted the distance with amazement. Tubac was only fifty miles from Tombstone, which was fifty miles from the Burkhart ranch! She had lived less than a hundred miles from her father and half brother all her life and never suspected their existence. On horseback a mere two days' ride.

Johnny was still speaking. "…easy going once we get onto the valley floor."

A light wind blew from the north. Smelling of pine, fir, and cedar, the air was cooler here, tinged with mountain crispness. "How long do you think Steve will stay at the ranch?"

"A week or so, anyway. Until he can figure out some way to make peace between Judy and Andrea."

"Is that what he wants?"

"You ever known a man who wanted to get caught in the middle of a cat fight?"

Tía laughed. "Maybe. If he thought one of the cats would leave and not come back."

"Steve isn't dumb enough to believe that. He knows you can't keep a cat away from cream permanently."

"You think he's resigned to her staying?"

Johnny's dark eyes narrowed. "You ever think of anyone besides Steve?"

"Occasionally." Enjoying the chagrin on his handsome face, Tía urged her horse into a run, leaving Johnny behind. She didn't know why, exactly, but she felt wonderful. The sky was as blue as it could get and stretched from horizon to horizon without a single cloud. The air filled her with a feeling of power and hope. She forgot everything that had been bothering her and enjoyed the ride so much she barely noticed as one shamefaced, dark-skinned rider after another melted into the party's ranks.

Judy slowed her horse to fall in beside Tía. "What did Johnny want? When he came back to talk to you...what did he want?"

"Oh, nothing. He just asked if I was all right."

"You kill me," Judy said, smiling.

"Me?"

"Yes, you, Tía Marlowe! The best-lookin' fella in the territory is buzzing around you right in front of his mistress, and you still manage to look big-eyed and innocent."

Tía was no prude, but she had never heard a decent woman admit to being a man's mistress before. Even the fancy ladies in Tubac had feigned ignorance of their status. Among Mama's friends women who lived openly with men did not call themselves mistresses. They congregated, in Mama's parlor and kitchen and talked about any number of things, but they always pretended they were respectable. But Judy, who obviously was respectable, pretended to be otherwise.

"Hey, Tía, want a cigarette? I bought some in town...special blend and prerolled."

Judy loved Tía's expressions. At the moment Tía looked as if she expected lightning to strike them both. Judy could not resist. Leaning close to Tía and reining in both their horses, she glanced around furtively. Then, in a stage whisper, she said, "It's okay, Tía. God knows I smoke, and he hasn't said a word about it to me. He knows better!"

Tía glanced both ways. Also in a stage whisper, she said, "Then...it's safe to be...this close to you?"

"Course! We have a very workable relationship, God and me. He minds his business, and I mind mine. I don't tell him how to grow grass or make cows from scratch, and he cuts me some slack. Actually..." She paused, smiling. "He's as easy as any man I know. I can't help it if men find me irresistible."

Tía laughed.

Pleased, Judy continued. "Grant says I've always been able to charm my way through just about anything, and I guess he's right. Hey!" she said, frowning. "Do you *really* like me?"

"Yes."

"I thought so. I could see it in your eyes. You have nice eyes. Most women have eyes so cold they could make ice with 'em. I can't charm women, except for the old ones. They think I'm cute and sweet. I have a very innocent face, too, don't you think so? Even when I'm being sultry."

"I don't know. Be sultry."

Straightening her back and composing her features, Judy lifted her chin, eased her head back, then looked down her nose and gave Tía a smoldering look.

"Now that is sultry!" she said with admiration. "I would never be able to do that in public."

"It is sultry, isn't it? It works, too! Every time."

Tía was amazed. Judy must have been far more protected than she had been. In Mama's circle the goal was not to be dragged off and sold to *comancheros*. A woman did not have to be sultry to get a man. She just had to stop holding them off with a gun. But Tía didn't want to make Judy feel bad, so she played along. "You must be very popular with the fellas."

"Listen, sweet-face, I don't know where you came from, but out here in this desert, Lucrezia Borgia would be very popular. The only requirement is that you should have a pulse. But I did get to practice on real men once when we went to New Orleans. I flirted with six handsome young gentlemen at one time."

Holding her own wrist, Tía pretended to take her pulse. "I think I've got one," she said, feigning surprise and pleasure.

Judy leaned close. "Well, do us both a favor and don't tell Johnny. He'll find out soon enough."

Tía stopped smiling. "Are you in love with Johnny?"

"Yes. I've been in love with him for years."

"Are you truly worried about losing him?"

Judy kicked her horse into a walk, and Tía did likewise.

"No, not really! I just like to tease you. Johnny has always loved me, ever since he discovered I was a girl. I was twelve and he was seventeen. Goodness, eight years! That is a long time!"

"It is. When…when are you getting married?"

The distance between them and the other riders widened. Urging her horse a little faster, Judy laughed. "I don't know. I haven't decided that yet. Of course, there is the small problem of his being away for the last three years…"

"Away?"

"Yes! He got mad because he thought I was untrue to him, and he left, never to return. Tried to get himself killed, and all he succeeded in doing was getting a name for himself as a fast gun."

"When did he come back?"

"Almost three months ago. I can't believe he's been home that long, and we just now got things patched up between us."

Tía nudged her horse with her booted foot, and Judy followed. They rode in silence for several minutes, then Judy sighed. "Johnny's good at everything. But he's a little too bossy sometimes. And…he doesn't like for me to have friends."

"Why not?"

Judy grinned. "Because all my friends are men! Johnny's the jealous type."

"Oh." Catching a glimpse of a walled enclosure, Tía stopped her horse. "Is that Fort Bowie?"

"No, silly. That's home. Fort Bowie is brick and concrete, up by Apache Pass, about three miles. Home looks like a fort, though. Daddy was an army man before he came west. He built the walls to protect us from Indian attacks. Real Indians! We have a commissary, a *cantina,* three bunkhouses, and a cabin that Johnny built to be by himself."

As they rode closer detail became apparent. Rough, pink adobe blocks, stacked seven to ten feet high, encircled an area approximately an acre in size. Raised platforms at each corner served as sentry posts. Heavy closed gates hung between portals wide enough apart for a wagon to pass comfortably.

"Some Fort Bowie, huh?" Judy said. "I only wish!"

"Why do you wish?" Tía asked, kicking her horse to keep up with Judy, who had quickened her pace again.

"Because I like men in uniform. There's just something about thirty or forty men in uniform…"

"Who's Grant?"

"Grant?" Judy frowned. "How did you know about Grant?"

"You said that he said you have charm."

"Oh, that's right. Grant's my best friend. He's one of our riders."

"One of these?" Tía asked, gesturing to the men ahead of them now.

"No. He didn't come today. You'll meet him. How old are you, Tía?"

"Almost eighteen. I'll be eighteen in November."

"Seventeen?" she asked wonderingly. "You look younger."

Tía blushed. "Because I'm so skinny."

Judy looked at her with an appraising eye. "You're not skinny. You have nice soft curves…not overblown like some people I know," she said, glancing with disdain at Andrea, riding at the front of the ragged pack.

"She seems nice," Tía said hesitantly.

"Are you going to be a traitor and be on her side?"

"Do we all have to choose up sides?"

"How can we help it?"

"Johnny said the mine was making a lot of money."

"It's not the money. It's the principle of the thing. My father did this to get his revenge against my mother. I can't let him win."

"But he's dead. Why would he want to hurt you? What does that have to do with Andrea?"

"You weren't here for the reading of his will. My father, at least the man I always called Father, cut me out of his will. He split everything between Andrea and Steve. I didn't get any part of the mine or the ranch."

Amazed, Tía stared at Judy. "But why?"

Pain flashed in Judy's eyes. She shrugged and looked away. "I guess he didn't think I was his kid."

"What happened to your mother?" Tía asked. "Couldn't she stop him?"

"She left years ago," she said, not meeting Tía's gaze.

"She just left you? Why didn't she take you with her?"

Fidgeting with the reins, Judy looked away. "I was only eight. They fought over me, but my father wouldn't let my mother take me. He loved me too much. It broke my mother's heart to leave me."

"I'm sure it did," Tía said loyally.

Judy glanced over at Tía, an odd look in her eyes. It matched the baffled little laugh that escaped, but not the nonchalant shrug of her slim shoulders. "Sure," she said ironically. "Everybody loves pretty little Judy. Bet you wouldn't guess, just to look at me, that nobody has ever *really* loved me."

Confused, Tía frowned. "Steve loves you."

"Steve doesn't count. He's my brother. He *has* to love me. No one who doesn't *have* to love me has ever loved me."

Judy's eyes strove desperately for nonchalance, but the look didn't come off. Tía reached out and covered Judy's gloved hands with her own.

"Johnny loves you," she said softly.

"Oh, I forgot," she said quickly, forcing a smile.

"I love you, too."

Tears brimmed in Judy's eyes. Impatiently she shook her head fast to fling the tears away. "I'm terrible," she said finally, her voice thick with sadness.

"No, you're not!"

"You're sweet, Tía. Maybe if you help me, I can be good."

"What kind of help do you need?"

"All kinds! I don't know…things just go wrong…I don't know why."

"Then I'll help you."

"Promise?"

"Yes," Tía said firmly, meaning it. She would start by telling Judy the truth. But first she needed to talk to Andrea so they could do it together.

They rode in silence for a long while. A Gila monster—its black-and-yellow mottled skin looking like a beaded bag that had gone awry—sunned itself on a long slab of granite, its low-slung body and fat, stumpy tail an odd match for its reptilian head. Tía stopped to watch. It looked like a lizard crafted by a clumsy child with a bad sense of proportion. Its leather had a dull glow, like painted, fiery pottery. Little raised beads covered the body from head to foot, evenly spaced except on the legs, where the beads were crowded together in a solid mass, looking more like a cluster of grapes than legs.

Sluggishly the Gila raised its head and flicked its tongue at Tía. The round, beady eye on that side of its head looked as dead as any of the other beads on the odd creature. Tía realized she hadn't seen a Gila for months.

She smiled and nudged her mare into a canter. The sun dipped toward the western horizon. They must have been riding for seven or eight hours.

At the northern end of the valley, they rode up a long gentle incline to the Burkhart *casa grande*. The gates to what Judy had called the "compound" slowly opened. Tía rode through last with Judy. Another hundred yards brought them to the front steps of the house. According to Judy, the house had started out as a one-room adobe hut half-buried in the ground. Now it rose like a monastery. Four curved arches spanned the front porch. The first level was still buried in the ground, but another level—its adobe bricks a deeper pink—had been added above the first. The wood-shake roof hung out over the small, deep-set windows to shade them from the hot sun and soared high overhead to keep the sun as far away from the rooms below as possible. Heavy, weathered shakes, the color of dry straw, shone like silver in the late afternoon sunlight.

Two small Mexican boys ran out to take the women's horses. Leading their own tired mounts, Steve, Johnny, and the riders fanned out toward the barns and corrals. A beaming, round-faced Mexican woman, who yelled at the boys as if they were her children, opened the heavy oak door and motioned Judy, Tía, and Andrea inside.

Half-blinded by the transition, Tía could barely see the dim interior. A massive, blackened fireplace dominated one wall. A long sofa and three large leather chairs faced the fireplace. Hand-tied circular rugs covered the wood floor. In winter a crackling fire would warm this big, comfortable room.

"Oh, it's marvelous!" she gasped, glancing quickly at her sister. Andrea's face was strangely closed and carefully guarded. She did not look at Tía.

"Cruz! Lupe!" Judy yelled. As if they had been waiting just outside the room, two smiling Mexican women, shuffling their sandals on the wooden floor, appeared in the doorway, filed into the room, and lined up beside Carmen.

Judy pulled Tía forward.

"This is your new *jefa* and my friend, so take good care of her: Tía Marlowe. Tía, this is Carmen, Cruz, Lupe."

The women sobered instantly. Carmen was shaped like a brick. Her round face was open and smiling. Cruz looked as if she had been raised on lemons. Lupe, the youngest, probably popular with the young men on the ranch, ran her hands down her slender hips and tittered something in rapid Spanish to the other two. "*La jefa está muchacha pequeña solamente.*"

"*Sí,*" agreed the others.

Judy scolded them in Spanish. "She may be just a little girl, but she is a very powerful and formidable little girl. One word from her, and you will all be out on your lazy butts."

Cruz and Lupe looked at Tía with barely veiled hostility. Carmen smiled at Tía with the same warmth she had shown the children.

"And this is Andrea Garcia-Lorca, your new mistress, and half owner of all she surveys," Judy said. She started with a false brightness that she could not maintain. At the end, she couldn't seem to stop herself: she curtsied stiffly to Andrea.

Coolly, Andrea nodded to the women. "I think I would like to go to my room," she said.

Judy inclined her head. "Of course. Lupe, please show Miss Garcia-Lorca to the room next to mine." Judy seemed to recover momentarily, but the sparkle did not return to her eyes. "I hope that won't be too objectionable to you, having the room between the head housekeeper and the poor relation."

Tía felt Judy's pain keenly. Although the "poor relation" was struggling to seem unaffected by Andrea and the threat she perceived there, even Andrea seemed to sense her discomfort.

For the first time since entering the house, Tía realized she had probably been conceived here. Mama had told her a little about Bill Burkhart and how she had met him. A chill rippled through Tía. She thought it too bad that Judy and Andrea were so busy being uncomfortable with each other; all she felt was their misery.

"I find that quite acceptable, thank you."

Judy grinned suddenly, and this one seemed genuine. "Oh! You'll find no gun rack in there, either! Sorry, but we didn't expect a great huntress."

"That will be fine." In silence Andrea followed Lupe out the door that opened onto a common hallway that appeared to run around three sides of the roomy parlor.

"Do these women sleep in the house?" Tía asked, careful to keep her voice down so as not to aggravate an already tense situation.

"No, they have quarters in one of the bunkhouses, but you will have the room next to Andrea's. It is more fitting. And besides, I can keep a closer eye on you." Judy smiled knowingly.

Tía flushed. "You don't have to do that. I don't take things that don't belong to me."

"Men aren't like things. They sometimes take matters into their own hands."

"Well, what should I do first?" Tía asked to change the subject.

"We missed supper. But Carmen will fix us something. I'll show you to your room, and by then our supper should be about ready. We eat around six o'clock in the summertime, about five in the winter. You rest tonight. Tomorrow will be soon enough…I have lots of plans for this old house. After dinner, I'll tell you all about it."

CHAPTER TWELVE

"How's the new sister?"

Judy wriggled her slim body as if she were trying to make a permanent imprint on the narrow cot. They were in her old playhouse at the north end of the compound. Her father had had it built for her when she was seven. Now it was a sanctuary.

"Disgusting," she said, wrinkling her pretty nose. "She's beautiful and poised and talks exactly like a damned schoolteacher. She *was* a schoolteacher! Can you imagine? It couldn't be worse."

Grant laughed. Pleased at his reaction, Judy smiled coquettishly. Grant always made her feel good. There was something about the way he reacted to her, even when she was being outrageous, that made her feel good about herself. Grant was sitting on the ground between the undersized door and the cot that had cradled several of Judy's favorite dolls. A desert lily bloomed in the sand beside him. His hands, which almost could not keep themselves still, were busy making cone-shaped indentations in the dirt beneath the white blossoms.

"I saw her from a distance," he said tentatively.

"Well?"

"She is very pretty."

"And?"

"She looks like someone who might be a good friend."

"Not to me. I hate her."

"Because she looks invincible. But if you discovered that *she* has as many problems as you do, you'd like her. I know you. Inside, you're as soft as warm butter."

"She's about as vulnerable as an armadillo. We're talking about a woman with an income of three thousand a month."

"You gotta admit, it was a good try for a clown-faced runt," he said, tossing a flower at her.

Judy laughed. Grant had a wonderful smile. He called himself names because he was short and not handsome and because he had no pretensions. What he said was true, sort of, but it didn't matter to her. Grant was her best friend. Friends didn't need to be perfect specimens of masculinity; they just needed to be loyal and attentive and available. Grant Foreman was all three. She really hadn't looked at him in years.

"I'd be willing to stake a month's wages on it," he said.

"A whole month? Forty dollars?"

"Yep."

"Forget it," she said. "I'm destitute."

"Hogwash!"

"Well, close," she said, grinning impishly. Grant knew Steve made sure she always had money. She just didn't like being dependent on someone else. She had wanted her own money, her own inheritance. And she should have gotten it.

"What did you do, go shopping again?" he demanded.

"Cynic!"

Grant laughed. "Where did you get that word?"

"I read it in a magazine article. All about the new cynicism. I liked the sound of it. Don't you think it sounds elegant somehow?"

"I'm not a cynic. I just know women," he said easily.

Sighing, Judy squirmed her bottom into the cot. That was what she liked about Grant: he seemed to know so much about everything. And he was comfortable with himself, not like her at all.

"How did you get so smart about girls?"

"Did I say I was smart?"

"Well, didn't you?"

"No. I had three sisters. I made a life's work out of watching them. I noticed that it doesn't happen in real life the way they write it in the storybooks. Not one of my sisters found Prince Charming and then decided she wanted to marry him. They went out a lot and had a lot of fun until suddenly, one right after another, they decided it was time to get married. When that happened, each one of them looked around at all the fellas they were walking out with and took her pick of the litter. The best prospect suddenly *became* Prince Charming. He didn't know he was a prince until she told him."

"Pish, tosh! You are a cynic!"

"Me?" he asked, widening his eyes innocently. "The fella who suddenly gets elected Prince Charming should be the cynic. One day he is a happy-go-lucky bachelor, minding his own business, and the next this beautiful woman blinks her big brown eyes at him, and he can do no wrong. Until about three days after the wedding, anyway."

He laughed outright. "You watch that happen three times in a row—bing, bing, bing, to three perfectly ordinary men—and you realize it's not who you are that matters, it's being there at the right moment that counts."

"You really believe that?"

"How could I help it? My sisters couldn't be all that different from other girls. Besides, I saw their friends doing the same thing, except for one, maybe."

"Just all of a sudden, huh?"

"*Bing!*" he said in a stern, remorseless tone. "*Now you are Prince Charming.*"

Judy played along with him. "Who, me?"

"*Yes, you,*" he said sternly, trying to sound like one of those men in the medicine shows.

"But I'm not a real prince," she protested, pretending surprise. "I was only having fun."

"*That's what you think,*" he growled, delighting her.

"Is there any way out for me? I'm not ready," she cried.

"*Too bad. You have been chosen. You are Prince Charming.*"

"No. No! I'm a frog," she demurred.

"*Not any more,*" he said sternly.

"Ohhh!" She covered her eyes with a tragic moan.

Grant laughed. "You do that almost as well as they did. The only thing missing was the proper degree of panic when they found out it wasn't a game."

"Your sisters are all married?"

"Could you doubt it? Of course."

"Just like that, huh?"

"Bizarre as it may seem."

"Bizarre," Judy repeated. "You have the most wonderful words. Maybe that's why I like to talk to you." She stretched. "That would be a frightening thing for a man to watch," she said, smiling lazily at the ceiling of the small dollhouse.

"Like taking a shower from a mountain spring," he agreed, smiling.

"Hmmm." Sitting up, Judy looked at him speculatively. "What does a man do if he falls in love with a particular girl?"

The smile faded in Grant's eyes. His restless hand stopped moving. "He stays close," he said carefully. "Just in case."

"That's all?"

"Men have very little control over a woman's love."

"I don't think I would like being a man."

Grant grinned. "It has its moments."

"You like being a man?"

"Yep!"

Judy noticed Grant's eyes reflected satisfaction with himself and a sureness she had never felt about herself as a woman. "Are you...is it okay if I ask a personal question?"

"Sure."

"Do you ever do things that you feel...sort of ashamed of?" Grant's gray eyes were still warm and accepting, but Judy looked away. They might change. She didn't want to know it if they did.

"Not for a long time," he said gently. "But men don't have the same opportunities women have."

"What do you mean by that?"

Grant chuckled. "You don't see any women with gold coins in their hands lined up outside the men's bunkhouse, do you?"

He was referring to the men who paid Lupe for her favors. It wasn't that obvious. No one stood in line, but everyone knew nonetheless.

Grant picked a piece of straw out of his vest pocket and chewed on it reflectively. "Women have far more opportunities, *and* they are far more vulnerable to those opportunities. It's incredibly easy for a man who knows what he wants to take advantage of a young girl." He sighed as if he were remembering something unpleasant. "Nature provides, pretty one. The female of the species is physically weaker, more vulnerable. We are just now entering an era where a woman gets to choose her own husband—in most countries fathers still decide who gets to marry their daughters."

Judy squirmed playfully on the cot. "That sounds suggestive. Are you trying to seduce me?"

"Think about it," he said earnestly. "You'll see I'm right."

"I know you are," she replied, strangely affected. "You're awfully smart, Grant. You almost sound like Andrea. Where did you go to school?"

"New Haven, Connecticut."

"Oh, I remember," she murmured.

"I didn't learn much in school, though, except by accident. I had a friend who was sort of a maverick. I learned a lot from him."

"Why did you leave home?"

"It was time. I was twenty years old. I needed to find out if I could survive without my parents' help."

"What are they like…your parents?"

"Regulation parents. My mother serves tea at three-thirty sharp, and my father reads the newspaper and works hard."

"So now you know you can survive. What now?"

He didn't answer right away. He didn't know the answer. He had gone to Yale University for two years, taking the business courses that schools in Georgia didn't offer so he could take over the family business someday, but something inside him had rebelled. The summer before his junior year at Yale, he'd realized he didn't want the proscribed life. He didn't want a wife who was little more than a dainty bejeweled hand lifting her sparkling teacup to pale, precise lips. No matter how beautiful she was.

Until Judy, it never mattered to him how beautiful women were, they simply could not reach him in any significant way. He had felt lust for other women, but even his lust had been impersonal.

First in Atlanta and then at Yale, he had felt only partially alive. In Arizona he'd almost died six times, but he knew he was fully alive. And he wanted more. He wanted freedom and sweetness. Judy Burkhart was that sweetness. Being near her. Teasing her. Seeing her rosy lips, her flashing brown eyes…

His father owned three general merchandise stores in Atlanta. He made a lot of money, but he did nothing else. Grant had worked summers for his father for six years, and the two of them had agreed on almost nothing. Grant could have run his father's stores, but only in a manner that would give Grant Foreman, Sr., a heart attack.

Grant smiled. His father had taken a vacation once, leaving him in charge. He had cut prices and moved items three times as fast as his father did, but his father had been furious. It didn't matter that he had shown a greater profit. His father would not sell anything unless he could make a margin of at least as much as he had paid for the item. If something didn't sell at the price he wanted, he would use it himself before cutting the price. To Grant, that was sheer, obdurate stupidity. His father was one of the richest men in Atlanta, but all the time Grant was growing up the family had only owned things they didn't like or that didn't fit, because his father had decided nothing would be wasted.

"Grant…"

"Yeah?"

"Remember me?"

Sighing, Grant closed his eyes. There were a few girls in the world who—once known—were never forgotten. With her downturning lips and eloquent brown eyes, Judy Burkhart was one of those. No man who had known her, who had shared her friendship, heard her lilting, mischievous laughter, or seen her face light with joy or cloud with sorrow, could ever forget her. Her every nuance of expression was stamped indelibly on Grant's soul.

"Judy, right?" he never gave her the details of his enslavement.

Smiling, she hit his arm. "So what are you going to do?"

"Oh, I don't know. I'll stick around here until you pick your Prince Charming, and then I'll move on."

Dark eyes showing alarm, Judy sat up straight. "Why?"

"I'm only human, pretty one," he said gruffly. It hurt that she never thought of him as a man. Just a friend.

"I know, but I thought you were my best friend. Friends don't leave just because someone gets married."

Grant leaned forward. Judy was serious. There was real hurt in her eyes. The inevitable tightening in his loins caused him to ache.

"Judy," he said quietly, "I'm your friend because that's the only position available to me."

"You mean you could just up and leave if I got married?" A tear welled up and trickled down her cheek to the corner of her mouth. Her chin trembling, she pulled in a ragged breath, and Grant groaned silently. How much was he expected to endure in the name of friendship? Did she think him so unfeeling that he could put up a tent and live on the fringes of her life forever—her own private court jester?

"Dammit, Judy, I'm just a man—" Clamping his jaws tight against any more sniveling, Grant stopped. It wasn't Judy's fault he was hopelessly in love with her. He had known when he'd decided on this course of action that it would not be easy. "A man with a need to travel, to see the world, to climb that next hill.

"Hey, pretty one," he continued gently, "you aren't married yet, so what are we worrying about? Besides, when your time comes, and the little bell in your head goes *bing,* you won't even notice if I wander away."

"Yes, I will."

"A wager, then," he said challengingly. Anything to keep her from crying. Her tears ripped his insides to shreds. Some things about Judy were predictable: She paid her debts, she was loyal to her friends, and she was otherwise totally unpredictable. Who would ever have guessed she would be upset because he intended to leave when she got married?

"You're on," she sniffed.

"You're covered. How much?"
"Five dollars."
"Piker!"
"Ten dollars."
"More like it."

CHAPTER THIRTEEN

After supper Tía helped the women with the dishes and then started to leave the kitchen. She was tired. She had gotten up early that morning, ridden seven hours to the ranch, helped Carmen prepare their supper and clean up the dishes, and now she looked forward to collapsing in her own room. It seemed perilously close to her bedtime.

"Tía."

It was Johnny's voice, coming to her from the back door. Tía untied the apron she'd been wearing. "What?"

"Take a short walk with me. I want to show you something." He walked across the dining hall to stop beside her. His nearness seemed to invigorate her, to make the air against her skin cooler. She didn't feel nearly as tired as she had a moment ago.

"No, thanks. I can't."

Johnny laughed softly. "Your beau waiting?"

"No."

"Then you can." Without waiting for her reply, he took her by the arm and propelled her toward the door on the exterior wall of the dining room. Outside, the slightly cooler breeze on her hot face felt so good that the protests she'd been about to utter died in her throat. She had been so stifled in the house, so aware of the tension from every direction. It felt wonderful to be outside. The sun hung low above the horizon. A bank of clouds had turned red and purple above the setting sun. Soon it would drop behind the Dragoons, and darkness would fall. Already crickets and frogs chirped a ragged backyard chorus.

"See how nice it is out here? Much cooler than sitting in that stuffy parlor. I want you to see something."

Without waiting for her to answer, he took her by the hand and led her into the barn, past the stalls occupied by snorting, snuffling horses to the east wall, where rungs had been nailed at intervals on the two-by-four upright supports to make a rough ladder up the hayloft.

"I can't climb that in this gown," she protested.

"I'll go up first and pull you in."

"I don't want to go up."

"I want you to see something you can't see from down here."

Noiselessly Johnny ascended the rungs to the top, lifted himself up and to the side, and disappeared for a moment. Tía thought about leaving, but curiosity was too strong in her. Johnny's face appeared at the hole, and he motioned her up.

Tía gathered the hem of her skirt and stuffed it in her mouth to keep the fabric out of her way while she climbed. At the top Johnny clasped her by the waist and lifted her up and over. "You look mighty pretty with your mouth full of your gown."

She started to retort, but he shushed her and took her hand. Tía followed in silence. Johnny knelt behind a haystack and motioned her down beside him. Once she was sitting, he turned and looked at her. "You need some straw." Before she could stop him he picked up an armload of straw and covered her with it.

"Are you loco?" she demanded.

"Hush, they're coming." He picked up a load of straw and covered himself with it, then another armload to cover their heads.

"Johnny, I'm not interested in becoming a haystack!"

"Shhhh! Aren't you curious? Listen."

Tía listened. After a moment she heard the murmur of children's voices coming from below. The voices were getting louder. She peered through the straw at Johnny.

"We have to be quiet," he whispered.

The children scampered up the same ladder Tía and Johnny had climbed. They were only children, no threat, but Tía's heart pounded with excitement at the thought that they might discover her here, hiding.

As they climbed up into the dimly lit loft, their voices took on hushed, conspiratorial overtones. She could barely make out what was being said. They settled themselves within twenty feet of where Tía lay.

One of the children, a boy who sounded like Carmen's son, Navarone, took charge. "If you want me to tell you a story, then you have to be quiet."

"Shhhh!" a voice hissed. Feet scraped and small bodies wiggled around for a moment, and then silence fell.

"Once upon a time..." Navarone told them a story about a ghost who lived at the old mission south of the ranch. As the story ended, Johnny made a low sound in his throat.

One of the kids shushed the other. "What was that?"

"Probably a rat or a chicken."

"I bet it was the ghost."

"Ghosts don't come out in daylight."

"Sure they do."

Tía counted six different voices, undoubtedly Navarone, Lupe's three children, and Cruz's two little ones. When she'd met them that afternoon, she had been told they ranged in age from five to twelve. Navarone started another story. She liked his voice. He was a good storyteller—he seemed to know how to adjust his story to keep their interest and make them laugh occasionally. As he told tales about the ghost from the mission, each one grew scarier and scarier. Tía wanted to see the children's faces. She too was spellbound. It called back memories she had forgotten. Andrea used to tell her stories. Sometimes she could prevail upon her sister to tell ghost stories. Then all the kids sat around in a circle, and Andrea told a ghost story that would go on and on and get scarier and scarier. Tía didn't know why that had been such fun at the time or why she should now remember it with such pleasure, but it had been and she did.

The boy's voice droned on, and she gave her imagination free rein. The ghost became a headless horseman who punished evildoers.

Once, a long time ago, Tía and a dozen children had climbed up into old man Mackelhenny's barn and sat in a circle around Andrea, who'd told ghost stories until full dark. There had been something delicious about sitting in the fragrant hay, smelling the barn smells, the animal smells, surrounded by other children as scared as she was. Tía could not believe she had forgotten until just this minute. She felt eight years old again.

Through the loose covering of hay, she glanced over at Johnny. His eyes were closed, and a dreamy look transformed his face. She smiled.

"What are you smiling about?" he whispered.

"I thought your eyes were closed."

"Closed but still working."

One of the children gave a little screech. "Aiiii!"

"I heard it, too!"

"What was it?"

In her mind's eye, Tía could see the children, all straining for some sound, half hoping it would be a rat or chicken, but half hoping it would be proof of a ghost.

Johnny tapped his hand on the wood floor.

"There!" one of the children yelped.

"What was it?"

The storyteller's voice shushed them. "It is only the ghost of the headless horseman," he crooned. "Be silent. Let him speak to us."

Johnny let out a low, moaning sound.

"Aiiii!"

"¡Caramba!"

Children scampered for the ladder. In the commotion they screamed and fought to be the first one out of the loft.

Finally they were all gone. The barn door slammed shut, and outside they yelled and ran. Gradually the usual barn sounds resumed. A chicken clucked as if it had just laid an egg. Horses in stalls snorted and blew. A pig squealed.

Tía sat up and brushed the hay off her. She wiped her face. "I'm going to itch all night. We better get out of here. They'll bring everyone in the compound."

Johnny laughed. "Nobody listens to kids, especially when they say they heard a ghost."

Tía brushed at a piece of straw that defied her. It was true: nobody would believe them. "That was a mean thing to do," she said, suddenly made crabby with the knowledge that he was right. "You spoiled their fun and fixed it so they'd get yelled at by Carmen for telling lies."

"Was not mean."

"Carmen, Lupe, and Cruz'll swat 'em and make 'em go to bed early."

"Not Carmen. Cruz will, though. She'd swat 'em no matter what they said to her. But they won't tell her."

"They will, too."

"Nope. I betcha a kiss they won't go near their mamas."

"Why would I want to kiss you?"

"The kiss was for me. I'll give you something else."

"Like what?"

"Like this." He slipped a bracelet out of his pocket. It was silver and jade. The silver had a nice polish on it, and the jade was an aqua color that she liked.

"Where'd you get that?"

"That whore I saved from *El Gato Negro*'s man gave it to me for saving her life."

"I better not wager."

"Why not?"

"Because you're Judy's beau. I don't want Judy to think I'm trying to cut between her and her beau."

"I'm not Judy's beau. I courted Judy three years ago, but she threw me over for another fella. I rode off in a fit of temper and stayed gone until old Bill and Steve asked me to come back."

"Well, how come she thinks you're her beau?"

"Maybe 'cause she wants me to be, but I'm a free man. Judy cut me loose three years ago. I ain't been tethered since."

That made sense to Tía. And she did want the bracelet. It was the prettiest piece of jewelry she'd ever seen. And she had enjoyed kissing him that day in Tubac. "How would we find out if they told or not?"

"You could ask Navarone."

"Then he'd know it was us."

"Don't ask him direct. You got to trick him into talking about it."

"I'm not good at tricking folks into anything."

"Then I'll trick him, and you listen."

"Okay."

Johnny shushed her. Down below, the barn door opened. It sounded as if the children were coming back. The thought of getting caught made Tía want to laugh out loud. She put her hand over her mouth.

"I'm not going back up there," a boy said.

"It's broad daylight, silly goose." That sounded like the storyteller.

"I don't care. We should have told Mama."

"You want to get a lump on your head, you go tell her."

"We still should have told her. What if she comes out here some night and the ghost gets her?"

Johnny let out a low moan, like a barn owl, and the kids screamed and slammed the barn door.

Outside, from a distance, other kids yelled and laughed. Johnny grinned from ear to ear. Tía felt like going into a sulk. She wasn't going to get the bracelet.

"Well, here's your kiss," she said, leaning over to give him a peck on the cheek.

Johnny shook his head. "This is an expensive piece of jewelry. I didn't wager it for something any kid can get just by promising to sit down and shut up."

Her sulk lifted a little. Somehow trying to cheat him out of something he felt he had coming made her feel better. "I can't imagine what you could do about it," she said. "Not many men would be dumb enough to trade anything of value for a kiss."

Johnny laughed out loud. From a distance a child yelled, "It's laughing! It's laughing!"

Johnny snapped his mouth shut. His eyes still lighted by mischief, he raised his arms and pretended he was going to grab Tía.

"If I scream, they'll figure out it wasn't a ghost."

"Why would you scream?"

"If you try to take too much of a kiss."

Johnny lowered his arms and frowned. "You were going to take my whole bracelet, weren't you?"

"Of course."

"Well, I've had one of your kisses before. I know what a whole kiss feels like. I'll just take one of those."

Tía thought about that for a moment. He had a way of making it seem so logical. Before she could make up her mind for sure, he lifted her chin and looked into her eyes. He had stopped smiling, and he seemed to be searching for something. "You've got the prettiest blue eyes I've ever seen," he said, his voice as low and husky as a barn owl's hoot.

He pulled her into his arms, and Tía's heart started to pound. Her mind filled with pictures of Mama being choked by Papa. She felt uncomfortable suddenly and tried to wiggle out of his arms. Johnny tightened his grip on her, then thought better of it and let her go.

Tía stepped away from him.

As soon as she did she felt upset that he hadn't kissed her and gotten it over with. But it had been her fault for turning so balky at the last minute. He'd made it plain he wasn't willing to fight her for a kiss. And he shouldn't have to. A deal was a deal. Maybe if he just wouldn't hold her. She didn't want to be held. She could feel herself growing upset again just thinking about it.

Johnny looked hurt. He turned and started for the ladder. Tía grabbed him by the arm and stopped him. "Don't be mad at me."

"I'm not mad at you. If you don't want to kiss me, I guess you don't have to." He'd had some experience with women, and he'd learned that usually if a man made it easy, most women would kiss him—if she wanted to anyway. He had made it easy for Tía, but she still didn't want to. He turned again to walk away.

Tía felt mad at Johnny for making a wager that would cause so much trouble between them. But she felt madder at herself for not being able to give him a simple kiss. She had in Tubac, and nothing bad had come of it. She hated it when she owed somebody something. She didn't want to see Johnny day after day, him knowing she owed him a kiss. Better to get it done and over with.

He was still facing away from her. She stepped up close behind him and put her arms around him the way she had with Papa so many times. Johnny was as tall as Papa. Somehow that surprised her. He felt as sturdy as Papa. She hated comparing Johnny with Papa, but she'd never hugged any other men. Elmo didn't count. He was too scrawny.

Johnny expelled a heavy breath. "If I turn around, are you going to run away?"

Tía didn't like him thinking her a welsher. "I will not. You've got a kiss coming, and I'll see that you get it."

"That won't be necessary," he said stiffly.

Tía wanted to shake him like a dog shook a bone. Now, somehow, he'd gotten his dander up, and he didn't *want* her to kiss him! Wasn't that just like a man? Tía had heard Mama and her friends say that so many times that it just naturally popped into her own head.

Johnny turned around and faced her. He looked stubborn now. "You're going to be kissed, Johnny Brago, whether you like it or not."

"I am, am I?"

"Yes. You can close your eyes or not," she warned.

Tía pulled his head down and pressed her lips hard against his. Somehow nothing much happened this time. His lips felt sort of wrinkled and hard. She pulled back and looked at him. His eyes were open, and he looked like a man waiting for her to be done. "Are we even now?" she asked.

"Even steven."

"You're still mad as a hornet, aren't you?"

"If you want to welsh on a bet, why should I get mad?" He turned to leave.

Tía grabbed him by the arm and jerked him back around. "I'm no welsher!"

"I wouldn't have paid you with an imitation bracelet, Tía Marlowe. I would have given you the bracelet I showed you."

He was right. Tía felt a sudden urge to cry. She didn't know how to re-create the kiss they had shared in Tubac. It hadn't been something she did, it had been something magical that had seemed to happen because they'd touched.

Maybe she wasn't the same person he'd kissed in Tubac. She didn't feel like the same person. Something had gone wrong with her that day, and she couldn't for the life of her figure out what it was, but she just didn't want to be held down and kissed. She felt at a loss to know what to say to him, what to do.

"Then you kiss me," she said, her voice nearly failing as she spoke.

"I already tried that, and you acted like a rabbit caught in a snare."

"Well, you held me too tight!"

"If a man can't do nothing right, it's time for him to go to bed."

"It wasn't you."

Johnny looked all around the barn. "Who was it?"

"It was me." Tía felt so miserable she could barely speak.

"Fine," Johnny said. "You don't want to be hugged when you're kissed, you don't have to be." He turned to leave again.

Tía stamped her foot. "You kiss me right this minute, Johnny Brago!"

"How am I going to do that without touching you?"

"Your mouth can touch my mouth."

Johnny sighed. Somehow his simple game had gotten out of hand. She was as agitated as a hen with an egg caught crosswise. "All right, but if you back off, that's it."

"I won't back off."

Johnny almost walked out. He couldn't see himself kissing a girl who had to screw her courage up so tight that her face lost its color. He didn't want his kissing her to be such an ordeal. Somehow this had worked around so that he couldn't win. Either way she was going to hate it, but he could see she wasn't going to let him leave without paying him what she thought she owed him. He might as well get it over with.

He leaned down and stopped. "Is it okay if I touch your chin?"

"Yes." Tía closed her eyes and waited. His warm fingers touched her chin and tilted it up slightly.

"Open your mouth," he whispered.

Tía let her lips part. Then she felt nervous and had to lick them. His lips touched hers and sort of insinuated themselves inside her mouth and around her tongue.

A wave of dizziness washed over her. She reached out to steady herself, and his body underneath the cotton shirt he wore felt so solid and warm and good that she didn't want to let go of him. And once she got started kissing him, she didn't want to stop doing that, either.

Johnny forgot his promise not to touch her. She seemed to have forgotten it, too. She was kissing him the way she had in Tubac. She sort of sagged against him, and he laid her down on the hay and kept kissing her until his own head was spinning like the merry-go-round he'd seen in Phoenix one time when a traveling circus had come to town.

Tía felt as though she might black out. Johnny was kissing her face, her throat, and her mouth again. Finally he just held her close for a long time.

She sighed with contentment. "I reckon that ought to be worth a bracelet," she murmured, so pleased with herself that she could have popped a freshly sewed button.

"They don't make bracelets that are worth that much." He reached into his pocket, took out the bracelet, and put it on her wrist.

"You weren't supposed to give it to me. I lost the bet."

"Well, I'm not going to wear it. I guess I can give it to you if I want."

Tía smiled and snuggled close against him. "I'm glad you're not still mad at me."

The sun had set behind the Dragoons. Through the lone window at the east end of the barn, a solitary star shone in the sky. He pointed up at it. "See that light there? You know what that is?"

"It's a star."

"Nope. It's Venus, a planet."

"How do you know that?"

"I saw it in one of Steve's books."

"Just like our planet?" Tía wanted to let him know that she had gone to school and paid attention.

"But colder. It's farther away from the sun."

"How do you know it's not a star?" She hadn't listened all the time. Now she wished she had.

"It doesn't twinkle. See how steady the light is?"

Tía peered intently at the tiny light hanging above the mountains. "Could you be wrong?"

"Never been before. Venus has been moving around up there since before I was born."

"You must think I'm pretty dumb."

Johnny shook his head. "I was testing you."

"For dumbness?"

"To see if you'd ever had a steady fella."

"How would that tell?"

Johnny laughed. "Because that's one of the first things a fella tells a girl he wants to impress."

Tía sat up and wiped the straw off her. "We better get back. I don't want to get into trouble with Steve my first day here."

"I hope I'm not going to have to answer any more questions about Steve," Johnny said, his voice changing. Tía started to tease him, but his face was such a thundercloud suddenly that she didn't. He stood up and pulled her up beside him. He walked her to the back door and stopped. "Don't lose that bracelet. It's probably worth a lot of money."

"Maybe you shouldn't give it to me."

"We already chewed that over." Respectfully, he touched the brim of his hat. "Good night."

Tía turned and walked inside. The house was dark except for lights in the parlor. She wanted to slip past and get to her room without being seen, but Steve stepped out and saw her.

"Do you have a moment?" he asked.

"Yes, sir."

"Could you come into the parlor?"

Tía followed him back to the parlor. Andrea sat on one of the leather Morris chairs. A book lay open in her lap. Judy stood up and excused herself. "I just wanted to talk to the two of you for a minute."

He looked uncomfortable. Tía glanced at Andrea. "Yes, sir?"

Steve cleared his throat. "I'm not good at saying things to women, but I wanted to mention that there are a lot of men living in this compound. I don't expect you to have any trouble of any type, but in case you haven't lived in quite these circumstances before...you may have noticed that we have a *cantina*."

Andrea caught Steve's attention. "You sell alcohol?"

"On Saturday nights I allow the men to buy as much beer and whiskey as they want as long as there are no fights. We're isolated here, and many weeks go by when they can't get into Fort Bowie or Tombstone. In years past, there was no Tombstone."

Steve looked at Tía. "Sunday is the men's day off. They work till noon on Saturday unless we're having Indian trouble, then sometimes they don't go outside the walls. During spring branding and fall roundups, the men camp out. The women have Sundays off except for breakfast. The men fend for themselves, usually eat canned goods and the like."

Andrea glanced at Tía, then looked up at Steve. "Are the men likely to bother—"

"I don't expect any man in my employ to force himself on either of you, but under the influence of drink, men are capable of making mistakes. Especially if a woman is attractive and friendly. I know you're both ladies, and I'm sure you know how to handle yourselves among men, but I just wanted you to know how we operate here."

"What do they do for fun?" Andrea asked.

"On Saturdays, the *vaqueros* play music, and anyone who wants to is free to dance and drink. Things get a little loose. If you go out, just try to stay with the crowd. That way you can't get in too much trouble. I know all the men, but occasionally a drifter will come through and work awhile. Some men are pretty hard cases."

Steve looked as if he had embarrassed himself. He stopped speaking abruptly, and then excused himself. Tía and Andrea walked in silence to their separate rooms.

When the house seemed quiet, Tía slipped out of her room and into Andrea's. In her long flannel nightgown, Andrea was just climbing into the big feather bed. Andrea held the covers for her sister to scoot under with her. "Where were you tonight?"

"Johnny asked me to take a walk with him. Are you all right? I was scared to death for you today," Tía whispered, shivering at the feel of the cold cotton sheets. So close to the mountains, the valley was refreshingly cool after sundown.

"Stay away from Johnny Brago," Andrea warned.

"How come?"

"Because he's nothing but trouble."

"He is not."

"Of course he is. You want to turn out just like Mama?"

"Yes."

"You don't mean that. Johnny Brago is just like Papa. He'll never amount to anything. He'll make your life a misery."

"Papa didn't make Mama's life a misery."

"Of course he did. Mama was a lady. Because of him, and marrying him, she had to live like white trash."

"Mama did not!"

"Of course she did. You think respectable white women live like we did? Do you think they work in saloons? Or befriend fancy ladies and saddle tramps?"

"Mama likes all kinds of people, if they aren't phony."

"Mama would have preferred to like people who were looked up to by folks around them. She had no choice."

Somehow it unsettled Tía to have Andrea talking about Mama as if she'd never been happy. She decided to change the subject in hopes of getting Andrea in a better mood.

"I was scared for you today. I rode up to tell Judy that I was Teresa, but I got there too late. You'd already shot off the gun."

"I'm glad you didn't say anything. I was fine. The Indian attack was more pitiful than anything else. I was a bit shocked when I came inside the house. Now I remember when we were here."

"You do? When? I don't remember anything."

"That's because you weren't born yet."

"Oh, well, that makes sense." They were silent for a while.

"This is the kind of place we'd have grown up in if Mama hadn't married a wild man like Papa."

Tía didn't know what to say to that. Mama had married Papa, and they had grown up in Tubac, which had seemed good enough at the time. She didn't know why Andrea was always saying "what if." It didn't make sense to her to worry about how things would have been if someone thirty years ago had done something other than what they'd done. Uncle Tyler worried about that all the time, and all it had gotten him was a sour look on his face and a dyspeptic stomach.

"Andrea, isn't Steve handsome?" she said.

"Yes, very." Andrea tried to decide if she wanted to tell Tía about the episode in the hotel room. But she worried that Tía would let on somehow and Steve would know she had told her.

"He seems nice, doesn't he?" Tía asked. "I love him."

Andrea ignored her last remark. Tía loved everybody, whether they deserved it or not. She was in love with the idea of having a brother. She had talked of nothing else the whole trip from Albany. Andrea was sick of the subject. "He may be nice to you. He resents me."

"But he spent dinner sneaking looks at you," Tía said.

"He barely knew I was alive," Andrea protested.

"That was when you were watching him. The rest of the time he was staring at you."

"He thinks I'm his sister. He's probably looking for some family resemblance." The subject made Andrea uncomfortable. "Johnny Brago watches you like a chicken hawk with his first pullet. If you're smart, you'll avoid him entirely."

"I don't see why."

"You haven't listened to a thing I said. Judy appears to be quite affected by him, and I think he's a cheat. And I can't stand a cheat!" Just thinking about Johnny Brago and Tía made Andrea angry. Tía would end up just like Mama: tied to a man who would be nothing but trouble!

"I thought you loved Papa," Tía whispered.

"I do love Papa, but that does not mean that I have to be blind where he is concerned. He made Mama's life a misery. At times she hated him, and so did I."

Tía didn't know what to think about that. She hadn't known Mama hated Papa. She hadn't know Andrea did, either.

"Well, I didn't—"

"You didn't care to know. You loved him so much you couldn't see anything else."

Tía frowned at the ceiling. She wasn't sure she liked growing up. She was learning all sorts of things she didn't want to know about people.

"Tía, are you asleep?"

Tía pulled the covers around her and snuggled closer to Andrea as if that could somehow rearrange the unsettling memory that had already lodged in her mind. Andrea was talking. Had she been talking long?

"Did you know Steve is a mining engineer? Judy bragged that he was the one who convinced their father to buy into the mine. He knew or guessed that the rock formation there meant the vein they found was going to go deeper and get bigger, not peter out the way so many of them do."

"Steve says he's here at the ranch to keep you and Judy from killing one another."

"Or maybe he wants to watch the fun."

"You're too suspicious, Andrea."

"She plainly resents me."

"She's nice. I think we're going to be friends."

"Sure. Until she finds out who you really are."

"Maybe we should tell them right away."

Andrea thought about that for a moment, then discarded the idea. She wanted to get to know more about Steve before she told him she wasn't his sister. "Couldn't we wait a week or so, until they get to know us? It won't hurt anything."

Tía sighed. She didn't like pretending to be someone else. Every time someone spoke to her, she had to try and remember who they thought she was. It was wearing on her nerves. And she didn't feel honest playacting at being someone else. She was sorry she'd thought of the idea, but it pleased her that Andrea was so happy with her role. Andrea liked to play at being the lady of the spread. She brought dignity and grace to the role. It was no surprise to Tía that no one doubted her.

Tía didn't see what good waiting a week would do, but she couldn't see any graceful way of telling the others they had been tricked. To her way of thinking, she should have confessed after the Indian attack. To let it go on longer seemed to be looking for trouble, but if it was important to Andrea, then she would go along with it. They would either forgive them or not, and when they told probably wouldn't make a big difference. She just hoped she wouldn't have to listen to Andrea talk about how different her life would have been if only they'd told at a time different from when they actually did tell.

Andrea turned over and put her arm around Tía. "Judy has to be the most nervous girl I've ever known. After you and Johnny went outside, she talked without a breath the whole time. I think she was hoping either we wouldn't notice or she wouldn't."

"Oh, no," Tía moaned. "Judy is in love with Johnny. Now she probably thinks I'm trying to take him away from her."

Outside, crickets whirred, and a dog barked. Tía wondered if Johnny listened to them make their screechy little sounds, or had he already gone to sleep? Beside her, Andrea plumped her pillow and repositioned herself. "It's nice here, isn't it?" Tía whispered. "I found a place out back where someone planted jasmine and wisteria and a lot of different flowers. Maybe Judy did that."

Andrea punched her pillow with her fist. "I might like it better if I didn't have to worry about Judy."

"I like it a lot," Tía murmured, snuggling close to her sister. "Are you sorry we changed places? I mean because of Steve?"

Andrea closed her eyes. All day she'd been thinking about Steve Burkhart and how she had let him kiss her. She had always thought herself different from Mama's friends, who talked about men constantly. In Tubac she had worked at being different, because if she got a chance to get away from Tubac, she wanted to make the most of it. She didn't want to be tied down by a man who thought he had some claim on her or by a houseful of babies. *No one ever got rich having babies,* Mama had said, and Andrea had believed her. Now she was twenty-five years old and a virgin. She had thought until her eye-opening experience with Steve it was because she didn't have the same feelings about men other women felt. Now it appeared that none of the men she had been exposed to had appealed to her.

The grandfather clock over the mantel in the parlor chimed nine times. Nine o'clock. Tía stirred. That was late for her. She kissed Andrea's cheek and slipped out of bed.

Tía stopped at Judy's door on the way to her own bed. She wanted to go in, but she didn't know what she would say to Judy. No sound came from Judy's room. Perhaps she was asleep.

Undecided, Tía slipped back to her own room. She had to be up at five the next morning. She took off her dressing robe, turned out the lamp, and walked to the window. Through the wrought-iron bars Steve had fashioned and installed over the windows to protect against sneaking Indians, silhouettes of the outbuildings were visible. Slowly, Tía's eyes adjusted. The building to the left was the Mexican women's quarters, the one opposite hers was Johnny's cabin.

A vision of Johnny lying in the haystack made her smile.

The building to her right was the main bunkhouse. Lights burned brightly there. Occasionally a man laughed or shouted some unintelligible remark. For the *vaqueros* who liked to be separate, another, smaller building had been built south of the bunkhouse.

Tía wondered why Johnny had to have a place of his own. She studied his cabin in the semidarkness. A female shape materialized out of the shadows and paused for a second in front of the door, then slipped inside.

Judy! Going into Johnny's cabin. She'd be right out. Johnny would send her to bed. With a mixture of dread and anticipation, Tía watched for a few minutes and then turned away from the window. It was bad enough to change places and lie to people; she shouldn't be spying on them as well. She walked to the bed and lay down. Maybe she was coming down with something. Her head ached, and her stomach felt queasy.

Tía closed her eyes, but sleep did not come.

Judy entered Johnny's cabin without knocking. Inside, she scanned the small room. "Well, what happened? Did she manage to get away from you?"

The lamp on his table was turned low. Surprised by Judy's walking in so unexpectedly, Johnny sat up and ran his fingers through his hair. He had hoped to put this off or avoid it all together.

"She's supposed to be my friend," she said, her brown eyes flashing. "If that little maggot is chasing you, I'll tear her apart."

"Rein in your temper. She's not chasing me."

"You're chasing her?"

Johnny stood up and opened the door she had just closed. He didn't want to fight with Judy about Tía. But he had learned women did things according to their own timetable, no matter what a man wanted sometimes.

"I'm not jealous, you know," Judy said vehemently, standing in front of him, her chin up, her slender young body poised in that stubborn posture he knew only too well. "I'm mad! I will not be made light of in front of my servants. I won't have my man chasing the hired help right in front of my eyes. It's humiliating! Besides, you don't need her. You've got me. We'll be married soon." She stepped close to him, put her arms around his waist, and burrowed her face against his chest. "Oh, Johnny, it feels so good to be in your arms."

Leaning away from him suddenly, she smiled. "I really love it when you look so fierce. You have the most beautiful eyes when you're trying to figure out what to do. I can imagine you doing any number of things to me when you look at me like that..."

"Judy, dammit." Things were moving too fast for him. Judy had a way of assuming a whole bunch of things, and if he didn't have enough time to sort them all out, she'd be working on another bunch of assumptions based on the last bunch he hadn't had time to call her on. Johnny picked the one that riled him the most for his challenge. "We ain't lovers."

"Of course we are."

"No. Maybe we could have been at one time, but not now," he said emphatically. "You're like a sister to me."

Judy's laughter drowned him out. "Sister!" she cried. "That was not brotherly devotion the other night, Johnny Brago. That was lust, just like the preacher yells about on Sunday morning, real hell-fire-and-damnation lust. I could tell."

Johnny reddened with shame. Judy had the damnedest way of saying things. She could turn a few kisses into a worrisome piece of business. He decided he might as well get it all out on the table, show his cards. "I might as well tell you this all at once. I was a worse bastard than you think. I came back here to get even with you."

"I told you you loved me. That's the act of a man in love."

"I was in love. But I got over it without noticing."

A stricken look clouded her dark eyes. "But you..." She faltered into silence. Tears spilled over and made shiny tracks on her lovely, curving cheeks. Johnny writhed inside. He didn't want to hurt her, but he forced himself not to turn away. He deserved anything she did to him.

"You love me, Johnny. You've always loved me," she said.

"I still love you. Only now I love you in a different way. Like a sister..." Johnny inhaled deeply. "I guess I loved you so much I went a little crazy with it," he said, his voice strained. "I thought I wanted to hurt you the way I got hurt. But I don't want to hurt you, Judy. That probably sounds like so much hogwash after what I said, but it's the truth."

"Is that why you avoided me, made me come to you?"

Johnny nodded. For a moment nothing happened. She seemed to be considering his answer, then her chin went up and her eyes flashed.

Before he could figure it out, she stepped back and slapped him hard across the face. "You liar!"

Johnny took the blow calmly. And most likely would have taken it again. He wanted to be free to spark Tía.

"You have to love me," Judy cried, her eyes anguished. "You have to."

"I do," he said gently. "I love you like a sister. I don't want to hurt you any more. I want you to be happy."

"Then love me the way you used to," she said, tears spilling down her cheeks.

"I can't."

"This is your revenge, isn't it?" she whispered.

"You give me too much credit."

"Do I?" Her voice sounded oddly brittle. She twisted at her skirt with hands that trembled. "I love you, Johnny. I was good today. I got up early, and I cleaned my room. I ate all my dinner, and I didn't do anything bad…"

Johnny couldn't figure out what she was talking about. They had been in Tombstone that morning. She hadn't gotten up early. She hadn't gotten to the livery stable until eight-thirty. She hadn't cleaned anything. Even her voice had changed, coming out in a piping, childlike singsong he'd never heard before.

"Judy…"

"I know what you're doing," she said. "You're just saying this to punish me, because you think I've been bad, but I haven't. I've been good. So you don't need to punish me."

Her bottom lip began to tremble. Her fingers dug into the soft skin of her arm. Again, she had changed more quickly than he could keep up. The confident woman he had known and loved and hated had been replaced by this stranger with the pleading eyes of a child. He didn't know what to do or say.

"Stop! You're hurting yourself." Johnny pulled her into his arms and held her close, feeling the terrible trembling inside her, racking her body. She cried softly. When she finally subsided he lifted her chin and wiped her eyes with the handkerchief he had taken out of his hip pocket.

"Feel better?"

"Yuh…yes," she said, trying to smile. "You won't be sorry, Johnny. I'm going to be so good. You'll be proud of me. You'll see. You'll love me more than ever. I'm going to be the best little wife in the territory. Everyone will be so jealous of you. They'll come from miles around just so they can tell their friends they stayed at the Brago house. It's going to be—"

"Judy, I can't marry you. I want us to be friends—" He stopped. Dilated and unfocused, her eyes told him she was rejecting every word he said.

Helplessness washed over him, the same sort of helplessness he'd felt when he'd found his parents dead—his father with an arrow through the chest, his mother with a tomahawk in the back of her skull. He had sagged down on the ground and not wanted to see or smell their bodies, as if not seeing again and not smelling would somehow change what had happened.

Now he wished he'd never come back to Rancho la Reina. He had the feeling that something just as final had happened here tonight.

Gently, Johnny disengaged himself from Judy's clutching hands, put his arm around her slim waist, and walked her to the back door of the *casa grande*.

CHAPTER FOURTEEN

Seeing Judy at the door of the bunkhouse, Grant Foreman, who had been playing monte with three other riders, passed his cards to one of the kibitzers, pushed his chair back, and strode quickly to the front porch.

"Hey, pretty lady, you all right?"

The smile she gave him was forced. "Of course."

"You look pale." He took her arm to lead her off the porch. She looked worse than pale. A hard look of strain pinched her features and darkened her eyes. "Did you fight with Johnny?"

Judy looked like a fawn surprised by a hunter. In the dim light from the window, her pretty face had a luminous glow. Grant was sorry he had asked. She would lie to him; he knew it instantly.

"Johnny and I don't fight," she said firmly. "You know how I am, though. When I'm bad he punishes me."

Concern furrowed Grant's brow. "What do you mean, he punishes you?"

"It's not important," she said vaguely, waving her hand. "It was all my fault. Besides, nothing matters as long as he still loves me…"

"Did he hurt you?" Grant demanded, anger rising in him.

Startled, Judy looked at Grant and then turned away quickly, her eyes clouded with some painful memory. "Johnny would never hurt me. Johnny loves me. He's always loved me."

Confused, Grant tried to control the rage building within him. "What happened?"

"Nothing."

"You're lying to me."

Staring at the bunkhouse lights behind Grant, Judy frowned. "Am I?" Then, taking a deep breath as if trying to throw off something unpleasant, she asked, "Will you walk with me, Grant?"

It was past the usual curfew that Steve imposed at the *casa grande*. The house would be locked when they came back, but Grant didn't care. Judy climbed in and out her window all the time. The only thing that mattered was she needed him. "Sure, any time, you know that."

Slowly they walked to the playhouse at the back of the orchard. Inside, Judy sank down onto the small cot. Grant sat Indian fashion at her feet. They talked for an hour, about anything Judy wanted to talk about. As always Grant was the perfect gentleman. He played his part the way she had outlined it to him long ago: he was her friend, which meant he could not expect romance. He knew she had others among the riders she flirted with and some she kissed and toyed with, but that only lasted until they pressured her in some way. There may have been one or two that she had allowed other liberties, but he loved her too much to dwell on that.

Close to eleven o'clock, they started back.

Judy took his hand and walked alongside him, swinging their hands between them. She stopped at the back entrance and let herself in as if she knew the door would be open. Steve always locked up the house about nine.

"Thanks, Grant."

"What are friends for?"

"See you tomorrow."

"Good night."

Judy faked a smile, waved at him, and then closed the door. She waited there until she saw Grant step up onto the bunkhouse porch and go inside. Then, quietly, she slipped back outside the way she had done when Johnny had left her earlier. She was already lonely for Grant, but she knew he needed his sleep. Johnny took the riders out early and worked them hard. She should go to bed, too, but she was too restless to sleep. The night was cool and crisp. Her room would be stuffy, stifling. She shivered. The terrible things Johnny had said to her kept bobbing around in her head like apples floating in water. Every time she pushed them down, they popped back up. And each time they bobbed up, the pressure increased in her head.

She had done it again. She had driven Johnny away the same way she had driven her mother away—by wanting too much. Her hands were sweaty and cold. Maybe she was going to be sick. Whatever it was, she didn't want to be alone. As she turned and started back toward the bunkhouse to get Grant, a shadow stepped out of the other shadows and caught her arm.

In the pale starlight she recognized the rider. "Oh, Slick, you scared me!"

Slick grinned and leaned against the adobe.

In the moonlight his resemblance to Johnny was stronger than usual.

"You want to sit and talk a spell?" he asked.

Judy started to say no, then stopped herself. Slick was safe. He wouldn't hurt her, and she didn't want to be alone now. She nodded. "Walk out to the playhouse with me."

Slick could not believe his good fortune. He fell into step beside her.

Five o'clock came much too soon for Tía. Groggy from unaccustomed sleeplessness, but excited about her first real day at Rancho la Reina, she tumbled out of bed. By the time she'd dressed and combed her curls, the eastern sky was streaked pale pink and gold with a hint of dawn.

Her room was next to the kitchen. The clang of iron pots greeted her before she opened her door. She couldn't believe her ears, but it sounded like even Andrea was up, moving around her room.

Tía walked into the kitchen. Kerosene lamps gave the room a cheery glow. Carmen was poking at the firebox under the oven.

"*Buenos días*," Tía said as she stopped behind Carmen. "What can I do?"

Smiling, Carmen looked over her shoulder. "*Buenos días, Señorita Marlowe*."

"Humph!" Sullen with sleepiness, Cruz eyed Tía and Carmen with gloomy impassivity. "No day that begins without mass can be a good day," she said emphatically.

Tía frowned. "Is there a chapel within the walls?"

"*¡No, por supuesto!* Would infidels build a chapel?" Cruz demanded, her high-pitched voice caustic. "Infidels tear down chapels. They do not build them. There *was* a chapel, down by the cottonwoods, but infidels burned it, too. Just like they burn everything of value. If it won't burn, they knock it down, brick by brick if necessary."

Smiling, Carmen motioned Tía to her side. "Don't worry about Cruz. She is only happy if she is complaining."

"Thanks," Tía said, grinning. "What can I do?"

"*Señorita*, if you would not be offended, there are many potatoes to be peeled and sliced," she said.

"I forgot where I saw the knives."

"Here," Carmen said, pointing to a drawer under the wooden bench beside the cook stove. From catalogs, Tía recognized the three stoves that lined the wall as Acme sterling-steel ranges, the best. With forty men to feed, and at ten thousand a week, the Burkharts needed and could afford the best.

Tía reached for the knife and the potatoes. If all the women had to do was cook, it was still going to be a long, busy day.

Cock a doodle, doo. Cock a doodle, dooooo! Andrea covered her head and tried to ignore the insistent crowing of that damned rooster, but the sound started all over again. She tried to mash the pillow over her ears, but the sound was so piercing she could barely tell the difference. Groaning, she staggered out of bed and over to her window. The offender was a small, red banty rooster, alternately crowing and pecking at the sandy soil.

She shushed him away and staggered back to her bed. Within seconds he was under her window again, crowing at the top of his lungs. Andrea threw her pillow at the open window, but it only hit the wrought-iron bars and bounced onto the floor. The rooster crowed louder than before.

"I'm going to suggest rooster for dinner!" she yelled. The rooster squawked and beat his wings and squawked louder. "Shut up!" Three hens rushed over to stand under her window and add their voices to his. At last Andrea sighed and gave up. "You win, but I warn you, I'm not going to take this lying down."

She sponged herself off in the bowl next to the water pitcher, combed her hair, and dressed herself. She would have liked to lie down again, but the chickens seemed to be louder than ever. She walked to her door and started to turn the knob.

A loud yell that sounded as though it came from the parlor caused Andrea to stop. The next voice was undoubtedly Judy's. Steve and Judy? Frowning, she opened the door and walked as quietly as possible into the hall.

"Leave me alone! I'm twenty years old. I don't need a wet nurse!" Judy cried, her usually melodious voice harsh with anger and passion. "I couldn't sleep, so I found Grant, and we walked for a while. That's all!"

Steve's voice was tight with suppressed fury. "I asked Grant not ten minutes ago, and he said he hadn't seen you this morning."

"You have no right running around like some prison warden spying on me. I hate it! I absolutely hate it! You treat me like a six-year-old child!"

Andrea could not make out Steve's low-voiced reply.

"If that maggot says one word to me, she's going to get a mouthful of knuckles, you hear me?"

Andrea flushed. He had been talking about her.

"Leave Andrea out of this."

"Then you leave her out of it. You're the one ganging up against me! Now you'll have Miss High and Mighty with her shotgun and her damned schoolteacher mouth on your side! She's a maggot! I hate her!"

"Hush!" he whispered fiercely. "She'll hear you!"

"You even like her! Traitor. I thought for once you were going to be on my side."

Andrea slipped back to her door, opened it, stepped through again, slammed it, and walked briskly and loudly toward the parlor.

As she stepped through the doorway, Steve frowned Judy into silence. The tension between brother and sister was palpable. "Well, good morning," Andrea said carefully. Now that she was here, she could not imagine why she had barged in.

"Good morning yourself!" Judy said, flouncing past her.

"Brat!" Steve said under his breath. A moment later they heard Judy's door slam hard.

"Problems?" Andrea asked.

"What the hell would you do if your sister came straggling in at six o'clock in the morning?" he demanded, forgetting Judy was her sister, too.

"That depends," Andrea said.

"On what?"

"On whether I loved her."

Caught off guard, Steve frowned. "And if you did?"

"I'd cook her breakfast, if she was hungry."

Steve looked at her as if he'd never heard anything so ridiculous. "Oh great! You'd cook her breakfast. How the hell is she going to learn right from wrong?"

Andrea raised an eyebrow. "Judy's a twenty-year-old woman. She's doing what she does because she either wants to or needs to, not because she doesn't know the difference between right and wrong."

Steve shook his head in frustration. Andrea was saying pretty much what Judy herself had been implying one way or another for years, ever since she'd been doing what she wanted instead of what she was supposed to do. "She'll hunt with any dog that'll run with her," he said bitterly.

"That's a pretty harsh accusation." Andrea watched him closely.

Wearily, Steve shook his head. "Well, dammit, if you walk like a duck, and you quack like a duck, people will call you a duck, and treat you like one, too."

"You have a point, but I don't see what good it does for you to yell at her. Doesn't that just announce to the world what you want to keep secret?"

"Don't you think an unmarried woman should be punished for living like a strumpet?"

"Not by you."

"Who's going to do it?"

Andrea felt a sudden surge of despair. She was thinking of her mother and all the ways the world had of dealing with a woman who broke the rules.

"You don't really want to punish her, do you?" she asked at last.

Frowning, Steve mulled over her question. "No. I'm just trying to save what's left of her reputation. I don't give a damn if she wants to live her own life, but I do want her to have a life left when she finally comes to her senses. She's got to learn there are serious consequences when a woman behaves badly."

"Yelling at Judy now isn't going to save her from anything else. All you're doing is ruining the closeness that you two already share." Andrea paused. "Has Judy always been willful?"

"Yes."

"Then you aren't going to change her at this late date. I would rather see you on her side so if she does get into real trouble, she has someone to turn to."

"She knows she can turn to me."

"Not if you're always condemning her. The world is full of people who can't wait to judge her. Do you really want to be one of those? Judy loves you. You're all she has. She's not acting out of malice. She's doing the best she knows how."

Too frustrated to speak coherently, Steve made a fist, then let it drop to his side.

Andrea felt like a fool defending Judy, but she couldn't seem to stop herself. "You love her. Don't shut her out."

"I don't want *anyone* to hurt her…" Pausing, Steve regarded Andrea more thoroughly. "You sound like you've had some experience with wayward sisters. Did you have one, too?"

"A wayward mother."

"I guess I should have known that. You must love her a lot, to be so understanding. What was she like?"

"A lot like Judy. Very pretty and very restless—she has to live every minute to the fullest. In spite of that, she was a good mother. She loved us and took care of us."

"You had brothers and sisters?"

Andrea blanched. She had almost given herself away. "One half sister. No brothers."

"Where's your mother now?"

"I don't know. She left me in Albany. Then Mr. Furnett's letter came…I didn't have any place else to go, so here I am."

"Where's your sister?"

Andrea sighed. "I'm not sure." That was almost true. Tía could be anywhere. The house, the barn, the garden…

Steve shifted uncomfortably from foot to foot. "Seems strange a woman as pretty and intelligent as you didn't get married."

"That sounds like a polite way of calling me an old maid," she chided gently.

Steve jammed his hands in his pants pockets self-consciously. Andrea smiled. "It's all right," she said softly. "You're right. I'm too old to be single, but I lived in a small town. The men I knew just didn't interest me. Or I them. The men I could have liked were fenced off from me."

"Because of your mother?"

"A number of things." Steve was forgetting she was a half-breed. He must have been seventeen or eighteen when she and Mama had come to Rancho la Reina. She hadn't seen him. Where had he been? What had he been doing then?

His lips tightened. "And you are encouraging me to let Judy—"

"No! Judy is going to live the way she wants to live no matter what you say or do. All I'm suggesting is that you not judge her so harshly. My mother is a good woman. With the right man we would have had a normal life. She loved us! She would have done anything for us. From what I've seen of Judy, she may be cut from the same cloth. What good does it do to make her feel badly about herself?"

Steve frowned. The way Andrea said it, it almost made sense. Was he befuddled by the fight with Judy or by this passionate, meddling woman befriending his sister? She was surprisingly persuasive and very appealing. Her lavender cotton gown was crisp and clean, and it hugged the soft curves of her body in such a way that he felt certain she was not wearing stays. His mind made a picture of her breasts, with their small, dark rose nipples. An irritating heat quickened in his loins.

Andrea started to put forth another argument, then stopped. His eyes had changed—the pupils were dilated so much they looked almost black. Suddenly she was remembering the incident at the hotel. Her body tingled with the memory of Steve's hands on her skin, the way his skin tasted and felt against her lips. Her throat constricted.

"Did you go away to school?" she ventured.

"Went to MIT. Before that I lived in Illinois for a while."

When Mama brought her here, Steve had been ten or eleven. Andrea remembered hearing from one of the housekeepers that Burkhart's wife had banished Steve to relatives in Illinois...

The clang of an iron pot startled Andrea. She looked away. "I guess I'd better go help the women with breakfast."

"You don't have to. Judy doesn't, and neither did my mother," he said quietly. His body signaled hers in some mysterious way. Andrea's knees felt strangely weak. He had shaved, and one small place on his chin looked raw. Her fingers tingled with the urge to reach out and soothe that spot.

She swallowed. "Thanks, but I like to keep busy."

Strangely subdued, Steve nodded.

Andrea joined the women in the kitchen and tried hard to become engrossed in their activity and camaraderie. They had breakfast on the table for the first shift by six-thirty—bacon, fried chicken, flapjacks, gravy, mashed potatoes, biscuits, pitchers of milk, hot syrup, and coffee.

Tía noticed Andrea's preoccupation, but she had problems of her own. Johnny Brago was one of the first to the table. He sat next to the door, so she had to pass by him each time she came through with another platter of food, removed empty dishes, or refilled a coffee cup. His dark eyes followed her every move. Carefully, she avoided looking at him until she felt his hand on her arm.

"Yes?" she asked politely, looking into his eyes for the first time.

"Hi, Tía."

"Hi."

Johnny frowned. The smile that had started in his eyes turned to puzzlement. "You okay?"

"I'm fine. What do you want?"

"Any more coffee in the kitchen? Our pot's empty."

Tía looked down at his hand on her arm. He flushed slightly and dropped his hand. She knew she had embarrassed him; confusion added to her problem. She had no ties on Johnny Brago, and Andrea didn't want her to have anything to do with him anyway, but she ignored Andrea's advice as often as she took it. She had purely loved kissing him, and she had thought he liked her. So what had he been doing with Judy, and what did knowing he had been with Judy entitle her to? Among Mama's friends, some women got mad, others sulky, one tried to shoot the man, and some didn't seem to do anything. Tía just felt confused.

She took the empty pot, refilled it in the kitchen from a bigger pot, and carried it carefully back to the table. Johnny looked up at her. His dark-eyed gaze held hers; he lifted his cup and held it out to her. Tía had to steady the pot. Part of her wanted to pour the hot coffee on his leg, but common sense won out: she poured it only in his cup.

"I've got a horse I want to let you ride," he said so softly she nearly missed it over the din of men eating and clanging dishes and forks.

Tía wanted to ride more than anything else. But she wasn't sure she should be riding with Johnny. At least not until she figured out what he was doing with Judy. "No, thanks." She moved on to the next man, the next empty cup. Johnny's eyes burned holes in her back. As soon as she could, she escaped into the kitchen and helped Carmen until he was gone.

At seven o'clock the second group came in. By seven-forty the dining room finally emptied out. Cruz, who seemed as tireless as she was grumpy, carried out fresh platters of food for the women's breakfast.

"Where's Judy?" Tía asked when they were all seated around the table.

Rolling her eyes, Lupe snorted. "You won't see Her Highness until noon, if then!"

Carmen clucked her tongue at Lupe. "For shame!"

"Less bad to speak truth?" Lupe demanded. "*La Excelencia* was out all night with her *caballero*," she sneered, glancing at Cruz for confirmation.

"Hush!" Carmen hissed. "*El patrón* deserves better than that his own people should speak in this fashion about his sister."

"*El patrón* deserves a better sister." Lupe looked to Cruz for support.

Tía rapped her fork on the table. "Lupe, please do not say rude things about Miss Burkhart. We work here, but it is not our place to judge the actions of our employers."

Lupe flashed Tía an angry look. Before she could speak, the outside door burst open, and Steve strode into the room.

"Sorry I'm late, Carmen. I was down at the barn helping Mahogany foal. Can I use a pan of your warm water and some soap on these hands?" Holding out bloody hands for their inspection and without waiting for a reply, he shouldered his way into the kitchen through the swinging doors.

"*¡Sí, señor!*" Standing up quickly for so heavy a woman, Carmen clapped her hands at Lupe. "Get another plate and utensils for the *patrón*, quickly!"

Lupe shot Tía a speculative look to see if she resented being ignored in the chain of command. Tía nodded, and Lupe flushed as if she regretted looking askance. Tía noticed, but she was too distracted to care. Her mind was still grinding on the remark about Judy spending the night with her *caballero*.

Lupe came back with plate, cup, and flatware. Looking at the table, she paused in the doorway. Andrea tapped the place next to her own. Begrudgingly Lupe set a place for Steve across from Andrea.

Steve emerged from the kitchen. Andrea caught his gaze and nodded at his plate.

As if he had seen her for the first time, the open, friendly look left his face, leaving it guarded and wary. He was not particularly happy to see her. Ignoring his lack of enthusiasm, Andrea smiled.

"And how are mother and foal getting along?"

"Fine. She did very well for a first-timer," he said, slipping stiffly onto the chair across from Andrea.

"Did you breed her yourself?"

"Yeah, by Velvet Warrior, an Arabian I bought last year."

"I'd like to see them," she said.

"I guess we can arrange that." He ate mechanically, methodically, with very little conversation. When he leaned back to pour another cup of coffee, his plate was clean.

"Seconds?"

"No, thanks."

"What do you do all day?" The other women were moving back into the kitchen, carrying dishes and platters.

"I'm usually at the mine. I only came out to help you get settled."

"How thoughtful of you," she murmured.

"I'm practical. I don't want you tearing Judy to pieces."

Andrea laughed softly. "I'm having difficulty keeping up. A couple of hours ago you were busy taking her apart."

"That's different."

"Oh, I see. Well, then, let me assure you that from what little I've seen, Judy looks like she can take care of herself."

"Looks can be deceiving. Judy has been a little thin-skinned since Pa died. I don't want her hurt any more than she has been."

"Perhaps you haven't noticed, but I'm the one in the vulnerable position. I'm the outsider. I have to make all the adjustments and concessions."

"But that won't be a problem for you," he said.

"Oh, I see. Was that a left-handed compliment?"

"Call it what you like. It's obvious you can take care of yourself."

"And Judy can't?"

"Not like you."

Frustrated, Andrea fell silent. Somehow Steve even managed to make her competence seem like an undesirable quality. Judy seemed to inspire an abundance of masculine protectiveness. Undoubtedly Steve still smarted from what had happened in the hotel room. Like the responsible man he so obviously was, he would not risk a repeat of that embarrassing and upsetting experience. That was expected, but somehow it piqued Andrea's vanity that he was so successful at it. A true engineer, he had chosen the safest and most proper attitude for a brother to take toward a sister. Part of Andrea knew that he could do nothing else, unless he *wanted* to play the fool, but his easy success at keeping distance between them hinted that perhaps he did not like Andrea after all—that if he hadn't been tricked initially, he might have shown his real feelings from the very first encounter.

"Well, at least I managed to get your attention," she said softly, unable to stop testing his reactions. "You were ignoring me yesterday."

"Not as much as I should have been." Muscles clenched beneath his smooth, suntanned cheeks. Andrea remembered how his lips had felt and tasted, how his skin had smelled.

"Can't we at least be friends?" she asked, watching him closely.

Steve looked at her and then around at the dining hall that had emptied to the point where only he and Andrea shared the big room. "I don't think so," he said bluntly. "We have a conflict." Andrea looked at him as if asking what it was, and anger raced through Steve. She knew as well as he did that he wanted her. She had to realize that with lust between them, friendship would be all but impossible. "You are determined to stay here at all costs, and I'm determined to protect my sister," he said lamely.

"Perhaps we could accomplish both without inconveniencing anyone."

It further angered Steve that she chose to speak to the problem he mentioned rather than the one motivating them. "I don't want you here, Miss Garcia-Lorca."

Andrea struggled for control. "Why? Because of yesterday?"

CHAPTER FIFTEEN

"I'd like to make a deal with you," Steve said. "I gave this considerable thought last night. I want to buy your half of the mine and Rancho la Reina."

Andrea Garcia-Lorca—or Andrea Burkhart—was the epitome of intoxicating femininity. Her dark eyes absorbed his statement without rancor.

Steve had had some experience with women when back east at school. But the only thing he had learned for sure was that it made good sense to pay attention when dealing with them. Women were not like men. Women had their own way of thinking, and it always surprised him. Watching Andrea now as she absorbed his offer, he had the worrisome thought that she might be even more different from him than other women. Andrea could beat Judy at her own game one day and then defend her the next. He did not know any woman who would waste time defending a woman who had crossed her.

Steve had no cause to trust women. His own mother had died and left him. Then Pa had married another woman, who had seemed to like him some of the time, but hadn't, not really. His stepmother, Judy's mother, had been pretty, but she'd played tricks on him when Pa wasn't around.

Andrea was pretty, too, as pretty as a dream woman. He couldn't believe she could have come this far in life without finding a husband. All the women around here had been married at least once by her age, some three times. Men died or got killed pretty regularly in Tombstone. And women needed protection. He pondered why she remained single and put it down to her being so different. Andrea might not suit anyone else in the world, but she suited him. He wasn't sure how he could be so certain of that, but he was. He'd never felt so provoked by a woman before and could not imagine what he had done to deserve a dream woman who turned out to be his sister. He knew that if he wanted to keep himself from wanting her, he was going to have to get rid of her. Soon. He could not imagine living the rest of his life with such worrisome desires. His thoughts were uncontrollable. They came in a continuous sheet, like water falling over a dam. And lately a great number of his thoughts were about Andrea and downright disturbing to him.

He had lain awake half the night thinking about the problem his sister posed for him. And all he had for his labor was excuses. He had been angry since the reading of his father's will. He still grieved. He had been unsettled by Judy's taking his razor and even thinking about hurting herself. The past two months had been difficult for everyone, but none of that was Andrea's fault. In all honesty, not even the near disaster in the hotel room was really her fault. Nothing like that had ever happened to him before. He was twenty-nine years old, and he had never felt like that before.

He had assumed that someday, somehow, he would marry, if he found someone who met his basic standards for cleanliness, seemed easy to get along with, and didn't play tricks on him. He sometimes dreamed about how nice it would be to have a woman of his own, but that was mostly because he got lonely. He'd been too busy to court a woman, and neither the university nor the Arizona Territory was exactly overrun with women willing to risk a baby under their apron before the benefit of a wedding ceremony. He didn't feel comfortable going to the whores. He liked to look at them, but he didn't like the idea of dipping his wick in a community pot. His father had been openly bitter about women. Perhaps some of that had rubbed off on him.

Andrea was waiting for details. He didn't have them. All he had to do was see her from a distance, and his heart pounded like a schoolboy's. That morning she had brushed against him in the hallway, and for an hour his guts had been knotted up like a tangle of barbed wire. If this didn't stop, he'd be a wreck. Too bad he didn't have Morgan Todd's complacence about women. Morgan would never fall in love or even moon over one woman. Morgan made it plain that lust was one thing and love another, and no woman wanted both. He took his lust to the whores, and he courted a number of young women, Judy among them.

"Is your offer legal?" Andrea asked.

"I talked to Jim Furnett when I was in town, and Pa's will did not preclude that possibility. We have an appraisal. Over twenty years we expect to take several million dollars out of the Lucky Cuss. One-fourth of that would be yours, but in order to obtain full value, you'd have to live here. As you can see," he said, waving a deprecatory hand, "it is primitive and dangerous and lacking in many of the comforts you are no doubt accustomed to. There are Indians; the weather can be intolerable at times."

"Please come to the point."

"All right," he said roughly. "I am offering to buy your half for fifty thousand cash now and fifty thousand a year for five years."

"Isn't part of that money already mine?"

"No. After my father's—excuse me, *our* father's death, Furnett set up separate accounts. The fifty thousand I'm offering you is in addition to a little over a hundred thousand on deposit for you at First National."

Hiding her surprise, Andrea nodded coolly. "I'll let you know my decision."

"Keep in mind that there's always the risk that the silver vein could peter out at any time. Each month the amount of silver being taken out of the Lucky Cuss has decreased."

"I heard in town that the mine is producing over ten thousand in silver each week," she protested, altering her source slightly to protect Tía and Johnny.

"That's gross, before payroll, materials, and cost of smelting. We get one-half of the net. Our share has been running four thousand a week."

"That's over a hundred thousand a year each. Over twenty years that's approximately four million dollars total."

Steve spread his hands. "I admit my offer may seem low, but there is an excellent possibility that we'll never be able to get all the silver out of the mine, even if we know where it is, even if the vein doesn't peter out unexpectedly."

"Why not?"

"Water," he said tersely.

"Pump it out."

"We do! But each year, as we dig more shafts and go deeper into the mountain, the expense of pumping becomes greater. We will reach a point one day where it'll cost more to pump than we can get paid for the silver."

"You *must* know when you expect that to happen."

Steve smiled. He was beginning to enjoy himself. She was not only prettier than any female had a right to be, she was damn smart. She knew the right questions.

"I do, but depending on the activity in the other mines, I can be off by one to ten years. If someone does something stupid, he could ruin it for all of us."

"And if no one does?"

"The Lucky Cuss could last the full twenty years, maybe longer. An outside chance."

"And the mine is two years old?"

"A little less."

"So you're offering me three hundred thousand dollars for a one-fourth interest in a mine that could be worth two and a half million."

"If you count the hundred thousand in the bank, your share of what's in the vault at the mine and what I offered you, you can walk away today with almost a half million dollars. Most women never see that kind of money in a lifetime. Men with families earn less than five hundred a year. If you spent four times that amount, you would have enough money to last two hundred and fifty years."

Andrea laughed. "I'd still rather have a couple of million."

Steve grinned, admiration sparkling in his blue eyes. "You're talking gross again," he chided her.

"Am I?"

"Sure. Each year recovery expenses are mushrooming. Right now one of our biggest expenses is getting the silver out of Tombstone. Wells Fargo charges near a usurer's rate to ship our cargo."

"How do they get away with it?"

"Insurance. Road agents are taking a heavy toll on silver shipments. We've done everything we can to help. We pour silver in two-hundred-pound bars to discourage robberies. We ship at unspecified times. But nothing seems to work. We haven't moved any silver for six weeks, and the robbers are getting so brazen they hit every stage that leaves town. We're afraid their next move will be to ride into town and steal the silver right out of our vaults. Sheriff Johnny Behan doesn't keep a tight rein on the criminal element."

"Why doesn't someone do something?" Andrea demanded.

"Russ Sloan, a friend of mine, is one of the owners of the Contention and the Tough Nut mines. He's going to make a stab at taking his own silver out. If he makes it, we'll all be trying it, probably."

"This is more complicated than I expected." Standing up, Andrea straightened her gown. "Now may I see the colt?"

The barn was a hundred feet southwest of the *casa grande*. The morning air was still crisp but warming quickly. From the trees in back of the house, birds sang noisily. A catwalk rimmed the inside walls of the fortress. The thick adobe enclosure had a walled platform at each corner. Even now men were on duty, watching.

"Do you keep men in those lookout posts all the time?"

"Geronimo is still on the warpath. And since Victorio was reportedly killed by Colonel Terrazas's forces, the lesser chiefs, among them Nane, Chatto, and Loco, are raiding all up and down the Mexican border. They strike and run, hardly ever staying to fight once settlers get organized. Lightning raids that are over in a matter of minutes. Then they show up maybe a hundred miles away. Same strategy. Two thousand troops cover his whole territory. Cavalry patrols spend weeks on forced marches and never see an Indian. They're like smoke. They disappear into wild canyons and mountain retreats. The Mescaleros are the worst. Outlaws for years, ever since Victorio left the reservation, they have an abiding hatred for whites."

Smiling to herself, Andrea wondered if he was trying to legitimize that phony Indian attack with a little local color.

The colt and new mother shared a stall near the front barn door. Still shiny and wet looking, its coat roughed up from its mother's ministrations, it walked stiffly, on brisk, spindly legs, but its breeding was already apparent in wide-set eyes, wide, deep lungs and sleek lines.

"He's beautiful!" she cried.

Steve's eyes were shining, too. "You know horses?"

"Some. I can tell good from bad. That goes for men, too," she said, facing him. "You're a good man, but you're doing some cold things."

Muscles moved under the smooth skin above his jawline.

"Really cold things," she continued. "Like going along with that phony Indian attack yesterday and trying to buy me out today. You act is if I'm so repulsive you can't bear to have me in your family."

Steve shoved his hands into his pockets. She was right. But how the hell could he tell her that knowing she was his sister hadn't kept him from having thoughts about her that were more than a mite improper? Shame kept him quiet.

"Well," she demanded, eyes bright with unshed tears, "aren't you even going to defend yourself?"

"No," he said quietly.

A standoff. Frustration boiled within her.

A gunshot startled them both. Steve had already turned and was running toward the house as two more shots rang out.

"What?" she cried, running after him.

"Indians!" he yelled over his shoulder. He ran for the house and came out with a rifle. Men yelled and ran toward the gate. Andrea picked up her skirts and followed Steve. *If this is another phony Indian attack, I'm going to kill him!*

She had thought the compound deserted since the cowboys rode out after breakfast, but several men ran toward the wall with rifles in hand, yelling at each other. Women spilled out of the house.

Steve was the first to reach the lookout who had sounded the alarm. "Where?" he demanded, climbing up onto the platform. Panting with exertion, Andrea climbed up beside him.

About half a mile down the long gentle slope that led up to the compound, two groups of riders trailed dust comets. Grabbing the field glasses, Steve watched for several seconds.

"Open the gates!" he yelled.

Men rushed to comply. Slowly the heavy gates swung open.

"What are you doing?" she demanded, not trusting his motives.

"That small group in front is ours," he said grimly, handing her the field glasses.

From this distance gunshots sounded like corn popping. Down the slope, six cowboys were being chased by a dozen Indians. One of the cowboys turned in the saddle and fired. An Indian fell from his pony. Two Indians appeared to have carbines, the rest arrows. One of the cowboys in the back of the pack began to sway in the saddle.

"Cover them!" Steve yelled. "Open fire!"

A hundred yards from the open gates, the injured rider's horse slowed. Three Indians in the front of the pursuing pack quickly closed on him. Andrea recognized Johnny Brago riding at the front of the pack. Johnny slowed his horse and dropped back. He reached the swaying rider just as the man's feet left the stirrups and he pitched forward.

Another few seconds and the Indians would be on top of them. "Cover them! Hit something, dammit!" Steve yelled, firing. Andrea craned her neck and tried to see.

Riders at the front of the pack pounded into the fortress, raising a dust cloud that almost blinded Andrea. Seventy-five yards from the front gate, Johnny dismounted, dragged the limp rider to his own horse, and tossed him over the horse's haunches. There was no time to mount himself. Slapping the horse and sending it toward the gates, he turned to confront a knife-wielding Indian. A spear of sunlight gleamed off the blade as the Indian threw himself off his pony onto Johnny, knocked him down, and rolled on top of him.

Only seconds behind Andre, Tía ran from the house, climbed the ladder to the catwalk, and peered over the wall.

Johnny was surrounded. All around her, instead of firing to help him, men watched the struggle, held their fire lest they hit him, and aired their lungs with more than one string of cuss words. A puff of smoke indicated Johnny had fired. The Indian with the knife buckled forward and slumped into the grass, but three other Indians swarmed over Johnny.

Tía turned to Lindy Parker. "May I borrow your gun?"

Lindy smiled. "You know how to shoot it?"

"Yes!"

Lindy unsheathed his .44, handed it to her, and turned back to the wall to raise his rifle to his shoulder.

Less than twenty feet away, Johnny struggled with two Indians. The third stood and raised his lance over his head to plunge it into Johnny's chest. Tía fired, and the Indian yelped and dropped the lance.

"I'll be dad-gummed," Lindy muttered. That little slip of a girl had shot the lance out of the brave's hand. Five men had been waiting for an opening to help Johnny, and she had just eased in there the second the brave showed himself and done it.

Tía fired twice more, and the remaining attackers fell back and ran for their horses. Johnny ran for the gates, which closed after him with a thump that shook the wall. Rifles shots cracked. Indian ponies screamed and fell.

"Man the walls!" Steve yelled at the men who had ridden in. "They're coming back!"

The next wave of Indians was greeted by a volley of rifle fire that added one more lean brown body to the count.

Johnny climbed up beside Tía, took her hand, and pulled her to a vantage point several yards from the nearest man.

"That was some good shooting."

Tía smiled. "I'm surprised you noticed."

"I always take time to notice when someone saves my hide. How come you did that?"

"They," she said, gesturing at the riders on the wall, "were cussing a blue streak instead of shooting."

Johnny laughed. "That probably saved my life. These fellas ain't too handy with firearms. I was praying none of 'em forgot that and tried to pick off one of my opponents. They musta been kinda excited. They don't generally try to bust any of the Lord's commandments."

"I heard some words a mule skinner would be proud to repeat."

Johnny laughed. "You're my good-luck charm. You stay right here beside me."

Tía wanted to stay away from him until she figured out how she felt and what she wanted to do about Judy, but she could tell by the look in

Johnny's eyes that nothing short of the .44 in her hand was going to get him to give up his tomfoolery.

Johnny must have seen her answer in her eyes. He turned to add his rifle to the volley of gunfire. Another Indian fell. Tía sidestepped over, gave the heavy gun back to Lindy, and returned to stand near Johnny.

Finally the yipping braves pulled back. Johnny leaned back against the wall and looked at her intently. "You okay?" he asked. "You look pale."

Excited by the fight, he looked cocky and handsome. His narrowed eyes seemed to see inside her. As if he knew how attractive he was with his shiny black hair and his healthy bronze skin, set off by a slash of black eyebrows and mustache.

"I'm right pleased you cared enough to save this ornery hide of mine," he said, his voice husky.

"How could I not?" she asked irritably. "I don't want anyone to be killed."

"Nothing personal in it, huh?"

Tía shrugged.

"Would you cut that deck a little deeper for me?" His hand brushed her cheek and caused a strange weakness in her knees.

"No, I won't," she said, stepping away from him. Her foot slipped off the edge of the narrow catwalk. She clawed for the wall that somehow had gotten out of reach, and his left arm snaked out and caught her, stopping her sudden fall.

"If you'd just quit trying to get away from me," he growled. Tossing the rifle up a little and catching it by the barrel, he eased it down beside him so he could hold her with two hands. "You're lucky. You could have been hurt."

He held her safe, but well away from the catwalk so she was at his mercy. "I'm used to being a sight luckier than this," she said dryly. She tried to swing her self around so she could touch the catwalk, but he merely smiled and eased her over so he could hug her full against him. His heart pounded against her breast, confusing her.

Tía stopped struggling. Her hands on his chest tingled with awareness and feeling. Beneath his shirt, his skin felt damp, warm, and pulsing with life. Through narrowed, dark eyes, Johnny slanted a look at her. Heat flashed in his eyes and acted on Tía like a drug. Her mind forgot to function. She just hung there in his arms, her feet dangling, her body pressed hard against him.

Steve yelled, "Here they come again!"

Johnny's mouth opened as if he were going to lower his head and kiss her. Beneath his mustache, his lips looked pink and soft. But slowly he swung her to his right until her feet touched the catwalk. He lowered her carefully into place.

"Get down," he ordered, kneeling with her and pushing her head down until she was huddled into a ball at his feet. "Stay there. Don't move."

His hand on her head felt warm and masterful. Part of Tía wanted to do what he asked, but she was too curious. He stood up to raise his rifle, and she straightened, sidestepped out of his reach, and stuck her head up to see what was happening. The Indians were circling, yelling, and shooting guns and arrows. A dampness against her breast caused her to look down. A bright red stain wet the right shoulder of her gown.

Outside the walls, the Indians had begun to flee. Johnny lowered his rifle and turned to look at her. His dark eyes seemed to blaze. Then he saw the red stain on her gown and paled. His lips tightened into a hard line. Fear transformed his usually amiable countenance. "I told you to stay down. Now you're hurt," he growled hoarsely, angrily.

"You're hurt!" she countered, pointing at his left sleeve where blood had soaked through his cut shirt.

Johnny looked down at his arm. The Indian must have gotten him with that knife. He remembered the sting of it. Relief that it hadn't been Tía made his knees weak as water. "It's only a scratch if I am."

Nearby, Lindy Parker broke his rifle and reloaded. "Should we kill all of 'em, or do you want us to leave some for seed?" he asked.

"You musta finally hit something. You sound awful cocky there, Parker," Johnny said, winking at Tía.

"Johnny!" Steve yelled.

"Yeah?" Johnny's gaze never left Tía's face. His dark eyes mesmerized her, kept her still and quiet and watchful.

"They're pulling back. Think we can parley with 'em?"

Johnny nodded to Steve but spoke to Tía. "I don't guess it'll do any good to order you to stay down."

Tía shook her head. "Guess not."

Johnny sighed as if his burdens were near unbearable with her being so disobedient. "I'll be back."

He caught and mounted one of the horses ridden in and abandoned in all the excitement. *Parley* meant Johnny, who spoke a little Apache, had to ride out there alone with only a white cloth on a rifle. He rode slowly toward the braves, who had regrouped on the flat valley floor; Tía barely breathed.

A good two hundred yards down the slope, Johnny rode right up to the Indians. He sat his horse with his back to Tía, talking to them for what seemed like an eternity. Tía knew that if the riders on the wall hadn't been able to hit anything before, they would be entirely useless now. Fear for Johnny turned her hands to ice.

At last Johnny turned and led two Indian ponies back up the gentle slope and into the compound without a shot being fired. Weak with relief, Tía listened to the warm sound of Johnny's husky voice as he reported to Steve. "I was wrong. These aren't Apaches. I shoulda known. If it was Chatto, he would've waited until dark to get his dead. Then they'da crept over the wall and killed anyone they could find, stolen anything they needed, and probably burned us out. These're just hungry renegades from Bosque Redondo. They want flour, sugar, salt, a couple head of cattle, *and* the right to reclaim their dead and wounded."

Steve yelled to the men beside the gate. "Get two packs for their ponies." He turned to Johnny. "We'll take it from here. Go have that wound dressed. You're losing blood."

"I'm okay," Johnny said. "Where's Grant?"

"That blasted horse of yours wouldn't stop running. Slim is still chasing it." Steve motioned to Tía. "Take him to the kitchen and get Carmen to help you dress that cut before he gets blood poisoning."

Tía and Carmen converged on Johnny. Grinning, Johnny fell into step beside Tía.

"Does it hurt bad?" she asked, feeling foolish. Of course it hurt bad.

Johnny considered telling her about extreme suffering to see if she would care, but he resisted the urge. "I haven't felt it yet. Check with me later. About nine o'clock tonight."

Tía turned to Carmen, trotting along beside them, panting at the exertion. "He's delirious already, Carmen. Do you have something for that?"

As if Johnny was one of her favorites, Carmen smiled at him until it looked like her face would split. "*Sí, señorita,* castor oil. It is very good for all sorts of cowboy maladies."

CHAPTER SIXTEEN

The wound was longer and deeper than Johnny had expected. Carmen held the bottle of spirits over the gash in his arm. "If you have a God, *Señor* Johnny, now is the time to ask him for strength."

"Just pour. You can gloat later," he muttered. Anything else he would have said was cut off by the sudden flash of pain. It felt as if a white-hot poker had been inserted into his flesh and held there. He concentrated on breathing as Carmen used her needle and thread to take eight stitches, then tied off the thread and poured fresh whiskey over his arm.

At the sight of his blood sizzling under the whiskey, a heartbeat of compassion throbbed inside Tía. Blackness started closing in on her from the periphery. She reached out to steady him or herself, she could not tell which.

A sweet, familiar voice jolted Tía.

"How touching!" Judy said from the parlor door, her voice taut.

Tía started to defend herself, but one man pulled open the outside door and two others carried in the rider who had fallen from his horse.

"Grant! What happened to Grant?" Judy cried, rushing forward to where they were laying him facedown on the table. An arrow protruded from his back. Johnny stood up and placed himself between Judy and Grant. He took both Judy and Tía by the arm and walked them forcibly out of the kitchen. Whiskey ran off his arm onto the floor.

"You'll be better off if you don't watch," he said firmly. Judy tried to protest, but Johnny stepped back inside and closed the door in her face.

"Bully!" Judy glared at the closed door. When Johnny did not respond she turned away. She wasn't sure she really wanted to watch whatever they would do to Grant. She'd heard terrible stories around the evening fireplace about how they poured gunpowder in an arrow wound and lit it. Shuddering, she turned and tried to concentrate on watching the activity between the house and the front gate, where men loaded supplies onto Indian ponies.

Tía walked over to the dining room window and peered inside. Carmen slipped a bandage around Johnny's arm, and he waited patiently while she wound it around a few times and tied it.

Johnny used a knife to cut Grant's shirt away from his body; in his capable hand the knife moved quickly, deftly. Blood dripped slowly onto the floor. It was like a dream. A wave of nausea washed over Tía. He could be dying. She'd only met him yesterday, but she remembered him because he was the only one with a real name. The others had short, convenient nicknames like Dap, Willie B., Leon, Robert, Lindy, Slim, Sandy, Red, High Card, but he was Grant Foreman. Alert intelligence sparkled in his gray eyes. She had liked his open, friendly smile.

Judy touched her arm. "Will he be all right?"

"I hope so."

"What happened? Shooting woke me. I climbed into the hayloft, but it was mostly over by then."

"Indians attacked…"

"Real Indians?"

Tía nodded soberly, hardly able to believe it herself.

"Well…" Judy sighed. "It was overdue. Things have been too good around here for too long. 'Sides, lately everything has gone wrong. Might as well be attacked by Indians, too."

"What else went wrong?"

"What hasn't? My father died, then he cut me out of his will and everybody in the world found out I was a bastard. Then Miss High and Mighty Andrea came, then my Indian scare backfired. Everything…"

Looking very earnest, Judy's wide brown eyes were clear; the sweet curve of her cheeks and the purity of her skin reminded Tía how easy it would be for Johnny to find her appealing.

"You kill me, Tía Marlowe! You should have seen your face when I caught you with your arms around Johnny!"

"I just reached out to steady him."

"Any port in a storm, as the old saying goes. Don't fret yourself! I had a talk with Johnny last night. I told him if he really loves me, and I really love him, waiting a little longer to get married won't kill either of us. He's so impatient! That's the only thing I don't like about him. He's always trying to pin me down. I'm still young. I enjoy dancing and flirting. He takes everything so seriously! Especially Grant! Grant has been my friend for ages. We're very close. He adores me. He'll do anything in the world for me. But Johnny seems to think that's bad. Do you think it's bad for a girl to have a friend who just happens to be a man?"

"No."

"Neither do I."

A knot formed in Tía's stomach. "When are you and Johnny going to get married, then?"

"Not for a while if I can help it. I'm not a girl who likes to be tied down. I told Johnny he should force himself to pay attention to other girls. Look around a little. Heavens! You'd think I was the only girl in the world. Grant loves me. Johnny loves me. Morgan Todd loves me. My head just spins sometimes."

"You're very lucky."

"Lucky! It's a curse! Sometimes I wish I weren't so pretty. But"—she giggled mischievously—"not really."

"Who's Morgan Todd?"

"Don't say that name so loud! Johnny sees red at the mere sound of it. Steve says if I'm not careful Johnny will kill Morgan."

"How awful."

"It is, isn't it?" A curious look came into Judy's eyes. "But it would be sort of romantic, wouldn't it?"

"For a man to be killed?" Tía asked.

"Don't be so serious! He won't really be killed. We're just talking."

Tía breathed a sigh of relief. "Of course, I forgot."

Judy lifted one corner of her skirt and swung it gracefully. "Do you think I look like a great lady?"

"Yes," Tía said quietly. "You're the prettiest girl I've ever seen."

"That's what Grant says, too. He loves me a lot. He would love me a lot more if I let him, but I won't," she said firmly.

"Why not?"

"He's my best friend! Besides, he's not handsome enough. If he looked like Johnny…" She paused, admiring her shadow. "Maybe if he had lots of money…no, not even then. Grant is my friend. He loves me no matter what I do. He'll do anything for me. Anything at all."

"Aren't you worried about him?"

Judy frowned. "He wouldn't dare die. Besides, he's as strong as an ox. He'll be fine." But she suddenly felt a strange sense of foreboding.

From her vantage point on the platform, Andrea watched the Indian ponies being fitted with *aparejos* to carry the sacks of staples Johnny had promised the braves—fierce brown savages on horseback, several of them on paints and pintos—who waited in a loose-knit group at the bottom of the long, grassy slope.

"Why are you giving in to them?" she asked.

Steve looked at her sharply, so sharply she thought he wasn't going to answer. "Because enough men have died or been wounded. The Indians have always kept their word to us in the past. No sense losing men if we don't have to. If they take our staples, they won't come back for a while," he ended curtly. During the fight, Andrea had stayed close to Steve. Now, because of his brusqueness, she stepped back. Chin high, she tossed the auburn mass of curls off her shoulders and pushed them back with a slender golden hand.

Any kind of fight always got Steve's dander up. But seeing that instinctive, totally feminine movement, he was unexpectedly filled with the memory of burying his face in Andrea's thick curls. Then shame capsized his reverie.

"If I were you," he said, "I would take the money I offered you and go back to Albany, where you'll be safe."

Andrea looked him up and down slowly, much the way a man would appraise a horse he was too smart to buy. "Perhaps you would, but you are only a man, aren't you?" she asked scornfully. "While I am a Garcia-Lorca! The blood of *conquistadores* runs in my veins, Mr. Burkhart. We are not cowards!"

Steve nearly laughed aloud. If she really were a Garcia-Lorca instead of a Burkhart, they wouldn't have this problem. He had the wild urge to drag her into his arms and show her what *only a man* could do. But this woman, the ultimate in grace and beauty, pulsing with intense and vivid life, was his sister, and that knowledge drained the blood from his heart and choked the retort in his throat. His anger turned to defeat and then to resignation.

Turning away abruptly, Steve skimmed down the rough wooden steps that led from the catwalk on the adobe wall. He stalked off toward the kitchen to see about Johnny and Grant.

"Keep a sharp eye out," he yelled gruffly to the man beside Andrea. "They may decide to come back."

In the kitchen Johnny was easing the arrow out of Grant's back. Arm bandaged now, Johnny handed the broken shaft to Carmen and sat down.

"How is he?" Steve asked.

"Lucky. We were able to cut it out instead of shoving it through," Johnny said, wiping the beaded perspiration off his forehead. "I don't think it hit any vital organs."

"Good. Let's hope he doesn't get an infection. How are the other two?"

"Flesh wounds. Carmen cleaned 'em good and wrapped 'em. We wasted a heap of good whiskey so's they wouldn't get infected."

"Too bad you weren't still together when they saw you."

"Yeah. I had just sent more than half the riders south into the brakes along the foothills when we spotted 'em. Hell, we'd only been outside the walls a few minutes."

"Let's have a drink," Steve said.

The parlor was deserted. Steve poured each of them a stiff shot, gave Johnny his, and then stared morosely at his own. Bad sign. Now he was drinking in the morning. He downed it as if it were water.

"Do you think you could manage here without me? I've decided to go back to the mine."

Johnny leaned against the doorjamb. "Bad time to be traveling. Rumor's that Chatto's all fired up, looking for scalps. Any time a scraggly bunch like these cut loose, you know there's a thousand Injuns around. Stragglers like them don't take on a fort like this unless they're feeling their oats."

Johnny decided to take a guess about what was bothering his boss. He had noticed Steve looking at Andrea, and he had noticed Andrea looking at Steve. "Andrea's quite a beautiful woman," he said meaningfully.

"She happens to be my sister," Steve said evenly. He wasn't surprised that Johnny had guessed about his frustrations. They had known each other a long time.

Johnny tasted the whiskey and set it on the mahogany credenza. He couldn't drink it, but he'd probably be sorry he hadn't. He felt a little tired, but he wanted to speak his mind to Steve.

Johnny teased other men, but he rarely teased Steve. Something about Steve's seriousness moved him to charity. Other men moved through life relatively unaffected, but not Steve. He took on little bruises that Johnny could almost see, like the bruise he still carried from losing his pa.

"When I was about fourteen, the year before my folks were killed, one of my mother's relatives came to visit. His name was Tatanga Mani, Walking Buffalo. He was a Stoney Indian from Canada. One of Ma's cousins had been carried off or got lost and wandered up there. My folks let us go off into the mountains to hunt. The second day out Tatanga Mani shot a moose. The arrow barely went into his hide. I saw it as clear as anything and told Tatanga Mani that it was a waste of time to follow him, but follow him we did.

"Tatanga Mani would stop every now and then and put his ear to the ground or to a tree and listen for the moose. He seemed to be slowing down, and as we followed we saw more and more blood. I couldn't figure it out. I'm too white, I guess. We followed that moose for three days. When we finally found him he was dying. I couldn't figure out how a moose could die from a little wound like that arrow barely sticking in his thick hide. Tatanga Mani told me that the arrows do not kill. The Great Spirit kills. The arrow sticks in the moose's side, and like all living things the moose goes to his mother the earth to be healed. But by laying his wound against the earth to heal it, he drives the arrow farther in."

Not understanding, Steve scowled at him. "Is there a moral to this story?"

"I don't know. I just had the urge to tell you an Indian tale, I guess."

Johnny left the room, and Steve shook his head. Sometimes Johnny was too deep for him.

Carmen opened the door and motioned Judy and Tía inside. Judy hung back, afraid. Tía took Judy's hand and led her into the dining hall.

At sight of Grant, Judy groaned. He looked dead. His face was ashen. His chest barely moved with his breathing. Part of her felt terrified by him. Another part of her wanted to pull him to her breast and rock him like a baby.

"How is he?" Judy whispered.

"God does not confide in housekeepers." Carmen shrugged. She had no hope for Grant. She had no faith in any man overcoming an arrow wound. She'd seen too many die of them.

Judy insisted Grant be moved to the small bedroom between the dining room and Steve's office on the west end of the *casa grande*.

They settled Grant on the comfortable feather mattress. As clumsy as they were, he did not wake up.

"Shouldn't we send for Dr. Potter?" Judy asked, frowning at how still Grant lay.

Carmen shook her head. "What can he do that wasn't done? I have seen many wounds like this, *niña mía*. Some heal cleanly. Some do not. It is not a thing that can be predicted. Not even by a doctor."

Judy moved a chair next to Grant's bed and motioned to Tía. "You stay with him."

Tía started to sit down in the chair, then thought better of it. "No, you stay with him."

"Me! I can't. I get sick at the sight of blood."

"He's your best friend. He needs *you*. It'll be good for you to take care of him."

"No, it won't. I hate it when people are sick. I especially hate it when it's someone I care about."

Tía took Judy by the shoulders and sat her down on the chair. "That's because you don't know anything about it."

"And I don't want to learn. He needs a doctor, not me."

"You heard Carmen. Doctors don't make people well. Folks make themselves well. Doctors either help or they don't, mostly they don't."

"What if he dies?"

"Then he'll be grateful you were here instead of someone he doesn't care for as much."

Judy stood up. "I don't want to be within a mile of this place." She stepped away from Grant as if he had already moved a step closer to death. She could not imagine surviving it if Grant died in front of her.

Tía took Judy by the shoulders and led her back to Grant's bedside. "Sit down and hold his hand. What man would want to die with you holding his hand?"

Tía had a way of making this bedside vigil sound like the only thing to do. "If he dies and I see it, I'll never forgive you, Tía Marlowe," Judy warned.

"Carmen and I will check on you," Tía said. "If you need help, yell."

Tía herded Carmen out of the room quickly. "*Sí*," Carmen called over her shoulder. "I will check again soon. Call Carmen if the bleeding starts again."

"Deserters!" Judy cried. The door closed behind them, and Judy slumped onto the chair beside Grant. Tía Marlowe would be sorry for this. Judy knew she would not be able to stand the waiting. She couldn't sit still waiting for her friend to live or die.

Nothing ever worked out the way she wanted it to. Grant would die; she knew it. She felt betrayed—almost as if he had gotten hurt deliberately. Her very best friend in the whole world would die and leave her. Then she would be really alone.

For hours Judy held Grant's hand and sat in a strange trancelike state. He breathed in and out, and she grew hypnotized by his breathing, willing him to continue. His forehead felt hot. She began making conditions. If he breathed three more times in the space of time she breathed three times, he would live. If a bird sang so many notes in the space of time he breathed so many breaths, he would live. She watched him breathe; occasionally she manipulated the numbers to make them come out right.

Could he actually just stop breathing? She would never forgive him if he did. It wasn't fair, anyway. She had been the one who wanted to die, not Grant. He was the epitome of life—so complacently alive he obviously expected to live forever. He never worried about dying.

The day dragged on. She decided Grant's easy complacence had been a trick to lull her into becoming his friend. She would never make that mistake again. Men always looked indestructible, but they weren't. It was just a trick a man used to get a woman to love him and depend on him, so he could leave her when she least expected it.

He stirred, and her heart lurched. His eyes opened tentatively and then focused on her. "Grant?"

"Hi, pretty one. What're you doing here?"

"Waiting for you," she whispered, her voice strangely hoarse.

"Was I gone somewhere?"

"I think so. How do you feel?"

"Like I've been nailed to the bed with a pitchfork."

"You took an arrow in your back. Johnny had to cut it out."

"Guess that must be it. Didn't feel exactly like hunger pains."

A small laugh came out of nowhere. Leaning forward, Judy touched him to reassure herself that he was really alive. A tear escaped, slipped down her face, and dripped on his hand.

"Hey, you all right?"

"Yes." She gulped, fighting for control. "How do you feel?"

"Grateful I missed the cuttin' it out part. I'm a genuine coward when it comes to pain."

"Sure you are," she chided him. Carmen had said they would know how the wound was healing by whether or not he got a fever. Shaking her head, she leaned forward and put her hand on his forehead. Her hand was so cold from fear that anything would have felt warm to her. "Damn!"

"I'm dead?"

Judy laughed. "No."

Mesmerized by her cool, trembling touch, Grant closed his eyes. When she touched him, he couldn't feel the pain of his wound—he could only feel Judy.

"Does it hurt real bad?" Judy asked, her dark eyes filled with compassion.

"Not when you touch me. I can't feel anything but your hand."

"You're teasing me, aren't you?"

"No, I'm serious."

Judy moved her hand away, and his face contorted with agony, which he only slightly exaggerated to mirror the pain he felt.

Judy's smile faded. She looked so strained and tense that Grant repented. "It doesn't really hurt that bad. I was just joshing you."

"Liar! Shhh, go back to sleep. I'll stay with you."

"You don't have to do that. I'm surprised to find you here."

"Surprised? You're my best friend! You'd take care of me, wouldn't you?" she demanded.

"Yeah."

"Then just hush and go back to sleep. You need your strength."

Grant sipped the water she offered him. He wanted to bask in this compassionate side of Judy, but too quickly his eyes closed.

At dinnertime, Carmen stuck her head in the door. Judy sat close to the bed, holding Grant's hand.

"Come eat something, *pequeña*. Lupe will spell you."

"No, thank you, Carmen. Grant might wake up." Judy had lost her desire to be distant from any calamity that might befall Grant. It felt good to be needed. Besides, Lupe's hands might not relieve his pain.

Grant seemed to drift in and out of sleep without any ability to control it. Every time he opened his eyes, Judy was beside him, offering liquids, soothing his brow, whispering words of comfort. Grant wanted to talk to her, to chide her for staying with him so long, but his eyes closed.

Even in his dreams, if they were dreams, Judy's anxious face floated before him. She was so pale with concern he felt obliged to get well as fast as possible to spare her feelings. But his body remained heavy and unresponsive. He had never felt that way before. Even his dreams were not his own. They were agitated, disjointed excursions that led nowhere. Perhaps they were Judy's dreams…

Once, in the dark of night, Grant moaned in pain. Tears of frustration at her own helplessness welled up in Judy, begging to be cried, but she couldn't. She made bargains with unseen, malevolent powers. She accepted their challenge. If she cried, he could die. She sat like a stone all night, refusing to weep, refusing to sleep, refusing to let Carmen or Tía take her place.

CHAPTER SEVENTEEN

In the sequestered coolness of the tall cathedral rocks that formed the Devil's Kitchen of the Chiricahua Mountains, Mateo Lorca sat motionless upon his sleek black Arabian. His face shaded by the brim of his flat-crowned black sombrero, he watched the slow progress of a smuggler train—its fine Andalusian mules loaded with booty. The train followed the trail that wound through a wild, deserted canyon between the Chiricahuas and the Peloncillos, running from the San Simon Valley in Arizona Territory to the Animas Valley in New Mexico Territory.

From his vantage point Mateo could sense his men who were concealed behind the boulders and trees that bordered the winding, overgrown path the mules would have to follow. Taking off his sombrero, he wiped his forehead. The sun was high overhead. On the canyon floor the sun would blaze even hotter on the men and animals.

Mateo waited patiently for the last mule in line to amble into his snare.

"Get up, you lazy so and so," Ed Smith said crossly.

Riding at the head of the train, Russ Sloan had learned a new respect for mules. They might appear to be the dumbest animals in the world, and sometimes they were, but these small, sturdy-limbed mules seemed smarter than the men who drove them. Especially smarter than Ed Smith, whose mule just sat down and wouldn't budge. Russ didn't think himself the most cunning man in the world where animals were concerned, but even he could see the mule was just toying with Smith.

Smith whacked the mule with his rawhide reata. The mule closed its eyes and brayed, but it didn't move. Russ had grown up around mules. He stopped his horse, fished into his pocket for a hunk of salt, and held it out for the stubborn animal to sniff. It licked the salt out of Russ's hand and then stood up to follow him. Every so often he would reach back and hand the little mule a salt chip. He liked doing it, because it irritated Ed Smith and pleased the mule. Salt was a little dear, but Russ was a rich man. He could afford to indulge himself.

With that problem solved, the mules—in single file, each with a jingling bell at its throat—moved steadily eastward. For each mule, half-hidden beneath its great rawhide *aparejos*—pack sacks—Russ had hired two armed outriders: hard-faced, swarthy men dressed as *vaqueros,* their sharp eyes alert for any sign of danger that might lurk in the wilds of the heavily thicketed canyon. The mules' bells tinkled reassuringly. Bandits or Indians would think twice before trying anything against these men.

Russ turned to Ed Smith. "I hate to brag, but I know a man who may just put Wells Fargo to shame. If *he's* not careful!"

Smith was used to Russ talking about himself as if he were someone else. He hardly noticed it anymore. "They ain't been doing too good, have they?" he snorted. "Losing the last three shipments to road agents. Reckon you had to take matters into your own hands."

Overhead, a shot rang out. Bounding off the rocky canyon walls, the reverberations cracked and echoed. Ed Smith was trying to decide if it was a .45 or a .44 or maybe a .30–.30. His hand was already reaching for his own gun. Unexpectedly a man leaped out of the bushes ahead of them, blocking their path.

"Rein in, *señors!*" he shouted.

"What the hell!" Russ cried, jerking his reins in a purely reflex action.

"You are surrounded, *señor!* Do not reach for your irons, or there will be much trouble."

Unlike Russ Sloan and the riders pulling up around him in stunned silence, the man speaking was a real Mexican, probably a real bandit. He wore a soiled, multicolored serape and a tall crowned hat with an extra-wide brim. His shaggy mustache covered his lips.

Responding slowly, Russ brought his hand up in a signal for his already motionless mule train to halt. No one moved. Perspiration trickled down the side of Russ's temple. He was in charge, and the responsibility confused him. By nature he wasn't a violent man. The men he had hired waited for some signal from him. When he had been thinking about this in his mind, he had assumed that if something happened, the correct action would automatically come to him, but now nothing came. What could be the right action if the bandit was alone would be wrong if he was heavily backed by others. Russ felt inexplicably paralyzed.

"Throw down your irons, *señors,* and no one will be hurt. You are outnumbered. If you do not comply, my men will shoot you down like so many dogs."

Russ Sloan could see no other men. He had a vision of himself riding into town without his booty or his silver. He would be a laughingstock. Word would spread all over Tombstone that with twenty men at his back, he had surrendered two hundred pounds of silver to one lone Mexican bandit. The sound of raucous, derisive laughter would follow him the rest of his life.

"He's…bluffing," Russ blurted, hating the way his voice cracked.

"You're nuts," Smith murmured.

"He's bluffing!" Russ said, stronger this time.

"No trick, *señor!"* the Mexican shouted, and motioned with his arm for his men to rise. From behind rocks, from behind bushes, from above them on canyon walls, at least two dozen men brandishing rifles and guns surrounded the mule train.

"Drop your weapons!" shouted the *bandido.*

Smith reached for his gun to toss it onto the ground.

"No!" Russ said under his breath.

"They got the drop on us!" Smith hissed.

"They're bluffing. They aren't going to kill twenty men. We know who they are. They kill any one of us, and they'll be hunted down like dogs."

"Throw down your guns, *señors!"* The shout came again.

"Fire! Fire!" Russ yelled. "They're bluffing!" He clawed at his own gun, cleared leather, and snapped off a shot. The man in the multicolored serape scrambled for cover behind a granite rock. Thus encouraged, Russ's men drew their guns and prepared to fight.

Russ Sloan gave a triumphant yell. In the next second light exploded inside him, and he was flung off his horse. He screamed and felt the ground curve up to meet him.

A cacophony of shots rolled one on another. Horses whinnied nervously. Russ hit the ground hard, but he didn't pass out. Riders fell. Soon only the mules were left, braying nervously in the hot sun. Russ felt himself lucky to have survived.

The scrape of boots walking toward him caused his heart to pound. He tried to see where his gun had fallen, but waves of pain exploded in his head. He seemed to hear a gunshot, but maybe not.

• • •

Mateo Lorca picked his way down the mountainside to the canyon floor. It took him less than ten minutes, but the shooting was already over. Slowly he rode the length of the fallen mule train, surveying the carnage. Patchy Arteaga rode up beside him and waited respectfully.

At last, *el general* looked at him. Patchy sighed. "A thousand pardons, *General*. It could not be helped. We gave them every opportunity to surrender the silver, but they would not."

Mateo shook his head in disgust. "My information about this one was correct," he said, dismounting to turn Russ Sloan's body with the tip of his pointed boot. "The padre called him a pompous ass. Now he is only a dead *gringo*."

"A very foolhardy man, *General*." patchy paused. "Shall we bury the dead?"

"Leave them!" Mateo said angrily. "Let their bones be a warning to others."

Judy woke with a start. Her dream had turned into one of falling. She hated falling dreams. She straightened and leaned over Grant.

His color was high and ruddy. Maybe that was a good sign. She leaned forward and touched his brow. It was so hot she groaned and sagged back in her chair.

"Oh, no," she whispered. Usually, if she talked, Grant would stir or show in some way he had heard her, but this time he lay like a stone.

Fear gripped Judy. He was going to die. Indian arrows were usually poisoned. She'd heard stories about people who died horrible, lingering deaths from being shot by Indian arrows. If they weren't poisoned, they were filthy.

A wave of nausea swept upward. Her stomach felt as if it were filled with rocks. Sweat broke out on her forehead, and she shivered as if she had taken a chill. A feeling of such sickness and self-pity grew in her that she knew she would be justified in leaving Grant. No one would blame her if she left him now. She'd made herself sick nursing him. That was all anyone could expect of her, even Tía.

Grant moaned. It was only a low sound, deep in his throat, but it caused her heart to constrict with fear. She leaned forward and placed a trembling hand on his forehead, which was so warm it felt good to her cold hands.

"If you die, Grant Foreman, I'll never forgive you," she muttered.

She sat there all morning, afraid to move. At midday Tía came in with a dinner tray.

"Judy, you need to eat something."

Judy pondered that for a moment. Her stomach still felt filled with rocks. "No." She shook her head. "Please, take it away. I don't like the smell of it."

"I brought some chicken broth for Grant. Why don't you rest, and I'll feed him."

"No. I'll feed him. He wants *me*."

Judy knew Grant was dying. She didn't tell Tía because saying the words aloud would devastate her, and she didn't want to cry in front of Grant or Tía, but she knew. Something had changed in Grant, slipped away from her. He was out of her control now. She knew when it had happened. It was only a matter of time now. But she would try to feed him. Maybe his body—the part that had decided to die—could be tricked.

Medicine box in hand, Tía left, and Judy raised Grant's head and put another pillow behind it. Then she brought a spoonful of broth to his lips and let a little of it trickle down his throat. He choked and coughed, and the pain of coughing caused him to groan.

"Grant...please don't die," she said, her hand shaking as she reached out to check his burning forehead. But she knew he would. And she didn't even. have the courage to leave him and save herself from watching it.

Medicine box in hand, Tía hesitated at the door of Johnny's cabin. She hadn't wanted to come, but Carmen's mischievous eyes had taunted her into it. Johnny was injured, Carmen had coaxed. But now Tía told herself nervously that if Carmen liked him so much, and he was in need of so much special care, Carmen should be taking care of him herself. In her opinion his wound was small and not that deep.

Unexpectedly the door opened, and Tía found herself gazing up into Johnny's handsome face. He smiled appealingly, and the dancing lights in his dark eyes made her forget her misgivings.

"Come in." He stepped back and let her pass into the relative dimness of the cabin. After the bright sunlight, the room seemed sultry and close. It even smelled like Johnny—a warm, dizzying smell that confused her senses.

He started to unbutton his faded blue shirt. The thought of being in this small cabin with him while he undressed unnerved her. She turned to leave.

"Tía!" Johnny reached out and touched her arm. "I'm only taking off my shirt so you can tend to my arm."

"Your shirt doesn't have to come off. You can just push your sleeve up."

"My arm's too big…"

So it was. Brawny and muscular, his arm was larger than the narrow part of the cuff. Tía flushed with embarrassment and walked to the table. She set down the box of doctoring supplies Carmen had given her. What was wrong with her, anyway? She had seen men with their shirts off before. Sometimes men bathed in the water troughs in Tubac, cupping the water with their hands and letting it run down their bare chests, soaking their pants. She should have asked Johnny to come up to the house, but it was too late now. He would only think her a naive girl who didn't know how to act with a man.

"Of course you have to take it off! I knew that!"

"Sorry," Johnny said, lifting his hands as if to ward off her blows.

At least he was not laughing at her. Slightly mollified, Tía rattled the chair at the small, rickety table and motioned him onto it. Looking completely subdued, Johnny walked over obediently, sat down, and waited for the next command.

Tía ignored his insistent eyes. His broad chest was covered with a furry mat of black hair. She untied the rags that held the bandage in place and was glad he couldn't see her fingers tremble. Once the knots were loose and she had exposed the area, her hands steadied. The gash in his arm was raw and red-rimmed, but it didn't look infected.

She cleaned the wound with a rag soaked in kerosene and felt grateful he didn't flinch away, showing the pain she knew he must be feeling. She expected him to kick like a bay steer, but he just sat there and stole occasional looks at her.

After she'd cleaned the wound, she rewrapped it and tied a freshly boiled bandage in place. There hadn't been time earlier for the niceties. "Should hold you for a while," she said, stepping back.

"Thanks. You've got a mighty soft touch."

"I hope I didn't hurt you too bad."

"You know, there's a small gate next to the wagon gates. Would you take a walk with me? It's nice after sunset. The Injuns won't bother us. Even if they tried, we'd see 'em coming."

"No, thanks, I better not."

Johnny, frowned and stood up beside her. His height intimidated Tía. She felt his nearness all the way to her toes. "How come you won't walk with me?"

"Maybe I don't want to."

"How come?"

Tía shrugged. His nearness confused her so badly that she couldn't remember what she had said or why.

Johnny scowled into her face a moment and then expelled a heavy breath. He had a suspicion, but he wasn't about to mention it. His pa had had strong feelings about a man shaming a woman. So he would not accuse her of anything, but he had seen Tía Marlowe three times that afternoon, and each time she had been either following Steve or trying to get him to talk to her. If she had fallen for Steve, it would do no good to try to spark her. Women couldn't be had for the chasing.

Tía backed toward the door. Johnny knew all about women, but he followed her anyway. Something irresistible about Tía Marlowe made him forget his common sense.

"You haven't worn that bracelet. I've watched for it."

"I didn't know I had to wear it immediately. I'll be happy to bring it back."

"You act like you think I'm bad medicine. Maybe I could change your mind about me if you'd just give me a chance. Just think about it, and chew it real fine, okay?"

Tía nodded and backed out the door, grateful he didn't follow her. Once outside and away from his disturbing influence, the slight breeze off the desert cooled her hot face. With the high-pitched screeches of fighting wrens and clucking chickens in her ears, she suddenly could not understand why she had refused to walk with him. A walk would have made her feel better. She had been cooped up inside all day.

All her life Tía had wanted to grow up, because she had thought life would be simpler when she had only herself to answer to. But that had been before she'd realized that she would have so many things to consider every time she turned around. She wanted to walk with Johnny. And not doing it made her feel cranky. But on the other hand, she didn't like the idea of walking with a man who had spent the night with another woman. She had half a mind to go right back there and ask Johnny exactly what had happened, but she knew that he'd probably tell her what he thought she wanted to hear, and she might not be able to tell if he was lying or not.

Judy had been out all night with Johnny Brago. It was no wonder she didn't consider his request for as long as it took her to listen to it.

Tía walked into the orchard, sat down under a peach tree, and put her head in her hands. A more pressing need existed in her. She should tell Steve and Judy who she was. Not telling was pure folly. The more water that flowed under that particular bridge, the more dangerous the current she'd have to tread to get back to where she'd started from.

In the distance Carmen yelled at the children, who were somewhere in the orchard, and they giggled and ran. Birds carried on their business—calling back and forth—arguing, singing, squawking.

In despair, Tía closed her eyes. It was one thing to know what to do and another to do it. She didn't deserve to be an heiress. She'd never felt any flinching away from anything good before, but now, strangely, she recoiled from her fate.

She almost wished Andrea was the lady of the spread. She enjoyed it. She was good at it. Tía was not. She wanted to work in anonymity—to work hard enough and long enough to get to the point where she would deserve it. She wanted to earn Steve's and Judy's admiration by her hard work. She wanted them to like her and respect her; she wanted them to depend on her…to love her. Then, when they found out the truth, they would…

What?

They'll know what you've done, a small voice within accused her. *They'll know you caused your papa to nearly die. They'll know it was your fault. They'll know you always wanted Papa to love you like he almost did.*

Tía trembled. *I didn't!*

Yes, you did.

"I didn't…I *didn't!*" she cried aloud.

But no one could hear her.

CHAPTER EIGHTEEN

Midnight. Steve stood up and stretched. Six o'clock would come too soon.

He turned down the wick in the kerosene lamp. The flame flickered and died. Steve walked through the dark office to the door. He didn't need a light. He knew every room in the *casa grande* by memory, right down to the placement of each piece of furniture. He'd lived in this house for twenty-six years. His father had started with a large, one-room adobe hut and had built on more rooms every few years. At one time the entire cabin had been no bigger than the parlor. Now a new parlor was surrounded by three bedrooms on the east, a large kitchen and eating hall to accommodate twenty or so riders at one time, and Steve's office on the north. The west side of the house provided two more bedrooms.

Built of thick adobe bricks, the house was relatively cool. With constant vigilance, a degree of safety existed inside the compound, but Steve followed his father's example every night before retiring. He checked the outside doors and flashed a signal at the sentries with a lantern. If all was well, they would take turns whistling an answering signal that everything was secure.

That done, Steve walked the length of the hall from his office to the women's rooms on the east and listened to be sure everything was all right. As he stopped in front of Judy's closed door, the hair on his neck prickled. On the surface, all was as it should be, but...

That nerve-end tingle of warning on his neck froze his steps. Frowning, he opened Judy's door and stepped inside.

There was enough moonlight coming in the window to illuminate Judy's empty bed. Unimpeded by bars, curtains at her window wafted gently in the cooling night breeze.

"Damn!" Instantly furious, Steve stalked to the window, reached outside, and closed the wrought-iron grillwork. The bars had been installed over every window to keep out intruders. At his father's request Steve had designed and built them himself. On a hot night it allowed the windows to be opened without fear of a surprise visitor. In case of fire they could be opened from the inside. Bill Burkhart had had a passion for security. Not even a child could squeeze through when they were locked in place. Unfortunately Judy had a bad habit of sneaking out and leaving the window unprotected so she could sneak back in without being caught. Why the hell couldn't she just go to bed like other people? When he found her, he would shake the teeth out of her head. There was no excuse for her to jeopardize the entire household…

Making a fist, he turned to leave. On the moonlit floor beneath the window, a small dark shadow caught his eye. Stooping down, he touched it, and alarm grew within him.

It was the top three inches of a warrior's feather. Steve picked up the feather and walked quickly across the room. In the hall he stopped to listen. A sound like creaking bedsprings came from Andrea's room. Steve walked to her door and opened it noiselessly.

Outlined against the barred window, a life-and-death struggle was taking place on the bed: moonlight gleamed off a muscular back poised above Andrea's slender, arched body. One hand covered her mouth while the other held a knife at her throat.

Steve yelled, threw himself across the intervening space to the bed, caught the warrior broadside, and tumbled him over Andrea. They hit the floor with a loud *thump*! and rolled toward the window, locked together in a death grip. The knife flew out of the brave's hand, hit the wall, and bounced onto the floor. The brave scrambled after his weapon and grabbed for the blade the same time Steve did. Steve got hold of it, too, but the brave, grunting and panting, forced him down and raised the knife over his head. It took all the strength he could muster to keep the warrior from forcing the knife into his chest.

As they strained against one another, Steve felt himself weakening. He used the last of his strength to try to force the knife loose from the brave's hand, but the Indian's grip was too strong. Behind the snarling face of the brave, Steve caught a glimpse of Andrea, huddled on the bed, clutching her torn gown around her body.

Steve was big and well built, but this warrior felt at least thirty pounds heavier than his own hundred and seventy pounds. If he didn't end this soon, the man would wear him down by sheer weight.

On top now and straddling Steve's chest, the warrior plunged the knife downward toward Steve's chest. Steve wriggled frantically, and the brave was forced to regain his leverage. Seeing his opportunity, Steve brought his right knee up hard between the man's legs. The Indian convulsed and lost his grip on the knife. Steve wrenched it away and swiftly plunged the blade into the warrior's heaving chest. The brave stiffened and slowly collapsed on top of Steve.

"Oh, God!" Andrea screamed.

Steve rolled the Indian off him. In the moonlight, Andrea watched the blood trickle out of the brave's mouth. Then his eyes rolled back in his head, and he went limp.

"Oh, Steve!" Andrea cried. "He tried to...to...he was going to scalp..."

Shaking uncontrollably, tears sparkling on her cheeks, Andrea started to sob. Steve moved close to the bed and pulled Andrea up, gathering the now hysterical woman into his arms.

"Hey! You're all right now," he whispered, awkwardly stroking her hair and back. She pressed against him, crying hard. Her torn nightgown slipped down, leaving her naked to the waist in his arms.

Like twin firetips, her bare breasts burned into his chest. He held her close, trying to ignore the flame that threatened to ignite in his loins. But after a while he could feel the sweat breaking on his forehead and hear the roar of blood in his ears.

"You're safe now. He's dead."

Andrea didn't hear Steve's words. She wanted only the protection offered in his arms. She pressed her face into the warmth of his neck and cheek, oblivious to everything except her need to feel safe again. His sturdy warmth coupled with his masculine, musky smell was a soothing balm to her shattered nerves.

She hugged him tight, and involuntarily Steve's arms tightened around her. She raised her head, exposing her throat to his lips, and without thinking Steve buried his face in the fragrant mass of her silky hair. Overwhelmed by her softness he crushed her against him. He meant only to hold her close enough to satisfy the fierce need that was raging against his willpower, but her lips were only a breath away—open, sweet, trembling...

Steve's warm mouth claimed hers at last, and Andrea's fingers stole under his shirt and pressed against the warm smooth skin of his back, still damp with perspiration from the savage's attack. His kisses made her forget everything except how good he made her feel. Once her hands had pressed against his flesh, she knew he wouldn't stop. His skin cried out to be touched just the way hers did. Her mouth opened to receive him, and his tongue slipped in and filled her as if he couldn't get deep enough inside her. As Andrea eased back onto the bed, she could feel his passion throbbing against her.

Moving with her as if they were one, Steve's lithe form pressed her more deeply into the yielding surface of the bed. His hips twisted against her as if he were already inside her. Andrea strained upward. He clawed at the restraining fabric of her nightgown, and Andrea helped him move it aside.

"Andrea, Andrea, Andrea..." She could hear his tortured voice and feel the urgency in his loins. His mouth found her again, and his legs forced hers apart. Arching, grinding against him, she moaned.

"Andrea, please let me love you..."

"¡Patrón! ¡Patrón! ¡Señor Steve!"

Steve bolted to consciousness and nearly collapsed with frustration. The clamor of feet running down the hall was not a dream. Men shouted his name. Someone would be at the door any second. Steve cursed softly and lifted himself away from Andrea's warm, soft body. He struggled into a sitting position. He wanted to kill the first man to burst into the room.

Dazed and disheveled, her naked flesh gleaming in the moonlight, Andrea sat up, swaying in the middle of the bed. Steve wanted to speak, but his mouth wouldn't work. Abruptly he stood up and stalked to the door, pushing it nearly closed.

"Señor Steve, we heard a scream," Carmen cried.

Half a dozen men and women crowded the hall. Shielding Andrea from their view, Steve quickly explained what had happened. "Search the grounds. If you find any more Injuns—kill 'em. Either this is a renegade of Chatto's, or those bastards didn't keep their word."

The men stomped away. Carmen remained in the hall, twisting the sash of her nightgown in her hands. "La patrona is injured, no?"

"La patrona's fine."

"I heard her scream. I call the vaqueros..."

"You did good, Carmen. She's fine. Just scared. She would probably appreciate a cup of tea to calm her nerves."

Steve knew Carmen desperately wanted proof of his statement, but she backed away and shuffled anxiously toward the kitchen.

Taking a deep breath, Steve stepped back into the bedroom and closed the door. Andrea was still on the bed, exactly as he had left her, her breasts gleaming like sculptured ivory cones in the faint moonlight. What the hell did she think she was doing? The chilling rage that had come over him when they were interrupted carried him forward.

Stalking to the bed, he caught her by the arm and jerked her forward. He had no idea what he intended to do. He was still inflamed by the desire to spread her satiny thighs and feel himself inside her, but even half-dazed he now remembered that this woman who had trembled and sobbed in his arms, opening her mouth and her body to him, was his sister.

"Get dressed, Andrea. Get some clothes on and keep them on! And if you know what's good for you, you'll stay away from me. Do you understand?" he asked, his voice harsh.

Finally comprehending her nakedness, Andrea reached down to cover herself. "That's not fair," she began, hurt that he was acting as if the whole incident had somehow been engineered by her at his expense.

"I don't give a damn what's fair," he threatened.

The look of anger on his face, and his cold, furious tone, convinced her that he was serious.

"You turn up in my arms and kiss me like that one more time, and I promise you, I'll take you, sister or not!"

Steve stalked down the hall toward his bedroom. Halfway there he remembered he had been looking for Judy when he'd surprised the savage's attack on Andrea. Grateful for the distraction, he now searched every room in the house. It served two purposes: it assured him there were no Indians lurking in the *casa grande,* and it diffused the intensity of his thwarted passion.

In the bedroom next to his, he found Grant Foreman and Judy. Judy slumped in the chair next to the bed, sound asleep, clasping Grant's limp hand in hers. In the dim glow of the lamp on the table beside Grant's bed, her soft brown hair framed her face.

Standing over her, seeing the exhaustion in every line of her body, he felt the fury he'd held against her drain out of him, leaving him cold and shaken.

He picked Judy up, carried her to the other side of the big bed, and laid her down next to Grant. She was too thin nowadays; she looked too vulnerable and young. He smoothed wisps of hair away from her face and then leaned down to kiss her warm forehead. He must be getting old. He couldn't remember ever kissing her so tenderly before. It had been a long time since he had really looked at her. Even in sleep, her face looked strangely ravaged, grief-stricken.

An unexpected sadness rose inside him and made him feel suddenly drained. He couldn't tell whether it was because he'd never have Andrea or because he'd wronged Judy by assuming she'd been out tonight. He'd better get some sleep.

Once in his bedroom, Steve fell across the mattress and buried his face into the quilt. Maybe he was losing his mind. Was this how it started? Everything caught you off guard? And you could no longer control your own body?

I don't give a damn what's fair. You turn up in my arms and kiss me like that one more time, and I promise you, I'll take you, sister or not! A heartless threat for any woman who'd been scared to death by a half-naked savage. Two savages, if you count me, he thought guiltily. Andrea had been terrified. He had been the one to pull her into his arms. But once she was pressed against him, he'd forgotten everything except how much he wanted her.

Andrea was as much his sister as Judy.

Too keyed up to sleep, Steve punched his pillow. For the first time in his life he felt hatred toward his father for putting him in this position.

Tensely Steve pressed his bent arm over his face. He loved his pa—how could he have guessed his son would lust after his own flesh and blood? He had to get rid of Andrea, or he would be doomed to spend the rest of his life wanting her. He'd pay her anything she wanted; do anything she asked. He had no choice.

CHAPTER NINETEEN

As Tía set the table for breakfast, Steve and Johnny tramped into the long dining hall, stamped a few times to get the sand off their boots, and then sat down at the end of the table. Steve nodded to Tía. Johnny's look was more intent and penetrating. Steve talked while Johnny's dark gaze followed her every step. After a while Johnny grunted a few replies to Steve's near monologue. Tía was so engrossed listening to the sound of his voice she couldn't remember what to do next. She surveyed the table, but nothing came to her. In frustration she walked into the kitchen and busied herself by the door, listening. She wished the sound of Johnny's voice weren't so compelling, but today she found herself hanging on his every word.

Steve started to talk again, then stopped. "Did you hear a word I said?" Tía searched her own mind and realized that she had listened to their whole conversation and didn't know what Steve had said, either.

"I didn't know you wanted me to listen to all that," Johnny answered, sounding surprised and innocent. Tía had to cover her mouth to keep from laughing.

"I can see if I want your attention I'm going to have to keep you out of the house. I said I want extra guards at intervals along the wall, and I don't want the riders to go out today."

Carmen picked up a milk pitcher and walked past Tía toward the table. Seconds later she walked back into the kitchen. "I was going to pour the milk for you, *pequita,* but perhaps you would like to do it."

Tía reddened. "Me? Why?"

"It might be a thing of more ease for you, since you no doubt understand where you have stacked the cups."

Tía flushed from her toes to her hairline. She took the pitcher from Carmen and rushed back into the dining hall. Johnny looked up at her, and she knew he'd heard Carmen. He winked. Tía's insides were so strangely affected that she almost dropped the pitcher.

Carmen waddled outside and rang the bell next to the house. It sounded like a church bell, except tinnier. Within seconds cowboys trooped into the dining hall, and Tía was too busy serving to let herself look at Johnny again. After the first rush, when most of the men had been served, Carmen came out and stopped beside Johnny. "Are those peaches ready yet?"

Johnny chewed the mouthful of food he had just taken and then swallowed loudly. "Green as gourds."

Dap Parker, a slim, wiry Texan with a droll look on his long face, chimed in. "Gourds look ripe next to them hard little knots."

Five of the Parker boys worked for Steve: Robert, Dap, Willie B., Leon, and Lindy. They generally managed to sit together. Willie B. Parker picked up a biscuit and slathered warm butter on it. "I et one of 'em yesterday, and that's probably what almost kilt me. My mouth puckered up so bad I thought I was going to have to kiss Dap to get it unpuckered."

Coming from Willie B., who had the most innocent face next to Lindy, the comment evoked general laughter. Johnny caught Tía's gaze and winked at her. Totally disconcerted, Tía forgot what she'd come out of the kitchen for.

"You *caballeros* have good appetites for men who just fought off an Indian attack," Carmen said, pausing at the end of the long table to spot a dish that needed to be refilled or a coffee cup that needed to be topped off.

Dap looked up from his plate, his eyes sparkling with merriment. "You call that a fight? Wasn't hardly noticeable. I'm surprised you remembered it."

"Dap's such a hard case, he don't consider nothing short of the Alamo a fight," Leon scoffed.

Carmen wagged her finger at Dap. "When men get themselves carried into my dining room with arrows sticking out of their backs, I remember," she retorted.

Dap nodded in sympathy and changed sides. "These hairy animals can forget anything. They got no shame at all, have they, Carmen? They'd eat on a grave."

Tía had already realized that Dap almost never said anything he meant. Everything that came out of his mouth was mostly just to agitate his fellow riders.

As the Parkers finished and left, others straggled in. When the last of the riders finally finished, Tía ate with the women and took her box of remedies to the bunkhouse to check on Slim Whitman, whose leg had been sliced by an arrow. She found him sitting on the edge of his bunk, strumming a banjo. The other men lolled on their bunks, some of them polishing leather, one braiding a rawhide reata.

Tía turned her back while Slim dropped his pants and wrapped himself in a blanket. When she turned back only one small patch of his wound showed. Tía unwrapped his bandage, carefully. Where the arrow had grazed his thigh, the skin looked raw and red, so she put on a fresh pad soaked in kerosene. As she was rewrapping his leg, she heard the scrape of boots and jingle of a certain pair of spurs on the porch.

Her heart gave a small, traitorous leap. She recognized Johnny's step. It seemed hard to believe that you could know a man by his spurs.

Steve and then Johnny stepped inside. "Well, how's your patient?" Steve asked. Johnny's dark-eyed gaze caressed Tía. He watched her intently, refusing to let go, and she learned how difficult Johnny Brago was to ignore. She smiled noncommittally. "He's fine, Steve. A couple more days of kerosene compresses should clean that wound up."

Steve turned to Johnny. "Did you have Tía look at your arm?"

"Last night."

"Maybe she'd better look at it again."

Johnny looked askance at Tía and stepped closer to look into her box. His warm body seemed to thin the air around her. It was harder to breathe. "I don't know. A man can't be too careful about women with medicine boxes," he teased.

"The box won't hurt you. All it has in it is quinine, calomel, blue mass pills, kerosene, rags, Epsom salts, tobacco for toothache, castor oil, a scarificator, some scissors, and a glass cup with a bulb."

"I never seen such a well-stocked medicine bag," Johnny said seriously.

Tía knew he was right. The Burkharts had something for every regimen known to man, which unfortunately amounted to only four— Mama called them soak, puke, purge, or bleed remedies. Or five if you counted blistering with hot poultices and plasters. Her own memory of some of the regimens she had endured was that the treatment, though dramatic enough to take your mind off the illness, was generally more dangerous than the disease.

"Reckon when it comes to doctoring I'm more Indian than white," Johnny said.

Dap Parker walked over and joined the group around Tía. "I seen that scratch on your arm, Brago. And I could almost see that nick on Slim's leg. Seems to me you boys're making a big fuss over such little bitty troubles. Why, I've had worst pimples than them."

"Seems little 'cause it ain't on *yore* leg," Slim retorted.

"Why, when I was a young-un' like you, a bear near tore my arm off, and I just wrapped it in a kerosene rag and forgot about it till it healed itself."

Johnny took Tía by the arm and led her toward the door. "I'd best get you out of here before these tales get so tall you won't be able to walk without it coming over your shoe tops."

The warm pressure of Johnny's hand on her elbow distracted Tía until they were outside. "Maybe you should look at this wound. Might be infected or something."

He led Tía to his cabin and followed her inside. Tía checked the cut and found it healing nicely—the skin was a little raw from the kerosene, but there was no sign of pus in the wound.

"Your arm is fine."

"Walk with me, Tía," he said earnestly.

Tía hesitated, but she had regretted not walking with him so much last night that she was too weakened to resist. "Where?"

Johnny took her by the arm and led her outside. The sun was so hot and the glare so bright that Tía's eyes watered. She shaded her eyes with her hands and squinted up at him. He turned her so the sun would be at her back. "You like peaches?"

"Yes."

In the orchard the air was cooler. Tía stayed in the shade, and Johnny stayed close beside her. In the distance a pig squealed. Sounds of children playing drifted up from the barn. Tía could imagine them up in the hayloft, telling ghost stories.

"I thought you said the peaches were as green as gourds."

"I did."

"I don't like green peaches. Which one of us are you lying to?"

"Carmen."

"How come?"

"'Cause Carmen likes to work better than anybody I ever seen. She'd take a perfectly good peach and cook it until it goes limp and then pour it into a jar so's we can eat it. All a man has to do is just pick it off the tree and eat it."

"You might be crazy. Have you ever had yourself checked over?"

Johnny stopped walking and reached up and pulled down a peach. He scrubbed it back and forth on his pant leg to rub the fuzz off and handed it to Tía, then reached up for another.

Tía bit into the peach. Juice ran down her chin. "Why, these are ripe enough to can."

Warm from the sun, ripened to a soft firmness, the peach tasted better than anything she'd eaten in weeks. It reminded her of being back in Tubac. She had loved to lie under a peach tree and gaze up at the clouds overhead and eat sun-steeped peaches.

"They're too good for canning. There's barely enough here for the Parker boys."

"If I know Carmen, she'll be out here cleaning them off the trees, too."

"She'd try. *If* she knew they were ripe."

Tía laughed. "Guess that's why you got away from *El Gato Negro*. You're just full of tricks. I'm surprised he didn't hang you."

Johnny frowned and bit into his peach while he thought about his answer. "I think he forgot about me. I hid until *El Gato*'s band rode out of town, and I stayed low for a while, waiting to see if they'd come back, but they didn't. How'd you get away?"

"We borrowed a couple of horses and caught the stagecoach on the road."

"Why'd you leave town so sudden?"

"Mama made me."

Johnny started to ask another question along that line, but Tía stopped him. "Do you believe in God?" It was the only question she could think of.

"God's kind of a highfalutin word. I have a cousin who's Sioux. The Sioux speak of the Creator as the Great Mystery. It's easier for me to believe in that way."

"Do you like being Indian?"

"I'm not full Indian. I'm just enough to make most men a little suspicious of me. Course it's taught me to shoot straight. Being Indian just means I have more fights than a man with no Indian blood. You like being white?"

"I'm not white." The answer came so instinctively that Tía didn't realize she'd said anything wrong until Johnny stopped chewing and looked at her.

"You sure look white."

"Do I?" Tía groped for an answer. "I'm part English and part Scandinavian. Is that white?" she asked as innocently as she could.

"I don't know what a Scandinavian is, but Englishmen are mostly white. Once I saw a black man with an English accent in Silver City." He lifted her chin and looked her over. "You don't look black."

Johnny's hand on Tía's face took her breath away. She wanted to turn and run, but she couldn't. His dark eyes softened and looked at her with such lambent purity that the birds seemed to sing louder and more musically, and the sky looked bluer. Even the heat seemed to cool. Johnny leaned down and kissed her lightly.

The warm softness of his lips sent a shaft of thrilling sensation more powerful than a horse ride between her thighs. Tía didn't know how it could happen, but each time she had contact with Johnny Brago, her body seemed to respond more hungrily to his touch, his kiss, the look in his eyes, the sound of his voice. Without her willing it, her arms were winding around his neck and her body pressed tight against his. Her mouth seemed intent on devouring him before he could devour her.

"Tía! Tía! Tía!" a woman's voice shouted at her.

At first Tía had ignored the command, but on the third shout her eyes opened. It was Andrea's voice. Tía disengaged herself from Johnny's kiss and drew in a steadying breath.

"Yes?" she croaked at the insistent voice.

"Yes!?" she said, louder this time.

"Where are you?" Andrea demanded.

"I'll be right there," Tía yelled.

"Come back," Johnny whispered.

"No, I better not."

"How come?"

"I don't know."

"Then come back." His lips were pink and smooth beneath the brush of his mustache. Tía wondered why she forgot to feel the coarseness of his mustache when he kissed her. He turned his head at a sound to the left of them, and Tía was struck again with the handsomeness of his sturdy profile. Coarse black hair, recently cut, barely touched the collar of his red plaid shirt. Her hands tingled with the desire to touch his hair, to stroke his sturdy muscles with her fingers.

Then an image of Judy slipping into Johnny's cabin surfaced in her mind. "I can't come back," she whispered.

Johnny watched the stubborn little blonde walk quickly back toward the house. Maybe she'd come to Rancho la Reina with the intention of consolidating her holdings by marrying Steve Burkhart. Was that why she couldn't make time for him?

• • •

Judy could not remember what day it was. She tried to count back but couldn't decide if three or four days had gone by since the arrow had entered Grant's body. Just as she realized this, Grant opened his eyes and caught her pressing a damp cloth to his forehead.

"Well," Judy said, amazed and relieved. His eyes were clear at last—focused and alert. She struggled to compose herself, to think up something ordinary to say. "The slugabed stirs. We thought you'd decided to cash in your chips." They seemed like words she would choose, but even to her ears they sounded strangely inadequate to express the gratitude she felt.

"I guess my money was no good. They sent me back."

Grant appeared not to notice how Judy struggled to seem normal, to seem as if she had expected him to be fine all along. The warm twinkle in his gray eyes was more than she could bear. Tears welled up from some deep place and spilled over.

"Hey, pretty lady! I didn't mean to work you so hard."

Grant pulled her head down and held her against him. Judy cried as if she would never stop. She cried so hard and so long she embarrassed herself and finally scared herself that she might cause him to have a set back. It was this thought that finally helped her to stop crying.

"I'm...sorry...I...didn't...mean to..."

"There, there," he crooned. "You're just plain exhausted. You've been here every time I woke up. You're worn to a frazzle. I want you to get in your bed and not get out until I send for you."

"You'd never send for me," she sniffed.

"Course I would. I couldn't stand to be without you for more than an hour or so. Now, you run along. I'll be fine, but you need some time to curl up in your own bed and sleep. A day or so I'll be up and around. You go, or I'll get up and carry you."

"I'll go. You just stay there where you belong."

Judy wiped her tears. Tremendously relieved, she kissed his forehead, straightened his covers, and kissed his forehead again, then walked to the door.

"You'll be all right, won't you?"

"I promise."

Finally convinced that Grant would survive, Judy walked out to the kitchen. Carmen lifted a stove lid and poked at the fire within. "Did that *indito* bring more wood?" she demanded over her shoulder.

"Don't call Johnny that," Judy scolded. She hated it when Carmen called Johnny *indito*, which was her way of saying friendly Indian as opposed to hostile Indian. The hostiles she called *indios*. "Grant is awake. He's going to be all right."

"Ahhh, that is good. You look tired, *pequita*."

Judy knew she was tired, probably more tired than she had ever been in her life, but she felt such virtuousness that her exhaustion buoyed her spirits.

"I am glad to hear Señor Grant is better. Now you go to bed. I will have Lupe sit with the *señor*."

"You sit with him. You need the rest," Judy said.

Carmen turned the stove lid over to Lupe and shooed Judy to her bedroom.

For the first time in days, Judy took off her gown and stretched out on the bed in her camisole. Lying down felt so good she sighed in comfort. Within minutes her eyes closed, and she couldn't open them.

Judy woke slowly. At first all seemed well. Then she remembered Grant. *Oh, God! He may have died!* Sitting bolt upright in bed, ignoring her state of dishabille, she ran all the way to his room, only stopping at the door to open it quietly, just in case.

The sight of his chest rising and falling with even breaths caused her heart to leap in joy. He was alive. *Thank God.*

Weakly, leaning against the door, Judy caught her breath, then walked over to stand looking down at him. His color was good. In sleep he looked so vulnerable that a small ache started in her throat. Reaching out, she felt his brow. It was cool. Gratefully she closed her eyes.

She walked back to her room and took advantage of the basin of water Tía had left for her. Seeing the clean washcloth and towel on the chest of drawers called up a vague memory of Tía, covering her, moving around the room like a wraith. Judy realized she hadn't talked to anyone in days, but she had been aware of Tía, her fragile face tight with worry, her round blue eyes hooded against showing the fear she must have felt for Grant. Judy remembered Tía bringing soup and trying to get her to eat it.

Finally, washed and dressed in a simple green gown, Judy brushed her hair, thanking the powers that decided such things that she didn't have unruly hair. Long and heavy, it curled just enough to look good flowing loosely around her slender shoulders. In the mirror she looked gaunt, tired, older somehow. What a hateful idea! Then she realized that she hadn't eaten in days. She'd sent back the trays Tía had brought almost untouched.

Judy walked to the window. The windowsill was wiped clean. Her whole room was clean. Marks that had been plainly visible on her walls were gone, no doubt scrubbed away by Tía's industrious hands.

Judy found Tía in the parlor, her head bent over Judy's pink gown, her left hand patting and smoothing as her right hand pushed the heavy iron. Tía had spread heavy sheeting over the table, using that as her ironing board, probably because the parlor was the coolest room in the house.

Judy stopped at the door, feeling so good she could forgive Tía anything. "I see you're still using your little magic wand to tidy up all my messes."

"Judy!" The welcoming light in Tía's eyes warmed Judy's heart. A smile to match Tía's flooded her face and made her mood suddenly soar. Judy swept into the parlor and plopped herself onto the heavy Morris chair left of the empty fireplace. "Would you lend me your magic wand?"

"Of course," Tía said, a mischievous sparkle in her usually innocent blue eyes. "But it does have its disadvantages."

"Like what?"

"Well, for one thing, you have to use it standing up."

Surprised and tickled at Tía's wit, Judy laughed. "Well, I'm willing to suffer a little, but that's too unreasonable. I hate even watching drudgery."

"Well, don't look, then, because I'm going to finish pressing your gowns." Tía giggled.

"Hmmm. Maybe I'll just bring my things out here and visit with you while you work."

"I'd like that."

It took four trips to the kitchen and her bedroom for Judy to make herself comfortable in the parlor. In the kitchen the women were already busily preparing the evening meal. They shouted to one another and banged pots and pans. With forty hungry men to feed, meal preparations started early and ended late. The routines had been disrupted since the Indian attack because of the men's injuries, so the ironing, normally done on Tuesday, lay stacked in tall piles.

Judy ate two pieces of chicken, distractedly tossing the bones on a plate on the floor beside her. Satiated, she turned her attention to her friend.

"Tía, are you ever lonely?"

"Oh, sometimes, maybe. Are you?"

"That's a strange answer. If you were ever really lonely, you'd know it."

"Are you lonely?"

"Sometimes I could die of loneliness." Judy felt a sudden pall, as if the mere mention of the feeling could somehow recreate it.

"Before I came here I lived with my uncle and his housekeeper," Tía said. "I couldn't do anything right. I guess I felt lonely then."

"Have you ever let a fellow kiss you and hold you?"

Tía's cheeks vibrated with heat. She'd rather eat cut straw and molasses for a week then answer that question.

"I love the way you blush!" Judy said, twisting the sash of her gown. "I don't blush at all. I've let men kiss me and hold me and sometimes more, but it only really helps me feel better when I'm with them. That seems unfair, doesn't it? It should help for a long time and leave you filled with sort of a glow. Maybe I shouldn't let them even touch me. Doesn't seem to help me feel any less lonely. But if you don't let men kiss you and hold you and things, then you'd be lonely *all* the time."

Judy glanced at Tía to see if her admissions had horrified her. Tía's round blue eyes mirrored only her desire to help her friend.

"Well," Tía said innocently, frowning at the skirt that wouldn't lie completely flat. "Maybe you just found the wrong fella. The world is full of the wrong people. Just thinking about them will make you feel bad. But other people, just thinking about them will make you feel good. Don't you know someone who makes you feel good?"

"Sure," she said easily. "Grant."

Tía smiled pointedly at Judy. Flustered, Judy looked away. "That's only because Johnny's been gone so long," she said defensively. "Or I would have thought of him." She shrugged. "Grant's always around. Why, he's my dearest friend. It doesn't mean anything, though."

Smugly, her wide blue eyes cool and knowing, Tía looked up from her ironing and smirked at Judy.

Judy squealed and covered her head. "Noooo! I am *not* in love with Grant Foreman."

"I didn't say a word!"

"You don't have to. I know what that look means. I know myself, too. I could *never* fall in love with a man who wasn't absolutely gorgeous! Grant's *nice*! He's a really good friend, but he's barely taller than me! I like him, of course. He's very understanding. He talks real proper—almost like a book or a newspaper. He knows just about everything, but he's not…not…I love Johnny," she said wistfully.

"Grant has a really wonderful looking chest, doesn't he?" Tía asked, glancing sideways at Judy.

"I don't know. How do *you* know?" Judy challenged.

"I saw him through the window before they bandaged him. He's got a marvelous build for a small man. Broad shoulders, narrow waist," Tía said, flushing, "and long smooth muscles."

"Why, Tía Marlowe! You're positively indecent!" Judy cried in mock alarm.

"That's what everyone says," Tía said smugly, "but they're wrong."

"Are you sure?" Judy asked doubtfully.

"Of course," Tía said firmly.

"But," Judy challenged, "there are thousands of them and only one of you. How do I know I can trust you to tell me the truth? If you were an indecent woman, you wouldn't admit it, would you?"

"Of course I would. I may be many things, but I'm not a liar. If I were completely indecent, I would tell you," Tía said, her face resolute.

"Well…" Judy laughed, enjoying their discussion. "I'm glad that's settled."

When Andrea walked into the parlor Judy was wandering away to check on Grant, and Tía was pressing the last gown. Seeing the clutter on the floor—a plate with chicken bones and bread scraps, another plate with cake crumbs, a half-empty glass of milk, three magazines, two books, a comb and brush, three hair ribbons, and a cold cup of coffee—Andrea sighed.

"You're losing ground, Tía. Now the rest of the house looks like Judy's room has sprung a leak," she said dryly.

Tía laughed. Judy did have a way of spreading her world around. She had dragged her whole assemblage into the parlor. She was the only person Tía knew who could eat and read and talk at the same time.

"She's a busy little thing, isn't she?" Tía asked, smiling. She was enjoying having a little sister. All her life, she had been the little sister. Judy was older, but only in years. Tía felt very maternal with her.

"How can you smile about it? All you do is clean up after her."

"I don't mind. She reminds me of Mama."

Andrea frowned slightly. "She does a little, doesn't she?"

"She's not a mean-spirited person, not really. She's just trying to live her own life as best she can."

"It's no wonder it takes her all day and all night, then," Andrea observed, shaking her head at the wake of Judy's "living."

Dressed in the traditional brown cassock of the priests who had first settled this land, Esteban Amparo rode all night and most of the day to reach the pueblos of *El Gato Negro*. He trembled with his own importance. The news he had for *el general* was so personal and so outrageous that only a relative could carry it and speak the words without fear of death. He reached the pueblos in later afternoon, grateful for the coolness of the mountains after the deadening heat of the valley he had crossed.

"¡Esteban! Welcome. Much time has passed since you came here," Alanestra greeted him at the natural rock entrance to the pueblos. "I get off duty at sunset. We can have a drink, no?"

Esteban's cousin by marriage, Alanestra had been with *El General* for two years, ever since the week before his seventeenth birthday.

"*Sí*, that will give me much pleasure, but for now I have important business with *el general*," he said proudly. "Is he here?"

"*Sí*. He is here," he said with a significant look at the other sentry who half dozed with his back against a rock. "If you would speak to him of bad news, go with God."

"A foul mood, heh?"

"The most foul," Alanestra agreed, shaking his head sadly. *El general* was at best a moody man, but since his *rubia* wife had mysteriously disappeared, he had only one mood—black. The men who rode for *El Gato Negro* were not supposed to know Rita was missing, but after the stab wound *el general* had moaned in his delirium. The woman who cared for him had pieced together the story and shared it with Alanestra because they slept together, but, wisely, Alanestra had said nothing. *El general* was a proud man. And women—even though they belonged to the most famous of men, were still women—and capable of great treachery. If he repeated the confidences of his mistress, it could cost them both their lives. Though no one had suspected it, it now appeared that *el general*'s marriage to the most beautiful *gringa* had been a tempestuous one. Whatever the problem between them now, Alanestra prayed it would soon be over. He had been with the rebels three years, ever since he had turned seventeen, and one of the first things Patchy Arteaga had warned him about was the *señora*. *If you value your worthless life, you do not speak of* el general'*s wife. For you she does not exist,* comprende?

Sí, Capitán. *She does not exist. But…*

No buts. She comes and she goes as he wishes. Keep out of it, even with your eyes, especially with your tongue, if you value it.

That command had been easy to follow. The few times the *gringa* had come to the pueblos, *el general* had sent an escort so she would have no problem with the sentries—no matter who was on guard. Fortunately for him no one ever tested his ability to keep his mouth shut. A conspiracy of silence surrounded *el general*'s private life.

"I will see you after my business is complete with my cousin, *el general,*" Esteban said, waving good-bye, pleased at the shock on Alanestra's face.

"*Vaya con Dios,*" Alanestra replied, lapsing into the idiomatic Spanish of the Arizona border.

Sitting the saddle proudly, Esteban passed through the natural rock portal and into the canyon of the pueblos. The sides of the canyon were built up with small adobe huts that perched on the canyon walls. Once, a long time ago, Indians had built most of it. The story was that they had abandoned it because their gods had been displeased with them, but apparently their gods did not mind if the rebels made use of it. In twenty-five years no Indian gods had ever bothered them. Esteban's father, Antonio Amparo, was *el general's* cousin and one of his lieutenants; he told many stories of *El Gato Negro's* exploits. Esteban was one of the few people remaining who still knew *el general's* given name. Only the oldest of his men knew it, and they did not use it—to protect the *señora's* identity and thus *el general.* Only in that way was he vulnerable. Esteban was very proud of his inside information, his relationship to *el general.* Knowing *el general's* family name, even though he had never spoke it to any living man, had put him in the enviable position now of being able to perform this service. Perhaps someday he would follow in his father's footsteps and be a leader in *el general's* army instead of a lowly spy. Spies were necessary, even *el general* said *muy importante,* but in *el general's* army they were not as important as *capitános.*

The pueblos hummed with activity. Men, women, and children came and went, some nodding and smiling at him as they would have in any town, others ignoring him. The air was filled with the rich smells of evening meals simmering over hot coals: tamales, corn cakes, meat pies, tortillas sizzling on greased skillets, stews bubbling in heavy iron pots, coffee brewing. Esteban's stomach growled. In his urgency to share his news and bring glory to himself, he had eaten very little this day.

Wisely, he walked his horse through the narrow street so as not to make a dust cloud to irritate the housewives whose windows opened onto the boulevard. In the quad below *el general's* quarters, another sentry lounged in the shade, his rifle across his knees. Not even stopping to lift a glass of tequila to soothe his parched throat, Esteban left his horse in front of the *cantina* and approached the *guardia* in the quad. Chewing on a stubby cigar, his arrogant eyes slashing out at Esteban, the man was ready for hostility.

"Esteban Amparo to see *el general,*" he said, his tone and formality matching the importance of the news he carried.

"Is *el general* expecting you, Father?"

Hiding the satisfied smile at the reminder that he was a very convincing padre, Esteban nodded. "He is. I have important information, requested by *el general* himself in Tombstone."

"Wait here." The *guardia* climbed the long row of stairs to *el general*'s, quarters—two rooms high above all the others. Apparently *el general* did not enjoy frequent visits from feeble ones, or perhaps from anyone.

Returning, the *guardia* motioned Esteban to proceed. Esteban took the stairs two at a time in his eagerness, crossed swiftly to the door the *guardia* had indicated, and knocked softly.

"*¡Entra!*" El general sounded angry. It was a good thing for him he was a second cousin. Swallowing, Esteban opened the door.

El general was seated at a small table in the middle of the room. A half-empty bottle of tequila sat in front of him. He did not look up. In profile, his face looked ominous. Always the arrogant perfection of his medallion-sharp features rested on the edge of a snarl. Hiding his fear, Esteban waited to be acknowledged.

At last, as if resenting the intrusion, *el general* sighed. Surprisingly, he spoke with the voice Esteban remembered from his childhood—a voice patient and not unkind.

"Sit, Esteban. Help yourself to food and drink. You have information?"

"*Sí, General,*" he said, squaring his shoulders with pride. He had far more than had been requested. Far more. Eagerly he seated himself across from his general. Leaning forward, he waited for the general's nod.

"The girl, Teresa Garcia-Lorca, left Tombstone that same day…for Rancho la Reina." He paused to let the significance sink in. His voice low and firm, he continued in a tone befitting this momentous occasion. "She is the new owner," he said quietly.

El general's stunned dark eyes lifted to Esteban. A prickle of fear started on Esteban's neck and sped along his spine until his whole body shook with alarm. Thank the Virgin Mother he was only the messenger *and* a second cousin. There was fury in that look—fury and disbelief.

Mateo Lorca did not move or breathe. The blood drained from his heart. Rancho la Reina! The white man's parody of a name for what had once been the lands of the Garcia-Lorca family. As soon as he was well enough to ride, Mateo had gone to Tombstone, the origin of that letter to Rita, and asked questions until he'd learned that Burkhart had died. But he had not known that Burkhart's Rancho la Reina, the ranch on which Mateo had been raised, the ranch Mateo had expected to inherit one day, was Burkhart's possession.

"The new owner?" he asked, the words choking him.

Esteban could feel the cold sweat breaking on his own brow. This part he did not enjoy so much.

"*Sí, General.* Señor Burkhart, who was the owner, claimed Teresa as his daughter and left half of the ranch to her."

El general did not move. Like a stone, he sat for so long that Esteban began to sweat profusely. He had been a fool to carry such a blasphemous lie to *el general.* Everyone knew that both girls belonged to *El Gato Negro.* No one had ever questioned it. The blondness was of no import. *El general* could father gods if he chose. Bill Burkhart had been the fool. Patchy Arteaga and his own father attested to the fact that *el general's* own mother was a blue-eyed blonde. Blondness ran in the Garcia-Lorca family.

El general's face darkened, and Esteban could feel his hold on life becoming fragile indeed. He should have sent a boy. *El general* loved children. Everyone knew that about him. Almost as much as he hated *gringos.* If his *rubia* wife had lain with a *gringo, el general* would have killed her instantly. He would have wrung her neck like a chicken. No one had ever questioned *el general's* paternity. He could father albinos and gods if he chose. If Esteban could find the words to tell this to *el general,* perhaps then he would be spared…

But Mateo Lorca had forgotten Esteban's presence. He wanted to reject his second cousin's information, but his good sense told him it was true. No doubt Bill Burkhart had bought almost three-quarters of the land granted to the Garcia-Lorca family by the queen, after that fat pig who had stolen it had died in a suitably horrible fashion. Bill Burkhart had sired Teresa. The two Burkharts were one and the same. He should have made that connection when he saw Burkhart's name on that letter to Rita.

But it was too implausible that the Burkhart who had bought the Garcia-Lorca lands had fathered Teresa. Bill Burkhart, whom he had spared so long ago, because he'd come later, after the fat colonel had died for his sins…

Mateo shook his head. He had spared the man who had cuckolded him, the man who had lain with Rita. Bill Burkhart had desecrated the land with his walled enclosure and planted his seed in *El Gato Negro's* wife, and he had died without paying for his treachery.

Rage turned black as bile in him, became a torrent of emotion from which no escape was possible. Bill Burkhart was dead, Mateo reasoned. But his son was not. Not yet.

But at least now Mateo could begin his revenge. He knew where to find Teresa. He would not have to find Rita. Once word reached her that he had taken Teresa as his woman, Rita would find him, and then she would die—Andrea or no Andrea...He did not need love conditioned upon his accepting the unacceptable.

"¿General?"

"Sí, Esteban?" asked Mateo, his voice hoarse with rage.

"Is there anything I can do, anything to help?" he asked lamely.

"No, Esteban. Eat. Rest. I am leaving. I have business at Rancho la Reina."

CHAPTER TWENTY

Every day Johnny Brago rode out to scout for Indian sign. The afternoon of the third day after the Indian attack, Johnny returned from his search and found Steve in his office working on a design for a more efficient water pump.

"Looks quiet out there," Johnny said, dropping onto the chair opposite Steve. "I found the remains of a big camp…maybe two, three hundred Injuns, including squaws and young'uns. The tracks went south, then east into the Chiricahuas. Maybe to their Tres Castillo mountain camp. I followed 'em for about thirty miles and saw no sign of another camp…not even a stray war party around."

"What do you think it means? Are they going to rest for the summer or take us on in numbers?"

Johnny shook his head. "Hell, Apaches don't wage war like the cavalry, 'paches slip in like snakes and kill a man, slip out again. They harry loners. A half dozen of 'em will kill a lone settler and his family. They'll lurk in deserted places and shoot from ambush. That's their style. Only Captain Rutledge would expect murdering Apaches to do close-order drills," he said with disgust. "It's a cinch they aren't gonna take their womenfolk and young-'uns into war."

"Maybe that Apache I killed was a stray," Steve said slowly. "Probably one of Chatto's braves out to earn himself another coup."

"They don't earn coup by killing," Johnny corrected. "They earn coup by touching the body of their victim after they killed him. To their way of thinking, it takes courage to face a man you've killed."

Indians were so strange to Steve that he didn't even try to figure out how they thought. "What do you recommend?"

"I think we might as well get back out there and do some ranchin'. The boys are gettin' on each other's nerves. We built the new corral you wanted, put new shingles on the bunkhouse, cleaned the barn, and weeded Carmen's garden. They've played cards until they're on the verge of gunfights. I broke up two fistfights between a couple of featherheads yesterday. Besides, Dap won everybody's money, and the *cantina* is almost out of beer. Horseshoes are out. Leon tried to wrap one of 'em around Robert's and Willie B.'s necks. Even Lindy, usually the quietest, best-natured man on the place, is looking cranky." Johnny sighed. The Parker boys were his favorites. They were good, steady workers, which was essential to his way of thinking, and they were good-hearted. Droll and playful, they rarely said what they meant. Their comments were meant to entertain, not to be taken seriously.

"And those are just the best of 'em. The rest of the men are skittish as a colt in a grizzly's cave."

Red came into the room with his particular claw-tapping walk and stopped beside Steve's chair. Steve reached down and patted the dog's shiny, rust-colored coat. "Sounds serious. Well...take 'em out tomorrow and see if you can wear off some of the rough edges."

Johnny informed the bunkhouse that work would resume the following day.

"Hey, Brago!" High Card Slocum yelled from the table where he was playing solitaire. "You ain't played a hand of cards with anyone. You as lazy as they say or just savin' your money?"

"How lazy do they say?" Johnny drawled.

"Heard tell they had a man check to see if you was still breathin' once a day ever' day."

When the howls of laughter died down, Dap adjusted the wad of snuff in his left jowl and added his two bits. "My papa always told me that if you got a hard or 'specially complicated job to do, you should find the laziest man you know and give it to him, then watch how he does it. Maybe that's why Burkhart hired you, Johnny. Figures you can show us the easy way to do ever'thang."

The men howled. Keeping his face impassive, Johnny merely shifted into a more comfortable position, confirming their opinion of him.

"Wal," Dap drawled with deliberate slowness, exaggerating his Texas accent, "my papa told me that laziness may not be curable, but then it ain't fatal, neither."

Callahan hooted. "Hell! Who wants to cure it? I jus' want'a get in on it."

"Hey, Brago," Leon yelled from his bunk. "I heard a rumor that you ain't dark-skinned a'tall."

Johnny leaned back against the wall and grinned. "Oh, yeah?"

"Yeah. Heard that's just rust makes you so dark."

Rollicking laughter followed that sally. Johnny smiled a slow, good-natured smile.

The next morning the hands went out early and came back late. They straggled in to eat and then collapsed across their bunks, too tired to undress.

At seven o'clock, only half an hour after dinner, Johnny walked in, strolled the length of the bunkhouse, surveyed his devastated crew, and then walked back to the door, not bothering to hide the disgust on his face.

"I'm looking for a dozen volunteers to help me build a new corral."

"We just built a corral three days ago. What the dickens you trying to do, kill us?" Willie B. asked once the racket of protest had died down.

Johnny smiled a slow, innocent smile. "You boys are a mite disappointin'. Only yesterday you were complaining about how we don't work hard enough around here."

"Ah ha! So that's it!" Lera yelled. "He's trying to kill us to make a point."

High Card shook his head disgustedly. "What do ya mean, *trying* to kill us? I'm killed," he said tragically, "and just look at Brago. Fresh as a yaller daisy. Hell, you ast me, he made his point."

"Brago, you closemouthed son of a gun, was that what you was doing?" Dap asked.

Johnny cast one long, appraising look at the sad lot sprawled on their bunks. "Y'all were telling me what your papas said, and all the racket reminded me of what my papa said."

"Uh-huh, and what might that'a been?" High Card asked, looking from Johnny to the others.

Casually Johnny stepped close to the door. "He told me that men learn by doing, but that they learn better by being done to." He stepped quickly outside and pulled the door closed. A heavy boot thudded into the door. Laughing, knowing they watched from the window, Johnny strutted across the porch and down the steps.

• • •

For Tía the second week on the ranch was the most hectic of her life. On Monday after breakfast the men carried their dirty clothes and linens to the wash area north of the house, where five heavily blackened wash pots squatted, and paid by the piece to have them washed.

Steve had designed and built a system to carry water to the pots from the tank beside the kitchen. Carmen turned on the spigots to start the pots filling with water, took the men's money, and put it in a jar to be divided among the women who helped.

Johnny and three of his men carried wood and started the fires, without which the laundry would have been left overnight to soak.

Tía and Lupe gathered the dirty clothes and linens from every room in the house and added them to the mountains already piled on the ground beside the pots. The four women sorted laundry: white linen, collars, sheets, and body linen into one heap; fine muslins into another; colored cotton and linen fabrics into a third; men's heavy pants into a fourth; and the coarser kitchen and other greasy clothes into a fifth.

Each woman tackled a pile. Every article had to be examined for spots and treated with sal ammonia, then placed in a wash pot. Smoke and fumes swirled up and drifted over the house. It smelled like the place in Tubac where Tía had taken their laundry. Tía did not explain to Carmen that she had never washed in this fashion; she just watched what the other women did and tried to do the same. Andrea offered to help, but Tía shooed her away. It was hot, sweaty work, and it suited her need to earn her place. She did not want Andrea doing it.

Tía examined and spotted the gowns entrusted to her, carried the pile to the pot Carmen pointed out to her, and dumped them in. When the clothes were covered by the lukewarm water pouring in from overhead, she mixed soda and water to Carmen's instructions, poured the mixture over the clothes, and stirred. Then, again prompted by Carmen, she shaved a bar of lye soap and let the shavings drop into the pot.

Tía alternately struggled with her skirts to keep them out of the fire, stirred the clothes with a wooden paddle, and wiped her hot forehead. The smell of lye soap singed her nostrils. Tears ran down her cheeks.

Johnny stopped some distance away, in the shade. He leaned against the side of one of the legs that supported the water tank and rolled a smoke. Then, holding the cigarette in his right hand, he stuffed the fingers of his left hand under his belt. With his legs crossed at the ankles and his dark eyes shaded by his hat brim, Tía couldn't tell if he watched her or not. He could just as easily be looking at Lupe, who had a ripe young body and used every opportunity to flaunt it. Lupe had taken off her sandals, hiked up her skirts, and pinned them to the waist of her gown to reveal her shapely legs all the way to her knees. She made no secret of the fact she found the handsome foreman to her liking.

Tía was glad of having clothes to stir. Johnny's presence agitated her. He hadn't seemed to notice her for days, but every now and then he would position himself in her vicinity and just watch. He looked indolent and unconcerned on the surface, but something about his lithe body seemed to hint that even his nonchalance was a trick. Occasionally, before he walked away, he would raise one of his heavy black eyebrows at her and send her heart racing.

He had stopped asking her to walk with him, but at least once each day she would catch his dark eyes following her.

Steve walked out the back door, waved at Johnny, and strode purposefully toward Tía. He stopped beside her, and Tía smiled up at him. Any contact at all with Steve thrilled her, filled her with hope that he liked her.

"I forgot to tell you. I brought a new catalog back from Tombstone last week. I want you to look through it and let me know what you need for the house."

Tía was so pleased he had actually sought her out that she flushed with gratitude. "When do you need to know?"

"As soon as you can get to it. I have an order, but it's not urgent."

"Who usually does this?"

"For the house? Judy did it last time. Sometimes Carmen. I think whoever does it always asks around to be sure she gets everything."

Steve walked away. Tía was so pleased, she closed her eyes, took in a deep breath of the noxious lye soap, and exploded into coughs, which reminded her that this was no time to get dreamy. When she stopped coughing and glanced surreptitiously at the spot where Johnny had lounged, it was empty.

Somehow his leaving like that, without even quirking an eyebrow at her, seemed a condemnation. She didn't know what she might have done to cause it, but she felt like kicking the ground, in complaint, except that doing so would send a fine spray of sand flying everywhere.

The water finally got hot, and the clothes cooked for a good long time. Finally Carmen pronounced them finished. Tía ladled the clothes out onto a long wooden counter, bleached almost white from soap and water, so they could cool enough to be scrubbed on the rub boards.

By the end of the day her knuckles and the knuckles of every woman who helped had been scraped raw where hands had accidentally rubbed against the roughened ridges instead of the clothing.

It was hard work, but Tía found she liked it. The women shared stories and complained the whole time, but as hot and miserable as it was, they too seemed to like the change. Tía hung clothes on the line between the orchard and the back of the house and could practically see the waves of moisture rising as the sun dried the wetness out of them. Nothing could stay wet in this dry heat. It was probably the wetness of the wash that Tía liked best.

She hung out the last colored garment and came back to help wring out the sheets. Carmen and Lupe rinsed the last white sheet in blueing and lifted it, sopping with water, onto the counter.

"We've washed everything in the world. The only dirty thing left is that gown you're wearing," Lupe said to Carmen.

"We have to save something for next time," Carmen said, smiling.

"No, we don't. Those filthy cowpunchers will see to it we have plenty."

"I thought you liked those *filthy* cowpunchers," Carmen teased.

Lupe picked up a handful of blueing water and splashed it on Carmen's gown. "Here, scrub that."

Carmen laughed and picked up a handful of water from the rinse tub sitting on the ground and threw it at Lupe. "I don't want to be the only clean one."

Lupe responded by picking up a handful of water and throwing it at Tía, who was so surprised her mouth dropped open. Lupe pointed a finger and laughed, and Tía picked up a bucket of clear water and sloshed it at Lupe, who jumped back screaming. Carmen and Cruz doubled over in laughter. Lupe, soaked to the skin, grabbed Cruz and tumbled her into the big rinse tub. The look on Cruz's face as she struggled to get out of the blueing water was so funny that Tía and Carmen doubled over and howled.

Lupe grabbed Tía's hand and tried to pull her into the water. To save herself, Tía grabbed Carmen, and Cruz took sides against them. The two pairs then squared off on opposite sides of the tub. Lupe and Cruz pulled so hard, and Tía and Carmen laughed so hard, that Tía lost strength and she and Carmen tumbled into the water with a big splash with Tía on bottom. Even sitting in the rinse tub with Carmen on top of her, Tía still laughed until her belly hurt.

Soaking wet, they all finally gathered behind the water tank, where the combination of trees and tank offered a shelter, and took off their wet clothes and rung them out.

Johnny climbed the hill behind the house, found a level rock about halfway up, and stopped to rest. A flicker of light caught his attention. He scanned the valley. The wet season had failed this year. Usually the summer would be cooled by frequent rains, but this year the rains hadn't come yet, and the grass had turned yellow.

Light flashed again. It came from the ranch house. Johnny lifted his spyglass into place.

The women were having a water fight. Grinning and enjoying the thought of her being that playful, Johnny focused on Tía. She had seemed different since he'd first seen her in Tubac. There she had seemed relaxed, confident, and sassy. Here she seemed as tight as a new growth of bark.

The sight of Tía floundering under Carmen's weight caused him to laugh outright with pleasure. She seemed the same girl he had met and kissed in Tubac.

Dripping and laughing, the women walked into the shelter provided by a growth of trees on one side and the water tower on the other. Encircled by the back of the house, the water tower, and the trees, they were safe from all eyes except Johnny's.

They started to disrobe. Sobering, Johnny lowered the glass. He was no Peeping Tom. But even without the glass, given this clear Arizona air, he could see for miles. Tía unbuttoned her gown, slipped it off, and stepped out of it. She slipped the straps of her undergarment over her shoulders. Johnny tried to turn away but couldn't seem to.

Sweat broke out on his forehead. As if it had a will and mind of its own, the glass positioned itself, found Tía, and would not leave his eye.

Tía slipped the garment down. For a moment she faced Johnny, naked as a babe, then reached a pale, slender arm for the towel Andrea held out to her. The sight of her naked body surprised him and heated his loins.

The glass burned Johnny's hand. He laid it on the rock beside him, careful to keep the sun from flashing on it and giving him away.

He'd done it now. He *had* spied on Tía. He'd never done anything like that in his life. He felt like a sneaky schoolboy.

Now the memory of her slender body with its triangle of honey-colored hair would haunt him forever.

. . .

Tía bathed, washed her hair, and dressed in her room. Then she went to check on Grant. Judy was stretched out on the bed beside him, sleeping. One hand rested on his forehead.

Grant's breathing was deep and even. His skin felt cool to the touch. Taking liquids for two days now, he had sat up for a while this morning. The fever had not come back. To Tía it seemed a miracle. She had been convinced when his fever soared three days ago that he would die.

Judy had saved Grant's life. Tía knew that as surely as she had ever known anything. Judy alone had saved him.

That night at supper Johnny kept his eyes on his plate. He didn't look once at Tía. He talked with the men about things Tía knew nothing about, ate very little supper, and appeared distracted.

It was so unlike him that Tía felt the void instantly. Instead of being relieved by his lack of attention she was unaccountably piqued. She carried the coffeepot down to his end of the table twice. He did not look up or ask for more coffee. Usually he would drink his coffee quickly, smile at her, and lift his cup to summon her. Tonight he barely touched his cup.

At last Tía carried the pot down to his end of the table and poured coffee in all the cups of all the men around Johnny. Still he did not look up at her.

Finally she stopped beside him. "Coffee?" Suddenly her heart was pounding hard.

"No, thank you." His voice sounded so strangled, so disinterested.

Tía walked back into the kitchen and stayed there until the meal was over.

Tía threw herself into the housework to take her mind off Johnny, but she heard reports of his unaccustomed industry from Dap, who had apparently taken a liking to her. *That boy even volunteered to dig post holes.* To Dap everyone was a boy, even if he was the same age. *A foreman don't dig nothing. He must be off his feed.*

Tía couldn't imagine what had happened to change him from a young man who looked like he couldn't spit without leaning against something to a man who dug post holes. It was out of character. She began to worry that Johnny would cut his picket pin and drift on to another range, but she told herself she'd be better off if he did.

Each day, in addition to cooking, the women tackled one other chore or set of chores. Tuesday they darned, ironed, and sewed on buttons. Wednesday they put fresh linens on all the beds in the house and bunkhouse. In the house, the feather mattresses had to be beaten into a state of freshness and turned. Carmen informed Tía each bed was made a little differently. Steve preferred his mattress perfectly flat. Judy liked hers swelling slightly in the middle. In the bunkhouse, the cotton mattresses were dragged outside and hung over the lines to air, then fresh sheets were applied.

Thursday was cleaning day. Everything in the house was dusted, scrubbed, or mopped. Combs were brushed and wiped. Hairbrushes were dipped in a solution of soda and hot water until they came clean.

Friday was set aside for canning. Navarone supervised the children in picking cucumbers from the garden. Carmen supervised Cruz and Lupe in pickling them.

Andrea had finally given up trying to fight her own nature, even to impress Steve and Judy, and slept in until nine o'clock every morning. Steve didn't seem to mind. And Judy didn't get up in time to notice, but when she learned about it from Lupe, she was pleased Andrea didn't outdo her in that area.

Steve was an early riser. Sometimes he spent the morning in the barn. Sometimes he saddled a horse and rode out of the compound. Carmen said he liked to sit on the mountainside and think in the early morning hours. He would come back and spend the day in his office designing things. He had designed every improvement on the ranch. He only came out of his office to eat or take care of one of his horses. He shared Tía and Johnny's love of horses.

As the lady of the spread, Andrea spent her time as she pleased. She read books and old magazines, walked everywhere inside the compound, and familiarized herself with everything and everyone. Judy claimed Andrea was like a queen familiarizing herself with her kingdom. *I hope she knows I'm not one of her subjects.*

A week went by so quickly that Tía didn't realize it until it was over that she hadn't been near a horse since the ride to the ranch. Rancho la Reina's handsome foreman stayed away from her. She was bewildered by Johnny's withdrawal, but too busy learning all that was expected of her to do anything about it.

Friday afternoon she told Carmen she had something to do, slipped out the back door, and walked to the barn. She found the easy-gaited mare she had ridden to the ranch, saddled it, and led it toward the door.

"You need a good workout, don't you, girl?" she asked, patting the sleek mare's neck.

A familiar masculine voice stopped her. "You planning on taking that horse outside the walls?"

Tía turned slowly to face Johnny. He leaned against the wall beside the barn door, his muscular arms crossed over his chest, his eyes carefully hooded. Dressed in dusty black vest, blue-and-white-striped shirt that emphasized the darkness of his face, and dark trousers, he seemed to be daring her to fight with him. Matador, the horse he had been leading into the barn, sniffled at Tía's horse.

"Does that meet with your approval?"

"You don't need my approval. I'm nobody to order you around. But it might not be safe out there alone."

Johnny looked hot and dusty, as if he had been riding hard. She'd heard from Steve that Johnny was working harder than any of the other men, longer hours, more onerous tasks. Matador looked tired. Tía smiled. "You were out there. Was it safe?"

"Appeared to be, but I got to feeling uneasy about it and sent the men back in. I took a look-see, but didn't find anything too alarming."

"So you're recommending that I not go."

"Not alone, anyways. Not for any distance."

Tía walked almost up to Johnny. In the dim light of the barn his dark eyes regarded her with his familiar, careful expression. She had the urge to reach out and stroke his face, to feel the brush of his mustache on her fingertips. In Tubac or up in the hayloft she could have done it, but now he looked intimidating and unapproachable. Maybe she was just now seeing him as he really was.

Tía hesitated. She had been cooped up in the house all week, ever since arriving at the ranch. She needed to ride, to feel the wind on her face.

"I guess you're too tired to ride with me," she said. Her heart raced, and she immediately wished she hadn't spoken. He would probably refuse her.

Johnny's dark face seemed to pale. He looked like a man struggling with a weighty problem. Finally he sighed. "I'm not tired."

"You look tired." Tía could not imagine what had made her say that.

His lips compressed in a wall of stubbornness. "You want me to go or not? Just say so."

"I asked you to go. Why would I *not* want you to?"

Tía could not imagine how everything had become so difficult. Things had been easy between them from the first minute he'd stepped foot in Mrs. Gaston's dress shop. At some point that had all changed, but she had lost track of where and when it had happened. All she felt for sure was the heat radiating from Johnny Brago's lean body. She suddenly hated the cocky slant of his deep-set eyes. Anything could be going on in him—though if she had to guess, she would think he felt remorseful. But she couldn't imagine why he should, unless it had finally dawned on him that she knew he had spent the night with Judy.

As if he had made up his mind, Johnny levered himself away from the wall with his elbows. "Let me toss my saddle on a different horse."

It proved to be a lengthy process. He unsaddled Matador, brushed and curried him, turned Matador over to Tía to walk him, then strode out into the corral and roped a big red mare, another horse from his string, and brushed and curried her before throwing on a dry blanket and saddling her.

Tía was content to walk Matador around the corral. She didn't mind the delay, even though she was anxious to be riding. She enjoyed being with the horses, watching Johnny's deft movements, the obvious care he took with them. She knew which horses he rode, and they were all well groomed. His equipment was mended and polished. No one would ever accuse Johnny Brago of mistreating his animals. Somehow that warmed Tía toward him.

Navarone walked into the barn, and Johnny yelled for the boy, who came running.

"Walk Matador for me, will you?" Johnny asked, taking the reins from Tía's hands.

"*Sí, señor.*"

"When he cools down, give him water and oats."

The guard at the front gate was surprised to see Johnny going out again so soon. Tía had put on a divided riding skirt she had made herself in Albany before she'd realized she could not wear it because it would not be acceptable. In Albany decent young women did not ride astride in divided skirts. They wore elaborate riding habits that confined them to a sidesaddle.

Tía rode astride. Johnny let her set the pace. Tall and lithe in his saddle, he rode in silence beside her.

On the north side of the compound, just a few feet from the adobe wall, a peccary rooted in a tin can. Cans—some burned and some with paper labels—littered the sandy soil beside the wall. Some of the cans had bullet holes in them. Tía guessed the riders stacked them on the fence and shot at them.

The wild boar was a dark charcoal-gray color with a yellow circle of bristles around the musk gland on its back where a tail would normally be. Other pigs had tails, but peccaries just had that bright yellow crater of stiff bristles that surrounded the musk gland. The boar gave up on the can and walked over to a prickly-pear cactus, mouthed the pad of cactus until it blunted the spines, and gobbled the pulp. It didn't even look up at them. Tía looked around for his companions. Peccaries rarely traveled alone.

Johnny pointed to a spot where one of the peach tree limbs hung over the wall. A dozen boars rooted at the ripe and rotting fruit that had already fallen. Desert peccaries didn't have a horn on their foreheads, but they had been known to charge a horse if they were mad enough. These didn't charge or even seem to notice, however.

West from the compound, Tía struck quickly into gray-green sagebrush—miniature trees two to three feet high—tufts of bunch grass, and stands of greasewood. Thirty feet from where they rode, a rattlesnake coiled in the shade of a six-foot boulder. It lifted its head and watch them ride past. Tía kept a tight hold on the reins just in case, but the mare didn't seem to smell the rattler. Tía smelled it after they were past.

They rode toward the hills to the west. A thin black-and-silver coyote ran along beside them for about a mile, then loped off.

"Want to see the creek?" Johnny yelled over the sound of their horses' hooves.

Tía nodded. Johnny angled northwest, and she followed.

The creek was narrow. Clear water ran downstream to a point, and then the water disappeared into a wide pipe that lay atop the sand and angled toward the compound, its pink walls glistening like sugar in the sunlight, its water tower looking like a gray coffee mug on stilts.

Tía dismounted and loosened her saddle cinches. Johnny did likewise. His was a big, sturdy cow saddle, its seat completely covered by rattlesnake skins, from the finest diamondback rattlers. The yellow-and-black-patterned leather shone in the sunlight.

"Did you kill them yourself?"

"Yes." He turned back to his horse and fiddled with the cinches some more. Facing his broad, tapering back frustrated Tía, made her want to aggravate him into talking to her.

"Are you mad at me?" she demanded.

"Nope." Johnny knelt beside the stream, cupped his hand, lifted water to his lips, and drank. Tía walked away.

Johnny drank his fill and looked up at his companion. Tía Marlowe gazed beyond him at the mountains. She wore a thin white lawn blouse

and a brown riding skirt. Her wispy blond curls were mostly hidden
under a broad-brimmed black hat she must have borrowed. It came
down over her ears and emphasized the fragile grace of her neck and
shoulders and the tenderness of her slender arms. From where he knelt
by the stream, the sun coming from the side and behind her outlined one
small, cone-shaped breast—a swell of firm flesh capped with a smaller
swell of pouty nipple. He could see the outline of her camisole inside her
blouse. It was edged with lace, and square-necked.

Johnny forced himself to look away. He shouldn't have ridden with
Tía. That look had been a pure accident, but it reminded him of the
other, which hadn't been. Embarrassment flushed through him.

He needed to be doing things to get his mind off Steve Burkhart's
future woman, and here he was loading grist into the mill so he could
spend another miserable night thinking about Tía and questioning
his sanity.

"Well, you don't seem like yourself," she persisted.

"Maybe you don't, either."

"What's that supposed to mean?"

Johnny stood up slowly and hooked his thumbs in his pocket tops.
The look in his dark eyes was probably meant to intimidate her, but it
didn't. It raised her ire.

"What's that supposed to mean?" Tía repeated.

"Hoping you might tell me."

"How would I know?"

"You're the one that got too busy to see me." Johnny did not know
where that reply had come from. It had not been on his mind, which
seemed intoxicated with the nearness of this sassy young woman.

"I did not."

"I asked you three times to walk with me."

"I don't like to walk. I like to ride."

Tía dropped her reins and walked north along the creek. Johnny
stood, kicked at a rock as if to stand his ground, and then followed.

"Does this creek dry out in August?" Tía asked.

"Sometimes. Not always."

"What do we do for water when it does?"

"Lower a bucket into the well."

Tía blushed. She should have known that.

She was sorry she had come with Johnny. She had no idea why *he*
had consented to come. She felt more miserable than she had all week. At
least having him look at her from a distance, she had her own thoughts

about how it would be if he approached her. But now he had, sort of, and nothing had changed. He was just as distant, only doing it while he walked right beside her. She was glad she had decided not to like him anymore.

Tía turned and headed back to her horse. She'd picked up the reins and started to mount when Johnny's voice stopped her.

"Wait."

"What?" she asked, turning.

"Look over there."

Tía scanned the stretch of desert between them and the compound and finally saw what Johnny pointed at.

"Be quiet. Follow me," he said, reaching into his saddlebag to take out his spyglass.

Tía followed Johnny ten yards, then stopped beside him. He lifted the glass to his eye, then handed it to her.

"What am I looking for?"

"A roadrunner and a rattlesnake."

Frowning, Tía put the glass to her right eye. Johnny moved behind her and lifted the glass slightly. "See it?"

"No." Then she did. The glass brought the bird so close she could make out the tiniest detail. The roadrunner was brown, with a pattern of white-tipped feathers that made it look almost striped. White tips formed broken stripes from the roadrunner's neck down to a few inches above the tail at the end of its pear-shaped body. Its tail feathers were brown, edged in white also. At the moment it stood still, alertly facing a rattler, its broad, flat head lifted, swaying.

"What's going to happen?"

"I reckon that rattler's going to have a bad day."

"How can you tell?"

"See that cholla cactus laying around the rattler?"

Tía adjusted the glass. "You have good eyes."

A moment later she murmured, "Yes, I see it. What does it mean?"

"The snake can only move one direction without sticking himself. He must have gone to sleep, and the runner broke off those chunks of cactus with its beak and laid 'em around him."

"Are you sure? I thought that was an old wives' tale."

"He didn't finish. Rattler isn't completely penned in."

"Good." Tía had a weakness for underdogs. "What would happen if it was?"

"Legend has it a snake will bite itself to death if it gets trapped. I'd like to see if that's true, but it isn't quite trapped. Course it's at a disadvantage…"

As Tía watched, the nimble bird ran around to the side of the rattler, which struck at the bird and missed. Then the bird ran around to the other side, and the rattler missed again.

A young one, judging by its size, the rattler struck again and again, every time the bird darted in, but each time the fleet-footed bird just danced out of reach again. Finally, when the rattler slowed down, the bird ran around behind it, pecked it hard in the back of the neck at the base of its skull, and walked away with the snake impaled on its beak. The snake writhed for a while. The bird put one claw on the rattler to hold it down, then pecked it a few more times until it stopped writhing. The road-runner opened its gullet and took the snake in headfirst.

"What a crafty bird."

"Probably just hungry."

His voice had dropped to a lower, more sensuous tone. Tía's heart thumped in her breast. Carefully she handed the glass back to Johnny. "Thank you."

"Welcome."

Usually he would have smiled or even grinned at her, but now he did neither. His dark face remained impassive. She'd seen more expression on a cigar-store Indian. "I guess I'd better go," she said.

Tía walked to her horse and started to mount. Uncertain and tempted to tackle Johnny again to find out what was wrong with him, she hesitated. He must have misread her signal because he walked up behind her, put his hands on her waist, and lifted her effortlessly into her saddle.

With her seated on her horse, Johnny's handsome head reached up to her shoulder. In the sunlight it appeared every pore on the bottom half of his face was darkened with the stubble that made it look as rough as sandpaper. He had the most relentless beard of any man she'd ever seen. Indians had no beard at all. Indians had the same dark skin he had, but few of them had the richness of his eyebrows, mustache, and sideburns to lure a woman. Johnny's features were so distinctive that Tía could spot him from hundreds of yards away.

His warm hand still rested on her hip. Tía looked at it. She should thank him for helping her mount, not that she'd needed any help. For no reason she wanted to cry suddenly. His passive black eyes, narrowed and squinty from looking into the sun, made her so lonely she wanted to put her head down on her hands and sob.

Abruptly Tía turned the mare and let her prance sideways. Johnny walked to his own horse and mounted. Tía turned the mare back toward the ranch. She had lost her desire to ride.

At three o'clock on Saturday afternoon gunshots rang out. Tía's heart leaped into her throat. Outside, men ran for their rifles. Dropping her dust cloth, Tía lifted her skirts and ran out the door toward the front gate, grateful Steve had decided to keep the riders in the compound.

Because of the Indian scare, they had discouraged riders from going into Tombstone or to the fort.

Johnny ran ahead of Tía. He hadn't seen her. Steve had reached the south wall first and was watching through field glasses. "Open the gates!" he yelled. "When he gets into range, give him some cover!"

"Who is it?" Johnny asked, climbing up to join Steve.

Tía clambered up between Steve and Johnny. Johnny glanced once at her and then swung his rifle up and lowered his ruddy cheek onto the rich mahogany barrel.

"Looks like Morgan Todd," Steve said.

Johnny made a wry face and lowered his rifle. Steve brought his rifle up and yelled, "*Fire!*"

Johnny ignored the command. He merely watched the lone rider's frantic flight.

Whipping his horse into a frenzy, followed closely by a dozen yipping braves, Morgan Todd rode pell-mell toward the open gates. Rifles cracked as men all around Johnny fired to give cover.

Without warning, Johnny took Tía's wrist and led her down the ladder and away from the wall.

"Why aren't you helping?" she demanded when they were far enough away to hear over the gunfire. She was so surprised by his action that she was too distracted to control the leap of her heart.

"Some of these boys are not too sure with a weapon. If Morgan Todd gets shot, I can't afford to be pointing a rifle in that direction," he said, propelling her along beside him.

"Oh." So darkly attractive against the light blue of the sky, Johnny's manly profile filled her with a strange queasiness. Pink and slightly moist, his bottom lip was smooth and inviting beneath his crisp black mustache. He slanted a look at Tía. His narrowed eyes ignited a strange warmth inside her that spread up to her cheeks.

"How's your arm?" she asked, looking away, ignoring the fact that they were far from the others and he was still forcing her toward the house. She could not imagine what had gotten into Johnny. Yesterday he had taken her for a ride and practically ignored her. Today, in front of fifty people, he was holding her arm and dragging her along beside him.

"Reckon it could use a new bandage."

Tía wasn't sure what had happened to her, either. She had been so miserable last night after that short ride that she had gone directly to bed after supper. It had been all she could do to keep from crying. She had decided that Andrea was right: Johnny was just like Papa. He'd end up on a Wanted poster himself someday. He was no fit husband for any woman. He didn't have anything, except his horse and saddle. And he probably didn't want anything else.

"I thought your arm was healed," she said.

They reached the steps that led up to the curved arches of the *casa grande,* and Tía stopped. She didn't want to go inside and be alone with him; besides, he hadn't turned loose of her arm. He would no doubt follow her in, and everyone else was at the front gate or somewhere on the wall.

Tía glared down at her arm where his hand still held her. Reluctantly Johnny let her go.

He didn't know what had gotten into him. Maybe it was just knowing that Morgan Todd was coming; he would probably take this woman, too. It caused him to forget all his good sense, if he had any.

"I guess you're too busy to change my bandage."

"Does it need to be changed?" Tía didn't wait for Johnny to answer. "Well, come along, then." She could not believe she'd said that. She probably would have said anything under the influence of his intent, dark eyes. Anyone would.

She led the way around the side of the house instead of through it. When they reached the back door, Tía stopped. Her medicine box and supplies were in the kitchen. She didn't want Johnny Brago to follow her inside, but she wasn't sure what to say to him to get him to wait outdoors for her.

Johnny must have seen or guessed her confusion. His smooth lips twitched and flattened into a smile. His dark eyes flickered with tiny glints of amusement. His old reckless humor seemed to be back.

"I'm housebroke," he said, his rich voice husky.

"It's not those habits I'm concerned about." Tía had no idea why she liked to see him grin like that, but when he did all her resistance dissolved. She wanted to try their aborted ride all over again, to be on horseback, racing across the desert, free as a tumbleweed. She turned to go inside, but he moved at the same time and stopped her.

"Are you in love with Steve?" he asked.

"No."

"But you want to marry him?"

That was so ridiculous Tía laughed. Johnny watched her a moment and then abruptly pulled her into his arms. The heat of his hard chest surprised her and took away all desire to laugh.

"We're gonna have to shorten your stake rope," she said. She'd meant it to be funny, but her voice failed in the middle.

"You talk more than any woman I ever knew." Without waiting for her permission, he ducked his head down and brushed her lips with his. This time she felt his mustache. It sent a little tingle through her body that felt like a sidewinder crawling down her spine. His mouth kissed her lightly, sweetly, and her body flushed with a strange dry heat.

Like the rush of wind through tall pine trees, a *whoosh*ing sound buzzed in her ears. Of its own accord, her mouth sought his. The buzzing sound in her head grew louder, more intense, and then she was lost, lost to everything except the taste and feel of him. His hands bit into her waist and back, pressing her close to him.

"Tía, Tía, Tía," he groaned, his warm breath rustling the hair at her cheek. Had he stopped kissing her, then?

"Tía, I need you so bad."

Her mind formed a picture of Judy Burkhart working night and day to save Grant Foreman's life. That was need. Tía opened her eyes, pushed against his chest, and freed herself from his strong arms.

"What's wrong?" he asked.

"I can't kiss around on you, Johnny Brago."

"Why not?" he asked, his hands encircling her arms like slaves' bracelets.

"There's someone else," she said. Even to Tía that sounded false, but she realized it was true. Judy was someone, and Judy had already staked her claim.

"Tell him you changed your mind."

Judy had completely forgiven her and even tried to cover for Johnny, but Tía was not willing to accept a sacrifice like that...

"No. I can't."

She stepped back, and Johnny let his hands drop to his sides.

"I don't want to," she lied.

CHAPTER TWENTY-ONE

Walking slowly, swishing one side of her gown with a careless hand, Judy glanced at Grant. He was moving very carefully. His cheeks were unusually pale. He shouldn't be up walking around. He should be sleeping. Why had she agreed to this? He'd insisted he was too restless to lie in that bed another second, but she suspected he'd only been saying that to get her outside. The house *had* been stuffy and hot.

It did feel good to be walking, to be free again, to be relieved of the fear of his dying. Grant always surprised her. He seemed to anticipate her needs and arrange for them even before she realized them herself. She didn't deserve such a good friend, but she was glad she had him.

Judy shuddered at the thought of Grant dying. She wouldn't have been able to bear it.

"What's wrong, pretty lady? You look so sad."

"Look who's talking. Two weeks ago we could have used the arrow in your back to hang coats on. You still look a tad green around the gills."

"If I weren't made of cast iron, I wouldn't have come west."

"I must admit you do *appear* to be as strong as an ox. A lesser man would have died immediately." Judy sighed. "All I did was have one tiny glass of wine, and I have a headache."

Grant chuckled. "One tiny little glass too many, you mean."

Grinning impertinently, Judy shrugged. "You'd call me a liar for two little words."

"I would never call you a liar," he said firmly. "The world can adjust itself to your words."

Judy glanced at him sharply. Catching the adoring look in his eyes, recognizing it for what it was—acceptance and loving concern— she looked away guiltily, as if seeing it could somehow commit her to something she didn't want. But it was too late: she had seen into Grant's heart. A feeling of mingled fear and joy rose up in her. Impulsively she took his hand and swung it between them.

Judy fairly bubbled with happiness. She liked him better than most men she knew, even if he wasn't as handsome as Morgan or Johnny. He wasn't half bad looking, she realized unexpectedly. Dark-complected like Johnny, but shorter, he had a muscular, compact frame that was very reassuring. He was a man who could obviously take care of himself. His mouth was a little too wide, but his eyes made up for everything. He always looked as if he were thinking about something he enjoyed, something she would enjoy as well. But most important, he always looked as if she made him proud to be with her—no matter what she did or said to him.

A frown knit Judy's eyebrows. Feeling the strain there, she forced her face to relax. The thought of making a permanent wrinkle horrified her. Even with Grant she had to be careful about how she looked, about what she confided to him. No sense making it hard for him to keep on loving her and treating her special. A girl needed someone constant in her life. The thought of Grant ever leaving had brought a strange pang to Judy's heart, but she refused to entertain dreary thoughts today, so she pushed all weighty concerns aside.

She smiled to dispel the sudden pall that had befallen her, stopped walking, and faced Grant. She could never many him, but she wanted desperately to give him something for being such a good friend to her, for getting well. It shamed her that she couldn't marry him, that looks and position were so important to her.

"I like you so much, Grant. You're the only man in the whole world who understands me."

Grant smiled. Her brown eyes were earnest and filled with a desire to please. "The man who understands is indispensable."

A cloud flitted across her usually sunny face, and a tiny ache seized his heart. He'd said the wrong thing, apparently. He would have cut his tongue out if it would have put the smile back where it belonged. He wanted to take her into his arms and wipe that forlorn look off her face forever. She'd worked so hard to keep him alive, she'd worn herself to a frazzle. Other days she could be impossible, impertinent, playful, but today she needed him to cheer her...

"I'm getting a headache. I think it's connected to something I haven't eaten yet."

Caught off guard, Judy giggled. "You're one of a kind," she said.

"God did do one thing right, anyway."

"But you notice, he stopped before he repeated his mistake," she said, her expression arch.

Pleased she had recovered, Grant chuckled. "Yeah, yeah. Just wait until you need me again." Another man, especially if he were good-looking, might feel he was wasting his time loving a woman who couldn't even see him, but Grant didn't mind, not really—especially when the only girl that made him happy was right at his side.

Distant rifle shots scattered birds from the trees overhead. Judy turned toward the sound, which seemed to be coming from the front gate. "Just what we need. Another Indian attack. This is God's way of telling me not to cry wolf, isn't it?"

"Let's find out." Taking her hand and forgetting how badly injured he was, Grant started to run toward the house.

"You're in no shape to run," she said, holding him there, refusing to let go of his arm. "We're going to walk. Slowly."

The slight pressure exerted before he could stop himself sent pain ripping through his back, almost bringing him to his knees. Darkness closed in from the periphery.

"Here, lean here," Judy insisted. "You're going to pass out, aren't you? Oh, damn!" She looked around frantically for someone to help her. They were about thirty yards from the kitchen door, under the shade of the orange tree nearest the *casa grande*.

Fighting the darkness, Grant forced himself to take a series of deep breaths. "I forgot," he said, panting, "that someone drove a wagon through my back."

Filled with anxiety at the way the color had drained from his face, Judy touched him gingerly. "I'm glad you don't exaggerate."

Listening to the scatter of gunfire, watching Grant out of the corner of her eye, Judy almost didn't see Johnny and Tía. She might have missed them completely, except she saw the change in Grant's face. Instinctively she turned to find what had caused his reaction.

Tía Marlowe and Johnny had stopped by the back door. Tía started to go into the house, turned back, and bumped into Johnny. He pulled her into his arms and kissed her. Tía's arms slipped up, and they looked like they would kiss until snow fell. Somehow it wasn't the kissing that hurt Judy. It was the way Johnny's dark hands cupped Tía's pale face. He touched her as if she were the most precious thing he'd ever felt, and he kissed her as if he would devour her. And Tía. Tía, of all people—Tía, who seemed so sweet and loyal—strained up on tiptoe, pressing her slender body into Johnny's. She was holding him so tightly that individual tendons stood out in her slender arms. Johnny was nearly crushing her in his embrace.

Judy started forward, but Grant, always the cautious one, took her by the arm and led her behind the spring house, out of sight of the two lovers. She would have struggled against Grant, but she was afraid of hurting him again. Fighting for control, she turned away angrily.

"Damn him!"

"Easy, pretty lady."

"Easy! You want me to take it easy?" she hissed, pulling away. "He belongs to me! That little maggot!"

"Maybe she tempted him," he said loyally.

"Of course she did. Johnny wouldn't risk losing me for a little twit like her. Johnny loves me," she said, wiping at a tear that trickled down her cheek. "Johnny has always loved me. Everyone knows that."

"How could he help it?" Grant asked, meaning it.

Remembering something Johnny had said, Judy felt the corners of her mouth puckering. "He loves me, but maybe he still wants to get even with me for the way I once hurt him."

"Get even?" Grant shook his head. The other riders were talking about Johnny and his all-too-obvious attentions to the new housekeeper. After Johnny had done whatever Judy wouldn't talk about, she had showed up at the bunkhouse, white-faced, numb, in need of comfort. Since that night, a slow rage had been building in Grant against Johnny Brago.

Hiding his rage, he faced her squarely. "Why would Brago want revenge? What for?"

"He thinks I cheated on him. I didn't, exactly," she said quickly. "But he…I mean, it might have seemed like I did. I wasn't exactly promised to Johnny then. But he acted like I was…"

Judy looked up at Grant, and her pale face slowly changed. "Do you think Johnny would make up to Tía to punish me?"

Inwardly Grant squirmed. He didn't know Johnny well enough to answer that. The bastard had left Rancho la Reina shortly after Grant had arrived there looking for work. No man worth a damn would be mean to a woman like Judy Burkhart.

"He would, wouldn't he?" Judy persisted. "He even told me he came back to take his revenge, but then he kissed me just like he had before. He's so rotten!"

"The shooting's stopped," Grant said, feeling unexpectedly helpless.

Judy turned and saw the gates swing shut. Men shouted and waved, cheering wildly as a lone rider slowed his plunging horse just inside the compound walls. Even from this distance she recognized the man who had ridden in. There was something unmistakable about the arrogant way he sat the roan. Judy turned back toward the house and expelled a purposeful breath. Tía and Johnny were gone.

"I'll see you later, Grant." Lifting her skirts, Judy ran toward the front gate and the rider who had just arrived.

Curiously saddened, Grant watched the woman he loved running away. He would do anything in the world for Judy, but the one thing she needed, he couldn't give her. He didn't have it.

Morgan Todd caught sight of Judy Burkhart, dismounted with a flair, flipped his reins at the man who had run forward, and smiled, enjoying the sudden rush of adrenaline that quickened within him at the sight of her vibrant form.

"Morgan!" she cried, rushing forward happily.

Morgan grabbed her and swung her around. "How's my little filly?"

"Morgan, you madman, put me down," Judy protested.

"No kiss, no put down," he threatened, a smile lighting his hazel eyes.

"Robber! One kiss, then," she offered.

Morgan Todd was not a man to waste an opportunity. He gathered Judy into his arms and pulled her hard against him. He was a gambler, a womanizer, and an opportunist, but he was not prepared for the passionate response he got for his efforts. Judy molded her slender softness against him, her sweet, down-curving lips opened under his, and her tongue lit quick, hot fires in him that he could not control.

"Ahem!" Steve Burkhart's less-than-pleased utterance brought Morgan out of the sweetness of Judy's kiss. With painful reluctance, he allowed her to step away from him. Her eyes were alive with mischief. It was all he could do not to curse aloud. Realizing the meaning of his expression, Judy quickly gave him a cool, triumphant smile, which hit Morgan like a bucket of cold water. She'd caused an ache in his loins that had damn near crippled him, and she stood there smiling! Damn her seductive brown eyes!

He held out his right hand to Steve. "Thanks for your help."

"What're you doing out here, Morgan? We're a little off the beaten track," Steve said, accepting Morgan's hand, a little put off and angered by the kiss he had just witnessed.

"Came out to see you. Russ Sloan made it through with his silver by now, and I wondered if you'd like to make a stab at it with me."

"Russ made it through, huh?"

"He must have. If he lost it, we'd have sure heard by now."

Men who had clustered around them began to disperse. The Indians had veered off, heading south, probably to harry other lone riders. For lack of anything better to do, Judy stayed near Steve, watching Morgan with eyes that were strangely dark and challenging.

"Let's go up to the house. You could probably use something to cut the dust," Steve said.

Following him, Morgan scowled at Judy. "Thanks, I'm spittin' cotton. It's hotter'n Texas chili out there."

Judy walked most of the way in silence, between the two men, listening as they talked about things of no interest to her, but enjoying their maleness. She felt so well protected that she even forgot about Johnny and his cheating. When they reached the shade of the front porch, Tía pushed the massive front doors open to let them in. They had been keeping the doors and windows secured since the first Indian attack. Under the curved arches it was noticeably cooler. Carmen followed Tía out onto the porch. Morgan smiled at the new woman.

"Carmen, some water for Mr. Todd, please," Steve said.

Tía looked as though she were about to melt back into the kitchen, but Steve stopped her. "Tía, I'd like you to fix up the room next to mine for Mr. Todd."

"Yes, sir."

"Well, who's this?" Morgan asked expectantly, smiling into Tía's embarrassed face.

Determined to show no jealousy, even if Morgan bedded the maggot on the spot, Judy lifted her chin and took the initiative. She caught Tía by the hand and pulled her in front of Morgan. "Tía Marlowe, Morgan Todd. Now Tía, here's a man who's a real good catch. Mr. Todd is the owner of the Contention mine. He's one of the richest men in the Arizona Territory and a great dancer. You watch out for him, though, he's a heartbreaker!"

"How do you do?" Tía smiled.

Morgan took Tía's hand and raised it to his lips. Judy felt confused impulses of anger and satisfaction. Let the little maggot try her hand at controlling Morgan. That should keep her busy.

"You heard from Russ already?" Steve asked, frowning.

Morgan made a deprecatory face. "Well, no, but like I said, you can bet we would have if he'd lost that silver. Every lawman in the territory would have been notified."

"Unless something happened to him."

"There were twenty men with that silver. It would have had to happen to all of 'em."

Steve pondered his scuffed boots. Morgan's bold gaze traveled down Judy's body. Judy glanced at Tía to be sure she was noticing *who* Morgan was looking at.

"I suppose that's possible," Steve said evenly. "Isn't it?"

Morgan scowled. "Ain't happened before! Nobody kills twenty men for four bars of silver. Hell, you sound like an old woman! That pompous bastard put one over on us. He beat out Wells Fargo. They'll think twice before they triple their prices again."

"Can't really blame Wells Fargo. They've been losing a lot of shipments to road agents. Their insurance would have to go way up when that keeps happening."

"So they're incompetent," Morgan said impatiently. "But we don't have to sit still for it. Russ proved that. I'll bet he's in Silver City right now crowing like the only cock on the walk."

"So what's your plan?"

"Same as his. Outfit a pack train and take our silver out same as he did."

"You don't need me for that."

"Hell, you haven't shipped since before me."

"What's the rush? It'll keep."

"Like hell it will. Three men robbed the Gold Nugget last night. Sixty thousand in payroll and almost two hundred thousand in silver gone! Even if it was safe, it's not earning any interest sitting in your vault. If we each bring fifteen men, we can be in Silver City in five days, even allowing a day to get to Tombstone, get outfitted and the like."

"What about Indians?"

"Geronimo is heading for the Pinalenos up north. Word came from Fort Huachuca yesterday. Major Hart at Fort Bowie is joining up with Captain Rodgers from 'chuca. They're gonna run Geronimo and Chatto out of this valley for good. They'll go back to the reservations whipped so bad they won't dare show their faces around here again."

"I've heard those stories before. Personally, I'll wait until we see how Russ Sloan's trip worked out before I risk fifteen men and a hundred sixty thousand in silver," Steve said firmly.

"Jesus Christ! You'd let a pompous bastard like Sloan be the only one to pull it off?"

"Would you mind spelling that for the ladies?" Steve asked, taking exception to Todd's rough language.

"Sorry."

"I'm an engineer, not a smuggler. We may not be as lucky as Sloan."

"Hell! Anything that stuffed shirt can do, we can do better," Morgan snorted.

"I'll talk to Johnny and let you know," Steve said, stepping back to make room for Carmen, who carried Morgan's water.

"Brago!?" Morgan asked, stealing a look at Judy. He didn't need Steve's nod. The look of victory in Judy's eyes was confirmation enough.

"What's he doing back here?"

"Pa and I sent for him."

"Let's go find him. I'm curious as hell to see what that ba—half-breed...has to say. Excuse me, ladies."

Morgan followed Steve across the room. Their heels were loud on the wooden floor, more muffled on the carpet in the middle of the room. Tía waited until they were gone.

"You wanted to see me?"

"Don't be scared. I'm not upset because you were making eyes at Morgan."

Tía wasn't scared, but with Judy the implications came faster than she could sort them out. "Morgan? I wasn't...I swear..."

"Oh, Tía! You're such a little tease! I saw you giving Morgan the eye. And I don't care. Morgan Todd is less than nothing to me. As a matter of fact, I think you should get to know him even better."

"Better? I don't know him at all."

"I know, but Morgan is a very fast worker. I have an idea. I'll forgive you if you grant me one favor."

If she hadn't just kissed Johnny, Tía would have blurted out that she had no reason to need forgiveness, but Johnny kept clouding the issues between them. And now something unfamiliar sparkled in Judy's pretty brown eyes that caused the hair on Tía's neck to bristle in warning. "What's the favor?"

"I'll tell you after supper. If you do it, maybe I'll forgive you. If you don't," she baited, "well, you can find yourself another friend, can't you?"

Abruptly, Judy turned and left. Tía watched her until she was out of sight. Judy *had* seen her kissing Johnny! Nothing else could account for her behavior.

Regret washed through Tía. She had seduced Johnny away from Judy—and Judy knew.

CHAPTER TWENTY-TWO

Steve found Johnny in the *cantina* sipping a bottle of beer.

"Johnny, you remember Morgan Todd." The introduction was sheer formality. Steve knew it as well as they did, but the enmity between Morgan and Johnny went back too many years to say anything else.

Johnny looked up from his beer. In the darkened *cantina* his eyes were as shiny as ebony. Except for that movement, his only reaction was a wry twist at one corner of his lips.

"How could Johnny forget me?" Morgan challenged. "He cut and ran rather than meet me."

Johnny rose from his chair and turned to face Morgan Todd.

"Your memory has some convenient holes in it, Todd." Johnny knew he should restrain himself. He had no reason to want to fight with Morgan Todd, but Tía's rejection made him want to strike out at something. Morgan would do nicely.

"Meaning?" Morgan asked, squaring his shoulders.

"Meaning *now* I have no reason *not* to kill you," Johnny said quietly. All sound stopped in the small saloon.

Morgan eyeballed Brago with icy hostility. "You *never* had an excuse not to kill me."

"Fortunately for you, I didn't know that," Johnny replied coldly.

"Then you got a problem, don't you, you half-breed son of a bitch," Morgan taunted.

Johnny'd heard the word "breed" in relation to himself many times. It held no magic power to incite him. It was just that anything less than complete respect from Morgan Todd seemed like a good reason to hit the bastard. Steve tried to move between them. And even if he hadn't been part Indian, Johnny would have been able to outmaneuver Steve.

Johnny's right fist hit Morgan's stomach with a meaty thud. As Morgan doubled forward, Johnny's left fist connected with his jaw.

Too dazed to remain upright, Morgan sagged to his knees. Johnny stepped back, panting, fighting the urge to kill the bastard.

"Get up!" he demanded, his voice taut.

"Killing me…won't get Judy back," Morgan gasped, struggling to his feet. "She's mine! She's always been mine. All I ever had to do was be there. She didn't want you. You were the only one in the whole damned territory didn't know that!"

Johnny *had* known it. That's why he'd been so mad when he'd ridden away three years ago. Now he was mad because Morgan's way of talking about Judy made her seem cheap. If he'd been the killing type, he'd have pulled his gun and shot Morgan dead, but even as mad as he was he couldn't see killing a man. But he could see beating Morgan to a pulp for taking advantage of Judy.

He threw himself at Morgan, and they tumbled down in a heap on the floor.

The two men rolled around and took turns walloping each other until both were bleeding. Steve yelled at them, but they ignored him. Finally he pulled a gun out of Dap Parker's holster and fired it into the air. Johnny and Morgan both looked up at that. "Get up from there and stop fighting!" Steve ordered, and pointed the gun at them.

"You want us to just stand up and quit fighting?" Johnny asked.

"That's right."

Johnny stood up, pulled Morgan Todd to his feet, and directed a half-swollen smile at Steve. They looked like a couple of beat-up drunks. Blood ran down Morgan's bruised face. Johnny didn't have any open cuts, but his cheek looked as if it would soon be black. Johnny reached over and straightened Morgan's collar, let his right fist drop to his side, smiled that silly-assed smile again at Steve, and without any more warning than that swung his fist upward with all the force he could put behind it. Steve saw it, cussed, and lowered Dap's gun. Morgan saw it coming, too, and tried to sidestep it, but Johnny had corrected for the movement. Morgan hit the wall and slid all the way down, as stiff and ungainly as an overfilled sack of oats.

Johnny watched for several seconds. Morgan was slumped into the corner. Around them the noise level rose as men found their voices. Shaking his head, Johnny turned to Steve. "When he wakes up, tell him I'll meet him in Tombstone, and we'll settle this once and for all."

He stalked outside. Steve gave Dap's gun back to him and stomped out of the *cantina*. "Johnny, wait!"

Angry and impatient, Johnny stopped and turned to face Steve. They were outside, alone now except for the men who peered from the dim interior of the *cantina*, out of earshot. Taking Johnny's arm, Steve steered him farther away.

"Dammit, you're my friend. We grew up together. You know I love Judy. I'd do anything for her. But I won't let you kill Morgan for telling the truth."

"He made Judy look cheap in front of those men. It doesn't matter what she's done or hasn't done. She has to face them day in and day out. No man has a right to cheapen a woman who loves him, especially not a bastard like Morgan Todd."

Steve had gotten so accustomed to criticizing Judy, he had forgotten she might need a champion. Maybe Andrea was right…

"You knew?"

"*I always knew.*"

Frowning, Steve shook his head. "Why didn't you kill him before you left?"

"Because I thought he would do right by her."

Andrea waited until she saw Steve go into his office, put down the dust cloth she had been wielding, and followed him. His office door was open. He sat behind his desk, staring out the window at the empty corral behind the barn. Sounds of two mockingbirds in the tree behind the *casa grande* filtered in through his open window. Short, confused notes and then a melodic song cut the air.

"May I come in?"

Cowed by his own self-condemning thoughts, Steve raised his hands as if to say "I give up. Do what you want." "Come ahead," he said ruefully.

Andrea sensed his turmoil and stopped. "Maybe I picked a bad time."

Steve stood up and stalked to the window. "There may not be a good time, the mood I'm in."

"Is there anything I can do to help?"

Steve sighed as if his burdens were more than he could bear. Andrea's fingers tingled with the sudden, irresistible urge to touch him. She wanted to slip her arms around his waist and rub her face against him.

"No." Steve wanted to tell Andrea that about the only thing she could do was to age fifty years overnight. Or keep her distance. And part of him couldn't stand it when she did. At least once a day he went looking for her because he couldn't help himself.

Steve turned and faced Andrea. "You came here for a reason. What can I do for you?" He controlled his eyes, kept them steadily on Andrea's face, but even so, they managed to take in her lush curves beneath the simple, high-necked, peach-colored gown. Short sleeves revealed firm, graceful arms. Her shiny auburn hair was pulled back from her high forehead with a peach-colored ribbon. She was so fresh-faced and enticing, he felt the jolt of reaction the entire length of his body. Thank God she didn't flaunt her many charms.

"I heard about a fight in the *cantina*. I wanted to find out—"

"Hardly a fight," Steve said, embarrassed that his voice sounded unusually low and raspy. He cleared his throat. "Morgan Todd shot his mouth off, and Johnny wiped the floor with him."

"Why?"

"Goes back a ways. I guess it started over Judy."

"Is it serious?"

Steve resisted the urge to laugh. Any altercation between gun-toting men was serious. A confrontation over land, cows, gold, or women was the most serious. "Could be."

"Is there anything we can do to stop it?"

"I could agree to accompany Morgan to the railhead at Silver City."

"I don't understand how that—"

"It might distract them."

"Could I go along?"

"No." There was no hesitation in his voice.

Angered, Andrea lifted her chin. "Why not?"

"Because I don't want you along," he said flatly.

Andrea couldn't believe how much his rejection hurt. He wasn't even pretending to be accommodating.

Steve saw her flinch, but it wasn't enough to dissuade him. He was still smarting from disappointment in himself that Morgan Todd had insulted Judy in his presence and he hadn't even noticed. As inadequate as he was feeling, he was in no mood to be reminded that his attentions to this sister had been far more than brotherly…

Stung more than she would admit, even to herself, Andrea tossed back her hair and pretended to be engrossed in looking out the window. "Aren't you supposed to go through the motions of politely considering my request and giving me a list of carefully thought out excuses to salve my pride?" She turned and let him see into her eyes, no doubt sparkling with tears.

"No," Steve said, his voice harsh with the effort at control. "You know the only excuse that matters."

A rush of emotion made Andrea dizzy. The huskiness of his voice, the tension radiating from him and vibrating within her, all combined to disarm her. She turned away.

Steve couldn't help himself. He stepped close behind her. Unbidden, his hands touched her bare arms. A jolt of electricity shot through him. His desire to touch her grew more intense. He should have let go of her, but his hands gripped her tighter instead, pulling her closer.

"Oh, Steve," she murmured. She leaned against him for a moment, then lifted her lips to be kissed.

CHAPTER TWENTY-THREE

Steve's lips touching hers blinded Andrea. His mouth tortured her with its closeness and its inability to get close enough.

Suddenly he wrenched his mouth away, took her face in his hands, and whispered, "Wait."

Whimpering a soft complaint, Andrea moved to regain his embrace. "Hush!"

Then she heard it. Feet pounded down the hall toward his office. Steve rubbed his thumb across her swollen bottom lip and reluctantly let his hands drop to his sides.

Lupe appeared in his doorway.

"The cavalry is coming," she said anxiously.

Steve turned to Andrea despondently. Her mouth looked too well kissed, her eyes appeared as dazed as he felt. He wanted to push Lupe from the room, close the door, and kiss Andrea until he'd had his fill of her. Maybe if he could do that, he wouldn't be so obsessed with the thought of her.

Andrea found her voice first. "Are we expected to prepare meals for them as well?"

Steve cleared his throat. "No. Usually the cavalry camps inside the walls and fends for itself. When my mother was alive she always invited the commanding officer up to the house for dinner. But you can suit yourself about that. I've never figured out why they stop here. Their fort is only three miles away."

"Should I change?"

Steve viewed Andrea's peach-colored gown. She had been working in the kitchen, which even on cool days was hotter than hell. Another woman might look wilted, but Andrea was radiant. Her cheeks were flushed with color, and her skin glowed. A moist sheen had dampened her gown between her breasts.

"Thank you, Lupe." He nodded at the young woman, and she turned reluctantly and walked back toward the kitchen.

A pang of guilt surprised Steve. Andrea was trying hard to fit in. It probably wasn't as easy for her as she made it appear. She had left loved ones and familiar surroundings to come here. So far all she had gotten for her trouble was trickery, rudeness, and two painfully aborted seductions. When he could think about her rationally—which wasn't often—he realized she hadn't sought him out and tricked him into almost making love to her. If her reactions were any indication, she was as caught up in passion as he and as helpless to stop it.

Once Lupe had left them, Andrea sagged onto the windowsill. She was so shaken that her knees felt like rubber. She had to tell Steve the truth. She couldn't imagine why she had let the charade go on this long... except that part of her enjoyed being the lady of the spread.

"Steve, I have to tell you something."

"I want to propose something completely insane to you. I know it may not work..."

Curiosity stopped Andrea dead. "What?"

Steve looked at the door as if he expected the cavalry to ride through it any second. "No, it's too crazy."

"What?" she demanded.

He touched her arm, golden and heated, and the magnetism of her skin weakened him to the point where he could have said anything.

"Meet me tonight after the others go to bed. Let me kiss you. I know this is crazy, but I have the feeling that if I could just kiss you...I promise I won't do anything else."

"Yes."

Steve drew in a ragged breath. "God help me...Come. We must meet our guests."

He took Andrea by the elbow and led her toward the front door. What he had asked of his sister was pure insanity, but it was the only chance he had to rid himself of his obsession for her. He would sate himself with her kisses tonight, and tomorrow he would take the silver through himself.

Going with Morgan would serve three purposes: It would get rid of Morgan Todd before Johnny killed him, it would remove *him* from temptation before Andrea turned him into a gibbering idiot, and it would get the silver to the railhead, where it would be safe and could start earning its keep.

"Is this appropriate? I mean, will Judy think I'm trying to usurp her position? I don't want to step on her toes."

Steve was unexpectedly moved by her concern. He hadn't worried about stepping on her toes. He'd been so damned busy being mad at her for causing him to lust after his own sister…

"Judy's not concerned with etiquette, especially where the cavalry is concerned. We're hardly your picture-book family."

"I'm hardly the product of a picture-book family myself," she reminded him.

He opened the door for her, followed her out, and paused at the top of the porch steps. Two abreast, with the United States flag and their company banner flying in the slight breeze, a column of blue-clad soldiers rode smartly through the gates.

Andrea squinted against the brightness of the sunlight. Probably in his fifties, the captain sat tall and straight in the saddle. He led the column, in full battle gear, up the path toward the *casa grande*. When he was ten feet from the steps, he raised his gauntleted hand, and his aide barked, "Company halt!"

The smartly uniformed company halted amid the creak of saddle leather and the clank of sidearms. Spread out, the line of horses, cannon, and wagons reached halfway to the gate. Horses stamped and snorted. The flag and red-and-white banner proclaiming *Company A* floated down and hung limply from lack of a cooling breeze. The soldiers sat their horses at attention. The captain adjusted the sword on his thigh and dismounted. He looked back at the column, tucked his hat under his left arm, and removed his right gauntlet as he climbed the steps. At the top he extended his right hand to Steve.

"Welcome, Captain Rutledge." To Andrea, they shook hands with what seemed great formality. Steve turned deferentially to include her. "Captain, I'd like to present my…sister, Andrea."

Clearing his throat, smoothing his dark, silver-streaked hair and impressive handlebar mustache with his hand, Rutledge stared in astonishment and then mustered a smile. "This is a great surprise and pleasure for me, Miss Burkhart, an unexpected bonus! My men and I always enjoy stopping at Rancho la Reina. Now our pleasure will be doubled. I only hope you will not mind being the recipient of so much avid appreciation from the opposite gender. Respectful, surely, but avid nonetheless."

Glancing at Steve, Andrea wondered if she should accept the appellation—"Miss Burkhart"—without explanation. Steve didn't even appear to notice. Surely everyone in the territory had heard about her questionable heritage by now; no need to belabor it. She was, in fact, grateful to Rutledge for not embarrassing her. Smiling, she accepted his remarks with gratitude. "Would you join us for supper, Captain?"

"I would be most delighted, Miss Burkhart. If you would excuse me now, I must see to the needs of my men." Rutledge bowed to Andrea and then addressed Steve. "You'll have to bring your beautiful sisters to the fort. No sense hiding them here, where all this beauty can't be appreciated."

"I'll be sure to do that," Steve said.

From the firm set of his jaw, Andrea guessed Steve was biting back some comment. Was it because of the *capitán* or because of her? Was he already thinking about marrying her off?

"Major Hart will be eternally grateful as well. He has a discriminating eye for beauty, Miss Burkhart. We see far too little of it in this territory."

"You don't sound like a westerner, Captain. Do I detect an eastern accent?"

Rutledge preened visibly. "West Point, Miss Burkhart. You have a discerning ear."

"How long have you been in the territory?" she asked. "I didn't think Fort Bowie was that old."

"It isn't. Fort Bowie is here for the duration of the war against the Apaches. I have been stationed in different parts of Arizona for almost twenty-two years: Yuma, Prescott, and Camp Verde to name just a few. But my heart has always been here in the Sulphur Springs Valley. I was one of the few soldiers who stayed behind to guard the settlers during the Civil War. Those were rough years. In spite of everything we could do, we were spread too thin; settlers died by the thousands."

"Perhaps you can tell me more about it while we dine, Captain. Dinner will be served at six o'clock. Will that suit your schedule?" Andrea asked.

"Absolutely, Miss Burkhart. If not, I would fit it forcibly. I shall be prompt." He walked quickly down the steps, remounted, saluted, and then led his men back toward the front gate. Andrea watched them leave.

"Now you know why he stops here."

"I do?" Steve asked, frowning.

"His heart has always been in the Sulphur Springs Valley," she said, mimicking the captain. "Perhaps in the form of Judy."

Steve chuckled. "He is the one man I would never accuse Judy of practicing her charms on. She thinks he's an old pervert who comes here only to spy on her."

The table at the far end of the parlor, which had been covered by three sheets to keep out the dust, was mahogany. Carmen uncovered it, and Andrea knew immediately that she would be using this table frequently. She had fallen into the habit of eating with the women in the dining hall, but she would not make that mistake again. The table had been built by a master craftsman. The top had a high sheen to it that would look wonderful in candlelight. Excited, Andrea scoured the compound until she had picked an assortment of wildflowers. Then she located candles and washed the good china Carmen said Judy had ordered from a mail-order house but had not used after the first week.

Once she'd washed and polished the table with furniture oil, it glowed a deep burnished red that set off the blue-and-white floral pattern on the china. To add to the ambience, Andrea had Dap and Leon clean the lanterns over the table.

By the time the table was set, Andrea was excited. She rushed to her room to dress for dinner. She had missed the formality of the East. She pulled out her prettiest gown. Uncle Tyler had begrudgingly bought it for her because he entertained occasionally. It was deep purple with black satin accordion-pleated ruffles. The white chiffon bodice cupped her breasts. Tiny cap sleeves left her arms and neck bare. Gathered fabric at the back fell in a cascade from the fashionable bustle. Andrea chose a black velvet ribbon to wear around her throat. After trying her hair in a dozen different ways, she decided to wear it up for a change. Arizona was so hot, even after sunset, that she would appreciate the coolness of having her hair off her neck.

She bathed in the kitchen because it saved carrying water all the way down the hall. Then, wrapped in her dressing gown, she passed Tía in the hall on the way back to her room to dress.

"Come in here, please, Tía."

Tía stepped inside and closed the door.

"What's happening out there?" Andrea asked.

"Judy is dressing for dinner. Mr. Todd is flirting with me, and Johnny is nursing his wounds. I think Steve is in his office."

"How is Johnny?"

"I have no idea." Tía clamped her mouth shut. However he was, he deserved to be even more battered. She hadn't really believed that Johnny belonged to Judy, after he'd said he didn't, and she had believed him and acted on it. Even though Judy had told her all along that Johnny loved her somehow Tía knew someone had to be lying, but she hadn't figured out who it was until today. Even then she knew it only in her head, the way she knew how to add and subtract. She hadn't known it in her heart, until she'd heard about the fight from Lupe. *La Excelencia! Puta, if you ask me! They fight over her like dogs over a bitch in heat, and she loves it. Tonight she will sleep with the winner; tomorrow who knows? Maybe they will have to fight again…*

Stop it! Don't talk about Judy like that! Tía had ordered. Lupe had tried to dismiss her with laughter, but Tía had persisted. *Shall I ask Señor Burkhart to make out your last paycheck?* Tía had expected to lose Carmen's support over that threat but she had not. Carmen had nodded her approval. And Lupe had lowered her defiant black eyes, at least for the moment.

Fortunately Andrea was too distracted to notice that all was not well.

"I would like you to dine with the family tonight," Andrea said, not taking her eyes off her own image in the mirror. She turned to see herself from a different angle. She had a startling figure, a classic profile and masses and masses of thick hair. In the purple gown she looked like a queen.

"No, thanks. I'm not the grand lady you are. I hate dinner parties."

Ten minutes later Steve summoned Tía into his office. Thrilled at the thought of contact with her brother, she dried her hands on a tea towel and rushed down the hall.

His door was open. Steve looked up from his rolltop desk and smiled. "Tía, I want you to join us tonight in the formal dining room."

The smile died on Tía's lips.

Steve saw the disappointment and confusion and stood up. "I assure you it will not be an unpleasant exper—"

"It's not that. I just don't do very well in formal circum—"

"Neither did I, until I had opportunities to practice my manners and become comfortable with them. No one will notice. Just follow my lead."

"Couldn't I please be excused?"

"No. Not since I know your reason. A young woman with your many attributes needs an opportunity to shine occasionally. I would be remiss if I did not provide one."

Johnny, who undoubtedly had been ordered by Steve to be present, seemed only slightly damaged by the fight, but he appeared as reluctant a guest as Tía.

Tía had been surprised to look up and see Johnny, his broad shoulders filling the doorway, his lithe warrior's body clad in unaccustomed good clothes. His dark eyes had sought hers out, not Judy's or Andrea's, but hers, and something happened in Tía. He gave her that special look—the look that signaled her alone. Still unwilling to forgive his fighting over Judy, Tía acknowledged him and than looked pointedly away. When Johnny tried to speak to her, she managed to ignore his overture.

Steve took Tía's arm and walked her to the table, then motioned his guests to be seated.

Andrea sat at one end of the table and Steve at the other. Johnny and Tía sat on either side of Steve while Captain Rutledge and Morgan Todd flanked Andrea. Wearing a red silk gown that brought out the vivid coloring in her cheeks and the sparkle in her eyes, Judy sat between Rutledge and Johnny across from Tía and Morgan. Surrounded by candlelight from the table, the glow of the lamps overhead, and the gleam of fine china and crystal, Judy looked sophisticated and at home.

Seated on Andrea's right, Captain Rutledge was jovial and expansive. "You're a lucky man, Steve. Two beautiful sisters and a beautiful housekeeper! Just look at them. Such loveliness! Ahhh. How I miss that woman's touch in my own life. A soldier's existence is austere at best."

"I'm dying to hear the news, Captain," Andrea said.

"Ah, yes. Shall I begin with Lillie Langtry or the phenomenal spread of the telephone?"

"Lillie, of course," Andrea smiled. She had become fascinated by the Jersey Lily in her short immersion into Albany society. She had been amazed to find that the otherwise staid women of Albany had been as fascinated with Lillie's exploits as she herself was. Lillie cut a wide swath through riches and royalty. She lived with the freedom of a man. Her affairs were as public as if they had been condoned by the Church. Crowds followed her everywhere.

Rutledge smiled at Tía. "I recently returned from New York, in case you are wondering why I have news that would interest Miss Burkhart."

At Tía's murmured reply, Johnny glanced up. She was wearing a yellow gown in a richer fabric than he had seen on her before. It made her skin seem gold in the lantern light, her soft blond curls even more appealing. He hadn't wanted to sit at this table tonight with Morgan Todd, not after fighting with the bastard that afternoon, but Steve had insisted. He could have refused to come, but he'd guessed Tía would be enlisted to round out the table as well, and he had wanted to see her, to talk to her. So far, however, she had skillfully avoided his eyes.

Tía tried to concentrate on the food before her, but her mind kept making pictures of Johnny. He had put on a frock coat, a clean white shirt, and a string tie. Beneath the overhead kerosene lanterns, his hair was so black it looked blue. He had shaved and trimmed his mustache. Of all the men at the table, Johnny was the most inviting. Just seeing him caused Tía to remember how he felt and tasted. His lips were smoother than any man's there. He had tried to slick his hair back, but it had fallen forward on his forehead, too thick and unruly to be tamed by a simple pomatum.

Johnny glanced up at Tía, caught her gaze, and the unreadable look in his dark eyes was replaced by something else—something challenging.

At the end of the table, Rutledge continued with Lillie's exploits. "Half the women in New York are wearing Langtry knots in their hair. The rest are wearing Langtry shoes and hats. I believe she's even had a bustle named in her honor. I actually saw the Jersey Lily riding in the park one evening with the Prince of Wales. I did not recognize him myself, but two of my companions confirmed that it was indeed the prince."

"I read in a newspaper before I left Albany that she was keeping company with the king of England. Is that true?"

"The king of Belgium, Prince Rudolph of Austria, and other royalty as well."

Carmen bustled in from the kitchen and poured wine in the goblets.

Rutledge lifted his glass and smiled. "Good thing we're not having dinner at the White House. President Hayes would not allow this."

Andrea laughed. "Lemonade Lucy has had quite an impact on that poor man."

"Temperance is as old as the hills."

"But so is wine," Andrea added.

Rutledge raised his glass. "Here's to both."

Judy leaned close to Johnny. "I wonder if he knows his cinch is getting frayed?" she whispered.

Johnny grinned. "If my hooves weren't hobbled..."

Morgan leaned toward Tía. "They don't keep any tornado juice around here, do they?"

Tornado juice had to be whiskey. Tía leaned closer to Morgan. "I believe Steve has some. May I get it for you?"

Morgan sighed. "No, thanks. I'd better behave myself or Rutledge'll spread some of that tongue oil on me."

Morgan looked up, caught Judy watching him, and winked at her. Judy felt slightly mollified. Rutledge talked incessantly to Steve and Andrea. He tried to talk to Judy, but for once Andrea came in handy.

They were all boring to Judy. The captain was probably nice for an older man, but she wished he'd stop coming around. Like a gossipy old maggot, he was always hanging around her, wanting to know all about her: what she was doing, whom she was walking out with, which young man she liked best. He was an old pervert who probably peeked in windows or something equally disgusting.

There was a sudden lull in the conversation. Rutledge glanced at Morgan and then at Johnny. "You two young bucks fighting on the same or opposing sides?"

Johnny glanced at Morgan and then at Tía. Steve cleared his throat and spoke. "Opposing."

"Ahem." Rutledge glanced quickly at Judy, then at Morgan Todd.

Judy could not resist the opening. "I don't know why they keep fighting over me. I hate men with bruises."

"If you had 'em both *lady broke*, you wouldn't want either one of 'em," Steve said.

Judy laughed. "We'll never know. Not much chance of breaking either one of these stallions."

Rutledge forced himself to keep silent. Breaking wasn't what they needed. He glanced at Johnny, who managed to remain arrogant in spite of his bruises, and at Morgan, who was starting to show the effects of too much booze and too many women. Men like these two should be gelded, he reflected soberly—save the world a lot of trouble.

"What tribe are you from, Brago?" he asked.

Shocked at Rutledge's insensitivity, Tía glanced quickly at Johnny.

"I never lived with a tribe. The Cherokee didn't want anything to do with my grandmother after she married a white man." His voice was deceptively mild, but Tía sensed the iron underneath.

"Ah, Cherokee. From Oklahoma?"

"No, sir. Originally from South Carolina." He sounded polite and unruffled by Rutledge's questions.

"You speak any Indian?"

"No, my father was a Texan who never mastered the Iroquoian tongue. My mother stopped speaking it when she married him."

"Your mother was full-blooded Cherokee?"

"Half."

"Humph. I guess that's not as bad."

"If I didn't lack one part white blood, I'd be almost human, wouldn't I?" Johnny picked up his knife and cut off a bite-sized piece of his steak. "Reminds me of a man who was describing Arizona. He said all the territory lacks is water and society or it would be heaven. His friend agreed. 'Yep,' he said, 'water and society is all they lack in hell, too.'"

Rutledge cleared his throat and looked as though he were about to say something.

Johnny lifted his fork to his mouth, waved it under his nose, and sniffed the fragrant aroma of beef. "There's no such thing as a little bit with child, a little bit dead, or a little bit Indian," he said, his eyes crinkled with laughter.

Carmen walked back into the room carrying a vegetable platter. Tía was tempted to order her to dump the whole thing down the front of the captain's uniform to see if he would scrape the peas and carrots off in formation. She couldn't imagine why she should care if Rutledge embarrassed Johnny in front of everyone, but she was outraged and glad that Johnny had turned the tables.

"Well," Steve said, glancing around at his guests, "I guess we can all be grateful this is still a country where a man can switch his tail."

Andrea picked up the conversation with a question, and Johnny resumed eating. Dinner seemed to drag on forever. At last Steve pushed back his chair. "Would you join me in a drink by the fire?" he asked the table at large.

Andrea, Rutledge, and Morgan followed Steve to the large, comfortable chairs by the empty fireplace.

Johnny glanced once at Tía, saw no welcome in the look she flashed him, and excused himself.

Judy motioned Tía to her side. "Will you do me a favor?"

"If I can."

Judy smiled conspiratorially. "Oh, you can. There's no doubt about that." Pausing, she pulled Tía around until they were both facing Morgan Todd, across the room. He tossed his whiskey down and then stood up to make his excuses to Steve. As they watched, he nodded at Judy and Tía, walked out of the parlor, and headed down the hall toward his room. Judy waited until his door closed.

"Did you see poor Johnny? He must love me a lot to take a beating like that," Judy said softly. "He can't even stand it when Morgan looks at me."

"You wanted a favor?" Tía reminded her.

"Before they fought over me, I promised to walk in the moonlight with Morgan. I'd be crazy to do it now. Those two might kill each other."

"So?"

"So…I want you to walk with Morgan…for me."

"Me! That wouldn't help," she protested. "It's you he wa—"

"Don't be silly!" Judy interrupted. "I saw Morgan looking at you.

He's easy. He'll court any pretty girl. Heavens! Don't you know anything?"

"I guess not," Tía said darkly.

"Well, it's time you learned. You promised me one favor, and this is what I want."

"I didn't promise."

"No welshing, Tía Marlowe. A promise is a promise. Besides, you could save Johnny or Morgan or both from getting hurt or even killed," she said sternly. "Will you?"

Inwardly Tía recoiled. She shouldn't do it. They would kill each other sooner or later anyway. She was sorry she had ever met Johnny Brago. Sorry she had ever let him kiss her. Any woman stupid enough to harbor soft feelings for a man like him deserved to have to walk in the moonlight with Morgan Todd. Maybe it would teach her a lesson.

"I'll do it," she said, reluctantly. She would regret this, she knew. But nothing much could go wrong that hadn't already gone wrong. All she had to do was walk in the moonlight with Morgan Todd. He was half dead already. Johnny had seen to that.

"When?"

"I'll let you know."

CHAPTER TWENTY-FOUR

For once Tía did not help the women clean up; she went to her room instead. She was tired, angry at Johnny, and in no mood to be nice to Morgan Todd, but the thought of taking a walk with him in front of Johnny did have a certain appeal.

Exquisitely melancholy and very Spanish, strains of a Mexican fandango wafted from the other side of the house, near the *cantina*. Tía knew who would be playing—she had seen the impromptu band of smiling *vaqueros* practicing on the porch of their bunkhouse. Sounds of people clapping and shouting "*¡Olé!*" made her impatient. Someone must be dancing. Perhaps Lupe. Men seldom sounded that excited and happy without female companionship. It sounded like Tubac on a warm balmy Saturday night. She was suddenly homesick for Mama, and her feet fairly itched to dance. Mama might not have taught her to be a great lady, but she had taught her to dance, ride, and take care of herself.

From the back door, the music was louder. It ended unexpectedly, and a new song was begun, this one with a quicker tempo. As she walked around the house, Tía's flat slippers barely touched the sandy soil. Paper lanterns had been hung from posts, illuminating a circle in front of the small *cantina*, where men crowded around, shouting and clapping their encouragement. Someone *was* dancing!

Straining, Tía stood on tiptoe, but she could not see over the heads and shoulders of the men. She pushed her away into the crowd. The music rose to a sudden crescendo. Stamping and shouting, men threw their hats into the air.

"Pah!" Angry and disgusted, a female voice caused a parting of the crowd near Tía. Lupe followed that curse to Tía's side.

"Lupe! Who's dancing?" Tía asked, amazed to find the girl beside her so suddenly.

"I hate that *puta!*" she snapped, her face sullen. "*La Excelencia—la patrona!* She dances like the teasing *puta* she is! She—"

Loud music and shouts of excited men drowned Lupe out. The crowd parted for a moment, and Tía saw Judy, her slender body swaying provocatively to the rhythm of the pulsing music. She danced beautifully.

The men clapped and shouted their enjoyment. How young and pretty and full of life she was! And how much joy her dancing gave these hardworking, fun-loving men.

A warm hand on Tía's arm startled her.

"Oh!"

It was Johnny. Narrowed against the lantern light, his dark eyes seemed to pin her to the spot, impairing her ability to breathe.

His hand slipped down her arm, burning a trail as he laced his fingers between hers, creating a warm, adhesive tingle in her palm that sent threads of hunger into her body and kept her hand unprotestingly snug in his.

"You owe me a walk in the moonlight," he said softly.

Now or never, Tía thought crazily. Johnny Brago was a man who could kiss one girl and fight over another, practically in the same breath. He obviously belonged to Judy, he fought over her as if he did, but that didn't stop him from wanting to walk with Tía. Now she understood what Mama and her friends had said about men being different from women. They did odd, amazing things that left a woman filled with confusion and uncertainty.

"Some other time, Johnny," she replied after a moment's pause. "I want to dance now, and later I've promised to walk with Morgan."

Johnny's warm smile faded to be replaced by that handsome, cocky slant of lips and eyes that projected an impenetrable facade. For an instant Tía regretted her words, but the part of her that still wanted to punch him as hard as her fist could punch didn't regret anything.

Johnny lifted Tía's hand. Now it all made sense to him. Taking this job had been a way of getting out of Tombstone. She was one of Morgan Todd's harem, but she was smarter than most. She had gotten Morgan interested and then ran off and waited for him to follow. And he had.

He had to admire her ingenuity, if not her ability to be a straight shooter. He turned Tía's cold hand palm up, forcing it when he had to, and then, with deliberate solemnity, pretending to be a swell like Morgan Todd, he lowered his head and pressed his lips into her palm.

At the touch of his warm mouth and tickly mustache, a shudder of desire rippled through Tía.

Johnny didn't seem to notice. "I sure hope you can forgive me, Tía. I haven't figured out how to recognize Morgan Todd's women in time to keep from getting attached to them."

He lifted her other hand and placed one in the other. Then he turned and walked over to the musicians. "The young lady wants to dance," he said. "Tía, what would you like?"

Tía was so frustrated she wanted to pick up something and throw it at him, but she restrained herself. "A Mexican waltz, any one will be fine."

Johnny raised an eyebrow at her, and Tía stuck out her tongue. One of the musicians yelled "*¡Olé!*" and they all stamped their feet and strummed their guitars until they found a chord they liked. Within seconds they were playing a *chiapanecas*, a sprightly Mexican waltz. Men paired off into couples, with bandanas tied on the arms of the men chosen as the female partners, and scrambled to form a double circle. Johnny stepped close and took Tía's hand. She started to pull hers away but inexplicably changed her mind.

"I thought you wanted nothing to do with one of Morgan's harem," she said.

"Bad as my pride's been trampled, I reckon I can't afford to eliminate women on that basis. Wouldn't be any left. I'm just going to have to remember not to get so high and mighty, expecting a woman to just drop everything because I come around. I know you must hate wasting your time with me, but he's dancing to Judy's tune right now. Maybe us two rejected suitors can show them we know how to entertain ourselves while we wait our turns."

Without waiting for her to say yea or nay, he pulled Tía into the inner circle and got into position. Men were on the outside of the circle, the make-believe women and the few real women sprinkled among the dancers on the inside. The musicians hit their stride, and Tía and Johnny joined inside hands and placed their free hands on their hips.

A group couple dance, it started with partners stepping on the outside foot and then swinging the other foot across and in front of the outside foot. As she got into the swing of it, Tía became sure she had chosen this so she would have an opportunity to kick Johnny. Cruz, Lupe, their partners, and Judy and Morgan were in the outside circle. Carmen was in the inside circle.

"I didn't know you could dance," Johnny said.

Tía stamped in place on her inside foot and aimed her outside foot in front, over and across, but she missed Johnny again. Either he was sprier than he looked, or his timing was too good.

Ignoring him, Tía stamped in place on her outside foot, released Johnny's hand, and clapped twice. Johnny grabbed her hands, swung them twice, and then they placed their outside hands on their hips and repeated the same sequence of steps, claps, kicks, and foot stampings again.

Tía felt immediately better. Dancing did that for her. No matter how bad she might feel, dancing made it better. This particular Mexican waltz was fun. Johnny seemed to know it well. He kicked and stamped and clapped and held hands at all the right times. When they came to the part where they had to embrace and clap behind their partner's back, he kissed her on the neck.

"Stop that, Johnny Brago."

Her voice must have lacked conviction, because he only laughed, grabbed her around the waist, and swung her into the next position. The firmness of his hands caused her heart to beat faster and her pulse to quicken in response. It didn't seem to matter that Johnny Brago had been as mad as she; he danced as if he purely enjoyed it.

The *chiapanecas* ended, and the men yelled for more music, but the musicians were ready for a tequila break. Nothing could induce them to play again immediately. Tía saw Judy and Morgan slip away from the crowd and glanced sideways at Johnny to see what he was going to do about it. But he was looking at her and seemed unaware of Judy. For the first time in Tía's life, she felt like a full-grown woman.

"Your girlfriend's getting away," she said.

"I told you she ain't my girlfriend anymore."

"You were fightin' over her today."

"Is that what you're so mad about?"

"Of course not," she said, quickly, probably too quickly from the look in his eyes. She walked away from the crowd, toward the back door of the house.

Johnny followed. "If that's all it was, you didn't need to get your feathers all ruffled up like that. I wasn't fighting over Judy. Morgan Todd insulted her, and I hit him."

"How'd he insult her?" Tía stopped walking, reached up, and picked a long, slender leaf off what was probably a peach tree. She couldn't tell in the dark.

Her fingers caressed the leaf and then, almost as an afterthought, ripped it in half. Johnny felt there might be some kind of warning in that for him. He wanted to reach out, take her in his arms, and hug her, but of course he couldn't do that in front of half the people in the territory. Then she'd have herself a reputation. He had to struggle to remember what she'd asked him. "Well, come to think of it, Morgan insulted me first, then I hit him. Then he insulted Judy, so I hit him again. Then he started trying to hit me back…" His voice trailed off.

"How long you two been fighting over Judy?"

The silky smoothness of Tía's sweet voice did not deceive him for a second. If she'd had a gun, he reckoned he'd be dead by now. "We've been fightin' since before he ever saw Judy. Morgan used to be a whiskey drummer, going from fort to settlement to railhead, selling whiskey to saloons and shopkeepers and Indians. He never stayed in one place this long before. 'Course Tombstone ain't that old. It's only been sitting in them hills a little over a year. Todd bought into one of the mines, and it hit pay dirt. So now he's rich, and I'm still poor."

Tía could not imagine why Johnny's complacence about fighting with Morgan Todd over Judy could make her so angry, but it did. She reached into the pocket of her skirt and pulled out the bracelet he had given her. "Here, Johnny. Maybe you can impress Judy with this."

She slapped it into his hand, turned on her heel, and ran toward the house.

The dance ended with exultant shouts for another encore. Laughing and disheveled, Judy leaned weakly against Morgan Todd.

"Bravo!" he shouted. "Well done! I used to think you had a wild streak…" He pulled her into his arms, still responding to the almost painful flush of pleasure he'd felt watching Judy dance that solo before the *chiapanecas*. "But I was wrong. You're wild all the way through."

"I thought you liked blondes." Leaning back in his arms, aware of the heated bulge of his sex pressed against her thighs, Judy smiled provocatively and reached up to let her long brown hair down. She had been fuming ever since she'd seen Johnny kiss Tía. It felt good to be wanted. And Morgan Todd did want her; there was no mistaking that. His desire was obvious and intoxicating. She felt good. Good and desirable and beautiful—the way only a man could make her feel. Johnny could go to hell! She didn't need him or his narrow-minded hypocrisy or his cheating with that little maggot Tía Marlowe!

Maybe Morgan *was* a womanizer, and maybe he would never marry her, but at least he didn't play games with her. He had his other women, and he didn't care what she did when she wasn't with him. They never questioned one another. He was almost as accepting as Grant—but far more attractive. And he was all man, from his expensive leather boots to his sun-streaked brown hair. He knew exactly how to make a woman feel like a woman.

With roughly possessive hands on her waist, Morgan turned Judy and walked her toward the orchard.

"Lead the way," he said, his breath rustling against her cheek.

"Why should I? That would be aiding and abetting the enemy, wouldn't it?" Judy teased.

"Because if you don't," he whispered against her ear, "these men are going to get the thrill of their lonely lives when I bed you here." His lean fingers pressed against her waist. Her feet barely touched the ground as he propelled her, laughing, in front of him.

"Poor baby! You sound so—"

They had reached the trees. Pulling her roughly into his arms, Morgan leaned against one of the tree trunks. His mouth claimed hers, cutting off the rest of her teasing remarks. A warm lethargy settled over Judy. She seemed to float in his arms, pleasantly aloof from his passion, untouched by it, and yet pleased and comforted by his heated attention and his obvious need for her.

Morgan kissed her urgently. His hard male intensity was a testimonial to her feminine desirability. Pleased and validated by his lust, Judy sighed and relaxed against him.

He relinquished her lips only to press hot kisses against her throat and breasts. She strained blissfully against him. This time when he insisted that she lead the way, she did so without protest.

She led him to the old playhouse at the back edge of the orchard. The roof shone with silver moonlight, but the inside was dark and forbidding. Judy hesitated. Morgan moved close behind her, grinding his hardness against her hips. His pulsing warmth caused her to moan softly.

His hand forced her downward. Lost in the bliss of his need for her, Judy complied. His hands found her breasts and squeezed until she cried out. It didn't even matter that he was rough, insensitive. Morgan always hurt her, and he never seemed to know it. She accepted him heedlessly, unthinkingly. She needed him.

Judy was kneeling on all fours. Morgan's hands were impatient, almost angry as they lifted her skirts, groped at her pantalets. Shuddering in anticipation, Judy waited. He entered her, and she whimpered like a lost child, enjoying the helpless sound of her surrender, inexplicably relieved by the feel of the coarse dirt under her hands. She reveled in its coolness, its grittiness. Not like the smooth, slick heat of the man...

"Oh, God!" Morgan groaned, arching against her forcefully, then becoming still. The sharp intake of his breath and the way his fingers dug into her hips pleased her.

"Judy, love…" He turned her, then pressed her down onto the mattress. To her surprise, he didn't fall heavily on top of her. Propped on one elbow above her, he stroked her cheek, kissed her throat, held her close.

Reveling in the unusual attention, Judy sighed.

"Judy, baby…"

Slowly he undressed her, then began to suck and kiss her small, cone-shaped breasts until her nipples burned. Judy surged with an excruciating fire. Usually, even the second time, Morgan took her quickly, but this time he lingered, showering her breasts, her waist, and her belly with kisses. Caressing her slowly, tantalizingly, he ran his tongue down her belly, and Judy's body buckled forward. "Don't do that!" she cried.

"Lie still," he commanded.

"No!" Confused, her breath coming faster, Judy squirmed under him. She was feeling things she had never felt before, as if he were on the verge of ripping away the protective mantle of her aloofness. She could not let that happen. He frightened her. She didn't want to feel anything herself. The passion was for him, her gift.

Hoping to distract him, to arouse him to some other action, Judy spread her thighs and wiggled her hips, crooning softly, "Now, baby, now…"

But Morgan would not be sidetracked. Ignoring her efforts, he lowered his head to kiss her damp warmth.

"No!" she cried.

"Hush!" Ignoring her, he lowered his dark head and kissed her breasts, her throat, her mouth, his hot lips burning into her, causing a trembling in her that added to her fear. His mouth moved back to her breasts, and he lingered there until she was moaning, then his lips slid back beneath her belly, teasing her, slipping into her navel.

"No…please…"

"Oh, yes," he whispered, his hot breath moving even lower. "I want you to know how it feels to be teased and tortured. We'll see how well *you* hold up."

Holding her wrists so she could not protect herself, Morgan lowered his head and made hot little licking motions in the nest between her thighs until she was thrashing wildly.

"No! *Johnny!* No! Please…"

Morgan stopped. His head raised. Relieved, Judy started to struggle up into a sitting position.

"*Slut!*"

Stunned by his sudden fury and bewildered as to the cause, Judy heard the hiss of his indrawn breath and felt his hand like fire against her cheek.

"Whaa..."

"You little whore. Call me Johnny!"

Gasping, Judy cowered away from him, covering her head, expecting more blows, but Morgan stood up and backed away from her, his face a mask of fury.

His hands dropped to his sides. He wasn't going to hit her again. Relieved, Judy tried to cajole him. "Hey! Call me Sadie. Or Juliana. Call me anything you like."

"Don't you dare laugh at me. I..." Morgan clamped his jaws against the words that almost spilled out. *I love you.*

Horrified at himself, disbelieving, he backed away. The little whore had almost gotten to him. He laughed—a short, shaky jeer that ended in a grimace. To hell with Judy. Nobody got to Morgan Todd. She had called him Johnny. Him!

Morgan ran a shaking hand through his hair. He couldn't believe the way she'd had him going there. It was a good thing he'd found her out. Next he'd have been wanting to marry her. That was a laugh. Morgan Todd marrying a faithless little jezebel like that!

Turning away in contempt, he ran all the way back to the house, stopping only once to adjust his trousers before he left the trees.

Captain Rutledge was a bit long-winded. Andrea could barely force herself to sit still. Hearing the strains of music from outside, she glanced toward the back of the house, envying Morgan, Judy, Johnny, and Tía. Morgan Todd had made his excuses and disappeared after one drink. Tía, Johnny, and Judy had not even waited for that.

Rutledge was vague and expansive, saying far too much and at the same time far too little. If Steve hadn't been held captive, too, the after-dinner conversation would have been deadly. As it was, Andrea contented herself with watching Steve, smiling at all the right times, barely listening to her companion's words, until Rutledge hit on a topic that interested her.

"Todd mentioned the two of you are planning to take your own silver out. That's a bit risky, isn't it?"

Instinctively Steve bristled. He had never particularly liked Rutledge. Anything the man opposed instantly looked more desirable. "Russ Sloan took his shipment through last week with no problems," he said stiffly, reminding himself that he was the host and Rutledge his guest.

"Well, I don't see the need for it. You could never justify a harebrained scheme like that to my satisfaction," Rutledge said, leaning back in his chair.

"We're not asking for military sanction, Captain," Steve murmured.

Winking at Andrea, Rutledge smiled. "Frisky young buck, your brother. Typical of his generation. They think they're invincible and act on it. No interest in listening to older, saner heads. Reminds me, Steve, there's a young lady asked me to give you her regards: Sara Jane Melrose, used to be Stagner. I'm sure you remember her. Fine-looking blond woman. Family was Scandinavian. You remember the Stagners. Had that ranch south of St. David years ago. Parents are dead now. Both of 'em. Sara Jane's husband was killed a little over a year ago in a brush with those murdering swine of Chatto's. Apparently you made quite an impression on her last month when you came to the fort. She sent an invitation for you to call on her."

Steve's face remained impassive. "Thank you, Captain. Tell Mrs. Melrose I'm honored she remembers me."

"Your brother is quite a ladies' man, Miss Burkhart. Sara Jane is the prettiest young widow in the Arizona Territory. Every unmarried buck I know is lining up to court her now that she's out of mourning. I'd be lining up myself except that Mrs. Murdock and I have set the date."

Steve murmured his congratulations and went on to say something complimentary about Mrs. Murdock. Around a sudden ache in her throat, Andrea murmured what she hoped was a suitable reply. This was an eventuality she hadn't counted on—another woman. She could almost feel the cogs turning in Steve's head. He would no doubt jump at the chance to divert some of the frustrated energy he had expended on her.

Andrea squirmed in her chair. Jealousy and frustration burned within, but she tried valiantly to keep it out of her eyes.

Steve squared his shoulders and looked at Andrea. His blue eyes level and strangely ruthless in his handsome face, he directed his words at Rutledge. "Tell Mrs. Melrose I will call on her as soon as I can arrange it."

Andrea lowered her gaze.

"I'll do that," the captain said, smiling, completely unaware of the turbulent undercurrents that swirled between Steve and Andrea—making her dizzy, making him furious.

"Soon as I see her. She's in Tombstone visiting her uncle for a few days. Well! I guess you'll be seeing her before I will if you're going that way with Todd tomorrow."

"We're leaving first thing in the morning if the Indian trouble has cooled off."

"You can count on it. You'll not be bothered with Indians after Major Hart, Captain Rodgers, and myself get through with them," he said, leaning forward. "You may see a stray or two, but no force of significance can withstand Major Hart's drive."

"Good," Steve said quietly, glancing meaningfully at Andrea.

"I can't discourage you from taking this trip?"

"On the contrary, Captain, the information you've just given me makes it both feasible and attractive."

CHAPTER TWENTY-FIVE

Shimmering on the windowsill, moonlight made the room seem bright as day. Andrea was sorry she hadn't pinned Steve down as to the time she should meet him, but it was too late now. The musicians had played until almost midnight. Steve had finally gone out and cut them off.

The house felt silent. Everyone would be asleep.

Andrea lifted her robe off the chair, sat up, put it on over her light lawn nightgown, and swung her legs over the side of the bed.

The parlor was dim. Moonlight streamed in the two barred windows on either side of the front door, casting light and shadows into the massive room. Only the dim outlines of the furniture were visible— foreign dark shapes.

She stopped beside the door that led into the parlor. Steve might already have fallen asleep. He might have changed his mind. The sound of cloth on cloth alerted her to another presence.

"Steve?"

"Over here."

Her heart leaped. She would recognize that low-pitched tone anywhere.

"May I join you?"

"Yes."

Was that resignation in his low voice?

Andrea moved closer. His face—tense and strangely unfocused stopped her. She felt too uncertain to proceed. He might have changed his mind. "Am I disturbing you?"

Always, Steve thought. "No," he said quietly.

"I couldn't sleep."

"It's hot."

"Steve…" Why had she used his name? Something had happened to her voice. Something revealing. "Do you think I could go for a walk?"

"I'll go with you," he said, standing up. "You might not be safe otherwise. These riders come and go. Half of them stay less than six months. Some of them are on the dodge when they come. And"—he stopped beside her—"there's always the threat of a stray Indian."

He must have changed his mind, Andrea thought. He spoke as if they had no agreement.

Even so, it felt good to be outside. The stars were bright. The moon—only a day from being full—illuminated the compound and silvered the treetops. Andrea walked north to the well near the spring house. Steve followed. The perfect brother, he was careful not to touch her or look at her.

"Do you miss Albany?"

She stopped by the well and leaned against the adobe brick base, enjoying the faint smell of water and the sound of crickets that chorused like a squeaky wheel from the orchard. "I miss my mother. I never realized until a couple of months ago how much I loved her. I hadn't even thought about her until you asked, but…" She paused. "The most awful feeling of loneliness came over me."

"What's your mother like?"

"She's too pretty to be a mother. I saw her in town once when she didn't know I was watching her, and I was embarrassed because she wasn't pinch-faced or dowdy like other mothers. I must have pestered her for a week trying to get her to look less attractive. I told her how pretty her hair would look in a bun. How much I liked black gowns on her. I even pointed out all her wrinkles and the tiniest little flaws. I talked about how old she was. My niggling didn't even faze her."

"Did she know how you felt about her looking so young and being so independent?"

"She knew, but she said it probably saved me a lot more unhappiness than it cost. At least I didn't end up married to some man who would make my life a misery. To her way of thinking, the worst thing that can happen to a woman is to get married to the wrong man. My father was a little difficult."

"Your father?"

"I mean my stepfather."

"What was he like?"

"Oh, very dashing and handsome."

"Was he…Mexican?" he asked gingerly.

"Spanish, very old Spanish aristocracy."

"Is it unpleasant for you to talk about your parents?" Steve asked, sensing the turmoil beneath her placid facade.

"Does it show?"

He nodded. Andrea was so damned lovely. It showed most in her eyes—the most expressively beautiful he had ever seen. All he had to do was look at her, and he sensed what she was feeling. He hadn't realized when he'd suggested their meeting that it would be impossible for him to just fall on her and start kissing her.

"Judy told me that you are a mining engineer."

"Engineering seemed to fit my compulsive nature. I hate cows. Johnny should have been my father's son. He fits in here. I'm as lost on a ranch as a deaf dog in a cave on a dark night."

"Sounds desperate."

"It would have gotten that way. My father was getting sick and tired of waiting around for me to start acting like a rancher. He didn't really understand engineering. If you can't grow it and feed it, then he was suspicious of it. He felt if God had wanted men to have silver, they would have been born with little pouches of it hanging around their necks."

"Why did he buy into the mine?"

"Darned if I know. I recommended it, and he did it. I'll never know why. Maybe he thought it would legitimize me in some way. He was a strange man. Very strict. My mother died when I was four. Then Pa married again, and that one ran away when I was seventeen."

Steve and Judy didn't have the same mother or father, Andrea reflected. They weren't related at all, yet Steve was extremely loyal.

"It was hard on Judy, mostly. She was only eight, and she wanted her mama."

"How dreadful. And then the man she believed was her father disowned her. He must have been a very bitter man."

"You chose kinder words than I. The night after Furnett came out to read Dad's will, Judy tried to hurt herself. It didn't amount to anything, but it woke me up to the fact that she was hurtin' real bad."

"I didn't know…" Andrea turned away. "What kind of man could betray a young woman's trust so heartlessly?"

"Truth?"

"Please."

Steve expelled an exasperated breath. "One time Pa entered a contest, something judged on skill, and he came in second. Second prize was a piano, a nice piano. I remembered thinking how nice it would be to have a piano for Judy. She always liked to fool around with the keyboard when she got near one. Anyway, his friends started talking to him, telling him how he should have won first prize, that second prize was an insult to a man with his talent. He listened to them and refused the piano, and he was proud of himself for refusing. And Judy never got her piano."

"Did you love your father?"

"Yeah," he said quietly. "I wasn't a true Burkhart about that, either. When Doc Potter told me he was dying, I felt like someone had kicked the foundation out from under me. I was so disconcerted by my reaction I couldn't even let him know."

Sadness edged Steve's words. Instinctively Andrea reached out to comfort him. Her warm hand touched his chest. And just as instinctively Steve clasped her hand to stop her. But once he had touched her she was like a magnet, pulling him close, stripping him of the shield he usually clung to. Dazed, he wondered what his father would have said about his lusting after his own sister.

"Steve...please..."

"Don't," he said harshly. His hand gripped her wrist, fingers biting into the creamy softness, but he couldn't seem to stop himself. "I was wrong in what I said this afternoon. I wouldn't be able to stop myself."

"I'm not your sister, not really..."

"Hush. Don't make it any harder than it is," he said, releasing her wrist. "Let's go back."

"Let me stay out here. Stay with me."

"I was wrong, dammit. I had no right to ask you here, and you have no business being here with me."

Andrea struggled to find words to explain.

His hands slid up her arms and shook her slightly. "You don't belong here. Go back to Albany. Take the money I offered you."

"If I can't?"

"I'll stay at the mine. You can have the ranch."

"So you can have your Sara Jane Broomstick?"

"Can you think of another alternative?"

Before she could speak, he took her arm and led her roughly toward the house. At the back door the moonlight beamed on his face, highlighting it into unaccustomed harshness.

"Steve, I'm not—"

"Judy used to tease me about our getting married someday. I always thought it was just a girlish game. How could she feel that way about her brother? I knew I didn't feel anything like that for her..." He opened the door and motioned Andrea through it. "Get some sleep. We'll be leaving early, but you don't need to get up."

PART TWO

But if in your fear you would seek only love's peace and love's pleasure.

Then it is better for you that you cover your nakedness and pass out of love's threshing-floor,

Into the seasonless world where you shall laugh, but not all of your laughter, and weep, but not all of your tears.

Love gives naught but itself and takes naught but from itself.
Love possess not nor would it be possessed;
For love is sufficient unto love.

When you love you should not say, "God is in my heart," but rather, "I am in the heart of God."

And think not you can direct the course of love, for love, if it finds you worthy, directs your course.

The Prophet
Kahlil Gibran

CHAPTER TWENTY-SIX

Andrea lay awake for what seemed hours. She couldn't let Steve ride away tomorrow thinking she was his sister. She was tired of this lie. This time she would make him hear her.

She stood up and put on her dressing gown, opened her door, and walked down the hall to his door. It was open. She stepped inside and closed it behind her.

Steve sat up in bed, leaning against a pillow propped against the brass headboard. He too had been awake.

Andrea was glad he didn't ask her any questions. He stood up and she walked into his arms.

"My God, Andrea, do you know what you're doing?"

"Yes." She buried her face against his warm chest.

His arms tightened around her as if they would never let her go. "If you stay here, I won't be able to keep myself from making love to you," he said, his voice filled with torment.

"I know," Andrea said. She needed to tell him the truth, but she didn't yet know how. Her mind worked in slow, methodical ways. Things had to happen in the proper sequence for her to reach the right conclusion. Besides, she had no idea what Steve would do once he knew the truth. It had taken such courage for her to come to him, to let go of false pride and all the other fears that could get in the way of surrender...

"God help me," Steve whispered. He took Andrea's face in his hands and stared into her eyes. "God help us both."

A tremor rippled through Andrea's body at the proof of his need, reluctance, and inability to resist. She felt his torment deeply, but she could not risk losing this moment to relieve him of it.

When Steve kissed her—Andrea was lost. She had been athrob ever since he'd kissed her in Tombstone. Now his touch ignited her senses. She was giddy and breathless—a woman afire. His tongue coaxed its way into her mouth and became maddened with what it found there. Her twenty-five years of being "virginal and careful" tapered to a quivering point, then dissolved in a frenzy of mutual possession.

At some point Steve picked her up and carried her to his bed. "I know better," he said, "but nothing will satisfy me unless I absorb every part of you."

Andrea knew he wanted her with the same intensity with which she needed him. That knowledge freed her. Now she could spare him. No matter what his initial reaction might be, she knew that together they could weather the storm.

"Steve…"

"Hush, no more words. There've been too many words between us already." He smoothed her hair away from her face. "I love you, Andrea. I may burn in hell for this, but I love you, and it doesn't matter what they do to me. If you hadn't come to me, I'd have ridden off and tried never to come back. Don't talk. We're beyond words. It's too late to change your mind now."

He silenced her utterances with his mouth as his hands groped futilely at her nightgown. Finally he levered himself up, and then, with a small gesture that Andrea would never forget—the sensation was keenly erotic—he spread her open with his fingers and entered her.

The feel of him inside her was a small, fierce, hungry flame that caused her to strain against him, to wrap her legs around his taut buttocks, to go wild with need.

His hand stroked her hip and thigh slowly as if he could not bear to be separated from her flesh. Their breathing had returned to normal, but still he held her close. She hesitated to spoil the moment, but it was time to take away his burden of guilt.

"I love you, Steve."

Sleepily Steve stroked her hip. "And I love you."

"Will you remember that, even if you get mad at me?"

Steve made a small rueful sound. "If I could forget it, we would not now be in this position."

Andrea sucked in a long breath and let it out carefully. "I'm not your sister. I'm an imposter, Steve. The one you know as Tía Marlowe is your *real* half sister."

Steve remained silent so long that Andrea sat up in bed to look at him.

"This is a dream, isn't it?"

"No. I'm not your sister."

"If I'm awake, that's the best news I've ever heard."

Andrea leaned down and kissed him. "You're too lazy at this moment to be mad…"

"Too stunned and content. I've been given too many gifts in the last hour." He looked into her eyes cautiously. "Why should I believe you?"

"Because it's true. We changed places after Tía walked in on Judy when she was preparing her Indian attack. We thought it would be fun to change places, but then we couldn't figure out a good place to stop."

"Until now…"

"Until now," she said softly.

"Then who are you?"

"I'm Tía's sister, I mean half sister."

"Someone will have to tell Judy."

"I know."

They lay in silence for a moment. "Steve?"

"Yeah?"

"Please don't go tomorrow."

"I have to."

"But why? You can't need that silver turned into cash that desperately."

"We don't, but I've given my word to Morgan, and the plans have been made."

Steve frowned at the ceiling. Silver had never been the most important thing in his life, but his word was his bond. He was slow to give it, and he never took it back. He'd made mistakes in his life, but he didn't regret them as long as he'd made the best possible decision with the information at hand. And he was not a man to keep chewing the same cud. He'd thought this out yesterday, and he saw no reason now to change his mind.

"Stop worrying," he said at last. "I promise I won't look up Sara Jane Broomstick."

Andrea laughed. "At least you remembered her name."

"How could I forget?"

"We'll have to tell everyone."

"Start with Judy. The others can wait." Steve thought about Judy for a moment and sighed. "I don't envy you or Tía that chore."

"What about Rutledge? We'll see him first. I doubt Judy will be up and around until after you've gone."

"Don't worry about Rutledge. We can square that anytime. Make your peace with Judy." Steve chuckled. "I'm glad I won't be here for that."

"Coward!"

"You're darned right. I'd rather face Chatto any day."

Steve rolled on top of Andrea, and his mouth took charge of hers. He grew heavy and swollen again, and his knee nudged its way between her thighs. Andrea closed her eyes and forgot everything except the pleasure of loving her man.

From the porch, Andrea watched Steve's preparations to leave. Morgan Todd and Johnny Brago looked like two tomcats: they watched one another as if each expected imminent attack.

Steve had convinced Andrea to leave his room before the women came to the *casa grande* to cook breakfast. He had checked to be sure the halls were clear, then she had slipped back to her own cold bed. She didn't feel sleepy the way she usually did when she got up before her body was ready. She was too excited. She felt wonderful, even hopeful.

Horses snuffled and stomped, and sabers clanked as the soldiers slowly pulled their mounts into formation, two abreast. The blue-uniformed riders with their slouch hats and red-striped pants looked surly after a night of sleeping on the ground. Andrea pitied any Indians who attacked this bad-tempered crew.

The sun was bright and hot overhead. The slight chill she and Steve had enjoyed in the early morning hours had quickly become only a memory. She felt sorry for these men in their buttoned-down uniforms. How stifling and hot to be riding overdressed in the relentless heat.

Steve watched from his horse. Andrea glanced at him, and he started forward, but Rutledge saw that his men were ready to ride out, rode over to the porch, and dismounted in front of Andrea.

Andrea had been lovely last night, but somehow today in her white lawn blouse and black skirt she looked even more beautiful. Steve wasn't given to noticing detail, but the flounces and ruffles on her blouse gave the impression of such soft femininity and purity that he had the urge to prostrate himself at her feet. She epitomized a woman at one with her power.

Rutledge spoke loud enough for Steve to hear over the stamp and shuffle of horses impatient to be moving. "Good day, Miss Burkhart. Please give my regards to Judy. Your gracious hospitality was most appreciated."

"Thank you, Captain. Go with God."

For a moment Rutledge actually looked very mortal and human. Then he recovered, bowed, and clicked his heels. "That is always one of my first priorities, especially when there are beautiful women to come back to."

He mounted his horse and waved his right hand. Andrea waved. Some soldiers saluted smartly; a few grinned and lifted their slouch hats. Rutledge led off, and the horsemen at the front of the column peeled off behind him. It looked momentarily chaotic, but as the captain and the front of the column reached the front gate, the riders had snaked around and formed the column behind him.

It was a relief to Andrea to watch the blue-clad column—red-and-white banners flying against a bright, cloudless sky—ride through the wide-flung gates. The company's wagons, cannons, and extra horses followed them out, and the sentries pulled the gates of the compound closed.

Now only Steve, Morgan Todd, Johnny, and a dozen riders fussing over six pack animals remained. The prospect of Steve making this trip evoked a strange foreboding in Andrea. She wished he would change his mind. But she had exhausted all her arguments this morning before she'd left him, to no avail.

Morgan Todd's sensuous face was bruised and surly. Even Johnny, who was not going along, exhibited a forbidding truculence that did not encourage conversation.

"Rutledge says the Indians have all moved north," Steve said to Johnny, who was smoothing the breeching in place on the pack he had cinched onto one of the mules. "I guess if that's true, it should be safe to go back to doing some ranching tomorrow."

Johnny grunted his assent. Steve mounted Sand Biscuit, a gray mare with sleek, racy lines. Johnny squinted up at him as if he purely resented having to speak. "I'll scout around this afternoon and see if I agree with him," he said curtly.

"If you take the men out tomorrow, leave a heavier guard on the walls, even if it looks all right this afternoon."

Johnny nodded. "Chatto's never been an enemy of ours particularly, but maybe his competing with Geronimo will change all that."

"Could be," Steve said. He looked at Andrea, and a smile started at his toes and worked its way up until he felt sure his whole face was involved.

Johnny Brago took his cue and moved away to speak to one of the other riders.

Steve couldn't touch Andrea, because he didn't want to spend the trip explaining to Morgan that she wasn't his sister, but he could look at her. Though he probably shouldn't. He might not have the strength to leave.

A question sparkled in Andrea's eyes. She needed to be reassured, told once more that he loved her, and Steve knew he would not have the opportunity to do that. All he could do was look at her and hope that she could take her assurance from his eyes. If he didn't see her again for ten years, the very next time she lifted her gaze to his would be as satisfying as it was this moment.

Andrea held him there with the power of her need, and slowly the truth dawned in her eyes. Ever so slowly, as a flower opens to the sun, her face changed until it reflected what he had sensed within himself, until her face blossomed with love.

The wind swirled her skirts, men shouted their readiness, and Steve's vision blurred, then cleared. Andrea was a shimmering enchantment in the simple white blouse and black skirt: warmth and fineness shone through her uplifted face and made him ache all the way down to his knees.

She skimmed down the steps and reached up to put her small, dainty hand into his, and the shock to his system was absolute.

"Be careful, Steve. Come back to me," she whispered, squeezing his hand, giving him one last look into her bewitching dark eyes. Then, her black skirts floating out around her slim ankles, she whirled and ran into the house.

CHAPTER TWENTY-SEVEN

The racket of men and horses and wagons and drivers out front drew Tía to the parlor window. Johnny Brago came walking around the side of the house with an *aparejo* over his shoulders. He tossed the pack saddle, a large leather pocket already stuffed with two or three inches of cushioning straw, onto one of the mules and began cinching it down, working quickly and efficiently. Next to Johnny, Leon Parker got his *aparejo* cinched around his beast of burden, but he could not get the breeching snug enough. Johnny finished, then helped Leon check the cinches and breeching to be sure the pack saddle would not slip under an awkward load. Then he walked his animal around to the side of the house, out of sight.

The soldiers were ready to leave. Judy's Persian cat Tiffany rubbed against Tía's ankle, and she reached down to stroke its plush fur. Tiffany purred insistently and pushed herself closer to Tía. Johnny reappeared, leading the now heavily loaded mule.

Tía lost interest in the bustling activity around the front porch, but she waited a few minutes to see if Johnny would return. She didn't even like him anymore, but with Judy's disaffection still stinging her, she wanted to see if he still liked her.

Tiffany meowed at Tía. A voice behind her, Johnny's voice, startled her so badly she jumped.

"That's got to be the most pitiful excuse for a meow I've ever heard," Johnny said dryly, looking from Tía to the face of the dainty female Persian Judy had ordered from back east.

He walked across the parlor, squatted down, and held out a small piece of bacon. Fascinated, Tía watched as the elegant fluff ball, hopelessly prissy by barn cat standards, lifted the offering from Johnny's hand without touching him.

Grinning, standing up, Johnny hooked his thumbs in his belt and leaned against the Morris chair next to Tía. She could not imagine what he was so pleased about. It irritated her that all she had to do was see his hands, so dark and broad, tapering into manly wrists and muscular forearms, and she remembered instantly how vibrant with life they felt cupping her face or pressing into her shoulders.

"Don't pay any attention to him, Tiffany, he doesn't know a really good meow when he hears one," she said, refusing to be intimidated by Johnny.

"Good!" he scoffed. "I've heard better meows on three-day-old barn cats. She doesn't meow, she squeaks. For fifty bucks she should sing the 'Star-Spangled Banner.'"

"She meows exactly like I taught her."

"It figures that she'd have to be taught how to meow."

"She didn't meow at all when I came here. She just opened her mouth and pretended to make noise."

"Do you sing, too?"

"No," she said sadly, forgetting for the moment that she was furious with him. "I would love to be able to sing, though. If I could sing, I'd be so good at it."

Tía had rejected him last night, but Johnny smiled in spite of himself. Her cheeks flushed as pretty as a ripe peach. Her lips were smooth and rounded, perched in a blushing half-opened pout that reminded him of a blossom waiting for a honey bee…

Johnny took another scrap from his pocket and squatted beside Tiffany. Daintily Tiffany lifted it off his fingers and carried it a few steps away. Johnny straightened, leaned against the wall again, and grinned at Tía, enjoying her flash of resentment. At least she noticed him.

"I thought you had work to do," she said irritably.

"I'm doing it."

"You are not."

"Foreman does the watchin'. I'm watchin' you."

"Well, I don't need to be watched, thank you."

"Seems to me you need a lot of watchin'," he said, a scowl darkening his face.

"Well, you don't get to decide what I need, Mr. Brago."

Johnny made some reply, not listening any longer to her banter. He should leave her alone. She obviously preferred Morgan Todd or Steve Burkhart, or maybe she hadn't even decided which one yet, but it wasn't him she wanted. Unfortunately, as long as she kept responding to him like she did, he didn't seem capable of walking away from her. He'd probably never had good sense.

Johnny flushed with anger at himself. Like a young buck caught halfway between hay and grass, he was still hanging around, teasing Tía into noticing him. It maddened him that he couldn't just walk away and leave her to whichever man she wanted. His pride and stubbornness would not permit him to do more than taunt her, so he contented himself with that.

"Your innocent little friend Tiffany's breeding, you know."

"She is not," Tía flared.

"She is so," he crowed, enjoying her chagrin.

"How do you know?" She stooped to pick Tiffany up, covering the cat's ears as if she understood every word and would be scandalized.

"Easy. Opportunity," he said. When Tiffany had arrived in her wooden cage—spoiled, pampered, combed and brushed until her fluffy silver-gray coat fairly gleamed—the other cats had taken one look at her mincing steps and her perfect coiffure and kept their distance until she'd gone into heat. That was something they understood.

"We have some very capable tomcats around here. She went outside every night she wanted to. You wanna wager on it?"

Tía flushed from collar to hairline, making her even prettier—if that was possible. As if the cat had burned her, she put Tiffany down. Johnny laughed, but the laughter faded as another dark thought came to him.

"I thought you'd been out there this morning, crying your eyes out because your beaux were leaving."

"I don't have any beaux."

"Don't expect sympathy from me," he said dryly.

"If your sympathy is as scarce as your good sense, it's rarer'n sunflowers on a Christmas tree," she said, shaking her head in disgust. "He didn't touch me."

"My condolences," he drawled, enjoying her anger and taking hope. "Maybe next time."

Lifting her nose, looking like a haughty, pedigreed kitten herself, Tía sniffed with such disdain that Johnny almost howled with laughter. Admiring the pale, golden glow of her skin, the rounded smoothness and swell of her lips, parted and beckoning to him, he fairly burned to touch her. Was it possible she truly did not know how pretty she was? If she did, would she stand there daring him to prove she could respond again, the way she had in the barn?

"I don't need your condolences, Johnny Brago. I'm fine. Never been better!"

"I'm glad you don't get all broken up when your love affairs don't work out right away. I like a woman who can bounce back."

"At least I'm not a cheat and a liar," she said, her blue eyes flashing.

"You want an award for not sneaking around?" Apparently since Tía had told him first, that made it all right to her way of thinking. The joy he'd felt when she'd seemed to respond to him dissolved. Maybe if some Indian didn't stick a dogwood switch in his back or Morgan Todd's bullet didn't find its mark in his chest, he would live long enough to understand women. But he doubted it.

Johnny picked up his hat from the back of a chair, jammed it on his head, and stalked out.

Tía could not believe her eyes. His lithe form moved faster than she would have thought possible. Nothing of indolence showed in the angry, purposeful way he walked. In a fury, she searched for something to throw at him. He had no right to come around, acting like she was the one at fault. And he had no right to leave when she still had a mouthful of angry words to say to him. It was no wonder she hated him.

Andrea found Tía in the kitchen and pulled her aside.

"I told Steve last night."

"What did he say?"

"He was relieved. We're in love."

"I doubt that was much of a surprise to either one of you." Tía expelled a deep breath. "Now, the hard part begins."

Andrea nodded. "We tell Judy."

"I guess I'd better be the one to do that," Tía said.

"Do you want me to help you?"

"No. This is between us."

"Is she still angry with you?"

"I reckon so."

"You could wait."

"No. The sooner the better. I'm tired of riding under the wrong banner."

Tía knocked lightly, slipped inside Judy's room, and leaned against the door she had closed after her. Judy slept in a tangle of covers. "Judy, are you asleep?"

Groggily, Judy turned toward the sound of Tía's voice. Her dreams had been bad, and she should have been grateful to be saved from them, but when she opened her eyes she recognized Tía Marlowe and remembered instantly that she was still angry with her because she hadn't kept her promise to walk with Morgan Todd. "Welsher."

"I didn't welsh. I forgot."

"You got me in more trouble than I've ever been in before in my life."

"I did?"

"Morgan Todd hates my guts. If he could, he'd probably kill me."

"How did I do that?"

"By welshing on our agreement. By not walking with Morgan."

Tía doubted that she could have caused all that, but she didn't want to correct Judy and put her in an even worse mood. "I need to tell you something real important."

Judy turned over and punched her pillow into a more accommodating shape, then lay back down. "What?"

"I lied to you in Tombstone."

"About what?"

"My name is Teresa, Teresa Garcia-Lorca."

"Teresa?"

"Yes. Teresa Garcia-Lorca."

Judy couldn't fathom all the ramifications of Tía's confession. If she was really Teresa…

"Then who's Andrea?"

"My sister."

"You can't be Teresa."

"How come?"

"You're not Mexican."

"Mama gave me my stepfather's name. My mother is white. So was my…Mr. Burkhart."

Judy faced away from Tía and stared out the window. A cacophony of sound rose from outside—hens clucked, a dog barked, men argued.

Judy had trusted Tía, and Tía had been laughing behind her back. A wave of disillusionment flooded her so completely, she thought she would suffocate from it. She had been right about Tía being a little maggot. Tía had tricked her, taken her beau, and abandoned her to Morgan after she'd promised herself to stay away from him. Tía had been laughing at her from the first minute they'd met.

Tía's voice was tentative. "Judy…"

"Go away!" Judy yelled. "I don't want to see you ever again!"

"Judy, please don't be mad."

"Mad! I hate you, Tía or Teresa or whatever your name is." A thought came to Judy, and she sat bolt upright in bed. "But I guess I'd better be nice to you, hadn't I? Else you'll kick me out of *your* house, won't you?" She jumped out of bed and curtsied. "How's that, Your Majesty? Please may I be excused? Or must I get up now?" Fury sparkled in Judy's scornful brown eyes.

Tía pressed her lips together in frustration. "I didn't betray you. Except for that one little lie, I was straight with you! I was your friend!"

"You tricked me!"

"Because you were going to trick me!"

"That was in fun! We wouldn't have hurt you!"

"That was in fun, too!"

"Making a fool of me and Steve for two weeks?!"

"If you'd run me off, I'da been gone forever." Tía scowled and turned away. "Once I'd lied, I couldn't figure out how to tell you; then you got mad at me…"

"You're a maggot, Tía Marlowe or whatever your name is."

"Remember what you said to me? Can't you take a joke?"

"You've lied to me every day since I met you, and now you want me to see the humor! You slither in here like a snake, take my man away from me, trick me into getting in trouble with Morgan Todd, take away my inheritance, and now you have the gall to be disappointed because I can't take a *joke*!"

Judy raised up and surveyed Tía as if she had just crawled out from under a rock. "Get the hell out of my room, Teresa Garcia-Lorca, while you can still walk!" she roared.

Thoroughly cowed, Tía opened the door and stepped outside.

Judy covered her head with the pillow. Morgan hated her. Johnny had gotten completely over her. Tía had betrayed her from the day they'd met. If Tía weren't such a maggot, Judy would be elated that Andrea, the schoolteacher, was not Steve's sister. Grant was injured and could still die. Steve had never had time for her. Her father had hated her so much that he'd given her inheritance to that little maggot he'd secretly loved when he should have been loving Judy. Her own father, if she'd ever had one, cared nothing for her. Judy realized that no one loved her. She didn't even love herself.

Life was trickier than it appeared. She seemed to have everything and actually had nothing. She had lost Johnny years ago. When she'd left the dance with Morgan, she hadn't realized she was making a choice, but Johnny had held her decision against her for years.

Her limbs felt leaden. She told herself to get out of bed so she wouldn't torment herself with all these losses, but she had no strength to move.

Her eyelids drooped, and it was too much of an effort to lift them. She didn't remember sleeping, but something was tickling her nose. She woke blurrily, fighting the dream and the encroaching reality with equal strength.

Grant Foreman leaned over her, tickling her nose with a feather. "Go away," she groaned, pushing at his hand.

"Wake up. I saved you some coffee. Besides, it's time to get up. I need someone to talk to."

"No. Please go away," she grumbled. Before his injury he wouldn't have been allowed near her bedroom. But because he had been injured and Carmen had taken a liking to her "cheerful *caballero*," he now had all sorts of privileges. Carmen had probably been the one to let him in her room. Glancing at herself, Judy was relieved to see that she was covered from the neck down. Usually she slept in naked disarray.

"What time is it?" she asked, feeling hot and sweaty. She hated sleeping this late, because it meant she'd missed the coolest, best part of the day.

"Almost noon. It's a beautiful day. Hear that? Birds are singing."

"Birds are so stupid they sing at anything."

"The sky's blue, and so am I," he coaxed.

It was so amazing to see Grant up and about, looking almost fully recovered, that Judy sighed, swung her legs over the side, clutched the covers around her, and sat up. Grant handed her the robe off the chair beside her bed. But when she reached for it, he suddenly jerked it back.

"No, don't put this on. Get dressed, and we'll take a walk. I feel so good I can't lie down."

Judy pushed Grant out the door, took a sponge bath from the basin on the bureau, sipped at the coffee he'd left for her, brushed her teeth with the wash rag, then pulled on her ugliest gown, a brown one that she hated.

He was waiting for her at the back door. "This better be good," she said sullenly. She was in such a grumpy mood she didn't speak again until they were hallway through the orchard, almost to her old playhouse.

"I don't want to go to the playhouse," she said, her mouth suddenly filled with a bad taste at the memory of what had happened there the night before.

"Then we won't, milady," he said agreeably. They changed direction and walked for several minutes in silence.

"You're looking spry today."

"I'm feeling better. Fortunately, the arrow went in my shoulder muscle, not one of my legs, or I wouldn't be walking."

"I hate Tía!"

Grant guessed this dark passion had something to do with the dancing he'd heard last night. Everyone who wasn't half-dead would have been out there. Men who couldn't walk off a horse still thought they could dance, himself included, but he'd been so sleepy it had felt good to just lie in his bunk and listen to the music until he'd fallen asleep. He'd moved back to the bunkhouse because of Morgan's arrival. "Did Tía dance with Johnny?"

"Every dance. You know what she told me this morning? That little maggot is Teresa Garcia-Lorca."

Grant stopped and checked to see if Judy was joking. "Tía is Teresa?"

"That little maggot lied to me from the day I met her."

"Why?"

Judy pressed her lips together. "How should I know?"

"Then who's Andrea?"

"Her sister."

That puzzled him. The two girls did not look like sisters. He would have to take a better look at them next time he saw them together.

"I hate men!" Judy said suddenly. "All men!" Grant's mind was still grinding on the problem of Tía, but Judy seemed to have forgotten her already. Her face darkened like a storm cloud.

"Hey, I thought with all that dancing last night, you'd be in seventh heaven."

"Because of Johnny and Morgan? Those worthless varmints! I hate both of them. I hate everybody!" Stopping, Judy stamped her foot, and great round tears spilled out of her stormy eyes. Her downturning lips trembled with exquisite wretchedness.

A knife twisted inside him. Grant had always been blithely indifferent to feminine wiles. Until he'd met Judy Burkhart, he'd had some shield that kept him from feeling emotions or responding deeply when he did, but now he writhed.

"Hey, sweet lady, nothing could be that bad," he said, his voice raspy with emotion and the effort to sound casual.

Sobbing, Judy swayed. Grant stifled a wave of sheer anguish and gathered her into his arms. As Judy cried, he held her—a slender, quivering wand of feverish intensity. He wanted to hold her forever. A thought that ambitious reminded him how unlikely the prospect was,

JOYCE BRANDON

and he prayed instead for the strength to play his role—the role she had outlined long ago in her sweet voice with matter-of-face precision. *You will be my special friend. I like you better than anyone I know. If I ever need anything, I will come to you. If you ever need anything, you will come to me, but you can't be my beau. Sooner or later I hate all my beaux. Friendship can't mix with love, so you can choose. I want you for my special friend, but if you'd rather...*

Since that day he had watched other men buzz around her, accepting whatever crumb she tossed them until she lost interest and flitted to the next flower, like a butterfly. He did not fool himself. There was nothing magic about him that would attract and keep a girl with Judy's passionate nature. He could have one or the other, so he had chosen the role calculated to keep him near her for the longest period of time, even though he desperately longed for even a brief immersion in the blinding rapture he knew she could give him. He had been sorely tempted to gamble. If he'd been blessed with even a dab of blind egotism, he would have tried it, but he saw himself too clearly—a plain-faced runt who would never be anything to her except a range bum. He loved her far, far too desperately to risk losing that shimmering gift of intimate friendship—to exchange it for a few moments of passion, then have it withdrawn with casual disregard when she fluttered off to tantalize the next man who caught her fancy.

Now, unnerved by Judy's unaccustomed desolation and the sheer wonder of holding this proud young beauty in his arms, Grant floundered in a rough and wicked sea. Holding her close, wallowing in self-pity, wonder, and finally resignation, he felt his strength return at last. He lifted her chin and wiped gently at her tears.

"Feel better?" His throat was painfully tight.

"No," she sniffed, her lips trembling.

"Sure you do. A cloud that dumps that much rain has got to feel better."

"No I don't!" she said sulkily, but before he could reply, her face trembled into a slow, shaky smile.

"Liar!" he teased, smoothing soft brown curls from her damp face. He still felt dazed, strangely light-headed. Her lips should be damp from his kisses, not her tears, but he had never once tasted that expressive, sensual mouth.

A slow smile lifted that exquisite pout, and she sniffed loftily. "I am not!"

He was unable to stop himself. "I love you, Judy."

She stared back at him with eyes that were infinitely sad. "Sure you do."

284

"I mean it."

"And you will keep meaning it, until I do something you don't like." Judy smiled, knowing without question that his love, like the love of others on whom she had depended, was tied with a lot of strings.

"No," Grant said, his fine gray eyes solemn. "I love you no matter what you do, no matter what you've done."

He looked so earnest, but she couldn't believe him. *He* believed what he was saying, but that was only because his limits hadn't been tested. The same destructive impatience that caused her to throw away a chipped dish before it could break was driving her now. She began to laugh recklessly.

"Try me before you condemn me," he said fiercely.

Then she stopped laughing as abruptly as she had started. "All right," she said, gauging his reaction. "Suppose I told you that I let Morgan Todd make love to me last night."

Grant knew that these words meant to hurt him were really aimed at herself, but he didn't know how to respond without making her think it mattered to him. Part of him had always known Judy was likely not a virgin, because it wasn't in her to hold anything back. She was intense and giving and lived by impulse in everything she did.

"It doesn't matter," he said.

"Suppose I told you I let him treat me like a whore, and it wasn't the first time, and that I liked it?"

It confused Grant to know that Judy thought it was her fault if a man treated her badly.

Hurt crept into his eyes and caused an ache to start in Judy. He had beautiful eyes. Why hadn't she noticed that before? They were clear and gray and filled with light.

"It doesn't matter," he said.

"You're just saying that because you can't stand to lose face after shooting off your mouth." Inside Judy pleaded with herself to stop.

"I love you no matter what," he said stoutly.

"Okay," she said, looking as though she had come to some momentous decision. "Do you know why Morgan Todd isn't speaking to me today?"

"Because he left before you got up," Grant quipped.

"Wrong. Because the second time last night, the time he undressed me and kissed me all over and..." Judy paused, staring at him like a defiant child, waiting for the strength to continue.

Tía was the only woman she had ever loved, and Tía's betrayal had left her feeling raw and exposed. Part of her wanted to tear at herself, to rend herself in some horrible way that would make them all sorry. Grant was waiting for her to continue, but she could not.

"Go ahead," he whispered.

"I guess you wouldn't know what a stud Morgan is, would you?" Judy forced a derisive laugh. "No, you wouldn't know that, but you can take my word for it. He would put one of Steve's Arabians to shame," she said admiringly. "Well, here's Morgan Todd making love to me, kissing me like he can't get enough of me, and you know what I did?"

"No what?"

Judy rolled her eyes. "I did the unforgivable. I called him *Johnny*. Can you imagine?"

"What did he do?"

"What would *you* do? He knocked me silly," she said as if that were the least he could have done.

"He hit you?"

"I'll say," she said, rubbing her cheek where the memory of his blow tingled.

Rage bubbled inside Grant. For the first time in his life, he saw red.

"That'll teach me to keep better track of who I'm with," Judy said savagely. "Some men are such nitpickers!"

Grant reached up to push his hair back from his face. "Yeah," he whispered, his hand trembling.

"Well, Grant, I gotta go back now," she said brightly.

Unable to move, he watched her walk away. A red haze distorted his vision.

Judy walked all the way to the house to be sure she was out of Grant's sight. Once inside her room, she collapsed across the bed. Holding her stomach, she pressed her face into her pillow and sobbed uncontrollably.

CHAPTER TWENTY-EIGHT

The trip to Tombstone was long, hot, and dusty, but undisturbed by Indians. They reached the town sprawling over the squat, ugly Tombstone Hills just after the noon hour.

Morgan Todd had barely talked at all during the long ride. Now he rode up beside Steve.

"I'm going to stop at Sadie's."

"That ought to put you in a better mood." Steve grinned.

Morgan looked away. "Care to join me?"

Steve shook his head. "No, I'll make the arrangements we talked about. We'll be ready to go before nightfall if all goes well. If we leave at five in the morning we should be in pretty good shape."

"Fine," Morgan answered, turning his horse, distracted.

A warm smile lighting her heavy face, Sadie opened the door herself. A tall brunette with hair dyed flaming red, she was no beauty, but she was buxom, jovial, and an expert at relieving all kinds of tensions. The gaudily decorated parlor was empty. A cat slept atop the piano. The women who usually adorned the room slept upstairs.

"Morgan, honey! Come in! Come in! Let me fix you a drink. I missed you last night."

"I was away on business."

"Glad you're back, sweetie." One arm around his lean waist, she hugged him and led him up the stairs and past a row of closed doors to her own room. A glaring display of opulence, her room was done in yards and yards of baby-blue satin: bedcovers, bed canopy, draperies, everything was blue satin.

Motioning him to a chair, Sadie poured a straight shot of whiskey and carried it to him, smiling archly. "You look like your saddle's cinched too tight, sweetie."

Morgan took a long pull on the whiskey and sighed tiredly. "It might be. Take your damned clothes off."

Smiling, making a show of it for his benefit, Sadie complied. She had a full, hourglass figure and shapely, tapering legs that she showed off by strutting archly from bureau to clothes closet.

"Now you," she said, beginning to undress him. That done, she moved into his arms for a kiss.

"What's the matter, honey?" Usually by the time she kissed him, his response was as immediate as it was predictable. This time, nothing. His face mirrored her concern.

"Here, you lie down, sweetie. Let Sadie take care of this." Sadie lay down beside him and began stroking and fondling his limp organ. No response. Scooting down, Sadie sucked it into her hot mouth, teasing the tip with her tongue. Enjoying how soft and smooth it felt, she kept her ministrations up for a long time, but it remained flaccid.

At last she scooted up beside him. "What's wrong, sweetie?"

"Nothing's wrong, dammit!" he growled. "Maybe I'm just tired."

Embarrassed that she had pressed him when she damned well knew better, Sadie retreated. "Why didn't I think of that?" she said soothingly.

Angrily Morgan dressed himself and reached for his wallet.

"It's on the house, sweetie."

Morgan pulled out a ten-dollar bill and tossed it on the bureau. "At least my damned wallet still works."

He stalked over to the Alhambra Saloon and had two drinks, but frustration and fury were driving him. He wanted to get his hands around that bitch's throat. It was all her fault. If she hadn't called him *Johnny*... He should have killed that bastard a long time ago. An image of Judy Burkhart swam before his eyes: her sweet angel face and that lissome, taunting, white body...

A tingle started in his loins. Glancing down, Morgan was stunned to see that he had an erection. And all he'd done was call up her image.

Well, she'd done him a favor at last. Morgan slammed down his glass and stomped out of the saloon. Ignoring the open-mouthed stares of the men who watched him, he walked through town to the Cattle Baron Hotel, sent a boy for Sadie, and took the stairs two at a time.

Sadie stuck her head in the door in record time. She saw the unmistakable bulge along Morgan's thigh and her eyes lit up.

She never wore much in the way of underclothes. All she had to do was slip the gown down past her shoulders, wiggle it over her hips, and step out of it, but by the time she did Morgan had shriveled to a skinny carrot.

"Damnation!" she swore feelingly. "You sure got a problem."

"And what the shit is it?" he demanded through gritted teeth.

Sadie shook her head. "I don't know." Her eyes widened. "Unless…"

"Unless what?"

"Unless…you're in love…"

"Bullshit!"

"Well…" She shrugged. "You'd know best." She paused, staring at him speculatively. "I did have this customer once in Kansas City… he was like you, strong and willing and always able. That feller was a real problem, even to himself. If he couldn't get a woman, he'd screw anything—sheep, small cows, even chickens—don't ask me how he did it. Anyway, then he fell in love with one of my gals. All of a sudden he couldn't do it with anyone except her." Sadie stared off as if remembering all that lost revenue with great sadness.

"How long did that last?"

"About three weeks. Then it was okay again, except by then he was married. Lost one of my best girls and one of my best customers."

"Shit!" Morgan exploded. "I don't love the bitch. I hate her!"

Frowning suddenly, Sadie put her hands on her hips and stared at Morgan. "That's what he said, too. Until she tried to leave him."

"She didn't leave me. I left her!" he roared.

As if she could see the money spilling out of her till, Sadie shook her head sadly and patted Morgan's hand. "Well, sweetie, take my advice and go back to her. It's better than being limp for three weeks, getting no sleep at all, and *then* going back and marrying her."

Morgan closed his eyes and repeated every curse word he could think of.

Sadie kissed his forehead, walked to the door, looked sadly at Morgan on the bed, and let herself out.

Determined to sleep, Morgan tossed and turned on the bed. He hadn't slept the night before. That was probably what was wrong with him. He was tired. He'd be a new man after a nap.

If it hadn't been for Judy…Judy's face appeared on the inside of his eyelids, then the image of her softly yielding body. He couldn't forget the seductive pout of her lower lip, the way her lips parted when she opened her mouth to kiss him, the pinkness of her tongue as it waited, just behind her teeth…

A painful tightening started in his loins. Morgan sat up as if the bed had caught fire around him. Sweat beaded his forehead as he looked down. He had swollen to the size of a fist.

"Shit!" Panting with frustration and desire, Morgan cursed Judy Burkhart and the day he'd met her. Was it possible that after enjoying her casually for three years he had fallen in love with her?

What a joke! He hadn't even bothered to see her the last time she was in town. As soon as that thought seeped into his mind, he rejected it. He wasn't so bad off that he had to lie to himself. Not seeing her that time had been a test of his willpower. And as long as he was being honest, he might as well admit that his trip out to the ranch to talk Steve into transporting the silver had been trumped up primarily so he could see Judy. He didn't give a damn about silver or paying Wells Fargo's exorbitant rates. He'd wanted to see her...

Groaning, Morgan rolled over and stood up. Sadie was right. There was no sense at all in spending three weeks like this.

"What?" Steve asked, his expression incredulous. "You're going back to the ranch? For what?"

"To see Judy," he said grimly.

"You just saw her."

"Dammit! We had a fight. I have to talk to her. If I'm not back, start without me. I'll catch up. You're going the northern route through Apache Pass?"

"No, southern, the way Russ went. It's shorter, and Rutledge says we'll stay clear of Indians. We'll leave at five tomorrow morning. Hell, you might as well meet us. No sense coming all the way back here. Just head south from the ranch and intercept us."

"Thanks, Steve."

Morgan stalked out the door, mounted his fresh horse, and whipped him into a gallop. Steve turned back to the bar and remembered the real reason why he shouldn't have allowed Morgan to go back to Rancho la Reina: Johnny Brago. The two of them would likely kill each other.

Frustrated with himself, Steve stopped at the beer hall for a bottle of Costello's famous St. Louis beer. As usual the place was doing a land-office business.

Martin Costello, the owner, clapped Steve on the back.

"Well, I heard the news. You and Todd are going to take a shipment of silver out. Word gets around fast in this town, boy. Your papa would be proud of you. I hear the folks at Wells Fargo are already having second thoughts about the prices they're chargin' folks."

Steve frowned. "How'd you find out we were thinking about taking a shipment out?"

"Hell, Russ Sloan didn't make no secret of it when he went. Todd told me about your trip. Course I didn't tell nobody. What with all the road agents hanging around Tombstone, when they ain't actually workin', that is."

"Johnny Behan is too friendly to be a good sheriff. Even the Clantons like him. No wonder there's no law here," Steve said with disgust.

Costello lowered his voice. "Heard tell Wyatt Earp is planning on running for sheriff against Behan."

"Might be a better man. Heard he cleaned up Dodge City. Maybe he can clean up Tombstone, too."

"That'll be the day," Costello snorted. "When you leavin'?"

On the other side of the table, a tall Mexican in the somber brown cassock of a padre moved casually away and slipped out the front door.

Andrea waited for an opportunity to see Tía, and finally found it when Judy was outside with Grant and the housekeeping staff was peeling potatoes for the evening meal. Steve had been gone for hours, but her nerves were still jumpy from lack of sleep.

"Did you tell Judy?"

"Yes."

"What happened?"

"She hates me."

"What did she say?"

Tía looked as though she might cry. "Just the truth. That I betrayed her by lying to her, and she isn't going to forgive me." She turned away and wiped at her eyes.

Willie B. Parker flung open the kitchen door and yelled into the house. "The soldiers are back!"

Wiping their hands on their aprons, Carmen, Lupe, and Cruz rushed out of the kitchen and scurried along the parlor at the front of the house. Andrea and Tía raced them to the porch.

The soldiers riding in through the opened gate were in a state of disarray—bloody bandages had been wrapped around injuries, dead bodies sagged across saddles. One of the covered wagons had caught fire; the canvas was blackened and sagging over the wagon bed. Injured men had been piled into it like kindling.

Tía turned to Carmen. "Get bandages ready."

Andrea ran down the steps and stopped beside Rutledge's horse. "Captain! What happened?"

"Geronimo! We were ambushed. His braves must have eluded Rogers's sweep. There must have been two hundred of those murdering swine. We barely got away with our scalps."

"Are they following you?" Andrea asked.

Rutledge looked behind him uncomfortably as if searching for Indians. "Hard to say. Something untoward is happening out there. I got the impression we were swatted away, like a bear swats at a gnat. Otherwise we wouldn't have made it this far. My men and horses took a beating. If you have no objection, we'll rest here tonight and go the rest of the way in the morning. I recommend you and all your people come with us. You'll be safer at the fort."

Andrea looked at Tía, who had come up beside her, then turned back to Captain Rutledge. "I'll talk to Johnny and let you know."

Rutledge shook his head in consternation, but Tía didn't wait to argue with him. She turned and ran to look for Johnny. Andrea picked up her skirts and followed.

Tía found Johnny Brago stretched out on his cot. He sat up and came easily to his feet. His dark eyes, narrowed against the sudden brightness, were unreadable. His gaze stayed on Tía so long that she felt heat flushing into her cheeks.

Andrea explained as succinctly as she could. "I'm terrified for Steve," she ended breathlessly. "He has no idea. Rutledge assured him they were driving the Indians north, back to the reservation, that there was no danger. They'll all be killed. He's riding into a hornet's nest."

"Steve has lived in this valley all his life," Johnny reassured her. "He knows what that kind of talk is worth."

"He seemed to believe it, though."

A wry look of consternation tucked in the corners of Johnny's lips. His gaze slid over to Tía and seemed to be probing her soul.

"Steve could be r-riding into a trap," Andrea stammered, not bothering to hide her feelings. Nothing mattered except that Steve be safe...

"Could be," he said slowly. "More likely Geronimo has bigger fish to fry."

"Like what?"

"Maybe tribal rivalry. Chatto and his daddy been a thorn in Geronimo's side for years," he said. "Or maybe he's got some target picked out to show Chatto up. Could be anything as long as it's daring. Something not just anybody would do. Could have nothing to do with us. Could be Fort Bowie. If I was Geronimo, I'd do something useful, like try to stop the railroad from coming through. But I doubt if he's farsighted enough to figure that out."

"Should we go to Fort Bowie?"

"Can't hurt. If the fort falls, we ain't gonna be able to stay here. If they're the target, they'll need all the help we can give 'em."

"Rutledge wants to wait until morning. Is that wise?"

"Not if he's right about the number of Indians."

"I'll tell him that, unless you would rather."

Johnny laughed softly. "If you want him to go tonight, tell him I recommend waiting till morning."

"Why?"

"He hates my guts. If he was starving, he wouldn't take my recommendation to eat."

Tía pulled Andrea outside. "He's right, you know. You go talk to Rutledge since he still thinks you're Teresa, and I'll make sure Carmen and Cruz are doing what they can for the injured soldiers."

Andrea obeyed. She should have believed Johnny and Tía. But she told Rutledge Johnny recommended going at once, and he puffed up like an adder. Logic forgotten, he was huffy and then adamant. "Morning will be soon enough, Miss Burkhart. Our horses are exhausted. I'll lose half of them if we don't rest them. The cavalry can't afford that kind of loss."

Andrea found Tía in the dining hall where she, Carmen, Cruz, and Lupe were tearing sheets into bandages and shared the news with them. After the initial reactions and excitement died down, she pulled Tía aside.

"I hope Steve made it to Tombstone," she said, a frown creasing her forehead. "He could be dead or injured."

"Don't borrow trouble. He made it fine," Tía said firmly. "I hope he stays there. Carmen, can you get along without Lupe for a while?"

"*Sí*, I was thirty years old before *patrón* hired her."

Tía laughed. "I meant as your helper with supper."

"*Sí.*"

Lupe flashed Carmen a look of consternation. She was accustomed to cooking meals. Changes could be good or bad. She would rather Tía had asked her if she wanted to be spared.

"Please come with me, Lupe. We will take the bandages to the soldiers and see if they need help."

Cruz snorted. "That should wipe the look off your face, Lupe. All those men around you."

Lupe picked up a stack of bandages and followed Tía. Injured men littered the south end of the compound near the front gate. Some had managed to take care of their wounds, others had not. Tía put Lupe to work and then moved from man to man, making them as comfortable as possible. She fashioned a pillow for one, covered another to stop his shivering in spite of the relentless heat.

Lupe decided she liked playing nurse and flirting with the healthy soldiers. She stayed to do what she could for them. Tía went back to help Carmen and Cruz serve supper.

Compared to the jovial atmosphere of Saturday's dance, Sunday's supper was a tense affair. The riders ate in relative silence, then tramped outside to talk in hushed tones or take their turns at keeping a lookout. Carmen and Cruz came out of the kitchen and sat with Judy. Andrea sat across from Tía. Lupe, who had never missed a meal and who had always been jealous of Judy, showed up after they had all seated themselves, decided that she liked no one, and sat by herself.

After the dishes were washed Andrea settled down with a book, although Tía suspected she wouldn't be able to read.

"Do you want to go to the outhouse?" Tía asked.

"No. Use the chamber pot."

"I'm tired of being in the house."

Tía excused herself, took a lantern off the hook by the back door, lit it, and walked to the outhouse. She knew she should use the chamber pot after dark—it was safer and less scary—but she needed to get outside. Besides, there weren't any Indians inside the walls, not with so many soldiers, cowhands, and *vaqueros* around.

On the way back to the house, she dawdled. She resented the Indians and the threat they represented. Although she was terrified for Steve, she felt sorrier for Andrea, who was in love with him and could only sit back and pray he would survive. If only there was some way to warn him.

Suddenly Tía stopped. Well, why couldn't they? A messenger on a fast horse could make it—easier at night than any other time. Why not? Steve wouldn't have left Tombstone yet.

Whirling, she ran to Johnny's cabin. The windows were dark. Disappointed, she stopped on the porch. She hesitated and then turned to leave. The door opened, and Johnny stepped onto the porch.

Licking her suddenly dry lips, Tía set the lantern down. "I…" she stammered. "I'm sorry. Did I wake you?"

His eyes reflected back the lantern light like mirrors. Their opacity taunted her. What was he thinking behind his mask? Why didn't he say something?

"I wanted to ask you if we could send a messenger to warn Steve about the Indians."

Johnny smiled—a slow, cynical curving of his smooth lips that confused her. "To warn Steve? Don't you mean Morgan Todd?" His husky voice was low and full of scorn.

"I mean Steve!" she protested, too flustered to be truly angry.

"I may look like I couldn't drive nails in a snowbank, but I do have some sense, Tía Marlowe," he said, his gaze raking over her.

Now the anger that had been seething in her ever since she'd heard about Johnny's fight with Morgan Todd brought her chin up defiantly.

"I'm not Tía Marlowe. I'm Teresa Garcia-Lorca."

"So Carmen told me. I'm surprised you bothered to mention it. After all, I'm just hired help."

Confusion almost overwhelmed Tía. She couldn't decide whether to fight with him about Morgan Todd or about her being Teresa or about his being mad that she hadn't told him.

"I'm sorry if I'm not exactly what you had in mind when you set out to make your girlfriend jealous, but unfortunately you forgot to tell me all the rules."

Johnny blinked. Of all the answers she could have given, that one stumped him. "The first rule is not to spread a lot of corral dust around."

"I didn't lie because I wanted to! And don't you act so superior to me, Johnny Brago. You spread some corral dust about Judy."

"I did not."

"You fought over her!"

His dark eyes narrowed. They looked like little half-moons, curving downward. Combined with the cocky slant of his lips, they seemed to taunt Tía, to remind her of things about him she'd rather have forgotten.

"Is that what's wrong with you? You got mad because I hit your boyfriend?"

"He's not my boyfriend. If you want to fight over women in saloons, I couldn't care less."

Johnny frowned. Tía had been mean to him for two days, but until that comment he hadn't felt that he knew why. He had no idea why it should enlighten him so—she'd said similar things before—but that comment clicked into place, like the last, missing piece of a puzzle.

She had been jealous. Joy rose up in him. If she was jealous, that might mean she really did care for him. He had the mad impulse to throw back his head and laugh.

"Come here," he said, stepping toward her.

"No." Anger and the jealousy she had denied boiled over. She didn't know why she should be so mad at Johnny, but the thought of him fighting over Judy put her in such a bad mood that she didn't want him to touch her. His touch had always aroused special feelings in her, and she didn't want to feel anything with the mood she was in. He reached out his hand to her, and for some reason she could not fathom she hit it.

Johnny looked stunned. Tía turned and walked off the porch without her lantern. She didn't say she was sorry or anything. She just walked off the porch and kept walking as if she couldn't stop herself. Johnny called her name, but she walked past the lighted windows of the women's quarters as if she hadn't heard him.

And somehow, once she had done that, she could not stop or go back or acknowledge even that she had walked away. So she had to keep walking, even though part of her knew that it made no sense.

Once she reached the orchard, where she felt safe from Johnny's eagle eyes, she broke into a run. It didn't matter that it was dark. She needed the exertion of running to still the terrible energy in her legs. And once she got running she couldn't seem to stop herself. She leaped every obstacle, as fleet-footed as a deer, and exulted in the sheer freedom of it. It was inconceivable that anyone could catch her. Certainly not Johnny Brago, who was known for his laziness. She had heard the jokes the men told about him.

She loved the orchard. Darker and cooler here, it smelled of overripe peaches. At last, panting, Tía stopped to listen. The sounds of people receded and were replaced by the skittering movements of unseen animals.

She would walk to the playhouse and then go back. She had never seen the playhouse after dark.

A hundred yards into the shadowy orchard, surrounded by weird, suddenly intimidating shapes, something skittered to the left of her. An image of Johnny in the hayloft, moaning to make the kids think he was a ghost, flashed in her mind. It might be Johnny trying to scare her. She would not give him that satisfaction. She strode forward confidently, tripped, and fell headlong in the dirt. Something moved nearby. Tía strained to hear it again. Her ears picked up the distant sound of careful footsteps. An Indian? Probably just Johnny, looking for her in the dark.

The compound was big enough that it was possible to get into trouble, even with all the soldiers camped by the front gate and riders standing guard around the walls. She was a hundred yards from the nearest wall and probably three hundred yards from the nearest guard. She could scream and bring everyone running, but then she would only embarrass herself. She would get up, brush herself off, and walk back to the house.

Tía stood up and started to brush herself off. Sand crunched as if under a foot. Suddenly she was remembering how easily that Indian had gotten into the house and almost killed Andrea.

Heart pounding, ears straining for any sound, Tía took a careful step. Was that a twig being brushed aside by a careful hand? Every nerve in her body strained at the inky darkness—she heard crickets and frogs; a horse whinnying, one of the women letting out a spurt of shotgun Spanish in the distance; but no footsteps on her path.

The sounds reassured her. She was only seconds from the back door. A mixture of emotions—fear that Johnny had followed her, foolishness that she was overreacting, and lastly defiance that she should care what he thought—gave her the courage to head back to the house. She could walk away if she felt like it. It didn't mean she was jealous. Maybe she just felt like walking away.

Forcing herself to breathe quietly, Tía moved forward cautiously. A bird trilled a few short notes. Startled, she turned and looked behind her. Nothing moved except the shadows made sinister by a light breeze. Tentatively she took a step backward.

A hand covered her mouth so tight she couldn't make a sound. A strong arm pulled her back against a warm chest.

"Don't be afraid," Johnny whispered next to her ear.

He held her immobile until her panic subsided, turned her slowly in his arms, and replaced his hand with his warm mouth. Tía's wild urge to struggle lasted only a moment. The kiss was sweet and dizzying. At last he relinquished her lips, but he did not move away. He held her close. She buried her face against his neck and pressed her lips there.

Johnny sighed. "Why do you keep running away from me?"

"I didn't run away," she whispered, feeling wonderful. She had never felt more alive. Her body tingled with power and awareness. His lips found her mouth, and she strained against him, not fighting him now, letting him kiss her, taste her, explore her. His body felt so good to her, so warm and solid and necessary. She hugged him hard and close. But it was not enough.

Johnny picked Tía up and carried her through the trees to his own favorite spot—stumbling only once, catching himself quickly—to place her on a blanket he had left there a day or so ago.

"Is this the playhouse?"

"No, this is where I sit when I need to get away from those lunkheads in the bunkhouse."

"You scared me," she whispered.

"I didn't want you to scream and bring the whole blamed compound down on our heads."

"I should have."

Johnny kissed her mouth, her eyes, her throat. His lips so close caused Tía's breast to burn. She longed to feel the warmth of his lips and the stiff bristle of his mustache on her breasts. She slipped her tongue into his mouth and wondered if doing so would cause the same reaction to him that his doing it caused in her. It must have. Johnny deepened his thrusting into her open mouth, but he didn't try to touch her breasts. His mouth nearly devoured her, but still his hands remained chastely on her back, kneading her hungry flesh.

Tía was on fire. Her whole body flamed. She wanted to feel his hands on her. His fingers pressed her spine, dug into the soft flesh of her thighs, but they didn't move threateningly close to anything he shouldn't be touching. At last, in desperation, Tía took Johnny's hand and guided it up to cup her breast. Johnny's hot fingers held her and squeezed her tight, as if their hunger to touch her equaled her hunger to be touched. Then his fingers teased and pulled at her nipple. His kiss deepened, making her crazy all over. Finally his teeth nipped through two layers of her clothing at her breast. Soon even that was not enough.

"Help me," Tía whispered.

She struggled with her gown, and Johnny unfastened the buttons and helped her free it over her head. It felt wonderful to be free, and she still had the safety of her camisole and undergarments. It was cooler with more of her skin exposed to the warm night air.

"You're going to get me shot," Johnny whispered.

"Do you care?"

"I guess not."

Tía laughed softly. "Then what are you complaining about?"

"Damned if I know."

Tía stretched her arms overhead and pressed herself against the length of his warm, hard body, reveling in the feeling of power it gave her.

Somehow she knew Johnny would go only as far as she wanted. She trusted him in that. He kissed her mouth, and while his lips and tongue set up a tumult within her, his fingers slipped the straps of her camisole aside and released her bare breasts to shower her there with kisses. Tía cried out with the wild, sweet sensation that swamped her at the feeling of his hot lips surrounding her. As if out of her control, her hips ground against his, and suddenly even that was not enough. She wanted to feel his bare skin.

Tía pulled his shirt out of his pants and ran her hands over his hard-muscled back. His skin felt hot and damp, the muscles taut. She wanted him to kiss her forever. Unfortunately, as soon as her body adjusted to Johnny kissing her breasts, it demanded a new sensation. Now it wanted to feel his bare thighs against hers.

"Take these off," she whispered, tugging at his pants.

Johnny opened dazed eyes. "I might not be able to keep the stallion on a lead rope if we do," he panted.

"I just want to feel your skin."

Johnny unbuttoned his pants and slipped them off. He lay back down beside her, and Tía wrapped her arms around his waist and hugged him hard.

It felt so good to feel him completely unfettered. She loved the warm, hungry feel of his manhood pressing against her hands, against her thighs. It was warm and smooth, and she could feel it throbbing in silence against her. Johnny just held her and kissed her and didn't seem concerned, but Tía kept worrying about his manhood. It felt so smooth and helpless with no arms or anything. She wanted to make it feel better. Or maybe she just wanted to feel it.

Johnny kissed her in that hungry, urgent sort of way, as though he were in terrible pain and couldn't cure it except by kissing her as hard as he could. Tía almost couldn't stand it. "Can I touch it?" she asked.

"You better not. I might not be able to—"

"I'll be good."

She slid her hand down between Johnny's thighs and fondled him. Touching his rigid shaft relieved a terrible pressure in her, and she withdrew her hand immediately. Johnny rolled away from her to lie on his back, and Tía scooted over to snuggle as close to him as she could. Johnny kissed her so hungrily that she just had to get closer to him. Still kissing him, she sat up and pulled her camisole over her head. Johnny groaned like a man whose burdens had just doubled. "You better not tempt me. I'm hanging on as best I can already."

"It'll be okay. I just want to feel you against me."

"Dammit, Tía…"

Tía stopped his protest with her mouth. She just wanted to feel him heavy and naked on top of her. She kissed him for a long time and then pulled him over on top of her. It was wonderful. He even kissed better that way. She let go of him with her hand and wiggled around until she had him between the tops of her thighs. It felt wonderful there. Johnny was breathing so hard and his heart was pounding so hard that Tía felt the life force in every pore of her body. She loved the feel of him between her thighs. She wanted this moment to last forever. Then, suddenly, even feeling his skin against hers didn't seem like enough. She wanted to feel how it would be if he just slipped a *little* inside her. But poor Johnny was having such a hard time with her last request that she hated to ask for more.

She let him kiss her until he seemed too blind to notice, and then she slid her hand down between them and took hold of him. Johnny groaned, and Tía found his mouth to quiet him.

Johnny dragged in a breath and took her hand in his. He forced it away from him and up to his lips, where he pressed warm kisses to her fingertips.

Tía whimpered. "But I want to…"

"No," he whispered against her cheek. "And don't give me a hard time about it. We ain't married, and we ain't gonna do married things until we are."

Tía felt confused. In Mama's circle of friends, women did married things all the time, and none of them had been married.

"What makes you think I'd marry you, Johnny Brago? A man who fights over other women in saloons?"

"You behave yourself, Tía Marlowe."

"Garcia-Lorca."

"Burkhart," he countered. "You still don't know who you are, do you?"

"I know as well as most."

"You're my woman. And I reckon to marry you."

"I won't even wear your bracelet. What makes you think you could get me to marry you?"

"You might want me to kiss you or something."

"I doubt I'd want it bad enough to marry."

"You might."

The warm light in his eyes caused Tía to smile. "I probably wouldn't tell you, even if I did."

"Probably wouldn't." Then Johnny stopped teasing and stroked her hair as if he expected to calm her to sleep. "Will you marry me, Tía?"

"Do you want me to?"

"Wouldn't ask you if I didn't want you to."

"I don't know."

"How come?"

"I got something else on my mind."

"Like what?"

"I have to tell Judy first. See if I can make her understand."

"You've got to be the dangedest woman I ever met." He took her face between his hands, kissed her lips, and then looked into her eyes. "I love you, Tía."

At his words, something settled quietly into place. That was it! So much joy rose up in her that she almost couldn't breathe. Her heart seemed to swell with it. "I love you, too, Johnny."

"I never thought I'd hear those words from you."

"Fighting over Judy, you don't deserve to hear them," she challenged.

"For the third time, I told you I wasn't fighting over Judy. I was fighting with Morgan Todd because I hate the bastard enough to kill him in his sleep."

"You do not."

"I know it, but you make me so danged mad."

Tía leaned up and covered his mouth with hers teasingly. She pulled Johnny back on top of her. "If you're so smart, let's see if you can kiss your soon-to-be fiancée."

CHAPTER TWENTY-NINE

Wearing a trail in the gold rug she'd ordered from a Chicago mail-order house, Judy paced between her bedroom door and window. Even as distracted as she was, she glanced occasionally at her reflection in the mirror. She was never completely unaware of the picture she made, a pretty girl in a yellow gown nervously pacing from bed to door in her white-and-yellow bedroom.

Judy paused and looked around her at the room she had grown up in. She liked its bright colors, especially when it was clean and orderly, as it was now.

Since Tía had been in charge of the house, the women had taken special pains with her room. Thinking about Tía filled her with confusion. Tía had claimed to be her friend, and she'd looked truly upset when Judy had accused her of betrayal. But the fact remained that Tía had taken Johnny away from her within minutes of arriving at Rancho la Reina, even though Judy had told her plainly that Johnny belonged to her.

Johnny had loved her, and his love had seemed as endless as water coming over a spillway. She had only to look at him to know he had a lot of love to give, so she had depended on it. But she had forgotten about Johnny's ability to build things. When she wasn't looking, he had built another spillway.

Grant had gone to bed early—supposedly to nurse his injured shoulder, but Judy didn't believe that for a second. He had been shocked by her revelations today. He would pretend that he still loved her for a while, just to save face, but soon he would drift on to another job, another ranch. It was better that way. Grant was too decent, like Johnny used to be. She wanted to be decent, but sometimes her life just got away from her. She didn't understand it…Somehow she got so distracted doing things that she forgot to consider the consequences.

At least she could be grateful that Andrea would not be living on the ranch forever. She would probably get married and move away.

Men seemed to find her attractive. Judy couldn't imagine why; she hated schoolteachers.

She also hated Indians, Morgan Todd, Johnny Brago, Tía, and herself. Only Steve had continued to love her, but even his love was measured out in stingy little amounts. Between pointing out her transgressions.

Judy grinned. Well, why not? It would take a lot of time to explain her inadequacies. That's the way she was. Steve had said it best. *You could get away with murder if you could talk to the man in charge, but if they ever judge you on your record, you're dead, because you're record is insurmountable.*

Steve had a way with words. That was the classiest insult she'd ever gotten. The ones her father had used were a lot less classy. They hurt more too, because she understood the words: *Just like your mother, aren't you? It's in your blood. You look like her. You act like her. You'll never be true to any man.*

How many times had he said those same words to her—one way or another—hated her for what she was? She could recall the exact tone of his voice: gruff and harsh and condemning: *You'll never amount to anything looking the way you do...*He had backed out of the room as if it had been filled with snakes.

Once when she was seventeen...

Before Tombstone even existed, she had gotten all dressed up for a big dance at Fort Bowie. She put on her prettiest mail-order gown and new shoes; she had a special grown-up hairdo with ribbons wound around the curls on top of her head. Carmen had worked for over an hour on that hairdo. She wore her mother's earbobs—the amber and gold ones. Johnny stopped beside her window and said she was the most beautiful girl in the world. She'd been so proud of the way she looked, the things he'd said. She'd been so much in love with Johnny. Unthinking, she had rushed to show herself off for her father.

She had pirouetted, swishing her crinolines in a very grownup way. *Pa...*She'd twirled in front of him. *How do I look?*

He'd looked up from his week-old newspaper and grunted. Then he'd blinked in disbelief and his eyes had filled with unmistakable revulsion...

All the joy drained out of her, and her insides hardened to granite. Her nerveless fingers dropped her skirt. Hot tears welled up inside her, but she swallowed hard, then turned to go.

"Judy, wait! I'm sorry. It wasn't your fault. It wasn't you..."

She tried to look at him but couldn't see through the haze of tears that flooded up in spite of her best efforts.

"It's all right, Pa. I understand."

That night Judy went to the dance with Johnny, but she flirted with Morgan Todd, and she sneaked out of the dance and let him take her to his hotel room to show her his whiskey drummer case. She'd never seen one. They stepped quietly up the back stairs so no one saw them. Morgan started to kiss her, and it felt so good to be held, to be made a fuss over, that she wasn't able to make herself stop him. Because Morgan was big and rough, he hurt her. He hurt so bad she couldn't stop the tears that squeezed out, but somehow she was glad.

"Why didn't you warn me you were a virgin? I have to admit, I thought that bastard Brago had been here first."

"Is that why you like to fight with him?"

"Naw, I just don't like the way he looks."

"I do."

"Then why the hell aren't you with him instead of me?"

Judy hoped Johnny wouldn't discover her deflowering, but he knew as soon as he saw her. She saw it in the flat brown opacity of his eyes; he could hide everything except his pain…

All Johnny had to do was look at her, and she could hear her father's mocking voice: "It's in your blood…you'll never be true to any man."

"Did you have fun at the dance?" she asked Johnny hopefully.

"Until you left, I did."

"I had a great time."

"Before or after you left?"

Like a turning kaleidoscope when the colors darken and spread out, little slivers of light flashed in the centers of Johnny's eyes.

"Who were you with?" His voice was filled with dread.

"Morgan Todd. I think he likes me."

"How do you feel about him?"

"Ohhh, I think I like him, too. He's so strong and handsome. You're handsome, too, Johnny, but he's just so…"

"Don't fret, Judy. I can find my saddle without a stick. I don't need a lead rope."

She hadn't seen Johnny again except from a distance. A week later, when the riders rode into Fort Bowie for supplies, Morgan insulted Johnny, and they fought until both dropped from exhaustion. The next day Morgan issued a challenge, and Johnny rode away rather than meet him. In the barn the day he left, trying to stop him from riding away forever, Judy taunted him into kissing her. She hadn't seen him for three years after that, until the week her father died. And then he'd only come back for revenge.

304

Fighting back tears, Judy walked out of her room and down the hall to Tía's. No answer. She would find Tía. Uncertain, though, she hesitated by the back door. What could she say? *Give Johnny back. He belongs to me.* Burning with shame, Judy bowed her head. Tía already knew that was a lie. Everybody probably knew. Johnny didn't love her. He had built another spillway.

Overwhelmed by her loss, she rushed back to her room and lay down on her bed. Johnny was lost to her. Morgan Todd was lost to her. Even Grant Foreman was lost to her. The only thing she was good at was driving away the ones who might love her.

The pressure was building up in Judy's head. She couldn't think. From some deep reservoir, her mind tormented her with flashes of her life: Morgan's face filled with revulsion; Grant's eyes, looking like Johnny's had that night…So much torment. Was there some hidden evil in her that attracted all this misery? Maybe Bill Burkhart had been right all along.

Once, a long time ago, she had been peeling potatoes with Carmen—mindlessly peeling, not really paying attention. She'd cut into a potato and found a blackish-gray mold inside. She'd cut deeper and then deeper yet, hoping to save it, but the whole insides were gnarled and malignant. She had shuddered violently. On the outside the potato had looked like all the others, until she'd cut into it. Were people like that? Could their perfect outsides hide something gnarled and putrid inside?

Mumbling some excuse to Carmen, strangely disoriented by so much hidden ugliness, she had slipped out of the kitchen. Was she like that? Was that what her father saw when he looked at her with hatred in his bright blue eyes?

Judy tried not to be like her mother. She prayed to banish all her evil thoughts. Her mind was innocent, trusting…but her body…

She loved Johnny so much. She had always loved him. *"I want you…tonight."* His quiet words seeped into her bones, and cold spread out from her chest. He'd been trying to warn her, but she hadn't listened. He didn't love her anymore. Her mind refused to accept it.

Judy curled into a ball. Then a sound drew her attention. How long had she lain there? Had she slept? Shakily, she uncurled and sat up. It didn't matter if Johnny didn't love her. She needed him.

She stopped at the mirror and tried to peer through the darkness to see how she looked but quickly gave up and slipped out of her bedroom.

Outside, the stars shone like diamonds in a velvet black sky. The cooling night air was fresh and dry on her face, but it was not powerful enough by itself to heal her heart. The night sounds were louder than usual. Judy listened until she realized that the soldiers had added their racket to the already noisy night; men were snoring.

She hurried past the women's quarters to Johnny's cabin. No light showed in his window. She knocked but heard only the hollow echo of an empty room. The faint hope turned heavy inside her. Her legs felt weighted with lead. The heaviness grew worse. She needed Johnny. Where could he be? In the old days he sometimes went up into the hayloft. At the thought of finding him her mood lifted, and she ran toward the barn.

The barn was still lit. Someone must be there. One lantern hanging on the center support post cast a gold luminescence over the drowsy horses that stood in the stalls.

"Johnny!" Softly she called out and waited, but only the animal sounds—the soft snorts and stampings, the creaking of a stall as a horse leaned against old wood—greeted her straining ears. Smells of dry hay and fresh manure, horses and leather, were all strangely comforting, but they made her miss Johnny even more poignantly. She could wait for him. It would be better that way. Waiting wouldn't seem so bad in his cabin.

Judy left the barn and ran across the compound.

Dap Parker hated guard duty. When it was his turn he generally bribed someone to stand in for him, but tonight no one had been willing. Sunday nights were bad for that.

A horse appeared down the slope; he heard it before he saw it. The moon wasn't up yet, and it was near pitch black out there. He watched mostly with his ears, which had to strain to hear anything over the racket inside and outside the compound. Anyone who thought the plain was silent hadn't spent much time on one. Between the stock and the horses and the cats and dogs, he barely had time to listen to crickets and other pests. Add to that the continual snoring of men.

The rider was halfway up the slope before Dap picked him out. He waited a spell and then called out.

"Might want to stop right there." The horse halted. "Good thing you did that, 'cause you come any closer this scatter gun might blow a hole in you we could walk a dog through."

"It's me. Morgan Todd. Open the gate!"

"How'd you get through them Injuns?" Dap had known Morgan Todd when he was only a whiskey drummer.

"Didn't see any Injuns."

Dap shook his head as he climbed down the steps to comply. He swung the gate open just wide enough for Morgan to ride his horse through. "Well, if it ain't old petty shadow. There must not be a blamed 'pache anywhere around, or he'da smelt your prime scalp and gone after it."

Morgan rode in, and Dap climbed back up onto his platform. Morgan rode up toward the *casa grande*, and Dap settled down to watch again. But the edge had been taken off for him. If a man as careless as Morgan Todd could get through a countryside supposedly peppered with killing-mad Injuns, Dap didn't need to be standing no guard duty while other men slept.

Leon stood guard less than a hundred yards away. Dap walked over to borrow some snuff. "Who came in?" Leon asked. He'd been able to hear the rider coming, but he hadn't been able to hear who it was.

"Old pretty shadow hisself, Morgan Todd."

"What's he doing back here? There trouble?"

"Reckon he wants to continue that fight with Miss Judy." Every man in the bunkhouse knew Morgan Todd had looked like he'd been raised on sour milk when he'd left that morning, and they knew the reason had to be Miss Judy Burkhart. She was the only reason he ever came to Rancho la Reina.

Leon grinned. "Can't imagine why a smart woman like Miss Judy would put up with a slick like him for two minutes."

"He's built kinda far away from his corns. Women like tall men. They ain't given to short little shits like you."

"Why, you ain't half an inch taller than me," Leon protested.

"Never said I was."

"Well, I hope they're not too blamed noisy."

"I'll tell 'em not to wake you," Dap drawled, and walked back to his post.

To Morgan Todd, walking his horse from the front gate, Judy's yellow gown was easy to see in the moonlight. Morgan reined his horse and started to call out to her, but something stopped him. Maybe the direction she was headed. If she was running after that bastard Brago again...

He watched as Judy ran straight toward Johnny Brago's cabin. Rage flushed through him, and he kicked his tired horse into a gallop.

A few feet from Johnny's porch, Judy heard the sound of a horse and turned. Who could be riding a horse inside the gates at this time of night? The bunkhouse was dark.

Unafraid, she walked forward to meet the rider in front of the casa *grande*. She stopped in surprise.

"Morgan, is that you?"

"It damned sure ain't Brago."

"Why did you come back?"

The fury that had been driving him ever since she'd called him Johnny—aggravated by his catching her sneaking toward Brago's cabin—bubbled to the surface and erupted. "I'll be damned if I know," he sneered. "I guess I forgot what a little tramp you are."

Judy turned to leave. Morgan leaped off his horse, grabbed her, and jerked her around to face him. "I'm not through with you yet."

Judy looked from his angry face to her arm, where his steely fingers were bruising her soft white flesh. Mindful of the injured soldiers sleeping a hundred yards away, she kept her voice low. "Well, I'm through with you," she said. "If you came back here to tell me how rotten I am, I don't need it. You can go to hell, Morgan Todd!"

His face contorted with rage. She had never seen him this angry. Fear rippled along her spine.

Swallowing, strangely intimidated by his silent rage, Judy tried to back away from him, but his hand held her fast. "So…don't go to hell," she said. "It was only a suggestion." Hoping to distract him, she ventured, "You going to amputate my arm with your hand?"

Morgan didn't answer. He walked toward the barn, half dragging her. Judy tried to hold back, but he was too strong. When they were inside the barn, with the door closed behind them, he faced her.

"Why did you come back, Morgan?"

"Because we have unfinished business."

Feeling as if he had called her a tramp again, she flinched at his reference to business. Was that what she was to him? Business?

"Take it to someone else," she said defiantly. "I don't want your business anymore!"

"Like hell I will! I brought it to you, and you're gonna take care of it." This wasn't what Morgan had planned, but Judy had a way of infuriating him so bad that he forgot why he had come back.

Judy jerked furiously on her arm. "Let me go!"

Morgan's grip tightened.

Striking out with her other arm, Judy hit him a stinging blow. The pain that flashed in his eye almost blinded him. He hit Judy twice, jarring his arm with the force of his blows. Like a cornered bobcat, she slashed out at him with one taloned hand. Fire tore down Morgan's face and chest. Before he could catch her arm she hit him in the eye again. This time the pain was excruciating.

Blinded, Morgan clutched his face. Judy darted toward the door, but he wasn't about to let her get away from him. He leaped after her and caught her by the hair. When she turned to come at him with those claws again, he hit her, and she stumbled. He hit her again, and this time she fell and lay still. Morgan staggered to the door and leaned against it, panting. For the first time he noticed the agitation of the stamping, snorting horses in the surrounding stalls. One banged against his stall door, another reared and whinnied.

Staring blankly around him, Morgan realized what he had done. Dazed, he walked slowly back to Judy's side, knelt down, and touched her cheek. His hand trembled. Already swelling and bruised, the sweet curve of her neck was cool to his touch. Frightened, he searched her wrist for a pulse but found none.

Hands over his eyes, he stumbled to the door and then outside. This was all that bastard Brago's fault! He ran to Johnny's cabin, banged on the door, then lifted his face to the sky and shouted into the night: "Brago, you half-breed bastard. Come out and fight like a man!"

Johnny heard his name called and knew immediately who it was. At first he resisted knowing, because he didn't want to leave Tía's side, but he knew he had to.

Sighing, he coiled up into a sitting position. Fumbling in the darkness, he found his pants and pulled them on.

"Stay here," he said to Tía, touching her thigh.

"No!" Tía reached up and tried to pull him back down beside her, but he only kissed her hand and placed it firmly back on her chest.

"I have to go. I been puttin' this off too long already."

"Fighting over Judy?"

"It's gone way beyond that," he said, his voice grim.

He stood up and stuffed his shirttail into his trousers but didn't bother to fasten the buttons.

"I don't know why men have to prove they know how to die standing up. Morgan Todd sounds mad as hell, and you don't have any more weapon than a toothless gopher snake. If the Lord had wanted you to fight like a dog, he'da given you longer teeth and claws."

Johnny ignored Tía's angry chatter and walked away.

If she'd had something in her hand, Tía would have thrown it at Johnny's receding back. He disappeared into the dark shadows of the surrounded trees. Frustrated, half-angry, she picked up her crumpled gown, discarded so carelessly only moments ago, and pulled it over her head. *I was a fool to give in to him. One second he's making love to me, the next he's running off to fight over Judy...Ohhh!*

Buttons that had been opened easily under Johnny's deft fingers defied her trembling attempts to close them. Straining her ears for any sound, she struggled furiously with the buttons, wondering what would happen if she walked up to the *casa grande* buttoned up wrong after Morgan and Johnny awakened the entire compound with their brawling.

Out of nowhere a hand covered her mouth and nose. Once in place, it clamped like a vise, cutting off breath and sound. Tía struggled wildly.

"Hush! Do not cry out. Do you hear me, little tramp?"

Papa's familiar rough voice sent a shiver of fear down her spine. Heart thudding like a triphammer, Tía nodded vigorously. The suffocating pressure diminished, leaving her nose free so she could breathe. The part of Tía that had loved him so well and so long leaped with joy. He was alive! But her fear took precedence, and she remained silent.

"I did not pay for your upbringing so you could give yourself to some *gringo* at the first opportunity," he hissed, shaking her hard.

"Where is your sister?" he asked, releasing the pressure on her mouth.

"In the house..."

"And Burkhart?"

Tía hesitated, and immediately the painful pressure was back. This time his powerful hands circled her neck and began to squeeze the life out of her.

"Tell me," he commanded. He realized with surprise and a certain amount of pride that he could kill her if need be.

Blackness flooded her senses. From a distance, Tía heard a shot. The sound broke the stillness so suddenly that birds, sleeping in trees overhead, were startled into flight. The pressure on her throat was gone as suddenly as it had come.

"I have no time. Tell me quickly."

Tía's mind was curiously occupied. She could think of nothing except Johnny! Had Morgan killed him? Was that what the shot meant?

"Tell me!" he growled, shaking her.

"He...he is in Tombstone," Tía stammered. Surely it was all right to admit that much. Before Papa could reach there, Steve would be gone.

His hand fell away from her neck. "So, *you* have inherited Rancho la

Reina. It is ironic that now we are both rich beyond our wildest dreams, you with your white man's stolen ranch and me with the pompous *gringo*'s silver...Too bad you will not be able to enjoy it, *niña*."

Papa's tone was casual, almost as if they were old friends discussing items of common interest. A chill of apprehension sent a shiver through Tía's body. Mateo's dark eyes glittered in the dim light that filtered down through the trees. She'd been a fool to run off at the mouth. Papa would kill Steve if he found him. It would be her fault.

Mateo took her by the arm and dragged her toward the back wall of the compound. Tía struggled against him. "No...Papa!"

Unexpectedly he stopped. Listening, he shushed her with a warning hand and waited. Too close to them, a heavy masculine voice shouted, "Spread out!"

"I heard something just now!" a voice answered.

The sound of men running toward them caused Tía's heart to lurch. Papa's hand dropped away from her arm.

Tía turned toward the sound, then back toward Papa, but he was gone; the shadows had engulfed him.

Other men shouted. Suddenly they were upon her. Surrounded by soldiers, all asking questions at once, Tía was filled with fear and the realization that to cause all this commotion, surely someone had died. Johnny hadn't been wearing a gun. Was it Johnny, then? Were they looking for his killer?

Weak with dread, Tía allowed herself to be lead back toward the *casa grande*.

CHAPTER THIRTY

Reaching the clearing around the *casa grande* and its companion buildings, Tía broke away from the soldiers. Ignoring their yells, she ran until she reached Johnny's side.

Facing Captain Rutledge, his hands manacled behind his back, Johnny stood between two soldiers who held his elbows.

Pale of face and hugging her dressing robe, Andrea stood at Johnny's side.

"I didn't shoot him," Johnny said firmly. "He was already down when I got here."

"I suppose this isn't your gun, either?" Rutledge asked gruffly.

"I picked the gun up off the ground because I wasn't wearing one. I thought I might need it. Then I saw it was my gun."

"Captain," Tía blurted. "He was with me. He didn't have a gun."

Rutledge turned sharp eyes upon her. He seemed to see everything— her state of dishabille, her fear—but somehow nothing could cower her now.

"He was with you when the shot was fired?"

Tía swallowed. "Well, no, but—"

"Miss Marlowe, we all heard Todd yelling. There was a good two minutes between the yell and the shot. Brago had plenty of time to get his gun and shoot Todd." Satisfied, Rutledge motioned his soldiers to take Johnny away.

"No...please," Tía began, glancing at her sister for support. Andrea shot Tía a warning look.

"Take him to our camp," Rutledge said to the men on either side of Johnny. He turned back to Tía. "I appreciate your willingness to help, but it isn't necessary. We'll hold him for Johnny Behan in Tombstone. Don't concern yourself with Brago. He's a bad penny. I'm sure this isn't his first break with the law. Behan probably has a warrant for his arrest."

"Please, could I speak to him privately?"

"No. It's late, miss. Better go inside," he said brusquely. Rutledge gave Andrea a look that clearly said Tía was being foolishly headstrong and should be given a talking-to.

"Captain, there was another man here," Tía blurted. "A man who doesn't belong here. He…he…threatened me. He was going to kidnap me. Only your men frightened him away. Maybe he or one of his band shot Mr. Todd."

Sighing at so flagrant a fabrication, Rutledge shook his head. "Miss Marlowe, Brago and Todd were sworn enemies. This was a long-standing feud. Todd came here to kill Brago. Unfortunately, Brago got him first." Impatiently he turned to motion his men away with Brago. "Take him."

"Captain," Andrea interposed, "please let her speak to Mr. Brago. I also need to discuss some matters with him. He is my foreman. With my brother away, you can see my problem." The lies came easily out of her mouth. It seemed wiser not to confuse Rutledge with the truth at a time like this.

Rutledge liked quick resolutions, but he didn't want to alienate the Burkharts. He turned to the soldiers flanking Johnny. "Stay with him," he said. Bowing to Andrea, he stalked over to where two soldiers knelt beside Morgan Todd. Andrea followed him.

"How is he?" Rutledge asked.

The soldier looked up. "Bleeding heavy. He needs a doctor."

"Captain," Andrea said quickly, "Carmen is good with injuries. Perhaps she could take care of him tonight."

Puffing out his chest, Rutledge shook his head. "These men are professional soldiers, Miss Burkhart. They've seen an injury or two in their time. I appreciate your concern, but I assure you it isn't necessary."

Andrea watched as the men placed Morgan on a makeshift stretcher and carried him off in the direction of the soldier's camp. If all he had between him and death was Rutledge's concern, Andrea knew he didn't stand a chance. Rutledge didn't like Morgan any more than he liked Johnny.

Masking her growing anxiety, she returned to Tía's side. Strain apparent in her face, Tía stood close to Johnny. Andrea didn't like the way her sister pressed so close to Johnny. To her the man looked too much like Papa. He would be nothing but trouble to Tía. Poor misguided child. She wanted to reach out and pull her sister into her arms, but she only stationed herself between Tía and the soldiers who guarded Johnny from a distance of five feet.

At Andrea's approach, Tía stopped whispering in Johnny's ear and looked over, pleading for more time. Andrea ignored the unspoken request. She had to know.

"Tía, you said someone tried to take you away."

The look of mingled fear and shame Tía shot her was answer enough. "*El Gato Negro*," she whispered.

Johnny, his dark eyes narrowing, turned to look at Tía. "He came here for you?"

"I don't know if that's why he came here, but he tried to take me with him. The soldiers ran up, and he took off, probably over the wall."

"Should we tell Rutledge?" asked Andrea.

"I doubt he'd hear it," Johnny reasoned.

He turned to Tía. "Tell me what happened."

Tía told him everything she could remember.

"He said silver, not just money?" Johnny asked.

"Yes."

"He said pompous *gringo*? You're sure?" He turned to Andrea. "I think Steve is in grave danger."

"But why?"

"Russ Sloan is the one man in these parts who perfectly fits the bill. And he was leading a mule train carrying a lot of silver. If Sloan didn't make it, there's a good chance Steve won't, either."

"Oh, no!" Andrea cried, realizing all her apprehensions about the trip were validated. "What can we do?"

"We can try to warn him," he said, remembering Tía's earlier suggestion.

Andrea blanched. The thought of sending a lone rider out at night…"Is it safe? I mean…"

"I don't know. Morgan made it through. It's our only chance."

"What about you?"

"There's nothing you can do for me now. This is the chance Rutledge has been waiting for."

"I'll send to Tombstone for an attorney. Steve can bring one back with him. We'll…"

A smile flitted across Johnny's dark face. Cold fingers wrapped themselves around Tía's heart. Rutledge *did* hate Johnny. She'd seen proof of that at the dinner table. Helpless and manacled, Johnny didn't have a chance. Rutledge could keep him, and if Morgan Todd died, they could hang him.

Defiantly, Tía stepped close to Johnny, went up on tiptoe, and pulled his head down to kiss him. All that mattered was that he was in danger. Holding his head, moving her lips softly against his, trying to memorize that fierce, sweet thrill that washed through her when he touched her, she lost track of where they were, the soldiers watching, Andrea…

"Hell!" One of the men grabbed Johnny by the arm and pulled him away. "Come on, Casanova!" he growled. Turning Johnny roughly, they led him away.

Andrea put her arm around Tía protectively. "Come inside, baby. He'll be all right," she said. "Come along now. I need to write a letter to Steve. We'll get that done, and then we can send a messenger to warn him."

Andrea surprised Tía with her apparent understanding. Maybe her sister had decided Johnny wasn't so bad. Or else being in love had mellowed her.

At the back door Tía stopped and looked around the empty dining room. A strange sense of foreboding prickled at her consciousness. It wasn't like Judy to miss any type of excitement. "Have you seen Judy?"

"She's probably in her room." Glancing around to be sure they were alone, Andrea pulled Tía inside and closed the door. "It was Papa, wasn't it?"

"Yes! He terrified me! He was going to take me with him." Tía shuddered, remembering her fear.

"If he hurts Steve…" Andrea stopped, too weak to continue. Once, a long time ago, Mama had fought with Papa, and he had pushed her into the bedroom. Andrea had listened at the door to what had sounded like a fight. Ever since that night she had feared her father.

"He knows everything."

"What did you tell him about Steve?"

"Only that he was in Tombstone."

Fear and helplessness warred for supremacy in Andrea. It wouldn't matter what anyone said now. If Papa wanted to kill Steve, no one could stop him. He was a madman. "It doesn't matter. Go see about Judy."

Tía checked Judy's room and rushed back to the parlor. "She's not there. I'm going to look for her." She ran to the bunkhouse, where two dozen men still lounged on the long porch.

"Have you seen Judy?" A chorus of replies, all negative, greeted her. "Help me look for her, please!"

Grumbling but excited, the men spread out. Tía ran to Johnny's cabin, but it was empty. Everything was as it had been earlier when she'd stood so uncertainly on the small porch, fighting with him. She glanced in the open door of the Mexican women's quarters, then, hearing the clamor of men's voices as they spread into the far corners of the enclosure, she remembered the barn.

Tía ran across the compound to the barn. Panting with exertion, she tugged the sagging door open enough to slip inside. The air was still and warm. The barn was dimly lit by a lantern that hung on a support post. *The door had been open.* Alarmed, Tía stopped. Steve always kept the doors closed and the lanterns out after dark. Frightened, she started to back outside, then stopped. Maybe Judy had left it ajar…

"Judy?…" Her voice sounded hollow.

"Over here."

Tía jumped. Her eyes scanned the darkness outside the cone of light, groping for the source of that low voice.

In the shadows at the outermost edge of a dim lantern's light, she saw Grant Foreman, kneeling beside a crumpled form in a yellow gown. Tía rushed to his side.

"She's dead," he said, not looking at Tía.

"Oh, noooo." Holding her stomach, Tía doubled over and moaned. Now that her eyes were adjusting to the dimness, she could see Grant's stunned face. Judy couldn't die. Tía's mind rejected the possibility. Her trembling hand reached out to touch Judy, to deny the truth of his statement.

"She's dead," Grant said quietly.

Tía's hand pressed against Judy's throat. A tiny pulse throbbed beneath her fingertips. Eyes widening, she took Grant's cold hand and forced it against Judy's throat. "She's alive! Feel it?"

"Thank God!" he gasped. Forgetting his own injury, Grant gathered Judy into his arms and stood up. Blackness almost filled his head, but he dragged in air as fast as he could. Gradually his head cleared. Tía ran and tugged the door open, and Grant followed her out into the cooler night air.

"We found her!" Tía shouted, running ahead of him toward the *casa grande.* "We found her!"

For a few minutes pandemonium reigned as Carmen and Cruz—crossing themselves, muttering prayers—gathered the needed supplies to deal with the evening's third emergency.

Silently cursing his own wound, which had weakened him, Grant staggered in and laid Judy on the long couch. Kneeling beside her, he carefully parted Judy's blood-soaked hair to peer at her scalp.

"Why doesn't she wake up?" Tía asked anxiously.

Andrea stepped close and placed her hand on Judy's forehead. "Concussion, maybe. Where was she?"

"In the barn. Do you think Morgan Todd...did this?" she asked, pointing to Judy. "And that's why Johnny..."

Sharply, Andrea looked at Tía. "I thought you said Johnny was with you."

"He was, but he could have found her and then gone after Mr. Todd."

"That doesn't make any sense. Why would Johnny run past Morgan, across the whole compound to the barn?"

Organized at last, Carmen and Cruz waved them aside. They worked over Judy quietly and efficiently. Grant sagged into one of the Morris chairs. Tía paced. Andrea finished her letter to Steve, placed it in an envelope, and then walked quickly to the bunkhouse.

Stepping onto the porch, she stopped at the door. In various stages of undress, men scrambled for their pants, shirts, shoes. Turning her back, Andrea counted to twenty and then stepped inside. She wasted few words in telling them what she needed and how dangerous the mission could be, but immediately a slender young towhead stepped forward.

"I'll go, Miss Burkhart," he said, hastily buttoning the shirt he had just pulled on, his southern drawl quite pronounced.

He looked too young for such a dangerous mission. "What's your name?"

"Snake Peterson, ma'am."

"You realize this may be dangerous."

"Yes, ma'am." Sheepishly Snake scratched his head. "But you see, ma'am, I got this gal in Tombstone, and I ain't seen hide nor hair of her in nigh onto three weeks. I'd ride through Chatto and Geronimo both, beggin' your pardon, ma'am. They don't call me Snake for nothin'. I kin slip right through, no problem at all, ma'am."

Andrea joined in the laughter. "Hell!" Dap called out. "They call you snake 'cause you're always slippin' outa work!"

That caused another uproar. When the room quieted, Andrea smiled at Snake. "Thank you, Snake. I'm very grateful to you. Please give this letter to Steve, and you may stay in Tombstone until you can safely come back with him. Warn him that it may not be soon."

"Thank you, ma'am!" Snake gathered up his hat and a gunbelt and bolted for the door. Yipping his excitement, he ran all the way to the barn.

CHAPTER THIRTY-ONE

The women were all clustered around Judy. Tía glanced up. Seeing Andrea, she left the group to meet her sister at the door.

"How's Judy?" Andrea asked.

"I don't know. She doesn't move or blink or anything. She just lies there. Carmen and Cruz have tended every bruise and cut, but none of them seems bad enough to keep her out like this."

"That's the way a concussion acts. It swells on the inside instead of the outside."

"How's Morgan? Will he live?"

Andrea sighed. "I don't know. He was bleeding heavily, and the man who was supposed to be taking care of him looked as scared as I felt. I hope he knows what he's doing…"

"Can't we do something? Take him to the fort?"

"I heard Rutledge tell one of the men it was too risky."

"I thought Apaches didn't attack at night."

"Maybe that's an old wives' tale."

"Probably." Tía sighed. "Now what are we going to do?"

"Pray."

The women took turns sitting beside Judy's still form. Grant Foreman paced with Andrea until Tía asked him to walk her down to see how Morgan was faring. Grant found a lantern.

His face shiny with sweat, Morgan lay on a blanket. When Tía knelt beside him, he opened his eyes. They were dark and glazed. Taking a handkerchief out of her skirt pocket, she wiped Morgan's face. Grant set the lantern on the ground nearby.

"They aren't doing anything for him," she whispered angrily to Grant, flashing a wrathful look at the man who was standing guard over the sleeping soldiers.

Morgan smiled weakly. "They can't…it doesn't matter," he whispered. "I'm dying…"

"You're not dying!" Tía said fiercely. "We're taking you to the fort in the morning. There's a doctor there. He'll fix you."

Morgan shook his head. "No. I won't make it till morning. Doesn't matter anyhow. I don't mind dying. I just wish to hell it didn't hurt so goddamned bad, even if I do deserve it."

"Did you hurt Judy?"

Morgan's eyes closed. Grimacing, he swallowed. "I killed her."

"No. She's alive."

His eyes opened, and he searched her face for deception. Finding none, he cried out, "Thank God!"

"What happened, Mr. Todd? Can you tell me?"

"I came back…to ask her to marry me, but I caught her going into Johnny's cabin. We argued. She ran, and I caught her…she hit me in the eye. I was so furious that I started hitting her hard…and couldn't stop…I didn't mean to hurt her."

He stopped. Pressing his hands to his stomach, he shivered with the pain that tore through him.

"It's okay. Don't talk."

"I thought I killed her. I blamed Brago, because we fought over him. I went after him. I guess he got me first."

"Are you sure it was him?"

"Who else?"

"Did you see him?"

"No." Shivering, he gritted his teeth. Tía lifted the lantern high enough to see. The bandage they had wound around his middle was soaked through with blood.

"Grant, I'm going to stay here with him. Go up to the house and bring more blankets and a pan of water with a washcloth."

The desert had cooled enough and the ranch was high enough that after midnight the nights were almost as cool as the days were hot. He was shivering as much from cold as shock. Stupid men! While Grant was gone, she held Morgan's hand and wiped the dampness from his face. The perspiration was from pain, not heat. Grant returned, and she covered Morgan with the blankets and used the wet cloth to moisten his dry mouth.

"Thank you, ma'am."

"Try to sleep. You must conserve your strength." Morgan Todd must not die, because if he died they would surely hang Johnny.

Rutledge walked over and stood above her. Tía came to her feet.

"How is he?" he asked. His tone was tinged with anger, as if she were defying him.

"He's bleeding to death, that's how he is."

"Uh-huh. Well, that's too bad," he said a little more kindly. Cursing the meagerness of the flickering lantern's light, Tía peered into the captain's face. An idea came to her. Judy had said Rutledge was always trying to talk to her, asking her questions, following her around. Maybe he was secretly in love with Judy. It was worth a try.

"Too bad we can't make it to the fort. A doctor might be able to save Judy."

"Judy?" Startled, Rutledge leaned close. "What's wrong with Judy?"

"We don't know. She's in a coma. We don't know how to help her."

"A coma? How did it happen? Was it Morgan Todd or Johnny Brago? By God, I'll—"

"No…no!" She hadn't meant to lie, but his sudden anger frightened her into it. "She fell out of the hayloft." She prayed he couldn't read her guilt on her face. But Rutledge had already turned away and was striding toward the *casa grande.*

"Todd got a bargain in you," Johnny said softly.

Tía's heart leaped into her throat. Johnny! Oh, no! He had been there the whole time, listening to her and Morgan Todd. Since she'd lied to protect him, now Johnny probably thought he'd been right all along in his suspicions about her and Todd.

Another thought took precedence over her feelings for Johnny. At the *casa grande,* they'd tell Rutledge the truth. Why had she lied? Rutledge wouldn't have killed Morgan on the spot.

Then she remembered that fortunately they didn't know the truth. No one outside herself and Grant knew that Morgan Todd was the one who had beaten Judy. By the time everyone found out, Morgan would be in Fort Bowie where he could get medical help, Judy would be conscious, and Johnny would be safe.

"How's Judy?" he asked.

Tía walked to Johnny's side and dropped to her knees. Johnny was lying in a bedroll, one arm under his head. Even as a prisoner he managed to look relaxed. In the dim lantern light his eyes were flat black and as unresponsive as a brick wall.

"She's in a coma. At first we thought she was dead. She was hit pretty hard."

"Why did you lie to the captain?"

"I don't know," Tía groaned. "I was afraid he would kill Mr. Todd and you'd get the blame."

Johnny shook his head. "Thanks for the thought, but if he killed

Morgan, most likely he'd get the blame. I'd be off the hook, Morgan would be out of his misery, and I'd be free and a sight happier." The lantern flickered in the wind and almost went out.

Johnny was mad. Tía wouldn't have been able to tell by his words, which even mad were carefully chosen not to embarrass her, but she knew. Frustrated, she scowled into the darkness. "Well, I don't want anybody to kill anybody!"

"Especially not your lover…"

"He's not my lover! You should know that by now."

The sentry walked over and stopped beside them. "The captain don't allow no consorting with the prisoner, ma'am."

Tía had the urge to plead with the man, but his face was almost as closed against her as Johnny's. Defeated by Johnny's stubbornness and too tired to argue with either of them, she stood up and stalked back to the house.

Judy was still unconscious. Everyone else was running around packing. Andrea stopped to explain. "We're taking Judy to the fort."

Tía started to ask a question, but a shout from outside interrupted her. Andrea rushed to the front door.

"Rider coming in!" Voices along the path from the front gate picked up the message. Tía and Andrea rushed out the front door and ran as fast as they could, covering the distance to the front gate in record time.

As Tía panted to a stop, the gates swung open. One of the sentries yelled for the women to stay back, but it was too late. Tía had already seen. Her hand flew to her mouth to stifle a scream.

Andrea turned away, reaching instinctively for her sister. Men ran forward to stop the runaway horse. Others clustered around the heaving animal, blocking the women's view. The silence was broken only by the blowing of the brindled dun.

"Is it?…"

"Stand back!"

"Reckon we don't want to send any more messengers."

"What does it mean?" Andrea asked of Rutledge over Tía's shoulder. "Is he…is he dead?"

Rutledge nodded. "Come away."

Dap was less considerate. "Wal, I reckon he's dead all right, ma'am. They sent us the hoss and the body, but them red devils kept his scalp. I almost volunteered to go myself. Sure glad I didn't. I was that close to going, too."

Andrea doubled over, retching. Tía gathered her sister's skirts and pulled them out of the way. After the spasms passed, she took Andrea's arm and tried to get her to walk back to the house.

"It's not your fault. It's not!" Tía whispered fiercely.

"Oh, Mother of God! Forgive me! That poor boy! I didn't know. I didn't think…"

"Andrea, you couldn't know."

"I was only thinking of myself…and Steve…"

"Please, Andrea, come inside."

"I sent him out there. I sent him…"

Rutledge cleared his throat self-consciously. "Miss Marlowe is right, Miss Burkhart. You couldn't have known. I hate to interfere when you're feeling so bad, but we have to leave now. There is no time to lose. They must be south of here. They may be moving this way right now. There is no safety here now. We must be going."

Andrea straightened with an effort. "We're no longer safe here?"

"No, ma'am. Bill Burkhart was too ambitious when he built this wall. Built it too big. He wasn't a military man, obviously. It would take two hundred men to defend this enclosure effectively. He's been lucky. Fort Bowie always protected him from any major attack, but if Chatto and Geronimo come in force…together…" Rutledge shook his head. "You've got a quarter mile of wall to protect. The only thing in its favor is that it sits at the top of a ground swell, and there's no cover to speak of outside the walls. Even so, it couldn't be defended against a determined attack if they come in numbers. If you want to save the rest of your people, you'll have them ready to move out in ten minutes."

CHAPTER THIRTY-TWO

Almost full, the moon was so bright it cast an eerie, silvery luminescence over the gently rolling landscape. A chill wind had come up; it made dry, rustling sounds against the occasional squatty trees and bushes as the party bound for Fort Bowie passed.

Tía rode in the back of the buckboard between Judy and Morgan. Judy was still unconscious, but Morgan was awake and in a great deal of pain. Every jolt of the wheels over the rutted path unleashed new waves of agony. He clamped his jaws tight and endured it as best he could.

Solicitously Tía leaned over him, wiping streams of perspiration off his shiny face, only to have new moisture break.

"Is there anything I can do?" she offered.

"Shoot me," he muttered.

The wagon hit a chuckhole, and Morgan groaned. Johnny glanced sharply in Tía's direction, making her wonder if she had made a noise as well. His horse's reins tied securely to the tailgate, he and his guard rode behind the buckboard that carried Morgan and her.

Even with his wrists manacled behind his back he rode with easy grace, his lean warrior's body becoming one with his horse. In that moment she would have given anything to be able to read the expression in his eyes. She cursed the darkness. But…perhaps it was just as well.

They traveled the three miles to the fort without incident. In the moonlight the fort looked deserted. It was not much bigger than the Burkhart compound, but the brick-and-mortar walls were twelve feet high and over a foot thick, with cannons mounted at strategic locations overlooking all sides.

Inside, the structure was surrounded on three sides by stores and buildings, and the final part of the quad familiar to many forts displayed a cannon and the flag. According to Captain Rutledge, Fort Bowie's barracks housed more than two hundred soldiers. The quad was so brightly lit by kerosene lamps that Tía could make out the general merchandise store, canteen, leather goods store, a shoe and bootery, and the post office. Sounds of hilarity and loud male voices rose from the canteen. The other stores were closed.

The driver stopped the wagon in front of a one-story barracks. A sign overhead read HOSPITAL. From inside, men raced to respond to the driver's yell. Grumbling, they came out with a stretcher. Their irritation at being disturbed dissipated at the sight of Tía. Clumsy and deferential, they were like little boys with an unexpected guest. Carefully, following Tía's instructions, they loaded Judy onto the stretcher and carried her inside. When they lifted Morgan onto the stretcher he finally blacked out. With a helping hand from the buckboard driver, Tía scrambled down and followed them inside.

Dr. Potter, a thin man with cold, dispassionate eyes, examined Judy quickly and carefully attended to Morgan Todd. Rutledge's wounded soldiers began arriving on foot and on stretcher. Potter scowled at the ragtag collection of sloppily bandaged men, then looked back down at Morgan.

"How long has he been bleeding like this?"

"Since about ten o'clock tonight." Tía bit her lip. "Can you do something?"

"I can go in and tie off the bleeders, but he may be too far gone to survive it." His completely indifferent response shocked Tía. How could he talk about a man dying with so little concern? Didn't he care?

"Then please do it," she said.

"I might as well," Potter said irritably. "He can't last this way." He felt Morgan's wrist again; his pulse was fast and thready. His chest barely moved. He hated gut wounds. He especially hated them at this time of night with a waiting room full of patients. Surgery was probably a waste of time, but the girl wouldn't understand if he just put him in a bed with a bowl under it to catch the blood. The bastard was unconscious now and probably grateful for it. At last Potter straightened.

"All right. I'll operate. He's pretty important to you, huh?"

"Yes, both of them," she said, pointing to Judy. Potter examined the girl again. He struck a match and watched her pupils. One contracted, the other didn't. Concussion all right. He took her pulse and examined the cuts and bruises on her face and head.

"Either a concussion or a cerebral hemorrhage from one of the blows to the head," he said dispassionately.

"Will she be all right?" Tía asked. Surely, if he knew what to call it, he should know how to save her.

Potter shook his head. "I don't know. It depends on too many things I don't have any control over: how bad it is on the inside. I have no idea," he said, his voice reflecting irritation.

"But surely—"

"There's nothing I can do for her. But I will see what I can do for him. Keep him quiet. If he comes to, let one of my men know, and he'll give him something for the pain. I'll get back to him as soon as I can."

Tía was shaken by the man's brusqueness. But at least he was going to help Morgan.

She stayed until all the wounded had been treated and the surgery on Morgan Todd had been performed. Except for the snoring men, the hospital was quiet. Outside, the fort was quiet as well. Tía leaned over Judy's still form, pressing a cool rag to her forehead. Potter walked tiredly into the middle of the barracks and stopped beside her.

Frightened, Tía stood up. Her eyes searched the doctor's tired face. "Is he?..."

"He's alive, but that's all. I tied off everything I could find, mopped out what I could of the blood, and took out the bullet, but I have to tell you I lose more than I save in surgery." Sighing, he shook his head and sat down on one of the beds. The soldier in the bed stirred slightly.

"How awful for you," Tía said softly.

Surprised by her empathy, Potter looked quickly away. By the time he looked back, a layer of impersonal efficiency had peeled away. He looked very tired suddenly. "Get some rest if you can, miss. I'll leave a man here to take care of them for you."

"I can stay."

"It's not necessary. An orderly has to be here anyway."

Tía gathered up her things. "Thank you for trying."

Potter nodded and turned away.

Tía fount Grant Foreman lying on a blanket just outside the hospital's front door. She was tired and hungry and drained, but she stopped beside him. The eastern horizon was already a pale, pearly gray.

"How are you doing?"

Slowly, as if he were trying to hide how difficult it was for him to move, he sat up. "I'm okay. How's Judy?"

"The same." Tía paused. She was wondering why he hadn't been inside with Judy. It wasn't like him to stay away when Judy was in need. Leaning back against the adobe wall, she slid down beside Grant.

"I guess you and Judy talk a lot...you're real close to her."

"What are you getting at?" Grant said suspiciously.

"You're Judy's friend. I want you to stay with her and take care of her and Mr. Todd, too, if you will."

"Why? You going somewhere?"

"If I tell you something in strictest secrecy, will you guard it with your life?"

Grant's gray eyes were level and clear. Looking into their depths, Tía knew she could trust him completely.

"Better not trust me," he said, looking away.

Instinctively she ignored his warning. Leaning close, she whispered into his ear, "We're going to break Johnny out of jail so we can go warn Steve."

"How?"

"I don't know, exactly. I just decided this minute to do it."

Grant searched her face and saw she was serious. He knew he should go to Rutledge and turn himself in before someone got hurt trying to break Johnny out of jail. "Well, if you need any help, let me know."

"You're not well yourself. We'll manage, if you'll stay here and take care of them for us. Will you?"

Avoiding Tía's pleading eyes, Grant stared down at his feet. He wanted to stay near Judy. He would give anything if he could, but he didn't have the right. Judy didn't want him around anymore. She had deliberately tried to run him off. If he had any pride at all, he would ride away, except he couldn't do that with good conscience. He had shot Morgan Todd for killing Judy, and he had kept silent when he'd found out they had arrested Johnny, partly because he resented the rotten way Johnny had treated Judy and partly because he was in shock from believing Judy dead. Now he knew he had to confess everything, but he couldn't.

"Grant, please?"

Baffled, sick with his own hurt, Grant closed his eyes. Judy was like a sickness in him. Ever since he had seen her that first time, he had been infected. She had become a part of him—like the color of his eyes and the shape of his hands. He loved her so much that if he rode away, he would probably die of it. Now he had probably killed a man for her— two men if Johnny died—and if he confessed, he wouldn't be there if Judy needed him. He would be in jail. Or hanged.

"Grant, will you?"

"Yes," he said, ashamed of himself, his weakness.

His fine gray eyes were bleak. Tía longed to do something for him, but she didn't know of anything that would help.

"Judy needs you now. She needs all of us. We can't let her down."

Grant looked confused. "Why are you suddenly so concerned about Judy?"

"Why not?" Tía asked, frowning.

"We saw you kissing Johnny."

"I knew she saw us."

"It hurt her bad. Real bad."

A hard lump swelled in Tía's throat. She looked away, avoiding his eyes. "I know."

Grant looked resigned. "I better go. Judy doesn't like to be alone in the dark."

CHAPTER THIRTY-THREE

"Hello, Captain."

Rutledge looked up to see Andrea Burkhart standing in his doorway, a warm smile on her pretty face.

"What...oh...excuse me," he said, coming to his feet. Hiding his confusion, he walked carefully around his desk. He had been in a daze ever since he'd found out Judy Burkhart had been hurt. Doc Potter had been little help. According to him, there was very little anyone could do for her; she would wake up, or stay in a coma, or die.

"Uh, yes, come in," he stammered, pulling himself together. "Sit, please. You look amazingly well for all you've been through last night and this morning."

Smiling, Andrea swept her skirts aside as she seated herself in the chair he had offered her. "Why, thank you, Captain. I must say, you look even more important in your office."

Rutledge preened visibly. "I'm a collector, actually," he said, waving his arm at the memorabilia from numerous campaigns. "But I'm sure you didn't come here to admire my collection. What can I do for you?"

"I need a favor. I have obtained the services of an attorney for my foreman. I would like permission for him to see Mr. Brago today."

"Today?" he asked, frowning. "There are no attorneys here. And at present no need for an attorney. I took the precaution of holding Brago, and I've every intention of sending word to Marshal Behan in Tombstone as soon as the Indians settle down, but there'll be no trial here. The military has no jurisdiction to try Brago. That will be taken care of by the territorial authorities."

"I'm sure that's all quite true, Captain, but it seemed to me that a good attorney could conduct the investigation on behalf of the accused. And I did happen onto an attorney. Are you acquainted with a Mr. Farraday, Captain?"

"Farraday. Not Jethrow Farraday, surely?"

"One and the same," she said, hoping she sounded tremendously pleased with herself.

"Excuse me, Miss Burkhart, but the man is disreputable. I hesitate to mention this, but Farraday was run out of Tombstone for public drunkenness. He only stopped here because his money ran out and he was forcibly ejected from the stagecoach. I would be remiss if I were not completely truthful in this regard. He is the last man in the world you should depend on if you are in need of an attorney."

Andrea lifted an elegantly curved brow, and Rutledge's confusion deepened. She smiled.

"But madam...if you wish to..." His words trailed off. He was hopelessly lost.

With a shake of her head and a gesture of her hand, Andrea tossed her hair back. Now she was glad that they had not told Rutledge the truth about their switch. "The man is important to my housekeeper, Captain, not to me. The girl must be humored, but frankly, just between the two of us, Brago has been nothing but trouble since he arrived."

"Ahhh!" he breathed, settling back into his chair and allowing his admiration to show in his eyes. Here at last was a female after his own heart. Too bad Judy was not as discerning a judge of character as this one.

"Ahem! Well! I will leave word at the stockade for them to admit Farraday whenever he is...umm...ready."

"Thank you, Captain. You have been most helpful," she said, moving her reticule from her right hand to her left. They rose as one. Rutledge took her hand in his, leaned forward to press his lips against it, then bowed again, deeply. "My pleasure, Miss Burkhart. You show rare good sense for one so lovely and so young."

Andrea smiled her thanks. For one moment they were co-conspirators. Then she turned, her satin skirts rustling. "Oh, Captain, I forgot to mention that we will be leaving today."

The smile died on his lips. "Leaving? That's hardly wise, Miss Burkhart," he said stiffly, all soldier again.

Andrea smiled graciously. "Please call me Andrea, Captain." She sighed. "I know you are right, but my brother is in a great deal of danger. I will leave Grant Foreman here with Judy to see to her needs. The rest of us are going to try to intercept Steve. I would appreciate it very much if you could use your influence to delay Mr. Brago's trial until we return."

Rutledge frowned. "As I've said, I have no authority in civil matters, Miss Burkhart. Of course, I have no idea when I will be able to notify Behan, nor when he may come for Mr. Brago. A great deal depends upon whether or not Mr. Todd dies. If he does, I'm sure the authorities will move rather quickly. The circuit judge has been known to respect my wishes on occasion. He may be willing to delay the trial if I asked him to, but I fear for your safety."

"Captain, we have reason to believe that the worst threat to my brother is not from Indians but from bandits."

"Bandits?"

"*El Gato Negro*," she said significantly.

"Good God! *El Gato Negro!* Are you sure? Damnation! Every soldier in the territory would be put at your disposal if that were true. *And* if we were not already engaged on a more pressing campaign. Unfortunately Captain Rodgers needs every man jack of us here. The timing couldn't be worse."

"I respect your problems, Captain. I only ask the same consideration for my own. My brother is in grave danger. We believe Mr. Sloan and his entire mule train were wiped out, every man killed. I do not want to risk a similar fate befalling my brother. I don't suppose you would consider releasing Mr. Brago, just until we find Steve?"

"Out of the question. I'm sorry," he said.

Disappointed, Andrea shrugged. "You know your job, I'm sure. Well, wish us luck?"

"You'll need more than luck, Miss Burkhart. You'll need a miracle."

"Perhaps…"

Rutledge shook his head. "Send the men, but do not go yourself. There is too much danger."

"I'm afraid I must go. With my foreman in jail there is no one else I trust to take charge."

"I see," he said grudgingly.

"Thank you, Captain. We will be heavily armed. Please do not worry. I have high hopes for our success."

"I wish I could share them."

Rutledge watched Andrea leave. He went personally to the stockade to give the instructions to admit Farraday whenever he presented himself.

Andrea returned to the room she shared with Tía and found her sister awake and dressed after a six-hour nap. "Feeling better?"

"Yes. I'm going to see about Judy and Mr. Todd."

"I was there an hour ago. No change."

"I know." Tía sighed. "I just have to check."

"Meet me here soon. It's almost time."

Morgan Todd was awake. His eyes were open and filled with anguish. Sweat beaded his face. His hands clenched and unclenched, only to clench again. Tía leaned close to him. "Have you been in pain long?"

Morgan nodded.

Tía found the orderly in a small office at the back of the ward and asked him to give Morgan something for pain.

The orderly picked up a bottle of laudanum and followed Tía back to Morgan's bed. Morgan sipped the bitter liquid, shuddered, and closed his eyes. The pain must have eased a little after a while because he flashed Tía a look of gratitude.

Two dozen wounded men occupied the beds in the long barracks. For privacy Judy had been moved to the front of the ward next to the window. They had curtained off a small area around her bed with light canvas draped over ropes. Except where the bruises discolored it, her face was as white as the sheet covering her. Her breathing was almost imperceptible. Grant Foreman sat beside her, his face glum.

"How's Judy?"

"Still breathing in and out."

"Why don't you go get something to eat. I'll stay with her for a while."

Grant remained motionless. Tía had lied about her identity, switched places with her sister to trick Judy, and kissed Judy's man. "I'm not hungry."

"You've been here a spell. I want to be alone with her for a few minutes, if you don't mind," she said firmly.

Tía was his employer, and that sounded like an order. Grant hesitated. His job meant nothing to him, but he couldn't believe she would hurt Judy. He stood up. "I'll take a walk."

"Thank you."

Tía waited until Grant was out the door. She knelt beside the low bed and took Judy's hand in both of hers. It felt dry and so limp it seemed boneless—so different from Judy's usual vitality that a pang pierced Tía's heart.

"Judy, I know you can't hear me," she whispered, "but I need to tell you something, because I feel bad. I'm sorry we tricked you. I didn't set out to lie. It hurt my pride that you wanted to be shed of me, even before you met me.

"I don't know what to say about Johnny. I get a cramp around my heart every time I think about giving him up. I didn't mean for it to happen, though." Miserable, she shook her head. "I've never known people I cared so much about so sudden, both you and Johnny."

Tía leaned forward to press her lips against Judy's warm cheek. "Morgan Todd loves you, too. He feels as bad as a cut wolf for hurting you. He came back that night to ask you to marry him. I don't know why you'd want him, but it's always nice to be asked. That's what I heard, anyway.

"I'm not saying this well at all. But I just wanted you to know that I love you, and I want you to get well. We've got a passel of things to talk about...when you can hear me..."

Tía kissed Judy's cheek and walked outside to join Andrea.

Sergeant Stone looked up from the deck of cards he was shuffling, noticed the time on the wall clock, two o'clock, and put his cards down. Accompanied by a young man Stone didn't know, a disheveled Jethrow Farraday dusted himself off, then aimed himself through the doorway. He crashed into the desk, straightened up, patted the lapels of his ancient frock coat, and clicked his heels together. "Mr. Jethrow Farraday to see my client, Mr. John Brago. My companion here has the unlikely name of Slick."

Farraday's knees buckled. Slick—a tall, well-built rider with dark hair, heavy black brows and a mustache—caught him before he hit the floor. Rolling his eyes, Sergeant Stone shook his head at the soldier standing guard in front of the locked door, which opened into the corridor leading to the cell where Brago was being held.

"You going to carry him into Brago's cell, or should we just splash him under the door?" Stone asked, disgusted.

His dark face lighting with mischief, Slick grinned. "I best pour him real gentle like if I want to keep my job."

"All right. This way." Standing up, Stone motioned to the soldier to unlock the door. Passing through that, he led Farraday and his keeper down the short corridor to the holding area. He stopped in front of a cell where the prisoner was sprawled on a cot, ankles crossed, hands behind his head, hat over his face. Stone unlocked the door, and Farraday stumbled partway into the cell. Then, as if all his bones had dissolved, he fell face forward. Cursing, Slick leaped forward, caught him, and dragged him the rest of the way inside, saying, "Okay, lock it." Lifting the skinny old man like a half-empty straw doll, he stood him in front of Brago.

Shaking his head, Stone complied. He stepped through the door to the office. "Don't reckon I'd keep a woman long if she sent me a lawyer like that," he said disgustedly.

Locking the door, the soldier grinned. "Maybe he works cheap."

"Yeah! By cricky, if he don't remember he's been here, he probably won't send a bill." Laughing, he sat back down at the card table and laid out another game of solitaire.

A discreet female cough caused the sergeant to come to his feet, almost knocking over the small table.

"Yes, ma'am?" he asked, flushing at being caught in so unmilitary a posture by such a pretty lady.

Andrea smiled. "Please, Sergeant, do not let me disturb you. My name is Andrea Burkhart." She smiled at Stone, then at the enlisted man, then back at Stone.

"Our pleasure, ma'am. Uh…what can I do for you?"

"Just a little forbearance, if you don't mind. My attorney is with my foreman. I must confess I'm too impatient to wait in my quarters. Would it be too much trouble if I wait here?"

Every word she spoke was entirely proper and ladylike, but a provocative sparkle brightened her pretty eyes. Her black riding habit revealed a slender but voluptuous body and complemented her fair skin and auburn hair. All in all, Stone found her irresistible.

Grinning, he bowed from the waist. "No trouble at all, ma'am. We don't run off ladies as pretty as you."

Andrea's eyes clearly showed her pleasure. "Why, Sergeant, how gallant you are!"

"Well, now, I wouldn't know about that, ma'am."

Laughing and teasing until Slick yelled for them to let him out, Andrea kept up a bantering dialogue. Still laughing and talking, she accompanied the sergeant back to the cell.

"Well," she said upon seeing Farraday, "how did it go?"

Farraday was being held upright by his companion, his arms around the lawyer's middle, his face out of sight. "That insolent young pup has rejected my help," he said, indicating the prisoner on the narrow cot, his hat pulled down over his face.

Shaking her head, Andrea cast Stone an imploring look, as if asking him to explain the irascibility of men. Enjoying her gesture of helplessness, Stone laughed.

"What now?" she asked. "Men are so stubborn! So necessary," she said, flashing a provocative smile at Stone. "But so stubborn."

Not taking his eyes off her, Stone held the door while Slick hefted the staggering Farraday out of the cell. Still behind him, Slick propelled the drunk down the corridor, through the door into the office, and out the front door. Lingering to offer Stone a flirtatious good-bye, Andrea followed more slowly.

"Good-bye," she said, giving the two soldiers one last smile. Stone hated to see her leave, but maybe when he was off duty…

Andrea was the last one back to her quarters. She walked casually up to the door, stepped inside, and closed it behind her, expelling a long breath of relief. Beside the table, Johnny Brago was buckling on his gunbelt. Flushed and nervous, her clear blue eyes unnaturally bright, Tía was watching him. Andrea saw the confusion in Tía's eyes. No wonder. Johnny looked even more dangerous now that he was a hunted fugitive. The latent violence she had sensed in him was more apparent now. Had she done the right thing, substituting Slick for Johnny under the very noses of the soldiers? What if she was wrong about Johnny and Rutledge was right?

Farraday leaned forward and poured himself another glass of whiskey. "The young pup didn't want my help," he said angrily.

Johnny smiled. Farraday was drunk as a lord. Andrea's plan had worked so beautifully that Farraday hadn't noticed when Johnny and Slick changed clothes and hats. Slick had laid Farraday facedown on the cot. Johnny and Slick looked enough alike that with Slick lying on the cot with a hat over his face and Andrea flirting with the soldiers, no one had noticed the small differences.

"I have to change," Andrea said. "Is there anything we've forgotten?"

"If what Tía tells me is the way it is, you've thought of everything. I just hope they don't hang Slick while we're gone," Johnny said dryly.

Andrea grinned. "I asked the captain to hold off on your trial until we get back. If Slick can lie still long enough, they'll never know it isn't you."

Johnny grinned. He was used to people complaining about his ability to relax.

Andrea stepped into the bedroom to change. Tía looked down at her hands, picking at the fabric of her riding skirt. Johnny had ignored her on the ride to the fort. It looked like he intended to continue. But it didn't matter. She didn't know what to say to him anyway. She was still stunned by Judy's condition.

"Tía…"

Her heart lurched wildly. "What?"

"C'mere," he said quietly. He stood with his arms crossed over his chest, an intent look in his dark eyes.

Feeling like a summoned child, Tía walked across the short distance and stopped. She could not bring herself to look into his eyes just yet. A short piece of string clung to the tan leather of Slick's vest. She was tempted to pick it off, but she didn't dare touch him. He might misunderstand. And she had had enough confusion for one day.

Johnny uncrossed his arms. After he had stopped being furious about Tía taking care of Morgan, he had realized that, tender-hearted to a fault, she could do no less. He had been a fool to suspect her motives.

Tía watched Johnny's dark face. His hand reached out, stroked the sensitive flesh of her inner arm, and then moved up to touch her cheek. Sighing, she closed her eyes and allowed him to pull her into his arms and hold her close.

"Tía," he whispered, his voice husky.

"Oh, Johnny…"

He held her tight. Like a tidal wave, emotion swelled within her. For the moment, Johnny was safe. His warm arms encircled her, and his heart beat loud and purposefully against her cheek. Johnny could save Steve from Papa and from Indians! Judy would recover; even Morgan would get well.

In gratitude and love, Tía strained upward, her mouth open and searching. Johnny's lips brushed hers, barely touching them, and she whimpered softly.

"Should I knock before entering?" Andrea asked, looking from them to Farraday, slumped at the table, staring at the whiskey. She did not approve of Johnny Brago as a suitor for her sister, but for the moment she had to depend on him completely.

Johnny released Tía reluctantly, stunned that so much female richness could exist in one small girl. He was torn by impulses of tenderness and lust.

Smiling blearily, Farraday lifted his glass in a salute. "Not on my account, good lady. A woman who serves good whiskey can come and go as she pleases."

"Why, thank you, Mr. Farraday. You may take that bottle with you."

Standing up uncertainly, Farraday nodded solemnly. "Good day, madam." He walked stiffly to the door, turned, bowed from the waist, and buckled into a dead faint.

Johnny lunged forward and caught him just before his head hit the floor.

CHAPTER THIRTY-FOUR

"Shouldn't we keep moving?" Andrea asked.

Johnny pulled off his saddle. They had reached Galeyville, skirted it, and he had decided to make camp on the leeward side of the mountain.

"No sense stumbling around in the dark. We're only two hours from the canyon Steve will be traveling through. If we get up before sunrise, we can be there before him," Johnny said, eyeing Tía's drooping form.

Andrea wanted to argue with him, to demand that they continue, but she knew from the look on his face that he would not. Tía and the other riders sagged in their saddles with weariness.

Sighing, Andrea caught the blankets Johnny tossed at her and carried them toward a grassy place off the trail they had followed. Johnny lifted Tía, who was so sleepy she could barely hold herself upright, off her mount. Andrea spread the blankets out for herself and her sister.

"Are you hungry?" Johnny asked Tía.

Tía snuggled against his warm chest and shook her head.

Johnny led her to the blankets, laid her down, and covered her.

"Can we build a fire?" Andrea asked. "I'd love a cup of coffee and some hot food."

The riders had dismounted and were unsaddling the horses and pack animal. Johnny walked to the little mule and rummaged around the saddlebags until he found the beef jerky and a hard biscuit. "Gnaw on this. Unless you want to die beside the campfire with an arrow in your back, you'd better settle for jerky and hardtack."

At last they were curled up together, lying spoon fashion under blankets, shivering from the chill breeze that whipped down from the north, which Johnny called the "high mountain chill." Andrea curled around Tía, trying to warm her.

Tía's breathing was soft and deep. Andrea sighed. She should be sleeping, too, but there was a bad feeling in the pit of her stomach—a cold, empty feeling. If there were any way in the world she could stop the events in progress, she would do so, but she knew she couldn't.

Johnny was an escaped prisoner. If Rutledge discovered him missing, they would hunt him down, maybe kill him. Morgan Todd hung to life by a thread. If he died, they would probably hang Johnny—if they could catch him. There'd been a look in Johnny's eyes as he'd strapped on his gun that afternoon that told her he wouldn't give it up again. They would have to kill him. Beneath his relaxed facade, a cold reserve dominated Johnny—a remorseless drive that reminded her of Papa.

Steve. Andrea's heart contracted with a flutter of fear. She knew *El Gato* too well. If he had a chance to steal a lot of money and kill *gringos*, too, he would do it—gladly. If what Tía had said about the silver and the pompous *gringo* was true, Steve was in extreme danger. Only one explanation would account for *El Gato*'s comments and the silence surrounding the first mule train—every man had been killed.

A gust of cold wind fluttered their blankets. Andrea shivered. The sky was clear and the stars bright and close to the mountains. The full moon was high overhead. She wished she had put their blankets under a tree. It was impossible to sleep with moonlight on her face. It made her nerves too jumpy.

A hard knot of anxiety had formed in the pit of her stomach. It would not go away. Somehow, she knew Tía was going to be the one to suffer…

It didn't make any sense! Steve was the one in danger—Steve, Johnny, and Morgan—but it was Tía she was worried about. Instinctively she cuddled Tía with her arm, taking a much needed comfort in her sister's sigh of contentment.

It had always been that way between them. Tía took care of Andrea in the morning, and Andrea took care of Tía at night. In so many ways, Tía was like her own child. Eight years younger and completely without guile, so full of trust and goodwill that she was almost defenseless, Tía inspired a fierce maternal instinct in Andrea. It raged in her now. She tried to deny it. She should be worrying about Steve, but her mind ground on Tía and the thought of Papa wanting to take her away. That was it. Papa was the threat to Tía. And to Steve.

Please, God, don't let anything happen to Tía. She doesn't deserve to be hurt again. Not by Johnny or Papa. Not by anybody. Please spare her. She's only a baby…

An eerie foreboding settled over Andrea like a cold fog, pressing against the darkness of her soul. No one listened. Tía Andrea had warned Andrea not to ask God for things. *God knows what we need. Surrender, Andrea. To do otherwise will only cause you grief.*

Defiantly Andrea burrowed close to her sister. "I'll take care of you, Tía," she whispered. Tía did not reply. Her deep, rhythmic breathing told Andrea she slept.

Andrea wished she could cry, but tears didn't come. It was just as well Tía slept. Her words of reassurance had an empty, hollow sound to them.

Johnny roused them so early the sun had not even brightened the eastern horizon. They were in the mountains. A thin film of frost—pale and crusty on the tips of bushes and tufts of grass that stuck up between rocks—whitened everything.

Stumbling through darkness and shivering from cold, they didn't take time to eat a meal. Johnny gave Andrea and Tía more hardtack and jerky. It stopped the hungry growling in Tía's stomach, but it didn't warm her.

Johnny saddled her horse. Under cover of darkness, his hands warm and masterful, he pulled her into his arms and held her close against him. Much too soon, he let out a sigh, gave her a little boost, and pushed her up into her saddle. His hand held hers for a second, then reluctantly let it go.

Andrea walked toward the couple. Tía couldn't believe how wide-awake her sister looked, how haggard.

"Did you sleep at all?"

Andrea shook her head and spoke to Johnny. "May I speak to you for a moment?"

Johnny nodded and followed her several steps away, out of Tía's hearing.

"I know this probably sounds foolish to you, but…well, I want you to stay close to Tía. If there's any trouble, take care of her."

Johnny tensed instinctively. He would have protected Tía in any case. "Is there something special I should look out for?"

"*El Gato Negro* might try to take her away or hurt her…" She could not bring herself to tell him that the famous bandit was her father.

"Why Tía? Why not you?"

"He seems…" Andrea floundered into silence.

"Attracted to her?" Johnny supplied.

Andrea nodded, too ashamed to say more.

They rode hard, always in an upward direction it seemed, through narrow ravines, over large granite slabs slashed and leveled by glaciers long receded.

With Tía behind Johnny and the other dozen men strung out behind Andrea, they rode in single file. By the time the sun came up, they had covered many miles. Johnny halted the procession at the edge of a long, steep drop. He pointed to a canyon far below them. A torturous, winding path cut through the center of it. Barely wide enough for one animal at a time, it looked almost impassable. There was no possible way down the steep incline to the canyon.

"We're lost, aren't we?" Tía said. "Can we go back the way we came?"

"This is it. This is what I was looking for."

"This?! We're going to leap off this cliff?"

"Look to your right a little."

Barely visible among the underbrush there was a narrow path. Tía smiled. "How long will it take us to get down there?"

"Half hour, maybe longer."

"Which way will Steve be coming from?"

"That's south," he said, pointing to her right. "He should be coming from there." He pointed west.

Andrea rode up beside Tía and looked over the cliff. She *must* love Steve Burkhart, she reflected. Nothing else in the world could induce her to tackle such a steep, narrow path.

"Could we be too late?"

"Not if he left yesterday morning. Mules don't move very fast. He should be here by noon, but we won't wait. As soon as we reach the canyon floor, we'll head west as fast as we can to head him off." Johnny paused.

Tía looked at his grim features. "And?"

"Nothing. Except…he could have gotten delayed in Tombstone… or after he left there."

"Then what?"

"Then we're on our own." The blood drained out of Andrea's face. Them against Papa. Or Steve against the Indians? It was hard to decide which would be worse.

Johnny led the way down the steep canyon walls. Because of the danger of a horse slipping and falling, the trip had to be made one person at a time. Johnny led his horse down first. When he reached the canyon floor, he waved his hat at Tía. Sure that this had to be the roughest, most impossible terrain she'd ever seen, Tía followed the path she'd watched Johnny take. Once she got her mare started down, she stayed behind her, just in case. It hardly qualified as a shortcut; it was more like a long drop. Tía slid most of the way on her backside behind and beside her horse, who skidded on her haunches most of the way. About halfway down, Tía slipped and almost went over a small ledge that would have dropped her to the canyon floor. She caught a handful of loose rocks and dug one of them into the dirt to use as a brake. She stopped just short of going over.

Panting in relief, she stood up and turned herself back around so she could continue the walk-slide down to the canyon floor. About ten yards from the bottom she could see she was actually going to survive. On the canyon floor, she half collapsed into Johnny's arms.

He waved to the group watching from the top of the cliff, then carried Tía to the shade of the wall and laid her down. "You all right?"

"I'm terrified for Andrea. I should have stayed with her. She doesn't wake up until noon."

"Don't look. There's nothing you can do now, anyway."

To distract her, Johnny asked, "Have you seen *El Gato* since you left Tubac?"

"Besides last night?" Tía stopped. "That might have been him in Tombstone, disguised as an old man."

"What makes you think so?"

"Even *El Gato Negro* has to get around somehow."

Someone yelled, and Johnny stood up to see what was going on. Tía scrambled to her feet as well. She followed Johnny and watched the last fifty yards of Andrea's descent.

Andrea's presence inhibited Johnny's questions. An hour later the last rider reached the canyon floor without major injury. They rested the animals and gnawed at the jerky while Johnny rode ahead to check the canyon for recent travelers.

They rode for hours. It was broiling hot on the canyon floor—a dry, still heat that made Tía pray for water. But the winding, brush-choked path was as dry as it was endless.

The sun seemed to trail them directly overhead. Still no sign of Steve and the mule train. At last Johnny held up his hand. He was surveying the topmost edge of the canyon wall. Andrea followed his gaze.

"What do you see?"

Reaching behind him, he fumbled in his saddlebag and pulled out a pair of field glasses. He lifted them to his eyes, the horse moved under him, and cursing, he dismounted.

"Well?" Tía prompted.

"There's a man up there. That's Devil's Kitchen."

Tía looked from Johnny to Andrea, but they didn't notice her. They both peered up at the tall sentinel rocks. Her nose wrinkled. What was that smell? Her stomach gave a sudden, hard lurch. She squinted into the canyon ahead; something fluttered in the slight breeze. It looked like a black shirt.

Andrea tapped Johnny on the shoulder. "Let me look through those."

Johnny handed the field glasses to Andrea. Just as her hand started to close around the black metal cylinder nearest her, a woman screamed. It could only be Tía. Panicked, Andrea looked around her, but her sister was not in sight.

"Oh, no!" Andrea cried, turning her horse toward the sound.

Johnny leaped on his horse and spurred it forward, past Andrea. Only seconds later Tía burst out of the thickets, crashing back onto the narrow path.

"Tía! Thank God! I thought you'd been hurt!" The look on Tía's face stopped Andrea. "Tía! What is it?"

Tía's hand covered her mouth. She doubled over and retched. Johnny walked his horse back to Andrea's side.

"What?" Andrea asked, not liking the look on his face.

"The first mule train," he said grimly. Then, carried on a wafting breeze, the stench reached Andrea. It was unendurable.

"Cover your noses!" Johnny shouted. "We have to go through."

It was a nightmare. Only the desperate need to reach Steve could have driven Andrea and Tía through it. The men had kerchiefs to keep the flies off their mouths and noses. Tía and Andrea pulled up their blouses. Retching miserably, they tried not to see the buzzard-torn bodies strewn along the path.

Their shiny black eyes glittering beneath hooded lids, the buzzards looked up from their feasting. Some flapped their wings, but none bothered to fly away. No wonder they hadn't seen buzzards circling. They were too gorged and busy to fly.

If the need for stealth and speed were not so great, Johnny would have shot the ugly black hulks and stopped to bury or burn the gutted bodies.

Tía wept as if her heart were broken.

Suspecting her father had either killed these men or ordered their killing, Andrea was awash in silent fury.

At last they were beyond it. Tía was pale and limp in her saddle. Andrea hurried her along, trying to distract them both with questions about Judy; but the memory of the graveyard of horror would not completely recede.

Johnny stopped them again. Even his sun-browned face looked pale. "I want you to stay at the rear. I think I know where the ambush is going to take place. There's one more spot up ahead where there'll be room to do what they did back there, to spread out, hiding in the rocks."

"How much farther?" Tía asked, her eyes still sick with the memory of death.

"Less than a mile, if I remember right."

"Let's hurry! Please," Andrea urged. "Don't worry about us. We have to save Steve!"

Nodding his agreement, Johnny spurred his tired horse. Tía and Andrea held back until the last rider passed them. Then they too fell into line. The heat, the stench, the discomfort—all were forgotten. The trap was set.

CHAPTER THIRTY-FIVE

Once again the lofty cathedral rocks that formed Devil's Kitchen sheltered Mateo Lorca from the heat that beat down like a stifling blanket on the winding canyon far below him.

His men dotted the canyon floor. From the west the mule train moved steadily toward the point of ambush. He could not make out features from this distance, but he had verified the identity of the caravan hours ago. It gave him great pleasure that the man so blithely riding into his trap was Steven Burkhart: the pampered blond son of the man who had cuckolded him. Even now, eighteen years after the deed, he felt intense hatred for Bill Burkhart. To kill Burkhart's son was some small satisfaction.

How many times had Rita cheated him in Burkhart's arms—soft and sensuous, her blue eyes slitted, her lips parted and sighing with ecstasy? How many times did it take for a woman to earn thousands of acres of land for her bastard daughter? Thousands of acres of land that belonged to the Garcia-Lorcas.

Where was Rita hiding? No one could elude him. He had a network of men the length and breadth of two territories. But three months after she had left him for dead, he had heard nothing. Not one word. Neither Andrea nor Teresa had tried to find out if he was dead or alive.

He would expect that from Rita, but not from Andrea, not from Teresa. He had loved the bastard Teresa even more than Andrea. Even now, at mention of her name, grief at her loss swelled within him. Rita had cheated him of his love for Teresa and turned Andrea against him. The monster within had also turned against him, made his nights a horror, demanding vengeance. The remorseless hatred he had used against the *gringos* would now be turned upon his *gringa* wife and her bastard.

Mateo shuddered. Only one other time in his life had he let his inhumaneness rule him, and that time he had avenged the Garcia-Lorcas against the fat colonel who had murdered his family and sentenced him to death.

At the thought of the colonel, a cold sweat broke out on Mateo's forehead. He gritted his teeth against the frustration and rage. *Wait*, he cautioned the rampaging beast within him. *Wait, and I will give you Teresa and Rita.*

Slowly, the trembling stopped. Mateo put his hands to his face and sagged in the saddle.

After a time he straightened. The mule train was close now. Soon the lead mule would be at the mouth of the trap. He closed his eyes to shut out the memories that had tormented him for weeks, for months.

A vision of the bed he had shared with Rita in Tubac flashed across the surface of his mind. *¡Dios!* Not their bed. Mateo wanted to bellow his rage. Eighteen years of blind conceit. That was the real humiliation. Because he had to take Rita every time he came home to her, he had believed she would not go willingly into any man's bed. Egotistical fool! All he had remembered was that when she finally surrendered to him she became a hungry wanton. After the initial awkwardness, they made love all night, every night they were together. It had always been that way. Short, intense couplings spread over twenty-five years. And even now, remembering her still slender, voluptuous body; her firm, thrusting breasts; her narrow waist and shapely hips, he could feel himself responding in spite of everything he knew about Rita.

The sound of rocks tumbling down a granite slab reined his attention back to the business at hand.

Squinting against the glare of sunlight that shimmered between him and the canyon below, he saw that the lead mule of the Burkhart caravan had already entered the trap. Only a little farther, and he would avenge himself. First the Burkhart whelp, then Rita's bastard, and then he would deal with Rita the way he should have years ago if he had been a man and not a lovestruck boy.

Rita finished packing the small valise and swung it off the bed. She carried it to the door and put it down.

Sitting at the small dropleaf table, sipping coffee and nibbling on a tea cake, Sherry looked from Rita to the valise then back at Rita's hair. "That blond mane of yours is a dead giveaway."

Rita glanced at the black wig Sherry had gotten from a musical company that went broke years ago in Tucson. These last few months whenever she left the house she had worn it; otherwise heaven knew what would have happened to her. She was sick of it. Her head got so hot she thought it would melt.

Rita's honey-gold mane caught the sunlight and gleamed. "I'm going to find Mateo. I no longer need it."

Sherry came to her feet, shocked. "Oh, my God!" she cried. "He'll kill you!"

Rita tossed back her long blond tresses with a dainty hand. Even at forty years old, nothing marred Rita's vibrant beauty. She moved with a lithe, animal grace, and her vibrant, richly colored cheeks, framed by thick gold hair, had a radiance that attracted masculine admiration everywhere she went.

"I got a letter from Tía Andrea this morning. I have to go to him and explain, before he finds Tía."

"Without the wig, you'll be recognized. He'll kill you on sight. You know what a temper he has. What good is that going to do you or Tía?"

"He won't kill me. At least not right away."

"No, he probably won't need to. You'll be killed by Indians!"

"Believe me, if there were any other way, I wouldn't go, but I have to." *Even if he kills me. Even if I kill him, and his men kill me. At least then Tía will be safe...*

Rita bowed her head, too angry and defensive to explain. The problem and its solution were hers and hers alone. She had made one mistake when she was fifteen, which had led her to make another mistake, and then another. And every time Andrea and Tía paid the price. Because of her impulsiveness, Tía had lost Mateo's love and incurred his wrath. Mateo was fully capable of extracting his vengeance on her daughters, and Rita could not bear the thought of it. She was tired of paying and tired of watching her children pay for her mistakes. It had to stop!

Sighing in resignation, Sherry reached out to touch Rita's hand. "You're so stubborn!"

"I'm a mother. No more, no less."

"When are you leaving?"

"As soon as my guide arrives. I contacted a friend of Tía Andrea's. He agreed to escort me to Mateo's hideout."

"You are insane!"

Helpless and resigned to her fate, Rita grew quiet. There was no sense talking about it.

"Rita! He will kill you!"

"Not right away," she said knowingly. "He always has a problem he wants taken care of first."

"At least you're as crazy as he," Sherry said grimly. Buxom, with a shapely figure that had expanded slowly over the years, she now only slightly resembled the girl she had been when she and Rita had met in Tubac twenty years earlier. She had been married to a soldier, one of three dozen who guarded the small border town from Indians. They'd met in the general merchandise store.

Rita had stopped beside the shelf where bakery goods were displayed and, hearing a strange lamentation, had turned to the plump stranger.

"Are you all right?" Rita had asked.

The woman had raised her eyes from the big glass jar of cookies to Rita's face. "Of course not! I'm starving to death! All my life I've been starving. How do you stay so thin?"

Enjoying the antic gleam in the stranger's eyes, Rita had laughed. "The secret is to chew your food for a long time," she had said, sounding completely serious.

"How long?" the woman had demanded, as if her desperation to be slim would give her the strength to do anything.

"Till it spoils."

They'd laughed, and then they'd talked. Rita learned that Sherry had only been in Tubac two days and that somehow no one had warned her yet about Rita. Before that could happen, the two became friends. Later, Sherry told her that one of the officers' wives tried to correct the oversight. She invited Sherry to tea and explained, china teacup in hand, that Rita was not fit company for decent folks, that she preferred the company of common Mexicans. Sherry listened politely, then went directly to Rita's house to tell her exactly what the woman said.

It took them only moments together to find out they were both from upstate New York—Sherry from Rochester and Rita from Albany. Rita was so homesick for a woman from her own world, that bond alone would have been enough.

Sherry's husband, Captain Howard Greenfield, had been transferred several times during those early years, but the two women always stayed in contact. The last transfer took them to Fort Huachuca, fifty miles from Tubac. Sherry was the only white friend Rita had, and Rita had told her the truth about Mateo only after she'd promised that she wouldn't talk to her husband. Rita trusted Sherry, but she did not trust Sherry's soldier husband. Sherry had never betrayed her.

Rita never quite understood why she kept Mateo's secret. She should have told the captain herself. Mateo deserved to hang, to have his head paraded like a trophy of war through towns and villages by the soldiers.

But she could not be the cause of it; she shuddered at the sheer barbarity of men. While she might fight Mateo on a purely personal level, she could not betray him to the soldiers.

"Why on earth did you marry him?" Sherry had asked after she'd learned the truth.

"I was fifteen. What girl has good sense at that age?"

Rita saw her guide, Abuelito, and picked up her valise.

Sherry saw him and closed her eyes in despair. "You'll be lucky to survive the first hour with that animal."

"Tía Andrea vouched for him."

Grudgingly Sherry pursed her lips together. "This makes as much sense as a barbed-wire fence full of knotholes."

"Wish me luck?"

"You're going to ride a hundred miles through Apaches with a man who looks like a vermin-infested escapee from Devil's Island to see a loco bull who may kill you in a fit of infantile temper, and you ask me to wish you luck? You're as crazy as he is."

Rita hugged her loyal friend.

"Rita, please be careful."

Rita laughed. After all Sherry had said, being careful sounded like a waste of time. "I will. I promise."

She picked up her valise, stepped out the door, and closed it firmly before Sherry could say anything else.

Rita didn't slow her pace until she reached her horse. She refused to think until she was mounted and unable to turn back even if she wanted to. It was all decided. She knew what had to be done.

The horse moved swiftly through the town and out into the desert. The blazing sun beat down on her head in spite of her wide-brimmed hat. The fear she had denied to Sherry prickled along her spine, coiled in her belly like a cold fish. The letter from Tía Andrea had begged her to stay away, warned her Mateo wanted to kill her and possibly Tía as well.

So why was she going? Did she think she could change his mind? Could anyone short of Mateo himself change that cruel, implacable mind?

Tía Andrea's letter had told her that Tía and Andrea were back in Arizona. But she suspected that Tía Andrea had not told her everything. If Tía was in Arizona, Mateo knew where they were. That was what drove her. She had to reach Mateo before he found Tía.

Leaning forward, she called out to her guide to hurry. If she was to save her daughter, there was no time to waste.

CHAPTER THIRTY-SIX

The Chiricahuas were behind Rita now. The Peloncillos loomed ahead like pale blue knuckles shoved up through the rust-colored earth. She began to recognize landmarks she thought she had forgotten. Things she hadn't seen in many years. Landmarks burned into her memory...

She had been fifteen the first time she'd ridden this way. Mateo and his men had swooped out of the hills, killed the men in the caravan, and spirited Rita and five other women away from the burning wagon train.

Because the bandits had been traveling fast, the women were tied onto stolen horses. Ankles chafing against bristly ropes tied underneath her horse's belly, clinging to the cantle of a horse led by a bearded, dirty Mexican who leered at her from beneath his wide sombrero, Rita rode until well after dark that first night.

From the looks on the other women's terrified faces, no doubt existed in any of their minds about what lay in store for them. But Rita was not paralyzed by fear, even when they were pulled roughly off the tired horses and dragged to a torch-lit central quad, surrounded by squat adobe houses carved into the walls of a steep limestone cliff. Screaming, sobbing, moaning, the women were poked and pinched and prodded by the animals who surrounded them. Only Rita did not cry.

"Get your filthy hands off me!" she screamed.

One of the laughing, half-drunk men lifted a torch out of its holder and held it close to her face, causing her to draw back. The men laughed boisterously.

"*Gringa* slut!" Menacingly, they moved toward her. The other women cowered, but Rita stood her ground.

"Filthy animals! Swine! Sons of brood sows!" she screamed at them. They laughed and grabbed at her breasts, making clumsy, lunging movements with their hands, not touching her, just threatening to. One of the men tripped her, and she fell. Another ripped her gown. Even tormented as she was, she noticed that they seemed to be holding back, *waiting* for something or someone.

A murmur started at the back edge of the crowd and spread forward. Men scrambled aside, fell silent. Her gown in tatters, crouching like a cornered animal, Rita looked up into the coldest black eyes she had ever seen. They were set in a young, smooth-shaven face that was so classically handsome it could have been called beautiful; under any other circumstances she would have been awed. Her pulse throbbing wildly against her throat, she looked into eyes so steely and cruel that her blood ran cold. Even his obvious youth did not mitigate the effect.

His gaze raked over her. For the first time she was aware that one of her breasts was exposed.

"Stand up."

Too terrified to refuse, gathering her tatters around her, Rita slowly came to her feet. Before she could step back, his hands lashed out and ripped her gown and the shift under it from neck to navel. One more savage, lightning-quick slash of his lean brown hands, and she was naked in front of five crying women and a hundred leering men.

For a moment no one made a sound, not even Rita. She was too shocked. Frozen, she watched his cold black eyes as he leisurely surveyed her body. A thousand thoughts could have formed in the space of his long and insolent scrutiny, but her mind was paralyzed.

Anger brought her chin up even higher. His cruel lips curled down into a wry smile. Shaking his head, as if shaming her for some act she could not even imagine, he snapped his fingers. Four men rushed to his side.

In rapid Spanish he spoke and then turned away, leaving her there, unaware of what he had said or what it would mean for her. The four men closed in on her, and now she screamed, a signal for the other women to panic, and they did.

Chaos reigned. Rough hands on her naked flesh, hurting, groping, squeezing her breasts, stroking her smooth white skin, filled her with violent energy.

Screaming, slashing out like a wild cat, Rita fought them. There was much yelling and cursing until they subdued her—one man for each wildly flailing limb. Others followed beside them to fondle the quivering, milk-white flesh. They carried her in the most humiliating way possible— legs spread, arms outstretched, bucking and kicking all the way, her eyes glued closed to blot out some small part of the horrors that awaited her.

Quickly they carried her up a long flight of stairs. She sensed the upward movement. They stopped, and she ceased her frantic struggles and opened her eyes, relaxing down into a swing between the men. The man holding her left leg knocked on the door before them.

"Enter!" It was that cold, arrogant voice she remembered from the quad. Fear rippled through her in waves.

They opened the door and carried her to the low bed in the center of the room. Bowing to the young man who was surely their leader, they swung her into the middle of the bed and dropped her like a rock. Ignoring her, they laughed and spoke in rapid Spanish to the tall, slender bandit who watched in silence, hands on hips, lips twisted in arrogant impatience. Rita scrambled into a more dignified position.

Finally, still guffawing, the men shuffled out and closed the door behind them. A rifle leaned in the corner of the room opposite the door. Rita mentally measured the steps to reach it.

They were alone. Rita's heart beat so hard she could feel it, like a hammer at her temples, hurting her head.

"Take your shoes off," he commanded in English.

"Take them off yourself! You savage."

He chuckled softly—the coldest, most frightening sound in the world—and Rita panicked. Lunging off the bed, she grabbed the rifle and brought the barrel up, aiming it at his broad chest.

Smiling just as coldly, he walked toward her. "Do not pull the trigger," he said softly, "or you will be very sorry."

Gritting her teeth, closing her eyes tight, Rita pulled the trigger. The hammer fell. Only a disappointing click broke the silence. Rita opened her eyes, screamed, and turned the rifle to grasp it by the barrel. With all the strength she could muster, she swung it at him.

He caught the stock with one steely hand, jarring her all the way to her toes. Before she could save herself, he slapped her a hard, stinging blow to the cheek.

Rita came at him like a tigress, and she kept coming at him; but slowly, methodically, relentlessly, he mastered her: he allowed her to fight him as long and as hard as she wanted, but always he hurt her more than she hurt him—until at last she went down and could not get up. They had not wasted time or breath for words. She lay on the floor, panting.

"Crawl to the bed, *gringa* bitch. You have earned your reward."

"Go to hell!" she gasped.

"Hell is reserved for *gringos*. I only make the reservations." Panting, he began to disrobe. There was no fight left in her. For the first time, tears slipped down her cheeks. Her humiliation was complete.

Tall, well built, slim-hipped, with heavy black curls running from throat to groin, he was a fearsome sight for a girl who had never seen a man without clothes. Her eyes widened. A hard knot of fear settled in her throat to burn there, choking off any words or screams. If she could have spoken, she would have begged him to spare her.

With deliberate roughness he picked her up and tumbled her onto the bed. Dropping smoothly to his knees, watching her horrified face, he caught her ankles and pulled her toward him.

"Scream if you like. It assures my men that you are receiving what you deserve, *gringa*."

Rita was bruised in a dozen places. By tomorrow she would be black and blue from the methodical punishment he had inflicted, but she didn't care. By tomorrow she would also be dead. With the last ounce of defiance in her body, she coiled forward and spat in his face.

With his left hand he grabbed her by the hair. With his right he slapped her across the face, back and forth. Finally, when he had reduced her to gasping, sobbing breathlessness, he let her drop back onto the bed. Only then did he wipe her spittle off his face.

She lay there, crying quietly, hopelessly. And, looking back on it, Rita understood that something must have stirred in Mateo Lorca; not kindness, but perhaps a grudging admiration. Had her futile attempts to fight him, a man with twice her strength and ten times her endurance, perhaps reminded him of his own past—that first year when he had reportedly fought the *gringos* alone, on their terms?

A lamp hung in the center of the room, casting a golden glow over her flesh, softening the bruises that would look stark in the light of day. His voice was harsh. "Too bad you demanded that I break you. Such purity of line should not wear bruises. Too bad you are a *gringa*."

Was it regret that caused him, unexpectedly, to lie down beside her and close his eyes? Or tiredness? He too had ridden all those punishing miles she had ridden. Was he human after all? Could his tireless young body be responding to the drudgery of riding to and from the wagon train?

His breathing was as uneven and weary as her own. Thankful for the reprieve, she allowed her exhausted body to relax next to his. Rita closed her eyes. Amazingly, sleep claimed her.

She woke by degrees. Her consciousness returned, but not her ability to move. A burning sensation drew her attention downward. A warm, feather-soft touch teased her thighs. A pulse quickened in her loins, a feeling so delicious, so incredibly heady, that she didn't breathe lest it stop.

She must be dreaming. Her heavy lids would not open.

A dog howled outside. That helped to place her in time and space. Then she realized that she was not dreaming. Someone was caressing her thighs, moving up her hip, pausing at the cleft between her legs, barely touching the sensitive inner flesh, moving slowly to her breast, lightly caressing the swollen peak. Warm fingers rolled the tight little bud of her nipple, and a shaft of heat spread down to her throbbing womanhood.

Slowly she regained the use of her sleep-drugged limbs. "No, please," she whispered, opening her eyes to look at the young man whose hand fondled her breast.

"Hush," he said softly. He leaned forward, and his lips brushed against her cheek until they found her mouth. His breath mingled with her own. His lips were hot, searching, his tongue soft and probing. She tried to push him away, but her hands had no strength. His hand found her breast again and caressed it until she squirmed beneath him. His leg nudged her thighs open, and by then her hips were already arching against him, already hungry for whatever he was about to do.

But he did nothing. He continued to kiss her. Clumsily his hand groped her thighs. When she should have protested, she was too weak, too defeated. He took her breast into his mouth, and she cried out softly. Let him do what he would. There was nothing she could do to save herself. There never had been.

The warmth of his mouth, the teasing movements of his tongue, stirred a response in her young and vital body, a reaction that seemed as inexorable as he. Breathless, her lips parting for his exploring tongue, she turned toward him.

In spite of her pain, or perhaps even because of it, all her responses seemed heightened, her nerve endings too close to the surface. Suddenly she remembered what he had said earlier, that since he had mastered her, it was his right to take her.

He positioned her carefully, holding her thighs apart with firm hands.

Silver shafts of moonlight illuminated the floor and bounced off it to light the bandit's quarters. Her slitted eyes opened, saw his handsome yet completely ruthless face, and then closed, but too late. As long as she lived she would carry the memory of his dark face, his lithe warrior's body, poised with inexorable intent in the V of her thighs—his darkness against her fairness, his hardness against her softness.

Panting, she tried to retreat, but his dark hands held her as easily as if she were a doll. He pushed into her. Surprised by the burning little pain, she tried to squirm away, but he held her tight, and, slowly, the pain seemed to subside, turning into an itch that needed to be rubbed against, touched. Her soft inner parts burned with desire.

With that terrible male wisdom available even to the youngest man, this bandit seemed to know that her body quivered with the same hunger as his.

Moving awkwardly at first, the bandit slowly found a rhythm he liked. Clinging to him, Rita half cried, half sobbed. Her body felt beyond her control. She tried to hold back, but it came out of nowhere: a vast, bottomless gorge. One second it was not there; the next she was teetering on the brink, her mouth opening to scream as the tension from his body coalesced in her belly, and the earth dropped away from her.

CHAPTER THIRTY-SEVEN

For a long time she lay quietly. When she spoke her voice must have startled him. Even to her ears it sounded rich and sultry. No bitterness marred its perfection.

"Now you must kill me," she said simply.

Shock that she knew and would actually say the words was quickly followed by flaring anger.

"No one tells Mateo Lorca what he must do," he said harshly.

With a wisdom beyond her fifteen years, Rita remained quiet and let him wrestle with the problem. He came to it with surprising ease.

"Your American brothers keep black slaves—I will keep a white slave."

He kept her for one month. She would never know what had prompted him to keep her or what had finally caused him to reject her.

One morning she woke up—her body pressing to his for warmth against the chill desert nights—and found him staring at her as if he had never seen her before. For a split second she thought she saw tenderness in his black eyes, then fear, except she knew Mateo Lorca, for all his youth, could not feel fear any more than he could feel tenderness.

That morning he did not make love to her. He told her to sleep. When she woke again he was bathed, shaved, dressed in a tight-fitting charo suit that was to become his trademark. Tersely he demanded that she dress herself—quickly.

So incredibly handsome that she trembled to look at him, his face was closed, unreadable. A stab of fear pierced Rita's heart. It was time. A month late, even crueler now, because she had begun to care, to hope. His cruelty must be more obdurate than even she had imagined. And more refined...

After he had talked at length with his lieutenants, they left camp alone. All day as they rode she waited for him to execute her, but her pride was absolute. She would not show by word or deed that she cared. Silent,

354

she rode beside him. An hour after dark they reached a small settlement. Mateo took her to the house of a middle-aged Mexican woman whom he called Tía Andrea and left her there without even a good-bye. No kiss. No words. The woman called him *patrón*. He spoke to this Tía Andrea in rapid Spanish, then, with as little ceremony as when he had taken her from the wagon train, he left her.

Relief that he hadn't killed her was quickly followed by outrage. When she recovered enough to ask questions, she learned that he had left money for her care and a ticket on the stage to her home, wherever that might be. But she couldn't decide where to go. She had no home. She had relinquished that when she ran away from Tyler, her tyrannical older brother.

Depression—and the fact that it took no effort to stay—kept her there. Two months after Mateo had left her, Tía Andrea asked her if she had decided on a name for the baby.

"What baby?" Rita asked, frowning.

"Your baby…the son of our *patrón*," she said matter-of-factly. "It must be a very special name, because our *patrón* is a very special man… *muy grande, muy bravo…*"

Tía Andrea waxed eloquently about the many fine qualities of the man who had kidnapped and abandoned her, but Rita no longer listened.

It could not be! It could not! But even as she seethed with sudden, hot anger, she knew it was so. She was not blind, only stunned for too long by shattering events.

She accepted the fact of her pregnancy on a Monday. On Tuesday she drank quinine, but Tía Andrea caught her and forced her to drink a glass of warm, soapy water. She wouldn't have done it except compliance was the only way she could keep from hurting the stubborn old woman.

Coughing, sputtering, she drank the soapy water and threw up and then lay on her pallet for a week, refusing to eat. Tía Andrea sat beside her and told stories all day long, all week long, about women who had given birth, about the joy of giving life, the innocence of tiny babies, the opportunity to give love and life to her own child. Wisely, she said nothing more about the man who had put this marvelous gift inside her. Finally, because she was young and hungry, because it was apparent that Tía Andrea loved her, but mostly because she herself needed someone to love, Rita relented.

The pregnancy progressed normally, but Tía Andrea seemed distracted, torn by indecision. One day, late in Rita's ninth month, Tía Andrea disappeared for hours and would not say where she had been.

Two days later Rita went into labor. She was on the small, narrow pallet, breathing with the hard, drawing cramps, when a tall figure—lean-hipped, broad-shouldered, dressed in a tight-fitting charo suit—appeared in the doorway. Oh, God! How many times had she seen that sinister, familiar silhouette in her dreams and nightmares?

That he should come now, when she was fat and ugly, when her face was shiny with sweat sheen, filled her with a sudden despair and then shame. What did she want? That he should make love to her? A filthy Mexican?

Wishing she could disappear or die, Rita turned to the wall. Her hair was uncombed, and her thighs were bloody. Damn him! Damn him!

"¡Patrón! You came!" Tía Andrea was joyful.

El Gato Negro embraced the thin, prematurely gray woman. "Of course, Tía Andrea. For you I will always come." His voice contained the first note of tenderness Rita had ever heard from him.

It was disgusting. While Rita gritted her teeth, hating them both for ignoring her, Tía Andrea gushed over her *patrón* for at least three minutes, thanking him profusely for coming. Desperately Rita tried to block their conversation from her mind, but she had picked up enough of the lyrical language to understand snatches of it. Finally, when she could stand it no longer, she turned over to watch the man who had abandoned her to this agony and fear.

"There were no others...after me?" Mateo demanded, his dark cheeks flushing in spite of his control.

"Oh, no! No one, *patrón*!"

In Spanish that Rita could not follow, Tía Andrea talked long and rapidly. When she stopped, Mateo sighed. He answered her in Spanish.

"I'm sorry, Tía Andrea. What you ask is impossible."

The woman's ancient, seamed eyes clouded with sudden guile. This time she spoke English. "You are right, *patrón*. The child is a *gringo*. It should be raised as a *gringo*." Heavily, she sighed and went to sit on the floor beside Rita, drawing his attention there.

Mateo fell neatly into her trap. His anger flared into a white-hot heat. "The child is a Garcia-Lorca!" he said furiously. "No child of mine will be raised as a *gringo*!"

"I will fetch the priest! There is no time to lose."

Tía Andrea was gone. They were alone.

Heart pounding so hard that she was sure it shook the room, Rita sat up on her elbows and faced him. "I will not marry you!" she cried fiercely.

Mateo smiled. Too late Rita realized that she had made it a contest—

one she could not possibly win—one from which he would not withdraw. If she did not want it, then it must be done. To protect *his* child.

With no knowledge of English, assuming that the bride's tears were from the agony of childbirth, the priest performed the wedding mass and the marriage ceremony, ignoring both her cries of anguish and her sobs of protest. The baby was born two hours later and in moments formally christened Andrea de Mara Garcia-Lorca.

Because he was fleeing from a posse, Mateo could not stay. Within moments of his daughter's birth he was gone. He left money with Tía Andrea. While Rita convalesced and fell in love with her daughter, Tía Andrea found a small house near her own and fixed it up for mother and infant. It had a parlor, two bedrooms, and a kitchen. It was ample for their needs.

When little Andrea was a month old they moved in. A strange contentment came over Rita. She no longer seethed with anger. The baby was beautiful—she had great dark eyes, a sweetly cherubic face, and a serene and loving disposition.

They had everything they needed. Surprisingly, Mateo Lorca turned out to be a good provider. Rita floated through motherhood radiantly. It was unlike her to be so complacent. Her figure returned, and men cast admiring sidelong glances at her, but there was no yearning anywhere within her, and she was grateful for it. She had feared she was cursed because each time *he* had come to her, the fires had leaped into brilliance.

Andrea was five months old when her father paid his first visit to their small home. Rita came back from the store to find him on the long sofa in the parlor holding his daughter. Her mouth dropped open, and she stopped. Through the door that opened into her bedroom, she could see his saddlebags draped over the foot of her bed. Apparently he had sent Tía Andrea away.

"No, no!" she cried, moving to put her groceries down so she could snatch her daughter from his arms.

Effortlessly stripping away her composure, his cool black eyes flicked over her. A shiver of anticipation defeated her protests. She stepped back. Andrea whimpered, but Rita could not take her daughter from him. With that one look he had reminded her that he was in control.

Rita started to back out of the room. Balancing Andrea in one arm, he stepped between her and the front door and closed it.

"We will have dinner first," he said.

It was incredible. Rita prepared dinner while Mateo held and jostled his daughter. After dinner Andrea fell asleep in Mateo's arms. Seeing the sleeping infant, a new wave of fear washed up in Rita. He couldn't possibly expect…

But he did. He expected, and he acted on those expectations.

Rita wiped the last plate and set it in the cupboard. Nervously she untied her apron and prepared to fight him, but in the dark recesses of her mind it was apparent to her, possibly to both of them, that this time her resistance might lack the necessary will to die, the total heedlessness of consequences. Either the memory of that night when he broke her, physically and mentally, was still too fresh, or her awareness of the baby, who slept in the other room and depended totally on her for survival, was too inhibiting. Tía Andrea could not nurse the infant.

Mateo walked across the room and stepped behind her. His hands settled on her shoulders. So warm that their heat seeped into her very bones, they moved lightly down her arms. Rita knew this was the moment to resist, but her body felt so heavy and unresponsive.

"You are my wife," he whispered. "The mother of my child." His hands distracted her, as did his softly uttered words. "She is a beautiful baby. You have done well."

Rita could not bring herself to stand so complacently under his stroking hands. But her body, starved for human contact for so long, yearned to immerse herself in his heat. Even her thighs quivered at the hint of approval in his words.

"She is not a boy," she said softly, gloatingly. At least she had not pleased him in that.

Mateo chuckled softly. "She is lucky. Boys have a harder life."

"She belongs to me. You can never take her from me."

"I have no desire to take her from you. What would I do with a baby?"

"Promise me," she whispered. "I have no idea what your promise might be worth, but promise me anyway."

"My word is all I have to give my people. It is worth my life, everyday."

Rita shuddered. She should hate him for what he had done to her, but her mind flashed pictures of the soldiers and the handbills they had passed out among the neighboring *peónes* last month, offering a reward for any word that would lead them to *El Gato Negro*. Tía Andrea had spit on the handbill and tossed it into the fire. *We should turn* el patrón *in so these pigs can cut his head off and put it on a stick?!*

Even with his soft words and his promise, Rita was determined that this time her body would not respond the way it had before he'd abandoned her. She would die before she pleased him in that way again.

CHAPTER THIRTY-EIGHT

Rita wanted to lie like a stone in his bed so that he would know how completely unaffected she was, but he would not allow it.

"Here, this is not like you, *paloma*. Go ahead, fight me if you like. I will endeavor not to hurt you."

It infuriated her that he knew she would fight and so gave her his permission. As if his making it a game put him in charge from the outset.

Enraged, Rita struck out at him. He caught her wrist so that the blow only jarred her own arm. She went crazy with the need to hurt him the way she had been hurt, but this time he refused to strike her. He carried her to the bed and used his strength to overpower her and his weight to tire her. Tangling around her legs, impeding her kicks, even her skirts conspired to sap her strength.

At last she lay spent and exhausted beneath him. He was not even breathing hard. She hated that about him—his damned arrogant strength and endurance. Raising up on his arms, he lifted himself off her gasping body, and with two savage movements of his brown hands he ripped her gown from high neckline to mid-skirt. His hands did not stop their work until she lay naked. Then, standing up, watching her with level black eyes that sent spears of fear into her, moving leisurely, as if no reason existed for haste, he undressed himself.

A year and three months had passed since he had touched her, but once again Rita was staring at his lean, hard body, framed in the pale V of her unwilling thighs. He was as ruthless and, if possible, even more invulnerable looking than when she had seen him last. For one crazy second she wondered what forces had combined to produce such impenetrable ruthlessness in one so young.

Was it possible he was only twenty-two? Barely a man by most standards? But if the stories whispered about *El Gato Negro* were true, he had been killing *gringos* for six years.

Rita stared down the length of her naked body, aware of the quick rise and fall of her breasts, the smooth white skin of her belly, and inexplicably, as if she had never felt it before, a keen and piercing awareness came over her. This man—*El Gato Negro*—was her husband. She was wondering how many other women he had taken just so. How many women had watched those cruel lips curl into that insolent smile? As if he knew her thoughts and mocked her...

If she'd had a gun, she would have killed him. Her slitted eyes darted around the room, searching for a weapon. Suddenly she was remembering that first time, when she had pointed his rifle at his broad chest. *You will be sorry if you pull the trigger.* She had pulled it and been instantly sorry, because no bullet had sped out of the chamber into his broad chest. How many times had she pondered that? Wondering if it were possible that a man like Mateo Lorca had a sense of humor.

Now he came to her. For the first time in over a year her body was alive! She hated him with a passion that was soul deep, yet as he kissed her and ran his dark hands over her trembling softness, there was no possible resistance.

Lowering himself on top of her, his hands stroking and searching as his tongue teased her mouth, he whispered incomprehensible Spanish words. Touching her softly in dark, secret places, his lean, brown hands were like fire. His body was like a furnace; only his warm, taut muscles protected her from the heat within. His hands moved tantalizingly over thighs, belly, breasts; his lips pressed her mouth open so his tongue could nudge at the inner recesses the way his probing flesh nudged at her thighs. The heated throb of his member pressing against her own throbbing imprinted itself on her nerves and tissues. Her heart beat with his. Her blood surged and receded at his touch. A strange, sweet bliss settled over her, blotting out everything except this need, this man, who knew exactly how to still her resistance.

They slept and made love again. When she woke in the morning he was gone. A small leather pouch filled with gold coins lay on the kitchen table. Screaming invectives so loudly that she woke Andrea, Rita threw it across the room.

Their life followed this pattern until Andrea was seven. Rita sought no other men, and she did not ask questions about other women. She knew he had them, because she knew him and his needs too well, but she did not want proof.

The summer Andrea was seven he came to her for three days, the longest he had ever stayed. When he was ready to leave, he asked Rita if she would like to bring Andrea into the mountains with him, to get away from the relentless heat of Tubac. To her own surprise, she accepted.

Hidden deep in the Peloncillos, the quad with its surrounding pueblos caused a thrill of remembered fear in Rita. It was beginning to take on the look of a small, secluded city. Now, instead of lonely, vicious men living in bachelor quarters, families with all their noises and paraphernalia filled every nook and cranny of the limestone city. The streets were clean. Women peered out the windows of small adobe houses at Rita and Andrea.

The coolness was refreshing. Andrea loved it immediately, and, slowly, Rita began to relax. There were children for Andrea to play with. Mateo was less tense. For the first time Rita felt truly carefree with Mateo—until one afternoon she returned from an excursion to Cave Creek with other women and children to find a woman in the apartment she shared with Mateo.

Too surprised to back away, she stopped in the doorway. The young Mexican woman was pretty and, at the moment, quite petulant. Mateo's face was closed, as unreadable as ever. They did not yet see Rita.

"Why did you bring her here?" she demanded, her full lips forming a pretty pout.

"It was hot in Tubac," Mateo said negligently.

"But you never brought her before! I thought you only married her for the child."

"I did," he said quietly, coldly.

Rita turned to leave, but at that moment Mateo glanced up and saw her.

She lifted her chin. "I will go back to Tubac now," she said, her eyes as cold as his.

Mateo stood up and walked slowly toward her, the other woman forgotten.

"You will go back to Tubac when I say so," he said.

She slapped him hard across the face, not caring in that moment whether he killed her or not, not caring about anything except striking out at that stubborn, handsome face.

Lips white with fear, the other woman scampered past them. Any triumph she might have felt was lost in the greater fear that, for witnessing such an act of impertinence, Mateo would kill her as well as the most foolish *gringa*.

In a silence so heavy it almost stopped Rita's heart, barely aware that the other woman had left, Rita and Mateo stared at one another, it was almost a relief when he hit her. Fear was replaced by a flash of light and an explosion of pain.

She awoke in another room and was held there three days without seeing Andrea or Mateo. She was being punished, and she knew it. She seethed with hatred for him. His mistress had returned to his rooms, and now she lived openly with Mateo. Rita did not care about that. Now she was filled with an overriding dread that Mateo would keep Andrea from her forever.

On the fourth day, presumably when Mateo had enjoyed enough of his game, Rita and Andrea were bundled up and escorted back to Tubac by four of his men. This was much worse than the first rejection. As soon as she reached Tubac and rid herself of her escort, she bought a ticket to Fort Bowie. The stage left at nine the next morning; she and Andrea were on it. She did not say good-bye to anyone, not even Tía Andrea. When they reached Fort Bowie, Rita intended to head east until her money ran out. Wherever that happened, she would find work. She would do whatever she had to do to get back to Albany, where her brother, Tyler, lived.

The stage was robbed just south of the fort. The bandit took all Rita's money. The hotel in town did not extend credit, but the clerk, seeing her desperation, remembered that Bill Burkhart was looking for a housekeeper and that he was in town.

"Keep body and soul together, ma'am. Uh, beg pardon, ma'am, but I'll need to know your name."

"Rita Caldwell," she said quickly, giving her maiden name.

"Fine. Fine. I'll send a boy for Mr. Burkhart. You sit right there and make yourself comfortable."

Bill Burkhart was only too glad to help out. He took them out to his ranch, three miles south. He had a two-year-old daughter, a son eleven, and a young wife who flirted with the men. Rita did not like Ellen Burkhart, but she liked Bill. He was hardworking, a gruff but gentle father, and not bad looking. He had regular features, coarsened by too much exposure to the sun and wind, a thick mane of straw-colored hair, and, like the boy Steven, whom she saw only once, nice eyes. At some point the bitterness and anger that still seethed in her formed a thought—not even a thought, actually, more like a vague recognition that seemed to grow like a mushroom in a damp, dark place.

Bill Burkhart was attracted to her. His eyes followed her everywhere, and when his wife was outside, he would often find an excuse to come inside where Rita was working.

The third week Rita was there Ellen Burkhart went to Tucson to shop. She would be gone a week. Four days after she'd left, Rita appeared at Bill's bedroom door after the children were all asleep. She was beautiful, and he didn't ask questions. He made love to her, and for the first time in eight years of sleeping with a man, she felt nothing. There was no urgency, no fire, and no sweetness, but she did not care. She closed her eyes and pretended that Mateo was watching. She felt instantly reborn.

She would defeat Mateo's blind egotism at last. She would show him that he could not treat her like property to be moved here and there and used at his will.

When she was sure she was pregnant, she told Bill. He gave her enough money to take her back to Tubac and keep her and the baby comfortable for a long time. His wife would not know, and he promised to provide for the child. When Teresa was born Rita wrote to Bill, telling him the date of birth, the baby's name, and that she was blond, with blue eyes like his and Steve's.

Then she waited for Mateo's return. He always came back. She didn't care if it took five years. She wanted to see his face when he saw her blue-eyed, tow-headed daughter and found out that she had named the child Teresa Garcia-Lorca.

But even in that he managed to defeat her. The cold-eyed bastard looked at five-month-old Teresa, and his eyes softened. "She looks like my mother," he said, bending down to lift the child into his arms. "I have not seen that particular color of hair in our family for many years."

The tone of Mateo's voice was reverent, and the look on his face was one of hunger and tenderness. Could he be serious? Didn't he know that the baby could not be his?

That was all he ever said about Teresa. But that night Rita had to be mastered all over again, and Mateo—guided by the blueprint burned into their passion—set himself to the task with surprising gentleness.

Rita had somehow missed her chance to tell him. And once she didn't tell him immediately, the opportunity to right her oversight did not come. She loved little Teresa, and she wanted everyone to love her, even Mateo, because Teresa needed his love so much. She wanted to be equal to Andrea in every way. If Papa patted Andrea, Teresa would crawl over for her pat. If Papa fed Andrea from his plate, Teresa would cry for a bite of his food as well.

Their lives ground along as before. Rita resumed her place as head of her little segment of Tubac society, and Mateo treated Teresa and Andrea with the same gentleness he reserved for all children and old ones. They never spoke of her parentage again. When Teresa was nine years old Bill Burkhart visited Rita and satisfied himself that Tía was his. Bill's wife had left him by then and Rita could have become Bill's mistress or his wife, but she wanted neither position. She enjoyed the liveliness of Tubac, which was now a military outpost. She had friends, odd as they were, and enjoyed being free from the daily drudgeries of married life. She implied to Bill that she had reconciled with her husband. Half-grateful, admitting that publicly claiming his child would be embarrassing for him at this time, he made no demands on her.

Rita gazed up at the Peloncillos, looming darkly. How would he receive her? It had been a long time since she'd gone to him of her own accord.

They were almost there. Late tonight, Abuelito had said grumpily when she'd refused to stop at sunset. Late tonight.

CHAPTER THIRTY-NINE

Movement as slight as the rising of a thin dust comet on the periphery of his vision caught Mateo Lorca's attention. He turned. A dozen riders, moving in a fast, tight knot from the opposite direction, were riding toward his ambush.

Mateo frowned at the complication. Fortunately they were not close enough to be effective in time. The most they could do would be to make a nuisance of themselves and to die for their stupidity. Mateo considered giving the alternate signal—three shots instead of one to bring all his forces into action—but he rejected the idea. The intruders would probably turn tail and flee once the shooting started. And he preferred to play his cards one at a time. Patchy was an able commander; he would know how to deal with interference.

Compared with the intruders, the mule train moved at a snail's pace. Even so, in another few seconds the entire mule train would be fully inside his trap.

Mateo brought his field glasses up to his eyes. He searched the fast-moving riders, trying to penetrate the dust and commotion. He recognized no one. They would be sorry they'd happened along at this particular time. Were they fleeing the corpses they must have found on the trail behind them? Or were they bent on some other errand? A posse, perhaps? To warn Burkhart? Had Teresa told them enough to tip his hand?

Another man with less confidence or more nervousness might have rushed and spoiled the effectiveness of the ambush. Another man might have abandoned the idea altogether. But Mateo Lorca did not even consider it. With the cool, calculating nerve of the born gambler, he waited until the last man in the mule train rode into the mouth of his trap, until every man, every animal, was ensnared. The intruders were still half a mile away.

Then Mateo raised his .30-.30 and fired the lone signal shot. He did not wait to see the result but urged his horse forward and began the long, steep descent. Details were unimportant. Now he wanted to be with his men.

On the canyon floor, Steve Burkhart heard the crack of the rifle and turned in his saddle, arm raised, preparing to shout a command. Where moments ago all had been quiet, with only the jingling bells on the lead mule and the sound of hooves on hard, dry earth to entertain the birds and animals in the canyon, now bullets tore into the ground beneath his feet. A searing pain strangled the words in his throat. Horses screamed, and mules brayed in panic.

Steve could feel himself falling and knew he'd been hit, but he felt no pain. The impact jarred him, but he did not lose consciousness. Horses' hooves stamped the ground near his face. Dust choked him, blinded him. He wanted to shout orders for his men to take cover, to defend themselves, but neither his voice nor his arm responded to his commands. He was either dead or paralyzed. That thought should have upset him, but it was only words.

A neighing horse fell next to him, barely missing him. He could not be dead. He heard the ring of ricocheting bullets, the hoarse braying of mules, the yells of his men, and the screams of terrified horses.

Blackness started at the periphery of his vision and closed inward but did not close all the way. He strained to get up, but his body didn't respond; he closed his eyes. A feeling of irreparable loss settled over him.

Down the canyon Johnny Brago heard the rattle of gunfire and knew he'd lost his battle against time. They'd been so close—so damned close!

Without slowing his pace, he turned in the saddle and pointed at six of the men thundering along behind him, motioning for them to leave the narrow path and swing around to the right to come out behind the bushwhackers. The remaining men he waved to the left to follow him.

The bandits were engrossed in shooting the men who had ridden into their trap. They did not see their attackers until Johnny and his riders opened fire. Unsuspecting bandits slumped and fell.

Patchy saw the counterattackers and shouted orders. Bandits not pinned down began working their way to the south, firing as they ran.

Where the floor of the canyon narrowed to a six-foot apex, half of the bandits regrouped and spread out behind rocks, their backs once more protected. Patchy caught his breath and waited for the intruders to rush them—if they dared.

"Take cover!" Johnny yelled. "Dismount!"

Bullets whined and ricocheted off boulders as men scrambled to comply. They dropped to the ground and ran to find shelter behind rocks. Gunfire slowed and became sporadic.

Andrea and Tía rode into sight. Johnny stood up and yelled, "Get down! Keep low!" Keeping low himself, he broke cover and ran toward them. Bullets fired into rocks and ricocheted off.

They scrambled off their horses and ran to meet him. Johnny pulled them down behind a boulder almost as tall as he. "Get down, dammit!" Without looking at either of them, he shouted for Dap.

"Take them back out of range!" he yelled.

Tía tugged on Johnny's sleeve. "I'm gonna stay with you."

"It's too dangerous. I want you out of here."

She started to insist, but Andrea stopped her. "Let her stay with you. I'll go with Dap. I have to find Steve."

"I thought you were worried about her."

"That's why I want her with you," Andrea said curtly.

"I'm staying," Tía said firmly. Johnny bit back his reply. Right or wrong, Teresa Garcia-Lorca was the boss.

Andrea slipped away with Dap.

Tía huddled beside Johnny and peered around at the men visible to her. She was looking for Steve.

"If these men belong to *El Gato Negro*, where is he?"

"I reckon we'll see. I imagine he's in these rocks somewhere."

Halfway to the canyon floor, Mateo Lorca reached a small plateau and halted so his horse could rest and he could survey the results of his ambush.

Taking off his hat to allow a sudden breeze to cool his hot forehead, squinting at the rocky gulch, he could see his men bunched together at the narrow, western end of the canyon. Facing them across a relatively barren stretch of level ground, *gringos* spread out behind creosote bushes and granite boulders.

A standoff. His men could protect themselves, but little more. Fortunately he had anticipated the most damaging eventuality. Now he peered closely at the canyon walls where he had directed Patchy to place their reserves. Smiling, he saw a patch of sleeve here, a head there, a rifle barrel there, an arm over there. Excellent. They were above and behind the men who faced his loyal *caballeros*.

Taking in the various positions of his enemy, his narrowed black eyes scanned the valley floor. At most twenty men opposed him. Mateo was suddenly impatient. It was time to put an end to this farce.

Raising his rifle over his head to give the signal that would send a hail of bullets down on the unsuspecting intruders and the surviving muleteers, he started to squeeze the trigger. A breeze whipped down from the steep canyon wall. A slender arm lifted a hat and tawny gold hair tumbled down and glinted in the sunlight.

¡Madre de Dios! His heart leaped at the sight of Teresa. At the knowledge he had almost fired the shot that would end her life, weakness flushed into him. Damn Rita to hell!

Mateo shoved the rifle into its sheath and urged his horse forward. As quickly as he could manage, he worked his way down to level ground. Moving with stealth until halfway between the two warring groups, he forced his reluctant mount through the heavy undergrowth that clogged the edges of the canyon floor.

Fortunately for him, the intruders' attentions were riveted on the bandits they had driven into the mouth of the canyon. Still unobserved, Mateo cut a long, straight limb from a bush, stripped off the small branches and leaves, and jerked his white handkerchief out of his pocket. Tying it to the end of the limb, he raised it over his head and waved it from side to side. Slowly the shooting subsided. Silence. Not even a bird broke the stillness.

Waving the flag, Mateo Lorca rode out into the open.

"Surrender, *gringos*! You are surrounded."

Johnny Brago shook his head and laughed softly to himself. *El Gato Negro*, the Black Cat—hunted by the military and every peace officer in two territories and feared by every white man who had ever sneered at a Mexican. And every half-breed who'd ever shot one of his men for trying to run off with a whore.

The white flag was a lie. *El Gato Negro* would give no quarter. That was apparent from his disposition of Russ Sloan and his men—one more incident in *El Gato Negro*'s tradition of dealing justice to his white neighbors. Surrender did not enter Johnny's mind.

"Go to hell!" he yelled, lifting his rifle to aim it at *El Gato Negro*'s broad chest. Remembering those buzzard-torn bodies, he lined up the sights. His finger tightened on the trigger. Moaning, Tía reached out and pulled the barrel of his rifle toward her.

"What the hell!?"

"No!" she said. "Don't shoot him."

"Why the hell not? He's their leader. We kill him, we've got half a chance of getting out of here alive."

Shaking her head, Tía looked up. Johnny's gaze followed hers. On the canyon wall above and behind them, men stepped out from behind rocks, stood up, and pointed their rifles at Johnny. As he watched, other men stood up from behind rocks and bushes. Johnny guessed fifty or more. The canyon walls appeared suddenly to be peppered with Mexicans. He lowered his rifle and faced the bandit leader.

"Now what?" he yelled.

"Surrender the silver and the girl, and you may leave in peace."

Johnny looked at Tía. "You understand that?"

Tía shook her head miserably. Before he could stop her, she stepped around the boulder and ran toward Mateo. She stopped beside his horse, shaded her eyes with her arm, and squinted up at him.

"Why do you want to take me away?" Tía asked. Hope still lived in her that he loved her the way he always had.

"To save them, you have to come with me."

"As your daughter?"

"As my woman."

A shiver of fear rippled through her, but Tía refused to give up hope. She could go along with him now and reason with him later. He could not forget how much he had loved her. "Will you spare them if I come with you?"

Mateo's black eyes flickered with sudden amusement. Tía understood: these men meant nothing to him. Even killing them would mean nothing.

"I gave him my word. I am not some *gringo* whose word means nothing."

"I will go with you, but let me talk to him first."

"Do it quickly."

Mateo motioned with his arm, and several of the men on the canyon floor scrambled from their hiding places and began leading the mules bearing the packs toward the west end of the canyon.

Helpless anger burned in Johnny. If they weren't so outnumbered and pinned down...

Tía ran back to Johnny and stopped well out of his reach.

"I have to go with him," she said blankly.

Stepping forward, he pulled her behind the rock. With the sun shining on her honey-gold curls and her cheeks flushed with bright color, she was so beautiful she made his heart ache. But he had nothing to offer her, except a bullet in the head.

"You know what he means to do with you."

Momentary despair flooded through Tía. "I know."

Johnny held out his arms, and Tía moved into them.

"I could kill you, if I had the guts to do it."

"No. If you do that, you'll all die. If I go with him, he promised he'll spare you."

"You don't believe that bastard, do you?" *El Gato Negro* would kill them the way he had killed Russ Sloan and the others. If Tía stayed with him, she would watch them die, and then, if she were not killed herself, the bandit would take her for himself or his men or both. If she went now, she might be spared watching the slaughter, but…He sighed heavily, his mind veering away from the thought: Either way she would be brutalized; if not killed, she'd be held captive and used until death would be a blessing.

He should kill her. One quick bullet in the temple. No pain. No suffering.

Switching the rifle to his left hand, slowly, Johnny reached for his handgun. The feel of the cool ivory handle against his palm was like a blow to his guts. Tía's eyes beseeched him, pleaded with him. To what? To let her go? To shoot her? A sudden hard cramp shivered through his chest and belly. Sighing, he slipped the gun back into the holster.

So…killing her was not possible for him. Not even to save her from *El Gato Negro*.

"Kiss me good-bye, Johnny."

Johnny pulled her into his arms and kissed her cheeks, her eyes, and finally her mouth. His lips warmed to the task, and all the fear in her body dissolved. She longed to tell him she loved him, but something stopped her. Better to end it now. She had made a deal with Papa, and she would keep it. Mama had told her once that a woman paid a high price for being a woman. She had to do things that came hard. Now, suddenly, Tía knew what Mama had meant. This was the hardest thing she had ever done, and it would probably get a lot harder before it was over.

"I love you, Tía. I'll come after you."

"No, it's over, Johnny. Let it go."

Tía stepped away from him. She held up her hand to keep him back, and then stepped around the rock and into the open. As if welded to her, Johnny followed. He looked from Tía to the bandit, tall for a Mexican—tall and straight-limbed and not half-bad looking.

"Why are you going with him?" Johnny demanded.

"If you ever loved me, don't ask me to explain. I'm doing what has to be done."

Bitterness flushed through Tía. Her whole life had worked like a funnel, pouring her toward this moment when she would have to leave Johnny. She should have told him about Papa that night. Now it was impossible. Too late. There were so many things she should have told him.

I love you, Johnny. Take care of Andrea for me. So much more burned in her heart to be said.

Aloud, she said nothing. Her throat wouldn't work around the lump that burned there. Johnny would take care of Andrea and Steve. He would do whatever had to be done—always—because he was decent and responsible. Now his dark gaze, so level and watchful, flicked over her again. The corners of his lips were tucked in. In disgust? Or despair?

It didn't matter. This part of her life was over.

Johnny's hand went back to the gun. It was apparent to him that Tía felt something for this bandit. Maybe *El Gato Negro* felt something for her as well. Once a long time ago he had heard a rumor about *El Gato Negro* and his lovely blond mate—supposedly a white slave he had taken in a raid on a wagon train. Perhaps Tía had been chosen as her replacement. Perhaps *El Gato* would keep her for himself. As repugnant as that thought was, it beat killing her by his own hand. Rage blazed through Johnny. He didn't want another man to touch her. The thought of *El Gato* using Tía, who should be cherished and taken only in love…

Tía motioned Johnny back as Mateo's men led the mules past her. It was time to go. Without looking back at Johnny, she turned and walked to her stepfather.

Already mounted, Mateo kicked his boot out of the stirrup. Tía put her foot into the wooden stirrup, and he swung her up behind him.

Johnny trembled with helpless anger, but his hand dropped away from his pistol. Tía's slender, golden arms tightened around *El Gato Negro*'s waist. Her proud, slender body swayed gently as the horse started to move away. Her shining golden curls blurred out of focus. He wasn't man enough to do the one thing that could save her. He would have to live with the knowledge of that weakness, but, he thought, looking around at the Mexicans aiming their rifles at him and his men, not for long.

CHAPTER FORTY

"You should get some sleep, young man," Dr. Potter said, stopping beside Judy's bed.

Grant sighed. "I don't want her to be alone, in case she wakes up. She doesn't like to be alone..." His voice drifted off.

Shaking his head, Potter walked away. Young people. Damned unrealistic. She'd have to be alone someday. When she was old and wrinkled—*if* she got old and wrinkled.

Judy lay on the edge of consciousness, drifting in and out as if in a dream. She heard Grant talking to Potter, and it touched her that Grant cared. He'd been there all night and all that day. Sometimes he held her hand. Sometimes he just sat beside her, sleeping lightly in the chair. Once he stretched out on the floor near her bed.

She drifted away and then back again. Slumped in the chair, Grant slept. Judy stared at him for a long time. He called his face a clown face. Suddenly she resented that. He had a nice face. The mouth no longer seemed too wide, the jaw too simian. They were generous, and they fit him perfectly. Actually she didn't really notice the outside of Grant much anymore. Lately she saw only his goodness and decency, beaming out of his eyes.

Her chest ached with a hot, crying pain, but she choked the tears back. Grant Foreman was a good man; he loved her, but something had happened to her when Morgan Todd beat her. Now she couldn't face Grant—him or anyone.

Morning? Afternoon? She must have slept again. An orderly came to check on her. His hands were warm and strangely impersonal; she liked the way they felt, so anonymous, so undemanding.

"How is Mr. Todd?" Grant asked as the orderly took her pulse.

"Woke up without a fever. The surgeon said the bullet hit his hipbone and stopped. The onlyest thing he could think of was that it must have been some wet powder or some such. The doc said he never seen a forty-five slug that didn't have the juice to smash bone. Usually a forty-five'll tear a hole in a man big enough to drive a steer through."

The orderly shook his head and grinned. "Course Todd must have the constitution of a loco bull. Even complained about being hungry. Asking about the young lady."

Grant grunted.

Judy woke slowly. Grant was sleeping again. Shafts of sunset gold slanted in the window, lighting the far wall. The air was drowsy and warm. It smelled of meat and potatoes and spicy, fruity pies. Judy's stomach growled. Footsteps shuffled close to her bed.

"Excuse me, sir. Didn't mean to wake you. Mr. Todd insisted he had to see the young lady. So I wrestled him into a wheelchair." It was the orderly. Judy recognized his voice. A moment's silence was followed by the sound of wheels rolling on the wooden floor. Grant mumbled something, and footsteps walked away.

"Judy," Morgan whispered. His voice was so close beside her. Her heart leaped with fear. "Look, honey, I know you can't hear me, but I got to tell you something." He sighed heavily. "You're half-dead because of me, and I'm thinking of myself. Guess that's just the way I am. No damned good. Anyway, I'm not good at this mushy stuff, you know that, but well, dammit, I'm in love with you, and I want you to marry me. I never realized it before, honey, but I need you. I need you to be pretty and cute and funny and to love me back. I need you to get well. I swear I'll never hurt you again, even if you treat me like the dog I am."

Morgan could not believe what he was doing. Proposing to Judy Burkhart! But she was so beautiful. Even bruised, a cool, sweet loveliness glowed in her face.

With his hands, Morgan covered, then uncovered his face. He opened his eyes; Judy blinked twice and stared at him. The look in her eyes staggered him. Her dark eyes watched him coolly, with intent and level gaze, as if she saw everything in great depth. He forgot to be amazed that she was awake.

"Judy?"

"I heard you," she said softly.

"Oh, Jesus! I'm so glad you're alive! I'm so damned glad I didn't kill you."

"Me, too."

Morgan flushed. "You heard what I said?"

"Yeah."

"Well?"

Judy shook her head. "No...I...I'm...grateful for what you said, Morgan, but I can't marry you." She shrugged. "I don't love you."

He bowed his head. "Can't blame you for that...after what I done."

"It has nothing to do with what you did...not really. I never loved you, Morgan. I always loved Johnny."

Morgan sighed, and pain stabbed into his chest, reminding him of his own injury. "He must love you, to shoot me..." His weakness was becoming more pronounced. He waved to the orderly. "Think about what I said...anyway."

"I will," she said gently, knowing she wouldn't.

The orderly came and wheeled Morgan away, and Judy wondered what had happened to Grant. He should be back by now.

Grant waited and watched by the window at the front of the hospital barracks. After a few seconds of watching Todd's face while he talked to Judy's still form, he turned away.

Morgan Todd was in love with Judy Burkhart. Really in love with her...the way she wanted a man to love her. And he was handsome and rich. And he had learned his lesson. Now Morgan could learn to cherish Judy the way she deserved...

Grant turned away from the window. Slowly, blindly, he walked away. At first he didn't know where he was going, but then, somehow, he did. It was time. He had put this off long enough.

Rutledge's door stood slightly ajar. Grant walked inside. The captain looked up; Grant saw recognition in his eyes.

"I shot Morgan Todd."

Rutledge's mouth went slack. Uncomprehending, he stared at Grant. "What?"

"I shot him. It was me, not Brago."

"Why are you telling me this?"

"Because it's true, and I need to get it off my chest. I can't let Brago sit in jail for something I did."

Rutledge sighed. The man looked like he was telling the truth. Damnation! "If you're telling the truth, I'm gonna have to lock you up, you know that, don't you? I have to let him go and lock you up. You want that?"

"Whatever I deserve, I'll take," Grant said.

"But you were sitting with the girl, with Judy…" Rutledge stopped. He was confused. He liked this young man. He liked the way he looked and the way he had stayed by Judy's side. The orderly had told him how Foreman had refused to leave her alone.

"Why are you leaving her?" he demanded, stalling.

"She has someone else now. She doesn't need me."

"Who?"

"Morgan Todd."

"That bastard! You'd leave her with him? He beat her. Didn't you know that?"

"I knew. That's why I shot him. I saw him drag her into the barn. I took Johnny's gun from his cabin. I ran toward the barn, but before I got there Todd staggered outside and started yelling. I let him go by and ran into the barn. I found Judy—dead, I thought. So I followed Todd and shot him."

"Mr. Foreman, you were not exactly alone in that compound. A dozen men stood guard around that wall. A company of soldiers slept within three hundred feet of where Todd was shot."

"The guards were looking out, not in. I didn't announce my intentions. I just walked up to him and shot him. By then people were running toward me, but I slipped into the orchard and climbed a tree. They ran right past." Grant hung his head. "I thought he had killed Judy. To my way of thinking he deserved to die."

"I could not agree with you more. The man's a scoundrel. He may have wealth, but that does not mitigate the fact that he is a worthless scoundrel. Judy Burkhart deserves better than him."

Confused, Grant sat down in the chair facing Rutledge's desk.

"The bastard should have croaked. Can't depend on a doctor. Usually they kill men in surgery, but Potter saved him. Blast it! Saving a stupid bastard like that. Can't depend on anything anymore. Nothing ever works out." Rutledge sighed.

"What do you want me to do? Should I go over to the stockade?"

"Stockade? No. No…go back to Judy. Stay with her."

"But I confessed."

"You going to run away?" Rutledge demanded angrily.

"Well, no, but—"

"Then do as you're told!"

Grant looked so thoroughly miserable that Judy stirred and pretended to wake up for the first time.

He jerked alert. "Hey," he said slowly, "you're awake. Thank God... Are you okay?"

"I think so," she said, looking about. "Where's Steve? Is he back yet?"

Grant didn't want to bother her with the details. "Not yet. Johnny went to get him. How do you feel?"

"A little dizzy. Not so unusual for me, huh?"

"You look wonderful."

"I'm a wreck. How long have I been out?"

"Two days."

Judy touched her face and winced. "Where's Steve?"

"You just asked me that," Grant said, but she looked at him so blankly that he realized she didn't remember his answer. "He left with the mule train. Johnny will reach him in time."

"How've you been?" she asked.

"Couldn't be better, now that you're awake. Does everything work? You know, hands, feet, liver?"

Judy wiggled. "Seems to."

Relief flooded through Grant.

Judy slept again, this time straight through until morning. She ate breakfast and sat up, and Grant felt so relieved that not even the cramp in his back could put him in a bad mood. Either that chair was getting harder or his back was getting softer.

"Grant, I need to talk to you about Morgan," Judy said, sounding softer, less sure of herself.

A sense of foreboding seeped into him. "I saw him talking to...I didn't know you were awake..."

"I was about half-awake. He said he was sorry about what he did. I think he said he wants to marry me."

Grant leaned back in his chair, studying his booted feet halfway under the bed. "He'll probably make a real good husband for you now that he's learned his lesson."

Staring at the ceiling, Judy fought down the hard lump rising in her throat. Why had she started this? Out of the corner of her eye, she was watching Grant. He wasn't even looking at her. "Probably," she whispered.

"Well," Grant said briskly. "See how well everything works out." He had meant to say more, but lies did not come easily to him. He plunged ahead before he could back out. "Funny how things work out. When I went over to the post office yesterday afternoon while Morgan Todd was visiting with you I found out I had a letter that's been sitting there for a couple of weeks. My mother needs me. My father...had a stroke..."

"Oh no! Oh, Grant, I'm so sorry!"

Grant colored with embarrassment at her distress. "It was only a minor stroke. He's going to be fine. It's just that now they need me to run the store. I guess he's thinking about retiring for good. I'll be number-one son—for a while, anyway."

"That's a wonderful opportunity for you, isn't it?" she asked, her voice breaking. She forced an apologetic laugh. "I'll have to learn to talk all over again. Bet you'll be glad to miss that," she said, gazing out the window. Her hands twisted at the sheet.

"It won't take you long. I'd stake money on that."

"Sure. I'll be fine. I'll write you letters. Tell you about what a wonderful time I'm having. Will you be leaving right away?"

Grant shrugged. "I'll wait till you go home. You can put up with me that long, can't you?"

"Sure," she said. "What are friends for?"

CHAPTER FORTY-ONE

"Wal, I'll be hornswoggled!" Red McElhaney said, shaking his unruly red hair to get out the sand and burrs he had picked up when he'd dived off his horse. Red had seen Steve Burkhart go down and hadn't waited for instructions. All his mother's sons had well-developed survival instincts.

Dap stood up and brushed at his clothes. "They left," he said.

Johnny surveyed the horizon, shaking his head. He couldn't understand it, either. *El Gato Negro* had spared them! He'd had them pinned down, outnumbered four to one, and he had ridden away with Tía and the silver exactly as he had said he would. It didn't make sense, but there was no time now to ponder it.

He turned to Dap. "I want you to take charge. Take the dead and wounded back to Fort Bowie."

"Where you going?" Dap asked. He knew the answer already. He'd watched Johnny looking at Tía for the past week.

"South," Johnny said, his eyes narrowed into slits as he glanced off in the direction the girl had gone.

"I won't need all these men to nurse a few cripples."

"You will if you run into Chatto or Geronimo."

"And you won't?" Dap growled.

"I move easier alone."

Dap lifted his eyebrows in consternation. "A smart cock-a-doodle-doo would send somebody else."

"Well, now you know why I'm going."

"Good luck."

"Thanks," Johnny said dryly.

• • •

Halfway to the pueblos, Patchy Arteaga pulled Mateo Lorca aside.

"*Un momento, General,*" he said respectfully.

It was time for a rest stop. Mateo raised his hand. The girl drooped behind him. Dismounting, he steadied her sagging form and then walked a distance away so Patchy could speak to him privately.

"We are being followed."

"How many?"

"One."

Mateo looked back over the trail. "The one who spoke for them?"

"*Sí.*"

Eyes closed, Mateo considered this information. Johnny Brago was well known to him: as the man who had shot one of his *caballeros* for a slight indiscretion, as the man who had lain with Tía, and as a man with a reputation as a fast gun, a man who killed his own kind. Mateo's lips curled with contempt. "Let him come," he said slowly. "Keep him in sight. I will tell you when to kill him."

"*Sí, General.*"

When they reached the pueblos, the sun was still high in the evening sky. Tía drooped with weariness. Mateo helped her down and turned her over to a short man with a sweat-shiny cherubic face. He led her up a long flight of stairs, put her inside a sparsely furnished room, and stationed himself outside the door.

The room had a bed, a bureau, two straight-backed chairs, and a table. Tía stumbled to the bed and dropped across it. She had slept only a few hours in the past forty-eight.

She should have been worried; she knew what Papa intended to do with her. But she was too tired to grapple with that now. Shutting everything out, she curled into a tight little knot in the center of the bed and fell almost instantly into an exhausted sleep.

Mateo Lorca spent two hours seeing to the details that required his attention. He settled a dispute between two men who had both claimed the same woman in marriage. He gave directions for the conversion of the silver into cash. He ordered supplies from a town in the Animas Valley where his operatives could obtain anything from gold to shellfish. He ate with three of his lieutenants, and then, while the sun was still relatively high in the sky, he went to his room.

Teresa was asleep. With her face unguarded and her arm thrown back over her head in childish abandonment, she looked no more than ten years old. Mateo sighed heavily and turned away. He walked back to the door, but he could not bring himself to pull the latch key. He stood there feeling a hard emptiness in his stomach, cursing himself for his weakness.

The girl is a *gringa*, he reminded himself. The daughter of that bitch and her *gringo* lover! Female captives must be treated as the women of my family had been treated by the hated *gringos*.

Mateo said the words in his mind, but he did not respond. Tiredly he leaned against the door. *You are getting old, Mateo. Old and senile and soft. Like a woman. For years now you have been avoiding the taking of female prisoners. Now, instead of a war camp, you rule a small city. Because you have encouraged your men to keep women of their own kind, because you are soft.*

A sickness rose up in him, filling his chest and tightening his throat. No matter how hard he resisted, the images kept coming. He saw Teresa as she had been at five with her oversized childish head on her slender, round little body. She had been the most beautiful, magical creature he had ever seen on the back of a horse. The look in her blue eyes as she slowly overcame her own fears and realized that she could master the animal by her will alone, her joy and gratitude when she looked at him— as if he alone had given her this gift. Even in memory, his pride filled him with intense joy.

He needed to put these images aside and remember that Teresa was his enemy. Her mother had hated him so much that she'd flaunted this blond bastard before him and the world.

Deliberately he concentrated on Rita—his bitch of a wife—seeing her as clearly as if she were standing before him. He smiled. She would be devastated. Inconsolable. Fighting for her cub, she would be a tigress. She would be as she had been that first night…

The memory of that night was bright and hard in his mind. He relived it all, every second of it. Mateo straightened. He was fortified; he could feel the heavy pulsation of his lust.

"Wake up, *gringa*."

Moaning softly, Tía rolled over, burying her face under her arms.

"Wake up. Or would you prefer that I offer you to my men?" he asked, his voice tight and harsh.

"Ohhh…" Tía turned over, blinking. "Papa?"

"Do not call me that unless you wish to die. You are your mother's bastard, nothing more."

Tía sat up in bed. Papa's black eyes were filled with coldness. Like an animal waking in the night, instantly alert, fear sprang alive in her. She scooted away until her back touched the brass headboard of the bed.

Mateo smiled. With fear in her wide blue eyes, she looked like Rita the night after he'd first mastered her.

In that moment she *was* Rita. Mateo stepped toward her.

Swallowing, her breast heaving with the sudden fear that gripped her, Tía looked quickly from side to side. A bottle lay on its side near the bed. She threw herself at it, grabbed it by the slender round neck, and broke the bottom against the brass headboard of the bed. The green glass shattered. Turning, she pressed the jagged glass against her neck under her ear.

Mateo stopped. They stared at each other in silence, the tension like a visible wall between them. Tía was aware of the throb of her artery against the cool edge of the glass.

As Mateo started forward, Tía pressed the sharp edge against her skin. "Wait!" he said.

Her eyes opened. Mateo held up his hand to stop her, noticing the tiny stream of blood trickling down her slim throat. She would do it, he realized in surprise. She would kill herself before she let him touch her. She was a *gringa*, but she was her mother's daughter.

He stepped back. Now he had something to stir him—a worthy opponent. Smiling, he bowed low before her. "You win this round, *niña*, but I will return. Next time, I will be better prepared."

The door closed. Shaking as if she had taken a chill, Tía dropped the bottle and collapsed across the bed.

Mateo Lorca found Patchy in the *cantina*, enjoying tequila with three friends. The two comrades walked outside, where the sinking sun was still hot in the western sky.

"All is not well?" Patchy said, studying his chief's face.

Mateo frowned aside the question. "Bring Johnny Brago to me... alive."

"The one who followed us?"

"*Sí*. Are your men still watching him?"

"*Sí*." Patchy paused. "I will see to it."

"Alive and unhurt. I would have the pleasure of changing that myself."

"*Sí, mí general*. It will be as you wish."

"*Pronto*."

"Within the half hour, *mí general*."

CHAPTER FORTY-TWO

Like a toy city beneath the billowing skirts of a female colossus, the pueblos sat at the bottom of a massive, smooth sweep of limestone. From the canyon wall opposite the pueblos, Johnny watched the activity through field glasses.

For all intents and purposes, it was a city he watched. Men, women, animals, children, came and went as naturally as if they lived in Fort Bowie and their existence was guaranteed by the full resources of the U.S. Cavalry. But why shouldn't they feel safe? No one had ever followed *El Gato Negro* to his lair and lived to tell about it.

Johnny knew enough about *El Gato Negro* to know that if the man captured him, he would not live to tell about it, either. The whereabouts of the Black Cat's mountain hideaway was worth his life. If the army knew where *El Gato Negro* was, they would come after him with a thousand soldiers. They wanted him that badly. As an intruder who carried this knowledge, his only chance, if he had one, was to sneak in after dark, take Tía, and sneak out again without her being missed.

Not a small order. Johnny drew his bowie knife and tested the edge for sharpness. Taking out a whetstone, he honed the blade long and patiently until the edge gleamed with deadly sharpness. Next he took one of his blankets and cut a hole in the middle for his head. It would serve as a serape. After dark, dressed like a Mexican, perhaps he could slip in and get close enough to be effective.

He ate three biscuits and some bacon he had squirreled away in his saddlebags and then stretched out to wait for darkness. He'd closed his eyes for only a moment when a sound beside him drew his attention outward. Slowly he opened his eyes. A dozen fierce-eyed *vaqueros* surrounded him, their rifles aimed at his chest.

"You will come with us." The man who spoke had a round, morose face with large, doleful eyes and full, tremulous lips. His clothes were hidden beneath a serape covered with once colorful patches. Now they were merely dirty.

Johnny frowned. It didn't make sense. They should have killed him on the spot. Slowly he rose to his feet.

"¡*Andale!*" The one in the dirty serape prodded him with the barrel of his rifle. Johnny moved with more alacrity, but not as much as they would have liked, just enough to stop the pain in his ribs.

They tied his hands behind his back, took his knife, guns, and rifle, and then they paraded him through the village streets. Men and women watched from doors and windows, much as they would have in Tombstone if the sheriff had brought in a prisoner: curious, impassive, but not personally concerned. As soon as he had passed, curtains dropped back into place and families returned to their dinners. Johnny smelled the rich, beefy aroma, and his stomach growled.

"Wait here."

"Here" was in the central courtyard at the bottom of a long stairway that led up to two pueblos that sat far above all the others. The man in the dirty serape climbed the stairs and knocked on one of the doors. *El Gato Negro* appeared, they talked briefly, and then the man came back and spoke to the men guarding Johnny. They called him Patchy.

Upstairs, *El Gato Negro* walked to the other door, opened it, and disappeared inside. Patchy rattled off orders in rapid, slurred Spanish. Then all the Mexicans walked away until they were out of earshot and talked together in low tones.

What were they up to now? Uncomfortable, Johnny strained his ears to hear, but it was no use. Damn! He hated surprises.

Mateo Lorca walked next door to the room where he had left Teresa. As soon as his hand touched the door latch, a scuttling sound started inside. When the door swung wide, he saw Teresa crouched in the far corner of the room, the broken bottle pressed to her throat.

He chuckled softly. "Still prepared, I see."

Tía licked dry lips but did not reply. Her eyes were hard with determination. That was good, thought Mateo. Her stubbornness fanned the flames of his own resolve.

"A friend of yours has come to call."

"A friend? Who?"

"Or should I have said a lover?" he asked softly, his lips curling in contempt.

"No. I don't believe you."

"Johnny Brago," he said, enjoying the fleeting look of fear, disbelief, and finally hope that darkened her eyes.

"I don't believe you."

"Look for yourself. He is in the courtyard below."

"It's a trick."

"No trick. I will step outside."

He did so, closing the door after him and moving far enough away so she would feel safe in walking to the window set high on the wall beside the door.

Tía walked to the window. True to his word, Papa leaned against the far wall, watching her. Keeping him in her field of vision, Tía cautiously dropped her gaze to the quad. She saw Johnny at once: standing bareheaded, flanked by a dozen bandits, and managing somehow to look imperturbably at ease.

Tía turned away. They had him! Her heart leaped to a painful, erratic rhythm. Papa had Johnny.

Mateo walked back to the door, paused as if he would give her a chance to back away, and then opened it, but Tía did not move away. She was beaten, and she knew it. He would know it, too. That was why Johnny still lived. Now she remembered her stepfather's words: *Next time I will be better prepared.*

Mateo smiled. The girl's defeat darkened her eyes.

"Give me the bottle," he said softly.

Slowly, Tía complied. Mateo took the bottle and smashed it against the wall.

"And now you will behave yourself, *niña.*"

Tía walked back to the window and looked down at Johnny. "I'm not a fool. I know you have to kill him. You can't let him go back and tell the soldiers how to find you."

"He only found the way because he followed us."

"How do I know I can trust you?"

"If I give my word, you can trust it. I am not a *gringo* that I would give my word and go back on it."

Tía covered her face. She should have killed herself when she'd had the chance. Let Johnny fend for himself. He wouldn't appreciate her doing this for him, unless he had never loved her…

Tía pushed the thoughts away. She loved Johnny. Anything would be preferable to watching him die in some horrible way Papa would undoubtedly decree.

"If you promise me on your word of honor that you will spare him and let him go free, and that you will not hurt Mama, not ever, then I will agree," she said.

Mateo hid the smile that threatened to show on his face. Teresa was braver than he had dreamed possible. She did not cry or threaten. If she agreed to be his mistress, he would not have to kill Rita. Finding out Teresa had replaced her would be punishment enough—and more suitable than death, because Rita would die inside every day he kept Tía, or as long as Rita lived. His body flushed with the power of his revenge. He felt better than he had felt in months.

"I agree, *niña mía*! But," he added, smiling, "there is one other condition. You must convince your young *caballero* that you do not wish to leave with him. I do not want him coming back for you. Can you do that? If not," he said, shrugging, "then he must die."

Johnny watched *El Gato Negro* walk from one of the apartments upstairs, confer with the morose man in the serape, then enter a different apartment. Patchy hobbled down the steps into the courtyard, untied Johnny's hands, and motioned him to follow. They climbed the stairs, and Patchy knocked on the door.

El Gato Negro himself opened it. "Come! Come!" he said, motioning Johnny inside with bluff heartiness.

Slowly, his gaze darting for sight of Tía, Johnny stepped inside the room. *El Gato Negro* was alone, the room sparsely furnished. Johnny had expected to see Tía. His anticipation must have been reflected in his eyes because *El Gato Negro* laughed.

"You are a foolhardy young man, Señor Brago. Brave but foolhardy. No one else has ever followed the Black Cat into his lair...and lived to tell about it. You must want to see me very badly. To what do I owe the pleasure of this visit?"

"You know that as well as I. I want the girl. I want Tía," he said grimly.

Mateo threw back his head and sent up peals of cynical laughter. Still laughing, shaking his head, he waved Johnny to a chair.

"We made a trade, Señor Brago. Does this mean you have decided to welsh on it?"

"It was your trade, not mine. I didn't agree to anything."

"Ah, but you have your life, and I have the girl and the silver. If we reverse that..." He shrugged as if he could not understand how Johnny could even consider it. "Please, I am a most abominable host, am I not? Sit. We will have a drink, some dinner. You must be famished, Señor Brago. You have had a long, hard ride." He wiped his eyes to dry the tears of laughter. "As for the girl, she belongs to me. But," he said, smiling with easy grace, "if she wants to go with you, she is free to do so."

"And if I believe that, you've got this horse you want to sell me. Not more than twenty or thirty years old, right?"

Mateo laughed. "You are very young, Señor Brago. Have you ever tried to keep a woman prisoner? I'm a very careful, thorough man, and I do not believe it could be done. A man has to sleep sometimes, does he not?" Two bottles sat on the table. He shoved a tumbler and the whiskey bottle toward Johnny. "Perhaps it could be done, but I have better things to do than to worry about unwilling females. As you perhaps noticed, there is no shortage of women in my camp."

"I want to see Tía. Where is she?"

"Next door. We were, as you would say, engaged, when we were rather rudely interrupted. She will repair whatever damage she can, and then I will ask her to join us. Would you like a drink? Some wine if this is not to your liking?"

Johnny did not believe a word *El Gato Negro* said. But he would play this out: he had no choice. "Whiskey," he said.

"Ahhh! A real *gringo*. Wine is too slow for real men, isn't it? I will have wine." *El Gato Negro* lifted the cork out of the whiskey bottle and poured for Johnny, then poured wine for himself.

Johnny took a quick sip and set his glass down. "When can I see her?"

"Ahhh! The young are so eager. So impatient. Come. We will see her now."

On the bureau rested a bowl and water pitcher she hadn't noticed before. Tía poured water into the bowl and washed her face. That helped a little. A small piece of mirror tacked on the wall at head height beckoned her. Using the towel, she rubbed some of the dust out of her hair and pinched color into her cheeks.

Footsteps sounded on the adobe walkway between the two rooms. Panic momentarily filled her. It was one thing to talk brave and another to actually be brave.

"Are you decent, *niña*?"

The door opened, and Papa stepped in. From behind him, Johnny's eyes beseeched her. For a moment she couldn't breathe. She wouldn't be able to do it. Then her stepfather's caustic voice, saying words she could barely comprehend, angered her, gave her strength.

"I can understand why you want her, Señor Brago. She is lovely. Truly lovely," he crooned, pulling Tía close to him and caressing her. "Not too skinny so the bones get in the way, but young and firm. I like that. Do you like that, Señor Brago?"

Tía hated to think what Johnny thought of her now. Papa's words flowed around her like water around a rock in a stream. Their eddy caused turbulence in Johnny, who had stopped by the door a good ten feet away.

"You son of a..." As Johnny started forward Mateo drew his revolver and pointed it at his chest.

"Now, now, do not be harsh. Here. Feel her breasts. Exquisite, aren't they?"

"Get your filthy hands off her!"

Mateo laughed. "Aren't you being a bit presumptuous, Señor Brago? Or don't your women get to decide for themselves? Is she protesting? Does she look so unhappy? Or just a little dazed by an unfortunate interruption?" Mateo laughed at the look on Johnny's face. "You could tear me apart, couldn't you? Except that would not be wise. You would be dead before you got halfway across the room. And for what? Does she look so defiant?"

"What have you done to her?"

"Nothing, yet." He shrugged. "Well, almost nothing. We were interrupted. She will be fine as soon as I can take proper care of her, won't you, *niña*?" Papa's voice was as slick as bear grease. Calculated, no doubt, to make Johnny feel the fool.

Mateo sheathed the gun. Sighing at the look of fury on the young man's face, he gave Tía a seductive pat, pulled her close to him, and turned her around so she faced her young man. Then he pressed himself against her backside and stroked her from her belly to her breasts. Johnny Brago's face flamed brick red.

"Nice, eh? Nice ass, nice breasts. No wonder you want her, eh, Mr. Brago? Even *gringos* occasionally have good taste in women, eh?"

Johnny's heartbeat fueled a massive rage, but caution held him immobile. Tía's face gave nothing away. Looking at him through hooded eyes, she just leaned there, letting that bastard fondle her.

The look on Johnny's face was deeply satisfying to Mateo. Smiling, he turned the girl into his arms. Her eyes closed, her long lashes fluttered

JOYCE BRANDON

and then lay still on her flushed cheeks. He turned her slightly so Johnny could see the rise and fall of her small breasts as she sighed and leaned against him. Her lips were soft. At his touch they parted, trembling, as she lifted them to his without resistance.

"Not now, *niña*. We have company."

Mateo turned her back to face Johnny. Unable to help herself, Tía opened her eyes and looked at him. His face looked strained. The corners of his lips were tight and grim. There was no sigh now in the cool, contemplative look he gave her of what she had once thought of as vulnerability. He looked detached. Somehow that made her part easier to play. She summoned an image of Judy being sultry and tried to imitate her. She must have succeeded because Johnny looked struck to the core. Mateo ignored Johnny's obvious distress and smiled at him as if the two men were co-conspirators.

"You'll stay for dinner before you start back, won't you, Señor Brago?"

Slowly, amusement erased the anguish in Johnny's eyes. He lifted one straight black brow and shrugged, managing to remind them in that one slight, sardonic expression that he was still very much a prisoner and of course would do whatever they wanted him to do.

"Unless you're in a hurry to be going?" Mateo asked with heavy solicitousness.

"Well, I do have to be getting back," Johnny drawled. "Unless you have other plans for me."

"Ahhh! You are a very astute young man," he said admiringly. "There is a time for killing and a time for drinking. I'm all through killing for today. Tomorrow, perhaps, but no more today." Mateo was enjoying this more than he had expected. Teresa was a better actress, too. He pushed her forward. "If she wants to go with you, take her. You have my blessing."

Johnny held out his hand to Tía. "Let's go."

Everything within her urged her to take Johnny's outstretched hand. Her heart thundered, but she remembered in time and affected a sulky, pouty look, which she flashed at her stepfather. "I'm not ready to leave yet. I just got here."

Johnny looked from Tía to *El Gato Negro*. Even when he heard it from her own lips, he did not believe it.

Mateo threw back his head and laughed. "What's the matter, Señor Brago? Are you surprised? Is this your first experience with women? Haven't you learned what fickle little things they are?" He shoved Tía toward Johnny, smiling benignly. "Go with him if you want, *niña*. I have lots of women."

388

Whirling on her stepfather, Tía stamped her foot and put her hands on her hips. "No!" she said softly. "I must stay with you. Please don't send me away again."

Mateo shrugged, contempt sparkling in his black eyes. "What can I do, Señor Brago? She is crazy about me."

Feeling the fool, Johnny stepped forward. "Tía?"

At last Tía turned and looked at him. "Go away, Johnny."

Tía's blue eyes filled with despair—the sort of look a mother might give to a child who had pestered her too long. Johnny realized she didn't really want to hurt him, but this was where she wanted to be. He had misunderstood again. He should have let her go.

Tía turned away from him, and her hand reached out and touched *El Gato Negro*'s vest. It fluttered there a moment and then slid up to caress *El Gato*'s jawline. The bastard leaned down and kissed her possessively. Tía pressed against him. *El Gato* looked at Johnny, triumph sparkling in his black eyes. Feeling sick inside, Johnny turned away. He wanted to tear Tía from *El Gato*'s embrace, but he did nothing...

CHAPTER FORTY-THREE

Mateo released her and turned her in his arms so she faced Johnny. His eyes searched hers, as if trying to see into her soul. It was almost a relief when Mateo pulled her back against him. He turned her so she faced him instead of Johnny and stroked her arm.

"You will forgive us, Señor Brago, if we seem eager to be alone, but you do have a prior commitment. You see, I have arranged for my men to, shall we say, watch over you. Your horse has been placed at the north end of the canyon. You will walk to your horse. A simple thing, no? Unfortunately, several of my men have a grudge against you for shooting their friends, and it would be foolish of me to let you go so you can lead the soldiers back here, would it not? We would have to find another hideaway. That is not an easy thing to do. There are so many of us."

Spreading his hands and smiling apologetically, Mateo paused to give Johnny the opportunity to make a fool of himself, as all hostages were quick to do. But Johnny remained stoic, his expression unreadable.

Conceding that point to Johnny, Mateo continued. "But I am a magnanimous man. If you do not hear a signal shot, you will know I have decided to move my camp and give you your life."

"*Gracias*," Johnny said dryly.

"It's a five-minute walk, Señor Brago. Five minutes in which to contemplate your life and, if you are so inclined, to make peace with your God. You do have a God, do you not?"

Nothing in the world could keep Tía from turning to look at Johnny. He quirked his eyebrows at her, stuck his hands in his pockets, and sauntered to the window.

Leaning forward, he looked out in both directions. Men with rifles lounged on either side of the path he would no doubt be walking. Who else but *El Gato Negro*, with his legendary cruelty, could have thought up such an effective way to torture a man without ever touching him?

Johnny turned back to face Tía. She wanted to look away but could not. Grudging admiration sparkled in his dark eyes, and a bitter smile twisted his lips. He walked across the small room and took her hand in his. Then, with a challenging half smile to *El Gato Negro*, he raised Tía's hand to his lips. At the last second he turned it slowly and pressed a kiss into her palm.

"Good-bye, Tía." For one fleeting second real emotion broke through his careful facade; his narrowed eyes darkened with pain. If not for Mateo's powerful hands on her shoulders, holding her securely and possessively, she would have collapsed.

"*Adios, señor.*" Papa's rich voice vibrated with enjoyment.

Johnny nodded. He sauntered to the door and closed it quietly behind him. His husky *Good-bye, Tía* aching inside her, Tía watched him walk past the window and down the steps. Furious, she turned on Mateo.

"You promised to spare him!"

"Is he dead?" he taunted.

"Not yet, but those men…"

"If I am too busy to give the agreed-upon signal, they will do nothing." His mouth adjusted itself into a meaningful line.

The blood drained from her face. "Now?"

"First we watch your lover walk to his horse."

"But you said—"

"I lied. There are men waiting along the first two miles of the path he must ride to leave this canyon. They will not shoot him until he is on his horse. And not then…unless I give the signal." He laughed. "I wanted you to watch him, *niña*. With five minutes to ponder when I will give the signal, a man's true character has a chance to surface. Will he crawl and whimper, or will he accept the inevitable with dignity? Or perhaps you will fail to keep your part of the bargain, and he will die anyway. Or, if he crawls, perhaps that will make his death more acceptable to you."

"Johnny's no coward!"

"We will see, won't we?" Smiling, he tilted her head up so he could watch her expression; he stroked her cheek. "Or perhaps you are the coward, *niña*? Maybe we will learn something about both of you…"

Holding her firmly by the shoulders, he turned her so she could see out the tiny window. He moved close behind her so the length of his body touched hers. Testing her resolve, his hands glided from her shoulders to her breasts. His warm fingers made small squeezing motions around the nipples. It pleased Mateo that his plan for retribution absolved him from any attachment he had to Teresa as his daughter.

His body responded to her as it had to Rita or to any attractive woman.

Fighting the despair that closed like a mantle around her senses, Tía shut her eyes. Papa's hands on her breasts fairly burned her. She felt such intense shame that she could not think. Papa's hands made her ashamed of her body, disgusted by it. She didn't ever want to be touched again, not by anyone. Papa seemed indifferent to her shudder of revulsion and confusion.

She could not imagine how she could live with herself after letting him defile her. Or how he could live with himself...

At the foot of the stairs, Johnny paused. Tía's attention riveted instantly on him in spite of Papa. She imagined herself calling out to him, telling him he was safe, that it was all a trick, but she said nothing. Suddenly the room seemed hot—dizzyingly hot. Her nerves fairly screamed to fight back, but she did nothing.

Johnny stepped out of the quad and into the narrow street. He looked so determined, so thoroughly absorbed in playing his part. Tía imagined this was the way all men went to war. Blindly? Resolutely? Heedless of the women they left behind? Heedless of death?

"Once, a long time ago, I made another man walk that path to his death." Papa's words were quietly spoken, but strange and harsh.

"He was a fat *gringo*—a *rubio*—like your mother."

Mateo kissed the back of her neck. Tía could no longer control her anguish, but the thought of causing Johnny's death kept her from giving herself away.

"He had a fat red face and white-gold hair. He was a colonel in the American army. We captured him and tried him for murder. I was his judge and jury. I sentenced him to be hanged, drawn, and quartered. Do you know what that means, *niña*?"

Grateful to have something else to think about, Tía shook her head.

Remembering Rita and how she had reacted to this story made his words husky and caressing. "Hanged, drawn, and quartered," he repeated. "Hanged by the neck, then disemboweled and quartered—cut into four pieces..."

Tía gasped with revulsion and twisted around to face him, her features contorted with disgust.

Mateo chuckled. In that, also, she was like her mother. Rita had been horrified when she'd read the story, printed on the tenth anniversary of the fat colonel's death in an old newspaper that turned up in Tubac. He could still see the disgust and loathing on Rita's pretty face when she'd confronted him with it. Unwilling to be intimidated for dispensing necessary justice, he had laughed at his wife's squeamishness.

"Relax, *niña*. That punishment is reserved for very special enemies. Your young man will die quickly, if you wish him to die."

"No. Please…"

"You moved away." He shrugged as if she had already willed Johnny's death.

Tía rushed to stand in front of him, pressing her body back against his. "I'm back, see?"

His breath warmed her cheek and neck. "So you are." His hands moved back to her shoulders. Possessively his fingers played with her trembling flesh.

Every nerve in Tía's body screamed, urged her to strike out at him, but Johnny's life depended on her. She stilled the urge to explode in rage at Mama for getting her into this, for lying with Burkhart instead of Papa. But she did nothing. She had vowed she would let him set her on fire to save Johnny. And she would not go back on her word.

"Where was I? Oh, yes! The *rubio* colonel. He could see the gallows at the end of the path. A grim reminder that when he reached them he would die a horrible death. The symbol of death is important, *niña*, and very demoralizing. That is the reason for placing Señor Brago's horse in plain sight. The symbol of both freedom and death. Ahhh. Back to my story. The fat colonel could not walk. My men had to drive him there with clubs. The colonel was no man. He cried, he begged, he slobbered." Mateo sighed. "*Gringos* do not die well. Thinking themselves worth immortality, they lack the necessary objectivity. They have no training for death. Just as they know nothing of honor or integrity."

Tía shuddered uncontrollably. Her senses reeled. A man she had loved and worshipped all her life was violating her body, talking to her as if she were someone else, and Johnny was about to die. If anyone at all fired a gun, they would shoot him down…

Johnny reached the bottom of the long, steep stairs and paused, scanning the path he would walk. His horse waited a few hundred yards away. He couldn't see the sun because of the steep canyon walls, but the western sky was aflame with sunset—a dozen shades of purple and gold.

Closing his eyes, he dragged in a full breath. He must be crazy. Kissing Tía's hand. Playing word games with her lover. Now, about to be executed, he was admiring a showy sunset sky.

No wonder she had played so hard to get. It all made sense now. He smiled at the irony. He had said the same thing when she'd told him she was going to walk with Morgan Todd.

Leaning against walls, smoking cigarettes and watching him with their smug eyes, Mexicans with rifles rested idly on the tops of buildings on either side of the narrow street. Except for them and the absence of normal activity, this could have been a street in Tombstone, flanked by pueblos instead of tents.

One of the Mexicans coughed discreetly and raised his rifle to his shoulder. The others followed suit—three dozen men—ready and waiting.

This was real. *El Gato Negro* would pick the moment, these men would take careful aim and squeeze very gently, and a dozen bullets would rip into him...

His knees were suddenly weak, his hands cold and clammy with sweat. Remembering the advice his friend Billy Breakenridge had given him that day in Galeyville before his first gunfight, Johnny took a few deep breaths, let them out slowly, and felt some of the tension leave him. *First thing you gotta do is admit you're scared. Only a fool ain't scared to die. So think about being scared and why you're scared. Then think about your cold hands, your sick belly, and your knockin' knees. Think about it and accept it, 'cause once you accept it, you can control it. Now dry your hands, brace your knees, and lean over and lift your ribs off your belly. That'll get rid of the need to puke. Now take a few deep breaths and mouth a silent yell. That'll get the old juices flowing. Hell, that's why them damned 'paches always yell when they're getting ready to attack. That yellin' is for them; gets the old blood moving—theirs and yours.*

Billy had been right: only a fool wouldn't admit he didn't want to die. Breathing hard, Johnny steeled himself to accept his death. Startled by the request, his mind recoiled with resentment and veered away from the idea. There was no time. He didn't know if he accepted death or not, but he went on to step two. No choice. These *bandidos* weren't going to wait all evening. He put his hands in his pockets and tensed his legs.

To Patchy, chewing on his cigar, the *gringo* looked cocky and insolent. He motioned for Johnny to get moving.

Johnny glared at Patchy and mouthed a silent yell.

Startled, disbelieving, Patchy glanced from Johnny to his man leaning against the next apartment. Had he imagined that? Surely the *gringo* hadn't...Uneasily, Patchy glanced back at the *gringo* prisoner.

Feeling foolish, Johnny shrugged and twisted his mouth into a lopsided grimace. The dolorous Mexican glanced sideways again.

Confused, he took a nervous drag on his cigar, then gestured with the rifle barrel for Johnny to walk.

"What's your rush?" Johnny muttered to himself. "I'm damned sure not going anywhere you don't want me to go."

Quirking his eyebrows in what he hoped was a devil-may-care look, Johnny hitched up his pants and slowly started to walk. Too bad Judy couldn't see him now, he thought. She had accused him of being a killer, one of the dread gunfighters who terrorized scattered western towns. In his entire life he had engaged in two gunfights. The first time he had stopped a man from tormenting a mere boy, trying to goad the unfortunate youngster into drawing on him so he could kill the kid and add one more notch to his gun butt. Some men did that—went from town to town, looking for victims. Billy the Deuce had been one of those until Johnny had killed him and picked up an instant, full-blown reputation. It hadn't mattered that he'd been scared half out of his pants. His arm and his eye had worked—Billy had died before he hit the dusty main street of Galeyville. One bullet through the middle of his chest. The talk in the town had been admiring—about how cool and controlled Johnny Brago had been. No one knew he had gotten sick afterward.

The second time had been in Yuma. Three drunken cowhands had started shooting at him. He hadn't aimed to kill them that time, only to stop them. Unfortunately, once started they didn't stop until they were dead. He'd found out the next day they were three of the meanest, most cold-blooded killers in the territory. They had looked so ordinary. Who would have guessed that beneath each man's unspectacular facade lay an urge to kill strangers—men they hadn't known an hour or a day before?

So his skill with a gun had been a gift. Too bad it wouldn't help him now. He cursed himself for letting them get the drop on him.

Purposefully concentrating on his breathing, ignoring the men who watched him over rifle barrels, Johnny sauntered across the quad and stepped into the street. Tía and her lover watched to see if he would break under the pressure of the bastard's sadistic little gauntlet. He had been a fool to pursue a female who obviously had no interest in him.

He took no satisfaction in remembering how the color had drained out of her soft, downy cheeks when he'd kissed her hand, no pleasure at all in the answering pang her look had caused in him. It didn't matter what she had done or planned to do, he saw her pain and would have done anything to take it away. Just proved he didn't have good sense.

Now she would watch him die...unless they had already moved to the bed. Johnny had the overwhelming impulse to look up at their window, but he wouldn't give her the satisfaction.

Death wasn't so bad—not this way. When *El Gato Negro* gave the signal, there would be only one split second of warning, and then—nothing. He could imagine the leap of fear that would send his heart pounding, but with any luck at all, he wouldn't feel the bullets.

There was an instinctive shrinking within, as if to ward off the bullets that would slam into his body. Willing his taut muscles to relax, Johnny concentrated on trying to stop the thoughts that didn't make a damned bit of sense anyway.

It'll soon be over. He walked slowly, his eyes narrowed at the irony of the thought he used to comfort himself. He'd only known he was going to die for a couple of minutes, and already he couldn't wait to get it over with. He could either live or die, but he could not live waiting to die. Better to get it over with.

Halfway there. What were these bastards waiting for? Probably enjoying themselves, if they were anything like their leader. Or maybe waiting for that cold-eyed bastard upstairs to give the signal. *El Gato* would probably drag it out till the last possible second.

Well, two could play that game. A few hundred feet from his horse, Johnny stopped and rolled a cigarette. Sweat rolled down his temples and into his eyes. With his sleeve, he wiped his forehead. He lit the cigarette, shook out the match, and then, unable to stop himself, searched out the window to *El Gato Negro*'s lair.

Beside the bold, dark shape of her lover, Tía's face was a tiny, gold-framed oval. She was too far away to make out her expression, but his mind imagined, her face twisted with grief. Unbidden, the urge to comfort her overwhelmed him.

Disgusted with himself, Johnny spat into the dust. He was almost five hundred yards from Tía now. How could he think he saw any expression at all on her face? Cursing himself for a fool, he dropped the cigarette and ground it under the toe of his boot.

Mateo Lorca chuckled softly. "He has sand, your lover. See how he waits, like a cougar, caged now, perhaps, but never a harmless pet. He is a good *hombre*—a little too cocky, but I would not fault him for that. He would make a good husband for you."

Tía closed her eyes. Johnny hated her now. He would always hate her—even the memory of her. Whenever Judy mentioned her name, his eyes would darken with pure hatred.

Abruptly, as if he had sensed her turmoil and was impatient with it, Johnny dropped his cigarette, turned his back on her, and started to walk again—that same relaxed, loose-limbed amble she had watched so many times before.

Johnny stopped walking ten feet from his horse and turned, scowling at the men he had walked past, staring at them with hostile, challenging eyes. He dared first one and then another, but no signal shot rang out to break the strange stillness. They looked back at him impassively, nonchalantly. Furious, he faced that window again, but nothing.

He had the urge to yell curses at the bastard. He had walked *El Gato Negro*'s damned gauntlet. He should not be toyed with like a mouse.

At last he strode toward his horse and mounted. He presented his chest to the riflemen, waited a few seconds, and then nudged Matador forward. Still nothing.

The dusty, cobbled road curved. Once he'd ridden around that bend, *El Gato Negro* would not be able to see him. And he would not be able to see Tía. And Tía would not be able to see when they shot him. Perhaps this was *El Gato Negro*'s way of sparing his woman.

Johnny should be grateful, but he wasn't. Childishly he wanted her to see him die, to think that he had died cursing her. Even if he couldn't. Especially because he couldn't. Slowly, reluctantly, he rode around the bend in the cobbled path.

More than a score of men were stationed on the sides of the canyon, their heads cocked to one side as they squinted over shiny barrels.

Then he knew. The game they were playing with him was only just beginning...

CHAPTER FORTY-FOUR

When Steve woke up, he was lashed to a makeshift stretcher, bumping along behind a horse. A canvas shield blocked the sun. Hot. The pain in his head was bad—very bad—as if he had sheets of tin in there, being whipped about by powerful blasts of air from a furnace. Even with his eyes closed he saw the blinding flashes of light and heard them: black and rumbling and painful. Overheated under the blazing sun, his mouth was swollen with thirst. Painfully he swallowed and opened his eyes.

"He's awake! Stop! Please!" The voice sounded like Andrea's, but where had she come from?

The rough, plowing motion stopped, and Steve was grateful. Cool hands rested on his face. Andrea?

"Steve?"

"How did you get here?" he asked around his thick, swollen tongue.

"With Johnny. You were ambushed by bandits," she said, grateful that he was at least conscious. "They took Teresa...and your silver..."

"Teresa?"

"Tía." Andrea reached for the canteen and wet his lips with the water.

Steve closed his eyes. Andrea had said something important. He tried to concentrate in spite of the pain.

"The other men...how are they?"

"Six of them died. Three are injured besides you."

Steve closed his eyes. He had been a fool to expose his men to these dangers.

"Here, take another sip. We must get moving."

Sitting their horses in silence, men crowded around him. Steve sipped the water and then looked from face to face, noting who was there and who was missing.

"Where's Johnny?" he asked, dreading the answer. Of all the men, Johnny was the one he would most hate to lose.

"He went after Tía."

"How many men did he take with him?"

"None. He wanted to go alone. There were fifty bandits. He said one man would be more effective."

"Which way did the bandits go?"

"South, then east." Andrea realized she'd made another slip, but it didn't matter. Soon Steve would either be strong enough to hear everything, or he'd be dead. She watched to see if he had caught the significance, but he didn't show any signs of wondering how she knew that later they'd gone east.

Andrea had been to her papa's hideout three times over the years. She wouldn't know how to get there alone, but she remembered they always traveled in an eastward direction from Tubac. They were far south of Rancho la Reina now; it figured they had to go east from where they had been.

Steve considered the information and decided to trust Johnny's judgment. If any one man could bring Tía back alive, Johnny was the man. A good tracker and a deadly shot, he wouldn't give up until he'd rescued Tía or knew she was dead.

That thought jarred Steve. He had liked Tía...Teresa. She was earnest and charming in a quiet, steady way he appreciated. He and Johnny didn't talk much about women, but he had suspected Johnny was sweet on the slim blonde. Johnny would save her.

They made better time now. By nightfall they were halfway home. One of the canyons surprised them with a small stream. They camped beside it and filled their stomachs with water and the last of the supplies purchased in Fort Bowie.

Steve had suffered from the long ride. He lay in his blankets, too exhausted to move but in too much pain to sleep. Because he had refused food, Andrea made broth with a piece of beef jerky and brought it to him.

"I'm not hungry," he said, waving the broth away.

"This isn't food. You need liquids, and this will warm you."

"I ran my stepmother off when I was seventeen," he said meaningfully.

"I'm not applying for that position."

Steve sipped some of the broth and then slept. He woke later to find Andrea kneeling beside him. The moon was directly overhead. A coyote pup howled, a leaner sound than that made by a full-grown coyote.

"What position are you applying for?" he asked as if they had only talked seconds ago.

Surprised to find him awake, lucid, and asking questions about something they had talked about hours before, Andrea reached for the water. "Drink this."

He looked at her intently, and she could sense a struggle going on inside him. As if trying to wipe away pain and confusion, he rubbed his hand across his forehead.

"Was Morgan Todd killed, too?"

"Morgan Todd has the constitution of a Texas longhorn. But he wasn't with you. Don't you remember?"

"He was going to meet us."

"He came back to the ranch, fought with Judy, and beat her unconscious. Someone shot him. He's…in pretty bad shape. They arrested Johnny for it, but we broke him out of jail."

"Have I been gone that long? How's Judy?"

"I don't know."

Overwhelmed by these complications, Steve lay so strangely lifeless that Andrea's heart lurched with fear. Could he survive two bullet wounds and a long ride back to the ranch?

"Come here," he whispered.

"I'm here," she said.

"Lie down beside me. I want to feel you next to me."

Andrea moved to comply. All day she had ridden in a daze. Now, his tenderness threatened to release a torrent of tears. At times like this she was sure she would be better off if she could cry like other women. She had never been able to cry.

"Please, don't be nice to me," she sighed.

"Because you're so terrible?"

She nodded, chin quivering.

"You're wrong. Judy and I get the credit for that."

"You don't know everything yet."

"Then tell me."

Shivering, Andrea snuggled close to him. His warmth gave her the courage she needed. Partly to keep him quiet and partly because she needed to confess, she told him about *El Gato Negro:* how he had tried to kill Mama, how she had stabbed him, and all her fears now that he had taken Tía away.

She did not tell Steve she had watched Tía bargain with Papa to save their lives. She had let her sister ride away with Papa to save Steve, and she would carry that guilt and shame alone.

Andrea stopped speaking. Steve was too quiet. A terrible dread filled her. His eyelids fluttered closed. He looked gaunt in the moonlight—so still and limp. Could he survive another day of being dragged in the hot sun?

She covered her face with her hands. Steve would die, and Papa would ruin Tía. "I hate you, Papa," she declared. "I hate you! I hope Johnny kills you!"

She was young and healthy. A few bruises, but they were nothing. Potter examined Judy Burkhart quickly, letting her see his disapproval. He didn't give a damn that she was young and pretty.

"I want you out of here tomorrow."

"What?"

"You heard me. I'm releasing you."

Anger flared in Judy, but she was too off balance to show it. "Sounds like you're evicting me."

"Same thing, I reckon."

Surprised, Judy looked quickly away. It wasn't the same thing at all. She should call him on his rotten attitude, but her heart was pounding hard and she was raging inside with what felt like rejection.

Potter cursed himself. He had overstepped himself, but, dammit, he resented her. He had patched up enough young men who didn't have any better sense than to fight over women. Her dark brown eyes glanced quickly at him and then away again. She knew. He was glad she didn't know why. She deserved to wonder about it. It sickened him that men worshipped her. She wasn't worth their time.

"I'm a doctor, Miss Burkhart. My job is to save lives. I got no truck for a woman who doesn't appreciate the value of life. Who encourages the wrong kind of men and gets 'em to fighting over her."

As quickly as he could, he finished his rounds and walked outside, pausing on the porch. The moon was already up, but dim against the slowly darkening sky. At the western horizon the sky was dark red, fading into pale blue. A warm breeze made his skin feel fresh, alive. He was getting too damned cranky to be a doctor. The Burkhart girl had looked like he'd gutted her. Damn!

A hundred yards away Rutledge left his office and headed toward the officers' quarters. They met halfway.

"Evening," Potter said gruffly.

"Doctor." They fell in step.

Rutledge glanced sideways at the doctor. "How's Miss Burkhart?"

"I have ten men in that hospital with more serious problems than that girl."

Potter and Rutledge had known each other for ten years. They were close enough and trusted one another enough to be honest—at least in minor matters. "She misbehaving?"

"No, dammit. She's a perfect lady. As long as I'm looking at her. The minute she leaves here she'll probably get two men fighting over her again and get 'em both killed. Someday one of 'em is going to get smart and kill her instead. That's probably what she wants, anyway."

Alarmed, Rutledge stopped walking. Potter didn't slow down. His long, angry strides were putting distance between them. "Potter, wait a minute."

After thirty years in the army, Potter was accustomed to taking orders. He stopped.

"Care for a drink?"

Potter shook his head. "That's all I need, a hangover."

"One drink. Loosen you up."

Potter squinted in irritation.

"Good. Come on. I've got some twelve-year-old brandy."

Rutledge waited until Potter had drunk most of his brandy. "You… uh…really think Judy Burkhart wants to get herself killed?"

"I don't think it. I know it. I had a twin brother, until a woman got him into a fight he couldn't get out of alive. It meant nothing to her. She sashayed off and found herself another man to fight over her." Potter scowled. "Besides, women who want to die find some way to live, even in the middle of a war. Women who want to die find some way to do that. Judy Burkhart's still the talk of the territory. She's still sassy-mouthed as all get-out. What I can't figure is how a woman with everything most women ever wanted in the way of looks, money, and young men flitting around her can get so lost that she lets a man like Morgan Todd within a mile of her."

He put his brandy snifter on the table and stood up. "I don't know why it galls me so. Guess she's determined to prove Bill Burkhart was right…must be her bastard blood showing through."

CHAPTER FORTY-FIVE

Uncertainly, Rutledge walked in and stopped at the foot of Judy's bed. After talking to Potter, he had spent a miserable night.

Irritated, Judy rolled her eyes at Grant, sitting on the opposite side of the bed. He stood up. "You wanted to see me, sir?"

"Will you excuse us a moment, please?" the captain asked, his voice hoarse.

Judy looked as though she was going to protest, but Grant flashed her a signal to behave herself. He excused himself politely and walked outside.

Judy considered falling unconscious but gave up the idea. Oblivion never came when she needed it.

"How are you feeling today, young lady?"

"Fine, thank you." He always called her that—"young lady"—as if he didn't know her name.

"I…uh…wanted to bring you something, some flowers or something, but I was afraid that might not please you."

Judy frowned. "And you want to please me?"

Her level brown eyes completely disconcerted him. "I should imagine you would be quite accustomed to people wanting to please you…" He stopped. He was botching this badly. His face felt beet red.

"Why do you want to please me?"

The blood seemed to drain from his heart. Twenty years he had fumbled around with this scene in his mind, always dreaming of how he would tell her—her reaction and his joy. Now he was speechless. It barely seemed real to him, but he plunged ahead. He was accustomed to following orders to do difficult or near impossible things.

"I have a confession to make. I am going to need all of your understanding." His voice was functioning, but his thoughts were strangely disconnected. What if she rejected him?

"A confession…to me?" Judy felt like telling him she was no priest, but something in the unnatural redness of his face stopped her.

"A long time ago I did something that may have caused you pain. I was young and thoughtless…"

A pulse began to throb in her temples. She was seeing Captain Rutledge now, really seeing him: brown eyes, brown hair, the same exact coloring as her own. Ever since she'd found out Bill Burkhart was not her father, she had imagined one man after another walking up to her and telling her that he was the one. Now, when she had forgotten it… "You…you're my father?"

Grateful he didn't have to continue, Rutledge nodded.

Judy moaned softly. Anyone but him!

Rutledge's eyes skittered away. He looked so miserable, so contrite. It was almost comical. All these years of watching her. Asking stupid questions; making a nuisance of himself. Probably longing to tell her…

"Why now?"

"I didn't want you to be alone if you ever needed anything or anybody." He cleared his throat. "That young man…Grant Foreman… he said you don't like to be alone. I…" He stopped.

Judy blinked in sudden emotion. Her mouth trembled. He really meant it! He felt something for her. All those years, hanging around the fringes of her life, wanting to do something for her, wanting to tell her, worrying about her, maybe. She could sense all that now.

He cleared his throat again. "Please…Miss Burk—uh, Judy…I'm sorry…I never meant to hurt you…to let you carry the brunt of it…but I didn't know what to do. I thought Burkhart didn't know that you…that Ellen…drat."

Strangely liberated by this sudden intimacy, this confession, Judy reached out and touched his hand.

"If you ever need anything, anyone…We don't have to tell the world…I mean, if you don't want to…I'll leave that up to you…"

Judy stared blankly.

"Do you want to marry Johnny Brago? I mean, are you in love with him?"

Her eyes widened, and he thought she wasn't going to reply. Finally she answered. "I was for a long time, but, well…I still love him as a friend." She was groping now, recognizing her feelings as she found the right words. "But no, I don't want to marry him."

"Are you in love with Morgan Todd?" he asked, embarrassed and gruff, but inside secretly pleased that she was answering him, that she wasn't laughing at him.

Judy looked down at her hands. "No."

"What about this young man, Foreman?" he mumbled. "Are you in love with him?"

Her head dipped even lower. He could barely hear her reply. "I...I don't know...maybe..."

"He loves you."

"No...not anymore. He might have. Once."

Rutledge frowned. "If he ever loved you, he still does."

"No, I did something...something terrible..."

He had no answer for that. He had heard the rumors about her, and it was his fault. He had abandoned her. Even after Ellen left and he had suspected things were not rosy between Judy and Bill, he hadn't stepped in and offered her his protection.

"He tried to kill a man to defend you," he said empathically.

"No. He's just a friend. I wouldn't be a good enough wife to him."

"Nonsense!"

"When men get married, they want a woman who is good. From day one. I'm not like that," Judy lamented.

"Dr. Potter said it's time for me to go home," Judy said, glancing quickly at Grant. "He was nicer this time." She mimicked his voice, making up words: "'We're going to miss you, Miss Burkhart. Not too often we have such a pretty patient...' The old goat. I don't think men should keep living after they get a certain age." In truth Potter *had* been a little nicer this morning. He had apologized and told her to wait one more day before leaving.

Grant laughed. He was accustomed to Judy's view of the world—as if people had no value except to please her, to play their small part in her melodrama.

He could not look at her. *Judy Burkhart will marry Morgan Todd and live happily ever after.* This morning, only days after he had made up a story about having to go home, he'd received a real letter from his mother asking him to come home, telling him that his father had suffered a heart attack.

Impending doom spread like a blanket over him, and he hunched in his chair. Tomorrow Judy would go home, and he would probably go free also. Todd was recovering. Rutledge did not seem interested in turning him over to Johnny Behan. The taciturn captain had hedged when Grant brought it up. Last time he'd said, *There's no rush. Johnny Behan's got his hands full right now, what with the 'paches on the prowl. I can't imagine anyone wanting to go to jail the way you do.*

Judy stirred, and the slight movement relieved some of her tension. Seeing how quiet Grant was, and too nervous to be still, she said the first thing that came into her head. "So, you'll be leaving, too. You'll go back to Atlanta to some knock-kneed southern virgin who'll give you perfect babies." She had meant to laugh, to sound merry and unconcerned, but the laughter got stuck in her tight throat. She would never see him again. He would marry some nice girl, someone brand new, like he deserved, and he would never even write to her. "It's hot and stuffy in here," she said suddenly. "Can we take a walk?"

The sun was setting, filling the sky with yellow, red, and purple clouds that looked like watercolors smeared together by a skilled hand. Walking slowly, she listened to the rattle of a trace chain as a buckboard clattered past, people at a distance laughing. The air smelled of dust and meals cooking. She didn't know why she had suggested a walk. Her mind filled with a thousand worries: about Steve, Tía, Johnny, Andrea, the riders.

Chatto and Geronimo had not attacked the fort. Did that mean they were out harrying travelers? Grant had kept her informed of the news. Patrols scouted in all directions. The Indians had apparently pulled back. But to where?

"Where do you sleep now?" she asked suddenly.

"I rented a room over the commissary. Generally you couldn't get a room in an army garrison like this, but the store operator is a civilian, and his wife died and his son left home. So he rented me his son's room."

"Could we go there?"

"No. Rutledge might shoot me."

"He seems to approve of you."

Grant looked at her curiously. Usually she would have said, "That old maggot!"

"He seems to approve of you, too," he said, glancing at her perfect profile. Against the colorful sunset sky, it was pale and lovely.

"Everyone approves of me...until they don't."

Grant had gotten so attuned to her moods he knew something was amiss. He started to ask her about it, but she didn't give him time.

"Take me there? Please?"

"You trying to get me hanged?"

"Who'll care?"

"The congregation of the First Baptist Church. Every man in the compound. Rutledge. The entire Apache nation. The attorney general. My landlord."

"The worst that can happen is either he won't let me in, or he'll kick me out, right? What else could he do to me?"

"I don't even want to find out."

"Can we get in without being seen?"

"If we went up the back stairs, and if he didn't happen to be up there, I guess we could, but it certainly isn't worth it if you get branded as a young woman of questionable morals."

"I am already branded a young woman of questionable morals. That's no longer an issue."

The alley behind the store was deserted, the door propped open to encourage the breeze. Six steps inside the door a stairway went up to the left. Voices of men added an element of excitement. Judy almost laughed aloud. Grant shushed her and led the way. She followed on his heels.

He opened the door to his room, motioned her inside, and then closed it and leaned against it. "They're probably forming a posse this very minute," he said. For years he had dreamed about taking Judy to his home, presenting her to kings, buying her jewels, but never bringing her to some dingy, faded rooming house with only a sagging bed, warped dresser, and rickety chair.

Glancing sideways at her lovely profile, Grant was aware his heart beat much too fast. Hands shaking, he lit the lamp.

"I like rented rooms. They seem so anonymous. No memories to upset you." Judy walked to the bed and bounced on the edge of it. The springs made a rusty, screeching noise. "Did you make this bed yourself?" she asked, her dark eyes filled with some strange light he'd never seen before. Her soft brown hair was pulled back with a ribbon, making her look younger, more innocent. A bruise on the soft curve of her cheek marred the perfect purity of her skin. Grant flushed with rage that any man could treat her so despicably.

"Yes." His voice sounded strange, hoarse. He wasn't sure if he could maintain his air of casual unconcern. Judy did terrible, weakening things to his resolve.

"You're very talented, Grant." Her expression was solemn.

He couldn't answer. The look in her dark eyes disturbed him—created a turbulence in his chest, a hungry ache in his loins.

"We'd better go now," he said, his voice thick, almost unmanageable.

"No." Her whisper was like a caress—warm and velvety. He could feel it the length of his body, from his hair to his toenails. Judy was doing it again: forgetting he was a man—a man with limits, like any other.

"No?"

"I'm leaving tomorrow," she said softly. "And you'll be going home. I'll never see you again…"

The pulse at his temples was suddenly throbbing uncontrollably. At first he was confused, but then, as if a light had been turned on, he knew what Judy was doing. It was payoff time. Judy Burkhart always paid her debts. Now, apparently, she thought she owed him this…this…

The enormity of the situation froze him. Like a vision in one of his wildest dreams, Judy stood and slowly walked toward him. Her eloquent eyes intent, her slender, downturning lips beckoning; she stopped much too close to him. Sighing, she lowered her lids and raised her dainty hands to burn his chest. Slowly they slid up and locked behind his head.

"No!" His breathing was sharp, his voice harsh.

Judy's eyes opened, gazed at him for seconds, minutes, hours, it seemed, saw that he had no will to oppose her, and ignored his entreaty. Only inches shorter than he, swanlike, she rose up and set her mouth over his.

Her kiss was different from anything he had ever imagined. She kissed him, and the urgency now was to become more deeply immersed, as if there were degrees of annihilation…

Grant started to protest, to tell her he didn't need this sacrifice from her, but he wanted her more than anything he'd ever wanted before. It would be a memory to cherish as long as he lived.

He seemed to change. The kiss stopped being her gift and became something he took. His hands came up and cupped her face, then slipped down to crush her to him. He kissed her until her head was spinning, then remorselessly and yet gently, his hands moved down to unbutton her gown, strip away her chemise and petticoat.

Guided by his warm hands, Judy stepped away from her fallen garments, and Grant stepped back to look at her. She moved away, to cover herself, but his eyes held her motionless. She tried to hide herself, but he forced her to stand quietly while he looked at her as if he would imprint every inch of her into his mind forever.

At last his hands guided her down onto the bed.

Judy had never been shy in her life, but now she felt strangely vulnerable. At first she didn't know what was wrong with her. It felt as if the first layer of her flesh had been stripped away, leaving her raw nerves exposed to his touch. She'd never felt so aware of her body—the way it felt when he touched her. Always before, when she'd given herself to a man, she had watched from behind a screen, which insulated her from real feeling, saved her from any real connection. Now, she was painfully aware, painfully shy. Somehow, she transmitted this unfamiliar demureness to him.

"You're exquisite, Judy."

His lips on her skin felt different from other men's—they felt more real, more satisfying.

"Kiss me. Don't stop," she pleaded.

His lips resumed their slow, hungry feasting. They worshipped her mouth, her breasts, her secret places, until she felt sure she would die of the sweet, delicious sensations.

At last he lifted himself away from her, and with his fine gray eyes intent on her face, exulting in her every gasping, indrawn breath, he positioned himself and took her.

Judy moaned until she was writhing in blind ecstasy, her blood clamoring with strange, sweet terror.

Tears scalded her eyes. She hated Grant suddenly. He was the most heartless traitor of all. She had never suspected he could become so filled with masculine power and mercilessness that his lips and hands could start such wild trembling and desire.

It wasn't fair that Grant—who would leave her tomorrow, never to return—should be the one to touch her to the depths of her soul.

This must be what possession meant—the lean hardness of his body wiping out everything except the fierce, urgent need to be one with this man she had never really known before.

CHAPTER FORTY-SIX

"Now, *niña*, it is time to let us see your courage…or lack of it…"

Tía turned to face Mateo. If Johnny could walk so bravely, appearing indomitable and stalwart, she would not grovel.

Mateo took off his shirt and tossed it on the single straight-backed chair in the corner.

Tía walked to the bed and sat down. Johnny was gone, and now this man who once had been her papa demanded that she lie with him as his woman. The thought overwhelmed her. But she had promised this exchange for the lives of Johnny and her mother. An unexpected calm descended over Tía.

She had promised, and now she must go through with it.

In spite of her newfound calm, she wasn't sure she could go through with this. Her mind simply would not accept the image of her lying down in bed with the man who was no longer her father. Just the image of it made a lump start in her belly and roll upward like a knot in a rope being pulled through a tight sleeve. The knot caught at her throat and came bubbling out as a sob. It was followed by another knot, and another. Once started, the sobs echoed faster and faster until they were spilling out of her in a continuous stream. She was helpless to stop them.

Mateo watched in amazement and horror. In a matter of seconds, Teresa had gone from the capable young woman who had fooled her lover to a howling child. She curled one leg under her, clutched her hands under her chin, and cried as if she were three years old—great, gasping sobs that filled the room.

And for the life of him Mateo could not figure out how she'd tricked him into watching it, but once seen, the picture could not be erased from his mind.

When Teresa was six years old, a kitten had followed her home from town and appeared ready to stay. Rita had asked him to get rid of it. Teresa had guessed what he planned to do and had cried exactly like this—openmouthed, louder than a train whistle, and with total abandon. He had not been able to kill the kitten.

Now, tricked into watching, all the lustful vengeance that had flooded him earlier mysteriously diminished. His arms hung like weights from his shoulders. His back ached with sudden tiredness. If he stayed, he feared he would be reduced to holding her while she cried. Already his hands longed to pull her into his arms for comfort, but he would not go that far. He forced his feet to walk to the door, his leaden hand to turn the handle.

In panic Teresa leaped off the bed. "Papa!"

On the verge of slamming the door behind him, Mateo stopped. "Don't Papa me."

"Ple…please don't…don't…" she sobbed.

Strangely, Mateo could not remember what he had threatened to do if she did not make good on her end of the bargain. But apparently Teresa did. She ran across the room, got between him and the door, and pushed him toward the bed.

"I'm here, see?"

Mateo gritted his teeth. He had no energy for this. All he wanted was to escape.

"Come to the bed, Papa. I'll honor my word. I promise."

She scampered into the middle of the bed, and pulled him down beside her. "See?"

"The only thing I see is that you have learned nothing."

"About what?"

Mateo almost groaned aloud. Her eyes were round and frantic with her desire to please him, to save her cocky young *caballero*. She had no idea that she had destroyed him. "About being a woman. You didn't cry with that *gringo*," he said bitterly.

Tía looked at him as if he should have known better but obviously didn't. "That's different, Papa. I love Johnny. He asked me to marry him."

As if her words had reminded her of things too painful to endure, she broke into a fresh fit of crying. Mateo watched in alarm and consternation. The child was going to damage herself with all this crying. Sweat broke out on his forehead. His hands itched to push the hair off her flushed face. Finally, when he could stand it no more, he pulled her into his arms and held her shaking body.

At some point her crying stopped. But it didn't matter. Mateo was too tired to move. It seemed that all the tiredness of a lifetime had pooled in his body—the tiredness of trying to right a lifetime of wrongs, of being stabbed, of losing Teresa and Andrea, even the tiredness of losing Rita. He turned over onto his stomach and let the sound of Teresa's breathing and her occasional gasping, indrawn breaths lull him to sleep.

It was well after midnight when Rita arrived at the pueblos. Her guide, Abuelito, not nearly as threatening once she'd gotten used to him, was worth every penny she had paid him. Joking at length with the sentries, he gave all the proper signals and responses and delivered her without incident to the guard who stood at the foot of the steps leading up to Mateo's room.

Her heart had been pounding ever since she'd seen the small sleeping city built into the limestone cliffs. She was insane to come here, she realized. Truly insane. Mateo *would* kill her. Fortunately, or perhaps unfortunately, it was too late to turn back now. Rita unsheathed the revolver she now wore at her hip, inserted a bullet under the hammer, and snapped the cylinder back into place. She would not go alone.

Guarding *el general's* rooms, bored by the long night that stretched ahead like the desert itself, Andano Madrigal was not alarmed by the *señora's* appearance. It was obvious in the way Abuelito acted that she was expected by everyone except himself. That was the way it always was. With no warning, a young woman, rumored to be *el general's* daughter, had arrived with *el general* that afternoon. Now, also with no warning, *el general's* wife.

Ceremoniously, showing his deep respect, Andano bowed low and let the *señora* pass. Straightening, he saw a smirk appear on Abuelito's face. Andano cocked an eyebrow.

"Perhaps now *el jefe* will be in a better mood, eh, *amigo?*" Abuelito growled, winking.

Andano laughed. "She looks capable of producing it, does she not?" he asked, mimicking the gruff comments he had overheard in the *cantina.*

"*Sí*, if he can keep her still long enough. That one has too much energy for her own good. My butt aches from riding too many miles in too short a time." Rubbing his aching buttocks, he turned away. "If the *señora* needs me, I will be at Juanita's."

Heart beating faster, Rita climbed the stairs. Thank God Mateo was a proud man. She had never had to make explanations to his people. Each and every one of them accepted everything about his family. Once a long time ago she had heard Patchy Arteaga telling one of the younger men, probably in relation to Tía: *El general can do anything he wishes. Gold coins could spill from his loins if he so desired.*

A knife had glittered and flashed in the sunlight, and the young *vaquero* had gulped back any reply he might have made.

Rita paused at the top of the steps. She had no idea what Mateo would do. Her heart lurched sickeningly.

No matter. She had to see him before he took out his wrath on Tía. Stepping forward slowly, reaching out for the latch key, she lifted her chin defiantly. If Mateo *was* with another female, he would just have to get rid of her. This was important. His *wife* was here on business.

As usual the door was not locked. A lamp burned on the bureau, the tail of the wick barely reaching the kerosene. For a second the light flickered and then slowly settled down again.

On the bed next to the dark, broad shape of Mateo, a slender golden arm gleamed in the lamplight. A tangle of gold curls caused Rita's breath to catch in her throat. Weakly she leaned against the door.

She was too late. Hands shaking like an aspen leaf in a high wind, she drew the revolver out of the holster at her side. Slowly, taking care not to wake them, she walked to the side of the bed. Mateo was lying on his stomach, one strong arm draped over Tía. Rita pointed the gun squarely between his shoulder blades, then moved the barrel to his left slightly to find his heart. In the lamplight the raised ridges of scar tissue gleamed white against the darkness of his skin. A long time ago she had risked asking him about the scars, but he hadn't answered her. She had dropped it by saying that perhaps once in his life he had gotten exactly what he deserved. Mateo had only laughed cynically.

Looking at his broad, tapering back, she found that her finger could not work the trigger. Even now, shaking with the desire to send bullets slamming into his hateful body, seeing the weals, she unaccountably remembered the way his skin felt under her hands, the way the long, smooth muscles of his back rippled as he moved in the rhythmic throes of lovemaking.

Another thought came to her, and she stared at Tía, searching for the answer.

No. Tía's fine pale skin showed no bruises. Curled in on herself like a morning glory closed for the night, she lay quietly—passive with sleep and exhaustion. Shirtless, Mateo slept, but he did not look limp or exhausted. Even in sleep he looked arrogant and lithe. No softness or fat marred that lean, manly frame. Like the cat he was named for, he slept lightly, and Rita, better than anyone, knew how quickly he could go from sleep to complete awareness.

Rita closed her eyes. Tía had no bruises, and she nestled against Mateo like a kitten against its mother. The sight was like a thorn pressing into a wound that had been festering inside Rita for eighteen years. Tía had loved Mateo without reservation, for seventeen years of her life. *Had she come to him willingly?*

Rita's stomach turned queasy. Tía had known for weeks that Mateo Lorca was not her father. Perhaps she had been driven to give herself to Mateo to keep his love.

Once the question was there, like a barb in her tortured mind, she had to know, before she killed him...

Turning the revolver in her hand, grasping the barrel, Rita swung it at the back of Mateo's head. He grunted—a small, surprised sound— and lay still. She grabbed his shirt off the chair, tore it into strips, and tied him to the bed at foot and headboard. Moving with urgency now, she rushed to Tía's side of the bed and covered her daughter's mouth with a firm hand. Gently shaking her awake, she watched as Tía's eyes blinked open. Sleep slowly gave way to surprise. Rita's fierce maternal instinct took over, and she leaned forward.

"Tía, *niña*, are you...all right?"

Rita relaxed the pressure of her hand over Tía's mouth as recognition registered.

Struggling up to a sitting position Tía glanced down at Mateo. The confusion in her eyes pierced Rita's heart. What had she done to this child? What had ever possessed her to stay complacently accessible to that man—to risk Tía's life to prove to him that she could be as independent and as cruel as he?

Flushed with guilt, Rita gathered her daughter into her arms and held her close. "Did he...force you?"

"What?"

"Did he rape you?"

"No." Tía flushed with shame to be asked such a question. It seemed to condemn her in some elemental way.

Rita breathed a sigh of relief and replaced her gun in its holster. She would probably wish she had killed him, but she was grateful she didn't have to. "We have to leave…before he wakes up."

Tía rubbed her eyes. They felt tired and gritty. "He has men everywhere."

Rita stood up. "I am his wife. They let me in. They will let me out. Apparently he did not tell them otherwise. Come. Get ready. I will watch him to be sure he stays out."

"I'm ready."

"Good. Now…can you laugh?"

Not understanding, Tía shook her head.

"Never mind. Smile. I will handle everything. Follow my lead."

Arm in arm, whispering and smiling as if they shared secrets only women would understand, they skipped merrily down the stairs. Andano smiled knowingly.

They reached the bottom of the steps and walked quite close to the guard. Giggling like a half-drunk schoolgirl, Rita walked Tía straight into him.

"Watch where you are standing, *peón*," Rita said in a low, forceful voice.

"A thousand pardons, *señora*," he said quickly.

"Only if you will be so good as to summon a man to bring our guide and our horses around."

"Now, *señora*?" he asked, frowning as he looked up at his general's bedchamber.

Rita laughed softly. "Unless you would like to receive the order from *El Gato Negro* himself, after disturbing him when he has a toothache. I am sure he can arrange a suitable punishment for such insolence, especially when I tell him you were disrespectful to his wife."

Andano flinched. When displeased, the anger of *el general* was legendary. When it involved his wife…aiyee! There were stories of volcanic explosions. And these last three months after *el general* had been attacked and stabbed by the soldiers and had been forced to send the *señora* into hiding while he recuperated, they had all walked on eggshells. This day, apparently because he knew she had been coming to see him, he had been almost like himself again. Andano would not be the one to upset the new tranquility.

"*Un momento, señora.* I will bring them myself," he said quickly.

Rita nodded her satisfaction, and Andano hurried away.

"How did you know he had not told them I was a prisoner?" Tía whispered.

Rita smiled, "*El general* has far too much pride. He would never admit that one of his women would run away."

CHAPTER FORTY-SEVEN

Andrea paced outside the door to Steve's bedroom, oblivious to the sounds of women talking in the parlor, the rattle of pans as Carmen, Cruz, and Lupe cleaned up the mess they had made helping Andrea care for the injured men.

They could have gone to Tombstone. Johnny said they were as close to the town as they were to the ranch, but Steve had wanted to go to the ranch.

Dr. Potter had been with Steve for what seemed like hours, and still the door remained closed. It was a dread barrier. Once she crossed over the threshold, the words he uttered, the words she heard would change her life.

Agonized, she could only remember Steve's face—slack with sleep or tight with pain. Either way, she was exhausted from feeling his pain with every step of the horse. With her eyes closed she could see his hands, white with the effort to hang on so they could move more quickly. Even half-dying, his first thoughts had been for the safety of the others...

The door opened. Andrea's heart chugged down like a locomotive engine under pressure, then accelerated. Tired from three days of tending badly wounded men, running his fingers through his thin, gray hair, Potter stepped out into the hall.

"How...how is he?" Her voice was timid, fearful. "He's...going to be all right, isn't he?"

"Not much good at reading the future. Never had the gift."

"But he's not dying," she protested weakly, more afraid that he would confirm her fears than hopeful he would deny them.

"He wants to see you."

Her heart sank like a lead weight. She turned away from the doctor's tired face and stumbled through the door.

Steve's face was averted. His hands lay on his flat belly. His eyes were closed, but his chest lifted slightly with each shallow breath. His broad chest was wrapped with a clean white bandage. His head was swathed with more bandages. Shaking all over, she sagged into the chair beside his bed. Needing assurance, she touched his warm hand. His head turned toward her, his eyes flickering and opening at her touch. He recognized her.

"You're going to be okay," she lied, brightly, squeezing his hand.

Licking his dry lips, he shook his head. Momentarily, his eyes closed then opened. "If I don't make it, will you take care of Judy for me?..."

"Of course." Tears streamed down Andrea's cheeks.

"Where are we?"

"You're home now. You're safe."

His voice was barely more than a whisper. Andrea had to lean close to hear him. "Where's Judy? I want to see her."

"She's fine. Rutledge will bring her home today. She's on her way now. I can't imagine what's taking her so long. Red said she was leaving as soon as he got there to get the doctor." She was repeating herself.

"If I don't get to see her..." Pain closed his eyes. Muscles in his jaw clamped hard against it. Slowly it eased, leaving him white, his face wet with perspiration. "Tell her that my half of everything belongs to her. There's a will in my desk...to make it official..."

"You're going to be fine...please don't talk like this..."

"Any word from...Johnny?"

"No...no."

"Tía?"

"No...no."

Steve's hand tightened around hers. "Johnny will find her. He's a good...man."

"Oh, please, don't talk. Save your strength."

"Lie down next to me. I need to touch you."

Fear and grief swelled inside Andrea with every word he uttered. She slipped onto the bed; she was afraid to touch him.

"Closer," he whispered. His warm hand found her lips. Slowly his feather-light touch burned to the core of her.

"Steve, you need to save your strength."

He smiled weakly. "This is how I do it. I feel better already."

Andrea forced herself to forget everything except that Steve was alive this moment and that he needed her. She scooted closer to him and concentrated on sharing her body heat with him.

If he died, nothing would matter anyway...

CHAPTER FORTY-EIGHT

The last rifleman had disappeared behind him. They hadn't killed him. It made no sense.

Turning in his saddle, Johnny gazed back over the path. He had ridden two miles under the rifles of *El Gato Negro*'s fierce-eyed, indolent *vaqueros*, and no shot had been fired. Weak with the effects of prolonged fear, he kicked his horse into a canter. It was a long descent into the Animas Valley—if he could find the way.

Johnny rode until dark and found a sheltered place to make a cold camp. Under the sheer face of a cliff, in a small indentation that sheltered him from the cold night winds, he spread his blankets and lay down. He was exhausted, but even bone-deep tiredness could not save him from his thoughts.

An image of Tía appeared in his mind. Her fine golden curls shimmered between him and the stars winking overhead. Her guileless blue eyes mocked him. In torment, he watched again as she lifted her lips to *El Gato Negro*. The warmth and color in her cheeks had receded. In that second before the bastard had claimed them, her lips had trembled, caused a wild turbulence around his heart.

Had he imagined it, or had Tía's face twisted in anguish as he'd kissed her hand? Because she hated him? Because she didn't want him touching her? Or...because she had cared? At that thought, an exultant flame warmed him. She had wanted him that night in the orchard— almost as much as he had wanted her. She had been as lost as he. Perhaps she *had* cared.

Surrender the silver and the girl, and you can go in peace. Tía's eyes had filled with anguish when he'd tried to shoot *El Gato Negro*. And then shame when he asked her about the man who had tried to kidnap her at the ranch.

Tía—soft and warm and responsive in his arms. He wanted to feel his fingers pressing into that fine, light gold skin, forcing small, startled gasps from her half-opened lips, to feel her body resisting his. To hear her cries…to cause them…

He should be dead now. *El Gato Negro*, should have given the signal. Why hadn't he? Johnny's body felt clenched like a fist. He forced it to relax, but as soon as he stopped consciously willing it, he felt the tension return, like bowstrings pulled tight in his back and chest.

The moon shone with cold brightness. Tía was with *him*, with *El Gato Negro*. Grief and rage swelled in him. Johnny wanted to go back and drag her out of her lover's bed.

Stars twinkled like tiny fire lanterns in the dark sky. They had been there before he was born. They would be there long after he was dead, long after his passion for Tía was forgotten.

He hated her. He hated all women. Love was an accident. It came unexpectedly and completely—as accidents did. Tía had looked at him with that self-assured sweetness in her eyes, and he had loved her, not because he had been touched by the rare beauty of her soul or even by the rare beauty of her sassy, sardonic eyes, but because he had been struck by the accident of love as if it were lightning striking at random or a knife thrown by a madman.

The shining blade of love had been thrust into his chest like a dagger thrown at a target. The point bit deep. The shaft and hilt quivered, vibrating since the first day he'd kissed her in Tubac. Now the sharp edge cut into the tender rawness of his insides. He could feel the blade rusting, taste the sour, cold metal poisoning his body and mind.

Johnny paced under the stars. Tía was in her lover's arms. He hated her. He had never really loved her.

He paced for hours, thinking his bitter thoughts, searching for the switch that would allow him to turn off his grief and pain. At last he admitted that he did love her—had loved her, he corrected himself.

Judy had left her scars. Tía would leave hers. Someday his insides would become tough, and he would no longer feel the bite of love. Someday. But not now, not this day. This day he would bleed.

Long before dawn, Johnny saddled Matador and headed west, working his way back toward the ranch. He rode all day. At the edge of the valley, only two miles from the Burkhart compound, he stopped and made camp. It made no sense to do so, but logic and reason did not seem to matter. Seeing the ranch off in the distance, Johnny realized he couldn't go back there.

On the one hand he wanted to be sure Steve had survived. On the other hand he didn't want to see or talk to anyone. He didn't want to explain. He was wanted by the army. Rutledge would order his men to shoot him on sight. His escape had given them the right to do that. The bastard would enjoy exercising that right.

He'd been a fool. He should have headed east or north—maybe into Utah or Colorado. He hadn't been there yet.

Jerking the saddle off Matador, he laid it on a level, shale-covered shelf and spread a blanket. He hadn't been thinking straight. Well, it wasn't too late. Tomorrow morning would be soon enough. He would strike out for Wyoming. Rutledge wouldn't follow him there.

Rita and Tía didn't stop until they were three hours away from the pueblos. The eastern sky was a dull gray. Soon the sun would be skimming back the darkness.

A small creek trickled through a ravine, surprising them. Abuelito had led them out of the labyrinthine canyons. The way was clear.

"Whoa!" Rita said, turning to look at her daughter. "We'll rest here. Don't unsaddle the horses."

Abuelito shook his head in disgust, but he obeyed. *El Gato Negro's* wife could do as she pleased, even to the point of cruelty to dumb animals.

As soon as their guide's snores assured them he slept heavily, Rita roused Tía. They filled their canteens, mounted, and made their escape. They did not stop this time until the sun was high overhead.

When they came to a wide, swift-running creek, Rita dismounted and let her horse drink. Tía gave them the last of the grain, drank her fill, and lay down to stretch her muscles.

"Tía?"

"Yes, Mama."

"How do you feel? Are you all right?"

Tía did not look at her. "Yes."

"Then why did you take a piece of that broken bottle?"

Tía looked away. She didn't know why.

Rita felt nauseous. Mateo had done something to the girl, something that had left her feeling vulnerable and trapped. Rita remembered how it was to be young, to feel things so deeply that every wound could kill. Gently, she touched Tía's chin, forced her daughter to look at her.

"*Niña*, you know that I love you."

"No, you don't!" She turned away quickly, but Rita had seen.

"Tía, tell me what's wrong?"

Anger flared in Tía's eyes. "You lied to me! You've lied to me every step of the way. You knew Papa was *El Gato Negro*! You knew he wasn't my father. No wonder Papa went crazy. The truth would be as out of place in your mouth as a polecat at a picnic..."

A corresponding anger flared in Rita. "At what point do you recommend that I should have made my confession? When you were two years old? Five? Ten? How could I tell anyone anything without risking all of our lives—just the way I did when Mateo found out the truth? How could I tell *you*, Papa's favorite, that your father wasn't your father? I envy you your simple idealism and pious morality, Tía, but life was different for me."

"Morality!" Tía screamed. "How would you like to stand in front of the man who's just asked you to marry him and let the man you had thought was your father fondle you!? Is that morality, Mama! No girl should ever have to bear such shame!"

"You're absolutely right! No girl! Not you and not me! But I had to put up with much worse! Life was harder for me! More..." Rita could not continue. Unexpected tears welled up in her eyes. Anger that she would cry now made her tone harsh. "I would have killed him to save you, you little fool! I've protected you every step of the way—the best I knew how. I didn't have anyone to protect *me*! I had to survive!"

Rita glared at her daughter. Tía glared back in stubborn silence.

The horses finished drinking, moved to the grain, and munched it in a few noisy bites. They walked out of the water and started to graze on tussocks of bunch grass growing along the creek bank. A breeze carried smells of pine and juniper.

"Sit down," Rita gritted. "I never told you how I met Mateo, but now it's time." Rita stalked to the shade of a mesquite bush and sat down on the sandy ground. Tía followed and sat down facing her.

"You knew that I ran away from Tyler when I was fifteen. I didn't just meet Mateo and marry him. He attacked the wagon train I was on, killed all the men, and took the women..."

Rita told her whole story. She left out nothing. When Rita finished, Tía's blue eyes reflected horror and disbelief.

"You never *loved* him?"

"I hated him."

"But you stayed..."

"I was pregnant and had no place to go. He took care of me. I was fifteen years old! Later, he was good to Andrea. He adored you."

Tía pulled up a blade of grass and tore it in half. "I thought you loved him. You were always *happier* when he was home. I could see it in your eyes. They sparkled."

"Mateo meant nothing to me."

"Mama, he was your husband for twenty-five years. He came to see you every two or three months." Tía glanced quickly at her mother to gauge her reaction. "Sometimes Papa stayed for days. You cooked for him, you had his baby, you must have felt something."

Rita was stunned by the force of her emotion. Shaking, she turned away from Tía. "He forced me to marry him! You don't know what it was like. He only kept me because he wanted a *gringa* slave. Now he has caused you to doubt yourself. How could I love a man like that?"

A lump in Tía's throat burned. It was entirely possible to love a man it made no sense to love. She'd had no business falling in love with Judy's handsome foreman, but it hadn't stopped her.

"Papa gave you a home and took care of you and your children. I'm not a baby, Mama. I know how it is between a man and a woman. You didn't hate him all the time."

Rita flashed with anger. "That doesn't make me guilty of anything!"

A sudden realization filled Tía. If her mother was guilty of anything, it was trying to survive. Perhaps even Papa had only been trying to survive, too. But it didn't help her. She could never face Johnny again. Even *if* Johnny *had* survived, it was still over between them. Grief welled up in Tía. Papa probably let Johnny ride out of sight and had him killed and buried somewhere. She would never know now.

Rita misread the grief on Tía's face, took her child's cheeks in her hands, and fixed her eyes on her daughter. "Forget Papa and what he did. Whatever happened back there makes no difference. The life you live from today on is the only thing that matters. All we have is today. Yesterday doesn't matter. Tomorrow doesn't matter. Mateo set me down in a dirty little town called Tubac twenty-five years ago, and I wanted to die, but I couldn't. Somehow, I got off my pallet and found a way to enjoy what little bit of life I had left, and I got so busy that I forgot to be miserable. That's what you've got to do.

"All that's happened was my fault. It was my fault Mateo took you. He did it to get back at me. I cheated on my husband in spite and anger, and I brought all this down on your head. Even if it had somehow been your fault, which it isn't, it wouldn't change anything—not you, not me, not my love."

"Who could love me now?" Tía whispered.

"I love you, Tía," she said firmly. "There isn't anything you could ever do to change that. There isn't any way you could stop it or change it or even make me regret it. Nothing you could do or feel, nothing that could happen to you would ever change my love for you. Do you understand what I'm saying? You did the best you knew how. Just like I did. I made mistakes with you and with Mateo, but I did the best that I knew how."

Mama's words twisted Tía's insides, but she could not fully accept her mother's absolution.

"I know you love me, Mama, but this isn't like a skinned knee or a cracked head. I'm a woman now. I guess I gotta work this one out for myself."

"Are you too grown up to listen to good advice?"

Tía shook her head. Mama couldn't understand that she had stood there and let Johnny watch her being handled by *El Gato*. Johnny wasn't like the men Mama and her friends talked about. Johnny wouldn't even make love to her until they were properly married. He darned sure wasn't going to just hang and rattle like a tied snake after what he'd seen. If he was alive, he'd take one look at her and hit the flats for Wyoming.

Tía's unwillingness to be instantly healed angered Rita. She had broken her wedding vows and left her daughter to bear the brunt of it. No shame borne alone could match the fierce pain of watching your child torn apart in your stead.

"We have to git," Tía said suddenly. She stood up and looked back over the trail they had traveled. A haze of dust caught her attention. Her mind was distracted with the worry that Papa would catch them and kill Mama. She held her hand out for her mother.

Rita looked at the cloud. Tía was no longer listening to her, but she couldn't drop it. "I guess we've all been booted out of the garden of Eden."

"Innocence can't last forever, can it?"

Rita sighed. Tía's innocence had been jerked away cruelly. Tía had lost Mateo's love, and she'd never had Bill Burkhart's. Rita knew the real shame was hers, and hers alone. There could be no life after Eden unless Tía survived.

Rita's anger had died. All she wanted now was Tía's assurance that she would survive her fall. "Tia…"

"We gotta git, Mama," Tía said grimly. "If *El Gato* catches us as mad as he is now, he's likely to trim a tree with our carcasses." They had a long way to go—fifty or sixty miles. But her mother's eyes were clouded with deep regret. Tía took pity on her. "I'm a woman now, Mama. I'll have to make my own peace."

Rita broke into tears. She could have handled anything except Tía shouldering the entire load for her.

"I can't run any more...You go ahead. Let him catch me. I don't care if he kills me."

"You don't really mean that, Mama. You're just real tired. I reckon the worst is over. Unless he catches us. Come along now."

Rita felt old for the first time in her life. She let Tía urge her gently toward the horse.

They rode until full dark, unsaddled the horses, hobbled them securely near forage, collapsed onto their blankets, and slept fitfully.

Rita woke first. The sun was about two hours into daylight, which meant they had lost at least two hours on Mateo. He would not oversleep. They saddled the horses, mounted, and headed north west. As they rode they ate the tortillas, beef jerky, and dried fruit Abuelito had procured.

The sun arced overhead, finally set, and still they fled, knowing now that *El Gato Negro* pursued them. Rita knew Mateo's tempers, and when he was angry, he would not come to her as husband, he would come as the avenger. When they rode on high ground she could look back and see his small army raising its dust comet behind them.

Tía could barely keep herself upright in her saddle. Night came. Mama found a place, and they rested fitfully until first light. The horses were suffering. The only comfort was that Mateo's horses would be as tired as their own.

It seemed Tía had just closed her eyes, but Mama roused her. Tía staggered to her horse, and they rode for hours, finally into a canyon at the western edge of the Chiricahuas. The eastern sky was turning from luminescent gray to dull pink. The mountains were finally behind them. Still shaded from the rising sun, the Sulphur Springs Valley spread out in front of them.

Breathing a sigh of relief, Rita exulted in finding the way. Fear had been a constant companion. A dozen times she had regretted leaving Abuelito behind. It had been a precaution that could have cost them both their lives.

In her excitement, tiredness sloughed off. Slowing her horse to a fast walk, Rita glanced at Tía to see if she recognized the valley and the tiny lights in the windows that signified the Burkhart household was up and stirring.

Riding mechanically, Tía's face was closed. Rita felt a sudden, angry impatience with Tía for reminding her, however passively she did it. Rita wanted to reach through her daughter's impassivity, to make the girl realize she had not been so irreparably damaged.

"We're almost there! Rancho la Reina," Rita shouted over the clatter of their horses' hooves. It meant safety from Mateo's wrath. Surely he would not pursue them in broad daylight, not into the compound.

"No!" Tía reined her horse, tried to stop its forward momentum. Alarmed, Rita looked behind them. Mateo's army was even closer. She couldn't see them, but a small cloud sifted up to the left of the rising sun. Mateo would marshal his horses and his men. And he knew better than she how to do that. She should have shot him when she'd had the chance. Rita reached out to Tía, then thought better of it and let the horses stop. They were blowing hard. Perhaps a short rest would work to their advantage.

"We must go on soon," she said. "Mateo and his men are too close."

Tía shook her head. "I'm not going back there now." She could never face Johnny again.

"There is no other place to go. We'll barely make it there. Hopefully Mateo won't dare follow us."

"I'm not going back there," Tía said firmly.

"Tía, please..." Rita paused. Her daughter's face was pale but determined. She meant it. For the first time Rita saw Tía as a separate person, not a child whose fears and hurts could be soothed away and dismissed. Even worse, Rita realized it had never been true—her false belief that the hurts of another could be erased. It pained her to see what she and Mateo had done to the girl. Tía had grown up overnight.

"Is there a young man?" Rita asked.

Tía looked away.

"Tía, nothing happened back there to make you unfit for him."

Tía's lips quivered. Her blue eyes flashed her absolute belief that Rita was wrong.

"Even women have a right to survive, Tía. I know first love takes you hard and deep, but it's not worth dying for."

Tears stung Tía's eyes, but she ignored them. And as she witnessed her daughter's fear, Rita grew angry and impatient. She used the only thing that might work. "Tía, I won't leave you. If he catches us, he'll kill me."

Tía searched her mother's eyes and spurred her horse. Rita breathed a prayer of gratitude. Temporarily at least, she had won.

CHAPTER FORTY-NINE

A promise of dawn turned the sky a pale shade of gray. Irritated by the frustration of inactivity, Johnny rolled up his blankets. He would climb to the top of the mountain. The exercise would be good for him. Taking his field glasses and some biscuits out of his saddlebags, he began to climb.

Enjoying the sweat of exertion, he climbed quickly. Halfway up he paused on a ledge and looked out over the valley below.

Almost a hundred miles long from south to north and twenty miles wide from east to west, the Sulphur Springs Valley faded into dreamy ghostliness. To the south the valley appeared endless—a pale gray ocean fading into the pale gray stillness of the predawn sky. To the west he could see the dim lights of the Burkhart compound. A tiny tendril of smoke curled upward—a pale ribbon rising on an updraft. Carmen had already started breakfast. To the north the pale, squat walls of Fort Bowie perched on a hill.

Turning east, he scanned the trail he had ridden to leave the mountains. In the path of the rising sun, the cleft between the two mountains glowed with light. He was almost ready to turn away when a movement caught his attention. Two riders entered the eastern end of the canyon, traveling fast.

Even in the first flush of dawn his sharp eye recognized Tía's silhouette. In his mind's eye he could visualize her golden curls, misty and ill defined around her plaintive face. He raised the glass to see who rode beside her. The slender silhouette indicated a woman, but he had never seen her before.

As he watched the two of them galloping their horses down the same path he had taken, a prickling sensation started in his neck: a nerve-end tingle that caused him to scan the terrain around him, the mountains behind him, the valley.

There. To the south. The lighter shading of the valley floor was dotted by the dark shapes of an army on the move. It looked like half of the Apache nation on horseback. Johnny lifted the field glasses to his eyes. He'd been right: every face was dark with war paint. Glancing back at Tía and her companion, he calculated their speed and whether he would be able to head them off. He was too far up the mountain. They would pass below before he could reach the canyon floor.

Probably timing their arrival to coincide with the rising of the sun, the Indians were moving steadily and slowly toward the Burkhart compound. No time to wonder why or even if he was right. Moving as quickly as he could, he raced down the mountainside. Afraid to fire a shot, he stopped when the two riders were almost directly below him and shouted, but they didn't hear him over the pounding of their horses' hooves. Tía and the woman passed without seeing him or his horse and rode out onto the gentle grade to the valley floor.

Johnny hurried as fast as the brush and chaparral on the mountain would permit. Tía was in danger. He had to reach her before the Apaches did. He could see Matador tethered in the small clearing where grass grew in odd little patches.

He reached the level breathless and panting. Because of undergrowth clogging the canyon floor, he lost sight of Tía and ran toward the spot where he had left Matador. Halfway there, the vibration of the hooves of many horses caused him to stop and listen.

What the hell?

Johnny saw them at the same time they saw him. Only minutes behind Tía, *El Gato Negro* and his army burst into view.

His nerves leaped, then settled down. It was too late to try to hide. He walked to the center of the path *El Gato Negro* would soon be thundering over and waited, using the narrow span of time to catch his breath.

They saw him. When they were fifty feet from him he held up both hands to stop them.

Scowling, *El Gato Negro* held up his left hand. The tight knot of surging, plunging riders halted ten feet from Johnny. Dust swirled into a blinding fog, then slowly settled. The sky behind *El Gato Negro* was like a bright gold halo as the sun, filtering through the dust particles, peeked over the mountain. A welcome breeze leveled some of the dust.

Hands on hips, Johnny affected his most challenging posture; *El Gato Negro*'s expression was contemptuous.

"Well, Señor Brago. I thought you would be in Tombstone by now."

"Burned some bridges in Tombstone," he drawled. "Reckon I won't be going back there. Thought I might make a deal with you."

El Gato Negro's smile was tight. "A man standing in quicksand is in a poor position to make deals, Señor Brago."

Johnny knew he was right, but he shrugged. Thanks to *El Gato Negro's* generosity, he had no bullets in his gun. There were more than fifty *bandidos* with *El Gato Negro* now, and more coming—if he always hedged his bets the way he had at the ambush.

"Señor Brago, I make no deals with you, except this: You will ride in and open the gates for us. I will take those who belong to me and no one else. Otherwise we will come in force, and we will spare no one. Then I will take those who belong to me."

Holding on while her horse skimmed the grassy plain, Tía used the last of her energy. The sky in front of them turned from dark blue to gray. Dimly, in the distance behind the compound, the Dragoons glowed with the rising of the sun. The labored breathing of the horses was a grim reminder that they might not make it. Leaning low in the saddle, hearing her mother's shout but unable to make out the words, Tía clung with all her strength to the horse's mane.

The gates swung open, and Tía and Rita rode into the compound. The guards shouted to alert the house.

Tía dismounted, looked toward the house, and saw Andrea on the porch, lifting her skirts to run headlong down the steps and across the fifty yards that separated them. Tía ran to meet her.

"Teresa! Mother!" Andrea hugged Tía hard. "Oh, *Tía!* I'm so glad you're safe. I was so worried. We were so afraid…" Andrea hugged her sister as if she could not believe she was alive.

"Rider comin' in!" one of the sentries shouted. "Looks like Brago!"

"Johnny!"

Tía ran toward the wall, scampered up onto the catwalk, and peered over.

"It's Johnny!" A feeling of joy almost overwhelmed her. He was alive. Her joy was followed immediately by a warning: *He might not want anything to do with me.* Johnny had survived, but his feelings for her might not have. He wouldn't even make love to her before they were married. Perhaps he'd find her too soiled now.

The gates swung open, and Johnny rode into the compound. Men spilled out of the bunkhouses, shouting as they pulled on pants, shirts, gunbelts. They loaded rifles on the run.

"Johnny!" Tía wasn't sure she had shouted his name aloud, but he looked up and saw her. His dark eyes held hers, and the blood coursed through her veins in savage spurts, making her dizzy. She searched his face for some sign, but the handsome, cocky slant of his eyes told her nothing. Men converged on him, and he turned away from her, abruptly.

"Hey, Johnny, we thought you was daid."

"Listen up!" he shouted. "We don't have any time to lose. There are two hundred nimble-blooded Indians heading this way, maybe more."

Johnny waved them toward the walls, and men scrambled to get into position. Tía looked as though she'd caught sight of something disturbing. She frowned and looked toward the *casa grande*. Suddenly her face changed from solemn to smiling.

Two men carried a stretcher down the steps. Recognizing Steve on the stretcher, Johnny left the riders by the wall and strode forward to meet the stretcher halfway and clasp Steve's hand.

"Glad to see you made it."

"Thanks," Steve said.

"Get ventilated pretty good, did you?"

"I won't die, but all the hinges and bolts got loosened a bit."

"There's no time now for explanations, but I made a deal with *El Gato Negro*."

"What kind of deal?" Steve asked, frowning.

"I promised to open the gates for him."

"Are you loco?"

"I know he is. I might be." Johnny cleared his throat and looked back at Tía. "We have someone he wants."

"Riders comin'!" shouted one of the sentries on the wall.

"Riders hell! Looks like Santa Anna storming into Texas!" yelled another.

"It'll be hot enough around here to scorch a lizard," growled a third.

Johnny borrowed a rifle from Willie B. Parker and ran for the wall. Aiming for a spot close enough to Tía to keep an eye on her, Johnny ran to the catwalk and leaped up. In front of a heavy cloud of dust, a close-knit, surging knot of dark-garbed, high-sombreroed riders were charging straight for the compound. *El Gato Negro* rode at their head, his lithe arrogance and slick costume setting him apart.

Steve felt his wounds deeply. He was reluctant to take charge, but too much hung in the balance. "Carry me up to the platform."

"You'll catch a bullet up there for sure," Dap Parker protested.

"Just do as I say."

Dap picked up one end of the makeshift stretcher and Leon picked up the other. They carried Steve to the foot of the platform. Then four other men lifted Steve and the stretcher up the stairs.

"Lean me up so I can see over," Steve directed. When he was positioned so he could watch, he motioned to Johnny. Andrea climbed up and stood protectively close to Steve.

"What are you going to do?" Steve asked, adjusting himself on the stretcher to lean against the back wall of the platform.

Johnny's dark eyes narrowed into slits. "Let 'em in," he said flatly.

Still groggy from sleep, Andrea turned to confront Johnny. Visions of hulking black buzzards tearing at the maggot-infested remains of the men in the canyon filled her with revulsion. "We can't let that man in here!"

"We need them," Johnny argued. "We can't hold off two hundred Apache all by ourselves."

"No!" Andrea cried. "You don't know that man! He'll kill all of us, the way he killed the men in the pack train!"

"We got no choice. Either we trust him to do what he says he'll do, or we all die anyway." Raising his right arm, Johnny shouted, "Open the gates!"

"Hold it!" Steve yelled.

The men poised beside the gate looked from Johnny to Steve. Frustrated, Johnny turned. From the south the Indians were closing much faster now. Soon they would spill over the Mexicans and around the compound.

At the head of the oncoming riders, within twenty feet of the gates, *El Gato Negro*'s horse reared and pawed the air. His dark gaze darted from Johnny to the dozens of men who peered over the wall from behind rifle barrels.

"Is this the way you keep your word, Señor Brago?"

Ignoring the stab of pain that shot through his chest, Steve yelled, "He was overruled!"

Andrea moved closer to Steve and put her arms around his neck in a way that was unmistakable. She lifted her chin defiantly and stared, with eyes cold and glittering with hatred at her father.

Seeing that look, Mateo Lorca's lips tightened into a grim line. He understood completely. His daughter had fallen in love with this blond *gringo* who had the power to overrule Brago. This must be the son of that bastard who had cuckolded him. His only daughter was rejecting him for this *gringo*. This particular *gringo*. A flame deep inside him flickered and died.

"*¡El general!* Indians. Hundreds of them," Patchy said, his voice low, urgent. Mateo turned in the saddle in time to see the Apaches rise up eerily on the horizon, less than two hundred yards from them, riding in a wide semicircle that would tighten to envelop them in a matter of minutes.

Flashing Johnny a smile, admiration mingling with the strange, deep coldness spreading into his limbs, Mateo started to turn away. Brago had led him into a trap. But nothing mattered now.

Johnny turned and pointed Slim's rifle at Willie B., who was standing beside the gates. He had known Willie B. for seven years.

"Open the gates!" Johnny yelled. "Open 'em!"

Willie B. looked from Johnny to Steve and back. Johnny cocked the rifle. Ignoring Steve's hard stare, Willie B. moved to obey. The gates swung open.

Burying her face against Steve's chest, Andrea stifled her cries. It was too late for tears now.

Watching from her own vantage point, sure she was the only one among them who understood clearly what was happening, Rita, too, was caught up in the strange unreality of this unfolding drama. Seeing that one flash of loss in Mateo's eyes, she knew instantly what he felt. He loved Andrea. Now Andrea had rejected him for the son of the man who had shamed him. Mateo might mask his pain from others, but Rita knew him too well.

Marveling at this revelation, and that she cared, Rita watched in silence.

At the head of his restive troops, Mateo scanned the wide, sweeping semicircle of Apaches, moving in rapidly now, tightening the death circle as they came. With a characteristic snarl curling his lips, he looked up at Johnny.

"Close your gates, Señor Brago. We want nothing from you."

CHAPTER FIFTY

Every nerve in Rita's body screamed for Mateo to ride into the compound, to ride into safety, but he would not relent, even in the face of death. The gates slammed shut.

Fewer than fifty men rode with Mateo. The Indians were closing in on them from all sides. Mateo saw them, and his fine black steed reared. Rita watched as he controlled the animal with the same steely grip he had used on her so long ago. He was badly outnumbered. He knew it, yet it made no difference to him. He had been born to be killed. Only the time and place of his execution had been in question. He was *El Gato Negro*, the maverick panther. Now it was his time to die, and he would do it his way—outside the white man's walls, at the head of his army, where he belonged.

He was prepared to face death in the same way he had lived: proudly, fiercely, with contemptuous disregard for the quakings of normal men.

An unfamiliar urging rose up in Rita—like a torch lifted in darkness. She jumped off the catwalk and ran for the small barred door beside the wide gates that had just slammed shut. Ignoring the yells of protest, she threw off the bar, dragged the door open, and, before anyone could move to stop her, ran through.

"Mama! No! No!" Tía yelled, her arms flailing above the wall as if to reach out and drag her back, out of danger.

Ignoring her daughter's plea, Rita ran forward. "Mateo! Mateo!"

Apaches had already engaged his men. They needed his attention, but hearing Rita's voice, Mateo turned, and as he did, he swung his heavy Colt around to point it at her heaving breast. Slowly he nudged his horse toward her.

Rita's senses dimmed so that she was aware only of him: his fierce black eyes; his handsome, arrogant, scowling face; and the drawn gun in his lean brown hand.

"It is fitting that I should kill you since you led us into this trap," he told her.

"Take me with you."

He would have laughed, but something shone in her face that he had not seen before. "We go to our death, no farther," he said harshly.

"I don't care. I want to go with you."

Seeing his general's preoccupation, Patchy Arteaga took charge and ordered his men outward to engage the enemy before the trap could be closed too tightly. Loyal *capitán* that he was, he positioned six men to guard *El Gato Negro*'s back and stayed close to be certain they did it well.

Without surprise or gratitude, Mateo Lorca noted these preparations and dismissed them quickly. His mind was occupied with Rita and his own response to her outrageous request.

Perhaps his ears were not hearing correctly. This was Rita, the tiger bitch who had fought him in every possible way, betrayed him, caused him to be stabbed, flaunted her golden-haired bastard in front of him, dared him a dozen times to kill her. She had even ridden into his camp and rescued her bastard child, half killing him in the bargain. His head still throbbed with pain.

Now, with tears shining in her wide blue eyes, she had the gall to stand before him and ask to go with him. She had never asked him for anything, not even when she had been great with his child. He had been the one to force her to marry him so their child would have a name and a place in heaven. He had known instinctively that he had to leave the money for their support on the table so she would find it only after he was gone.

Rita faced him squarely, her eyes shining with an impassioned light. His finger felt leaden on the trigger. He wanted to kill her, but not like this. For Rita, a bullet was too impersonal. Her life should end with his hands around her throat...

Mateo holstered his gun, leaned down, picked her up, and swung her into his arms. His men had engaged the enemy. The sound of battle was a din around his head. Tears sparkled on Rita's cheeks. Gently, his hand brushed at them.

"Why now, *querida*?"

It was this she had fought all those years—this doom of love—not him. She had tried so hard not to admit it even to herself, but now, when he was about to die, only now could she admit to herself and to him the truth.

433

Great blinding tears welled up in her eyes. "Because," she sobbed, "because I love you. You are my husband."

The shock of her words held him speechless. Never once had they thought or spoken of love. Their relationship had been based on his relentless hatred for her race and her stubborn unwillingness to submit.

Around them, the battle raged. Men fought and died, horses screamed and fell, but Mateo barely noticed. Shaking his head, ignoring everything except the fact of her surrender, Mateo lifted her chin and kissed her. For a long time he held her trembling body close. At last, remembering where they were, he turned, positioned her on the saddle in front of him, and lifted his fist into the air.

"Now we ride!" He had held his men in the trap too long. Putting spurs to his horse, he gave an exultant yell as it leaped forward.

On the wall, Johnny looked from *El Gato Negro* and the woman to Tía. She had called the woman "Mama." Tía's face was radiant.

Turning back to the battle at hand, Johnny shouted, "Cover them! Shoot, dammit!"

"Who the hell we s'posed to shoot at, the Injuns or them damned chili peppers?" Dap called.

"Can't you count?" Johnny yelled, firing. A bullet slammed into a wide, painted chest. An Indian jerked backward and fell off his pony.

"Playin' the numbers, huh?" Robert asked, popping off a shot at a tomahawk-wielding brave.

"When we run outa Injuns do we swap sides?" Willie B. joked, firing three times in quick succession.

"Don't run outa Injuns. Been here nigh onto ten years, and we ain't never run out yet," Dap drawled, reloading.

Sighting his rifle on one of a dozen warriors blocking *El Gato Negro*'s path, Johnny squeezed the trigger. One of the braves tumbled backward. *El Gato*'s broad back curved protectively around the female in front of him. He jumped the big black steed over the fallen brave. Bending low in the saddle, he broke through the ring of Mexican bandits and into a nest of Indians.

Next to Tía, Slim Whitman caught a bullet with his shoulder and almost fell off the platform. He set his rifle down next to Tía and jerked his bandana from around his neck. Tía picked up the .30–.30 and located Mama and Papa—she'd probably always call him Papa. Behind them an

Indian on a speckled mustang raised a tomahawk to send it flying after them, and Tía lifted the rifle to steady it on the adobe wall.

Andrea saw Tía and the direction she aimed the rifle and wanted to close her eyes. Tía would kill Papa, maybe Mama, too. They deserved it, but Andrea did not want to see it. Part of her wanted to cry out to Tía to spare them, but she had lost that right when she let Tía go with Papa.

Tía fired and recoiled from the kick of the rifle. The tomahawk-wielding brave fell off his pony.

El Gato and his female charge broke through the line of Indians and into a nest of *bandidos*. With Papa in the center, the Mexicans whipped their horses toward the hills. Indians abandoned their attack on the compound. Yipping wildly, they goaded their ponies into pursuit of the fleeing bandits.

Straightening, Johnny darted a look at Tía. She'd never been more beautiful. Her blue eyes shone with a strange triumphant light. Her teeth clamped into her soft bottom lip so hard Johnny wanted to stop her, to save that sweet lip from being damaged, but he was unable to move. A dozen questions formed in his mind. He promised himself he would get to the bottom of this later, but now he scanned the melee below to decide where to put his next bullet.

To the east, beneath the sun hanging above the mountains, an army of what looked like *El Gato Negro*'s men spilled out of the pass and spread out to engage the Indians and assist *El Gato*'s beleaguered forces. Reinforcements poured into the melee in an endless stream, hundreds of them. They swarmed like ants and overwhelmed the Indians by sheer force of numbers.

"Can you see? Are they all right?" Andrea demanded, shaking so hard she could barely maintain her footing on the narrow ledge. She had thought Tía would kill Papa. Unexpected relief that she hadn't left Andrea weak.

Taking the binoculars from the man next to him, Steve scanned the wild tangle of horses and men until he saw them. *El Gato Negro* had withdrawn from the battle in deference to his female charge. He watched from a distance.

"They're all right. Looks like *El Gato Negro*'s private army is in the process of breaking the back of the Apache nation. I expect Chatto will lead what is left of his warriors back to the reservation, if there is anything left. Those Mexicans are damned efficient."

Andrea flashed him an angry look.

"Sorry," Steve muttered, realizing he had spoken with less than respect.

"Don't apologize to me. I know Mexicans are not really gods. But if you're afraid you aren't good enough for me…" Smiling, Andrea let the mischief sparkle in her dark eyes.

Steve leaned forward and kissed her.

"You…don't look like you're dying," she said accusingly. "Last night you were, and today you're yelling all over the compound. You tricked me."

"Would you rather fight with me or forgive me for not dying?"

"Just like that?" she asked, her expression incredulous.

Steve nodded, his face serious. "Just like I forgave you for tricking me," he said softly. "Be as grateful that I'm alive as I am that you aren't my sister."

What Steve had done, letting her think he was dying, seemed much worse than what she'd done, but she stopped resisting and let him pull her into his arms. "You are a very good actor," she whispered against his shoulder.

"Potter said the two bullets did amazingly little damage. One just broke the skin on my shoulder blade, and the other—probably from a twenty-two—entered at midchest and exited near my spine. It looked and felt much worse than it was. If it had been placed differently, I'd have been paralyzed for life. As it was, Potter said I'll probably make a complete recovery."

"You're sturdy, for a *gringo*."

"Or you're a very good nurse." As Steve held her close, all desire to tease her left him. "I'm hurt bad enough to keep me down for a good long while, but I don't feel like dying. I've got more important business to tend to. Will you marry me, Andrea whoever you are?"

"Yes," she whispered, going on tiptoe to kiss him. "Yes, yes, yes."

Happy for Andrea and Steve, yet strangely unwilling to watch their happiness, Tía turned away. She walked past Johnny, brushing so close her body touched his, and started down the ladder. The sound of Johnny's voice stopped her in her tracks.

"You always place them lead plums right where you want 'em?" he asked, his voice low, obviously meant for her ears alone.

"Men were falling like wormy apples in a high wind. I reckon someone had to do something."

"You just do the least you can get away with, huh?"

"Seems to me I been doing more than my share as far back as an old Injun can remember."

Tía didn't wait for his retort. She scampered down the ladder. Andrea disengaged herself from Steve and followed.

"Tía, are you all right?"

"Yes." Tía did not slow her pace. There'd been a time when Johnny would have reached out and stopped her if she got that close to him. This time he had just looked at her, his dark eyes as unreadable as swamp water.

"Wait!" Andrea ran to catch up. "Did you understand what Mama did back there?"

"Yes."

"Would you mind explaining it to me?"

"Not here," Tía said. She glanced at Johnny, who had stopped to watch her. "Let's go inside."

In her room, Tía fell across her bed and groaned in pleasure. A feather bed after so many nights on the ground was sheer heaven. Andrea lay down beside her, and Tía told her sister the whole story, just the way Rita had told it to her.

"I didn't know," Andrea murmured when she'd finished. "I can't believe that he...actually took her off a wagon train and..." Her voice trailed off. "Did he?..." Andrea flushed. "With you...did he...hurt you in any way?" she ended lamely.

"No," Tía said firmly. She told Andrea what had happened at the pueblos between her and Papa and Johnny.

Angry and upset, Andrea cried and Tía comforted her. It was the first time Tía had ever seen Andrea cry. Somehow watching Andrea's tears flow loosened something in Tía, something that had been tight and constricted ever since Papa took her away from Johnny—she'd thought it was supposed to be that way. Whatever it was let go, and Tía could breath easier. Finally, Andrea wiped her eyes and pushed herself up on her elbows.

"I let you go with Papa. I could have stopped him," Andrea whispered.

Tía shook her head. "That's a dream. Papa wouldn't move camp for a prairie fire. If you've been flailing yourself over that, you can forget it."

Relief and a new flood of tears caused Andrea to double over. The storm passed and she lay weak and shaking in Tía's arms. At last her voice returned. "Tía, are you all right?"

"I'm looking for a dog to kick. Other than that I guess I'm right as rain."

"I thought you were going to shoot Papa," Andrea said, sniffing. "I'm such a coward. I'd have let you."

"If I'd wanted to shoot him, you couldn't have stopped me." They sat in silence for a moment. Off in the distance, the sound of gunfire was barely audible.

"I never know whether I want to kill Papa or not," Andrea said, wiping at her eyes.

"Sometimes he acts so low if he was a rattlesnake he'd still be ashamed to look his mama in the eye, but he's not as bad as he could be. I don't pretend to understand him, but the part of me that loved him when we thought I was his daughter didn't die. He could have taken me. He could have made me his mistress, but he didn't. He's the only father I'll ever have. He loved me enough to spare me, and I'm grateful."

"What are you going to tell Johnny?"

"Johnny knows all he needs to know about me."

"You have to talk to him…else he'll ride away."

"I'll saddle his horse for him, if he needs help."

"He already knows almost everything. You screamed 'Mama!' when the Indians attacked. He knows."

In theory Andrea was probably right. Tía couldn't think what else she could have done under the circumstances, but every time she thought of Papa, or of Johnny seeing how Papa had treated her, she felt shamed to the core.

At the closed look on Tía's face, confusion swamped Andrea. "Johnny loves you. He doesn't care about…"

"I care!"

"Tía, that's craziness. You love Johnny. You couldn't have done what you did for him otherwise."

"You're about as dependable as a rattlesnake for a coat hanger. Last time we talked you hated him."

Andrea wasn't sure she knew why she had changed sides. Hearing their story and realizing Mama *had* loved Papa, even after all he had put her through…

"I was wrong, Tía. I thought Mama hated Papa. Sometimes I hated Papa. But I knew you always loved him."

438

"So?"

Andrea grimaced. "So, if I was wrong about Mama and Papa, I'm probably wrong about Johnny."

"Then you fall in love with him. I don't want to see him anymore. Too much smoke up that chimney already."

CHAPTER FIFTY-ONE

On the plain, the Indians pulled back and allowed the bandits to make their escape. Turning in unison, Johnny and Steve watched Tía and Andrea leave. Steve recovered first and smiled at Johnny.

"So nothing much happened after all. Chatto is pulling out of the fight. *El Gato Negro* and his men will escape back to wherever they came from." He sighed. "Maybe now we can get back to ranching."

"I reckon you can," Johnny said slowly. "I'll be moving on."

Steve sighed. "Think we could talk about it?"

Engrossed in watching the two females disappearing into the *casa grande*, Johnny shrugged. "Nothing to talk about. I think I'll mosey up to Wyoming. See what's stirring up there." Tía was back, but she didn't seem interested in him. She had walked away without even a look at him.

"The fight's over for us. Come up to the house, and I'll buy you a drink."

"I could use a drink. I'd have to be primed to spit."

Dap and Willie B. carried Steve to the *casa grande*. In the parlor, they lifted him off the stretcher and into the Morris chair beside the fireplace, then drifted outside. Steve directed Carmen to pour generous shots. Johnny tossed down his drink and then stretched out on the long sofa. It had been a long time since he'd had a good night's sleep. He was feeling the lack of it.

"You took a hell of a chance opening those gates for that bastard."

Johnny shrugged. "Seemed to me, we'd a took a bigger chance not opening 'em."

Anger still burned in Steve that Johnny had overruled him, but it was water under the bridge now. He let it drop.

"You don't need to leave, unless you want to. Rutledge dropped the charges against you."

Frowning, his dark eyes demanding an explanation, Johnny coiled forward into a sitting position.

"Grant Foreman confessed to shooting Morgan. He saw Morgan drag Judy into the barn. He thought Morgan had killed her."

"Where's Grant now?"

"Fort Bowie. We found out yesterday when the Doc came."

"Is there anything we can do for him?"

"I'll look into it."

"He deserves a damned medal," Johnny said grimly. "But that bastard Rutledge will probably turn him over to Behan and the circuit judge who, depending on the mood he's in, might just hang him. Too bad Todd didn't croak. He must have a constitution like a Texas longhorn. How's Judy?"

"According to Potter, she's fine. Rutledge is bringing her home today. She wanted to come last night, but for some reason he wouldn't let her. Something about her not being strong enough yet." Steve shrugged. "Judy went along with him on that. Surprised hell out of Potter; I could tell."

Absorbed in their own thoughts, both men were silent for a time. The ticking of the clock on the mantel was the only sound in the room.

"I hope you'll reconsider and stay. I need you to run the ranch," Steve said finally.

"Looks like you and Andrea have consolidated your partnership."

Steve grinned. "Andrea has agreed to marry me."

"Congratulations."

Andrea kissed Tía's forehead, walked quietly across the room, and let herself out.

Tía slipped into a light sleep and dreamed vague, formless dreams that seemed more like shadows or dark silhouettes against a light gray sky. No one had faces or names. They moved in and out of her dream like ships sailing on a glassy ocean. They could have been all the same—one person or one ship used over and over again—or they could have been all different, passing through never to be seen again...

Slowly, Tía woke up with her limbs like lead weights, her breathing shallow and labored. She struggled into a sitting position. Panting from the heat, she took a few sips from the glass of water someone had placed beside her bed.

The water tasted stale. Hoping for a cooling breeze, she walked to the window, but the air outside was also still. Nothing moved. The orchard trees resembled statues or paintings.

Then, as if the painting had suddenly come to life, two figures appeared, stepping slowly into the wrought-iron laced frame of her window: Judy Burkhart and Johnny Brago.

Judy wore a stylish yellow gown with a wide-brimmed straw hat, trailing a wide yellow ribbon from the brim. Johnny had changed into a light-colored shirt and tan trousers. They made a beautiful couple—Judy so slender and lovely and Johnny so lithe and dark and handsome. They stopped under one of the plum trees. Hands in his back pockets, leaning against the trunk of the tree, Johnny watched Judy as she talked. Once she reached out to him, touched his shirt, and he pulled her close and held her. Arm in arm, they turned and walked into the orchard toward the playhouse.

Tía turned away. So...they had made up their differences. That was good—probably inevitable from the start. She was too exhausted today, but tomorrow she would pack and leave. Andrea would marry Steve. Judy had Johnny. Even Mama and Papa had found love, or had discovered they'd had it all along.

She would have a good future as well. Money would be no problem for her. Steve would buy her share of the ranch. She was lucky, actually. She would be free to travel. Maybe go to a good school and learn how to be a real lady, someone a man could really love...not something for a man to lay with when his true love was angry with him.

Tía shook her head at the self-pitying turn her thoughts had taken. Johnny Brago was not the only man in the world. With money and freedom, she would find her own happiness.

She tried to put him out of her thoughts, but she kept seeing him in her mind. Eyes opened or closed—it didn't matter. The languid violence lurking behind that cocky, reckless slant of eyes and lips. Eyes that could change so quickly from warm and laughing to cool and challenging. Johnny Brago was a mystery to her, nothing more. She did not love him. She had only been tricked by him, seduced by his smiling eyes and his cocky grin.

A knock sounded on her door.

"It's dinnertime, Tía," Andrea called. "Please come eat something."

"I'm not hungry."

Tía lay down on the bed. She felt tired, strangely listless. She closed her eyes for a moment and must have slept again. A sound wakened her.

The door opened and footsteps crossed her floor. "Tía?" whispered a voice.

"Tía?" the voice said again, louder this time. "It's me, Judy. I need to talk to you."

Tía roused herself with an effort. Disoriented at first, she could not tell, but it seemed she had slept too long. It felt like morning. Judy still wore the lovely yellow gown. Close up, Tía noticed it was a gingham print she remembered from washday. She had ironed that gown while Judy had lounged on the floor and talked.

"I'm so glad you're okay," Tía said after a moment, meaning it.

Judy smiled. "Me, too." Her smile seemed different, more authentic somehow. As if it came from a deep pool of self-confidence and hope. Probably because she and Johnny had settled their differences.

Tía wanted Judy to know she had expected it, actually wanted it. "I'm glad things worked out for you and—"

"I just wanted to tell you that I do forgive you for lying to me," Judy said, interrupting. "I'm sorry I waited so long to tell you. When I realized you had gone and might never come back, I felt awful. If you had died..." Judy shuddered.

"Thanks."

"Did *El Gato*...hurt you?"

Shame flushed through Tía, reminding her why she had to leave this place. Johnny had probably told Judy what Papa had done. Images of herself in Papa's arms would be burned forever into Johnny's mind. She seemed unable to see herself from any other perspective—only Johnny's.

"No," Tía said finally. "He didn't hurt me."

"I'm glad. I was afraid Andrea had lied to me so we could leave the ranch without worrying about you."

Tía tried to think of something witty and outrageous to say so Judy would know how unaffected she actually was by the thought of Johnny and Judy leaving Rancho la Reina.

Judy was talking, but Tía was so busy thinking of something to say she didn't listen. *Actually*, she thought, *I'm stronger than ever, far better equipped to deal with losing Johnny now that I saved his life. I owe him nothing. And he owes me nothing...*

Judy was animated, speaking. "...married this morning."

At last Tía heard her words.

"We're going to Atlanta to meet his parents. We'll probably stay there."

"Married?" So...Johnny had married Judy. It was done. Tía felt cold inside, cold and empty.

Judy laughed gaily, mischievously. "Yes. Isn't it amazing? I never dreamed I could make up my mind so quickly."

"I'm happy for you," Tía murmured.

Judy lifted her arms and stretched. "I can see myself now—mistress of an Atlanta town house…I hope Grant knows how to hire good help. I have the feeling I haven't changed that much. But I did warn him. It's not like he doesn't know me."

Tía could not imagine why Judy and Johnny would take Grant along, but then Judy could do anything she wished. Johnny would probably not object. Poor Grant…how would he feel living on the fringes of Judy's life?

Suddenly Tía's room was too bright. She would rather be in the barn surrounded by horses. She liked horses better than people.

Judy hugged Tía good-bye. "We aren't leaving until tomorrow. I hope you feel well enough to visit with me this evening. Of course, I suppose he's going to want to go to bed early…" Judy's back felt warm and damp, and her skin smelted sweet and fresh as she hugged Tía. Johnny would hold Judy like this, Tía thought. He would feel her shoulder blades under his hands…the warm, firm flesh alive and supple.

At last Judy left. Tía had promised to visit with her. She and Johnny would leave tomorrow, and Tía would no longer have to worry about seeing Johnny and being reminded of those tortuous moments in Papa's arms.

Tía felt stifled. The urge to get out of her room came over her suddenly.

She avoided the parlor, where she could hear voices, and slipped outside. Quickly she cut around the west side of the house to avoid having to walk past the bunkhouses, then headed north toward the orchard. She would slip all the way around…

"Tía…"

Johnny's voice stopped her. "Hi, Johnny. Sorry, I can't talk right now. I'm real busy."

"There's always something to do, but you owe me an explanation," he said quietly.

"I owe you my congratulations." The sound of her voice sickened her. She hated falseness, especially in herself. *He* was the one who had gotten married. *He* was the one who couldn't even wait a day. *He* was the one who couldn't even wait to hear her side of the story.

Johnny tried to hide his pride and pleasure at her wanting to congratulate him. If Tía was impressed that he hadn't fallen down and begged *El Gato* to spare him, then it had all been worthwhile.

"Aw, it was nothing," he said, grinning.

Tía shook her head, "Nothing, huh?" She wanted to ask him if he married every day. But she would not give him the satisfaction. "Reckon it changed your life."

"You think so?"

She wanted to pick up a two-by-four and hit him in the head. That should point out quite clearly that something had indeed changed for him. But she did nothing. "Why take Grant?" she asked.

Johnny frowned.

Tía flushed, realizing that she had let slip what was probably Judy's surprise. Obviously he didn't know about Grant. "You didn't know."

"Know what?"

"That Grant is going to Atlanta."

"I knew that."

Tía knew he was pulling a bluff now, cutting a typical cowboy shine. He didn't want to admit he hadn't known.

"Well," Tía said, "three's a crowd."

Johnny scowled in puzzlement. Tía had a way of saying things that seemed reasonable on the surface but didn't relate to anything he'd thought they were talking about.

"Why are you letting him go?" Tía demanded.

"Why am I letting Grant go to Atlanta with Judy?"

"That's real astute, Johnny Brago. That knob on the end of your neck ain't just a decoration after all."

"That's what you want to know?"

"Yes," she said as patiently as she could.

Johnny shrugged. "It's the least I can do. I figure since he loves her…"

Tía expelled a frustrated breath. "You think that's a good reason for taking him along?"

"And his folks live there…"

"Could you stand in the sunlight? I want to see if your head has holes in it. Maybe—"

"And he married her…"

Tía blinked. "Who married her?"

"Grant married her."

"I knew that," she said angrily. "Judy told me that this morning." The world jerked sharply into focus, and Tía felt instantly lighter. So *that* was what Judy had told her! A smile started at her toes and spread into every nook and cranny in her body.

Johnny was still talking. "Rutledge dropped the charges against Grant. He didn't even notify Behan about the shooting. Grant was the one who shot Morgan Todd, you know. They're leaving for Atlanta so Grant can take over for his father, who had a heart attack. His family has a store or something there."

Tía couldn't stop smiling. "I'm real happy for 'em," she said, meaning it. She'd never meant anything more in her life.

Johnny leaned back against the barn. Tía was smiling at him as if she didn't have a care in the world. She confused him so bad he had almost forgotten what he'd stopped her for. "I still think you owe me an explanation."

Tía felt so good she could easily have floated over the barn without a push. But Johnny's question sobered her. "What do you want to know?"

Johnny looked north, toward Wyoming. It was a hard question for him to ask. He wasn't sure he wanted to hear the answer. But he had to ask it, and he had to hear what she said. Anything would be better than not knowing. "Why wouldn't you come with me when he said you could?"

Tía leaned back against the barn beside Johnny. "That was a trick," she said softly. "He didn't mean it."

"You weren't free to leave?"

"Only if I wanted you to die."

"You stayed with him to save my life?"

"Yes."

"That's why he let me walk out of there?"

"Yes."

Johnny breathed a sigh of relief. The tightness in his chest relaxed. "I thought it was because I was such a cool *hombre*," he said, grinning.

Tía shrugged. "*El Gato* was real impressed with you. He said he'd never seen a man's pants dry as fast as yours."

Tía laughed, and Johnny swelled with pride momentarily and sobered. Tía had been willing to sacrifice herself to save him. The wonder of it was more than he could contain. This slim, magical creature had put his survival before the thought of her own life.

He wanted to say something to her, to thank her, but the enormity of what she had been willing to do for him left him speechless. He could not all at once comprehend it. Or her. Tía's long blond hair was tangled as if she hadn't combed it all day. Her face was sunburned from riding, but her blue eyes were round and sweet as she looked up at him. She was the prettiest thing he'd ever seen. He could never hope to deserve her, and yet she had risked everything for him. Johnny felt choked with love and gratitude.

At a loss for words, Johnny took her hand and led her into the barn, past horses in stalls, over to the ladder leading up into the hayloft.

"I can't climb up there in this gown," Tía protested.

"Sure you can. Just put your skirt in your mouth…"

Johnny climbed up and pulled her up beside him. He settled her on a pile of loose hay. "Andrea told me the whole story—yours and your parents. She asked me to give you time. Well, I'm not willing to give you time. I love you now. I want you now. Time may heal, but it robs you as it does. I've never waited for anything that turned out to be what I thought it would be when I started waiting for it. We have something now, something special. Maybe we'll still have it in a few weeks, maybe we won't. I'm not willing to take that chance."

"What if I don't want to get married?"

"Because you don't love me?" he asked.

"Maybe," she said, refusing to look at him. *Because I can't stand seeing myself from your eyes.*

"Look at me," Johnny commanded, forcing her chin up.

Tía sighed and lifted her gaze. His intent, plundering eyes stabbed into her. She felt exposed, to him and to herself. His knowledge shamed her, and she felt herself blushing.

"Since you aren't sure," he said, his voice husky, "maybe we'd better test the waters."

"No!"

Too late. His strong arms enveloped her. His lips found hers, and he kissed her softly, sweetly. The sensation was delicious and blissful. Tía wanted the kiss to go on forever, but too soon he lifted his head and pulled her into a warm hug.

"That doesn't change anything."

"Did for me," he said sighing.

It had for her as well, but she was terrified it wouldn't last.

He kissed her again. "Tía, Tía, Tía," he crooned softly, "I love you so much. I think I was born loving you, waiting for you."

Tía had to tell him. "You don't understand," she said guiltily. "The deal I made with him—I would have kept it."

Johnny shook his head. "I'm a man, Tía. I know what he wanted to do. I know what you believed you had to do...and now I know why.

"There's no way I can ever repay you for what you did. If I live to be six thousand years old, working every day in your service, I'll still be deeply in your debt," he said sternly. "You've put me at a terrible disadvantage. No woman should do that to a man," he said.

Tía searched Johnny's eyes. "I knew you'd be mad," she whispered.

"You actually believe a man would be dumb enough to be mad at a woman for saving his life the only way she could?"

"Maybe."

"I never saw a hostage that got to dictate the terms before. Of course *El Gato* didn't have but them two little guns and those five hundred or so *bandidos*. I realize that ain't nothing compared to a hundred pound woman with a mouth of her own, but tell me, how'd you get in charge?"

He scowled at her with mock seriousness and raised a questioning eyebrow. Tía blinked. Johnny knew she hadn't been the one in charge. She'd stood there in front of Johnny. He'd seen Papa...

Johnny read her confusion in her eyes. "The more he demanded of you, the more I have to pay back," he said gently.

Tía struggled with that.

"I want things right between us, Tía. What happened between *El Gato* and you has nothing to do with us."

Tía felt like crying. "But it had something to do with me, and I'm part of *us*."

Johnny took her by the shoulders and shook her gently, with restrained fierceness. "I love you, Tía. I love you so much I'm aching all over with it. I want to pick you up and squeeze you so hard you'll squeek. And another part of me wants to just sit and look at you because there's no way on this green earth I'll ever be fit to touch you. Not even the hem of your skirt."

His dark eyes filled with such fierceness and love Tía almost dissolved into tears. He meant it. He wasn't just saying it. A hard ache swelled and throbbed in her throat. She wanted to tell him she understood, but nothing worked. She just looked at him, mute and grateful and tear choked.

"I love you, Tía."

"Don't love me," she whispered.

"I love you, and you love me."

Tía tried to turn away, but Johnny wouldn't let her. "It's no use, Tía. I love you, and I'm not going to stop."

"How long you think you can keep it up?"

"Forever," he murmured, touching her cheek with his finger. "I've loved you since the minute I saw you in that silly bonnet you stole."

"I didn't steal it. I just forgot to pay for it."

Johnny laughed as his warm lips closed over hers.

Tía pulled away from him, searched his dark face. "How are you going to forget I let him kiss me? That he touched me?" she asked. She couldn't surrender herself to him without an answer to that question.

Johnny drew away in order to look down at her. "I don't need to forget. How are you going to forget?"

"I don't know if I can," she whispered.

She was so young! So incredibly young to think that a kiss or a touch could diminish her in some irrevocable way. Johnny wanted to shake her.

"You saved my worthless life, woman," he said gruffly. "And I'll never forget how much you had to love me to do that. To risk everything a woman holds dear to save me from certain death. You're braver than any man or woman I've ever known. How do *you* forgive yourself for that?" he asked gently, wiping the damp curls away from her face.

Her shaky laugh surprised Tía. "Blamed if I know," she said, sniffing.

"Tía?" he whispered against her cheek.

Slowly she opened her eyes.

He pressed his lips against her cheek and his warm breath caressed her temple and stirred the hair at her ear. "Do you know yet?"

"What?" she murmured, drawing away so she could focus on his dark, intent face.

"If you still love me."

She nodded.

"Well?" he prodded.

"I love you," she whispered. "You've always known that. That's why you kept badgering me."

Johnny laughed. "Badgering you? Girl, I've been dying of love for you. All you did was run from me. You've been as touchy as a teased snake ever since you set foot on this ranch."

"I suppose you've been nothing but light and sunshine."

"I don't like to brag, but…"

Tía poked him in the ribs.

"Owww!"

Johnny cupped her face in his hands. "And I thought Judy Foreman was the mischievous one." His tone was light, but the look in his eyes told her that she belonged to him, only to him, for always.

Johnny gathered Tía into his arms gently as if she were the most precious treasure imaginable. As usual, it took her a while to catch on, but at last she realized what he had in mind. He wanted to make her his, to wipe out all memories of the past forever.

But Tía knew she didn't need Johnny's embrace to do that. The warm smile of loving acceptance in his dark eyes had already done it. She *was* his—and his alone.

There *was* life after Eden.

THE LADY AND THE LAWMAN

Life on the Western frontier in the 1880s is filled with risks and danger—a fact Angie Logan quickly relearns upon arriving back at her family's Arizona ranch, home from college back East. To help quell the riots against Chinese immigrants that have settled in Durango, Angie relies on her education and wits in appealing to the governor for assistance. The governor sends help in the form of Lance Kincaid, a charismatic gentleman who became a ranger to avenge the murder of the woman he loved. While working to resolve the current upheaval, Lance catches the trail of the murderer. Nothing will stop him from catching the killer and bringing him to justice, except perhaps Angie, the mysterious woman who looks eerily like his lost love.

THE LADY AND THE ROBBER BARON

Jennifer Van Vleet is a woman who knows what she wants out of life and won't let anything stand in her way. She's dedicated herself to the art of ballet and becomes the prima ballerina for her company. When her costume catches fire during a performance, Chantry Kincaid III—a rakishly charming Texan builder whose family has as many enemies as it has properties—saves her. Jennifer finds herself drawn into a whirlwind romance with Chantry, where the passion between the two is undeniable, until she learns of the Kincaid family's hand in her parents' deaths years ago. Now she has a decision to make, one that will decide whether she can let go of the past and move forward from tragedy.

THE LADY AND THE OUTLAW

Leslie Powers has every reason in the world to hate Ward Cantrell, the devilishly handsome outlaw who kidnapped her. Instead she finds herself head-over-heels in love with him. When prompted by the sheriff to testify against Ward, Leslie firmly states that she was never Ward's hostage. Now a free man, Ward courts his way through the young ladies of Phoenix society, appearing to seduce them with wanton abandon. Leslie believes he is a rogue and worse, but she can't get him out of her mind or her heart. She's seen behind his mask and knows there is more to him than meets the eye; something in him has captured her heart.

ADOBE PALACE

After the deaths of her parents, Samantha Forrester was raised with the Kincaid children. She fell in love with Lance Kincaid as he protected her from childhood bullies. Now they've both grown up and Lance has married another. When the devilishly charming Steve Sheridan rides into Samantha's life, she sees her chance to build the house of her dreams, save her son's life, and claim Lance's heart for her own. But life doesn't always go according to plan, and fate will take them all on a journey as wild as the land they live on.

Printed in the United States
by Baker & Taylor Publisher Services